AGE OF EXPANSION

- -RISE OF MANKIND 7-

- JEZ CAJIAO

Jez Cajiao

CONTENTS

Jez Cajiao

THANKS

Hi everyone! Damn, well that's Age of Expansion done, and by the time you read this, I'll be hopefully nearly done with Age of Conquest as well, though it'll only just be entering edits at that stage, not, well, *complete*, if you know what I mean?

So, I'm working on a lot, as normal, but I was thinking about this, and as I last thanked my wonderful wife Chrissy, this time around I'm going to make it about my eldest son Max.

Now, many of you won't know much about my kids, which is as it should be, no need for you to know after all, but what I will say, is that he's incredible.

Max has started school, and every day, in some way, he makes me proud of him. Be that because of his kindness in helping his brother, be it his intelligence, and his determination, or just the little bugger's sense of humour.

He makes us all laugh, love and enjoy life a little more each day.

I had no idea how much better my would could be, until you were in it Max, I love you son.

Thank you,

-Daddy (Jez)
07/10/2024

PROLOGUE

Jean-Claude scrambled across the shattered stone, diving down the far side, whimpering in terror as his hair was whipped by the slipstream of the creature's near miss.

Claws, teeth, and bones. That was all he'd seen—the flash, as it arced around, screeching its fury at its failure, had moved so fast, everything else was a blur. That it was also some kind of demon—and one that a constant low-level stream of Hail Mary's his God-fearing grand-mère had hammered into him, was doing nothing to dispel—didn't mean he was going to quit his desperate attempts.

He slid down the slanted, shattered section of stone, fragments cascading loose and tearing his skin, then kicked off. He landed hard, rolling to lessen the shock, and staggered into a fresh sprint. His breath whistled in his ears as his heart beat fit to outdo any underground dance scene.

Ahead lay what had once been the greatest of national symbols, and it was seemingly now the last refuge he had, as he'd been systematically cut off from all other routes.

It was a mistake, though, and he *knew* it was a mistake.

Once he was on there, there was nowhere else to turn, nothing to hide behind, and yet... He glanced to the left. The fragments of broken stone rolled under his feet as he hopped, dancing through the debris, and started to alter direction...until a flash of movement and a distant clatter made him change back.

They were there as well!

He skidded and almost went down. The clacking of closing feet barely out of sight made him whimper again, the sound lost beneath the panting of his breath. He grabbed the remains of a tree, using it to redirect his scramble as he leapt a fallen branch that half covered the path.

He ran on, barely hearing the *hisst* that rang out. But when he did, his heart leapt. Frantically, he searched for her, knowing that the gods must have led him to her, and she had to be able to save him. She just *had* to!

The Avenue Silvestre de Sacy had been one of their favorite haunts before the end, and even recently, despite everything, they'd laughed and loved, looking back on strolling arm in arm along its gentle paths.

Sun-dappled pavements that had once been graced with the most beautiful of a nation's sophisticates were now strewn with ruined buildings, sundered trees, and the equally broken remains of those once wondrous artistes.

Now, as he frantically searched, his gaze flickering from broken cars to shattered windows that stared like the hollow eyes of a skull at the Parisian skyline, he couldn't see her! The remains of bodies lay everywhere, reduced to refuse; torn, bloody cloth flapped in the wind. But nowhere in sight was the one he'd come searching for.

She was here—she *had* to be!

He thought he'd lost her, thought that he'd lost everything, until the dreams had come, drawing him out of hiding, out of his last refuge to search the streets, only to find they were suddenly full of... of...

Movement to his left resolved into a pair of the terrible flying creatures, long dead, as were all the rest.

They drifted like balloons given maniacal will, half a human body from the waist up, tattered robes fluttering in the rising breeze as they cried out their perverse joy at his terror.

He gibbered, knowing she might very well be *right there*, just hiding out of sight, but he was out of time! The others, the smaller flying ones, all bones and claws, were fast—incredibly so—but he'd seen over the last two days that they were also dumb as rocks. They were as likely to attack a flapping sign or a tattered flag as a human.

Anything was a target to vent their hatred of the living upon, and he was as likely to be left alone as not, provided he managed to make it under shelter and stay out of sight again.

The wraiths, though? They were different. They took sadistic pleasure in hunting the living, in tormenting them. And since their arrival in the city, more and more of the survivors had fled, or vanished.

He bounced off the side of a parked car, shoving off it and around. His breath hissed as he snatched back a hand; fresh blood dripped from the broken window he'd inadvertently brushed against.

He started to run again, this time whispering a fervent wish that he could lead them away from wherever she was hiding, knowing that he couldn't lead them to her, that he would never betray her love.

Instead, he put his head down and ran.

He ran hard, feet slapping against the pavement as he picked up speed. Tears streamed down his cheeks as he mentally bade her good luck and whispered his eternal love for her, before leaping an overturned food cart, long since stripped and forgotten.

Landing on the far side, he broke to the right, weaving between a handful of trees, behind a concession stand. Dropping to all fours, he scrambled up the bank on the far side, grabbing at frost-coated bushes and trees, and hauling himself to the top.

He crested the short peak, then crashed down the far side. Stealth and any concern about leaving no tracks was long lost in the desire to ensure he led the accursed ones away from her.

A distant and earsplitting screech from behind him rang out, filled with hatred, then followed by a stream of words no mortal was meant to hear. Stumbling, twisting around to see what had made the cry, Jean-Claude staggered, tripped, and barely caught himself, before gaping at a green wash of energy that flashed past him. It passed in a blink, sinking into the bodies of the dead laid abandoned and forgotten here and there, but flowed across his flesh like water. As if he were an island in the sea, he was left miraculously alone, as the magical energy faded from view into the distance.

The once carefully manicured gardens at the base of the Eiffel Tower were now as rotten and abandoned as the rest of Paris. But as he leapt the ornate fence, with its proud fleur-de-lys and scrollwork, he saw the gated entrance ahead swinging gently in the breeze.

It was suicide to go there now. If he climbed the tower, he'd only trap himself on her multitude of steps. And yet, it was death to go anywhere else.

Even now, to the left and right more shivering spoke of the bushes being disturbed by others.

Hands long loosed to the dreamless sleep of death twitched and shifted, rising again as he hurdled them, running. Whimpering. Panicking.

On all sides, the bodies of the dead were suddenly starting to rise again. He had no choice now, and raced for the entrance. The steps ahead beckoned, and he cursed, but did as he knew he must, running for the gate.

Two floors…that was it—that was all that the public could climb in better times. But if he was fortunate, perhaps the gates would have been left unlocked, and he'd be able to climb higher.

What he'd do then? When there was no way but to climb higher and higher as they followed?

He didn't know. But if it gave her the chance to escape, then it'd be worth it.

He'd barely reached the gate when the first of the undead lunged out of the bushes at him. The setting sun made it harder to see it, where it'd lurked in the darkness and shadow.

It hit him. The pair of them half spun as his momentum met its lunge. They both crashed into the ancient iron fence and bounced off. He grunted then screamed in horror as what had once been an older woman, elegant and bedecked in stylish jewelry, snapped teeth closed a centimeter from his nose.

Half her face was gone; the white of bone showed through the putrefying flesh that remained. And yet still she lunged, fingers clinging to him as he shoved her back, then hit her.

It was a right cross, one that was instinctive from those long-ago—and he'd thought long forgotten and a waste of good money—self-defense classes.

Now, though, as the head snapped sideways, the flesh of the neck barely keeping it attached, he saw an opportunity, and he took it.

The ornamental fence nearby had sections that rose and fell regularly, rounded triangles that held the fleur-de-lys symbol protected for all to see. Between each of them were valleys that came to a narrow point.

He shoved her dead form backward, amazed at the lightness of it in comparison to a living person. He hit her head again, driving it onto the far side of the shoulder-high fence.

Her neck slid into the gap, and he pushed down on both of her shoulders, ignoring the scrabbling fingers that scratched and tore at his skin and clothes.

It worked!

The force on the shoulders, the speed, all of it! Her head snapped free, and the body on his side of the fence collapsed, lifeless again. Jean-Claude staggered loose and wiped at his face, his own fingers coming away bloody.

"What... I..." He whispered, before a nearby sound made him spin. Others were closing in.

He took off, grabbing the battered gate and lunging through it, dragging it closed after him, then finding the dangling chain that had once secured it.

There was a lock, cut free by bolt cutters and laid useless on the floor, but the chain was still there!

Dragging it through and into the far side with him, he looped it as fast as he could, through and around the bars, doing his best to tie a sort of rough knot with the short length as more and more of the undead closed in.

A single last loop, then he dropped the ends, backing away, staring, as the first grabbed the gate and started to pull.

It held! Shaking and crashing the metal gate against its posts, the monster clattered and chattered, teeth clacking as it tried to break through. Then it gave up and instead lunged for him, pressing reaching arms through the gaps, moaning.

Relief washed through Jean-Claude as he backed away even farther, before turning and sprinting for the first of the steps that led upward, ever upward.

There were over a thousand, he knew, but up there were also the restaurants, the museum, and the gift shops as well. Maybe, just *maybe*, he could find something to defend himself with, and he'd survive all of this yet...

He failed to spot the sight of his one true love, as now that the hated sun was vanishing from the sky, she dragged herself out of the sewer she'd been hiding in. She licked her lips; twin lengthened canines gleamed as she stared after him, and hungered.

Tonight, she'd feed well.

CHAPTER ONE

I blinked slowly, memory coming back as I stared at the ceiling overhead, working my way through the last things I remembered, before shifting and letting out an inadvertent groan as I realized where I was.

I was back in the dungeon, and specifically, in my bed.

Our bed, I should say, rather.

Both Kelly and Finn sat there, and there was a goddamn pane of solid glass that ran from one side of the room to the other, separating us.

"Kelly?" I mumbled. Both she and Finn were watching me. I sat up slowly. The blanket fell free to pool at my waist as I looked around, frowning and stifling another jaw-cracking yawn with the back of my right hand.

"Wha…what happened?" I managed to get out on the second attempt, feeling like hammered garbage.

"You got yourself drained by another woman." Kelly's voice was a mix of cold, annoyed, and frustrated.

"Eh?" I squinted at her, then shook my head vigorously and winced as the world spun. "I think I'd remember that, right?" I suggested. Indeed, the memories of the fight were returning fast now. The ogre, the taking of the Galleries' citadel, and…and Robin? She couldn't possibly mean…? "Whoa, hold the fuck up," I said quickly. "I didn't… I mean, I would *never…*"

"She knows you didn't cheat on her." Finn rolled his eyes and sighed, before gesturing at Kelly, who sniffed and looked away. "She's just salty about the whole situation, that's all."

"What situation?" I asked blankly.

"You bonded her to you," Kelly said grimly after a few seconds. "You don't think that's the kind of thing your girlfriend should have a little heads-up over?"

"Bonded…?" I muttered, as I tried to remember, before sagging backward as a wave of dizziness flooded me.

My head hit the pillow, and I stared up at the ceiling overhead, even as a distant and new bundle of emotions twitched as I mentally reached out and prodded at it.

"Bonded…" I muttered again, barely remembering the damn end of the fight and seeing it as almost a half-remembered dream. "Kelly, I… I don't know what to tell you," I admitted, struggling back to an upright position and glancing over at her. For me to be here, the glass separating us, and Finn to be here as well, there had to be more going on.

"Did you mean to do it?" she asked. "Or have any kind of warning?"

"Warning of what?" I rubbed at my face, then summoned a glass of water. I took a sip, then downed it and banished it; I shifted around and dropped my legs over the side of the bed before scratching at my unkept hair and beard as I thought.

"The last thing I remember was getting a prompt, asking if I'd accept Robin as a Paladin. The fight was going our way, and the ogre was getting close to falling. The majority of the prisoners were down, or out of ammo, and things were getting better.

"Robin had pulled some glowing shit with her new class and was beating the fuck outta the boss, but that was basically because we'd taken down all his defenses and he was on his last legs. The system asked if I'd take her as a Paladin, and I figured why not? I mean…no, that's not right." I broke off, thinking hard and trying to remember the last prompt and the way that everything had been going.

I pulled the prompt back up and stared at it, nodding as I read it aloud for the others.

Congratulations!

You are the first of your nascent brethren to have a Paladin pledge their life to your own. Do you accept the life bond of [Robin] as your first Paladin?

Yes/No…

"I'd not seen the 'life bond' bit, just that she was a Paladin, and that seemed like it was just what we needed, right? A warrior-cleric class. So I said yes."

"A warrior cleric," Finn murmured, glancing at Kelly knowingly. "Matt, mate, why did you accept that, though? Was there something specific, or was it on instinct?"

"Maybe instinct," I admitted slowly. "I mean, the warrior cleric was the cool part, but like I said, I figured we needed that, right? In all the games, Paladins are cool. Sure, they can be pricks with their oaths and so on, but that they can go toe-to-toe with the frontline fighters and lead a charge, or heal people…that's what we need more of."

"So it was instinct, and then you reasoned it out and accepted it?" Finn asked. "Matt, I need you to be as honest as you can be. This bit is important."

I glanced from him to Kelly, hoping I wasn't about to get grief for this one if I said the wrong thing. I sighed, then went for it anyway.

"Instinct," I confirmed. "When I thought about it and realized the powers she was showing, that was cool, and I guess I figured that was exactly what we needed, but I did it on instinct."

"Thank you!" Finn crowed. "Yes!"

"What?" I frowned, confused.

"Ignore him." Kelly sighed. "I'm sorry, Matt. I know you did what you had to do and your instincts haven't driven us wrong yet, but you basically married Robin. You see that, right?"

"MARRIED?!" I cursed. "Oh hell to the fucking no!"

"Glad you're as happy about it as I am." Kelly quirked a brief and grim smile.

"I'm not, I mean, I wouldn't…" I spluttered, searching for the words.

"Matt, don't worry. Kelly, stop giving him grief for something you know he had to do! You also know he wouldn't do that," Finn added in before shooting me a conspiratorial sidelong look. "She's just salty because she doesn't want to share you, that's all."

"I wasn't suggesting we share," Kelly said quickly.

"Hell no!" I agreed, then paused as a brief mental image popped into my head and I remembered a couple of nights in Zante with…*no*. I banished the thought as quickly as it'd come.

"Anyway, the point here is that you're bonded to someone we all barely know," Finn explained. "And once again, you did your whole 'I'm tired so I'll just nap right here' thing."

"I passed out," I guessed. "You know it's kinda an accident…I didn't plan for that."

"Yeah, we get that, but you also were basically out for the count, and it was right after the fight. Nobody saw what happened and they pieced it together afterward between the whole light show that Robin put on and that notification that went out."

"Notification…" I saw just how many of mine were flashing, then sighed as I pulled them up. "Give me a second and I'll see what I've got," I offered, getting a nod from them both.

Congratulations, First Lord of the Storm!

As the first leader of a Local Pantheon to raise and unlock your own Paladin class, you have been granted the following Boons!
- **+10 to a single Stat of your choice**
- **+2 Spells**
- **+2 Class Ability Points**

Followed by:

WORLDWIDE ANNOUNCEMENT!

THE FIRST LORD OF THE STORM HAS PUBLICALLY ACCEPTED HIS FIRST PALADIN, RAISING UP A NEW CLASS OF WARRIOR WORSHIPPER AND BEQUEATHING HIS ESSENCE TO THOSE HE LEADS!

KNOW THIS! THE ONLY LIMIT ON YOU IS THAT WHICH YOU PLACE UPON YOURSELVES. GROW, ADVANCE, *LEAD*!

***

Beware, First Lord of the Storm! Your Divine Core is unestablished, and as such, drawing on your essence to empower your worshippers can be fatal...

***

New Quest Discovered!

Establish your Divine Core:

As a Divine being, you may choose to gift your burgeoning Divine essence to those who please you. This can be done through the path of religion, through empowerment of artifacts, or directly, but beware!

The path of organized religion offers a safety net, a buffer, between the god and their followers, but currently you have no such protection!

Create and fill the first level of your Divine Core to gain access to the following rewards:

- *Unlock the Priesthood of the Storm Questline*
- *Unlock the Paladins of the Storm Questline*
- *Unlock the Defenders of the Faith Questline*
- *Level One Artifact Creation*
- *Survival...*

The others were less joyful, as I reread the prompts I'd gained already, then examined the new ones.

You have completed a new Sub-Quest!
Quest!
Ogres' repose...or is it dispose?

Jez Cajiao

Once a human, one who has fully embraced both the nature and nurture side of being an ogre, this remnant of humanity has utterly reformed himself into a terrifying example of what is possible.

The Ogre boss was eliminated, and although he certainly had it coming, his loss to the universe may yet have profound knock-on effects, ones that may not be felt for years to come.

You eliminated the Ogre Boss to receive the following bonuses:

- *+1 Class Skill Point*
- *Possible new Dungeon-Born*
- *5000 XP*

The other quest notification I'd not actually read before, not properly anyway. It'd come in while we were speaking to Robin for the first time and I hadn't made a decision. Then, by the time we'd started the ball moving, I'd just pulled it up and glanced at it, making sure it wasn't shite and I'd accepted it, before sharing it around.

Quest Complete! Stronghold Liberation (I)

A nearby fortress had fallen into the hands of escaped prisoners, who were using it as a base for their nefarious activities. These criminals had enslaved innocent people and posed a growing threat to the surrounding areas. As the master of the local dungeon and a powerful [Arcanist], your intervention was crucial.

You have liberated the stronghold, defeated the escaped prisoners, and freed their captives to complete this quest and receive the following bonuses:

- *+2 to top three Attributes*
- *+1 Class Skill Point to allocate*
- *Access to stronghold resources*
- *7,500 XP*

Objectives:

- *Capture the enemy stronghold 1/1*
- *Defeat the escaped prisoner's leadership 1/1*
- *Rescue and free the enslaved captives 7811/7817*

Beware, [Arcanist]! As your power grows, so too does the difficulty of the challenges you face. Prepare yourself for formidable opponents and unforeseen obstacles.

I read it over again, then snorted derisively, guessing that even the system hadn't been prepared for the sheer mind-numbing stupidity of the guards, who'd basically all just let us waltz right into the middle of the base before the fight had kicked off.

The end result was that the fight had been difficult—dangerous, even—as the combat classes had been a serious risk, as had been the ogre. But the rest?

I saw that we'd completed the rest of it while I was out cold, and I cleared my throat, then plowed on, ticking off the last notifications in the list, while banishing the rest. The usual minor skill-ups were dismissed, as nothing brought me an increase that was more than an unidentifiable or unnoticeable 1% here or there.

Congratulations!

You have killed the following:
- **11x Local escaped prisoners, Levels 2-14, 504 XP**

Total XP earned: 504 XP

You have assisted in the elimination of the local boss variant:

- **1x Ogre Boss, Level 17, 320 XP**

Total XP earned: 824 XP
Total XP awarded: 824 XP

Current XP to next level stands at 59,787/60,000

I snorted at that. I'd gained a load of benefits, sure, but I was so close! I could practically taste the goddamn level-up, and yet I'd not gained quite enough! Goddammit.

I glared at that notification, before quickly collecting all the bits I'd gained together where I could see them.

I'd gained two points to Agility and two to Intelligence, which was nice. I was over a hundred percent faster than a human should have been able to reach now, and I had a boost of ten points to assign to a single stat when I was ready, which I decided to hold off on for now.

Beyond that, I had two spells and a massive four class skill points to assign, as well as the dubious rewards of the captured citadel's resources, and the dead body of the ogre.

That one...well, I wasn't sure about that. If I absorbed it into the dungeon, I knew that I *should* get access to the dungeon-born version of him, but...

There wasn't one in there already, I knew. The prompts and the bleed-through of limited knowledge I had made that clear. With a little focus, a bit more of the details seeped loose.

When the fuckers had been made extinct, the dungeons either hadn't had access to the bodies, or they'd chosen not to add them to the roster. Considering they even had their most hated enemies, the orcs, on there, and the specific sub-breed that was currently conquering the galaxy as a valid, if restricted, option?

This was going to take some serious consideration.

If I chose to add them to my dungeon, I might get a completely new version of the ogre, one that I could then work to evolve again. Maybe I could even train them and bring back the nobler version of their race, making them a boon to the galaxy, as well as specifically something that could help in our coming battles with the orcs.

That was great, but there might also be a situation where I just got the same dickhead that I'd just fought, as he'd be the only version in the system. And even if I then refused to summon him again and he was forced by the dungeon system to obey me, I might end up fighting another dungeon that had gained access to the blueprint through some reward once I'd put it into the system.

Fuck, that was going to need to be thought through.

I quickly checked my stats, then banished the screen, blinking. Finn was now sitting back with both earplugs in and reading a book, while Kelly waited for me, legs crossed, one knee over the other and foot tapping the air impatiently.

"Uh, sorry, how long was I distracted there?" I glanced from one to another.

"Only a minute or so," Kelly assured me, sighing and sitting up before gesturing at her and Finn. "Look, Matt, this is what we came up with in the short term, when we weren't sure if that...if *Robin* had done something that was going to kill you."

"Go on..."

"I was worried that with us not knowing what was going on, that you were away from the dungeon and had been for a while, if that might have contributed to it."

"Uh, like I was tied to the dungeon and had to return?" I guessed, scratching at my chin as she nodded. "No, I don't think so?"

"That's a relief then." She sighed. "Look, I didn't know what else to do, but equally I wasn't willing to risk it all, so what we did was agree to a compromise.

"We allowed the others who came back with you to come in, but we kept them in the castle portion of the dungeon grounds. For now, they, and you, aren't allowed any physical contact with anyone. That's a hard rule."

She paused to look at me, making sure I understood, and I nodded for her to go on.

"Also, because we all know what people are like, a random second person is to be involved at all times in any meeting with those who might have been infected. That's why Finn is here. Although he's basically trying to ignore us, he's here to make sure I don't decide to open the glass or get a cuddle or whatever.

"It's both an honesty and a checks and balances system, but I didn't know what else to do. If it had been that you were somehow suffering because you were being kept from the dungeon as well as everything else…well, I couldn't risk it."

"I get it." I nodded. "Shit, yeah, it makes sense. And to be honest, I'd never considered that I might 'need' to be close to the dungeon, but I can see how it could happen."

"But you're sure you don't need to?" she asked me, and I shook my head. "Good, because as of this afternoon, you're out again."

"Why?" I asked, my head spinning.

"Because even you and the others just being here is a risk," she said softly. "Someone—two someone's, in fact—have to watch over you at all times, and that's people we can't afford to have doing nothing. Also, frankly, the Washington base needs to be sorted out. Robin came back here with you at my order, but she didn't want to. Her three friends are watching over the situation there now, along with Rhodes, Jo, Ashley, and Dante."

"What's happening?" I asked, and Kelly shook her head.

"No clue. We got a report about four hours ago that people were getting antsy and pretty demanding. Some want to leave. Others were insisting that they take over, or that we hold elections, for fuck's sake. Still more were stripping the place or had already set off for parts unknown. We need you there, but if you're too tired, then you might do more harm than good."

"I'll go." I reached up and dragged my fingers through my hair, before growling in frustration.

"Now what?" Kelly asked.

"Nothing."

"Just tell me, Matt. Don't make me drag it out of you." She sighed.

"It's stupid." I snorted. "It's just been like two weeks since I had a trim, and when I got it cut then? She insisted on it being a bit longer and styled differently from my normal."

"It suits you," she assured me.

"As it is now or as I walked out of the trim?" I asked her shrewdly, and she winced, then nodded.

"As it was."

"And that's why I'm getting frustrated with it," I said. "It's a nothing detail, not something that matters at all. It's just that my beard and hair are longer than I like, and that's with a few weeks of growth on a longer style than I'd have chosen

17

normally for myself anyway. I just feel unkept and untidy, and I just woke up. Do I have time for a shower?"

"You do, but be aware that Finn is going to be here the whole time, as am I."

"If teasing you by helicoptering means I tease him too, that's a risk I'm willing to take," I joked, watching Finn to see whether he could hear me. When he stayed seemingly absorbed in his book, I snorted and stood.

"Fill me in on anything else in a few minutes, okay?" I asked Kelly. "Just let me grab a shower and wake up properly."

"Go for it, but you'll need to keep the door open. We need to be able to see there's no vurms or anything making a break for freedom," she apologized, then grinned. "Did I ever tell you, you've got a pretty bum?"

I shook it, walking away, then stepped into the shower, feeling the almost instant caress of the hot water pounding the cares and stresses away, even as I tried to ignore the fact that Finn sat on the other side of the room.

It went against every instinct I had to know that Kelly was right there, and I couldn't invite her in to fool around a little. But fuck it, that was life, and I needed to get shit in order as quickly as possible, so that I could invite her in damn soon.

As I scrubbed away, I checked the details in the dungeon sense, still having difficulty doing physical things—like soaping up my ass crack—while I did it, but it was becoming easier, certainly.

The dungeon was working steadily. The core appeared stable, and was about two-thirds of the way to completion, with a rough guesstimate from me of another two days to complete the upgrade to Glass.

That was, if everything stayed as it was.

Trying to reach out further into the dungeon, I slipped as a leg gave way beneath me at my distraction.

I caught myself on the wall, grunting, then waved as Kelly called out, asking whether I was okay. I laughed to myself as Finn, apparently having his attention dragged by her lurching to her feet, then caught an unwanted eyeful and promptly buried his nose in his book again.

I toweled off quickly, explaining what had happened to Kelly, then dressed, pausing as I looked at my armor, then back at Kelly in question.

The armor we'd been using had gone through various upgrades of late. Hell, there was barely a week that passed that the damn thing hadn't changed in one way or another with Aly and her research teams working on mad shit. But mine was significantly different from the way it'd looked only a day ago, *again*.

The design hadn't changed much in appearance from the Bronze core version upgrading all the way to Steel; most of it had been clearly cosmetic, in the color changes to a matte-grey steel from the golden bronze. But now?

The chest, with its stylized stomach, shoulders, fore and upper arms, thighs and shins—not to mention the codpiece—were more or less plain, simple polished steel that was more functional than anything, with the goddamn cloak attached to the back of my cuirass to make a signature statement.

Now it'd evolved again, with the various plates picked out in steel but with the edges outlined with black lines to make it more impressive. The scales were a glossy black that I just knew were going to get me fuckin' noticed at the wrong point. And the middle of the cuirass?

A logo.

"What the hell is this?" I asked Kelly, and she shrugged.

"You've seen it before," she pointed out.

"Yeah, but…" I squinted at it, and tilted the steel, looking at it from various angles and then gave up. "What the hell is it?"

"It's the symbol for the dungeon." Kelly nodded toward it. "I don't know what it really means, but when Ashley went to the other dungeon? She said that theirs was different. Their doors all glowed with a set rune or symbol as well, but the dungeon itself has a single main one on the front door. She asked them about it, and the dungeon fairy admitted that each dungeon has one, and that it's unique to it.

"It seemed appropriate to have the symbol of our dungeon on things, moving forward." She shrugged. "Plus, it looks kinda badass."

I had to admit it did. It was a pair of glowing red, vertical lines that angled inward in the middle like they were stretched by a bow. Then they swept upward, with a third laid diagonally across them with a roughly twenty-degree decline from left to right. Lastly, there were a series of small symbols and dots beneath. It looked like a cross between Aztec and Chinese to me, with maybe a dash of Sumerian. Whatever it was, though, it was cool.

That was recessed into the center of my armor now, and it'd been made of mana crystal, I knew immediately as I touched it.

"You sneaky fucker," I breathed.

"Does it work?" Kelly asked me anxiously. "Will it, I mean?"

"Yeah," I guessed, touching it and tracing the crystal. "I think so, and the size… I'm betting it'll hold at least as much mana as I can."

"It's a reserve." Finn grinned, having seen that I now had pants on at least and apparently deciding it was time to talk about the creation. "It won't be refillable, or at least I've not yet figured out how to make it that, anyway. Drain it all the way and it'll shatter, but what it holds? If you need it, that could be the difference between life and death."

"You have no idea," I agreed. "Can we do this with all the armor?" I glanced over the other sections, noting that they were lacking the new ornamentation.

"Probably." Finn scratched at his chin. "Though I think it'd be a waste."

"Why?" I asked.

"To make that, just that section? A hundred and thirty thousand mana."

"Fuck me with a javelin." I cursed.

"Kinky bastard." Finn grinned. "Seriously, I know it's horrifically expensive, but I think it's because we've not got any magical artificers yet—not in armor or

19

dedicated artifacts anyway. Like the focal orbs…if we can get that sorted out, then the armor should be much cheaper. And frankly, as often as you need a new set? It's not worth it."

"Only if I want to live," I breathed. "This is a priority, Finn. This for all our people, because—"

"They're mana crystals," Kelly interrupted. "They're not specific to the dungeon, don't forget."

"So?" I ran a finger over the pattern. There was definitely something familiar about it.

"So if someone else touched it, they could use it, even if it's against you," Kelly said.

I winced, then nodded. "Fuck. Yeah, I didn't think about that," I admitted, before shaking my head sadly. "We can't use it, can we?"

"We can," Finn corrected. "We just have to treat it as any other weapon people are holding. I mean, if you're fighting some asshole and he gets your gun, then he might use it on you. This is no different, right?"

"Perhaps," I muttered, before shaking my head. "In the short term, though, no. We don't know enough about magic, so we need to do more tests first and be sure that it's not something that an enemy can do remotely. If it's limited to touch range, then—" I broke off. "Dammit, it's not."

"Dickless?" Kelly asked, and I nodded.

"What?" Finn asked, and I smiled sadly.

"It looks good, but it is what it is. I accessed and drained the mana crystals from a distance when I was fighting Dickless, so it is possible, but we'd need to experiment with it to see if that was in part because they were created through the dungeon and I'm who I am." I took a deep breath, then shook my head, disappointed. "So for now? I'll wear this, but it might be that we need to either plate over the top so that nobody can see it, or remove it entirely."

"Yeah." Finn winced. "Dammit, I'm sorry, Matt. I was thinking that it would really help…"

"And it will." I nodded. "If nothing else, I'll look the part with this when I go back to Washington. But for now, we don't do this for our people."

"Agreed." He pulled out a notebook and made some notes. "So, with you heading back to Washington, have you made any decisions about how you'll do it?"

"What do you mean?" I asked. "We've still got the vehicles, right?"

"We do." He nodded. "And I think that's how Robin and the others should return, but…"

"Oh gods, here we go." I groaned, letting the armor sag to the floor as I stared at him. "What maniacal bullshit have you got planned now?"

"I just think a little theatre is in order, that's all!" he replied innocently, holding his hands out to either side.

"And it keeps you out of a small, enclosed space with Robin," Kelly added darkly, before waving her hands in negation. "I know! I know, all right! I'm just annoyed. It's fine. I trust you, and I sort of trust her. I don't even think she swings that way, but I'm just…"

"Feeling a bit neglected?" Finn elbowed his friend, winking. "Me too! So let's get this upgrade sorted out, get your boy toy out to get the local area pacified, and get some loving back on the menu, all right?"

"Deal," she agreed, before glancing over at me as I stared at them, hearing my services being bartered so blatantly.

"What?" Kelly asked innocently. "We're all adults here and you know you want to play again soon."

"Damn right," I growled. "So what do I need to do?"

"Well," Finn grinned, "when I say 'theatre'…"

CHAPTER TWO

I stepped out into a cold, crisp morning, feeling Kelly and Finn, as well as the ghostly attention of at least a dozen others in the dungeon sense, as I closed the door behind me, then turned and took a deep breath.

The others had left about twenty minutes ago. Robin, Patrick, Kilo, Mike, and Chris had gone, and there was a plan for them to start making food runs.

The cost of summoning a clone of the truck or the reworked boxer military vehicles were horrific—again, because we didn't have anything to produce them from besides pure mana, and damn, that was frustrating.

We'd looked at the trucks in the area. Although it was possible to rework the design and rebuild just their engines to use the new crank starts and more, it wasn't worth it.

Instead, we'd decided that the northern dungeon would get another one working as quickly as possible, then send it south to us. The military vehicles were just massively superior when you looked at the need to regularly shove abandoned vehicles off the road ahead of us, and the rugged survivability they had.

For now, the truck would be escorted back and forth, with a dozen Scepiniir riding herd for protection. At the park, it'd be loaded up with as much food as it could carry; then it'd do a run back to Washington, unload, then back. Rinse and repeat, basically.

While Chris and the others were doing that, Robin would be dropped off at what we'd just taken to calling the Galleries, and I'd head there soon.

There was a hell of a lot that I could be doing with my time, including doing some much needed sexercise, some meditation, some training or sorting out the expansion that we all needed to address.

Instead, though, I was on "hearts and minds." And, as Finn and Kelly had hammered into me, for that to work, I needed to look the part.

I needed a goddamn haircut, but I'd made do with a self-administered trim of my beard, some oil and styling shit, and little luxuries like aftershave and deodorant.

Now, in my gleaming armor, cloak streaming behind me as I strode across the dungeon's roof, I lifted my helmet and slid it on before lowering my hands to my sides—feeling incredibly self-conscious—and I soared into the air.

I was tempted to do a "Superman" and have one fist extended, or both or…

Instead, I just relaxed as much as possible, lifting up and up, staring in wonder as I felt the others falling away behind me.

Up here, as I channeled the storm and slipped the bonds of the earth to fly free, I stared in shock at the difference that had been made to the area of late.

To the east, the high-rise buildings that had once dominated the close-in skyline of the city had—with the exception of the one we'd retained for overwatch—all been torn down.

That single building there, Cale Cross, had actually increased in size and was a very different beast from what it had been.

Glittering now in a fresh dressing of frost and with most of its windows sealed away by stone, it towered, grim and silent.

The upper floors had been narrowed in and supports added, ascending at least thirty floors higher than any architect had ever expected it to reach. Although it was now the highest building in the area by a significant margin, the gleam of fresh dungeon delivered construction shone atop it still.

It was to be an aerie, Kelly had said, rather than just a sniper nest as I'd intended. Once we had our own native fliers, that would be their home.

On all sides, where the walls of the dungeon stood tall on our side, around Cale Cross, there had previously been dozens of smaller buildings and storage areas, obsolete railways and bridges, parking lots and more.

Now, there was fresh earth. The stone that had once covered it was absorbed and new soil birthed, ready to accept what I'd been told would one day be an orchard.

In Newcastle, that seemed almost as insane as the monsters that now roamed the area . But fuck it, it'd be a nice addition for people fleeing the madness of war, I guessed.

To the north, there were more general structures: hotels, parking garages, shops… The pattern repeated for miles, but already a huge swathe had been carved free by the on-rolling undead army of processors.

They were incredible, not needing rest, and no risk of distraction or boredom. The changes since we'd started using them were amazing.

I took it all in with a single slow rotation, then set my sights on the Queen Elizabeth hospital at the top of Gateshead. The hill it perched atop meant it was visible, glinting in the distant sunlight, even from here, if only just.

I flew steadily, covering the distance at roughly twenty miles an hour. With the distance that separated the citadel and the park at approximately eight miles, it'd take me maybe twenty, twenty-five minutes.

I could have gone faster, but with everything that had been happening of late, I found that I needed a little time to be just…me.

As I flew, I saw random hints of movement everywhere. For the first time, I realized just how much we were missing as we roamed in the packs we'd formed.

Dozens of creatures—some I'd never even seen before—were in motion…running, leaping, flying. Life was everywhere, and no sign of David Attenborough to catalog it.

Flying across the lower areas of Gateshead, I frowned. A patrol of Scepiniir ran through a graveyard, chasing something that staggered and lurched as it fled them.

It looked something like a hairless gorilla, five meters high at the shoulder. It ran on its knuckles, bellowing something back at them, before changing direction to head toward a hidden dell.

I shifted slightly. The Scepiniir weren't running particularly quickly. In fact…the buggers were herding it? From above, I could see three more of the same creature were lurking at the end of the dell, poorly hidden and apparently lying in wait. For a second, I almost paused, thinking to give warning. Then I noticed that lying wait right behind them?

Four more Scepiniir.

It was only from above that I'd been able to pick them out, as three of them crept across the roofs to the right of the poorly hidden monsters, while another squatted in the trees above them.

I hesitated, watching; then I shook my head. Either I trusted them to do their job, or I didn't, and I had to take off the kid gloves at some point.

I reached out to Jack. He was roaming, as was his default, and currently clearing out the naturally occurring undead that seemed to always spring up in graveyards. Arend-Jan and Griffiths had asked to keep him on station, as he was impervious to the weather and lethal to most enemies. I'd agreed, though with reservations.

Soon I was going to need him, and badly. But for now, he was more useful there, I had to admit. Rather than twenty or more Scepiniir or soldiers freezing their asses off in the moors, there was just him, roaming on auto mode, hunting down anything that was a threat to the new northern dungeon.

For whatever reason he'd stopped feeding me experience for his kills of late, but that was around number three thousand and fifty on the list of 'why the hell is…' and I simply accepted that and moved on now.

Nodding to myself, I continued, flying in a roughly south-by-southeast pattern. I lifted higher, searching the skies for any threats.

The wind picked up. It was colder than a witch's tit up here, but the more I breathed, just…relaxing? The more I genuinely started to calm and relax in truth.

I was the storm, I was starting to accept, and my own natural aversion to water—not keeping clean, but the sea and more—was clearly something that had held me back too long.

As I drifted higher, the low clouds scudding past, heavy with incoming hail and sleet, I opened myself to them. I forced aside the instinctive desire to huddle in closer, to wrap my cloak tighter and to pick up speed.

I was wrapped in metal, a hell of a lot of it, and up here it was significantly colder than it was at ground level, but the deeper I breathed, the more I felt…right.

I climbed steadily, checking my mana. Instead of losing mana, I was starting to almost break even. Intrigued, I reached out, opening myself to the world around me, and felt...peace.

I didn't know how else to explain it. But the cold, the calm...it felt right and natural. And the deeper into the cloud layer I moved, the more it seemed to accept me.

Lifting my right hand, barely able to see it before my face, I clenched a fist, feeling the buildup of the ice that was forming. The water vapor was becoming a problem, I realized, as was the sheer cold that turned it into the ice that began to coat me. But a little focus, a little summoning...

As my own lightning rose in me, crackling to life in my palm, I felt a wash of heat. Lifting my left hand as well, I summoned more lightning, then sent it arcing between my fingers, dancing along my arms. It roamed up and across; my chest thrummed with the power as crackling lines moved up and down my body.

My mana dropped now, as the lightning sprung free, but all around me, the clouds swirled and eddied. Reaching my arms out to their full extension to the left and right, I ran lightning across them and into me, flooding my body with my power...before sucking down more and more mana with each breath.

As my lightning sank back beneath my skin, I felt invigorated. The mana loss dropped sharply now that I was no longer just allowing it to arc and sputter.

Lifting higher, I picked up speed, wanting to see it, to know it, and even when the mana all around me started to dip and reduce, I continued.

Water mana dwindled by the second, but now fresh bursts of Air and even occasional Fire came closer.

For the first time, holding myself between the physical world and the altered reality that I'd come to accept as the dungeon sense, I instead reached out, rather than in. I tried to envisage the mana all around me, much as I did with the mana as it streamed into me during meditation.

Inside, it raced and danced along my mana channels. I was normally flooded with thousands of different flavors, a mélange of different forms, many of which broke and shattered by the second.

Here, so high above the earth, I found dozens still. But instead of looking at the mana that was inside, I stared around and reached out to the mana that surrounded me, interacting out there, not internally.

Air was the highest concentration here, massively so, but Water battled for second place. As I lifted through layers, the darkest clouds gradually lightened.

As Water dropped away, and more and more Light and Fire picked up, my body started to warm again. As the seconds passed, I pushed harder. The dark grey shifted to lighter, which in turn gave way before fluffy white, until finally, I burst free, rocketing into the sunlit uplands.

I gasped. The shock of the bright sun compared to the cold and dark below made me squint for several seconds. But as I did, I swallowed and adjusted my arc.

I'd been pulling in mana at a hell of a rate, basically meditating on the move, I realized. Because I'd been nearly full already, instead of guiding it into me to be ready, I'd actually been pushing more and more into my ability.

In the darkness of the clouds, where I could see literally inches and then only just, I'd not noticed the speed I'd been going. But now? Now, I damn well did! I reached back, sensing for the dungeon, and found I must have overshot Washington by a hell of a distance. Hell, I could barely sense the *dungeon* in the distance now, and the northern dungeon beyond it?

Nope.

That was too far, making me instantly know that at least one point was going to be spent on the Reach Out and Touch Me class skill.

Regardless, though, even as I tried to do it again and found only the cold, I realized that my constant practice with entering the dungeon sense and doing things—working out at the gym, running…everything—it'd served far more of a purpose than I'd expected.

If I could learn to actively meditate while fighting? I'd become an unholy threat to anything with my magic.

Before I could look at that, though, I needed to deal with the shit before me, and that meant getting my arse back toward Washington.

Focusing on where the dungeon was, and knowing roughly where I had to be in relation to it, I turned, aligning myself, and dipped into the clouds again, pushing harder with my ability and wincing at the fresh buildup of ice and water vapor.

Literally, my armor was tingeing white as I dipped into the darkness. Only the pull of more lightning dancing across it helped to banish the cold again.

The mental image of me arriving, unable to speak through bloody frostbite, only helped to persuade me that I needed more. As I thought on the next stage of the plan, I dragged in a little more, and a little more.

Dipping free of the clouds again, I managed to suck in more Air and Water mana, feeding it into my channels, though nowhere near as much nor as quickly as I had been before.

I stared hard at the rolling hills and fields below, squinting as I tried to line up landmarks. I couldn't have gone *that* far, after all, and then I spotted a familiar sight.

It was a small town—though well spread out—by the name of Peterlee. The reason I recognized it? I'd once done a sponsored skydive here for charity.

It'd scared the bejesus out of me, and I'd basically been crippled by it. A tandem harness on a big guy to strap me to another big guy was never going to end well. By the time I'd actually landed? I was gloomily convinced that I'd done permanent damage to the meat and two veg.

Literally, I'd spent the entire trip down, not looking at the scenery or experiencing the wonder that my then partner had enjoyed. No, I'd spent it holding the harness for dear life and essentially doing pull-ups trying to save my testicles from bursting under the pressure of that goddamn harness.

Now, as I passed over the remains of the airfield, I remembered that viscerally, and I unthinkingly clenched.

That done, though, and the brief spike of remembered pain aside, more important and relevant details filled my mind.

First and foremost, that I had travelled at least twenty miles in a damn short period of time. And secondly?

The *airport*.

This airport was barely a runway and a collection of tiny craft, microlights, and small personal craft—all impressive to a non-flyer, but unimportant in the great scheme of things to me.

But, if I thought about *Newcastle* Airport? *That* was a hell of a point. A friend had once sent me a photo of the technology inside a large commercial jet, and although it'd been impressive at the time, and I'd sworn to never get involved with that side of IT, it'd stuck with me.

Now I knew why.

The inside of those things was incredibly complex, and each and every one had literally tons of dedicated computers. If I considered the hundreds of flights a day that took off from there, and the multitude of aircraft that were likely filling the sheds and hangars?

That could be a hell of a windfall right there.

I glanced down and adjusted my course slightly, unable to fly high enough to see Washington in the distance due to the clouds. I instead kept adjusting course as I went, before slowly drifting up and reaching out.

Now that I was looking for it, I could feel the strings that bound the others to me, and specifically the one that I recognized as Chris. The mad bastard, despite not needing to *at all,* had still sworn along with all the others.

So too had Robin. Her thread was gold, one that seemed to push and pull at me almost equally, letting me feel her uncertainty, her fear, and her...hope?

Fuck it, I'd deal with her soon as well. But the best bit here was that I could sense them through the clouds, and that meant that I could climb into them, then push out my lightning.

That was what Finn had meant when he said we needed theatre, and lots of it. It wasn't that I needed to wear makeup, tight pants, and pretend not to hear it when people shouted, "Behind you!" It was that I needed to make my entrance incredibly memorable.

He'd also called me a load of names when I'd used that comparison with him, as apparently I was such an uncultured swine that I'd mixed up theatre and pantomime.

Jez Cajiao

So sue me.

I picked up speed, deliberately pushing my lightning out. The crackles of power lanced and danced into the thick clouds, scattering in fractal patterns that were almost painfully bright.

As I descended, the pressures flowed and ebbed all around me. I longed to explore them further, especially the way that my lightning changed them. I could feel updrafts surging, ice crystals forming more densely around me, as I heated my immediate area but displaced other clouds and...

I could feel them just ahead, and I forced myself to stop, to just let the lightning be lightning. I started to lower myself back out of the clouds.

The last thing I wanted, if Chris and Robin had managed to gather a decent crowd together, was that I injured half of them with an out-of-control storm, after all.

I was, however, determined that if I could learn more about controlling the weather, then I would, as the power here was incredible.

Instead, I dropped from the denser layers. The dank fog resolved into wispy clouds, and then broke down further into faint blurring of the air at worst.

As I emerged fully from the clouds, I arced in around from the south to approach the western entrance, where we'd oh so recently stormed the place.

As soon as I saw them waiting, though, I felt that familiar twisting of my stomach in sheer panic. There were well over a thousand people out there, and at least half of them looked to be clutching some kind of a weapon.

"Well, fuck..." I muttered, shaking my head as I dropped farther, my body outlined in lightning and cloak flapping behind me in the steady breeze of my passage.

They'd gathered on what was laughingly referred to as the field, once large parking lots that served the shopping center and the surrounding buildings, but now had been half broken up to enable the people to plant vegetables.

The fields were currently full of people who ranged from waiting more or less patiently for my arrival—and the arrival of the food truck, I had no doubt—to fighting over the half-grown and now-frozen plants that had managed to take root. There were at least a dozen small scuffles that threatened to spread into much larger ones.

As I came in for a landing, I saw that Chris had managed to cobble together a raised platform for me to speak to the people from.

The boxer and truck had both left already, or one of them would have done, I had no doubt. Or the makeshift tower that had been built to watch over the fields would have worked as well, I guessed.

If the people hadn't torn it down as soon as they knew their former overlords were dead.

As it was, it seemed to be a collection of pipes and connectors that had been used for scaffolding and for events, then a simple set of planks had been put across the top. The whole thing looked incredibly unstable.

As I dropped lower, I sent out a single heavy blast of lightning across the sky, spreading fractally and smashing the air aside with a loud crash of thunder that broke up the fights instantly.

It also sent practically everyone to their knees in fear, hands raised to protect themselves, until they saw that Chris and the others were watching impassively.

Then it probably helped dispel the aura of ultimate power that I'd just created, when on landing—gently; it wasn't even like I landed hard, for fuck's sake—the central plank let out a great creak and then cracked under me.

I lifted myself into the air just as the plank split. An entire section broke loose, and I slowly revolved, drifting out and looking back as Chris winced and then shrugged.

"Sorry, boss!" he called up, and we both saw the way people moved away from him quickly, expecting him to be punished in some way.

I shook my head in disgust at that mentality and reached out, pulling my helmet off, and continued to fly, hovering and drifting as I did a wide arc, looking down at the people who surrounded me.

"People of Washington! I am Matt, the Dungeon Lord of Newcastle. We've come here today because one of your own, Robin, sought our help. We answered that call, freeing you from those who oppressed you. But our work here is just beginning." I tried to remember the speech I'd worked on a little as I dressed, and wished I'd damn well done more planning.

"The world as we know it has changed. Magic has returned, bringing both wonders and terrors. In these turbulent times, you face a choice—one that will shape your future.

"You can choose to remain here in the area and to forge your own path. If that's your decision, we'll respect it. We'll provide you with food and supplies for the next few days to help you recover and decide your next steps. But understand this: we won't return again, and the citadel that once imprisoned you will be torn down to prevent it from becoming a threat to others."

People turned, staring at the buildings, and the wall, clearly trying to decide what to do if the walls were taken from them.

"Or you can choose to join us in Gateshead, at Saltwell Park." I let that offer hang in the air for long seconds as I let the tension build. "In our dungeon, we've built more than just walls—we've built a *community*. A place where your children can sleep with full bellies, where your sick can be healed, where you can learn and grow. We have hot showers, abundant food, and as much safety as we can provide in this new world."

That got a few mutters, as well as a lot more focused stares from people as the thought of hot food and hot showers spread.

"But let me be clear: joining us means joining our cause. There's a war coming—a war for our very survival. In the dungeon, everyone contributes. Whether you become a mage like Dante, harnessing the power of Fire, a diplomat like Ashley, or a Druid like Chris who can make crops grow in barren soil—there's a place for you." I turned to Dante and pointed.

He grinned and lifted both hands into the air, then sent a blast of flames at least ten meters long straight up, with a roar like a dragon with intestinal issues.

"We have soldiers and scholars, teachers and traders. We're rebuilding what was lost—not just surviving, but thriving. And we're preparing for the battles ahead."

More and more people were nodding now, and smaller side conversations started up while others shushed those who spoke, wanting to hear what I was saying.

"If you join us, you'll have the opportunity to discover your affinities, to train, to become more than you ever thought possible. But it won't be easy. We all work hard—myself included. We have laws that protect and bind us all equally. Assault of any kind is not tolerated.

"The choice is yours. Stay and carve out your own future, or join us and be part of something greater. Help us build a new world from the ashes of the old. To those who choose to join: welcome to the next chapter of your lives. To those who choose to stay: I wish you the best of luck." I paused then, making eye contact with as many as possible before saying the last bit. "You're going to need it."

I let that hang there, then spoke again. "The future is in your hands. What will you choose?"

With that, I turned and flew back toward Chris and the others as questions started to be asked by the crowd.

"What do you mean we need to…"

"What kind of work?"

"Can I bring my husband?"

"I have children. Can they…"

"What gives you the right to tear this place down?!"

That last question was shouted at me, and I slowed, turning and fixing the crowd in that direction with a stare, my helmet held in the crook of my arm. People shuffled aside, making room for an older, red-faced man.

"I helped make this!" He gestured in the direction of the shopping center-cum-citadel and glared at me. "This should be our home—it can be! I say we stay!"

"Go for it," I called back. "You want to stay in the area? Feel free."

"Then you leave it be! You leave the building here!"

"No," I said firmly. "I won't permit another force to move in and use it as a base. Any other questions?"

"When will we get our food?" he shouted after a brief hesitation.

"What food?" I asked curiously, tilting my head to one side.

"The food you promised!" he spat. "Or are you already breaking your word?"

"I said we'd bring food for the next few days for everyone," I pointed out. "You'll get the same as those around you, and we'll do that for two days. At that point, we'll stop coming, and we'll tear down this building. As I say, I will not permit someone to use it to threaten my people. I'll leave the outer walls, though, so if you want to live in here then? Feel free. As I said, the choice is yours."

"I won't let you!" he roared. "You don't get to decide what we do. You don't get to force us out, or you're no better than the slavers, are you!"

"I'm going to leave you with a quote." I smiled. "I can't remember where I read it, and I'll probably bastardize it, but hey, here goes: 'If someone serves me dog shit on a plate, and tells me it's a steak, I don't need to taste it to be sure.' Do you understand what I'm saying?"

"No." He glared at me.

"It means I don't need to debate with you whether I'm better than the fucking slavers, and if you can't tell that already, then you go on enjoying your delusional dog shit."

With that, I started to move again, ignoring him as he shouted something that I guessed was probably abusive, right up until one of his companions grabbed him and dragged him away.

I landed close to Chris, and people moved hurriedly out of the way, as he snorted and shook his head.

"I never get people like that, you know?" he said conversationally, as we walked toward the main building. Jo, Kilo, Ashley, and Dante fell in close, with Robin and her friends trailing behind. "I mean, if he thought you were actually a bad guy like that, he'd never dare say that shit, because you'd rip his balls up and outta his mouth. But when he thinks you're a good guy? He has to try to piss you off like he's gonna gain something out of it."

"Assholes," I said with a disgusted grunt. "They're the same everywhere you go."

"Truth, brother," the big man said philosophically. "What's the first step then?"

"We get inside, do a quick tour so I can see what we're working with, and then we make a solid plan for the next stage," I said. "We deal with the locals, and we start the ball rolling with the dissolution of the building. Then it's down to you and me."

"What's that?" He cocked an eyebrow in question.

"You've got something to tell me, I'm betting," I suggested, looking him over. Unlike before, when he'd been looking like a recovering drug addict in the depths of going cold turkey, now he looked like he was recovering.

"Not much to tell." He shrugged, leaning in a little closer and dropping his voice as we moved through the crowds. "I got a class upgrade when I leveled after the boss fight. Changed my class from Druid to Primal Shaman, and well, you know how you said I'd been growing plants back there?"

"Yeah?"

"Yeah, I can't do that anymore." He grinned apologetically. "Sorry, dude. Part of the evolution was that my mana was turned inward, and now it's basically there to power my shift."

"Your shift? Like that tiger-man change that had Saros wetting herself?" I asked, and he nodded.

"Yeah, basically if I can get a token from any animal now, I can use it to power a shift to that form. Think of me as a shapeshifter, but one who needs a hit of the animal I'm shifting to, to make it work."

"And the one you used?"

"Simo's tooth," he admitted. "It was the last part of him I had, but I figured it was worth it."

"Thank you."

We both knew that we'd have won the fight without it. But we might have lost people if he'd not done that, and it sure as shit would have been a harder one. As it was, if I'd not tied all my Divine essence and Divine core to Robin, I'd have probably been fine, but it was what it was.

Thinking of her, I glanced back, catching her watching me, and she quickly ducked her head as soon as she saw me looking.

That was going to have to be addressed as well.

"So what now?" Ashley asked, just as Dante spoke up as well.

"Are you okay?"

"I am," I said, raising my voice as we broke through the nearby crowds, leaving them behind as we walked through now propped open doors of the shopping center. "Damn, this is fucking cold." I glanced around. "Why are the doors open?"

"People were forced into set areas if they weren't actively working," Robin replied, her face bright red as I glanced at her. "I, *we* thought it would help them understand that they can come and go as they want."

"And the kids?" I hadn't seen as many as I'd expected to, considering how many younger people were in the crowds.

"They're in the old tax building." She pointed across the parking lot to the black glass high-rise. "Everyone agreed we didn't want them out in the fields. But it was too cold in here to just let them roam, and the areas that were secure enough that could be made warm...well, there's a lot of bad memories in there."

"So you've got people watching over them?" I asked, and she nodded. "Fair enough. Robin, get your arse up here and talk us through what we're seeing. Then you and me need to have a chat at the end, when we've got things moving."

"Yes...Lord?" she said tentatively.

I snorted. "Matt is fine, or Dungeon Lord if you need to be formal," I assured her.

"But not God of the Storm?" she asked.

"The title is First Lord of the Storm," I answered after a minute of thought, then shook my head and sighed. "Fuck it, let's get this out of the way now. It'll just hang over the conversation anyway, and I'm not hiding anything from these people. They need to know what's going on to help us figure this shit out. Tell me about you being a Paladin."

"Ummm." She blushed even more. Her right hand dropped to caress the simple mace that I'd seen blazing with holy fire during the fight. She reached up, scratching the back of her neck with her left. "Well, I got a notification, in the fight, and it offered me a class choice, like you'd said it would."

We'd all been bringing her up to date with things when we'd been in the back of the truck, waiting to begin the assault. Thinking back, we'd all tried to give her and her friends a lot of general advice.

"So, first off, stopping to read a goddamn notification in the middle of a fight isn't a good idea," I said as diplomatically as I could. "Seriously, what were you thinking?"

"I was thinking that I was useless with the gun and I wanted to make use of the gear you gave me!" she snapped back, before apparently remembering herself and clearing her throat. "I mean…look, it gave me some choices, okay? Most of them, they were boring, but when it gave me a rare class, I remembered you saying that it was the path to real power." She looked at Ashley, who nodded encouragement.

"So, when I saw Paladin…it was the class I always played online," she admitted in a lower voice, as if ashamed and embarrassed by it. "I always wanted to be the Paladin, the knight who protected everyone. And the dungeon? The way you do things, it just fits. I want to help people, and it means I can do that. It gave me a boost to my Wisdom, my Constitution and Strength. It gave me two spells to start with, though they needed Divine essence to power, as well as mana."

"Tell me about that," I ordered. "That's why I passed out, because you essentially ripped all my strength from me."

"Oh God," she whispered, closing her eyes. "I know, and I'm so sorry!"

"Don't be sorry. You helped us win the fight, so that's good, but we need to know what and why before we can move on with things," I pointed out, and she nodded quickly.

"Okay, well, my Blessing of the Faithful is an AoE heal. It's a small one—a meter radius, that's it—but it means I can heal myself and anyone I touch. It costs a hundred mana per second active, and a single point of Divine essence, which I can hold five of at this level of faith."

"Yeah, I need you to explain that more." I shook my head.

"Ummm…" Robin scratched at the back of her neck again and bit her lip. "I don't know what to tell you, not really. It just said that I could use the power of my god to smite my enemies, and to power my heals, so I did?"

"Smite?" I asked. "That's the second spell you got?"

"Yeah, sorry. That's the second spell, and it's the same cost, a hundred mana and a single point of Divine essence. But it gives me a ten-second boost to my attacks, or I can channel it and it doubles the damage they do with each strike."

"Wait, double each time?" Dante's eyes went wide. "Linear or exponential?"

"What?" Robin frowned. "What does that mean?"

"I mean…oh gods, I need paper for this," he muttered, casting about, then giving up and trying to explain it verbally, now that we were outside the dungeon's reach and he couldn't just summon things. "So, let's say you did ten points of damage with each hit, right?" He nodded at her excitedly, and she nodded back, slowly.

"So, if you double that, you get twenty. So do you do twenty damage with each hit, or does it double again and again? Like ten, twenty, twenty, twenty for the ten seconds it's active, or ten, twenty, forty, eighty, and so on?"

"Oh, ummm, the second one when I channel it, I think." She looked embarrassed.

"Fuck me," Dante whispered, staring at her in shock, before looking at me. "Matt, I need Divine essence," he said quickly. "If I could do that with my flames, do you know what that would be like? I could make my Dragon's Breath melt through a bank vault in *seconds!*"

"Yeah, except it wiped me out," I growled; he blinked and then made an "Oh" face as he apparently remembered that minor detail. "In the fight, you were using the Divine essence, right? The first bits, when you were smiting the fucker. Then what happened?"

"I saw the damage it was doing, and I was suddenly so angry, so mad that…I wanted more and I just did it. I channeled it. The two points of essence I had vanished, but the power kept coming."

"Because it was being siphoned from me directly," I agreed dryly. "You nearly killed your 'god' to spread the good word. Now doesn't that sound like a great reason to avoid religion?"

"It would, if there hadn't been a handful of others learning to do it now that you've done it," Ashley agreed. "Since you passed out, the other pantheons started figuring it all out. You were the first to get a Paladin, but there's two more that got high priests and clerics."

"I saw them." I had vaguely glanced at them when I went through my notifications, but as I'd taken to, I'd filtered it into the "I don't care" pile because there were so many each day like that.

The notifications had started to become like spam emails, and I just didn't have the time to deal with that shit, though the discussion had prompted a new one.

New Evolving Quest Update: Divine Core Establishment (1)

***Congratulations, First Lord of the Storm! You've unlocked the initial stage of
your Divine evolution. Your nascent godhood has begun to take shape,
revealing the first steps toward establishing your Divine Core.***

Rise of Mankind: Age of Expansion

Current Objective: Master the Fundamentals of Divine Essence

Progress:

- *Establish your Divine Core 0/1*
- *Learn to safely channel Divine energy 0/10*
- *Explore methods of empowering followers 0/5*
- *Understand the risks and rewards of direct intervention 0/2*

As you delve into your newfound divinity, you're beginning to grasp the intricate balance of power and responsibility. Your choices in distributing your Divine essence will shape your path:

1. *Organized religion (slower growth, but safer)*
2. *Artifact empowerment (balanced approach)*
3. *Direct intervention (high risk, high reward)*

Warning: Your Divine Core remains unstable. Reckless use of your powers could be fatal!

Create and fill the first level of your Divine Core to gain access to the following rewards:

- *Unlock the Priesthood of the Storm Questline*
- *Unlock the Paladins of the Storm Questline*
- *Unlock the Defenders of the Faith Questline*
- *Level One Artifact Creation*
- *Survival...*

Continue to explore and master your Divine powers. Remember, First Lord of the Storm, with great power comes great danger. Choose your path wisely!

I read it over then banished it. It'd told me nothing new, though the phrasing had apparently changed slightly with the new information I'd learned.

I decided to reread it later, and pressed on.

"Okay, so moving forward, no channeling Divine essence until I figure this shit out, all right?" I said to Robin, who nodded quickly. "Great, now that's sorted, we'll figure the rest out, and I guess…wait, you're staying, right?" I asked, suddenly realizing I'd not asked her. "Joining the dungeon and staying, I mean?"

"Yeah, if I'm allowed?" she asked.

"Yeah, just wanted to be sure." I grunted. "Okay, what about your friends?" Glancing back, I saw them duck their heads and try to avoid my eye. "What's going on?" I asked them and her.

"You're a god," she admitted. "You can fly and do lightning and…"

"Fuck's sake," I groused. "Right, whatever. I'm a small god though, okay? Small *g* not big *g*…not yet."

"But you could be." Ashley spoke up quickly, and when I looked at her, she held my gaze, making me feel this was important. "Matt, if you're starting to develop powers you can share with others, and you're able to improve this? It could be huge. The Smite spell …imagine that was something that Chris could use in a fight, or Rhodes? If she could power it through her gun, and fire a full clip? Each bullet that does double the damage of the last before it? She could…what?" Ashley glanced from me to Chris as we both winced, looking at each other.

"Clip." I shook my head. "Sorry, Ashley. I used to call it that as well—movies, I guess—but the thing that holds the bullets for the gun is a mag or a magazine. A clip is what you use to load the mag."

"Is that *really* that important?" She glared at me.

"Considering it's the end of days and fall of civilization, it shouldn't be," I admitted. "But you know, speaking to people who know the difference? It really pisses them all off."

"Fine, I'll try to remember." She sighed. "You really need to work on the Divine side of things, though," she pointed out.

"I will," I assured her. "Okay, so we know what happened and why."

"I'm sorry," Robin said in a small voice.

"Don't be," I told her. "We learned something, and nobody was seriously hurt. It's not like there's a wiki, so we're all learning on the job as we go. Last question."

"Yes?"

"Why me?" I asked. "Was I all that was offered or what?"

"No, when I chose Paladin, I was told that all my magic comes from Divine sources, so I'd need to pledge myself to a god. And I couldn't just back up and choose something else, so when I saw your name on the list, I picked it."

"Glad I was such an important part of the decision," I muttered. "Okay, thank you, Robin!" I smiled, trying to take the sting of the dismissal out as I gestured around us. "Anything we need to know then?"

While we'd been speaking, we'd made it up the bank from the parking lot, and into the main building. Once inside, we'd seen the shattered security grates that had once held the doors to shops; we'd seen filth and cracked and scarred patches of stone.

There were areas where people had apparently just decided "here will do" and they'd made firepits, surrounded them with stone or metal, and then they'd lit them.

The walls, the ceiling...half the damn place was covered in soot. It was probably only that the doors were so poorly fitted and that everything was stone that had kept people from burning to death in out-of-control fires, or from smoke inhalation.

There were holes smashed in the ceiling here and there, but apparently without care for any kind of future the building had, as after what I guessed were torrential rains, they'd moved the firepits along and set up on a new fresh patch.

The marble sheathing that had covered the stone floor had shattered, leaving it spiderwebbed in cracks. Between them and the dozens of bullet holes, the apparent hits from random items, and then the random shit themselves?

There was a chair that had been half submerged into the wall, presumably by the stone mage for fuck's sake, a meter or so up, so that someone could sit up there and watch things.

I mean, fucking *why*?

I just shook my head and kept going.

The smaller shops on either side were made out as small apartments now, with beds and more in there, but they were also stripped of anything of value, which I guessed could have been done at any time, by the freed slaves or the former slavers' companions.

The larger shops, as we passed the entrances to them, had been reconfigured as massive barracks, and great fences erected inside them, complete with patched-together latrines that must have needed to be dug out each day.

"There's not enough room for everyone in here, surely?" I asked Robin, as we passed another larger barracks, and she shook her head.

"We were separated into smaller groups, and if your group was judged to have been shirking, then you didn't get to sleep."

"Right, they just did what?" I asked.

"They made us keep working."

"Through the night?" Ashley asked.

"We got a half an hour break every three hours to eat something, but that was it. And if we worked hard, we got to rest at night. If we didn't, we didn't," Robin replied darkly, making us all drop it.

The rest of the building was just...it was somewhere that I was determined to pull down, put it that way. The areas that were reserved for the boss and his cronies were places that would forever remain burned into my mind, as were the things we had to do to free people from the manacles, the stone restraints, the pit...

Jo had firmly shooed us all out at that point, only keeping Kilo, who was fairly fucking terrifying, I thought, to a normal human, but I got it. It was a time to make sure there were no men in the room, and definitely no weapons.

Whoever the Stone mage had been before the fall, the things he'd done after guaranteed him a place in the deepest depths of hell. And had he lived, I'd have made sure his passage was a painful one.

At the end of the tour, sickened and refusing to spend one more minute in the damn place, I stepped back out into the grey light outside, and stared up at the drifting snowflakes as they fell.

"Did that fucker know what the place was like in there when he wanted to claim it?" I asked Robin, gesturing vaguely at the group of people who still drifted here and there on the field.

She hesitated, then shook her head. "Probably not," she admitted. "He was on the wall teams, so never got to stay inside. They had to live in there." She indicated one of the warehouses on the outskirts of the site, and I let out a long breath.

"That's a relief then. Had he seen all of that and still wanted to live in there? It was hammer time." As I was resting my hand on the head of my hammer while I spoke, I think she got the message.

CHAPTER THREE

Outside, the mood was grim—of course it was, given the bodies that we'd just seen, the mutilations, and... I shook the thoughts loose. This area of the compound was raised, and I moved to lean on a nearby barrier as I thought, staring out across the field, seeing none of it.

There were easily half again the people there now that had been there when I arrived, and the buzz of conversation drifted even to us here, there were so many going on.

"So what do we do then?" Chris asked me.

I picked at a scale on my armor as I considered, not a hundred percent sure.

"I think we ask who wants to come, right now, and who wants to stay," I replied after a bit of thought. "We're at least two days from the dungeon being able to reach here. It's just too far, and that's even with the skeletons working constantly. But the trips for the truck to feed this many people? It's only twenty minutes' drive, right?" I glanced at Chris, who nodded.

"More like ten, but it's the weaving in and out of the stalled traffic." He scratched at his beard. "I mean, we could spend a few hours clearing all the traffic from the road, and that'd speed things up, but..."

"But it's a waste of our effort." I grunted. "Summon a few skeleton laborers, though. Get them to do it and to push the cars into the dungeon's radius. Then we absorb them and it offsets some of the cost of all of this."

"That works," he agreed. "So, we do that, but what do we do now? Like right now?"

"We offer them a chance to come with us," I repeated, straightening up. "If we even get a few hundred, it's a strain off the food supply here, and it gets the people somewhere warm."

"Saltwell Park?" Robin asked diffidently, joining the conversation, and I nodded. "I thought the dungeon was in Newcastle?"

"That's the heart of the dungeon," I explained absently as I squinted out across the people below us. "There's limited space, so we have the magic tower and the heart there, research and so on, though that's started being done at the northern dungeon as well now." I paused, thinking how best to explain it.

"Saltwell Park became sort of the main living area," I went on. "It wasn't intended to create two separate spots, but when we realized how many people there were there—and at first, they weren't part of the dungeon; they were a separate settlement—it just made sense to grow this way."

"It was organic," Chris added in. "It just sort of happened, stage by stage. If we'd started out with a definite plan, it'd have probably been elsewhere we set up things like that."

"Regardless, the park is now the bigger of the two, and there's more room for expansion, as well as a need for more things to be built there, so maybe we'll get that started right away. We can set off with however many want to go to the park now. If there's not that many, they can ride back in the truck maybe with each run, and then we start looking at the expansion of Barry's side."

"Barry?" one of Robin's friends asked—Laurence, I vaguely remembered.

"He was the leader of the community there," I said. "He's a good guy, though he's a bugger when he wants something. So no doubt I'll get an earful when we turn up with more refugees."

"Think he'll use it to get the park some upgrades?" Chris asked with a grin.

"Probably." I sighed. "Maybe a pool?"

"They could do with it." He nodded.

"A *pool*?" another of Robin's friends asked, goggle-eyed. Katee? I guessed.

"I told you we had some luxuries." I winked. "The pool is one of them. And yeah, it's nice, but it's at the Newcastle site, so it makes sense that we should build one there."

"And the lure." Chris nodded.

"The lure?" I pushed off the barrier and started to walk toward the ramp that led down to the lower area where everyone was congregating.

"Yeah, you remember?" he asked me. "We were talking about building the lure—not to draw in the monsters, but to draw in people. Like a fifty-floor-high tower block, but all lit and hard as steel."

"Ah." I nodded. "Yeah, that's what will probably have to happen if this many people move over eventually, or even half."

"How many to a floor did we work out?" Ashley asked, smiling at the looks on the newcomers' faces. "Two thousand, wasn't it?"

"About that," I agreed as we moved on. "So, before this gets out of hand, what we mean by the lure isn't a trap. It's..."

The conversation went on until we reached the bottom of the hill. People spread out to give us some room, falling silent as we passed, until I guessed I'd reached about halfway into the mass.

"Okay, give me a minute, and we'll see if anyone actually wants to join up," I muttered, before lifting into the air.

The murmured conversations on all sides fell silent as more and more of them stared in wonder.

"Hello again everyone!" I called out when I'd made it up ten meters or so. "Now I don't know if you can all hear me, and I'm not giving the speech again, but for now I'll reiterate the basics. In the dungeon, we have warmth, safety, and jobs for those who wish to come. You will be required to swear an oath, one that's magically binding, if you want to stay, to agree to work for a year and a day. But there's nothing dodgy in it. You can read the oath and my part of it, and come to me or my people if you think there's a problem.

"It basically says that you swear to be good, not hurt each other, not screw the dungeon over, and to help by working. My part swears that I'll not take the piss with the jobs I ask, that I'll protect you, and that I'll respect you. There's a lot more mumbo-jumbo, but that's the heart of it.

"If you're willing to take a risk on me, and you want to see what it's all going to be like, then you can come to our main site tonight. It's at Saltwell Park, so it's not that far, and we'll sort food, hot showers, and somewhere to live. If, in the morning, when I ask you all to swear the oath, you decide you don't want to? No hard feelings. You can leave and come back, or go wherever. At least you'll get a warm meal and a safe night's sleep on me.

"So, are there any volunteers?" I peered around. "If so, please head over to..." I squinted, seeing the truck with its escort approaching in the distance, and I grinned. "There!" I pointed to the far side of the parking lot, away from where the truck would be pulling up to disgorge its supplies.

"Over there, we'll be out of the way of the truck and everyone who's staying," I finished, thinking we might get a few handfuls of people moving over.

Then I started to wonder whether there was going to be space in the truck, as more and more people moved. But that was okay, because they were just shifting out of the way of the others, right?

Wrong.

Out of every hundred people who set off moving to the far side where I'd indicated, only perhaps three or four stayed behind to mill about uncertainly.

All the others? Yeah. I'd apparently really hit a nerve with the "hot showers" bit.

"Oh crap," I whispered, forcing the smile to stay on my face. I drifted down, landing next to a chortling Chris. "Don't you fuckin' say it," I warned him in a low voice.

"Oh no." He sniggered. "Wouldn't dream of it, oh high and mighty Dungeon Lord!"

"I will smite you," I promised him. "I have a Paladin, and I'm not afraid to use her." Then I saw the look on her face on the other side of him and closed my eyes, taking a deep breath. "Please ignore that, Robin...it came out wrong."

"He often engages his mouth without his brain." Ashley smiled, before going on. "If you're wondering about these two, you need to understand that they grew up together, and as much as they might look and act like they hate each other at times, they're actually the best of friends. Whereas with sensible creatures like women that results in us supporting each other, in simpler creatures..." She gestured to me and Chris. "That comes across as constant low-grade arguing."

"I don't know about your friends," Katee said after a brief pause. "But most of mine would have stabbed me in the back a lot worse than that."

"In a good way?" Ashley asked, and she nodded.

"Oh yeah, but you know, in public they were all 'OMG, you're so beautiful' and then in private, it was all that my ass was too fat and my tits too small. But in a good way, you know?"

"Said with love, and just a bit of cattiness." Ashley snorted. "Don't worry; I get it. Well, with Chris and Matt, it's because Matt just realized he now needs to explain to his partner Kelly, and her sister-in-law Aly, that they need to massively upgrade the living quarters. And instead of it needing to be done in a few days, as people gradually move over and join, it needs to be done today."

"And that costs mana." I sighed. "For this many people, a *lot* of mana, and it's mana that we're currently using."

"So, are you going to turn them away?" Laurence asked.

I shook my head, seeing the relief on his face at that.

"No, not now certainly," I assured him, nodding toward the families sprinting, carrying their kids from the old tax building, desperately trying to get into place in the mass before I did whatever I was going to do.

"Though I think some reinforcements would be a good idea, as I can't see marching this many people to the park going off without a hitch," I admitted. "I guess I'll start dealing with a few jobs. If you can start spreading the word we'll need to walk there in batches, Chuckles?" I asked Chris, who just grinned. I glared at him. "Seriously, will you quit that?"

"Yes, oh Lord!" he said theatrically, starting to prostrate himself as the truck came to a halt nearby.

The sight of Rhodes as she hopped down apparently reminded him of a conversation about not cutting me down in public, and he rapidly sobered up. "Sorry, mate. I'll get going," he promised, giving her a little wave. He grabbed Robin and the others, with a little shove to get them started.

"Come on, people, let's get spreading the word!" he said hurriedly. "We'll be setting off walking soon, so anything they want to bring with them, they need right now. Let's go!"

"What did I do now?" The new captain peered suspiciously at him. "Or more to the point, what did he do?"

"It's not important," I told her, deciding to throw Chris a bone. "So, I've got good news and bad…"

Ten minutes later, I sat in the passenger side of the boxer military APC, enjoying being out of the wind as I got comfy, before offering myself up for ritual sacrifice.

Also known as telling my partner I'd fucked up.

I thought about the best way to break the news, considered different phrasing, maybe ways to hide it, and then sighed and laid back. I closed my eyes and brought up my class skills, deciding to make one change before I "called" her and Aly.

I had four points to spend, and the very first one was going into Reach Out and Touch Me. It was an easy decision to make, considering I'd found that the radius that the dungeon considered "local" was about eight to ten miles, thereabouts, and the next level that was offered was a simple hundred miles, if I was reading the map right that I got on approving it.

It also gave me access to an expanded map, which was worth it by itself. But as I tried to zoom out and see more, or skip across to Sunderland and see just how wrecked and ruined the city had been, I got an error, with everything greyed out.

Apparently this was another of the things I couldn't do until the core was upgraded.

I'd recently gained access to the second level of Arcanist, and damn. I wished I'd looked at the class skills before now. I silently berated myself for my stupidity, before reading them over again from scratch.

Of course the goddamn things had changed with me reaching the second level of Arcanist! Of *course* they had!

Class Skills:

Class selection: Arcane Dungeon Lord

Imbue: You may choose to give freely of your own manapool to imbue an item or creature of the Dungeon with magic. This ability can fail, and spectacularly so; however, creations of wondrous might can also be brought into being. Be wary. (Selected)

Evolution: Foresight: No longer are your creations the chance things they were…now see the true potential of a creature! (Selected)

Arcane Fusion: Combine multiple magical essences or items to create more powerful and complex enchantments. This skill ranks from 0 (Basic Fusion) to 5 (Legendary Amalgamation).

Monster Master: No longer do the creatures of the Dungeon view you with apathy or irritation when you pass by. Now they are devoted to you! This skill ranks in levels from 0 (Interested) to 5 (Worshipful). (Current level: 2, Revered)

Evolution: Lord of All! The creatures of your Dungeon know their true master, and those who follow willingly can now receive arcane gifts that match their level of devotion! (Selected)

Evolution: Arcane Symbiosis: Form a deeper magical connection with your creatures, allowing you to temporarily inhabit their bodies or share

---

their senses. Ranks from 0 (Surface Link) to 5 (Perfect Synchronization). (Current Level: N/A)

Arcane Breeder: Some Dungeon Lords wish for only the purest strains to survive, while others enjoy the randomness of evolution…select the genes you wish to see and promote them!

Evolution: Elemental Infusion: Introduce elemental traits into your creatures' genetic makeup, creating hybrid beings with unique abilities. Ranks from 0 (Minor Traits) to 5 (Elemental Lords). (Current Level: N/A)

Artificer: You may gift magical artifacts to your creations, and when combined with Foresight, these creatures will gain significant bonuses to magical item creation and replication. This skill ranks in levels from 0 (Curiosity) to 5 (Legendary). (Current level: 0, Curiosity)

Evolution: Living Artifacts: Create semi-sentient magical items that can grow and evolve alongside their wielders. Ranks from 0 (Awakening) to 5 (Artifact Ecosystem). (Current Level: N/A)

Arcane Pets: Your sentient Dungeon inhabitants can gather and breed pets, but where before there was an element of random chance, now you may lure those you wish into the range of your tamers. This skill ranks in levels from 0 (Magical) to 5 (Legendary Creatures) (Current level: 0, Magical).

Evolution: Familiar Bond: Forge deep magical connections between your dungeon inhabitants and their pets, granting shared abilities and enhanced communication. Ranks from 0 (Empathic Link) to 5 (Spiritual Fusion). (Current Level: N/A)

Insatiable Curiosity: Random Sentient Dungeon Creatures will now have the chance to be spawned with an Insatiable Curiosity. These creatures can be put to work in your Research Nodes to increase Research by a staggering degree. This skill ranks in levels from 0 (Incompetent) to 5 (Genius). (Current level: 4, Gifted)

Evolution: Magical Researcher! Before, your researchers were generalists, plodding along at their task, be that a better toilet seat or a converter; now they stand a chance at developing true magical gifts, and at learning the secrets of creation! This skill ranks in levels from 0 (Novice) to 5 (Master). (Current level: 1, Apprentice)

Evolution: Eureka Cascade: Researchers' breakthroughs can trigger chain reactions of inspiration across your entire dungeon, temporarily boosting all research efforts. Ranks from 0 (Minor Ripple) to 5 (Innovation Tsunami). (Current Level: N/A)

Manafield: Your Dungeon's Manafield will now passively expand at 10% more than the previous rate, enabling greater growth in a shorter period of time. This skill ranks in levels from 0 (Restricted) to 5 (Expansive). (Current Level: 1, Limited)

Evolution: Tides of Mana! All life creates mana, as do elemental interactions. Now through the wonders of gravitational magic, you can start to draw more mana into the area of your Dungeon. This skill ranks in levels from 0 (Gentle) to 5 (Vortex). (Current Level: 1, Steady)

Evolution: Mana Crystallization: Convert excess mana into physical crystals that can be used to power artifacts, enhance creatures, or traded as valuable resources. Ranks from 0 (Crude Crystals) to 5 (Perfect Lattice). (Current Level: N/A)

Reach Out and Touch Me: Your Dungeon is no longer only controllable when you are within its own environs. Now you can interact with it at increasing distances. This skill ranks in levels from 0 (Local) to 5 (Interstellar). (Current level: 1, Regional)

Evolution: Gates! No longer is the Dungeon a distant creation. This skill unlocks the creation of the Gates, transportals that can be built inside the Dungeon and activated at a remote location to provide a stable link between the two points.
This skill ranks in levels from 0 (Single Gate) to 5 (Unlimited) (Current level: 0, Single).
Evolution: Multidimensional Anchor: Establish your dungeon as a fixed point across multiple dimensions, allowing for easier interdimensional travel and resource gathering. Ranks from 0 (Dimensional Echo) to 5 (Nexus of Realities). (Current Level: N/A)

I read and reread them. I'd had four points, and I'd just reached out and spent one of them without even bothering to look at the goddamn options.

As they were? They could be incredible! I hesitated, then forced myself into the dungeon, shifting to the control center and appearing before Aly and Kelly as they discussed something.

"Goddammit!" Aly hissed, jerking back. "I swear, Matt, I'm gonna find a way to put a bell on you!"

"I've got good news and bad," I said grimly, before glancing at Kelly and forcing a smile. "It's better news than the one you gave me last time, though."

"Bad news first; is everyone okay?" Kelly asked, and I nodded. "Okay, then what?"

"This place…" I shook my head. "Look, it's two pieces of bad news. First, I'm a fucking idiot. I spent one of my class skills without thinking about it so that I could access the dungeon from farther afield."

"And that's bad because?" Aly asked after a brief pause, watching me.

"Because I'd unlocked upgrades to my damn class skills and I didn't read them first!" I snapped, before closing my eyes and taking a deep breath. "I'm sorry," I said after a few seconds. "I'm not angry with you. I'm mad at myself."

"It's okay. So that's one set of bad news. Is it major? Like, will the dungeon collapse because you did this, or was it just a bit foolish?"

"Foolish," I admitted.

"Then that's all it is," Kelly approved. "You'll think in the future because you made a mistake…no great hardship. So, moving on, what's the *bad* news?"

"The site here is a fucking nightmare. These people don't want to be inside it, and there's apparently been little effort to subdue the monster populations in the area. We can't just let them go home. And they don't want to."

"And they can't spend another few nights in the citadel place?" Aly asked, and I shook my head.

"You know what it was like for you at the park before I came?" I asked, and she nodded. "Imagine that, but if those who were in charge gave up pretending to care about you or doing anything but rape, murder, and worse."

"Right." She took a deep breath, then nodded. "So they can't go into the building, not if there's another option. Go on."

"I asked for volunteers to come to the park," I said. "My plan was that even if we got a few dozen, it was less here who needed food and more shipped in." I looked from one to the other. "I underestimated the way people felt."

"Okay, how many do we need to move to the park?" Kelly asked, her eyes already distant as she considered options.

"About three thousand and climbing," I admitted. "There's no food, no heat, and just painful memories here. They're desperate to go anywhere."

"Oh…" Aly winced. "Matt, that's a lot of people…"

"I know," I said softly. "Like I say, I fucked up. But if we can't give them this…"

"Then they see us going back on the deal already and they won't trust us," Kelly finished for me, covering her face with her hands. "Oh, God. Okay then…well, we've got the undead stripping the area already, and anything that goes over a hundred thousand in mana storage is being used to power the dungeon's upgrade. If we keep it below there, we can build section by section on the accommodation block, I guess." She bit her lip, reaching up with an incorporeal hand to tug on her ponytail as she thought.

"Maybe if we do it stage by stage, and ask people to eat in their rooms, that'll free up space in the canteen and…"

"Matt, do you need to be here?" Aly asked. "Are you free to help or are you needed elsewhere?"

"I need to check these class skills. There might be something I can use to help. Then I'll need to do an escort run to bring them to the park."

"You'll need a few teams to help you. Scepiniir?" she suggested distractedly.

I shook my head. "No, there's enough here. What I'll do is do the trip by groups," I decided. "That way, you don't need to spend the mana, and it can help with the housing. If I do, say, five trips of two hundred people and then we see where we are, that keeps the park from being overwhelmed all at once as well. We'll need to tell Barry..."

"I'll deal with it. You sort your side. But you and your people need to stay outside of the park—" She broke off. "That's not going to work, is it? Dammit."

"What?" I asked.

"The vurms, the quarantine. All of it." She sighed and shook her head. "It's been breached in a dozen places already, we think, as much as we tried not to. I guess that's a concern for later. I'll speak to Barry. You go sort this, and then later we'll discuss the class skills, if you don't mind sharing?" Kelly asked.

"Oh no, I was planning on keeping it all a secret," I said with a weak grin, before sighing. "Honestly, I'm sorry, girls. I genuinely didn't think this was even a concern. Maybe a few hundred at most would have said yes to moving into the dungeon in the short term, and then we'd have to have Ashley busy as hell for the next few weeks doing a 'hearts and minds' campaign to convince them to move over and trust us.

"Instead, there's thousands here and more coming. They've been stashing their kids in other buildings so they don't have to be in there, but the buildings they're using are all glass walled, and a single monster attack—" I broke off. "I'm going to look my class skills over like I said; then I'll start running groups through to Barry. I'd rather use the truck, and I will for the smallest children and weakest people, but I'll have the majority running alongside me."

"Do it," Kelly said. "We'll make it work. Somehow."

I blew her a ghostly kiss, then ducked out, realizing as I blinked in the boxer APC that I'd never even got to tell her about the good news.

As much as all of this was a ballache, as much as we needed to get things moving—and goddamn was that a real and imperative need—and the next twenty-four hours were going to be frantic with running and possibly dangerous actions...we'd done it.

The people here were desperate to join us, and they'd accepted that there'd be an oath. That made it easier to enforce and to be sure all of them took it.

We'd found a way to be sure of new people coming in, and as much as it was going to kick our ass, we'd needed to start addressing the elephant in the room with the park anyway.

It was like looking at climbing a mountain. The hardest part was always getting started, because from there it was just step by friggin' step.

Jez Cajiao

I squinted out of the front windshield. The drifting snow was continuing, and I shook my head in amazement.

I'd lived in the area most of my life, literally ten or so miles away for the last few years, and all over in the various foster homes. I'd never seen as much snow in that entire time put together, as I had over the last week.

Literally, here it rained for fun.

The north of England was notorious for being too cold to be comfortable for most people, too warm for snow and a proper winter, and lashed by the constant rain and storms that rolled in off the North Sea. We were the narrowest point of the UK until you hit the central beltr of Scotland. And if the temperature had dropped far enough this year alone with everything that had happened?

The thought of the snowfalls to come as the winter really got started were seriously concerning.

Like "let's build a giant dome and live under it" levels of concerning.

I stared for another few seconds, then shuffled over and cracked the door, waving to get Ashley's attention as she was nearby, speaking to Jo.

"What's up?" She jogged over, her cheeks rosy red with the cold air.

"Five minutes and we'll move out," I told her, thinking quickly. "As soon as the truck is unloaded, see how many of the most infirm and the smallest kids we can fit in it, and get together with Rhodes. I want an escort for them and as many people as she believes we can reasonably support and protect. Probably no more than a few hundred on foot, but that's her area of expertise.

"As much as I'd like to just start shuttle runs with the truck taking people over and over to the park, these people don't know us, and they're not going to want to send their kids in the back of someone's truck if they can't go as well."

"We could send them in family groups in the truck?" she suggested, and I shook my head.

"I'd considered it, but if we do, we've got a load of fit and healthy people riding in the trucks, and the weakest will be waiting days to do the trip. This way, we can run alongside, or slog anyway. When we hit the park, we send them in and peel off to run back. The truck drops people and gets filled back up, then drives back with the food; we unload it, then rinse and repeat. I'm working this shit out in my head, and Dante will probably tell me my math is wrong, but if we can move three or four hundred per run, and we take fifteen minutes at the end to rest between runs, that should give us about five thousand a day, if we do it for a full twenty-four hours."

"That's…that's a hell of an ask," Ashley said after a few seconds. "That'd mean we'd…" She shook her head. "I don't think we can do that. A thousand, maybe two if we really push it, but no more."

"Get with Rhodes and Dante and figure out the details. The first batch, we'll take a smaller number of people so that we can work out any kinks. For the weaker people who can't keep up, as soon as we reach a section that we have influence over, we can erect a secure station," I said after a few seconds' thought, wincing as I realized my mistake.

I'd been thinking of the weakest and ill as simply cargo, and the rest running all the way. I—and the others with a few levels—could probably sprint it each way for most of the day without issue, and all the way around the clock with the frequent breaks on return.

The issue was the humans we were escorting. We'd be lucky to make a steady jog with them.

"I'll get with Rhodes and sort out a plan. Five minutes till we leave might be pushing it. If we can make it fifteen, we can do a lot more."

"Do that then," I agreed, before settling back and closing the door as she jogged back to rejoin the group.

I could see her waving to the others, pulling people in and speaking quickly. I snorted a laugh at the glare I was getting from Rhodes, and the horrified O of Dante's mouth as Ashley explained the plan, and that he'd be running alongside as well. Then I pulled up the class upgrade options.

I needed to get shit moving.

CHAPTER FOUR

I read my way through the class skills, working in order from top to bottom, and with an eye to the future more than right now.

Imbue was a good one. I really needed to start working with that more. The void blade, for example, was an incredible weapon, but the vague, unfocused imbuing of the blades I'd done before had left them unfinished and chaotic in reality.

Each had the potential to be incredible, but as the wielder bonded the weapon, the effects were unpredictable. I could create copies of the magic weapons once they were awakened, which was awesome, but until that point, I genuinely didn't know what we'd get.

I'd set them up and, as the prompt said, I could literally imbue a weapon or a living thing, and "creations of wondrous might" could be brought into being.

I'd also created a load of monsters that basically exploded, created a golem that was linked to my life force accidentally, and I'd shredded my skin while creating an exploding spear when I tried to pour in an insane amount of mana.

The most successful creations I'd made were the swords, and I'd done those by literally pouring my personal mana into the weapon and just stopping when it felt "full."

Then I'd forgotten about it, and I'd copied the damn thing into the dungeon's memory and I went on along my merry way.

It wasn't until later I realized that the basic standard-issue blade I'd been making for people was magical and could shift its properties depending on the person who activated it.

When I tried copying an awakened weapon? The cost was an order of magnitude higher than the unawakened version. They also tended to have unexpected benefits or costs.

The void blade, for example, required not just the power of muscle to swing the fucker—though it could cut through pretty much anything that wasn't magic resistant, as I'd found out with that bastard ogre.

The downside? It needed mana and *health* to power it. Go into a big fight swinging that thing and it might not be the enemy that killed you—it might be your own weapon.

Others had vastly different effects. One, I knew, left frostbite as an additional effect; another, burning. Some were light as a feather. Others couldn't be lifted by anyone who wasn't a bodybuilder. And the effect when a blow landed? It was like being hit by a truck, never mind the effect of the sharp blade.

I'd not been working on imbuing things in, well, *forever*. Just too many calls on my time. But the last time I'd taken a skill in this, I'd unlocked Foresight, which gave me the potential to see what the weapon would be when finished.

It was a great ability, and I'd not even tried it yet. Too damn busy. So, cursing, I resolved to do that as soon as I had five minutes to scratch my arse.

The new evolution of the skill was Arcane Fusion. Unlike the other two, it wasn't a yes/no skill. I didn't "buy" access to it and have it, only constrained by the skill I showed and focus in the crafting. No, for this I could buy up to six ranks inside that skill, making it possible to make a blade that dealt both fire and ice damage, or was manageable to swing and yet still hit like a meteor.

Probably.

Knowing my luck, if I tried to combine them, I'd end up with a sword that exploded. Or if I evened out the massively heavy and the weightless sword, I'd get a magical sword that was perfectly normal and weighed the appropriate amount for a sword.

Heh. Murphy's Law right there.

I put that one on the back burner, resolving to look at it once I'd had the chance to explore my other options.

Monster Master was a fun one as well. I'd taken two points there last time, taking me from interested to revered, and still the bastard wraiths had turned on me as soon as they were given the chance.

That gave me two ways to look at it. Either the skill was such a weak one and ineffectual that it was basically wasted, or…the only reason we were still around was that it was so powerful that using it I'd managed to overcome that shit.

I genuinely didn't know what it was. I'd taken Lord of All already, and that basically rewarded the loyal dungeon creatures with new abilities and more. I was fairly sure that Kilo's meteoric rise in power and spells was an example of that, but I also didn't want to ask him randomly "Hey, are you getting free shit because you like me or not?" considering that was guaranteed to either lower his regard for me because I clearly didn't know what was going on, or make him annoyed that no, he wasn't.

I'd work on that later, somehow.

Arcane Symbiosis was the new skill I'd been offered in that tree. It was a basic "see through my eyes" spell, as near as I could tell. I could trigger it and see the world through the eyes of my minions, but I was fairly sure that Kelly could already do that, and I'd be doubling up on our skills there.

It seemed a waste. Sure, it'd be cool if I had points to burn, but not right now.

Arcane Breeder hadn't been chosen yet. I didn't have the creatures of the dungeon "gettin' jiggy with it" and I didn't see the advantage there. But the new version, Elemental Fusion, was interesting. Basically, I could introduce enhanced

Fire elements to the kobolds or whatever, which was cool in theory, but if it meant they needed to be done as the next generation came along?

Either I was experimenting on their unborn embryos, or waiting for them to make the beast with two backs and sitting in the corner calling out, "Don't mind me, just keep going. You're doing great" while magically enhancing their sex lives.

It felt a bit like the old "God is watching you" sketches, where a hot couple are getting it on in the bushes and God was enjoying the view, cancelling his Pornhub subscription in favor of the real thing.

Hard pass.

Artificer was cool. It let my dungeon-born have a much better chance of creating magical artifacts, which were incredibly needed. The evolution to that was that the new version could create semi-sentient living artifacts. The description wasn't incredibly helpful, but it basically meant that my void blade would evolve and grow more powerful...if, you know, I'd created it with that skill.

Bit late now.

A plan for the future, possibly, though.

Arcane Pets? That's more like it. Not so much because I really wanted a pet—I didn't have the time—but looking at it as a method to get Chris—and others like him—materials? Or getting better pets for Beta and her kobolds?

Just the thought of the kobolds riding into battle atop a set of velociraptors was awesome.

Sure, this was saying Arcane Pets—I already had a level of it that had basically brought in fuck all useful—but that wasn't the point.

I'd barely unlocked it, and it went from magical all the way to legendary. And that wasn't even considering that the new evolution was "familiar bond," which would allow people to bond the creature as, you guessed it, familiars! We'd have witchy types with black cats, kobolds with kittens and giant war dogs, and of course, Chris with a goat or a sheep, no doubt.

Kinky bastard.

Then I snorted. If I chose that, and it ended up with the animals being able to talk? The tales the Welsh sheep would tell would be enough that an entire generation would run.

Insatiable Curiosity was the research option. We'd taken that all the way to level four, and considering that it started at zero, and was now gifted? I took the final stage in that without pause. Boom. Genius level attained.

That wasn't to say that all my researchers were suddenly geniuses. It just meant that there was a much better chance of a dungeon-born being spawned now with that as a perk. And the things they could achieve? It could be a game changer.

That was an easy choice to make.

Then the skill had evolved from that to include the option to unlock Magical Researcher. I'd previously invested two points in that so far, taking it to apprentice tier. That gave them a chance to discover new spells, artifacts, and more.

The new evolution option was Eureka Cascade. If my researchers had that skill, and they made a breakthrough? That breakthrough could inspire others. At first, that'd have been a cool idea but of limited utility, considering that Aly was the main, and only, dedicated researcher we had for a long time.

Now, though? We had two sites set up for it, and when we started upgrading the park, we'd be creating more there as well. The knock-on effect of this skill could be huge. I'd have to consider that.

Manafield was next. That was a game changer—or it could be.

The manafield was a curious thing. It was both the area of influence the dungeon had, and the area of mana it could pull from. So the more space we had, the more mana we could pull in.

The downside was that if we invested too heavily in there, it was in theory possible to actually starve the dungeon, by draining the local area of mana and fucking us all over.

Obviously, that was a nightmare looking to happen. But fuck it—checks and balances and all that.

The first two points I'd taken in this area in the past meant that the manafield was expanding twenty percent faster than it would have done naturally anyway. To combat any draining of the area, I'd then taken two more points in Tides of Mana, the first evolution of that skill.

That basically used a form of gravitational magic to pull in more mana from the surrounding area. It was still dangerous, but not, well, *really* bad.

For now, it was limited by the speed and the area it covered. At first, I'd thought that it was fine, that we'd just pull in more and more mana and keep reaching farther out. But that meant that eventually we'd hit that problem, even if we went for the full-on vortex option that lay at the end of the upgrade path.

I hoped I had a solution in mind to that, and it seriously involved Jack. But we weren't there yet, and I wasn't even sure I could really pull it off.

The evolution for that skill was Mana Crystallization, and that…that was tempting. Anything that was excess would be automatically converted into crystal; those crystals could then be used to power things and that could be a game changer.

It wasn't that we couldn't just create the crystals ourselves. We could—we had the ability now. We'd pretty much learned it back when I accidentally infused a spear with so much mana that it blew up.

We could create the crystals easily enough through the dungeon when we needed to as well. It was how Aly had made the power systems for the shotguns; they were essentially mana-powered rail guns.

We'd then further proved the concept worked for different shapes and sizes as well when Finn fucked about with inlaying the mana crystal in my breastplate, establishing that it wasn't just something that I could do, but that was possible for anyone to work on.

No, the game changer here was that the mana storage devices we had were limited, and they were for the dungeon. Once that storage was exceeded, the mana was just lost.

We regularly spent anything and everything we could get because we were always in the situation of having more needs than we did production. But every so often, that changed.

If we were to do this, we'd not waste that opportunity. Instead of the mana being bled off into the ether, we'd get crystals that could then be used to power things, and that seemed like a no-brainer to me.

Moving on from there came the final option, one that I'd already spent a point in today.

Reach Out and Touch Me was basically making the dungeon remotely activated. Even from here, I could now reach Kelly and the others, and as I went farther and farther afield, I'd increase the range.

Currently with the latest upgrade, I was thinking it was about a hundred miles. It wasn't exact; the system was alien designed, which was why it had reached eight miles in one direction and nine in another, with just under ten in a third, but it all evened out.

The first evolution of this skill was Gates, and they were literally what it sounded like: transportal gates that connected two fixed points and allowed transport between them. We had the most basic level unlocked right now, and that allowed us to join one other gate to the nexus portal we had back home.

The plan was definitely to have the northern dungeon connected using that, and that as we set up additional arms of the dungeon farther afield, we'd unlock and set up more.

The new evolution of this, though? Multidimensional Anchor.

That was fucking terrifying, frankly, as I already had enough shit going on here that I couldn't imagine adding more dimensions to the fucking mix.

"Establish your dungeon as a fixed point across multiple dimensions, allowing for easier interdimensional travel and resource gathering. Ranks from 0 (Dimensional Echo) to 5 (Nexus of Realities)."

That was the text that came with it, and damn. I was tempted to just stay the hell away from it entirely, but the "resource gathering" mention made me curious.

But curiosity was for when I had some goddamn spare points that weren't valuable anywhere else, not for here. Fuck it.

I had two points left to spend now, as I'd increased the range for access to the dungeon and the researcher level to genius. I also chose a single point in Mana Crystallization as the third point. It only unlocked the most basic, "crude crystal" level, but that was better than nothing, and anything we overproduced moving forward could be bled into them. Then, hopefully, if nothing else, I knew I could draw from them and it'd get us around the issue of not having mana potions still. Goddammit.

The last point was a hard one to spend.

There was so much that could help us, so many details that could be the difference between survival and not. But in the end, I assigned the point to Eureka Cascade.

With those skills upgraded and unlocked, I sat back upright, having slumped a little while I was working through the options. I turned to the passenger window, before cursing as I jerked back.

Chris had moved up to the window when I was distracted and had pressed his face to the bulletproof glass, smushing it and staring at me, waiting.

The bastard burst out laughing, and I kicked at the inside of the door, torn between calling him the asshole that he was, and thanking him for the lighthearted distraction.

As much as I obviously couldn't tell him that, because he'd be unbearable after, he was a hell of a friend. The comic relief side of things when I really needed them was wonderful.

"You know, if you're not careful, your face will get stuck like that." I jumped down from the boxer as he moved back out of the way, then I drew in a deep breath of the cold, crisp air.

"Joke's on you. This *is* my normal face." He rubbed his nose as he relaxed.

"Joke's on Becky, more like. Poor girl, having to wake up to that monstrosity," I replied.

"She does call it monstrous," he agreed easily, falling into step with me as I started walking toward the others. "But you know, it's not just the length, it's the girth as well."

"*Monotonous,*" I corrected. "Though the rest is right, I'd heard. She does call you dull and boring in bed, and yeah, she complains about how uninspiring both the length and the girth are."

"Good one." He nodded in respect. "That was quick."

"Thanks…"

"But then that's what Kelly always says to you, I hear. 'Wow, that was quick'…and it's generally with either her voice filled with despair that she'd barely gotten started, or elation that it's over already and she can paint her nails."

"Damn, dude." I shook my head. "How long you been working on that?"

"Awhile," he admitted. "You were clearly busy, and a few people kept trying to come and interrupt you. So I told the others to keep working on things and that I'd keep guard over you."

"Thanks, man. Any excuse to goof off work, eh?"

"You know it," he agreed happily. "So, what's the plan?"

"You fuckers run along in the snow, the refugees get carried in the truck and the boxer, and I fly above like the god that I am."

"Damn, I hate you at times, you know that?"

"I wonder if I could somehow manage to have a nap while I do it as well…" I mused, before dismissing the jokes, snorting and shaking my head. "Seriously, though, it's going to be hard. Us running the refugees back and forth is going to take a lot of time, and any monster nests in the area are going to unleash hell if they catch them coming."

"Then we just make sure we eliminate them all," Chris said firmly as we reached the others.

"Sir." Rhodes straightened, nodding to me. "We've got a plan for the evacuation. I need to go over it quickly, then have you sign off if you're ready?"

"Go for it." I glanced at the others, seeing the worried look on Dante's face and the determination on Ashley's. There were also similar looks on the faces around the periphery of the group, including a handful of Scepiniir I didn't know the names of yet.

"We can fit thirty in the truck rear, with one guard on the tailgate, one driver and four children in the cab. Using the boxer, we can have one driver and nine others inside. That gives us forty-three people. Utilizing the full complement of guards we have, that gives us a maximum number of two hundred people on foot who we can protect.

"We've got thirty guards, counting my team and your personal one, as well as the freshly arrived dungeon-born, but it means we're losing any control at this end. To combat that, we summon five corpse lords and have them set off with us from the park on the return journey.

"That means that there's a small chance of a mishap on this side when we're gone, but I judge it unlikely. With two hundred and forty-three, we take the most direct route. On the way back here, we use a further five corpse lords to clear a lane of the highway. They then push the cars into the path that the dungeon is expanding along, which means we can absorb them as we go. As soon as we've gained enough mana, we produce another boxer.

"This clears the sight lines, so that we can see farther as we travel, and limits the ambush points as well as enabling us to go faster. The new boxers are considerably more secure than the truck, and as we summon more and more of them, that'll increase our options significantly.

"The group will clear the path as we go, essentially trampling the snow and making sure that it stays as clear as we can make it. For now, there's not many options with regard to the distance and any rest points, but we can probably make it there in about an hour."

She paused, seeing that I was opening my mouth and went on quickly.

"Yes, *we* could run it in a lot less than half that time, but these people aren't us. Some will be wiped out running for five minutes, and that's not taking the snow into account. When we get to the park, we'll add kickboards and handholds to the side of the truck, and people can jump on and rest in relay as well.

"We alternate running and walking until we reach the park. Once there, we peel off and circle back, leaving Barry's people to take care of the refugees. Depending on how far the influence has reached, it might be worth setting up a rest point on the way, so that people can stop and catch their breath. What do you think?"

"It's barely a mile beyond the edge of the park that we've claimed so far." I shook my head. "By the end of the day, it'll be halfway, and there it might be worth it, but the cost is high for a single day or two of viable use as a rest spot. Better just to push through," I replied after checking.

"Very well. This plan should, if we're lucky, get us around two thousand from here today. We'll be able to add a few more people to the trip using the kickboards and so on from the second run. If we add another boxer later today, that gets us up to maybe three thousand a day if all goes great, though I think this is only the beginning."

"Why?" I asked her, glancing around at the masses of people standing, shivering in the cold still. "Can we move them back into a building?" I added. "There's no point in them all standing out here."

"They don't want to go and miss their place in the line." Rhodes sighed. "Believe me, I've told them several times to go back and rest, that this stage will take several days, but they don't want to hear it."

"Then let's make it clear." I lifted into the air and raised my voice; the crowd fell silent. "Okay, everyone! This stage, as Captain Rhodes has told you all, will take several days! You cannot stand here, in the cold, for that long. Please, go inside, relax and we'll load in relays. The way this will work is…"

A handful of minutes later, I landed. A small number moved off, looking uncertain, but the majority stayed exactly where they were, watching one another, waiting for one of them to leave, so they could move up the line.

"Fuck's sake," I muttered, getting annoyed when I saw how many kids were being clutched to their parents in the cold. "What the hell are they playing at?"

"Think we could use the markers?" Dante suggested. "You know, like we did for the teaching runs and to separate them out when we set up the various groups for the army?"

"They don't want to leave because they're worried they'll miss their place," Rhodes agreed. "A ticket or something would work, but it'd take an hour or two to write them all out."

"We'll spawn them at the park and bring them back," I agreed. "Good idea, Dante. For now, well, this is gonna take what, an hour?"

"About that, sir," Rhodes agreed.

"Then either they'll get sick of waiting by the time we get back or they won't." I sighed. "Let's load up those we can now, and I'll have one last try. Then they can do what they want while they wait for their turn."

With that, we started moving people out of the crowd. Literally, the oldest and weakest—which wasn't always the same thing—were separated out first and loaded aboard the vehicles; then their families were picked out to run alongside. The rest were ordered back.

After two minutes of people being asked, then told, then shoved back, I launched myself into the air and unleashed a huge bolt of lightning as thick around as my leg, into the air with a boom of displaced air.

"BACK!" I roared.

People scrambled backward, several being trampled as they lost their footing in the panic. Jo and the Scepiniir were moving already, as were others. They were quickly patched up, though the time it took made me furious.

"What the hell are you playing at?!" I shouted across the heads of the crowd. "You think this is the way to start your tenure with us? You think we *want* people who'll trample the weak to grab onto the side of my truck and *demand* to be let aboard?" I stared out across the crowd, glaring at them.

"We *asked* you to get back, then we *told* you. The next time I have to do that, we'll also be telling you that you just forfeited your chance at any life in the park as well!"

I shook my head. "Do you understand? In your panic, you could have killed people, all because you want to get a goddamn shower sooner than the person next to you! When we return, we'll be handing out tokens. They'll tell you where you are in the line. And no, it won't be the first in line who gets the token. So go inside, get these poor kids out of the cold, and rest! Each run back will be loaded with food, and you can relax around the fires, okay? Standing out here in the snow while we run back and forth is only going to provide a tempting buffet for any monsters that we miss, so don't do it!

"Remember that you're not animals, you might have been abused and mistreated, but your new life starts today! You'll need to work to earn it, and to achieve your full potential. So trying to threaten your fellow citizens is a shitty way to do that! For now? Go.

"Go inside, go home, go wherever, but you can't wait here. And if you ignore me and stay?" I asked, seeing a few people glaring back at me. "Well, that's your choice, because the people we want to come and join us? That's the people who understand patience, who can take direction and listen to goddamn orders. We'll be offering the tokens to those people first. So, waiting here? You're just going to get cold and miss your chance!"

With that, I turned my back on them, checking over the truck and boxer, the guards who were forming up and the two hundred or so who were nervously standing around in the area we'd told them.

"Okay, Captain!" I called out. "Let's roll out!" I'd always wanted to say that, but I managed to keep from doing it in a robotic voice. And no matter how good my magic was getting, I'd still not figured out how to transform myself into a truck.

CHAPTER FIVE

The single corpse lord that we'd brought to start the vehicles was put to work then. The crank handle turned with a level of power and smoothness, as well as monotonous determination, that only the undead could manage.

It took literally seconds, but seeing the effort that the damn thing had to put in, I couldn't help but curse. One of the first inventions we needed once the Glass core was up and running was a decent starter motor.

The sound as the starter caught rang through the air. The coughing roar of the engine as the vehicle started up was almost music to my ears. The massive construct yanked out the handle, then moved to the boxer, repeating the process with ease.

Ten seconds later, the wheels turned; the crunching of the snow under foot and wheel began, and the bedraggled mass of humanity started to walk quickly, headed for the exit.

It wasn't far, a hundred meters or so, and the corpse lord was put to work opening the gate…only to expose a road full of people who were struggling up it.

My first thought, as I'd flown higher, clearing the wall and seeing them, was that we were under attack. And then it was to curse inwardly at the realization that although it was great that we weren't, there were also enough people here who had clearly run off to find others and then had come back, that it was going to be a nightmare to get in and out at this rate.

The truck and boxer ground to a halt. People screamed at the sight of the corpse lord, and then I floated over the wall and hovered over them, giving the same speech again, making it clear that no, we couldn't just take the rest of them, and no, they couldn't just run along behind and hope to keep up, as we'd not be able to protect them and the others.

They were to move off the damn road, then move inside, get settled, and we'd take them to the park in groups over the next few days.

Inevitably, a bunch of people simply refused to listen, who believed that the rules didn't apply to them, and that nobody would mind just them trying to push their way into the ring of people we were escorting.

Once one of those had been grabbed by the scruff of the neck and hauled out, then thrown into the snow-covered bushes and told to basically fuck off and that he'd just lost his chance…well, that made people get the hell out of the way and hurry inside to rest and wait up.

I got it—really, I did—but if they weren't going to listen now, then I doubted they'd listen later when they were told that they needed to work and to help.

Robin was left behind with her people for this run, as I wanted her to help get them all organized and be seen as more of a leader in the community. So with that distraction gone as well, I lifted higher in the air and started searching.

It didn't take long to find our first visitor slinking through the trees: a goblin…a lone one, which I instinctively distrusted, and then a pair of others a few hundred meters back from him that crept along as well.

The road ran down the hill from the shopping center, then up onto the local highway. Both sides of the road were bracketed with trees—which, in my opinion, was bloody stupid, considering the group had been running low on wood, and they were reducing their sight lines—but the left side of the road then led out over Princess Anne Park.

The park was around five hundred meters across, and perhaps two miles long, bordered in turn by houses, the highway, and repeated small industrial estates. But that it was still there?

The goblins that were approaching through the narrow band of trees toward the road had clearly followed the mass of migrating people, and now they looked confused to all hell to find the huge vehicles and marching soldiers passing back in the other direction.

"Rhodes." I zipped back across and dipped down low; she raised a hand to show she'd heard me. "Off to the left, thirty meters ahead and ten or so to the side of the road, there's a small party of goblins coming in that direction."

"Want me to make them dead?" She was already peering ahead.

"A few." I dropped down lower and spoke in a normal tone. "Kill most of them, then send a Scepiniir to track them back to their camp. They look to be wild, but we need to know, and either way they'll be useful for training."

"On it." She barked out orders as the boxer hit the bottom of the declining road and started to pick up speed. The truck followed suit, and the people started to jog, then run, splitting into two columns that ran in the tire tracks of the vehicles.

I lifted higher into the air again, looking out over the trees, noting no more visitors coming, and flew in that direction. From there, the screams as two of the Scepiniir leapt onto the goblins from hiding were barely audible.

The screams did help the refugees to keep focus and pick up the pace, though.

The trip, beyond that, was pretty uneventful.

Ten minutes or so in, when we hit the main highway for the area, we saw more and more traffic, as well as more burnt-out cars and signs of recent attacks. But nothing was foolish enough to try to jump such a large group.

We were on the highway for perhaps half an hour, maybe a little less, but it was as soon as we came off it and started back into the residential areas that the next visitors came out.

Surprisingly, it was a small family, four people: a mum, dad, and two girls. The kids were about ten and four, and the sound of the approaching engines had clearly drawn them out. They started waving gaily covered flags and cloth to get our attention as they ran down the road from a side street.

I flew down to them, leading the column as I was, and saw the way they instantly backed up.

"It's okay," I assured them, holding my hands out to make it clear that I wasn't a threat to them, only to have the man—I assumed he was the dad—shout out to me.

"Leave us, demon!" he called, brandishing a cross at me…like that was going to do something.

"What?" I touched down and walked a few steps closer. "Hey, look, I'm Matt…"

"You're a demon!" The mother clutched her children to her legs as they turned their faces away, hiding in her skirt. "We want nothing to do with your kind. Let us pass!"

"You're trying to get our attention…" I pointed out.

"Not yours!" the dad replied. "The army!"

"My soldiers," I said. "We've managed to make some of the vehicles work again, and we have a camp nearby. Hot food, hot and clean water, and safety—"

"Demon worshippers!" he bellowed, before pulling a knife with one hand; he kept the cross in the other, starting on some long and complicated speech, in a voice that shook between terror and determination. "Exorcizamus te, omnis immundus spiritus…"

I stared at him in disbelief. "Are you…"

Then I shook my head and lifted back into the air, hovering a few feet off the ground, and spoke scathingly. "I'm no demon, and I'm trying to help people. If you want to come to Saltwell Park, that's where some of our people are. If you want to stay here? Fine. For the next few days, we'll be driving back and forth, bringing more refugees to safety. Then, after that, we'll pass by now and then. Step out, flag us down, and we'll take you in, as long as you'll help the community. If you try to attack us, it'll end badly for you. But if you stay here? I doubt you'll live much longer."

That was true. They all looked tired, filthy and half starved.

I lifted higher into the air and turned from them.

My instinct was to try to rescue the kids, to grab them and take them to the park, because I "knew better"; I knew what was really going on. But I couldn't do it. I was no kidnapper, and no parent would let what they believed was a demon take their kids without a fight.

I resolved to sort out a little hearts and minds mission with Ashley, sooner rather than later.

With that in mind, I made sure the perimeter was clear, then dropped down and filled her in, before returning to my post, as she made a note to reach out to them soon.

The trip to the park was perhaps another twenty minutes. We'd slowed more and more as we went, due to people collapsing from exhaustion as much as anything else.

These were people who were used to working the entire live-long day thanks to the slavers, but they were mainly doing stationary jobs, or moving short distances.

They had basically built themselves into physically strong workers, but they'd not run in months. By the time we were perhaps five minutes from our destination, we ran into the first roving patrol. They helped to escort us in, with my small team peeling off as soon as we'd handed over to Barry at the entrance to the park.

We all knew by now that the chances of us being infected by a vurm, any of us, was incredibly low. We "knew" that the vurms died when the queen did, but it was safer if those of us who had been to the camp still limited our interactions with people.

That meant that as people were escorted into the park, they were taken into a small building that had been summoned to one side of the entrance, and they were met by medical volunteers.

They stripped, washed, and were examined to make sure there weren't any obvious wounds that needed tending—or that signified a vurm accessing them—and then were provided with their clothing repaired and cleaned, and were escorted into the park proper.

While they were doing this, and the injured were being unloaded from the vehicles, ready to have food summoned in their place, me and mine were heading back to Washington as quickly as we could.

I'd landed for this part of the journey, running alongside the others, and seeing the way that more and more were flagging as we did.

"Come on, people!" Rhodes called a few minutes into the run. "Ten minutes and we'll be overtaken by the truck. Then we all jump in and get a ride back to start it all over again!"

With that wonderful encouragement, we kept going. The ten corpse lords that Kelly had summoned for us on arrival were following us in two groups as well. I sucked the cold air down, and I just gave myself over to the joy of good health and strong muscles.

The first set of corpse lords broke off only a few minutes into the run, aiming for the dead cars by the side of the road, and shoving them into the manafield as we went.

They collapsed into motes of light. Their essence streamed to the dungeon and fed it. But all too soon, we left the most distant point the dungeon had reached, and the corpse lords fell behind.

They knew what they were to do. Their job was simple enough, after all: clear the road, feed the dungeon. That's it.

The other five thundered along behind us, and I wondered whether it'd be worth creating a skeletal steed.

We'd done it with the trikes, after all, although they were so slow they really weren't worth the investment of time to try to improve on.

Soon enough, the transports overtook us, and we jumped up on the sides, using the kickboards and handholds, picking up speed a hell of a lot as I continued to consider and plot.

I came up with, and discarded, a dozen plans by the time we reached the old shopping center again. But in the end, I decided that the one that we had was the best for now.

The corpse lord reopened the gate for us, and once inside, we set people to handing out the tokens, unloaded the food and supplies using the other five corpse lords, and loaded up again.

Rinse and repeat, basically—hour after hour, we did this. It took around an hour to cover the distance from the shopping center to the park, then half an hour to return, unload and reload, then go again.

All told, by the time we dealt with the idiots, the new arrivals, and the occasional monster attack enroute, it ended up at two hours per trip, with the average of around two hundred and fifty people each time.

We "rested" in the back of the truck each time on the way back, or hung onto the kickstands. On the sixth trip, we'd managed to break down enough material for a new boxer without it costing us anything from the other pots. We even managed to keep going for the full twenty-four hours.

Twelve trips, each with around two hundred and fifty people now, and by the end, as Rhodes and I agreed that we could do no more without rest, we'd managed to evacuate a total of nearly three thousand people.

The most badly wounded and disabled were transported in the additional boxer. Although it didn't end up increasing our overall capacity for the lift, it did mean that we didn't leave any behind nor lose space.

I was damn proud of that, but by the time I awoke—I'd forced myself to stay at the shopping center in a room that was put aside for us—it was to some very welcome news.

"We think it'll be another three days, that's all," Aly told me, grinning as she said it.

I was laid on my back, my body still drifting through the last stages of sleep, dipping back in and out, as I'd appeared back in the dungeon sense, finding her and Kelly—no surprise there—working in the command center.

"Before the Glass core is active?" I asked, still trying to get my brain in gear.

"Yeah. The bigger changes in the core have reached the halfway point. Those to come seem to be minor now. And the way that the conversion has gone...honestly, I think it'd be sooner if we stopped drawing on it, but obviously we can't do that," Aly offered.

"No, we need to draw on the mana we're collecting," I said. "These people had a shitty enough time. If we offer them food and safety, then tell them it'll be a few days, and they have to wait longer? I don't see it ending well."

"We heard that some were ignoring you and trying to make it on their own," Kelly said softly, and I nodded. "How many did you find dead along the road?"

I sighed. "Too many," I admitted. "We found signs of them more than actually finding them. Clearly, whatever monsters are in the area are feasting well, and we now need to find the nests and clear them out."

"You warned them not to do this," Kelly pointed out, and I nodded.

"Yeah, we did. We also knew they'd not goddamn listen. There's always some fuckers who think they can just do what they want."

We'd found the first traces on the way back from the first run, though we'd not been sure. As soon as we'd left, there'd been those who had set off behind us, running along and deliberately keeping far enough back that they believed we weren't sure if they were there—we knew—and close enough that they could keep us in sight and run to us when they got scared or threatened.

Those groups hadn't lasted long. Most had turned back within the first few minutes as they fell farther and farther behind. But some individuals kept going.

By the time we were halfway, there'd been one of those individuals left in sight, and the others had all fallen back or returned.

We'd agreed that we'd take as many as we could safely monitor and protect, but if we stopped to wait for stragglers outside of the group, or we strung out the guards to watch over them as well, we opened the main group to being hit and much larger losses of life.

That was why I'd been so goddamn clear that people shouldn't do this.

On the way back, though, we'd passed splashes of blood. Torn clothing and abandoned packs of belongings.

What we'd not passed, at first, were survivors or bodies.

We got back, we warned people, and we went again, and again, and again.

Each time, there were always a few who decided to risk it. On two trips, people actually made it to the park. We passed them on the way back and we let them be; it was their right to risk themselves.

Now, though, as I looked back at it all and wondered what the hell possessed them to risk it, I sighed and pulled up the details on the dungeon. The core was as they'd said, getting closer to completion.

The core changed with each iteration, and currently, as it ascended to the Glass level, it was not only pushing out more conduits, it was also changing from the glossy steel of the last core, to a deep sea-green.

It looked to be made entirely of glass, inches thick, layered atop the earlier cores, with just a hint of them visible through in the smoky depths.

Where it'd gone to the size of a basketball last time—now, well... I didn't know what ball anyone played with that was that size, but the fucker was getting *big*.

It was half a meter across, basically a large beach ball maybe? But where the original core had hung suspended between two spikes of silvery metal, the core area had expanded, and now its room was significantly larger.

Those spikes extended from the floor and ceiling, and now more lifted from the walls on all sides, a square room instead of the virtual broom closet it'd been hidden in before. Four spikes jutted out from the compass points, pointing inward and generating a force that crackled and danced.

It called to me, that power, and I nodded in understanding as I realized that my affinities were now visibly interacting with the dungeon.

Lightning arced and danced down the pillars, leaping from one to another, and arcing out again from the core, bathing the chamber in light.

The lightning was a part of me, and I just knew that furry turd Thor would be purring himself into insensibility over this fucker.

What it meant for the dungeon long-term, I genuinely didn't know. But what I sensed straightaway was that for the Storm Titans that I was hoping to raise? This could be a hell of a boon.

I was the only one so far, the first and only member of my pantheon, and apparently my success was pissing a few people off, judging from the whole "we're watching and we hate you" message I'd gotten recently.

Regardless, though, what I really needed now that I knew the core was nearly upgraded, and that my elemental affinity was affecting it, was to spend some quality time with my goddamn ascension.

It went on the list, along with the other three hundred jobs for the day.

Moving from the core, I lifted up through the dungeon and out, appearing over the heart of Newcastle. I stared down, seeing the difference that a— Fuck me sideways with a chipmunk dipped in batter!

There were over a thousand skeletons working in relays now and… I paused, squinting as I double-checked that. A solid increase in the mana was being generated, but it seemed wrong, somehow.

A thousand skeletons were generating a million mana a day now, according to the details, but…there was something off with that. Something was massively wrong. I couldn't work out what it was, just that it wasn't right.

I dipped back to Aly and Kelly, finding them working silently, and I slid in, waving to get their attention, and waited as politely as I could.

"What's up?" Aly asked me after a few seconds, before shaking her head. "Kelly, I don't like that look."

"What I— Oh, fuck's sake," Kelly whispered, covering her eyes with one hand. "Now what?"

"I don't know," I admitted. "Look, this might be absolutely nothing, okay? It might be totally unconnected, but…something seems wrong."

"Go on." Aly sighed.

"Mana," I said. "We get what, a point of mana per brick we absorb?"

"About that." Aly nodded.

"Right, so we've got a thousand skeletons working on the project, right?"

"That many?" Aly asked Kelly, and she nodded.

"Yeah, well, it's six hundred on the expansion role, and four on absorbing, but yeah, why?"

"Okay, four hundred skeletons, and they break down a brick in how long?"

"About ten seconds?" Kelly guessed, not seeing the issue.

"Let's check it." I whisked us all to a nearby site where the undead were working under the supervision of a bored, and then terrified, lad who looked to be maybe sixteen.

"Sir, umm… I wasn't goofing off!" the boy said desperately. "Honest, I wasn't!"

"You were staring at the wall, zoned out," Aly said. "I saw it, and I hope we don't need to discuss this again?"

"No, sir!" he said quickly. "Uh, ma'am, uh…"

"Just pay attention," Kelly said soothingly. "We know it's boring, but it's an important job, so please, pay attention, okay?"

"Yes, Mistress!" He nodded frantically.

"Good lad." She sighed, as the pair drifted over in the dungeon sense to where I hovered, watching the nearest skeleton.

"What's up then?" Aly asked me as she came to a halt.

"Ten seconds," I replied tersely. "It's taking ten seconds, on average."

"Right? That's sounds about the same as a human, right? I mean, it used to be a little more, I think, for the lower-leveled cores, but…"

"It's wrong," I ground out grimly, reaching out and tracing the mana as it cascaded from the collapsing brick and then drifted in the direction of the dungeon.

"In what way?" Kelly asked concernedly. "The skeletons need some tweaking, I'm sure, but—"

"It's not just them." I saw more and more of the pattern and focused, following the mana as it drifted toward the dungeon.

I could see the mana density all around us—the areas that were made up of the strongest naturally generating mana, anyway. I'd always been able to see the way that the mana collapsed from an object, streaming into the dungeon to feed it. The issue?

The light of the mana streamed toward the dungeon core and fed itself into there—that was fine—but the stream of mana seemed to only be visible for a few meters, if that…and it just faded away as it went.

We knew we earned roughly a point of mana per brick absorbed. But if that was the case, with four hundred skeletons producing a single point per ten seconds…

"Fuck's sake, where's Dante when you need him?" I muttered, before forcing myself to just work it out, blurring the three of us back to the dungeon control center. The screen nearby blanked and started to print out the figures as I worked them out.

If four hundred skeletons produced a single point every ten seconds, that was four hundred every ten seconds, which was two thousand four hundred points a minute.

Sixty minutes in an hour, that was a hundred and forty-four thousand points in an hour. And in twenty-four, as they didn't need breaks...

"Don't forget the higher mana items," Aly added in worriedly as she apparently picked up on some of the issue. "We've been getting about one in twenty bricks, works out for an average of a hundred points extra per twenty bricks, or one percent gets five hundred on average. Makes it easier to work out."

"Okay, so...working this out from scratch..." I started again. "The skeleton has twenty-four hours of work in a day, so can—on an average of ten seconds per brick—break down eight thousand, six hundred and forty bricks a day. To break that down further, with one percent of that bringing in another say five hundred a day, that gives us..."

"Twenty million points of mana a day." Aly sat back and grinned challengingly at me before I could figure it out. "Twenty million, seven hundred thousand and one, four hundred and forty points."

"So where the fuck is all of that going?!" I almost shouted, before trying to calm myself and stop, to think through it logically.

"It's...it's sustaining the dungeon," Kelly said softly.

"What?" I squinted at her, then gestured for her to carry on.

"The mana...we know now that the connectors that run from the core to the converters stop the loss of mana from one end to the other, right?" She clicked her fingers. "What if...what if the breakdown of mana is the problem? There's no nearby connector, or at least not one that's close enough, so the mana is dissipating on its way to a point that can pull it in!"

"So we need conduits?" I muttered.

"Conduits!" Kelly groaned. "Not connectors, but yeah, you knew what I meant. What if the mana being broken down is failing enroute to the dungeon? That'd be why the ambient mana here is as high as it is, and why we've not really seen any issues from draining the area with so many converters. What if we should have run out of mana before now—what if that's the secret?!"

"What secret?" I asked.

"The...look," Kelly said, changing tack. "You know how the other dungeon fairies were pissed with you? You said they thought you've been harvesting dungeons and thought you must be doing something wrong, right?"

"Yeah?"

"And yet, despite not knowing what the hell we're doing, we're *still* one of the top six dungeons in the world?" she pointed out. "How the hell does that work when we're just bumbling along, making mistakes all the time?"

"Well, thanks for that resounding endorsement." I grunted.

"Matt, honey, I can blow smoke up your arse, or we can sort this out and maybe figure out something important. Which do you want?"

"I'd not say no to just the blow…" I muttered, then grinned. "I was only playing," I assured her.

"Good." She sighed. "Okay, so really, we should be one of the lowest-level dungeons, right? I mean, the Gateshead dungeon must have known about the ability to break things down, and integrate creatures into the dungeon sense to do that, but it didn't. Why not?"

"Maybe…it couldn't?" Aly wondered, suddenly sitting forward. As she did, she summoned a mug of hot chocolate in her right hand and slurped from it, leaving a splotch of whipped cream on the tip of her nose, before wiping it free and sucking it off her finger.

"What if the dungeons and the fairies are programmed to avoid detection?" she suggested. "I mean, that makes sense, right? Up to a point, they'll need to stay hidden, to try to get the place built up before they start doing anything else. You said that one of them had said they need to build to a certain point, then they do deals with the surrounding populations and enable one of them—or a pair—to become the new Dungeon Lord and Lady or whatever."

"So you're thinking they're all working on a plan of keep hidden as much as possible, while we've been fucking up but power-levelling by stripping the surrounding area?" I suggested, before grinning.

"So we're possibly the only one, or at least one of only a handful of dungeons that are free enough to do this," Kelly pointed out, before grinning evilly. "No wonder they keep wanting to do deals with us! It's not the tech, or anything that we'd been thinking they were looking for. It's the secret to the levelling we've been doing! I bet they'd have been sneaking it into innocuous chats! Just 'Walk me through the average day and we'll see where we can help…'"

"Fuuuuuck," Aly whispered, sitting back and shaking her head. "Damn, no wonder they're so happy to help! If they can figure out what we're doing…!"

"They could surpass us in days." I nodded. "We need to keep this quiet. But it also shows just how much we've been wasting our advantages."

"What advantages?" Kelly asked. "Shit, we're constantly trying to figure this all out and—"

"And we've been thinking it's the manafield and the Tides of Mana skill that's been helping us, but we were wrong," I said. "If we're looking at this as a way to expand? We need to figure out a new solution, because the mana that's getting lost, that's drifting toward us and that's just either breaking up in the ether or that's being lost to hang about, uncollected…that's all that's been keeping us going."

"So if we increase the converters massively, they're going to suck the area dry," Kelly finished for me, seeing the issue and nodding. "We'd win for a few days, maybe even a few weeks, but what we've been doing is dragging millions of points a day from all the matter we've been breaking up, and dragging it inward toward the core, keeping it fed."

"Not entirely," I mused, scratching at my chin as I thought about it. "Does the local area look any more saturated to you?"

"No…" Aly waggled her hand from side to side. "Well, maybe, but I'm not sure?"

"I think it's a darker blue," Kelly said after a few seconds of us all looking. "Does that mean…?"

"We've only recently stepped up the intake," I pointed out. "Originally, we were getting one point of mana per brick because we were processing them inside the dungeon. Literally a few dozen meters from the core. Now, as the skeletons have pushed outward, they've increased in numbers, but the mana they've been earning is dropping like a stone. Because we *know* we get a point of mana per brick, we just didn't consider the speed they were working at. If they were doing this, breaking down the mana, while inside the dungeon's immediate area?"

"You mean right next to a converter with a conduit attached?" Kelly sat back, tucking her legs under herself as she focused.

"Yeah." I nodded. "Let's test that."

The conduit was the longest part of the process to arrange, selecting it and the freshly summoned Earth converter that stood in the middle of the plaza outside the building that the skeletal army were working on, then growing the link out to that point.

It took nearly an hour, in which time I'd left the dungeon sense, grabbed some food, and busied myself with a trip around, collecting the others up.

No surprise that I was the tardiest of the bunch. Everyone else had been up for hours, and I'd apparently been left to sleep while Chris and the team did two runs.

I was torn between cursing him, as they'd sacrificed their overwatch ability by leaving me to sleep, and praising the fucker for thinking of it and letting me get some rest.

I'd not realized how much I needed it. I seemed able to go literal days now without sleep and it didn't affect me, until suddenly I crashed and burned.

Stupid human body.

I found Robin, who was in a small room off the side of the former "throne room" and knocked, getting a growl of impatience as she continued working, facing away from me and reading over some papers.

"If this is someone with a reason that they should be bumped up the list and allowed to go to the park in the next run instead of waiting their goddamn turn, so help me God, I swear they're going to regret it, and be moved to the last run of all!" she announced loudly to the air, before slowly turning to glare at me.

That glare drained off her face when she saw it was me, and she visibly gulped. "Oh God, I'm so, I mean, uhm…" Her words tumbled over themselves in her haste to get them out.

She lunged to her feet; her chair toppled over and struck the table next to her. A half-cleared plate of food crashed off the far side and shattered as a glass clattered to the floor, water running down the wall.

She jerked to a halt then seemed frozen, unsure what to deal with first: the food that was now being wasted, the chair, or the water that was apparently almost as valuable as the food.

I couldn't help but smile.

"Don't panic," I said as reassuringly as I could. "Look, I've been sleeping, and I apparently missed Chris taking a team and doing a few runs. Any chance of a catch-up?"

"Uhm...sure?" She shook her head. "I mean, yes, Dungeon Lord." She straightened. "What would you like to know?"

"What have I missed?" I asked. "Has anything happened?"

"Not really." She shrugged, clearly much more comfortable as I sank into another seat and gestured to her to do the same.

I reached out through the dungeon sense to absorb the mess as I always did...and remembered that they were nowhere near here in their expansion. Dammit.

"There's been another boxer added to the numbers, and I've asked for a truck next, but Chris said no." She glanced at me to see whether I'd overrule him.

"I agree, no to the truck," I said firmly. "It's about ongoing use, as much as value. The truck is a short-term benefit. It could be used to transport people or goods, but it's basically canvas covering it. It's not secure in any real way. The boxer costs half again as much as a truck, but it can take direct hits from an RPG. Monster attacks are going to be ineffectual against it unless it's a big fucker. A truck? It can be attacked easily. We're using it because we've got it and we're protecting it, but moving forward, we'll be phasing it out," I explained.

"Ah, okay, that makes sense, I guess," she mumbled. "Well, there's been nearly eight hundred who have gone this morning, and we've got people organized with the tokens. There's been some fights and some thefts—people stealing tokens—so I started a register. Now, if anyone gets a token, they write down their name, and if the token gets handed over with a different name, that person is kicked to the back of the queue."

"You're giving them a second chance?" I asked, surprised. "When they took the tokens from others?"

"Yes and no." She sighed. "Look, I don't have the authority to be telling people they can't come to the dungeon, so I've been making a note when people are particular assholes and why, or at least what I know about it. For example, one guy, Michael Moors, he apparently mugged a guy and stole his token, beat him unconscious and hid him, tied up with duct tape."

"Shit. Okay, we definitely don't want—"

"He gave his token to his ex-wife's new husband. His kids want nothing to do with him. They chose to go with the ex-wife in the divorce, and then they wanted to stay with their stepfather. He raised them from literally toddlers, while Michael was in and out of prison. The youngest has a degenerative disease, but no proof that he could show to get bumped up the list. The assignment of transport for her would have her moving out later tomorrow. Instead, she left last night, along with her stepfather and sister. They were healed by Jo before they left, about ten minutes of work on her part, and that little girl will never have to worry about it again. As soon as he'd heard that she made it to the park safely? He turned himself in, explained what he'd done and why, and led Katee to where the guy was he'd beaten up and hidden. We had no clue."

"So, he did the wrong thing, but for the right reason." I grunted, shaking my head. "Now what the hell do we do with that?"

"That's my point. He offered to join the army, said he'd do whatever we need, as long as we keep the girls safe. As near as I can tell, they had no clue what happened. And their stepfather? Well, he was told to take them by Michael, and he had a token offered. He didn't ask how or why…just did what he needed to do to keep his kids safe."

"Well, fuck." I grunted. "And before all of this? Before we freed them, was he one of the ex-prisoners?"

"No, he guarded his kids. They were on the outside of the camp. He kept them and the husband hidden, and he raided the supplies here daily, kept his ex's family and a dozen other people safe."

"And again, he was raiding and stealing…killing, I'm betting?" I glanced at her, and she nodded. "And yet we killed them all as well. Hell, I kicked off with the army for attacking us when they didn't know any better, complained that they didn't even try to make friendly contact, and yet I did the same here. Fuck."

"So…I put him at the back of the group, with the other volunteers." Robin nodded.

"Volunteers?" I asked, curious.

"There's seven so far." She sighed. "People who have done deals, threatened or stolen, but for similar reasons. They've all volunteered to be the last, to be here in case the monsters come when there's nobody else left, as long as we let their families go earlier."

"Dammit," I muttered. "All right, seven of them, right? Anyone else in a similar position?"

"Not that I can think of," she admitted, frowning. "There's been others, but some have been thrown out. I told them to wait and when the captain made it back, I brought them to her and she ruled on them being allowed into the park or banished. I tried to come to you, but Chris wouldn't let me interrupt…"

I'd seen that as well, I realized, Chris and Rhodes hustling her off to one side when she'd brought others forward when we'd gotten into the frozen remains of the parking lot and had been loading up again.

I'd seen it and, knowing people I trusted were on it, I'd let it be.

"Okay, these seven, are they leveled yet?" I asked. "Any classes?"

"Just Michael. Rogue," she said distastefully.

"Shit, really?" I asked, impressed. "Well, we can definitely make use of that."

"Really?" she asked, shocked. "I didn't think you'd want—"

"Think of him not as a thieving bastard, which they generally are, but as a scout and assassin combined," I suggested. "That's the basic level of a Rogue, but that's a hell of a lot more useful to us as well." I scratched my chin as I thought about it, then I nodded. "Okay, give me a few minutes. Have we got any confirmed monster nests in the area?"

"Two," she said. "The cat people—"

"Scepiniir," I corrected. "You don't want to offend them, believe me."

"Oh, uhm, okay, the Scvepi—"

"Scepiniir," I repeated, stressing it, and she sounded it out before nodding that she got it.

"Okay, the Scepiniir, they found the goblin camp. There's like thirty or so, they said, but they were mainly underground so they couldn't get an accurate count."

"Is it far?"

"Half an hour or so's walk," she said, then went on. "The other one is a pack of feral dogs, but huge. The goblins are apparently trying to tame them, but without much success."

"Probably why there's such a small number of goblins around." I grunted. "They close by?"

"About half an hour from the first group, maybe ten or fifteen minutes from here in a straight line. They're in the opposite direction of the park. The Scepiniir who found them, Saros, said that she followed the trail of blood and bodies until she found the second nest."

"Perfect." I grinned evilly. "Okay, last question, then I'll let you get back to work…" I paused. "Think you can escape from all of this and leave someone else in charge while we go kill something?"

CHAPTER SIX

"Hey, Chris!" I called up to him, as the truck pulled into the middle of the parking lot. "How was the run?"

"Well, look who *finally* dragged his ass outta bed!" He grinned as he swung down from the passenger side of the cab. "Damn, dude, I was starting to think you'd smuggled Kelly into the room and were hiding!"

"Damn, I wish." I grunted, clapping him on the shoulder as we moved back away from the truck. People were already streaming forward, the guards shouting at them to form an orderly line and to get their tokens ready.

"What's up then?"

I shrugged. "You know, the usual," I said. "We've found another area we've fucked up in with the dungeon, but..."

"But?" He squinted at me. "Come on, dude. Give me some good news for a change."

"Well, you know the skeletons were bringing in about a million mana a day?"

"Yeah?"

"Well, we were losing the majority of that, so a few little changes, a bit of tweaking, a bit of upgrading here and there..." I let it hang, before grinning at him. "Long story short, we just hit what's probably going to be five million a day, and that's with the issues still in place. If we can increase them, solve a few bits, and invest a lot more?

"Yeah." I shook my head. "With some serious luck, we'll be on about twenty million a day inside the month, and scaling rapidly up from there as well."

"Fuck me," Chris breathed.

"I'm fine, thanks," I said with a kind of massive dignity. "Not that I'd say you're ugly or anything, but you know, you've got a face like a sad bag of hammers."

"What's a happy bag of hammers look like?"

"A lot better than you. Come on, man, keep up!" I grinned. "The big advantage of this?"

"Yeah?"

73

"We're capped by space and reach, so we won't be leaping up to it in the short term, but it just made the little extras a lot more affordable…things like the next set of upgrades, better armor and weapons, and the ammunition factories."

"Oh, thank fuck." He grunted. "How long until we've got lasers?"

"A long time." I snorted. "Dude, *Glass*—which we've not yet reached—is basically the Information Age. All the shit that the most advanced humans had access to is about the level that we're going to reach in the next day or so. Oh, and that's a point as well. The core was going to take three more days. Instead, it should be done by about lunchtime tomorrow."

"That's a relief then. Dame Wrist and her five lovely daughters are barely speaking to me as it is." He grunted. "So we should be able to get scanned, prove that we're all clean and then go home…triumphant heroes return and the ladies love us again?"

"Basically." I nodded. "Though obviously it might be magic, but it's not *magic*, magic. You'll still be ugly."

"One step at a time." He sighed. "Showers, dinner with Becky, and a fucking hug. I miss her, you know? It's not the same in the dungeon sense."

"I know, brother." I sighed, all joking pushed aside. "Right, I can come with you on the next run if you need me, but…"

"But you summoned a shitload of gear and dumped it in the back of the truck for a reason?" he asked, and I nodded. "We don't need you on the run," he admitted. "There's been one attack in the last three runs, and that was a terminally stupid pigeon."

"A pigeon?" I asked, a sudden vision of the spawnskulls filling my mind.

"Yeah, it was about double the size of a normal one and it divebombed the boxer. Literally. Boom! Greasy splatter across the windshield. And because we're on the basic capabilities of the vehicle, no electricity and not even goddamn power steering, we had to pull over to wash it off."

"He means I had to piss on it!" Andre called cheerfully, jogging over. "Hey, boss, any chance we can go home soon?"

"Yeah, mate, hopefully a couple more days, that's all," I assured him, before glancing at Rhodes, who was steadily working through the lists of refugees. "Let's go talk to Rhodes," I suggested, heading over that way.

"What's up sir?" she asked briskly as I came to a halt.

I grinned, fighting the urge to salute the shorter woman. "Sorry to interrupt, Captain." I smiled. "I'm not going to be joining you for this run, and probably not the next one as well. You didn't need me the last few, and I think it's time to take our lower-leveled people out and get them a little experience. Do you think that'll work, or do you want me to fly overwatch?"

"That's fine by me, sir. You'll be taking how many of the guard with you?"

"None…" I started, only to see "that look" flash in her eyes. I went on hurriedly, "I'm taking Robin and a few of the troublemakers she'd identified. The ones who made the wrong choice for the right reason, not the shit birds," I clarified.

She nodded. "I understand, sir. And Chris?"

"He'll go with you. He's a hell of a fighter, after all, and if you actually get hit by something strong, you'll need him."

"Then you'll be taking the twins." She glanced from Andre to where Jimmy was sidling up to listen in.

"That's what I wanted to talk to you about," I agreed. "Frankly, I don't really need them, but—"

"But you probably don't need anyone. You're powerful enough to take out low-level nests on your own. This is a power-levelling setup, and my boys could do with it," she finished, brooking no argument.

"Yes, Sar— Captain," I said quickly, before grinning at her as she snorted.

"How long 'til you leave, and how long will you be gone?" she asked.

"Probably half an hour 'til we leave, and two to three hours," I said. "The plan is more to see what Robin and these few do, and see if we actually want them. They seem like the sort who'll stand firm and follow orders, but we won't know until they're tested."

"Best to test them in a controlled environment then," she agreed. "Will you be taking Kilo, Dante, or Jo as well? You'll need support."

"None," I said firmly this time. "If we need ranged, I can provide it. And we have the rifles. I'll take the healing focal orb, but Jo is by far the more powerful and versatile, and I'd rather you had her."

"As you say, sir. Anything else?" she asked, and I shook my head. "Then I'll see you in four hours at the latest, or I'll be bringing a team to find you. Robin, mark on this map the location of the nest you're aiming for, please."

Robin had just arrived and looked flustered to all hell as she tried to figure out the map and align it with an area she barely knew herself.

"Here, I think?" she said softly. "The Scepiniir—"

"Saros!" Rhodes bellowed over her shoulder.

A heartbeat later, the athletic Scepiniir leapt off the bonnet of the truck, landed and raced over to us, coming to a halt looking as if she'd just strolled over gently, not so much as a hair out of place.

"Yes, my captain?"

Rhodes gestured to the map. "You know where the nest of... What was it?" Rhodes asked me, glancing up.

"Goblins." I smiled. "The horrible little bastards."

"You know where the goblins are?" she asked, and the Scepiniir nodded, before looking at the map in confusion.

A few minutes of explanations later, and we had an emphatic claw mark where the goblin camp was, and a hopeful request to come with me.

"She could do with the levels," Rhodes pointed out, watching me. "She did well enough in the fight to take this place, but she needs more desperately."

75

"She does, and so do the other seven I'm taking," I replied dryly. "If I take them, plus Robin, and the twins, and then her...the XP isn't going to be worth the trip for them, though it'd still shut down a nest, I guess..."

"Take half," Rhodes suggested, then smiled. "Or better yet," she turned to Saros, "you said there were two nests in the area?"

Saros nodded emphatically.

"Excellent. You take all of them then, sir. Give them some advice and split them into two teams. Let them raid the nests one at a time with the other team held back to offer constructive criticism and support if needed."

"That..." I nodded, seeing that sense. "That works," I agreed. "Okay, so, you need us for anything?"

"No sir," Rhodes said. "Though, if you could collect your gear to let my refugees board, I'd appreciate it."

"Shit. Sorry, Rhodes." I sighed, feeling again like I was the rank amateur who she was putting up with a lot of the time.

"Not a problem, sir." She smiled. "Andre, Jimmy, get the volunteers sorted, the gear unloaded, and the refugees loaded. Then you're under the lord's command. Don't embarrass me."

"No, Captain!" they both chorused.

I snorted, remembering the "We'd totally do you" line when we were getting ready to raid this place. The twins had a gift for putting both feet in their mouths at the same time, and they were about as bright as a lightbulb running off half a potato. But they were brave, loyal, and honest. They were willing to throw in with me on anything, and that was something that could be neither taught nor bought. It had to be earned.

"I'll be a few minutes." I moved off to the side and sat, reaching out to Kelly in the dungeon sense, to confirm the tests had gone well.

What we'd done was create a converter near the skeletons as they worked to demolish the buildings; then Kelly had connected up a conduit but had left it turned off. She'd also thought to split off half of the team and send them to work on the next building over. That'd provided a valuable baseline. Once we were sure of the results we were getting, she'd activated the converter, and the longest conduit we'd yet made.

The result...was incredible.

The mana was no longer being lost at a significant rate, and as soon as the mana started coming in again, the three of us had made a new series of plans, including me finally bringing them on board with my idea for the next stage.

"You mad, mad bastard," Aly had whispered, as I finished outlining it. "What the hell is wrong with you that you came up with that? And do you have any clue how big that would need to be? Also, the cost? My God, the cost..."

"This has to be something they work on regularly," I'd pointed out. "I mean, what else do they do when the dungeon gets to that stage?"

"They probably work on consuming the planet," Kelly admitted. "Convert it into a dungeon world."

"And yet they sent over a hundred dungeons here, and the fairies said that more than one on a world is rare," I said. "They had to know that wasn't a viable option here."

"Well yeah, maybe, but this?" She stared at the blueprint that slowly rotated before her, and she shook her head. "If you do this? I mean, I get it, but this design? You're gonna get sued by the Mouse. They bought all the rights to this stuff—you remember that, right? George sold them."

"Most of them. And you think there's any lawyers left out there?" I shrugged, grinning at my maddest design yet, unable to take my eyes off it.

"If there's anywhere lawyers survived, it's there," Kelly said. "Hell, they probably have a dungeon, and just the thought of that is horrifying enough!"

"Yikes," I agreed. "Well, you know what they say—the first thing you do when you take over the world is line all the lawyers up and shoot them. Best thing for everyone."

"True, I worked with them for far too much of my working life," she agreed with a sigh. "Okay, we went off on a tangent. Long story short, the manafield is stable for now, more or less, but I don't want to add any more drain on it. So five million a day, plus the converters and the northern dungeon, is the limit. Call it six million. Three million for research, three million for production and maintenance."

"Wait, we could—" Aly started to say quickly, her eyes almost feverishly bright, before being shot down.

"If we're to manage this plan, and provide everything we need, then it's time to start working heavily on infrastructure," Kelly said firmly. "We need the forces, and the transport. You get three million a day and you can be happy with it."

Aly frowned, opened her mouth to complain, then saw the look in the Dungeon Mistress's eye and nodded.

"It's over two million plus more than I was getting yesterday." She sighed. "It's annoying, but I can deal with it."

"Glad to hear it." Kelly snorted, then glanced at me. "So, what are you doing here still?" she asked archly.

I grinned at her. "Nothing..." I assured her, holding my hands up in mock surrender. "I was just checking in, that's all."

"Well, now you know that it's all in hand, and the timescale has stepped up..." Kelly said imperiously, before waving in dismissal. "Begone, vagabond! Leave me..." Then she changed her tone and smiled, a twinkle in her eye. "But get your butt in gear and make sure things are sorted out, because you deserve a little treat for that, once you're home and all confirmed 'clean.'"

"Oh, and Matt?" Aly added before I could escape. "I know it's yours, and that's fine, but if you could send the bag of holding to the dungeon with Rhodes? Then Finn could get started on replicating it."

"I can just permeate it and—" I started to offer.

"Best not to," she said quickly. "That *should* work, but just in case it doesn't, I want him to have a look over it first, see what he can observe and learn."

"Dammit…" I muttered, before shrugging and nodding that I'd do it, as much as I didn't want to let go of it. I'd sweated blood for that thing.

"Okay, now get outta here!" Kelly ordered, smiling.

"Your wish is my command." I blew her a ghostly kiss, before opening my eyes and looking at the newly arrived small group gathered before me.

"Time to get it stuck in, I guess," I muttered, before taking a deep breath and stepping forward.

"Okay, everyone, I'm Matt, the Dungeon Lord of Newcastle. It turns out most of you are on the shit list, for one reason or another, so…"

The conversation with them all was a simple and quick one. Basically, I let them know that they'd all fallen foul of the rules in one way or another—the seven, anyway—and that what we were doing was giving them a chance, not just because it might be that they were dicks and we needed to know, but also because they'd all to a man volunteered for the army, and I'd like to know what kind of people they really were.

They'd all agreed, unsurprisingly, and had worked their way through the weapons, armor, and general gear that I'd had summoned for them.

I'd decided that I didn't know, nor trust these fuckers, so they weren't getting the good toys: no assault rifles, no handguns, no shotguns.

They'd need to do it all "old school," but they'd have the twins there armed to the teeth, Saros and me, with Robin as well. But she'd be armed as a Paladin should be, with a mace and shield, and she was relieved when I suggested it.

"Honestly, I just like the mace," she'd admitted, as we set off. "The rifle's good for getting at people out of range, but it's too easy to run out of bullets. And then it's just a weird-shaped club, and I'm not very good with it."

"Play to your strengths," I agreed, smiling to myself as we left the camp and I received a new quest notification.

Congratulations! You have discovered a new Quest!

Nest Cleansing: Goblins and Mutts

Two monster nests have been identified in the nearby area, posing a threat to local safety and dungeon expansion. A goblin nest of low-level creatures has established itself, while a pack of mutated dogs is preying on the goblins. The goblins, in turn, are attempting to tame these dogs as mounts.

Objectives:

- Clear the goblin nest (0/1)
- Eliminate the pack of mutated dogs (0/1)

- Assess the combat skills of the soldier trainees (0/2)
- Evaluate the Paladin trainee's potential (0/1)
- Determine the trustworthiness of the borderline recruits (0/7)

Trainee Team for Assessment:

- 2 x Low-level but experienced soldier trainees
- 1 x Paladin trainee
- 1 x Scout trainee
- 7 x Borderline untrustworthy recruits

Complete this quest to gain access to the following rewards:

- +1 to top three Attributes
- +1 Spell
- Improved regional security
- Access to potential new recruits or mounts
- 2,000 XP

I'd accepted it instantly, of course, and apparently the others got a similar quest, though for a different reward.

As I set off, I nodded at Katee, who stood to the side, glaring at me. She still looked annoyed, along with Jakob and Laurence. All three had originally come with Robin. They were more than a little pissed that they weren't being invited to come play today.

I'd had to smooth some ruffled feathers over this, but they accepted that someone needed to hold down the fort and that I'd make sure they got another chance at it.

It felt a little like I was rewarding bad behavior with the group I had with me, but it was also a good chance to see what they did. I had faith that the twins and Saros had my back. Robin...I wasn't sure of yet.

"Remember," I said to her as we left the safety of the walls. "If you're going to use Smite or anything, use it sparingly, and don't goddamn channel it! Has it refilled?"

"The Divine essence bar?" she asked, and I nodded. "It's up to three points." She glanced over at me and then away as I caught her eye. "I'm sorry, it just seems a bit weird that you have this, that you're somehow powering me and my abilities, but you don't know about it."

"You have no idea." I grunted. "Okay, people, let's pick up the pace! Saros, Michael there is a Rogue—you lead the way and see what you can teach him!"

Michael picked up speed unasked, and moved to catch up to the bounding Scepiniir, as we jogged down the hill and across the road.

Instead of following as the truck and the others went, along the road and up onto the highway that ran parallel to the shopping center, but raised, we took a left immediately and jogged into the scanty cover of the trees.

From ground level, I could see why the goblins had thought themselves well hidden. The low shrub bushes and arcing vines, nettles and thorns, blanketed in snow as they were, covered them well from the road. But the trees that rose overhead were bare and winter stripped.

Their leaves had long since succumbed to the severe frost, and now as we slogged through those same bushes the goblins had tried to hide in yesterday, I couldn't help but be glad about that.

We'd have had no clue they were there otherwise, especially considering their wild garb. They had been covered in patched leathers, all dull, earth-like colors and fluttering loose cloth that looked something like a ghillie suit, making me wonder just how advanced they'd been...until I passed the first body.

It was laid on its back, staring sightlessly up at the cold sky overhead. Snow half covered it, and I could smell it before I saw it.

Passing by, I barely slowed. The hilt of the metal shank-like blade it'd dropped in the fight stood proud in the snow. The wire, that looked to have once been a phone cord or similar, was bound loosely around the shaft to provide a grip.

The clothing...well, it covered the goblin enough that it'd be the smell that got it banned from anywhere, instead of because it'd been it exposing itself. That was about the best thing that could be said, really.

That was a massive relief as well. Remembering how broken up their outline had been, I'd started to worry that maybe this was a much more advanced group of goblins...but no, in the cold weather they were simply wearing multiple torn and oversized layers.

Fuckin' relief, really.

Through the scattered trees, barely a dozen or so wide, we emerged, and the bank that climbed ahead of us cut off all view beyond it. The winter-browned grass, frozen in place, crunched underfoot as we hurried to the top of the small rise. Once there?

We stopped, our breath fogging the air as we stared out across the small parkland.

It was a peculiar place; it really was. Hemmed in on all sides, it was barely more than a few hundred meters across at its widest, and in many places, it was less than a hundred.

It was filled with tall trees, though, and cleared areas where when the town was all planned out—it'd grown from the original home of George Washington's family into a large planned urban area—had been designated as picnic areas, as fields for children to play in and as pools to relax in, in the summer's heat.

Unfortunately, as many such projects had, it'd been stripped of all funding in the '80s, and what was returned in later years was never enough to combat the damage done by disaffected youths.

The small toddler pools had concrete bases to keep them from getting too gunky, and to enable them to be drained regularly. They'd also had concrete crocodiles and other creatures that were intended to rise above the low water and be fun for the kids...

They'd been targets for glass bottles thrown at adolescent alcohol-fueled late-night parties—glass which had shattered, then sunk to the bottom, unseen, and then maimed small children. The parents stopped letting their children use such places, as the limited park funds couldn't cover someone watching over it around the clock, nor daily cleaning, and that was just the start.

Lights were put out. The long subways that ran under the local highways connecting each "village" of the town to the park and one another became gang hangouts. Between the abandoned and used needles, the broken bottles, the shouts and abuse? Well, most people started taking detours.

With fewer and fewer people using the parks, the assaults, muggings, and robberies became commonplace, no longer mere shouted abuse. And given this was an era before the use of drones, and where helicopters were reserved for only the most important crimes...

They got away with it most of the time.

The result was a park that had, when my parents had taken me as a little one on playdates nearby, looked incredibly exciting, so overgrown and wild...had become a festering sore for the area.

The local government of later years would invest heavily in it, cutting back the trees, introducing more play areas—which would be vandalized by the end of the week—and generally trying to clean it up. But as time went on, it became clear that it was only a matter of time before the area was flattened and turned into just another housing estate.

Now, as we stood at the crest of the small hill, the highest point in the surrounding area, to stare down at the scattered trees, damn, it brough back memories. I stood, thinking about the times I'd walked, hand in hand with my parents through the grass here, running...

"We shouldn't be here." Saros crouched nearby, glaring at us all. "You are easily spotted against the sky. Come!"

And just like that, the mist of decades vanished, and I was back in the present, before sighing and running down the opposite side of the hill with the others.

"What's the plan then, boss?" Jimmy asked as we reached the flat area, passed along the cracked and broken asphalt road for a few meters, then followed a clearly beaten path down a second hill toward the thicker forest below. "Are we just here for backup or...?"

"You're here to get a little experience, as Rhodes suggested," I assured him. "The goblins are individually weak, or they usually are, and they'd be no match for real weapons like these." I patted the rifle I held as we ran.

"So…?" Andre's forehead wrinkled as he thought about it.

"So you're using the blunt ones and the shield," I finished for him, shaking my head. "In this situation, I'll be at the back, on overwatch. I'll not be involved, not really, as I'd massively lower the XP you'd earn. You two are to keep quiet unless you see really dangerous mistakes…" I said to Andre and Jimmy, before I raised my voice, making sure the others could hear, and ignoring Saros's glare when I did so.

"You'll operate as we said, in two teams. The less experienced get to go first. That's not because I'm a dick—it's because you'll learn a lot more when you understand exactly what it's like. Fighting for your life, when you can get hurt or killed, will earn you a fuckload more experience than fighting when you know you're safe and there's no risk.

"I'll be at the back, myself, but Robin will lead you, and I'll only get involved if you need me. Not if you get in the shit and you're trying to escape…not if you get close but you're okay. I mean if you *really* need me."

"What about me and her?" the guy introduced as Michael asked, nodding after Saros, and I smiled.

"Well, you both get the really fun job," I warned him. "You get to scout out the situation for both nests, and then you kill something—anything. You assassinate one of the enemy and escape unseen."

"Okay…" he agreed nervously. "You know I'm just starting out, right? I'm level five, that's it."

"I know," I assured him. "At that point, I was fighting the gangs in the park, all of them armed, while I had to take my guns from their bodies. These are goblins, fundamentally stupid creatures at this level of evolution, so I've got faith in you. Also, Robin and her team will be waiting to back you up. So…"

I glanced over then. Four of the shit detail were men who had mainly chosen short swords and shields, two women who had both chosen spears and shields, and one I didn't have a clue about—long hair and very feminine features but with a full beard—who carried a bow as their chosen weapon.

It was Andre who asked before I had the chance to, and it turned out their name was Xen, and their pronouns were they/them.

I didn't care, frankly, but to be able to split the people I had up into even teams, I checked their rough builds, splitting Andre and Jimmy between the two teams. Robin would lead them both; Saros and Michael would be on both teams. The archer was on both teams as well. That got some glares from those who only got to be on one, and a panicked look from Xen as they realized they were at risk twice over.

It was a simple decision, though. If we weren't using the rifles, and I wasn't using my magic or even getting involved unless the shit really hit the fan, then they were the only ranged option the teams had.

On realizing that, those who had been clearly uncomfortable around Xen suddenly grew much more accepting when they figured out it was their ass on the line if they didn't play nice.

We paused at this point. I realized that, as much as this was all second nature to me now, they were not only people who neither knew each other well, but they had never trained with their weapons before.

I had them run through a few drills in the snow. Simple stuff, like how to form a shield wall, how to angle the shield so that you could stab out, and how much room to give each other in the line.

"Turtling up" was covered. I made them spread out, then rush back to fight with their backs together a few times, just to make sure that they knew how to.

Then we set off again, and enroute, I covered the basics, like cutting with the sword and stabbing, rather than cleaving and getting the damn thing caught in the middle of the target body.

That was almost fun, as Jimmy explained that if you hit as hard as you could in training, then the training dummies that Rhodes had created ended up trapping the sword, leaving you open to a kick in the balls.

It'd almost sounded like a bit of general advice, until Andre admitted that he'd been walking with a limp for the rest of the afternoon, after he'd been warned not to do it twice, and he'd still gotten overexcited and had done it a third time.

At that point, Rhodes had deployed a far more memorable method of teaching, and had put any future children he might have in doubt.

The way he'd crouched around himself, even while running, as he tried to tell the story, made everyone laugh.

With that, we'd gone back over the teams, splitting them up and confirming what they needed to do when we found the enemy, who would be standing back to watch, and who would be kicking ass first.

So in the end, we had Andre, Robin, Xen, Michael, Saros, two guys and one of the ladies joining the first team. They moved up into position as we approached the lowest point of the little valley.

Saros had switched to hand signals, and because none of us knew what those signals meant, Andre was the first to speak up and ruined the surprise.

To be fair, I'd had no clue as well, and had been about to ask the same thing. But a half second after he opened his mouth, a goblin that had apparently been hiding under the nearby bridge started screeching.

"What's tha—" he started, and all hell broke loose.

CHAPTER SEVEN

The first goblin in sight was, as I said, the little shit that had been hiding under the bridge. We'd literally been approaching it, with Michael and Saros in the lead. The pair had been moving slower as Saros tried to figure out what the other Rogue knew. Her own dungeon-granted knowledge was enough to get her started, but little more than that.

She essentially had an aptitude for the role, but no formal training.

That was probably why the pair of them had been peering at the tracks on the muddy ground right before the bridge, instead of splitting up to check underneath the fucker, or roam farther afield.

The goblin that shot out of the far side of the bridge was short and hairier than any other goblin I'd ever seen. He looked like, although he'd always been bald, he was trying to back-comb his shoulder hair into a hair style and was extremely proud of the progress he'd been managing.

He was also a little under three feet tall, with a chest that—where it could be guessed at being, through the incredible hair that poked through the tattered rags it wore—was also slightly smaller than that of the average pigeon.

Combine it with spindly arms, an underbite that could have made an orc propose on the spot, and halitosis that it was apparently trying to weaponize? I didn't get how we'd missed it at any real range.

Mind you, we weren't the only ones surprised.

It leapt out, a short branch in one hand, and what looked to be the remains of a kid's plastic tennis racket in the other, the head broken into a point. It bared its teeth in what was clearly supposed to be a threat and challenge.

Then it saw our group, that we were heavily armed, armored, and all at least double its size, and promptly pissed itself.

Literally.

A wash of dark-yellow piss spread down its matted clothing, and then left a trail behind it as it spun and ran, throwing its weapons away and shrieking fit to wake the dead.

"Xen!" I snapped. "Shoot that fucker!"

They brought their bow up quickly, tugged an arrow free of their quiver and drew back, squinted along its length, led the target, and fired.

The arrow barely cleared the bowstring, however, before it dipped, clattered, and bounced off the ground. It then vanished into the long grass and snow by the side of the path.

The closest it'd been to the fleeing goblin was probably when the arrow was still in the quiver.

We all looked at Xen, at the bow, the path the arrow had taken, and the still fleeing and shrieking goblin...and I fought down a curse. My own first attempts with a bow and arrow hadn't been much better, and I damn well remembered that. But of all the times to fuck up!

"I'm sorry!" they whimpered, dragging a second arrow free and trying again. This time, they managed to clear half the distance between them and the goblin, before the arrow, again, vanished into the underbrush. "I'm still learning!" they cried.

I forced out a smile. "That's fair," I said loudly, over the rising mutters. "That's totally fair! Have you used a bow before?"

"No!"

"Okay, for those who don't know, if you use the bow a bit, and get some practice in, you'll get an archery skill. That'll level as you do, making the harder shots much easier for you. We've got incredible archers back at the dungeon, but none of them started out that way."

I turned back to Xen. "Did you pick the bow for a reason?" I asked more quietly.

"Am I a coward who wanted to hide at the back, you mean?" they countered, then shook their head. "No, I just... I thought it'd be cool to learn."

"That's fine," I assured them, reaching out and taking the bow, and drew an arrow free. "Believe me, I understand it. I was asking so that I knew if it was something you were interested in learning, or if..." I paused, drew the arrow back, lined up the shot, and made sure I was as ready as possible.

I led the target. The little bastard had turned around now, and when it'd seen that we weren't following—the scouts had stayed where they were when the first arrow flew, rather than get in the way of that—it'd slowed to a walk.

Now the goblin was backing up slowly, but had apparently decided after seeing the last two arrows fall well short that it was safe.

It paused in backing away, clearly annoyed that it'd run and flung its weapons aside, but too afraid to come and try to recover them.

Instead, it lifted the bottom of the long, ragged sweater it wore and exposed itself, waggling what was clearly supposed to be its man—or goblin—hood and hooting something in its language, a mixture of grunts and barks.

I hurriedly reviewed everything I could remember about firing a bow, including the system-granted optimizations, checked my aim, and released.

The snap of the bowstring was different to the *boing* of the failed fires from Xen. Instead of the arrow flying off in a random direction as they jerked the bow on release, mine flew true, though a slight miscalculation in trajectory meant that instead of the chest that I'd been aiming for, it hit just above the groin.

It was close enough, though, that when the tiny figure was sent crashing from its feet, the arrow lodged in the lower stomach, it looked as though I'd taught it a real lesson in keeping your privates, private.

"Holy shit!" one of the trainees whispered.

I raised my voice to be heard over the goblin's now much more pained and panic-filled shrieks. "That's the difference of practice!" I glanced around at the others as I handed the bow back to Xen. "And that, unless you've forgotten, is exactly why we're here. You're here to learn a little, and I'm here to teach you, as well as find out what kind of people you are."

"Uhm, there's more coming," Robin added diffidently. "Goblins, I mean."

That turned out to be a wild understatement.

The path had meandered down the sides of the valley, through a forest and at its lowest point crossed a small bridge, then climbed back up the far side. The rotting wood that made up the bridge was thick and covered in a mix of mud, runoff from where the stream had overrun its banks and the side of the bridge and then frozen, and the overall detritus of the area...meaning piles of leaves, general mulch, and random—and probably goblin—crap.

The stream ran to the left and right. A few dozen meters farther along to the right, where the bank had been eroded by the rising water, then exposed as the seasons passed, was a hole.

It was a little larger than the entrance to a badger's set, though not by much. I'd dismissed it when I'd glanced around as anything more important than just that.

That was apparently a massive mistake. Goblins came boiling out of it, slipping and sliding down the earthen bank and leaping the narrow stream. More were coming out of at least one other exit; that was clear as the shouts, shrieks, and hooting in the distance intensified as well.

The problem was, it was coming from all sides.

"Okay, people, fall back on Robin, backs to one another, and get ready," I said quickly, before crouching and launching myself into the air.

"What the fuck!" one of the men gasped. "He's leaving us?!"

"Don't be so stupid!" Andre snapped. "He can see more from up there!"

Unfortunately, they were both right.

I lifted into the air and flew up around thirty meters, higher than most of the small trees that stood on either side of the stream here, and turned in a tight circle, looking to see how many and where they were coming from.

"Okay, people!" I called down. "There's...well, there's a few of them. I'd not say a lot, but you can certainly manage this yourself. Forget splitting into two teams for now, though. I'm going to move over to the far side of the stream, and I'm going to watch over you. This is your chance to impress me. If in doubt, remember that the pointy end goes in the other guy...and good luck!"

With that, I moved off. This was going to be a hard fight for them, but there was little choice. At some stage, they needed to do this themselves, and better that they do it while I was here, able to step in and heal them should they need it, rather than just blow some sunshine up their arses and then see them fail.

I landed on the far side of the stream, halfway up the bank, close to the now slightly weaker shrieking goblin. I absently drew my hammer from the loop on my belt. Watching the others farther down the hill more than anything, I stepped to the side and crushed his skull with the head of my hammer, wiped it clean, then leapt into the air, travelling thirty or so meters to the side before landing again.

I now had a better view of the action about to unfold below, and wasn't as close to the stinking creature that I'd just killed.

Andre was obviously prompting Robin, who'd been frozen in indecision. As soon as he'd stepped in closer, saying something I couldn't hear from all the way over here, she started to snap out orders to the others.

I nodded, and Andre nodded back, clearly aware that I knew what he'd been doing.

The brothers had already moved into position. Their limited levels were due to the situation and lack of experience points awarded while hiding with Rhodes, as opposed to a lack of training.

The others were less impressive.

With the goblins apparently coming from three sides, all closing in on them, Robin spread people out. Xen was firing almost desperately and had apparently failed to hit anything beyond the ground so far. The others were cursing them, while backing in as close as could be together.

"First mistake right there." I grunted, making a mental note. "No room to maneuver."

That became apparent as the goblins swept from the trees and their hidey-holes. Robin had positioned the group on the bridge still. With its sides covered by thick posts and bars as guide rails, she clearly thought that'd limit the angles of attack.

Unfortunately, the goblins were small enough that a contingent of ten or so scampered along the side of the stream, headed presumably for the place the lookout had been hiding under the bridge, and would soon be able to swarm up and around to hit them in the ass.

As it was, she took the lead, her mace ready and shield in place, with Andre and Jimmy on either side of her. The others formed a tight circle around Xen, who was down to a handful of arrows now.

Most would probably be recoverable, as they'd hit nothing but grass and mud, but they'd only be able to do that after the fight.

There were three groups of goblins that I could see from my position here, higher on the side and looking down from above. The first swarmed through the trees to their left, or the south, now. There were about thirty of them, with another twenty or so coming in from the west, as they faced back the way we'd come.

The ten that were hurrying along the edge of the stream were going to cause serious problems, as the rear of the circle started spreading out, moving from a solid turtle formation into a wall. A wall that had its backs to them.

"Fuck's sake," I muttered. From where they were, they had to be able to see the goblins coming, surely?

I started chewing on my lip, watching as the ten vanished beneath the bridge, and waited as the first of the main gang...? *Infestation.*

That was a better term for a group of goblins, I decided. The majority of the infestation was still running, but the first few hit the line, and were bounced back by the defenders' shields.

That was great; several fell to the ground, practically beaten senseless by the impact. But as I watched, only Andre and Jimmy thought to actually stab theirs! The others were getting ready for more, and just bracing themselves behind their shields!

Saros was the literal exception. Her shield was a much smaller thing, a buckler rather than a tower design, more like something a rider would have, or a Norman in the conquests, rather than the massive oblong things that the legion had used.

She was off to the side, apparently unconcerned about the rest of the group, fighting on her own. Although she was good—and damn, she was—she'd clearly soon be overwhelmed by the sheer number coming.

I waited a few more seconds, growing more and more annoyed—while reminding myself that I had barely taught them the basics, and it wasn't entirely their fault—before I started walking.

I could have flown down in seconds; I could have just taken a knee and used my damn rifle. But I still harbored a little hope that Robin would be able to lead them effectively.

Spoiler: she didn't.

I drew my sword and broke into a run about thirty seconds later, when the goblins from beneath the bridge started to swarm up, rushing the group from the rear.

Saros had finally realized that the "I'll rush out and fight on my own" plan was going to get her killed, and was backing up, fighting goblins on three sides. While she was doing this, Andre and Jimmy, who had some formal training by Rhodes, were clearly trying to hold it all together and most of the group were now panicking.

"Fuck's sake!" I grunted, before launching myself forward, pushing hard to cover the last few meters to reach the goblins before they could hit the group from behind.

Although I could have used the rifle, that could have been even riskier for the group if they tried to retreat into my arc of fire while I was taking the goblins out. So, as I landed, I extended into a lunge. The tip of my sword impaled the closest goblin at the back of the group.

Nice; I'd stopped that one. As I reset, dragging the blade free, I stepped forward and lunged again, slicing across the back of the legs of the next in line, taking him down with a pained shriek.

That left me in the middle of eight of the little bastards, and as they'd now given up on stealthy sneaking, Robin and the others had realized they were there and panicked.

All in all, it was a right clusterfuck.

I spun, dipping down low and powering the blade around in an arc. I hacked through three more bodies at waist height, then straightened, now facing away from Robin and the others. I'd taken five of the goblins down: the first dead with a skewered heart, the second bleeding out with the thicker muscles in the back of its thighs severed as it rolled around, shrieking and spraying blood.

Goblins three to five were dead or dying, bisected laterally at the waist, while the remaining five were too close for anything fancy. I backhanded the one to my farthest right, spinning him from his feet. Then I caught one by the face as it leapt at me and threw him back at a friend.

He'd been entirely unarmed beyond claws and teeth that probably carried rabies and weaponized levels of halitosis, so the damage he'd managed, scrabbling at my armored forearm, was negligible.

I stepped back, straightened and flicked a finger at the middle of the remaining three, muttering "Incinerate" and focusing on his head; he went to the ground with steam erupting and his flesh charring. Then I skewered the one to his right and punted the remaining one on the left in the face.

He was sent flying, bones definitely breaking, and his skull, if not deformed by birth, certainly done in now.

Two quick stabs were all it took to ensure the battered and beaten survivors of this wave were no longer suitable for that moniker, and then I turned back to the others.

They'd seen that I was there and had—I guessed—trusted that I'd deal with things, as they were back facing forward. Robin shouted over the screams and shouts of the fight to "stab them," and Andre and Jimmy were doing the same. The others...were trying. That was the best that could be said.

One sobbed with terror, clearly having real difficulty in holding the shield up that the goblins were battering on. Saros had taken a dozen small wounds and was wading through the stream below, headed to get back behind me, with one hand clutched to her stomach and what looked to be an arrow sticking out of her.

Considering there was no way that I could see Xen having managed that shot—Saros had been facing in the other direction before this—I guessed one of the goblins had found it and decided it was a far better weapon than the improvised ones most of their kind were brandishing.

From there, well...

About half of the goblins were down, though most were either injured or semiconscious. The ladies with the spears were doing the best by far, if I had to guess, with Robin, Andre, and Jimmy accounting for the rest.

"Screw it," I growled and launched myself into the air, flashing over the battered line, before twisting and landing on the ground on the far side, sword held in both hands. I slipped into stance, the blade held upright by the side of my face.

I stepped forward, bringing the blade down in an overhand chop, then drawing it back and twisting at the hip, feeding a little mana into the sword and feeling it as it drew health as well.

What that sacrifice made happen, though, was the activation of the Void Blade spell. The blade no longer snagged on bone, muscle, and cloth. Instead, it slid through them with almost effortless grace.

I pivoted and swung, slashing the tip around in a wide arc that carved five more goblins in half. My left hand pointed and unleashed a lightning bolt that punched straight through another into his friend behind him and took the right arm from another on the far side before it slammed into a tree.

The tree exploded, splinters scything more from their feet, and in less than ten seconds, the goblins were running. I stabbed a last one that I could still reach, nodded to myself as Xen fired an arrow into the back of one that was fleeing, taking it to the ground, and then it was over.

"Well," I said after a few seconds, looking over the panting, battered group, and shook my head. "You'll understand when I say that I'm less impressed than I hoped I'd be."

Glancing from one to another, I sighed, then went on.

"Okay, up to you if there's anything you want to loot. But if you're not dying, then the first thing you need to do is make sure of your kills. Remember, this is *experience*, so if one of you goes around stabbing all the bodies and finishing them off, they'll get the majority of the XP from this fight. That's the last thing most of you can afford, so don't try to skip this!"

I said it, seeing the green look on a few faces and knowing that at least one of the group was sure to do it anyway.

"Secondly, Xen, you need to recover your arrows. Get them all rounded up and see which are reusable. You're going to need them, after all! Third? Did anyone get a level in that fight?"

There were a few raised hands, and I nodded.

"Glad to hear there was some benefit to it. Okay, who's under level five?"

Three hands stayed up.

"Anyone closing on ten?"

Jimmy and Andre lifted their hands, and I glanced at them.

"Level eight," Andre said.

"Just hit nine." Jimmy grinned at his brother, and I turned to Robin.

"Six," she admitted, and I nodded.

"Okay, first things first. Does anyone here want to be a healer? Any of you three specifically?"

One of them nodded, a skinny guy who looked almost panicked at the thought.

"Okay, now be honest, and there's no shame here, or wrong answer—I'll only be pissed if you lie to me. Are you wanting to be a healer because you don't want to fight, or because you want to fight and bring some healing to the front line? Again, no shame. It'll mean I know where to focus your training. We need both kinds of healers, so either is fine."

"Away from the fighting." He looked down, abashed.

"That's fine." I nodded. We did need more healers, after all, and they couldn't all be like Jo, who was happy to be wherever she was needed. "Okay, anyone else?"

"I'd like to know, but I can stay on the front line," Xen offered, and I nodded again.

"That actually works out well then," I said. "If you're happy with the archer build, you can use ranged first, then focus on healing others once the enemy are in close."

"I can do that." They nodded.

"Okay, be sure though. If you just want to go full healer, or multiclass in a different way, again, no issue. You need to do what feels right for you. First step, though, is this." I reached into my bag and pulled free the orb, holding it up and making sure they could all see it.

"This is a focal orb, one of only a few we have. It holds a healing spell, and that spell can be used by anyone who holds the orb and pours in their mana, provided your Life affinity is high enough. For most people it is, fortunately.

"In this case, as well as healing the target—which can be you or another—it'll also give you experience as a healer. That will, in turn, make it more likely that when the time comes, you'll be offered a healing class as one of your class choices. These come at level five, then again at ten, and every ten thereafter.

"We recently found out that if you match certain prerequisites—I don't know what they are, so don't ask—then you'll be given a specific class at any time. I recently unlocked Arcanist level two, which is great, because it increased my options without using up the class choice I'll get at my next milestone.

"Those who want to have healer as a choice, though, if you use this"—I hefted the orb again—"and heal your friends, then you're more likely to be offered that when you reach the class threshold. Remember: each level you gain matters." I paused, shaking my head at the sorry state of Saros, who not only looked like shit as she slogged over to the group, stopping to lean against the side of the bridge's barrier, but was also plainly half frozen.

"Right, Saros needs a lot of healing, clearly. I want a volunteer for this, as it's going to most likely max out your mana. Then the other will use theirs to heal everyone else of the minor wounds."

"I have three hundred mana," Xen admitted, almost as if they should be embarrassed about it, and I snorted, as the other man spoke up as well.

"I've two hundred and twenty," he said.

"Eleven Intelligence?" I asked him. When he nodded, I turned to Xen. "Fifteen?"

They nodded as well, and I smiled.

"Okay then, as you can see, certain things are easy to work out. The mana you get, for example, is worked out generally as ten times the level of your Intelligence until you hit ten, then each point becomes worth twenty. It means that as you get a lot higher, you can cast a lot more spells. The issue you'll have? The more powerful the spell, the higher the cost.

"One of mine is Incinerate. A hundred mana to raise a small area to a thousand degrees. Doesn't sound overly useful when said like that, but if I target the spell an inch behind an opponent's forehead? They're dead. As I am now, I could take out nearly fifty people with that spell alone. That sounds incredibly overpowered, if you're a gamer."

I paused at that, noting the nod that Robin had given. "Now you look at the other side of that, and consider the ogre that you were all dealing with. The boss of the citadel back there was gifted with magical resistance, and a high enough level that it meant that he could essentially ignore that spell completely. I hit him with a strong enough lightning bolt that he should have been reduced to his constituent atoms, and it barely gave him a minor burn. Once we'd passed the amount of mana he could shrug off? Spells started working on him again."

Looking around as I passed the focal orb to the guy and pointed to Saros, I went on.

"Now, you know what's going on here. I could have fought this group alone, killed the goblins with ease. Hell, I could have increased the size of the field for Incinerate to a few meters across and then spam it twenty times and have any goblin that ran into it burst into flames.

"No fuss, no muss. The reason I didn't is because until you get some levels under your belt, you're essentially not much more dangerous than they were." I gestured to the bodies. "That's why we're here, for you to get that chance, and to learn more. So, who can tell me what went wrong?"

Saros opened her mouth, then shut it and just glared at Robin and the others.

"Saros?" I prompted.

"They did not advance!" she spat, glaring at the guy as he started to heal her. "They abandoned me, out of cowardice!"

"No," I said firmly. "You attacked, you stayed out ahead of the group, and you almost paid for that with your life."

"Exactly!" she snarled. "They did not attack!"

"They were holding a shield wall, against a larger number of attackers," I pointed out grimly. "You chose to attack, and in that case, you were almost killed, weakening the overall group."

"But…" She looked from me to the others, clearly confused and pissed, not getting it.

"I think this is a cultural thing," I said. "The Scepiniir are aggressive fighters, as well as individualistic. Humans are more pack based. Regardless, though, your people have slotted into our formations well in the past…" I paused then grunted as I understood. "Probably because you've been in groups with a team of trained soldiers, but with me or Chris leading. We tend to be more aggressive, because we've got the experience to know when to switch tactics."

"So they should have attacked!" She nodded in satisfaction, then yowled as her healer apparently did something. "Fool!" she snarled, before taking a couple of deep breaths and shoving the arrow deeper into her stomach, then collapsing against the bridge as the pain nearly made her pass out.

"Wait!" I snapped, moving in close as quickly as I could. The healer moved aside, looking at me in confusion. I grabbed the arrow shaft, then drove it all the way through, grunting with the effort as I forced the head through her leather armor and out the far side. Then I reached around and dragged it clear, before speaking to her healer.

"What's your name?" I'd been told earlier but I couldn't remember, and as Saros hissed in pain, I didn't have the bandwidth to deal with stupidity.

"Carl," he whispered, looking sick.

"Carl, if you healed her with the arrow still in, you'd have to either shove it free, as we just did, cutting her up again, or she'd have been left with a damn hole all the way through her and healed up areas all around it. Think next time! If you can't think on your feet, healing is going to be a hell of a lot harder for you than fighting. You'll need to train to heal with bandages and splints as much as magic, because a healer without mana is useless otherwise."

"I don't…" He shook his head. "I don't want to be a healer."

"Then get your weapons ready, and back on the line." I nodded to him. "No shame in knowing your limitations, but the more someone heals, the better the chance they'll be offered a healing class. Any other volunteers before I heal her myself?" I asked, and there were several who hesitated. "Come on, people!" I snapped. "She's bleeding out here!"

"Me!" Jimmy said quickly, stepping in and reaching for the orb.

"Really?" I asked, surprised. But I let him do it. He clearly reached his limit before she was fully healed, but I was pleased he'd tried.

"We'll always need a healer, right?" He stood up as I finished her healing off. He winced at how bright the light was all around us, and I nodded, knowing full well just how bad the mana migraines could be.

"We will. Thank you, mate," I said, and I meant it. "Okay, Xen, how's the healing looking?"

"Two real injuries, three minor." They looked at the others, and then back to me.

I passed them the orb and directed how to use it, before helping Saros to her feet.

"Okay, while Xen heals the others, anyone else have anything they think I should consider for that fight?"

"We stayed behind the shields too long," Robin offered after nobody else said anything. "I thought we'd be better off breaking the attack, but when we just waited..."

"They got back up and attacked, and you ended up with more enemies in close than you could handle," I agreed. "Okay, that's true. Anything else? I've got one more that's really important."

When Andre opened his mouth, I shook my head at him. "Not you, mate. I want to hear it from the others."

Jimmy looked at him, then at me, then winced and glanced at the bunch of dead goblins behind them, before theatrically zipping his mouth as well.

"We didn't think about being flanked," Robin admitted, seeing the look they were giving and the bodies, then at last piecing it together.

"Yeah, that's the biggie." I gestured over the side to the stream below. "From where I was, I could see them coming easily, but had any of you looked over the side of the bridge, you'd have seen them too. You had two scouts—one's a Rogue, the other a Scout, sure." I nodded from Michael to Saros. "But they're both fast, have higher than average perception and sneakiness. They could be deployed to the sides, sent to flank the enemy or kept back just to hold the line, but they need to be used to their best advantage. Your shield wall at first was a turtle, right?"

"Yeah." Robin's voice was dropping from embarrassment by the second.

"That was a good choice if you were being attacked on all sides but you still had time to move. When you were as close in as you were, you had no room to maneuver. Spear wielders!"

The two ladies jumped and looked at me worriedly.

"Yeah?" one asked in a nervous voice.

"How long are your weapons?"

"Uhm, this long?" the one who'd spoken said uncertainly, holding the spear up so I could see it.

"I created it," I said. "*I* know how long it is. My question is, do you?"

"Uhm, a meter?" She tried again.

"One and a quarter," I corrected. "They started out as a meter, then the advanced kobolds and higher-leveled humans came along, and we realized that a slightly larger design worked better, but not the full-on pike length that was popular in days of yore. They're short enough to throw, and long enough to still work as spears, instead of pointy sticks. You two..." I pointed at her and her friend. "Stand back-to-back."

They did as I asked, and I nodded. "Okay, let's make this a little fairer. Step forward a step, then put your shield in position and try stabbing forward with your spear."

They tried, and both hit the shield or body of the person behind them. That brought some mutters, and they tried again.

"Okay, now try standing side by side…" They did that, both facing in one direction, with the dead goblins surrounding them. "And you two, step up behind them, backs-to-backs, then take a step forward." They repeated this as a group. "Now try it again."

Again the spears fouled it up, and the two men glared at them, before looking even more confused when I had them repeat the same exercise without the spear wielders and just swords back-to-back.

"You see now that you all need space to work!" I said. "The spears work best at this length from behind the swords, and the swords you're using as *short blades*." I held mine up for emphasis. "This is a longsword."

"We can see." Michael sighed. "Seriously, so Robin fucked up, that's fine. Can we go now?"

"No," I snapped, glaring at him as Robin looked at her feet, apparently feeling like shit. "No, because although I put her in charge, you're all in the wrong here. If any of you had tried getting ready for the charge like that, you'd have realized it. Instead, you were happy to hide behind your shield. I told Jimmy and Andre to keep quiet about things, to let you make your own mistakes because that's how you learn best. Apparently I took that too far because they then didn't warn you about things I considered to be common sense." I looked around, seeing the expressions that ranged from embarrassment to fury.

"At the end of the day, I'm giving you advice. Robin is leading the fight, but if she says cut your own head off, I expect you to use a bit of common-fuckin'-sense! Sometimes you might be in a position where someone is given an order that will result in their death no matter what. 'Hold the line' while your friends retreat, as an example, buying time for them to escape. That's a shitty situation, and I hope it never happens, but that's the reality of life as a soldier, as a *protector*! You all ended up here because you either broke the rules and fucked someone over, or you needed experience.

"When you fuck things up like that, there's consequences. In this case, it's that you're here. You're being given a chance, one that Robin put you forward for, instead of you being lumped in with everyone else. But, already having a black mark against you, she suggested that your situations were unique and that you deserved that opportunity."

Michael looked at her, then away, and I went on.

"At the end of the day, Jimmy and Andre here didn't have a great start with me. Frankly, neither did their wives."

Andre snorted at that.

I grinned, moving on. "But I also trust them with my life. And if they needed something? They'd get it, because they've earned that right. They know that if they came to me with a genuine need, not a want, a desire or whatever, but *needed*

95

something? I guarantee I'd try to sort it for them. That's because they've earned that trust from me."

That got through to a few of the others—the more materialistic—as I thought it might.

"You've got kids, families, and you've asked that they be accepted into my dungeon, protected, given all they need." I looked from one to another of them as I went on. "I agreed because it was the right thing to do. But you fucked up. You broke the rules, and you offered to serve in the army or elsewhere to make up for that. Not all of you had that exact situation, but regardless. This is how you prove you deserve that chance. So stabbing your leader in the back, expecting her to take all the blame when she's as green as you, does fuck all for you. Understand?"

"Yeah." Michael sighed. "Sorry."

I didn't make him apologize to Robin, even though I wanted to, mainly because I could see just how embarrassed she already was.

"Okay, so last point before we move on to finish the fight. You're surrounded by the dead because I stepped in before you could get really hurt. Pay attention to your surroundings, pay attention to your weapons, and for fuck's sake, think about each other's safety as much as your own. You're a squad, not just random fighters. You're all going to be fighting in a place I can't help you in a minute, so pay attention and hopefully you'll all live through this.

"Saros and Michael, you're scouts. Your job is to find out what's going on and report it to your squad leader. Spear wielders, you're defensive. Hold the line, but in close quarters, coordinate with a swordsman and get behind them! Your reach and the length of their sword means you can stab around them and past their shields. An enemy will have two arms—generally—and if they're focused on a shield before them and a sword, they'll never see your spear until it's too late.

"Swords! Where you're going, it's going to be cramped, so your spear wielding and archer companions aren't going to be much use if you don't help each other."

"'Where we're going?'" One of the swordsmen looked at me askance.

"Yeah, you didn't forget, did you?" I asked him. "I mean, you got the quest to eradicate the goblin nest, right?"

"Yeah, but that's what we did," he pointed out.

"No," I corrected. "You didn't. You broke their first wave, that's all. There's going to be at least this many more in the nest, probably more. They're vicious little bastards and cowards at heart, so if they ran, they'll have gone to wherever they feel safe. If you were three foot tall and had the charisma of a wet jockstrap, where'd you want to hide?"

"Home." Robin looked over at the nearby hole that led into their nest. Sure enough, a pair of beady eyes glared back at us.

"Home," I agreed. "And I can't fly and watch over you in there, so this time, it's going to be all on you."

CHAPTER EIGHT

"I...hate...goblins!" Robin ground out, dragging herself out of a small exit from the underground compound nearly three hours later. "I *hate* them!"

"Don't blame you in the slightest," I assured her, offering a hand to help her get up, and grinned at the disgusted, exhausted, and traumatized look on her face.

"Did you know there were kids?" She glared at me, and I blinked in shock.

"No." I said, aghast. "How many? Did you save them?"

"Save...?" Now it was her turn to look shocked. "The goblin kids? Are you insane? They're as vicious as the parents. They all attacked on sight!"

"Oh." I blew out my breath and shrugged. "Well, that's life, I guess. Shit, I thought you mean they had kids down there, human ones. Though, I guess it kinda makes sense. In the dungeon, we have an option to summon goblins and they're a bit crap, but that's just the lower levels. It's also possible to get a breeder's hut, though, to combine the various bloodlines, and to gestate specific variations."

"To...you mean, you breed goblins?" she asked me, horrified.

"No," I said firmly. "Not yet. And frankly, I don't see why we'd ever bother. We'd end up with weird babies and then have to wait for them to grow up to be of any use. But the goblins we've spawned in the past...summoned is probably a better choice of words, actually...but they've been useful. And *big advantage*, we didn't have them running around as babies!"

"I don't see how." She groaned, pressing her hands into the small of her back and twisting, grunting as an audible click sounded and she relaxed. "Oh, thank God..." she whispered, her head sagging. "My back was killing me."

"Here." I reached out and took the healing orb from Xen as they climbed out and nodded a greeting. I'd given them it as they went inside, and a bare lick of mana later, Robin stood a lot straighter as her aching back was healed. Ten minutes later, the last of the group was outside in the fresh air, still covered in muck and what I guessed had to be trampled goblin shit from the smell, and damn. They looked like they hated me now.

I pulled up the quest and read it over quickly.

Congratulations!

You have made progress in your Quest!

Nest Cleansing: Goblins and Mutts

Two monster nests have been identified in the nearby area, posing a threat to local safety and dungeon expansion. A goblin nest of low-level creatures had established itself, while a pack of mutated dogs was preying on the goblins. The goblins, in turn, were attempting to tame these dogs as mounts.

Your party of trainees, after a long and arduous fight, have managed to eliminate the goblin threat, though be warned! No goblin nest stays empty for long. Expect to regularly return to cleanse the area, or destroy it entirely, to prevent reinfection.

Objectives:

- Clear the goblin nest (1/1)
- Eliminate the pack of mutated dogs (0/1)
- Assess the combat skills of the soldier trainees (0/2)
- Evaluate the Paladin trainee's potential (0/1)
- Determine the trustworthiness of the borderline recruits (0/7)

Trainee Team for Assessment:

- 2 x Low-level but experienced soldier trainees
- 1 x Paladin trainee
- 1 x Scout trainee
- 7 x Borderline untrustworthy recruits

Complete this quest to gain access to the following rewards:

- +1 to top three Attributes
- +1 Spell
- Improved regional security
- Access to potential new recruits or mounts
- 2,000 XP

I nodded, glad that the notification had been received. I was fairly sure that it'd been cleared by the time Robin had crawled out, but still, I'd been worried for a while.

There'd been a lot of shouting, some distant cursing, some screams…and now as everyone stood, glaring at me, I forced myself to not say anything about the smell or the time it'd taken them.

I was fairly sure that I, or any of my usual teammates, could have cleared it entirely in less than a third of the time, but that was life.

"So," I said cheerfully. "Who's ready to take on the mutated dogs?"

The look I got…well, let's just say that it wasn't happy and excited.

I could feel the glares on me as I turned to Saros, offering her a hand as she clambered, shaking and practically frozen to the bone, from the river.

She batted it aside and glowered at me, slipping and sliding up the side of the stream's bank as she cursed and muttered.

She'd dove into the shallow water as soon as she'd gotten out. I was torn between being impressed by her bravery and horrified by the absolute madness.

It was cold here right now—hell, it was literally below freezing. The only reason it'd stopped snowing was that we were between the damn clouds, and the sky right now was a brilliant, icy blue where it could be seen.

The weather wasn't going to improve, not even a little; that was clear. Whatever had sparked the changes had dropped the average temperature in the area by at least five degrees. It usually rained for fun here, but now it meant that the same was true for snow.

I'd expected it to clear. Hell, I was actually getting concerned that it wasn't, it was that out of the ordinary. But that the damn Scepiniir had dove into the water and scrubbed herself?

She was at serious risk of hypothermia, if nothing else.

I debated with myself for a few seconds, then cursed and told Saros to lead the way, and that I'd just be in the middle of the pack while I checked something out.

The spells I had were a bit different from the normal Arcanist's variety, I knew. For one thing, they'd been offered as part of the Dungeon Lord selection, rather than as a "real" spell list that was more rounded. Pulling it up, I read through the descriptions quickly, figuring out the details I needed and how to do it, and still make it hopefully both survivable and useful.

Spells:

Class selection: Arcane Dungeon Lord

Summon Demon: Summon a Demon. Formed entirely of your power and imbued with terrible purpose, the Demon exists to see your will achieved, and will allow nothing to stand between it and its goal. (Selected) (0)

99

Incinerate: Cast a blast of terrible heat at a target, achieving up to 1000 degrees of heat in a single location. Note: This spell has lessening effects, depending on the area covered, and ranks from 0 (10cm) to 5 (1000cm). (1)

Evolution: Atomic Furnace: Select a location and summon the power of the sun to turn all inside that area to glass! Note: This spell has lessening effects, depending on the area covered, and ranks from 0 (1m) to 5 (1000m). (0)

Eternal Winter: The depths of space are places of terrible cold; why not share that knowledge with your enemies? It's likely to leave a lasting impression on anything that's caught inside the AOE. Note: This spell has lessening effects, depending on the area covered, and ranks from 0 (1m) to 5 (1000m). (N/A)

Tame: Tame a creature, adding it to your Dungeon lists. (Selected) (1)

Evolution: Affinity Boost! As you Tame a creature, you can now choose to imbue it with an elemental affinity. The higher your own affinity, the higher the chance the gift will result in a successful union. (Selected)

Conversion: Creatures you encounter out in the wild, be they sentient or not, should all be part of your domain. Convert the heretic to your side! This spell ranks in levels from 0 (Unfriendly) to 5 (Sworn Nemesis). (N/A)

Examine: This spell allows the nascent Dungeon Lord to divine details about a target that are hidden from the eyes of most mortals. This skill ranks in levels from 0 (Curious) to 5 (All-Knowing). (1)

Evolution: Secret Knowledge! Those you encounter frequently have their own agendas; why not make them share that information?

This skill ranks in levels from 0 (Fears) to 5 (Darkest Secret). (N/A)

Summon Elemental: Summon an Elemental to do your bidding. Note: This spell will summon a creature of the Elemental Planes, depending on your ability, to serve you for a short period of time, and ranks from 0 (Lesser) to 5 (Elemental Lord). (N/A)

Lightning Bolt: Cast a blast of Lightning at your target, stunning and possibly frying them with the power of electricity. Note: This spell has lessening effects, depending on the area traveled, and ranks from 0 (50,000V) to 5 (150,000MV). (1)

Evolution: Lightning Storm! Select a location and unleash the true power of the Storm! Note: This spell has lessening effects, depending on the area covered, and ranks from 0 (10m) to 5 (10km). (1)

I'd read through the spell descriptions enough that I knew them practically by heart in the first days. But since I'd taken Arcanist and I'd begun building my own spells, I'd basically ignored the list. More to the point, I'd fallen back on the basics.

Now, I looked them over again, knowing that although most spells, such as Incinerate, for example, were "personal" in nature, I could use them when out and about or whatever. The majority of the Dungeon Lord's spells were designed to be used for and around the dungeon.

Tame, for example, was a spell that was aimed at getting more creatures for the dungeon, things like the doggos I was aiming to be fighting next. Conversion, on the other hand? That was aimed at getting me new races, I figured.

Tame was for unthinking beasts, and Conversion for things like the goblins, kobolds, and Scepiniir.

That opened up some interesting possibilities. Really, I should have been using the fucker a lot by now. I had another spell coming; I had one as part of the rewards for this quest, which was what had probably prompted me to look at the damn thing again. But Conversion wasn't something I'd taken up till now.

If I had taken it? A damn good use would have been to use it when that first goblin had jumped out. Tame it, figure out what was happening, then have it bring out its friends one at a time. If it was like the Tame option, they had to be taken by surprise, though, which limited its usefulness, or when they were already beaten down and accepting their fate.

That being said? If I'd done it right, with over four thousand mana, I could have potentially claimed forty damn goblins.

Then the reality struck me, that they were stinky little fuckers and the last thing I needed was these particular goblins following me home.

I shook my head and got on with the reason I'd actually pulled the spell list up.

Incinerate: Cast a blast of terrible heat at a target, achieving up to 1000 degrees of heat in a single location. Note: This spell has lessening effects, depending on the area covered, and ranks from 0 (10cm) to 5 (1000cm).

(1)

The key point here was that Incinerate let me spread the heat out, but the levels were actually more about how much I could concentrate as a *maximum*.

As an example, I could, currently, effect a maximum area of ten centimeters with the top temperature of a thousand degrees. I could make the area covered a hell of a lot bigger: I could spread that heat out across that space, or I could channel the mana into it and in theory, warm an area quite nicely for a short period of time, thank you very much. The issue was that both it cost me a hundred mana a second to run, and I couldn't be sure how wide a section I needed to cover to spread the heat out and make it not only survivable, but actually useful to the others.

If I got it to a level that was, say, the equivalent of the noonday sun in Hawaii, that'd warm them all up a lot and start their clothes drying off nicely.

It'd still take about an hour to dry them if they jumped in the river and washed off all the crap, though. That would then cost me... I shook my head in bemusement.

I had a horrific amount of mana now in comparison to where I had been only a few weeks ago. But even with all of that, I could cast such a spell for less than a minute.

That meant that there was a single option, if I didn't want Saros to collapse through stupidity, or the others to stay as they were and reek for the rest of the day.

I needed to make up a new goddamn spell.

The lucky part was that I had the basics already down pat in channeling, so it couldn't be that hard, right? With that insane level of both optimism and stupidity combined, I pulled up the details for the apprentice rank quest and checked it over to make sure I was going to hit at least one of those with the spell as well. No need to waste my effort, after all.

Crafting the signature spells of the Apprentice [Arcanist] is a hurdle that many sapiens fail to clear, as each spell completed not only limits the paths available to the mage for their future growth, but is also correspondingly more difficult.

Choose to create three separate spells of any two of the following categories to reach Apprentice Rank as an [Arcanist]. Alternatively, create a single spell in each category to receive an increased boost to your selected affinities and a bonus magical item:

- **Animation: 0/1**
- **Blood: 0/1**
- **Divination: 0/1**

- **Elemental: 0/1**
- **Enchantment: 0/1**
- **Mental: 0/1**
- **Rune: 0/1**
- **Temporal: 0/1**
- **Spatial: 0/1**
- **Summoning: 0/1**

Realistically, there was no way that I could pass on the opportunity to get the elemental boost that crafting one of each of these spells would grant. But for now? The elemental one would do, and it'd have to be Fire.

Working through what I understood of creating the spells I already had, I checked in the group, finding them still the same: surly and mainly glaring at me, as Saros shook like a shitting dog.

She was the only one who had a chance of sneaking up on the mutated dogs as she no longer stank like a goblin, but still. If I didn't hurry up, she was going to collapse. Also, she was learning a very valuable lesson currently about the "joys" of bathing outside in the winter, while fully dressed.

Sure, she was clean again—which, judging from the condition of the others, was a massive relief—but the effect on her now as she roamed ahead? No. No matter what happened now, there was only one way that she'd be alive at the end of the damn day, and that was if she got some magical assistance. I could heal her and that would help a bit, but the damage was down to the cold seeping into her bones and organs, not to something physical.

I grimaced and got back to work, stumbling along in the middle of the group as I spoke quietly to Andre, who'd taken up station on my left.

"I'm trying to work on a new spell," I explained. "It's to warm you all up so that you can wash in the stream or whatever and then have dry clothes, but if I don't manage it and fast, Saros is going to collapse. So, get my attention if something happens. Otherwise, just keep me pointed in the right direction, all right?"

I didn't bother waiting for an answer and split my attention, a little of it toward keeping my body stumbling forward, and the vast majority to working with my mana.

The issue that I had—I knew how to split out different threads of mana now, after all—wasn't creating the fire. I knew how to do that, and I was fairly sure I could create, for example, that Dragon's Breath spell that Dante had been so proud of, even if it would cost me a lot more mana and effort than it did him.

The problem was engagement.

I needed to be able to set an area and have the effect happen there. With Lightning Bolt, I "threw" it out: I gestured; the lightning coalesced and ran through my mana channels, streamed down to the hand and then outside.

In effect, it was two sections for the spell. One was Air magic, a vortex that streamed from me and created a tube. One that ran a hundred meters or an inch, and that created a vacuum. Then the Lightning mana—essentially it was dragged or allowed to fall down that cleared, ionized path.

Now this was a bit more complicated because I couldn't just send out a stream of mana and hope for the best. I mean, the cost would be horrific, and the time taken? Insane.

That being said, though, how the hell did Incinerate work?

It had to be that either it was creating a path from here to there, and then pouring the heat to it, or...

Or maybe, just maybe it wasn't at all. The mana I was trying to use was all around me, after all. Even in the depths of space there was mana, even if there was barely a hair's worth over hundreds of kilometers that I'd recognize.

There still had to be different kinds.

Here, looking about and forcing myself to focus and work, I saw hundreds of thousands of strands. Selecting one, the Fire that I needed, and focusing on just Fire mana, the others faded slightly into obscurity. They were still there, just greyer and less vibrant.

The Fire mana was everywhere. At first, that seemed insane to me—it was cold as a witch's tit, after all—but it quickly came apparent two seconds later that was because although it was cold here compared to the summer, it was still a hell of a lot hotter here than it was on, say, Pluto.

That meant that there was a hell of a lot of mana here that I could use, and that simply by focusing on it, I could create a link from me to that point.

Once I'd done that, noting a strand that was hovering close to a tree off to the left as my target, I focused and added more to it. The mana that was in me burst free, more than I'd tried to use—a *lot* more.

I'd had no clue it was this easy, that the mana would travel from me to that point almost instantaneously. And when it did?

The effect was catastrophic.

The tree, half frozen as it was, with only the dimmest flickers of its hibernating life still registering, was suddenly exposed to a horrific amount of Fire mana.

That mana took the sap, which had already begun to crystallize—the trees in the UK weren't used to such rapid temperature shifts and it was already being damaged by it—and it subjected it to rapid boiling.

There was nowhere for the sap and the gasses to go...and as it was happening everywhere, with the surrounding wood unable to shift its position and adjust as quickly as the sap.

The explosion that rang out was probably heard for miles, certainly for hundreds of meters, and the wooden shrapnel made its presence felt as well.

I and the others dove for the ground, splinters falling everywhere. I tried to figure out what had happened, piecing it together in my mind, as they panicked and searched for the enemy that had apparently tried to blow us up.

"Calm!" I shouted over the rising voices. "Stop, all of you!"

"Keep your head down, boss!" Andre shot back, peering along his rifle and trying to pick something out. "There's someone..."

"It was me, dammit!" I snarled, getting an instant silence in response to that admission. "Me!"

"You blew up the trees?" Robin raised her head and looked into the distance, confused.

A half dozen other trees and bushes had been close enough to be cut down by the explosion, and that had contributed to the spell's destructive force. She clearly couldn't decide whether she was pissed, impressed, or desperate to learn the spell herself.

I pulled up the notification as I explained it, then cursed.

New Spell Discovered!

As an Arcanist, you have gained access to the secrets of creation itself, or at least the ones not very well hidden. Magic, mana, and mysteries fill your mind, and you are finally ready to move on and prove yourself.

You have successfully created a new spell: "Fuck That Tree!" Yes, that's right: you created a spell apparently designed to punish anything small and inoffensive that tries to live quietly in a tree. No more shall those damn squirrels go on simply laying about and avoiding work! Now they too will have to adapt, possibly by getting a job and paying a mortgage, just to escape your wrath!

Cost: 500 mana

Damage: Variable

I read and reread it. Not only had I created a spell that was, in effect, fucking useless, it hadn't even counted toward the class quest! Sure, it was Fire based, so it really could have counted as an elemental one, but it damn well didn't, apparently.

"Why did you do that?" Robin asked acidly.

She'd decided—I could see—to opt for fury, instead of awe. Sod's Law.

"I'm sorry, *sir*, but that just gave away any chance we had at secrecy and the damage! You could have killed one of us!"

"There was no chance of secrecy this close to the goblin nest," I pointed out tiredly. "They'll have heard the shouts and…" I blinked, twisting and peering around, then groaned as I finally caught my brain back up.

The changes in the ground, the ease of walking, the lack of goddamn deep snow, and moreover, the lack of the woods and bloody wilderness?

I'd lost myself in what had seemed like a few minutes of figuring things out, and instead I'd spent at least half an hour at it! We were bloody villages away from where we had been. And yeah, judging from the sudden barking and growls I could hear in the distance, I'd just butt-fucked the element of surprise.

I'd not even bought it dinner first.

CHAPTER NINE

I'd apparently picked a set of trees that extended down a nearby bank, and now, where we were half laid in the fallen snow, we were perfectly in view for the scout that raced over the top of the hill, skidding to a halt, before starting to bark furiously at us.

We were at the bottom of a hill, again, though this one was in the housing estates on the far side of the park. We'd apparently walked its length, through an underpass, and then had started up the far side from that underpass to climb into the middle of the next village.

The path now arced around to the right ahead of us, passing the now thoroughly beaten and battered trees, before climbing up to the left, going between a handful of houses, and then, if memory served me right, across a main tributary road.

The path was old and tree roots had broken the asphalt in dozens of places. But the funding to repair a back path was never a priority, while for some reason, trimming the grass and maintaining the edges had been.

Meaning that until the fall, this area had been marked by almost unusable paths, and neatly trimmed grass that ran from the right off down the bank and away into the distance.

Now, at the top of that curving path that led away, I could see the first dog, skylined against the scudding clouds that I'd also missed approaching.

It had once been a sausage dog, a cold part of my mind pointed out—probably, anyway—one of those ones that made you want to say "bless you" when their owner named the breed. But the change? Well, it was still long, and with a clearly flexible spine, as the rear had apparently missed the whole "we're stopping here" message that the front end had sent out.

It was about five feet tall, a meter plus at the shoulder, and when it'd seen us, it'd skidded to a halt, front paws bouncing as it barked and snarled. The combination of yips and savagery made it unclear whether we were about to be licked to death or torn limb from limb.

The rear, though, had snaked around and had to be at least a meter longer than any sane animal designer would have added on. Now it was scrabbling, nails digging through the snow and shoving off as it tried to get itself back around into

107

its assigned layout, while the front half, that had been dragged by its momentum, was suddenly flipped.

That started it off. The angle of the bank, the snow, the mad rear end that the front was only apparently giving suggestions to instead of orders…

It all combined to send the damn thing flipping end over end, rolling through the snow, biting and twisting as it barked, seemingly more furious with its own ass than anything else.

The problem, though? Less than three meters from it, lay the still form of Saros.

She'd gone down in the snow, and for a heartbeat, I actually wondered whether some of the shrapnel had killed her.

Then the weak raising of her head made it clear.

Nope, it was the cold. She'd fallen, and all that had probably been keeping her upright until then was pride and determination.

A few meters behind her was Michael, and then seven or eight farther down the bank, we all lay spread out.

The dog was bounding and rolling, though, and as it hit Saros, it twisted, apparently seeing her flaccid body as prey it could vent its anger on, and bit down.

That galvanized her, though she was clearly only able to weakly respond. The momentum of the dog then dragged her around, upright, and flung her off to one side as it lost its grip on her.

She hit the ground and rolled, blood splattering from the bite. The metal of her armor hit the path and caused even more of a ruckus as the sound of more approaching dogs came.

And that was when Jimmy arrived.

I'd never seen him move so fast. One minute, he was pressed to the ground a meter or so to my right. The next, he was running, skidding and bracing himself.

The dog flipped over, twisting its back end like a maddened ballerina, and snapped at him, only to be taken to the ground by him. He first took the hit, feet skidding back, and uncovered some of the path beneath him; then he dove forward.

He landed hard, the giant dog beneath him. One armored forearm wrapped around its throat kept the head trapped back, jaws locked closed. The other arm apparently gripped something else as the dog went instantly still and whimpered.

"Hold it!" I called, struggling to my feet and glancing at the crest of the hill. I had time, I decided; there was no—

The first dog bounded into view.

I cursed, unleashing a spell; then, half a second later, a second.

The first was Lightning Bolt. It was a spell I loved, one that seemed to just fit almost every situation, and I didn't regret it here. It slammed into the chest of the leaping dog—some kind of Alsatian crossbreed, I was guessing—and blasted it backward with a cascade of drifting hair and whimpers.

The other spell was Tame. Although I might not use it frequently—and I damn well knew it had drawbacks, such as the target not being actively able to express aggression against you—right now, in this situation, where a massive man had it pinned in place and its scrotum in one iron fist, it was very, very ready to obey.

The spell had barely licked out—its gold, black, and purple flowing lines of smoke latched onto their target's head, pouring in through the eyes, ears, nose, and mouth—before it sagged and whimpered again. Fully ours.

"It's okay!" I said quickly. "Let him go!"

"What?" Jimmy blinked and shook himself, checking that the smoke, whatever it had been, hadn't done anything to him.

"He's tamed!" I snapped, then cursed. "Up and at 'em, people!" I bellowed, as more dogs—fully half the pack at least, I guessed—burst into sight.

This time, Jimmy understood, and although he released the dog gingerly, he did do it. It bounded free of him, shaking itself and ducking its head down to check its undercarriage, before twisting around and growling at the incoming challengers.

"No time for this, I guess…" I muttered. "Fuck's sake, has a training mission *ever* gone this shitty?"

It was a rhetorical question, and yet someone behind me decided to answer it.

"Probably not."

"Yeah well, fuck it!" I snarled, choosing not to twist around and glare at whoever it'd been. "Lightning…*STORM!*" I pulled both hands back to my shoulders, as if I were doing an upright pushup, then thrust my hands forward and channeled fifteen hundred mana into it.

The plan was a bust. And as close as the enemy were, added to how battered my people were? There was just no point.

It was time to cut my losses and work on getting them back in one piece.

The smallest area I could cover with the spell was ten meters. Inside that radius, there was a hell of a lot of damage. But like Incinerate, it was possible to spread the effect and create a larger radius.

When I'd cast it against the goblins in the trial dungeon, I'd kept it to the original intended size; I wanted maximum devastation and destruction, after all. But now?

I lifted into the air and flew forward, the lightning storm aimed about thirty meters back from the brow of the hill and covering a solid few meters past the ridge toward us to make sure I got anything and everything beyond it.

The devastation was incredible, sure. Spread out over such a range, there was less than a third of the power invested into every impact. And those that did land were smaller in number as well. But damn.

As I'd lifted into the air, the clouds had twisted overhead, darkening. The wind picked up seemingly out of nowhere. And the light beneath its outstretching cover darkened to an almost green or grey color.

Then the first strikes came.

109

Each that fell pounded the earth and filled the air with the crack and boom of shattered peace. The pressure grew and the mutated dogs, grown impossibly large, most well over a meter in height—several reached two and more—reacted in absolute terror as nature herself unleashed her fury.

I rocketed forward. I activated my other defensive spell, one that transformed me into a living, breathing taser as I flooded my extremities with lightning.

I took the first dog head-on. It'd spun, snarling and backing away, staring up at the suddenly antagonistic clouds, and sensed me only at the last second, spinning and snapping as I reached out.

Its jaws closed on my armored forearm. The circuit was completed, and boom! It tried to howl, in the last seconds of its life.

I hissed in horror, cutting the power levels drastically as steam billowed from its eyes. The body convulsed as the muscles shriveled and tightened.

There was no way the dog could have survived that level of power. As such, now instead of a stunned and easily tamable dog, I had a rapidly charring hunk of meat—and yeah, smoldering hair—locked onto my arm.

I tore it loose, discarding it, and caught a second. I locked my hands onto its shoulder and head, twisting at the hip, and threw it sideways, out of the storm's radius even as I cast Tame again, blasting it and turning away.

They were all around me now, at least thirty dogs. Some were smaller, weaker, and less developed. But the larger and most powerful ones were clearly getting the lion's share of the food they'd found.

In an honest fight, they'd have been a nightmare, I guessed, but now? Stunned as they were by the sudden storm, panicked by the lightning that hammered down, multiple bolts on all sides, and the air filled with the sticky static discharge…they were terrified and going entirely on instinct.

That instinct was to run like fuck and get away.

I grabbed at anything that came within reach, making the most of the brief time I had left with the storm active.

Grab, taser, throw, tame.

That was it—that was what I'd reduced the world to, and in thirty seconds, I'd spent just over two thousand mana.

By the time the storm broke, its clouds suddenly streaming away in all directions as if as desperate to be elsewhere as the pack had been, I was panting, glaring around. My head throbbed as the last few mutated mutts sprinted in any direction but toward us, howling and whining in terror.

I turned, looking around, making sure the Tame spell had in fact worked. The lightning sunk to quiescence inside me again, as I released it and faced the others.

Robin was in the lead, as she sank to one knee.

"My lord," she said reverently. "I believe."

I stared at her, frowning, then bit back a curse as she lifted her head. Her eyes gleamed with fanaticism, even as a new prompt flashed into being.

Congratulations!

You have increased the faith of your follower [Robin – First Paladin]

Continue to increase your standing among your people to advance the path of religion.

I stared at the prompt, then the look on her face and damn well cursed internally. I'd just massively fucked that one up.

As luck would have it, that was when Saros groaned, flapping one hand weakly, as a giant Doberman—fortunately, one I'd tamed—started licking at her mangled arm.

Bright-red blood spattered the snow nearby and covered one bracer, standing out against the black and steel of the metal, and the grey and white of her fur. And the dog?

It was loving the smell of her, and apparently the taste of her blood.

"Back!" I barked, striding forward, and dragged the healing focal orb back out of my bag. As I reached her, I checked my mana and cursed. "Healer!" I called. "Whoever is training to be a healer, get over here!"

Jimmy was the first, and he powered the orb nicely. Saros hissed again as what was apparently an indented section of the armor gave her grief as the flesh tried to heal around it.

I reached down, wriggling my fingers around and underneath it, twisting it. I searched for the clasp, then popped it and ripped it free.

She whimpered, then glared at us both for hearing such an un-Scepiniir-like sound pass her lips.

"What do we do, boss?" Andre stood next to me, and I glanced from him to the state of her, the dogs around us, and the filthy, worn-out condition of the rest of the party.

"We head back." I sighed. "We head back to the citadel, and you all get some rest and recover. Tomorrow, we come back and sort out the remaining dogs, then head back to the park. This training run is over."

There weren't any complaints, which was both a relief and galling.

If I'd said that to my team? I'd have had half of them complaining straightaway, which was why I was relieved, but they'd have been arguing to complete the mission.

The job wasn't done until the job was done, they'd say. Or, in Chris's case, probably something about butt sex and a squirrel. But that wasn't the point. We'd gotten to where we were because we always got the job done.

Glancing around, though, I could see that although Andre and Jimmy were fine to continue, the others were massively relieved to not be going on. Robin just stared at me, star-struck…which I hated. Saros was barely aware of anything; even with the healing, she was half out of it. And the trainees?

111

They weren't ready for this. Or, at least, they weren't ready for the big league. The average row? Mid-tier at best? Yeah, they could probably achieve that, with training.

Andre and Jimmy, though? There, I realized it was me letting them down.

I picked up Saros and raised my voice as I glanced around, making sure everyone was listening, and projected my intention at the dogs.

"We're heading back to the Galleries. What's the fastest route?"

"This way," Michael said quickly, gesturing back up the bank and to the left. "It's about three-quarters of a mile that way."

"Lead on." I shifted Saros to lie more comfortably over one shoulder and started off. The others fell in around me, and I chewed at my lip as I thought.

What I needed to do was get her back and warmed up. I had no clue what the real effects of hypothermia were; I just knew that she was cold as shit and that wasn't good. She was also a Scepiniir, and my understanding of their reaction to the cold was limited to "Well, they've got fur and look a bit like cats."

She wasn't doing well. She could be minutes from death, already too late to save, or totally fine…just wiped out due to low blood sugar, for all I knew.

The problem was, for me to fly her back to the base, or better yet to the park, I'd need to leave the others. They'd already proved to me that they had nowhere near the natural drive that I'd be comfortable leaving them out here, and the dogs were only half tamed.

Sure, the spell had worked, but ten minutes ago, they had wanted to eat me. I couldn't trust that the spell would definitely hold, not until they'd had a bit of time. For now, that meant we were walking, though I made sure to set a fast pace as I did it.

That got a few complaints after a couple of minutes, but Robin and the twins stifled and shut them down before I could.

Ten minutes later, we could see the outer wall of the old shopping center. Five minutes after that, we were inside, and at last I felt that I had some backup.

The truck was there. Corpse lords were unloading it, food coming down and boxes of supplies, as people milled about, waiting on their turn to climb in.

I turned to the others and spoke quickly. "Robin, take the others and get food, rest, and cleaned up. We'll speak later. Andre, Jimmy, you're with me."

"Yes, Lord." Robin bowed her head.

I stifled a growl, turning away, and marched toward the vehicles. Before I could make it halfway to them, Rhodes was there.

"Sir, how can we help?" she asked briskly, carefully not wrinkling her nose at the goddamn awful stench that rolled off most of the party.

"Saros is in shock, or hibernating," I said without preamble. "She was in the water, and then walking in this cold for too long… The others are…" I paused, then took a deep breath, before admitting to it. "The majority are a shower of shite, and I'm a terrible trainer. I think I'm going to need your help, but Jimmy and Andre did well."

"Well, at least you learned something valuable, sir." She clearly tried to hide a smile. "A quick tip for you, though. You never tell the lower ranks they are doing well in front of another, unless it's in front of the whole company. Praising them now, after a mission, and to me, just says how much you need to learn."

"Dammit."

"I can work with this." She nodded, a twinkle in her eye. "Jimmy, Andre, get Saros to Jo. She'll know what to do."

"Yes, Captain!" they chorused, before taking the unconscious Scepiniir from me and heading off, grinning all the way.

"Seriously, how were they?" She glanced after them.

"Not bad, a bit too bound to orders," I said. "I told them to guide Robin but to let her make her own mistakes, and they nearly let her get them all killed. That was on me ordering them to do one thing and not countering it with more specifics."

"It's their greatest limitation." She nodded. "They're born soldiers, fast and strong, brave. Not the brightest, but they'd never make it beyond corporal, and that'd be more on time served than ability. At the bottom of the rung? They'll always excel, though."

"Yeah." I grunted. "I mean it, though—I fucked up."

"None of them died, and you look like you did well with the dogs?"

I glanced back at the pack that stood around, happily watching the world passing by.

"I got about half to a third of the pack, but by the time I did that, I'd used most of my mana, and I couldn't guarantee the safety of the trainees anymore." I blew out a long breath in frustration.

"You took care of the goblins?" she asked, and I nodded. "Then you got more than halfway. For a first training exercise, and one planned on the fly, that's not bad. When are you planning to go back out?"

"As soon as I've recovered my mana and had a goddamn shower."

"Tomorrow morning," she recommended. "At that point, we'll take a few others out, and I'll come with you—send Chris on the run to the park on his own. Then I'll be able to offer advice after I've seen you in the field," she proposed. "You forget, it's a sergeant's job to break in perfectly useless second lieutenants and make something that can shit thunder and piss lightning. I think I can make a passable officer of you yet."

"Thanks, Sarge, although, you're a captain now, remember?" I sighed, before grinning ruefully. "You know, I used to think about joining the army, instead of going down the civilian tech route."

"Why didn't you?" She sounded genuinely curious, before shrugging. "And I'll always be a sergeant at heart."

"I didn't think I'd be good with the discipline and the early mornings," I admitted. "That and I was too busy drinking and partying."

"You'd be surprised how much of that there is going on."

"I bet." I straightened my shoulders, then looked around again. "Where's Chris?"

"We left him at the park to deal with a few problem children, and so he could get a shower and some sleep. He'll be back tomorrow. Why?"

"Dammit, he's the fuckin' Druid!" I groaned. "I tamed the dogs, thinking he'd be great with them, and now…?"

"Well…" She smiled. "He's actually staying in a small building built outside the walls of the park. Everyone who came to Otterburn is doing their best to limit contact with everyone who didn't as much as possible, so when Ashley suggested a 'hearts and minds' offering outside the main camp, just so people could see what they were getting inside, Kelly agreed. He's staying in there."

"I don't get it."

"It's a building with bunks and showers, basically ten small separate bedrooms, all ensuite, and each with two single bunks in each room. If we don't want to let people inside the walls, and we want to show them that we still have access to civilization? They can go in there."

"And they'll never leave." I grunted. "If they're desperate and we decide we don't want them inside, they'll refuse to leave if that's heated and with hot water, etc. Who could blame them."

"True, except that we have control over the walls and so on." Rhodes grinned. "She thought of that and made it so that the rooms all back onto the outside world. All we need to do is grow stone over the door, and then take down the rear wall. Then they're moving on whether they like it or not."

"Devious." I nodded. "I like it."

"So, the others you took out?"

"The scout—damn…rogue, I mean—Michael was a bit average, as was…ah, hell, they *all* were. I'd hoped one of them would stand out for more than how happy they were to return here, but they didn't."

"Anyone you'd not trust?" She frowned, watching them in the distance as they hurried across the small bridge toward the entrance to the old shopping center.

"No, but none I'd trust either," I admitted. "Beyond the twins, I'd only keep Robin as useful, and that's more because of her class than anything else. The others…" I shook my head.

"Then we know where we stand." She nodded. "Okay, tomorrow, first light, we head back out and see what we see from them all. For now, I'd suggest you set your dogs up with a place to stay, give them some food and get some sleep, sir. Tomorrow, you're going to need to be on form. That or join the next caravan and take them to Chris?"

"Oh goodie." I sighed, before looking back at the dogs. "Goddammit, Chris." The option of feed his dogs or take them for a walk wasn't one that I'd considered. I forced a smile, thanked the captain, then set off, trudging across the uneven ground in the direction of the building ahead.

Between the mana migraine—thankfully, low grade, but definitely there thanks to the low mana I had—and the long day out in the cold, without food, I was damn well ready for a shower and sleep.

I made it into the building, got people to direct me to where I could have the dogs without anyone interrupting them or causing issues, and then cursed again.

I'd not been damn well thinking! Not only could I not have a goddamn shower here, but I couldn't create food, heat, or any of the luxuries I'd been wanting.

Cue ten more minutes sorting out a load of cans of food that the dogs could eat, water bowls and so on, and then getting myself something to eat, before I finally laid myself down and slid into the dungeon sense. I closed my eyes and let my body relax, as I searched for the next job.

I'd check in with the ladies, get some exercise in and then get some rest, and prepare for tomorrow.

CHAPTER TEN

"Well, all things considered, that went better than I was expecting," Rhodes assured me cheerily.

I glared at her, the grumbles of the rest of the group behind me clearly audible as Robin prattled on at them about how they should be searching for the secret to becoming a Paladin like her and devoting their lives to the "new gods."

I closed my eyes at that, dropping my face into my hands and groaning. That was going to bite me in the ass at the worst possible time, I just fucking knew it.

"Did you check your notifications?" Rhodes asked.

I lifted my head, taking a deep breath, and did so.

Congratulations!

You have killed the following:

- **17x Wild Goblins, Levels 2-5, 204 XP**
- **2x Mutated dog, Levels 3-8, 170 XP**
- **1x Axmoxiss, Level 17, 300 XP**

Total XP earned: 674 XP
Total XP awarded: 674 XP

Current XP to next level stands at 60,461/60,000

Congratulations!

You have reached Level 29.

Current XP to next level stands at 461/75,000

You have 9 unspent Stat Points

You have gained additional Stat Points in the following areas through constant effort.

- **+1 Agility**

- **+1 Charisma**

Continue to work hard to increase these or other stats...

Just seeing that was a kick in the tits—not that I'd achieved another level...well, not *really*. It was that the next one, which would bring a class choice for me, was at seventy-five thousand points! That felt like forever away, when killing those goddamn goblins had barely netted me more than a handful of points each.

The next prompt was a bit of a consolation, though that quickly turned sour as well.

Congratulations!

You have completed your Quest!

Nest Cleansing: Goblins and Mutts

Two monster nests had been identified in the nearby area, posing a threat to local safety and dungeon expansion. A goblin nest of low-level creatures had established itself, and a pack of mutated dogs was preying on the goblins. The goblins, in turn, were attempting to tame these dogs as mounts.

Though it took several attempts, you and your trainees have managed to clear out the local monster nests.

Objectives:

- Clear the goblin nest (1/1)
- Eliminate the pack of mutated dogs (1/1)
- Assess the combat skills of the soldier trainees (2/2)
- Evaluate the Paladin trainee's potential (1/1)
- Determine the trustworthiness of the borderline recruits (7/7)

Trainee Team for Assessment:

- 2 x Low-level but experienced soldier trainees
- 1 x Paladin trainee
- 1 x Scout trainee

Jez Cajiao

- 7 x Borderline untrustworthy recruits
- +1 Experienced Trainer

Complete this quest to gain access to the following rewards:

- +1 to top three Attributes
- +1 Spell
- Improved regional security
- Access to potential new recruits or mounts
- ~~2,000 XP~~
- 500 XP

Note: Due to the level of difficulty involved, the reward has been modified accordingly.

Basically, the system was saying "You're a useless trainer and you needed help, so no cookie for you." Damn system and its shitty rules.

I pulled up my character sheet and ran through it quickly, checking the details and seeing what and where I'd increased.

I'd remembered and made use of the bonus plus ten points to a single stat that I'd received and put aside earlier, using it to significantly close the gap between my physical and mental abilities, then slid the other nine stat points I had straight into my Intelligence. It leapt my mana all the way to six thousand points: sixty solid uses of a simple spell like Incinerate or Lightning Bolt, and four uses of a major spell like Lightning Storm. I couldn't help but be impressed by that, even if the second level of Arcanist that I'd gained hadn't improved the selection of spells at all.

Name: Matt, First Lord of the Storm				
Host Powers: 1 (Enhanced Regeneration)				
Species: Thunderstorm		Bonus: None		
Level: 29		Progress to next level: 961/75,000		
Stat	Current Points	Description	Effect	Progress to Next Level
Agility	55	Governs dodge and movement	Heightened chance to dodge attacks 110%+20%= 132%	4/100
Charisma	43	Governs likely success to charm,	72% more likely to succeed in events that require seduction, persuasion, or threats (10%+ (33x2) = 72)	2/100

		seduce, or threaten		
Constitution	53	Governs Health and Health Regeneration	HP: 53x60 = 3,180	23/100
Dexterity	45	Governs ability with weapons and crafting	+45% Increased chance of improved result +17 to melee damage	37/100
Endurance	47	Governs Stamina and Stamina Regeneration	Stamina: 47x50 = 2,350	14/100
Intelligence	75	Governs base manapool, standard intellectual capacity	Mana: 75x80=6,000	42/100
Luck	46	Governs overall chance of bonuses and critical hits	+72% increased chance of positive outcome	69/100
Perception	44	Governs ranged damage and chance to spot hidden items/traps	+34 to all ranged attacks	19/100
Strength	41	Governs damage with melee weapons and carrying capacity	+62 to all damage with Melee weapons	15/100
Wisdom	60	Governs mana regeneration	1200 mana regenerated per hour (Arcanist class 2 boost)	11/100

For whatever reason, my Wisdom had leapt by a point, as had both the Luck and Charisma stats, though I'd not felt like they were the most used stats recently. Fuck it, probably the damn system having a laugh. I grumbled about it under my breath as we stalked back along the road toward the citadel again.

Thinking back to my magic, though, and specifically my Arcanist class, it wasn't like I was planning to take it again moving forward. Instead, I'd work to unlock it the "real" way, I'd decided already. Learn the spells and understand them: ultimately, they'd be a lot more powerful, rather than learning them by rote unlocking and activation.

Goddamn standard user crap. I was an admin by damn, a super-user! I was when I worked in IT. I was as the master of the dungeon, and I damn well would be with magic as well!

After all, when you knew the rules, you knew how to break them better.

The fight had been easy, I had to admit. I didn't really see what had been done differently—not much, anyway. It was simply that *everything* had gone wrong last time. This time around, Rhodes explained the situation beforehand. She walked them through the likely results and the possible counters—just like I damn well had—and then she sorted them into their positions and led them in.

I'd tamed the dogs yesterday, and I did so again today, taking us up to thirty-seven of the hairy slobbering buggers that we had by the end of the day.

The fight to capture them was far easier than I expected, mainly because the dogs we'd already tamed worked in tandem as Rhodes ordered, fighting and pinning set animals, while I alternated taming them with my spell, or acting like a walking taser and then taming them.

We'd separated our target animals from the main pack, attacked, subdued and tamed, while most of the group drove the others off by setting off a few flash-bangs. Then we waited for my mana to return and went for the next small portion.

The trainees had catchpoles, clubs, and padded armor that had been brought back from the park by Rhodes last night. And when they didn't have to crawl around in goblin shite, they were a lot more sanguine about their life choices, apparently.

Really, the only thing that had gone wrong in the entire fight was that it'd taken Rhodes to order them about and not me…and that, from their point of view, they were being constantly pestered by an evangelist.

It was only that she was a heavily armed and armored evangelist of their new boss's own religion that was keeping her from being assaulted, I guessed. But if she kept this shit up?

I'd be helping them.

At the end of the day, though, the job was done; the quest was complete. Although I'd blatantly failed as a trainer, I'd achieved what I actually set out to do.

Andre and Jimmy got a little more experience, as did Saros, though hers was tempered with the whole "You're an idiot who nearly killed herself in an attempt to be clean."

The twins learned that sometimes you needed to read more into the situation than the orders you were given and adjust on the fly. They got two extra levels, and discovered that I was great at the big picture, but as Rhodes explained: "Officers need to stick to officering, and leave the actual work to those who know better."

Fucker.

I also knew who was worth the effort with the new trainees, which was to say that they were well worth the effort of the trainers to beat them into shape, that they weren't as near as I'd seen complete wastes of skin, but neither were they worth any extra effort.

That was fine. I was more interested in making them understand that they'd broken the rules and had to atone, than anything else. If they'd broken the rules and had been bastards with it—as some had been—then they'd just have been out the door, regardless.

Robin was…well, she was the exception.

She was annoying, she was frustrating, and she seemed to be determined that I was a "real" god and that she, as my first Paladin, needed to grow the religion.

I hated that in so many ways I couldn't articulate it. *But*…the potential? It was incredible.

I was fairly sure that a religion like this, having priests and paladins and shit, couldn't be entirely one way. They'd kill their god in their first major battle if that was the case, after all, but I just didn't know enough about the system yet to figure out anything else.

As it was, though, I finally had some time to work on it, and I wasn't getting distracted by anything else. The core should be done in a few more hours and then that was it. I could get the ball rolling with the tech side, get the medical, get the—

Fuck.

I forced the list of jobs aside and looked over at Rhodes, who was watching me and waiting.

"Sorry," I muttered. "Checking details and I had a lot of notifications that were…meh."

"Meh?"

"Kill notifications, level-ups, quest completions…that kinda thing. Were you expecting anything else?"

"Not really, but I wanted to be sure," she admitted. "So, what's your next step?"

"Do you need me here anymore?" I gestured to the citadel walls in the distance.

"We can manage without you," she assured me. "Any news on returning to the camp and ensuring the lack of any infection?"

"That's what I'll help with next," I said. "I'll take the dogs to the park, hand them over to the trainers Chris said he was sorting—"

They were called "beast-masters" apparently, and he'd already had a few in training, or who were looking at the Druid path. He'd gathered them up a few weeks back and they'd been the ones maintaining, checking, and operating the traps until now.

I'd not checked in on them, but with these dogs, this apparently would bring our numbers to up over a hundred now—more than enough for a respectable cavalry unit.

"Then I'll be hitting the showers, getting some hot food in me, and starting on the Glass core updates, as I know there's going to be an absolute fuckload of changes there. Then once we've got a handle on it? Magical shite."

"Better you than me, sir," she said. "So, ETA on being able to return? We should be finished with the evacuation later tomorrow, if not before…though some more civilians have joined of late, adjusting the numbers again. Is it likely that we'll be in a position to return to Newcastle or spend time inside the park at that point?"

"I don't know," I admitted. "I'm hopeful that as soon as we've finished the upgrade to Glass, we'll have the option to update the medical facilities, and then it'll be right from there that we can move on. Maybe a day, maybe less. If that's not the case, though…well, I don't know. Sorry, Rhodes. You know as much as I do."

"Understood, sir. It'd be nice to be able to tell the boys and girls the plan, that's all."

"When I know, you'll know," I assured her, before turning to the others. "Okay, people, I'm going to be leaving you as soon as we're back inside of the walls. I'll be taking the dogs and—"

"Sir, if we use the dogs as additional scouts, now that they're trained, we'll be able to take more people on the runs to the park," Rhodes pointed out. "It'll take a little longer for each run, but it'll significantly increase the number of people we can move."

"Fair point there." I sighed, hating that I was constantly changing the goddamn plan five minutes later. "Right. As soon as we get back inside the walls, I'll be leaving you. Robin, help maintain control over the citadel and get people moving. Use those you can and keep people safe. We'll talk more over the next few days about the whole Paladin thing.

"The rest of you are under Rhodes's command as usual—either like Andre, Jimmy, and Saros as part of our dungeon forces, or as new trainees. You put the hours in; you learned a bit and leveled a bit. You passed enough that, although you didn't impress me, you're into the dungeon, as you also didn't fuck up too badly. I'm sorry that my training for you wasn't as effective as I'd have liked. The situation was fluid, but we survived and the objective was achieved. Let's move on from that."

As speeches went, it was frankly right up there with "They couldn't hit an elephant at this distance" by an American general I'd been taught about in school, who was immediately shot and killed. It was shit. I knew it was shit, and they knew it was shit. I stared at them for a second, they stared at me, and I finally turned back to the road and stomped on.

The only thing that made it worse was when Jimmy and Andre tried to push the others into a cheer for me.

I hated my life at times.

Half an hour later, I touched down, landing lightly and jogging a few steps to slow. I approached the new building on the outer edge of the park.

I was also incredibly goddamn thankful to be away from *everyone*.

The small building was simple in the extreme, about ten meters wide, a hundred long, and built as an oblong, with a twenty-meter gap from its wall and roof to the nearby wall of the park, to make sure that nobody could climb on the roof and then use it to scale the park's walls.

There'd been more added since I learned of it, apparently. There was now capacity for twenty rooms on either side, each that could house—comfortably—two people. They had a small space in the room for eating, and then their beds, along with a shower and toilet each.

All in all, it was friggin' luxury compared to the way most of the human race was living right now. And after a few days in the citadel and traveling from Otterburn to here, then back and forth from the dungeon and the various running about I'd done?

I was goddamn ready for this.

I marched straight past the guard on the door, who saluted, and I barely gave them a nod, I was so ready for some peace and quiet. Moving along the corridor, I saw little markers on each door that showed whether they were occupied or not, and it only took a few steps to find one that was available.

Ducking inside, I double-checked it was, and then closed the door with a sigh and locked it. Five minutes later, I was naked in the shower, and I let the rest of the world just go fuck itself.

Half an hour, that was all I gave myself, but damn I felt better when I was done. Ten minutes in the shower, ten minutes sorting my gear—basically entering the dungeon sense, replacing some of it, repairing and cleaning the rest, and making a few minor adjustments like to some leather that'd been rubbing—and then food.

A steak, rare, a mountain of fries, some roasted carrots, greens with bacon and onions, and a nice, straightforward garlic cream sauce. That and a few buns to dip in it all, and I was at peace with the world.

Half an hour. That was all I needed.

When I finally laid down on the bed—being the trusting soul that I am, I got entirely dressed and armored again first—I was ready to get back to work.

"Kelly," I said in greeting, smiling in return when she turned and smiled up at me, then reached out and hugged her close.

I'd entered the dungeon sense as soon as I'd closed my eyes. Rather than have a look around and check on things myself, I simply blurred straight from my little room, right to the dungeon control center.

Once there, I found her standing over the table and checking details on a wall image. For the first time in ages, Aly was nowhere in sight.

"How are you doing?"

She smiled again, before sighing and shrugging. "I'm okay, missing my boy toy, and some real relaxation a bit, but I'm getting there. You okay?"

"Yeah," I assured her with a faint smile. "I needed a shower and some food when I returned, but that was all. Ready to work now."

"Returned?" she asked sharply, and I snorted.

"Don't worry, I'm at the housing outside the park," I explained. "I meant when I got back into the dungeon's reach, that's all."

"Ah, okay. Damn, you should have sorted yourself somewhere nicer than that..." Then she shook her head and corrected herself straightaway. "No, you were right not to. It'd be a waste. Hopefully, in a day or so, you'll be back in here and that'll be an end to all of this."

"Exactly. Any news?"

She shook her head, moving to sit down. "Not really. The increase in mana has massively helped speed things up, but we also don't want to drain the area, so we're taking our time. We're about an hour away, as near as I can tell. This upgrade seems more involved than the others, but it shouldn't be much longer."

"That's a relief then. What's happened with the hospital staff?"

"They're in." She smiled.

As soon as she said it, a massive weight shifted on my shoulders, getting ready to lift off. "Really?"

"Yeah, they're still wary of us, of the dungeon and you specifically, but that's not a personal thing. It's that it's a dungeon, and it's so far outside of their comfort zone, it's like getting Chris to teach algebra."

"What made the difference?" I asked.

"Honestly, I think it was a combination of things. Ashley made it clear that you and a team had rescued people from the Otterburn Camp and they'd joined us. That we were recruiting specialist people, like these doctors and nurses, and we respected their knowledge and training, and needed them still. It wasn't all just a matter of it all being handwavium or magic of some kind, and that there was magic to be learned and improved upon as well.

"The vast majority of the survivors they had were at death's door. They were the most severely injured, those who were limping along day-to-day and who they could see no way to help, or to improve. They were getting ready to humanely kill them, because they saw no alternative and were bound by their oath to do no harm.

To someone who's in constant pain every day, with almost no drugs left to treat, to then be exposed to this winter, dwindling food supplies, and more?"

She shook her head and gestured vaguely around at the outside world. "They were losing hope. They didn't know what to do. And when they first heard of us, they were worried that we were warlords or gangs like the other one, setting up, ready to take and take. That the army is supporting us and we'd not be simply forcing them to kill their charges, and then forget their training and go till a field or whatever? It was enough to make them consider it.

"Then came Ashley's 'hearts and minds' messages—the hot food, the safety and the warmth, as well as the healing tower and seeing their people actually getting better. Basically, we gambled that they'd like and trust us, and it's paid off.

"Don't get me wrong—there's a shitload of work left to do before they're ours and they're ready to be essentially trusted as members of the dungeon, or we're looking at having one of their group sit with Jo on the council. But it's coming."

"Thank the stars," I whispered. "That they're actually joining us is incredible. It means that we can..."

"You can come home," she agreed. "Soon, you'll be home with me again."

"That's what we need," I said with a nod, before going on firmly. "And not just because I need you and I need to damn well sleep in my own bed and have some sexy time, as much as I love that."

"Oh?" She arched one eyebrow. "And what, pray tell, is more important than being my boy toy?" she asked in a hoity-toity voice.

"Being able to open the nexus gate to the camp, and bringing all those people back to actually see some real life again. Letting them see that there's hope and that people are actually living, not just surviving." I tried to joke about it, and I'd known that Kelly was joking as well, but the thought of all those incredibly traumatized people from Otterburn Camp being able to walk in the park, to meet someone and have coffee by the lake, to go on a date or grab a burger and just...stop?

That was what I needed to achieve, and it'd been percolating around the back of my brain for days, I realized.

"Okay, that's the plan," she agreed. "But in working to achieve that, we need to find a realistic way to do it and not freak everyone out. The best way that I can see is..."

The plan was immense, but also badly needed.

Essentially, it came down to the construction and manning of three new medical facilities, with the largest being at the park, and the camp and the main dungeon hub both getting slightly smaller ones. People would be marched through them, scanned, evaluated, and then healed...day in and day out. They'd be given a marker when they were done; a list would be created in each section and updated

125

in the dungeon, and that master list would show who had been seen, confirmed as checked, and who hadn't.

There'd also be a census performed when we did that, with people being questioned as to their skills, and whether they felt they were being best utilized where they were, or whether they wanted to ask for a transfer, then what they wanted to do.

That section was simple, because most of these people had been working their asses off doing mundane absorption tasks. As the undead resource teams came online, they were becoming less and less needed.

The priority at first, of course, was going to be funneling the people who had come from Otterburn through the process. That way, we'd find out in short order whether any of us were infected.

If we were found to be, then there would need to be a solution found and boom, then we'd move on. If not, as I was damn well hoping and expecting, then the process could pick up speed, and we could start moving people to the different sites to relax a little, to recover and to go on with their lives.

By the time the Glass core finally clicked over, activating and unlocking the rest of the systems, Aly was back. We'd started discussing possible transfer zones by then, sites for the new hospital—as that was what it was going to become, after all, and we might as well start as we meant to go on—and the lesser medical facilities.

There was talk of redesigning the park, of making it not only the main medical facility where the "real" doctors would be located and where the medical appointments and midwifery, etc., was all being carried out, but also, yeah…

It was to become the new crafting, manufacturing, and research hub.

That was when I'd laid out the last details, and why the Newcastle dungeon as it existed currently wasn't going to be the main hub site forever.

Frankly, I think I scared the shit out of the ladies by the end. But they agreed: the Mouse and his lawyers—if any survived—would definitely be coming after me.

CHAPTER ELEVEN

The Glass core, as it activated, flooded the system with an incredible, deep sea-green tinge for long seconds, before it bled back to a more normal and almost unnoticeable level again.

As it did so, a thousand changes came online and faded, like waves coming in and out of the shore.

Data was there in far greater numbers than ever before: everything from the exact mana production rates, to the temperature, wind variance and speed, the mana flow…

To all Inhabitants of the Glass Dungeon!

Welcome! We, your distant allies, thank you, and stand with you through our gift of technology. We believe in you all!

To reward you for your advancement and dedication, your dungeon will receive an appropriate primary bonus!

Gah! Not *again*! Fucking aliens! I cursed again and again as another prompt appeared and refused to allow me to minimize it.

Congratulations, Dungeon Lord!

You have ascended even higher to the mighty rank of Glass, and your dungeon is now named as the First Glass Dungeon. Other Dungeons will be informed of your magnificent achievement, and will be made aware that your path is the most effective! Soon, additional dungeons will be able to be connected to your own.

The Primary Nexus Gates have now been created, though as the first to reach Glass, you will receive a secondary nexus gate as a bonus reward! Speak to your Dungeon Fairy for more details and to make the necessary arrangements, as well as to receive a bonus!

I continued to curse, over and over, banishing the goddamn notification and just hoping that, for once, nobody was going to be pissed that I'd managed to reach the next level ahead of them.

I shouldn't have bothered, as three more dungeons immediately declared their enmity and that they were joining the goddamn Pantheon of Unlife and their war against us.

I was just glad that none of the names were familiar. Had some of the Dungeon Lords and Ladies I'd met already joined them, I'd have been *really* pissed.

I dragged down a deep breath and forced the whole thing away, determined to get on with the goddamn job at hand.

Reams of data were suddenly available at my fingertips, and it was just too much. I was used to working in IT—though I had to admit I was enjoying stabbing things in the face far more than I used to enjoy that job.

I'd gotten through many a day by spending every user interaction mentally visualizing beating them to death with their keyboard, all while screaming the most commonly used passwords at them, and why they shouldn't think that "P@55w0rd" was a super-sneaky and incredibly inventive one.

Now, though, as I stared at the fields that surged up, populated and then died away, I shook myself. I'd seen in those brief glimpses a veritable smorgasbord of randomness. I'd seen things from predictions about population growth to soil composition and mineral content.

There were spaces for accessing seismic data to mana migration patterns, and satellite tracking facilities to goddamn genetic augmentation. The leyline tracker and prediction algorithm had distracted me for a half second, until I saw that it was an option, and one that I'd have to research, but that it sat at a hundred million mana in cost.

A HUNDRED MILLION.

I felt like Doctor Evil, reading and rereading that fucking number, before banishing it.

There were dozens of sections—hell, there had to be a hundred new lines that led off the tech side, and goddamn, they were…they were…huh.

I paused. I'd been moving on, planning on just a quick overview of each area to see whether there was anything that I needed to look at, but that I'd just get it sorted and fuckoffski, until I saw the new lines.

There were two new advancements now visible.

If I researched crystals, for example, I could now see that depending on the other paths chosen, they would unlock more and more paths that were complementary.

Through crystals and mana storage—which we'd unlocked a fair amount of now—I could see that crystalline-based memory storage was an option…provided I also unlocked data devices and precision glass-based manufacturing.

That last one was a headache and a half as it required a dozen other smaller level technologies, including…glassblowing.

Glassblowing and smelting were in there, as was advanced furnace technologies, high purity refinements, precision molding and shaping tools, and optical measurement systems, finishing with annealing and stress relief.

Stress relief wasn't even marked as a blowjob and a rum, either. Apparently, it was something to do with...

I blanked and pulled back, seeing the way that the suddenly flowing path of technologies flexed and twisted, shrinking back down as I stared in shock.

Essentially, I'd just discovered that we were no longer limited to "unlock this and then see what comes next" as a technological path. This was incredible!

The lower-level techs that led to the glass-based manufacturing were all things that we were already working on, in one way or another.

We had the lowest levels of these all unlocked as part of unlocking the glassblowing research. It needed its tools, it needed a method to heat and cool the glass, the purification, and the methods of looking at the results to see whether they were stable or cracked underneath and more.

All the most basic levels of these were already unlocked in that research tree, and as I blinked, I saw that it was a tree as well. That was what the change to Glass had unlocked: specializations!

These were levels of equipment, for example, that would need massive amounts of research and investment to get right. But, once they were done? They could then be used in so many ways!

The glassblowing tools, for example? They weren't limited to damn glassblowing! So many of the same tools were needed in high-strength manufacturing, in blacksmithing, in machinist's tools, in...

My mind shuddered away from trying to figure out the immensity of the knock-on effect this Glass upgrade had brought.

Not all tools would be useful to each stage or skill—of course they wouldn't—but there were so many that *would*, it was incredible. It was also low-key terrifying because the sudden jump in the mana that we'd managed to unlock had me convinced before that we were about to hit a kind of renaissance.

We'd have the mana to burn to carry out some of my madder plans, right? We could get started on it all and finally slow down with the panic. Instead, we were going to barely keep up thanks to that and the massive upgrades.

Fuck me, though—if we'd not invested before all of this? I could see exactly where we'd have been shafted right now.

If not for the seed growth ability, anyway.

I shook that thought aside and *shifted*, dragging the other two from their own spheres of influence with squawks and protests as I hauled them into the air with me, reaching up toward the previously highest point we'd been able to reach...and finding that it'd changed as well.

No longer was the view like this in the dungeon sense as blurry and far-reaching as it had been. Instead, it was crisp and clear, and I just knew we'd be capable of reaching low orbit through more research now. Hell, possibly much farther out!

"Matt!" Kelly snapped. "I was looking at things..."

"So was I," Aly growled.

I held both hands up in appeasement, nodding. "I know. I'm sorry. I know you were, and I'll let you get back to them in just a minute," I assured them. "You're right—I should have asked first, but you both need to stop for a second and look at what you were working on."

"Why?" Aly snapped. "I was looking at the new trees and the massive upgrades I can make to research for everyone!"

"And Kelly?" I prompted.

"The minion access logs." She frowned. "There's a whole new section that's opened up on my system that gives me access to much more in-depth data on the dungeon-born, as well as their growth and abilities."

"And how do either of those systems, specifically the sections you were looking at *right now*, affect the plan to get the dungeon's people examined with the new medical facilities?" I asked.

"Well, they don't, but I was just..." Aly shrugged, before pausing and checking something else. "Damn."

"Damn?" Kelly asked.

"Half an hour." Aly shook her head. "I'd been looking at things for half an hour, lost in the new potential."

"Oh," Kelly said, suddenly sounding a lot less annoyed and a little embarrassed. "Well, it was only half an hour, I guess..."

"It was," I agreed. "But I saw a thousand things I wanted to work on, and to unlock, and I was 'only' looking for half an hour. If I wasn't desperate to get back? I could have spent a week looking over all those details. But if we stop instead, and start the next phase? Then we can relax and explore once we've done that."

"Okay." Kelly sighed.

"I hate it when you're right," Aly grumbled.

I laughed. "Don't worry, I'll not tell Mike that you forgot about him."

She glared at me. "You do that, and I'll make sure Kell punishes you later," she said warningly.

"Kinky," I joked.

"Chastity belt," Kelly said. "Maybe I should wear one of those for the first few days when you get back, just to make it clear that you're not—"

"*Illbegood!*" I said in a rush, making both ladies laugh. "Okay, okay. You win, all right?!"

"Good boy," Aly murmured, and we all grinned at one another. "Okay, let's get back to it." Aly sighed after a second.

The air around us blurred for a moment, before we were back in the command room, standing over the table.

As Aly looked at it, a representation of the new medical facilities appeared, first in blueprint form, and then, as more and more detail was added, with the upgradable and unlockable additional facilities.

"I'll reach out to Jo," I said after a few seconds, bowing out and quickly searching for her. She was sitting at a table in a small office in the hospital, deep in discussion with a battered and clearly exhausted doctor.

It only took a few seconds to summon and drop a kobold next to them—though, in hindsight, I really should have considered just how much that would make the doctor shit himself before I did it.

As soon as the kobold appeared, the flash of lights dying away, Jo was on her feet, stepping between the doctor and the freshly summoned creature, one who was thoroughly confused as to why he'd been summoned there in the first place.

"It's okay!" she was saying. "It's okay!"

"What the hell!" The doctor gestured to the massive creature, which shook his head, tried to stretch his freshly created wings, and knocked a handful of medical tomes, a pair of binders, and a load of random crap off a nearby shelf. "What are you *doing*?!"

"Why am I here?" the kobold grumbled, twisting and turning, lashing the edge of the table and sending a coffee cup crashing to the floor.

"Out!" Jo snapped. "Get out!"

"But..." The kobold grunted, still totally confused.

"Just get out! Go on, scat!" Jo snapped, before picking up a book from another table and swatting the massive, heavily muscled, and well-armed kobold with it. "Go on. Get out. Go find the others!"

The kobold left the room, totally bewildered and fleeing the small woman and her textbook more than anything else, before she turned to the doctor she'd been talking to.

"I'm sorry, James. As I explained, communication can be a pain, and it looks like some moron decided this was the best way to let me know I was needed and that they were here in spirit form, rather than, oh, as a wild suggestion, summoning a brownie slice. That would have been a great surprise, and would have made it clear someone was here, but no. As I said, a moron."

"O-okay..." The doctor shook his head. "Why that creature, though?"

"Let's ask them," she said. "Okay, I know I explained the process before, but I'll give you access to the most basic level of the system and walk you through it now..."

Two minutes later, she stood before me, glaring, as James, one of the most senior surviving doctors, appeared.

"Hi, James," I said with a smile and a nod, trying not to look like I'd just practically had my skin flayed off by Jo's acid tongue while we'd been waiting on him.

"Hi," the doctor said absently, frowning as he glanced around, seeing the world around him in the dungeon.

"I'm sorry for giving you a scare," I said quickly. "My intention was that I'd summon a dungeon-born close to Jo to ask her to join me in here, to examine a new facility that we're building, and then, rather than that mana being wasted, the kobold could go and join his fellows outside and add to the security force here."

"But it just appeared!" He goggled, and I nodded, sighing.

"It did," I agreed. "And I'm sorry for that. As I said, it seemed a less wasteful method, and most people are used to the dungeon-born now."

"So, now that you've practically given my counterpart here a heart attack, and probably set back our discussions by a month through your foolishness, what was it you wanted to ask me, oh mighty Dungeon Lord?" Jo asked.

I glared at her, seeing the way that the doctor jerked around and stared at me now like I had three horns.

"Please ignore anything she's told you about me." I sighed.

"She said that you were nothing like we'd been expecting and envisioning, and that you were primarily concerned with protecting people," he told me slowly.

"Okay, yeah, listen to that…" I agreed.

"He's also an asshole who likes to give his friends heart attacks," Jo added helpfully, and I sighed. "So, was there something?" she prompted again.

"Fuck's sake, yes. *Here.*" I shifted us all to the control room and gestured to the table before us, where Aly and Kelly were in a full-blown argument, one that only ground to a halt at the yell of panicked confusion that James unleashed.

"Matt, I swear, you're not allowed to interact with people from now on for a full month after they've joined," Jo whispered, as Kelly and Aly glared from each other, to her, to me, and then blinked in confusion at the newcomer.

"Hi everyone, this is James," I introduced him, brightly. "Jo decided to bring him into the dungeon sense to show him a bit more of the system when I was getting her, and he's a *doctor*." The emphasis on that title might have been a little overdone, but when the ladies heard it, they instantly realized why he was there.

"Welcome, James." Kelly smiled, taking a deep breath and gesturing to the table and seats around it. "You've joined us as we're trying to decide where to focus on with this facility."

"Oh?" he said, clearly at a total loss.

"Look here." Aly smiled as well, before glaring at both Jo and me.

The image of the medical facility was impressive, clearly upgraded from the earlier ones, which had basically been easily wipeable surfaces with a Life converter in the corner to make sure that infection was kept to a bare minimum and to speed recovery.

There'd been all the usual comforts of home—bays with beds, curtains that could be dragged around them for privacy and cupboards full of bandages and so on—but most of the room had been taken up with a single large surgical suite.

We'd learned early on that healing magic could regrow limbs and more, but it wasn't specialized. It didn't know, for example, that if there was a section of metal in the body, that needed to be removed.

It could heal the injuries, and if someone had something in them like a parasite, that was damaging to the body, it'd remove it, healing the injury as well. If it wasn't? If, for example, someone had a badly broken bone that had a plate attached to it in the past, and now the injury was healed? It didn't remove that plate now.

That meant that we needed to have a place that we could perform operations to remove everything and seal people back up. Places that blood could be taken and stored and more.

That was the height of the medical facility so far, and it was impressive. The blood chillers, for example, kept the blood that we had nice and safe and at the right temperature, and people healed much quicker in there, but it didn't do much else. Certainly little that you'd have been overcome with awe and enthusiasm for, anyway.

That was where the new system came in.

The base layout was pretty much the same, slightly upgraded in terms of materials science, but that was about it. It was the next stage where it got really interesting.

The facility was available to be upgraded as a modular design.

The first few rooms in the blueprint that Aly had been working on had the basic layout: ten beds, five on either side, a main nurse/doctor station, and then an operating theatre at the back. But when we'd arrived, it'd been to find that was being scrapped, in favor of a ward design.

The ward would be where people were stored—I couldn't think of the proper word, so fuck it—until they could be worked on, or after an operation, etc., so they could recover in peace.

There would be five rooms to a ward—none of this open plan shite—and each room would be pleasant. They'd have a window, they'd have storage for things, and they'd have a nice bed instead of something that would have been refused by the army as cruel and unusual punishment under the Geneva Convention.

Then, behind the wall, the real fucking magic was set up.

The modular system meant that things could be added into the rooms, things like an operating system, a storage area for blood, an emergency biomedical contamination facility, and finally, a mana crystal-infused scanner.

These were the most fundamental things that the facility could be upgraded with. And in the case of the crystal scanner, it was basic, but achievable in perhaps three days.

That was it.

We needed two other technologies, and the building itself to be summoned and constructed, but that was it. Totally do-able!

All we needed was Light research (Advanced) and Mana Resonance (Uncommon) to unlock the tech for a mana crystal-infused scanner.

It'd be basic. The one that we'd get access to at first would be closer to an x-ray rather than a full-on MRI and scanner. But the upgrade to the core came with so much additional data now that it was ridiculous. We knew by focusing on what we needed, that it would give us access to this, and not that, but also that by unlocking these steps, we could see the potential.

It'd have been incredible for the lower levels if we'd had access to this kind of a cheat sheet, and I guessed this was what it was like for the fairies.

The best bit, though? Now that we had this, we could start evening the field a little bit!

As we were looking it over, Jo was already making changes: shifting walls, increasing one section, shrinking another, and opening out still more.

"We're going to need to develop triage areas... Look here, what if we remove this, and put in seating?" she muttered, before dragging James in to look it over with her.

"What is... Is this a...?" He started, gasping then moving something, or trying to, and getting a red pulse that warned him off touching it.

"Aly, I need his help," Jo said distractedly.

With a glance at me to make sure I wasn't against it, Aly upgraded his access, then sighed and started making notes on the tech that was needed.

As the medical professionals reworked the entire design, I examined the tech that was needed and why.

Light research was just what it said on the tin. Apparently, at this stage, it was now possible to do specific research into individual forms of mana and matter, and although the early levels were cheap, the later ones wouldn't be.

Twenty thousand mana for basic was fine, sure. A hundred thousand for common, okay...half a million for uncommon? Ouch. That was where the prediction grew too fuzzy to see anything else, and that was only after Aly had already dropped the twenty in and completed it in a matter of seconds. The hundred...she'd paused and checked with me, and I nodded, before wincing as that almost cleaned us out of the current available stores.

We'd be earning that back quickly—no stress there; less than an hour—but damn. If this pattern held true, that meant we'd need two and a half million for advanced, and from there it just got crazy.

The reason for it, though, was incredible.

Light was both a particle and a wave, apparently. Although that meant nothing to me, it came with a host of other information, some of which was amazing.

When we'd been looking at the various forms of magic, we'd been considering it as a separate thing, like spells are X and the research the dungeon could carry out were limited to things the dungeon could create.

So it could create a light bulb, or a magical light or whatever, but at most, the very best it could do with a spell was going to be something along the lines of a spell that could be attached to a tower and provide illumination to the dungeon.

That was it.

Hoo-boy, was I wrong.

I should have realized that as the dungeon created things, it could just as easily create a fucking *book*.

As soon as the first level of Light magic was researched and its basics unlocked, it opened up the options of Light-based facilities—lights, I guessed—and knowledge.

The knowledge? The basic level was a tome that I could summon for fifty thousand mana that had all the key information on Light, including the fundamentals of Light *mana*.

I'd been hung up on figuring this shit out, without ever understanding that in the Information Age, as the Glass core was analogous to, we'd finally be getting access to goddamn data!

Once Light-based knowledge was unlocked, I could sense a multitude of additional information beyond it, and I WANTED IT.

I wanted it badly.

The issue was, the tome was fifty thousand mana to unlock, and that was *per copy*. If that was the basic level, and then it followed the same pattern? The common level was going to be a quarter of a million per book, and then over a million per book for uncommon knowledge.

I wanted it so bad I could taste it, and that was for *Light*-based mana. It wasn't even for Lightning, which was a tier two and more advanced level and would therefore be more expensive. But goddamn, I wanted it.

From what I could see on the new foreknowledge base, the basic level had data on the mana spectrum itself, something we'd had to cobble together an imperfect understanding of as it was, and then?

It had illumination, refraction, elemental interactions, energy conversion, perception enhancements, photosynthesis, basic illusions, purification, and mana detection.

All of that...all of it was available—at the most basic level of understanding.

That was it, and yet...for the luxomancers in training? That tome could be literally game changing. That could open up entire worlds of magic for them, and it wasn't even what we were trying to do!

That we'd need to spend six hundred and twenty thousand to unlock the level of research was doable. That it'd be providing a lot of the research we'd need to be able to go down the tome route soon as well was great, but it only got better from here.

Resonance would build on this path nicely, as the sections that needed to be unlocked for mana resonance at common came with mana frequency identification, harmonic amplification, crystal attunement, and interference patterns. Then came resonance circuits, frequency modulation, energy transfer principles, resonant shielding, mana flow visualization, and the cherry on the top: diagnostic resonance.

That was the one that we really needed at this stage, along with the Light research's ability to create basic illusions to create an image of the target for the scanner. But the rest?

Mana frequency identification meant we'd be learning more about mana. In theory, we could probably use that to track certain types, further down the line at least, such as being able to track undead by their mana signature.

Harmonic amplification? Not a clue on that one, but a little focus came up with everything from mining to shields. And crystal attunement? Hell yes. That meant we could attune the mana crystals that we could create to the user. We could literally make it so that nobody else could use those mana batteries and that'd make them safe to produce!

Interference patterns was a step along the road to a different kind of shielding, and it was one that could be incredible. The undead were coming, there was no doubt about that, but if we did this? We could create areas that the undead were literally unable to step across. I didn't know how, but I sensed that I could, if I researched it far enough along the line, simply create barriers to Unlife mana.

That sounded interesting, but the place my mind immediately went to? Drains.

Drain that mana away, fracture it, break it up, and feed it into a dungeon core, and every undead that crossed a line would collapse to bones and dust, as its animating energy was ripped into my dungeons to feed their growth.

Resonance circuits dealt with the pathways that fed mana—or other matter and protons or whatever—along them. They were the basis of the conduits that ran through the dungeon. If I could increase my understanding of them? We could create more and more!

Frequency modulation would help with stopping the undead, and so would energy transfer principles. Mana flow visualization would enable us to track the mana of the world, and figure out more about how to use it. And last, and best of all?

Diagnostic resonance would work with the Light technologies to enable us to scan our bodies.

This was a tiny fraction of the potential, seriously it was, but knowing that just those two basic technologies—that were being upgraded in a few places and would be literally not specialized at all; it'd be accessing just the most basic, entry-level data on them in those paths—would be enough to do this?

I saw the same trap again then: the desire to make perfect scanners. It'd not take that much extra effort. Perhaps an extra day, and then we could upgrade the scanners massively, make them at least twice as effective, and much higher resolution. All we'd need to do was…

Was put off installing and working on the things for another day, then another, and another, as we found this perfect complement to the tech, followed by this, and one of those, and perhaps…

It went on and on. And that wasn't even looking at the bigger picture; this was just the scanners for the medical side.

Looking at it realistically, we could make a perfectly supported society with this level of tech and magic blended alone. We could create armor that would make our scouts functionally invisible, we could create illusions, lasers… The list went on and on, and I forced myself out of it, the seductive possibilities just too great for me.

"Aly, Kelly…" I whispered, before drawing them aside, leaving Jo and James to excitedly adjust and alter the plans over and over. "We need to focus. Get the basic scanner up and running, just that. A single-room version of the medical facility, a tester so that we can prove it works, and then we move on. Jo and James can plan out their perfect medical center for later, but for now, once we know this works, it's getting put into production. You have two days."

"Got it." Aly nodded.

"What's wrong?" Kelly asked me, and I snorted, before trying to explain as Aly left us to it.

"So…" she murmured a few minutes later. "You think this is dangerous?"

"I do," I said. "And not as in an intended trap, but you remember the conversation we had a few days ago? About me losing my focus and wanting to do too much?"

"Ah." She nodded. "And you think this research is like that. It could send you off on trying to find perfect solutions instead of ones that will get the job done?"

"Exactly." I nodded. "We have three priorities as I see it. First, the Orcan— they're coming and we need to get ready. Secondly, the incoming undead and whatever else is coming from the other Dungeon Lords and Ladies, and lastly, saving as many people as we can."

"Right." Kelly nodded. "You think that we need to watch the new shiny toys because they're going to strip us of our focus?"

"Yes and no," I corrected. "We desperately need it, and the mana that's coming in means it's not that big an ask to spend that much now, *but*…if we go down the research rabbit hole, we'll achieve nothing except research."

"So what's the solution?"

I took a deep breath, before blowing it out and smiling, feeling a little guilty, but knowing it was for the best. "I bow out of all of that side."

It felt a little like I was saying "I'm too important to deal with this; you do it…I don't want to." But, in reality, if I told them to get me X, and I didn't have to worry about the steps? That'd make it a lot easier. And it'd also make things a lot better when it came to magic as well.

I could focus on that, and what I did best—which, I was starting to see, wasn't leading the research, or commanding soldiers and more. What I did best was pick an objective and follow through.

I was good at dealing with the problem, and maybe—I hoped, anyway—providing a bit of leadership and direction. But when it came to the nitty-gritty individual side? I was a lot weaker than I thought.

What I was best at was learning my magic, finding solutions, and fucking shit up.

It was time to play to those strengths, I decided.

CHAPTER TWELVE

Chris, it turned out, had gotten bored of the constant shuttle runs as well. When I'd left the dungeon sense and sat down with a summoned meal, I'd not even manage to get the first bite to my lips before that bastard was rocking my door on its hinges with his fist.

"Come on!" he shouted through the wood. "I know you're in there. Stop playing with it and open up!"

I closed my eyes, swearing silently, before pushing the chair back and stalking over to the door, yanking it open just as he went to hit it again.

"About time." He grunted, shouldering his way into the room, and let out a groan as he dropped into my chair.

It barely held his weight; the creak was loud enough I thought it was going to collapse. But it was when he started eating my goddamn pizza that I finally slammed the door shut and stomped back over to sit on the second chair.

"Hey, Chris, great to see you, buddy. Why the hell are you in my room, *eating my goddamn pizza*?!"

"Love you too," he mumbled around a slice of pepperoni, before winking at me, then swallowing hard. "What, no drink? Shitty host you are, mate…"

"I…you know what, here." I summoned a drink for him and gestured. "Have a drink, have some of my pizza, then tell me why the hell you're not in your own room."

I summoned another drink for myself and a second pizza, deliberately choosing a ham and pineapple with pepperoni, knowing that he'd not touch it as it had pineapple on it now.

"You sick bastard." He grunted, seeing what I'd done, before attacking "his" pizza.

We probably looked ridiculous. I'd gotten dressed in my armor before I'd laid down to work in the dungeon, because I knew what my life was like for random events and shit going down.

That meant that if anyone was to see us, they'd probably laugh their asses off. We were big guys now, both seven foot or thereabouts thanks to the points in Constitution and Strength. Add on the armor, the weapons, and that, for all intents and purposes, we were basically sitting in a small hotel room, around a tiny desk that was barely big enough for one of us to sit under, with two massive pizzas, a beer each and soft drinks, rail gun shotguns, swords, shields, heavy armor, hammers, handguns…the works.

Then add on that Chris was covered in what had been snow when he'd come in—a light dusting, but still.

We looked daft.

"All the rooms are gone," he said around another mouthful of pizza a few minutes later. "Gods, I missed this," he grumbled.

"Pizza or sitting down?" I offered him the bottom of my bottle, getting a *clink* as he bumped his off it.

"Both," he admitted. "The fresh meat think I'm a god, the soldiers look at me like I'm nobody one minute then practically knock themselves out saluting when I ask them to do something, and every one of those fuckin' dogs out there wants to hump my leg." He broke off to glare at me. "Why the hell did you bring those fuckers here?"

I started, surprised. "I thought you'd want them," I said. "That's why I tamed the fuckers."

"Yeah, well, they're giant dogs, mutated. Some are brighter than the average, but the majority are about as bright as the inside of a black cat in a blackout. You know they're led by a fuckin' chihuahua, right?"

"What?" I blinked. "Chris, I didn't even tame one of those fuckers."

"You did. That thing with the massive ears," he corrected. "The middle of the pack always, doesn't get at the front…it hangs around the middle and just watches."

"The tan one?" I asked after a minute of thought. "Really damn hairy ears and sod all fur beyond that…looks like someone shaved the ugliest rottweiler in the world?"

"Crossbreed." He nodded. "Yeah, that's the one."

"Weird." I grunted. "What's that got to do with anything?"

"You ever see one of those that wasn't insane?" he countered. "That's a dog that's the size of a horse, with a brain the size of a pea, that thinks it should be carried around in a handbag. That's without getting into the aggression and unstable side of things. That's the base level of the damn dog, and it's the leader of the pack. The only thing I want to do with a dog like that is take it to the end of the pier and punt it off."

"Becky would murder you if you did," I pointed out, grinning.

"What she doesn't know won't hurt me," he growled, before sighing. "You know I'd never hurt a dog, really."

I nodded.

"But…they're not worth trying to use my abilities with. Seriously, they'd be a waste." He looked at me to make sure I understood what he was saying. "As a Druid, I can do a lot. I can help them to find their place here. I can talk to them and understand a lot more than is being said back. But, at the end of the day, they're dogs, and they're being led by one that's batshit.

"Best thing for them is to turn them over to Beta and her kobolds, train them up, absorb them into the dungeon, and use them to breed a decent cavalry. Shit, that's a point…you get any access to new creatures with the upgrade? I mean, it's done, right?"

"I didn't see," I admitted. "To much to deal with."

"Well, get your arse in there!" he snarled. "I could be wasting away here while my T. rex is sitting, bored, waiting to be summoned!"

"You're not getting a T. rex," I said firmly. "I'd not trust you with a duck."

"Hey, those little fuckers are vicious." He snorted. "They're like this far from a goose." He held up a hand and indicated an inch with his fingers pinched close together. "Pretty sure a T. rex is in those fucker's ancestry."

"Aren't they in all birds?"

"See!" He nodded as if this were a great win. "Knew it. Never trust a duck."

"I give up on you." I sighed, taking another slice of pizza. "Right, I'm getting back to work. You're taking the other bed, I take it?"

"Unless you want a goddamn cuddle, yeah." He squinted at me, and I shook my head.

"You know what, I'm good. I can wait for Kelly," I said with as much dignity as I could muster.

"See you remember that later. No stabbing my arse with it when I'm asleep," he ordered me, before standing and starting to shuck off his gear. "Gods, I need a shower."

I didn't ask him anything else—any answer might be as much abuse as truth—and left my friend to defrost. I finished my food and laid back down on the bed, closing my eyes. And, to the groaning of my oldest friend showering in the next room, I slid into myself—not in a kinky, perverted way…no, I accessed my mana channels—and relaxed, letting the cares of my body float away.

I had four jobs I needed to do over the next few days, now that things were more or less in hand again. They were, in no particular order: first to complete that quest on religion, second to complete the quest on my magic and get a more structured plan in place for magic moving forward.

Next, my own personal evolution, though I guess that also sort of tied in with point one and two. I was working toward my ascension as a Storm Titan. Although that was part of my Divine side, it was also something that had been stalled for a while. So, my plan was to figure out what the hell was going on with the Divine core and ascension, and then work through each stage as I went.

Then, lastly, I needed to start *the plan*.

I managed to keep from focusing on it. I'd kept my brain away from it for days, weeks even, and that was because I was starting to see that focusing on a plan only tempted fate and his prophet Murphy to take a steaming turd on my plans.

If instead I just kept it all to myself as much as possible, there was less to go wrong. But for now, I'd get the other two out of the way—or at least underway. And once the dungeon was back on its feet and we were all home? Then I'd have a proper meeting with those who were going to be involved in it, and get it started.

For now, though, it was time to try to find my goddamn Divine core.

Sinking into my mana channels, I picked an easy point to start: my right hand. Not because I had to start with something familiar and there was no part of my body that was more familiar, but because I knew that I had to start somewhere, and I wanted to see the channels as clearly as possible.

Mentally sinking through my skin and into "me" wasn't hard, not anymore, and certainly not after the hundreds of hours I spent working on repairing my mana gates. Dipping in mentally, though, there was always that disconnect between what I knew was there—flesh, blood, and bone—and what I also knew was there: a secondary capillary system that flowed around my entire body, that carried mana instead of blood.

That it was ringed over and over by great circular "gates" that took the mana as it flowed and compressed it, picking up its speed and cleansing it as well, was insane. For the first time in days, I wondered where that little furry turd Thor was hiding.

I dismissed the thought and picked up speed, flowing along through my mana channels and examining them. More and more were slowly starting to form, which made me smile to myself.

It was something that I'd been wondering about for ages. That the mana gates were helpful was clear, but they were also, as near as I could tell, both purely mental and entirely magical.

They had no physical form, though neither did the mana channels themselves. When I'd created my mana channels in the first place, I'd gained a boost to my mana regeneration that was significant.

When I'd damaged those same channels, I'd shredded the gates and I spent weeks repairing what Thor had done almost effortlessly.

Now, I saw that clearly I was evolving in ways beyond my expected ones, as here and there the start of ghostly gates could be seen, shimmering in and out of existence.

They were, I guessed, showing up equally about halfway between each of the established ones, meaning that when they were finally all in place—provided I didn't fuck up insanely—I could probably look forward to a fresh boost then as well.

I almost dropped out and started working on them, then forced myself to keep going instead.

The gates were all appearing at once, meaning that if I pushed ahead working on one now at this end, as likely as not, I'd fuck up a system that was intended to work in a certain way. If I activated a single extra gate when it was supposed to work in tandem... I already had experience of how much that could suck.

I remembered the constant vomiting and cramping from the unbalanced and corrupted mana in my system when I'd done that, and I moved away from that plan with a shudder.

Instead, as I picked up speed, I simply reached out, sensing the flow of my mana, and reveled in it.

Twice, I lapped around my body; twice, I blurred past my core, searching for a hint that it was anywhere else, that there was anything more to my system than the mana core at its heart. But as I came around for the third pass, I separated out and dove into the core, drinking deep of the silence and wonder.

My core was different from the way that others described theirs. I'd heard them compare their core to a spark, or to a guttering candle, which was just weird.

For me, the core was a blazing neutron star, one that sent fervent pulses out into the depths of space and that was surrounded by a great ocean of mana.

The central spire that rose from the star and that reached out into the depths of space was the pure mana, as near as I could tell, and I'd accidentally drawn on that before.

The power that came from it had been enough to contaminate and almost kill me. It'd screwed with my system and had massively fucked me over—but it'd kept me alive at the time.

Now, as I soared closer, I shifted my alignment, my perception changed at will, until suddenly I was no longer flying toward the star, but instead falling, staring down as I adjusted, and aimed to land on its surface.

The closer I got to it, the more that surface shifted. The rising and falling bands of flame, like spears of fiery nuclear whips that rose and fell into the mana ocean, diminished in brightness. By the time I touched down, they were simply huge, glowing strands.

Each strand had to be miles long. Hell, the way that reality seemed to bend here, they were both a few hundred meters across and infinite, like they went on forever, linked to the mana ocean, which was thousands of miles beyond their tips, but also "just there," almost within reach.

The whole system was almost impossible to confirm: length and width shifted as easily as I breathed, and yet, it was real. I knew it was real. So many times, I'd wondered about this, trying to decide whether this was in my head—or my heart— or whether it was really "out there" somewhere in deep space.

The truth was both, I somehow knew.

Inside me, as I stared out, I had an entire galaxy—though how, I had no clue.

Perhaps each of us had one...I didn't know. But for me, I could feel the great spire under my hand as I reached down, running my hands across its warm-to-the-touch surface. I could feel the pure mana that pulsed along it. If I was to reach out and pull? It'd come to me again.

Pausing, I thought about that as I straightened, turning without thought to the one that really called to me, even here.

Jez Cajiao

Lightning.

It took a mere flexing of my mind, and then I lifted through the air. My feet touched down atop the somehow narrower, and yet more welcoming surface of the Lightning spire.

There was something about it—there always was. Although the other aspects of the storm, such as Water that I'd disliked so much, were no longer an issue for me, I always desperately felt drawn to the Lightning.

That was how I felt now, crouching down and pressing my palm to it, and feeling the life stirring beneath my hand.

I drew several long breaths, before reaching out further. Fortified by the feeling of closeness the Lightning always granted me, I started to search again.

My core was here. I could feel that this was my core, somehow, though no more. And if this was my core, there had to be a reason that it was so different from everyone else's.

This had to be part of the Divine side of my core, and something to do with that. But as much as I focused, as I searched, and as I tried, I found nothing.

I searched deep inside, and lifted as far as I could from the spires. I tried to travel along their length, and to the heart where they all met, then erupted free.

I tried everything I could think of, and yet still, I found nothing.

Hours later, as I stared up at the dark ceiling overhead, the sound of Chris flat out asleep in the bed across from mine—snoring fit to wake the dead—I still had no clue where to go with it all. Finally, as I drifted off to sleep myself, I did so with a mental image of the core burnt into my mind.

The next day came and went with me being seen by as few people as possible. Chris got up and buggered off, attending to a dozen minor jobs; then, because he was apparently bored, he took a few tours of the magical traps. After that, according to the smell when he returned that night, he'd apparently been at a rave in a goblin toilet, but I chose not to comment.

I checked in with the ladies, and made sure everything was proceeding on track. I really wanted to check and go over them—but I didn't look at the upgraded dungeon creature lists, nor the upgrades that were available for Jack.

I didn't search the area, nor analyze the first stages of the hospital, nor the increases in the park and the new blueprints.

I didn't even go for a walk or to grab a drink and to get some fresh air.

Instead, I spent the next entire day deep within myself, searching for my core, desperately picking through every inch of my own internal reality, searching for something that stood out, something that was different, something that was *more*.

In the end, I was left floating over my core again, sure that this was the secret, that this was where everything stemmed from, and yet unable to figure out any difference.

After more than three hours just floating there, staring, a million sensations a second being churned up and discarded, tickled into life and let loose by the broken segments of mana that soared past in the ocean, I abandoned it all. I closed my eyes again, this time excluding everything but the silence of the soul.

All my achievements so far, everything I'd done, I'd done through a mixture of luck, sheer bloody-mindedness, and, most of all, instinct.

Now, closing my eyes, both mental and metaphorical, I listened to my instincts and simply *did*.

I felt the touch of something beneath my feet. I knew what it was, but I didn't allow myself to think about it. Instead, I simply trusted myself, and drank deeply.

Opening myself to the spire that I felt touching the underside of my feet could have been a horrific mistake, had I landed on the pure spire, as I always seemed to unconsciously be drawn to land on. I'd have been either seared internally to ash, or have been filled by a ghoulish version of myself. Instead, I felt the surge of power and life that I'd come to associate with Lightning.

That this was what it was, I felt a flicker of relief, that it could have been worse… I quashed the thought and returned my mind to as much of a flow state of perfect channeling as was possible and concentrated on the mana running through my body.

I had a second panicked thought that maybe out in the real world I was filling the room with lightning as well as frying Chris. But again, I doubted that, and I trusted my instincts.

Instead, I found myself drinking deeper, then deeper again.

Then…a second spire caressed my touch. My left hand was raised, pressed to it, even as my right was pressed to the one beneath me.

Another pulse of power washed into me. This time, I gasped, both buoyed and scoured by its cold majesty.

The Air mana that tore through me stole my breath away, filling my veins and battling with Lightning that was already there…until I felt something else suddenly beneath my right hand. I was standing, I realized, at almost the exact second I felt Fire rushing into me as well.

Lightning was me; it was part of me in a way that nothing else was. To be harmed by Lightning would be like being harmed by my own breath or my eyes being blinded by my own reflection. But *Fire*?

Air was in the high eighties now. I'd had it as my lowest constituent stat for Lightning, and it'd been boosted when I managed to learn my third custom spell. That was great, but it was only when that form of mana hit a hundred that the damage channeling it changed to healing.

Now, as Air and Fire mana ripped through me, I opened my mouth to howl in pain, and instead Lightning mana tore from it.

I vomited Lightning, both forms mixing and battling as they erupted free, cascading from me and crashing free, dancing across the infinite void before me…until it hit the spire.

The Lightning spire drew on it greedily. For a second, I felt relief…until suddenly I felt anything but that!

The mana was being pulled from me, and I was no longer in contact with the spire! Somehow, I'd been launched into the air. I still felt connected to the twin spires of Fire and Air, and was still drawing on them, but, I realized in horror, I couldn't break free!

I was being drained...*consumed*!

My mana was being ripped from me, and as Fire and Air were pulled in, I was converting them and feeding that in as well!

I...I didn't know what to do, and fear—as well as a rising burning—was starting to really make its presence known.

The only thing that kept me from really panicking at this point was that the burns that were being seared along my mana channels were actually being healed by the passage of the Lightning mana as well.

It was Lightning that I had the highest affinity for and...well, mainly, anyway. Mainly...because although Lightning was at a hundred and six, Storm was at a hundred and two.

A hundred and two, and I was a Storm Titan, or I would be, not a fucking Lightning Titan!

I forced myself to move, to twist. Reaching out blindly with one foot, I fumbled it onto the nearest spire that I could sense...Earth.

The connection felt heavier, which was stupid. Just because it was Earth didn't mean it was heavy, but I didn't know how else to explain it.

It felt heavy and solid, sluggish and...and slow to respond, like it was almost sleepy and couldn't be bothered. Water, on the other hand? That felt more willing to come. But when I felt it starting to channel into me, it seemed like it all wanted to come—like I'd sucked on the end of a high-pressure hose and I had no clue how to stop it, short of swallowing it all.

A stray thought reared its head then and was instantly banished, leaving only a lingering determination to be nice to Kelly later.

More mana started to flow in. Where Earth was sluggish to begin but I sensed could be almost impossible to slow once it built momentum and Water was terrifyingly fast at responding, I panicked seconds later when I felt the imbalance starting.

At first, it was subtle. But as the seconds passed, they grew increasingly out of alignment. The Lightning started to sputter and spurt, the connection growing more and more clogged by the second.

What the hell was I doing wrong?

The pain was building as well, as each form of mana tore through me and the Lightning grew less and less plentiful, and therefore less healing.

As more mana was torn free of the spires and fed into me, the pain ratcheted higher and higher. I could feel more damage being done, as the world around me split into two. The darkness of the room around me was suddenly lit by sparking links of lightning as Chris roared and leapt to his feet.

Then, on the other side, I could see the core before me and all around, vanishing into the infinite distance, as more and more mana roared in and was fed through me to that massive construct.

I felt the changes as the core grew increasingly unbalanced. Surges of power rocketed through me as blockages formed and were blasted through...

I didn't have long—no time to waste!

Whatever my subconscious had been trying to do on instinct, I needed to figure out, now. Otherwise, I was going to burn my core out entirely.

Mana... I was a Storm Titan, not just a fucking Lightning Titan or whatever the nomenclature was, so I needed to accept that and not just channel fuckin' Lightning! That was why I'd reached out to Earth and Water as well as Fire and Air. But where I was feeding Fire and Air together to form Lightning, channeling that into the Lightning spire, the other two mana forms were...

They were still intact! I was dragging pure Earth and pure Water through me, and not combining them. If anything, they were mixing themselves and forming Clay and Mud mana, two separate forms that were created by mixing the two with a different component in ascendency.

That was it!

Earth and...what the hell were the components of Storm again? Lightning was Air and Fire, Thunder was Air and Earth, and Water... Storm was Air and Water!

I had no clue why I'd had such issues with Water elsewhere, but when it was in the Storm component, I loved it. Fuck it, I didn't have time to screw around. If Air and Water made Storm, and I needed that at the very least...

I started twisting more Air into myself, pulling harder on it and forcing it into a new form with the Water mana. At first it resisted, trying to combine into something else. The Water meeting Fire in my mana channels tried to form steam; the Earth meeting Water wanted to be Mud; Fire and Earth sought to be Magma—thank you very much—and through it all, I swore and fought, battling and shoving the component parts into an alignment that matched...before it finally snapped into shape.

Air and Water formed the Storm, a storm that raced through me—fortunately not to come out of my ass or dick, but instead erupting from my chest in a stream that seemed to core me out. Lightning raced ahead of me, slamming into the Lightning spire. Storm tore around and hammered into another spire—its own Storm spire, I saw—and beyond that...

The spires were moving!

They were huge things. The Storm started to move, arcing around faster than the others, with the Lightning spinning after it and picking up speed. I drew a breath, pained and drained, yet for the first time feeling that I was making headway.

I knew what I had to do, though.

147

Jez Cajiao

The mana was racing from me, and now that I'd gained control over it to some degree again, I could have choked it off and escaped. Although I'd gain a little from the experience, I wasn't done...not yet.

I'd created the basic forms, combining Storm and Lightning within me. But as they roared on, the Earth mana was being torn along and discarded. That wasn't right.

There was a third composition that I needed to complete—this I knew, at an instinctual level, and that...that was Thunder!

Air and Earth slammed together, fighting for dominance in a way that Water and Fire didn't. I had no clue why...until I sensed that Thunder was only at fifty-eight percent, while the other two were over a hundred.

That meant that everything was at least twice as hard with that goddamn element, and yet...as the two forms of mana combined, they sparked and crashed, bouncing off each other. They fought on and on, until, in a fit of inspiration, I laid the two mana streams side by side, then twisted and funneled them forward. Then it was just a matter of compression and determination and...

The boom of thunder that rolled out from my supine form rattled the doors and walls, making Chris shout in pain and glare at me from behind the desk, where he was currently hiding—or so I distantly sensed.

Inside my core, though, it had a far more impressive effect as a third and hitherto unnoticed spire started to pick up speed as well.

The three spires spun faster and faster now. The faster pair left behind a glowing trail, blurring, and the third lumbered after.

The other spires twisted into a new configuration, one that left the basic elements spread out to form a cube-like lattice around the main three.

The other mana forms twisted, shortening and growing wider, stubbier, as the height lengthened, locking into place.

As they did that, somehow the three were spinning around and through the others, and yet they still never stopped nor impacted: a merry dance of death made up of mating skyscrapers and highways that seemed lit from within by terrible, wonderful light.

Thunder rumbled, lightning seared the heavens, and through it all the storm grew and the rain lashed down with terrible ferocity.

The snow was blasted away by rising winds, scoured as if from existence, and I knew that finally, it was time.

I opened my eyes, seeing the world around me and superimposed over it the building power of both my mana conversion and the storm outside. With a thought, I demolished the wall between me and the outside, staggering as I stumbled through the devastation that had once been a neat and orderly room.

CHAPTER THIRTEEN

I ignored the random worried abuse that Chris hurled after me, aware, distantly, that he'd done it, but unable to articulate words to counter or to assure.

Instead, as soon as I was outside, I lifted into the air. Sparks that I'd been suppressing for hours finally burst free as my power reached out to join with its ultimate expression.

"Matt?"

I sensed Kelly there by me in the dungeon sense, but again, I was too far gone to explain to her, to share beyond a need, a clear pull and…a sense of warning hunger.

She—or Aly; I never knew which it'd been—created what I knew I needed in the middle of the park then: a single spire of metal that rose higher and higher, tied into the mana grid as I corkscrewed into the thunderous clouds.

Crashes rang out on all sides; light flared in the clouds that spiraled in closer and closer. I knew what I had to do next—reaching out, desperately searching, feeling the building power…then cursing as I saw that I couldn't do it, not here!

To rise to the next stage of my evolution, I needed to grow. My mana manipulation had to evolve, from first-tier forms to more advanced. And I needed to master them, to use them as instinctively as I'd been using others.

For the next form that I sensed as needed, though, I required a hell of a lot more Water…

I had it here, so much of it in comparison to normal, but I needed more!

I drank deeply. The mana stored in the massive spires in my core reacted to my will, pouring into me. They fueled my ascension as I took the three building layers of the storm I was familiar with and bound them to myself, searching for the final fourth.

Inside me, the spires glowed brighter and brighter. The spinning ends of the greater three seemed to blaze with light; the next eight surged and dimmed, pulsing faster and faster with each beat of my heart.

As it hammered faster, so too did the light, until the core blurred around me, glowing with a bright, vibrant golden light. The minor spires—those that I could barely use, or that were ill-matched to me—seemed to melt. They cascaded away, sliding around into a rapidly hardening core…one that was layered over and over with volatiles.

All around me, the thunderous crashing of the storm rose in volume. Water, like vertical seas, poured free, and booms of lightning like heavy machine gun fire rent the clouds.

For miles on all sides, the storm grew. The wind rushed faster and more furiously by the second, screaming around and around. The tail of a rapidly forming twister gamboled wildly as it lowered farther and farther, enhanced by my Divine power.

Mana surged and danced. The spires in my heart fed on each other and then fed their greater compatriots in turn as more and more was drawn in.

Then, finally, as I drifted into the center of the building cyclone, I stopped dead. The water that had been lashing down frantically from the storm was spun up into the swirling winds, torn around and funneled into blurring waves.

Thunder rolled; lightning arced upward and down into the waters and lit the world for miles.

The cyclone, twister or hurricane—whatever it was—was barely being held a dozen meters from the ground as I compressed the upper and lower levels, pulling all of the pressure and force inward. My affinities started to tick upward. The pressure and force that was being exerted was enough to improve my mastery of the element as sweat ran down my body, only to be burned free in a cascade of light and power.

More and more, the power raced through me, and I felt the first racking, terrible pains of forced evolution that flared through me.

I almost stopped, I wanted to stop, but the pain…it was different. It wasn't just an "argh, that hurts"; it was more cleansing, more reformative. As the seconds raced on, I knew not only that I could, but that I *had to* hold it together.

The power rose. The compression that I was forcing was building toward something. As light flared faster and faster, my core began to shudder and shake; more and more melted as the light grew brighter and the heat intensified.

Tick, tick, tick… My affinities clicked along, and the sweat streamed free, only to be wicked away by the frantic winds, to erupt into gasses by the heat and flare of lightning, to be compressed by the pressure of thunder…and to reform into the spiraling cyclone.

All four elements of the storm were here now, and each one of them was desperately screaming to rise to rule. Instead, I bound them all to me even tighter, this time letting the lightning punch down into the space I'd created and connect to the dungeon below, forming a link between it and me.

Lightning was Air and Fire; Thunder, Air and Earth. Storm was Air and Water. Finally, as the first three forms of the storm were bound into submission, the first of its tier-three forms bowed to me.

The cyclone form was Storm, Air, and Pressure. That last was a form of affinity I'd hardly noticed until now. It was one I barely had any affinity with as well. But as I crushed the frantically screaming storm in around me, Thunder took its place, bullying its elder cousin into obeying and playing its part.

It finally locked into place as the pressure surged, as force built and power screamed through me. My core built to one last crescendo, and I arced my back unthinkingly. Power streamed out from me, reaching a final limit a dozen meters from me, and then reversing, as the storm all around me had its beating heart ripped free.

The massive surge of power crashed inward, annihilating any last barriers, and provided the final spark, as my freshly formed Divine core flared and began to beat with a solid, thunderous heartbeat that rang in my ears.

Light flared around me, golden and brilliant; then lightning flared and danced. Thunder rolled, but unlike before, where those peering out of windows and doors feared for their lives should the storm build more, now they watched in hushed awe as I drifted down gently, landing with bare feet on the sodden earth, that even now was cooling again, winter's icy grasp reasserting itself from the energetic release.

I drew in a deep breath, then another. My chest rose and fell with a gentle, yet pervasive warmth that ran through me, as prompts flared again and again.

Through it all, even with the main prompt that filled my vision and refused to be dismissed or hidden until it was acknowledged, I simply breathed, relaxing. The need and the power faded from me; the world returned to as it should be, with one slight change.

WORLDWIDE ANNOUNCEMENT!

THE FIRST DIVINE CORE HAS BEEN ESTABLISHED!

Matt, First Lord of the Storm, has ascended, and filled his Divine Core for the first time! Where others fear to tread, he races on ahead, gaining power and devotion. But who will be next?

As a one-off reward for the first to ascend, he receives the following bonus: 1x Divine Shard—Zeus's Master Bolt.

Three times more shall a shard be gifted to those who ascend. But once this is done, never again shall such power be unleashed in such a form upon your world.

151

Who will claim the next?

As the text faded and dimmed, pressure built around me, as some of the power that had been funneled into the dungeon now reversed, flooding out and coalescing into a single jagged shard of lightning that hovered before me, Zeus's Master Bolt gleaming in all its glory.

I took it, feeling the surge of power that ran from it into me. But when it offered me the choice to absorb it, I refused, knowing instinctively what a waste that would be.

The next prompt that popped up made it clear that yeah, others knew damn well what I'd just received.

Congratulations, First Lord of the Storm! You have established, forged, and filled the first layer of your Divine core, and as such, you stand now a full tier above your fellow godlings!

Through extreme methods, instead of meditation, you have surged ahead, scouring your path clean and making your soul ready to be greeted by the non-believer.

Beware, however: with great power, comes great vulnerability. Where others plotted and grumbled before, now come true declarations of enmity!

They feared you when you were the first to tread the path they coveted. They hated you when you drew the worship of those they never considered. But now?

ANATHEMA HAS BEEN DECLARED, and WAR follows!

Not only have the first steps been taken to godhood, the first ladders climbed, the first rungs forged, but now the first HOLY WAR has been declared!

Simon, Lord of the Mechanist, and his bonded Dungeon #47 declare their allegiance to the Pantheon of Unlife!

Clive, Lord of the Western Winds, his Dungeon Fairy and Wife [Identity Hidden], and their bonded Dungeon #4 declare their allegiance to the Pantheon of Unlife!

Sari, Mistress of the Sea declares her allegiance to the Pantheon of Unlife!

Petr, Lord of Darkness, his Dungeon Fairy Sin, and their bonded Dungeon #91 declare their allegiance to the Pantheon of Unlife!

You have received an updated Declaration of War from the Pantheon of Unlife...

Do you wish to Accept, Cede, or Negotiate?

Be aware: any response to this declaration will result in a formal Link between the Pantheon of the Storm and the Pantheon of Unlife. As the defending party, you will receive a second bonus—should you survive—and both sides will know the location of the other. You will receive a [10%] or [+10 boost] to a single aspect of your choice for your forces.

Please select from the following:

- *Ambient Mana Generation: Yes/No*
- *Mana Regeneration: Yes/No*
- *Health Regeneration: — Already Selected —*
- *Melee Damage: Yes/No*
- *Ranged Damage: Yes/No*

The boosts that have been selected by both sides will be awarded to the winner of the conflict as permanent boons!

Good luck!

I accepted the declaration of war. It wasn't like it was going to change anything. And as soon as I discovered that it did, indeed, change something, the three goddamn dungeons that had declared in favor of the dickhead of death suddenly flared in my mind, making me well aware of their locations.

I grinned when I found that one of the dungeons was in the UK, and it looked like Simon, Lord of the Mechanists, was today's lucky wiener.

That and the fact that although I damn well knew that the Lord of Unlife wasn't in the UK yet, but that this dickhead was? Well…I couldn't afford to let him get direct control of a dungeon.

The title of Lord of the Mechanists was a little weird and certainly mildly confusing, but fuck it. For now, at least, I was one of the highest ranked and most powerful Dungeon Lords, and as far as I knew, still one of only a handful to have established a secondary site. If I could deal with this Simon now? I could make things a hell of a lot easier for me and my people.

New Evolving Quest Update: Divine Core Establishment (1)

Congratulations, First Lord of the Storm! You've forged your Divine Core, unlocking new potential and challenges. Current Objective: Master the Fundamentals of Divine Essence

Progress:

- *Establish your Divine Core 1/1*
- *Learn to safely channel Divine energy 0/10*
- *Explore methods of empowering followers 0/5*
- *Understand the risks and rewards of direct intervention 0/2*

As you delve into your newfound divinity, you are beginning to grasp the intricate balance of power and responsibility. Your choices in distributing your Divine essence will shape your path:

1. *Organized religion (slower growth, but safer)*
2. *Artifact empowerment (balanced approach)*
3. *Direct intervention (substantial risk, high reward)*

Warning: Your Divine Core remains unstable. Reckless use of your powers could be fatal!

You have made progress in unlocking the following:

- *Unlock the Priesthood of the Storm Questline*
- *Unlock the Paladins of the Storm Questline*
- *Unlock the Defenders of the Faith Questline*
- *Level One Artifact Creation*

Continue to explore and master your Divine powers, First Lord of the Storm. Remember, with great power comes great responsibility…and greater threats. Choose your path wisely as you navigate the challenges ahead.

***Bonus: Your recent advancement has increased your Storm affinity by 5%.
Current Storm affinity: 107%***

All in all, it was a hell of a cascade of prompts—one that was only slightly ruined, all things considered, when Chris walked up to me holding out a singed towel and spoke the words that I'd secretly feared hearing my entire life.

"You know you're standing in the middle of the park with your tackle swinging in the wind, right? Stark bollock naked you are."

I looked down and sighed. Yup, that bastard was right.

Some days it just didn't pay to wake up.

***

So there he is..." The bastard chortled, half an hour later, to Barry and me as I glared at him. "Standing there, all high and mighty, First Lord of the Storm, god of lightning and master of all he bloody surveys, and he's not even got a chub on to make it look a little more impressive."

"Well, it's a cold night..." Barry offered, clearly trying to help, while stifling a smile behind a hand that furiously scratched at his thickening beard.

"It must be!" Chris agreed, grinning. "I mean, if it's not that, then I feel sorry for Kelly, and—"

"Matt, you're up!" Jo called from one side.

I climbed to my feet with a relieved sigh. That moment of inattention meant that I almost missed the sight of Rhodes stalking over and grabbing the massive man's ear, twisting and dragging him off to a corner to receive a dressing-down.

All I heard was something about the "...damage to morale..." and an indrawn, pained breath.

It made me feel a lot better, though, as I heard the gasps and promises that he was making, all of which I knew the bugger fully intended to break as soon as his ear was released and he could retreat to safety.

"So, 'Sparkles,' anything I need to know?" Jo asked me dryly, closing the door behind me while gesturing to the bed. "I'd ask you if it bothered you disrobing in front of myself and James here..." She gestured at the doctor, who gave me a nervous nod. "But let's face it...you're naked about as often as I eat warm meals, so one of us clearly has a problem."

"Love you too." I sighed, tugging the clothes off and settling onto the bed, feeling slightly self-conscious. Sure, they were medical professionals and they needed to examine me, both physically and using the freshly built scanners, but I was also naked. And yeah.

After the entire park seeing my meat and two veg, I was feeling a little off right now.

"We can leave the room if you want," Jo said seriously, seeing the look on my face, and I snorted, shaking my head and lying back as she moved in closer. "Are you okay?"

"Yeah, I'm fine." I sighed. "Just wasn't expecting that, that's all."

"Me to make a joke?" Her lips quirked in a smile.

"Nah, you always do." I smiled back. "I was working on magic, that's all, and got carried away."

"I noticed." She nodded. "I mean, it was hard not to. That whole 'hurricane and the mother of all storms' going on right above the park, then your armor exploding into ash and shattered links as you flew around, mooning the world. I mean, you leave a hell of an impression on innocent young ladies, you know."

"Innocent." I snorted. "You're about as innocent as the man behind the grassy knoll."

"Maybe, but I could have been." She grinned. "I probably was, once."

"The park is full of refugees from Sunderland," I pointed out. "There are people out there who have seen more cocks than a chicken farmer, so you'll forgive me if I'm not overly concerned by an honest mistake."

"'Mistake' he says." She shook her head, a pad the size of a table device held in one hand as she dragged it into position, at the end of a long metallic arm. "Matt, you were glowing like the sun. And as much as I joke about you being naked, the human body isn't designed to have its clothing, much less armor, detonated and turned to ash atop it. *You* should be ash, instead of looking like you just stepped off a tanning bed. Seriously, are you okay?"

"I am," I assured her, shifting uncomfortably on the cold bed. "Or I would be, if this damn thing wasn't so bloody freezing."

"Oh, there we go, god of lightning and he can't handle a chilly mattress," she distractedly said to the doctor, who chuckled dutifully. But it was obvious that the pair of them were really focusing on the scanner and whatever it was showing them.

The next few minutes passed slowly—the occasional comment or joke, a bit of light ribbing—but their focus was on scanning my brain, and my focus was on trying to tell whether I could feel anything there or from the scanner.

They shifted away from my head, moving to the neck, having me roll over and lie face down—I made a mental note that I needed to make beds with one of those cut-out face holes in them when we upgraded the suites next—but after a full hour, I was finally allowed to turn back over.

"Well?" I asked as they paused dramatically. "You gonna tell me that I've caught a Divine version of the clap or something?"

"Well, there's good news and bad news—" she started, only to be cut off by the doctor, who gestured for me to start dressing again.

"You've got a clean bill of health, Dungeon Lord." He fixed Jo with a disapproving look before turning back to me. "In fact, I've never seen anyone as healthy. Were this the old world, I'd be asking you to be a study for medical magazines. As it is? I simply offer my congratulations, and a recommendation that whatever you've been doing, you keep doing it."

"Fighting." I grunted, pulling my new pants on and then smiling at the look he gave me. "Seriously, I fight to the death on a regular basis, fly around in storms, and get shot, blown up, stabbed and worse."

"Then I guess immortality isn't for everyone, as I doubt I'd survive the first week," he replied dryly. "I'm sorry…" He turned to Jo. "But the first thing that we're taught is that when you have a patient in a position like this, you *cannot* make jokes.

"Reassure them instead. Be honest, and always be respectful. Teasing him that there might be something seriously wrong is incredibly unprofessional and—"

"I'm all clear to leave?" I asked quickly, interrupting the pair, and got a glare from Jo and a nod from the doctor.

"There's nothing there, Matt," Jo eventually admitted. "And I'm sorry. I guess I did that a bit wrong."

"No, you didn't," I assured her and the doctor. "We're living on the ragged edge every day. A little joking now and then gets us through, so don't worry about it. And when you get Chris in here…"

I summoned a handful of medical devices, including a speculum, something I'd been assured was a horrifically uncomfortable experience. Then I laid them all on the table to the side and grinned evilly. "I'm not saying use them…just give him a little scare, that's all."

Although Jo snorted, James glared at me and shook his head.

"It wouldn't be ethical," he said, and I nodded that I understood, then waited. "But…" He sighed after a few seconds and compromised. "Perhaps they could be left on the table, where he could see them."

"That's what I like to hear!" I grinned. "So, I can return to the dungeon?" I asked, again wanting it to be fully confirmed and knowing damn well that Kelly was going to be in the dungeon sense right now, watching.

"All clear. Go on—get out of my hospital and go chase Kelly around the bedroom!" Jo smiled, before walking to the door behind me and opening it up, whispering as I turned to leave. "Don't forget to look like it hurt."

"Oh gods…" I whimpered, laying it on a bit thick as I limped out of the room. "Seriously, why did you have to shove it *there*?"

"We have to be thorough," Jo said blandly. "Chris, your turn. Come on, big lad."

"Uh…what?" Chris stood and looked from the pained expression on my face, and the way I was holding myself, to the room beyond. "What did you…?" He started to back up until Jo reached out, grabbed his arm and hauled the massive man into the examination room.

157

"Come on, we've not got all day!" she snapped. "You know how many people we need to examine? Just getting you lubed up and ready for the probe takes its time…"

"PROBE?!" Chris wailed.

The door shut off the sudden panicked look on his face, and I chuckled, straightening up and winking at Barry.

"All clear. And don't worry…it's a little scan, that's all," I assured him.

"But you're clear and the others are as well?"

"We need to check everyone who came from the camp," I said. "But as long as they're all clear, then yeah, I don't see a need to have everyone in the park checked. If we're clean, then we clearly didn't bring anything with us."

"Glad to hear it." He grunted. "So, this here medical facility, it's a bit bigger than I expected. And Kelly and Aly were talking about extensions to my park?"

"You mind that?" I glanced over at him as he fell into step alongside me, the two of us heading to the exit.

"Nope, not at all. Bit sick of feeling like the poor cousin, actually," he admitted with a sudden grin.

"Well, the plan, last time I was involved in it, was to upgrade the park heavily, and to start building everything here. There'll be a smaller presence kept there, at the dungeon's heart, and the mage's tower and so on, but that's it. The vast majority of stuff will be here from now on."

"Good to hear." He grunted. "Manufacturing, research, and more, I hear."

"If you've heard it all, why you asking me?" I cocked one eyebrow, and got a snort in reply.

"Better to hear it from the horse's mouth than anywhere else." He smiled sardonically. "I know you've got a lot going on, what with flying around naked and flashing the entire park, so I'll let you get to it."

"I hate you." I sighed, crouching, then leapt into the air, soaring up and away, into the early morning, headed for Newcastle.

CHAPTER FOURTEEN

It was perhaps twenty minutes or so later when I landed atop the roof of the dungeon proper, back home in Newcastle and finally there both in the flesh *and* conscious on the way in.

I found the door unlocked to the upper level, and after glancing inside as I passed, I was pleasantly surprised. My gym thankfully didn't reek of cigarettes nor was it knee-deep in trash, though there was a general air of shabby abandonment and a whiff of sweat and uncleaned towels.

I sighed and moved on, adding it to the list of jobs to do tomorrow—or later today, as it were.

There were plenty to address. My spells, new armor and gear, learning more about my core and figuring some of that shit out, Robin and her place in things now that the dungeon would be open to them all.

Plotting for the dungeons that were allied against us would take a little time, making sure they were recorded and remembered, as well as where that Balthazar was, and his people. But it could wait. It could *all* wait, I decided.

The gym would be cleaned, lessons would resume at the tower, artifact creation would be looked into, as would the paladins and priests, the various research projects and the ongoing crafting, as well as the glassblowing and so on.

There was no end to the things that needed addressing, I knew, but as I jogged down the stairs, my soft-soled sneakers silent in the night, there was only one need that was going to get addressed tonight.

Kelly.

Reaching the bottom of the stairs, I turned and headed for the sealed second stairwell. The door at the top of it opened easily for me, encoded to recognize the dungeon's master.

I passed through and continued down. Thirty seconds later, I reached the lowest level—or, at least, the lowest *accessible* level, anyway.

There was a narrow hallway with rooms on either side, followed by a communal living area, and with a sharp turn to the right from that, a short final corridor.

The far end of the corridor held the core, hidden behind a very real wall, and reinforced now, but that was the closest point of access to it.

All I spared the hidden core was a glance, though. Instead, I turned right again, reaching up one hand and tapping lightly on the door, before pushing it open.

I had a mental pause as I considered that maybe I'd been wrong and that Kelly hadn't realized that I was coming, and maybe wasn't here…then the darkness of the room beyond resolved.

There were candles scattered around the room in small bowls. Their flickering, yet low wicks offered a gentle light that hid as much as it illuminated.

Our room's layout had changed while I'd been gone, the malleability of the dungeon playing its part, as now the bed itself was half recessed into the wall in the middle on the left, its headboard sitting flush against the stone.

The room was oblong—roughly—with the entrance, if seen from above, at the bottom. A glass panel at the top covered most of the far wall. It was frosted, with the dimness beyond showing the shower to the right, and the solid wall hiding the toilet and facilities to the left. A simple glass door led into the bathroom area, and a second door had always hidden the toilet.

Now that glass wall into the shower had been extended, and rather than a single pane that ran its length as we'd talked about to give a little extra light, instead there was a vaguely opaque frosted wall.

With the light right there, the view would be incredible, I knew. On the right, there was a table and chairs where we'd enjoyed many a meal, though now it was bare, its cutlery and crockery cleared away. Along the wall to the right was recessed storage for clothing, and on the wall on the left…our armory.

The layout had changed little, but it had changed. And a meter or so from the foot of the bed, where it extended into the room, there now hung a sex swing, one that looked clearly ready for all kinds of mischief.

I, however, had eyes only for the woman in a chair just to the right of it.

She had a small table set alongside the chair, and a footstool that she was resting her feet on. A cocktail glass was in one hand, and she was smiling at me, enjoying the way my eyes had locked onto her.

Kelly was stunning. For me, she was incredible in every way, almost classically Nordic in looks. She was slimmer and less busty than my usual tastes before her, with long blonde hair, high Slavic cheekbones, a small nose, and narrow ears that gave her an almost pixie-ish air about her. All in all, just gorgeous.

She was slim, yet strong, having spent time fighting alongside me. She'd spent points in Constitution and Strength, making her physically as strong as any athlete before the fall, and yet she could double as a model in most places, even if she'd never be able to walk a catwalk in Paris or Milan.

She was beautiful in a way that none of those models ever could be, because she was real. She had a thousand 'imperfections' and a million more reasons that she *was* perfect. More than that, I loved her.

Though, as she slowly uncrossed her ankles and stood, I couldn't help but shake my head and let loose a low whistle in admiration.

She knew what she looked like, that she was beautiful, and that despite the hours she'd spent outside, she'd never keep a tan long. Her skin was a pale, yet creamy white, and the blonde hair cascaded in a stream of golden yellow down one shoulder, where the straps of the black lacy lingerie flowed down.

Where she'd gotten the outfit from, I had no clue; it was definitely new, though. I knew that because there was no way that something that had that much lace and required so many small knots to be done and undone was ever going to survive what I was going to do to her.

Or *for* her.

Hell, the things she'd be doing to me and that we'd be doing together meant that there was no way that was going to be intact and undamaged in the morning.

"You like?" she asked in a slightly husky voice, before sipping her cocktail, and setting it down onto the table with a clink of glass.

"Oh, I like," I agreed fervently. "I like it very, *very* much!"

"Glad to hear it, because I'm starting to feel a little neglected." she said with a little mew, stepping forward.

I had to pause a heartbeat longer to take the rest of her in.

Whereas her top was essentially a collection of tiny straps that accented and uplifted far more than it hid, her knickers were…well, they were there, apparently, though again, very small and designed more with easy access in mind.

The suspender belt was a gossamer and lace creation that hugged her hips, while thin belts led down to the top of stockings. As she clicked toward me, her high heels granted her both a few extra inches of height and a swaying walk that sent her gorgeous hips rolling.

I stepped in, reaching down and kissing her, my hunger clear, only to have a hand on my chest pressing me back after barely a taste of her.

"I'm all clean, and ready, trimmed, waxed, and the works…but you? You're clean, just about, but you smell of soot and ash. Go get clean."

"But…" I whispered huskily, reaching for her again.

"It's only fair," she whispered back, before slipping past me. She gripped the sex swing, lifting herself into it, the braced seat clearly augmented to make sure it was more comfortable than these things generally were.

I loved the view, and I turned to make the most of it, before letting loose a groan of need as she laid back, settling into place, and placed her feet into their own loops.

The way that she spread her legs made it very clear that the underwear had been designed to stay on during our fun, and yet not get in the way. And when she plucked a toy from the table next to her and smiled evilly, I couldn't help but groan again.

"Don't mind me," she whispered. "I've been waiting awhile though, so I'm just going to keep myself going while you're in the shower…" She broke off as she slid her toy inside, and I stood there for long seconds.

"The shower…" she gasped after a solid minute of me just watching. My eyes flickered from hers, to lower, watching as she enjoyed herself. "Don't make me…wait…!"

"Oh, you're fucking cruel!" I groaned, pulling my clothes off, backing away slowly and staring.

"Don't forget!" she called after me. "Self-care…is the best care!"

"I'm loving watching your self-care!" I agreed.

She grinned, her face growing redder as she worked herself upward. "I mean…take your time, if you want me…to take…mine!" She ended on a gasp again, her orgasm clearly building, and making it obvious that she might have been waiting for me, but she'd not been idle while she waited.

I backed away, hating leaving the wonderful show, but knowing that she was right. I'd been running around like something not right for weeks. I'd not shaved, I certainly hadn't engaged in any intimate grooming, and yeah, my clothes and armor had erupted into fire only a few hours earlier.

I probably stank.

Hurrying into the shower, I found a second lovely surprise waiting for me. It wasn't just that the shower was hot almost instantly, nor that my razor, foam, and so on was set out, ready.

It was that with a simple sliding of the glass from what was marked as "position one" to "position two"—a little note was dangling from the handle with "pull me" on it—meant that the glass went from semi-opaque and frosted, to perfectly see-through.

I could see her clearly, and she could see me, watching as I lathered, rinsed, repeated, and nearly trimmed myself rather than hairs in my distractedness.

I probably managed a record in getting in and out of that shower. But by the time I strode free and headed for her, I had to admit, I was much cleaner, less smelly, and better groomed.

"About…time…" she gasped, clearly very, very ready for me, as I came to a stop, standing between her legs and looking down. "Please…!" she whispered.

I couldn't help but grin, knowing exactly what she wanted.

I took her face in my hands and kissed her—her hands were both very busy—then I dropped soft kisses down her body, sinking to my knees between her legs.

She stared down at me as I paused, then started to kiss the inside of her right leg, trailing gentle, lingering kisses along the inside of her knee.

The skin of her inner thigh was soft and warm, and she flinched as I kissed more and more, inching my way closer to where she wanted my lips, even as my fingers ran down the outside of both legs.

I reached up, grasping the swing, and pulled it close, looping my hands through and taking hold of her hips, before switching to her left leg and beginning to work my way up that side as well. Each kiss was having a very clear effect as she moaned and gasped. The closer I came to her, the more sensitive her skin became.

"*PLEASE*…" she whimpered, looking down at me. "So…so close…!"

"Shouldn't have started without me then," I replied, before grinning and pushing her toy aside. Then I breathed on her, slowly, letting my hot breath tickle and tease her as she groaned…before sliding my tongue across her, and beginning.

The next few minutes were spent rebuilding her need, bringing her to the point of climax, and backing away, deliberately changing my rhythm and method, until she was screaming.

One hand was free of the swing now and clamped onto the back of my head, pressing my tongue into her from lower down. Her fingers were working fast and hard, and we stared into each other's eyes as her orgasm built, climbing past the point of no return, and then scaling higher and higher.

She bucked wildly as she climaxed, losing all control. Her breath had been coming in short, sharp gasps, before a ragged last was dragged down, and the screams began.

By the time she regained control, I was there already, standing over her, holding her upright and to me. Her body quivered with the last pulses, and she clung on, her nails digging almost painfully into my sides.

Then, I felt her hot kisses, as instead of speaking, she shifted around, unhooking her legs and slipping almost bonelessly out of the swing. She dropped to her knees, reaching up for me.

I stood over her now, as she gripped my length and pulled me forward. One hand started to stroke me, lightly at first, then with increased vigor. Her hair was plastered to her face with sweat, her skin flushed with excitement and pleasure, and her breath still coming sharply.

That was when she dragged my tip downward, lifted slightly, and pressed trembling lips to it, kissing me at first gently, like the gossamer kiss of a butterfly landing, and then sliding her tongue along me.

She licked every inch. One hand worked my length, the other cradled and played lower, making me groan as my need grew harder to ignore.

"Tell me what you want…" she told me, and I glared at her.

"Kiss it," I told her, and she did. "Suck it," I ordered, and she smiled, before dragging her tongue along its length again, from base to tip, and then pressed another chaste kiss to it, before sliding lower and starting again.

"Please!" I groaned.

"That's better," she whispered, before kissing my tip, and then suddenly pressing her head forward. Her lips and mouth opened slowly. The increased pressure, the hot wetness of her mouth, and the way that she sucked it all at once made me gasp. My eyes widened as she started to work her way deeper with each bob of her head.

She worked me like that for a while, taking more than logic and any kind of reasonable belief said she could, and picking up speed and force.

She went faster, harder, and dragged her nails down my stomach, before taking the toy I had snatched from the small table and offered to her. Then I stared into her eyes, seeing it reflected there as she made use of that toy at the same time, the enjoyment that built in her at the same time as mine built in me.

She slowly pulled her head from me, swallowing hard, catching her breath, and stared up at me for a few long seconds, her eyes slightly unfocused as her breathing continued to come quickly.

"Do you…want me…to stop…?" she asked, before grinning. "Or keep…going?"

"BOTH!" I groaned. "I don't want you to stop AT ALL but I want so much more!"

"I know…" She gasped. "But…we can play…*again*…soon…?"

I looked into her eyes, seeing that she was building to a new crescendo, and I reached out, taking the back of her head and pulling her mouth back onto me.

I didn't say it, but I also didn't need to. Her hands were busy taking care of her own needs, and she maintained eye contact while I did the same, doing my best not to go too hard or too deep, building to my own climax as we stared at each other.

The end, when it came, was powerful for both of us, leaving us gasping, exhausted, and desperately wanting to relax, and yet both wanting—and needing—a lot more.

We'd done so little, and yet so much. As she slowly took my hand and stood, we exchanged a long kiss, before she led me to the bed, pushing me onto my back and kissing me more.

The kisses started out gentle, but as they lengthened, so did the passion. She slid up and straddled me, sitting over me and staring down into my eyes as she sat, and round two began.

CHAPTER FIFTEEN

The next morning arrived after what felt like about fifteen minutes of sleep. We were both lying on the bed, me on my back, a bare fragment of the duvet covering my upper left side and half my cheek.

She was on her side, facing away with the blanket wrapped tightly around her. As I rolled to face her, shifting her hair out of the way to press a gentle kiss to the side of her neck, she groaned and reached back, flipping the blanket away from her back and reaching for me.

I took the hint and shifted in closer, pressing my cold body against her warm one and making her stiffen in shock.

"That's..." She gasped. The welcoming hand that was inviting me closer suddenly pressed hard against my chest and shoved me back. "Too cold!" she finished, shuffling away, or trying to.

She didn't make it far as I'd wrapped my arm around her and I dragged her in close, pretending I didn't understand and that I thought she wanted to warm me up.

That started a bout of play fighting, a beating with a pillow, mock wrestling...and then more sex. This time, we didn't make it to the swing. Instead, it was the bed, followed by her dragging me upright and across to the small table.

After she'd climbed aboard and we'd almost broken that, we made it to the shower, and ended up getting cleaner while acting very dirty.

Half an hour after, we were back out of the shower, both pulling clothes on, and I stared down at what was left of my little armory, feeling remarkably depressed for a guy who'd had his world rocked so thoroughly so recently.

"What's up?" Kelly asked me, moving up to slide her head under my arm.

"Ah, you know." I sighed. "Just trying to figure out my weapons and more again." I kissed the top of her head.

She frowned, glancing at my gear, or lack thereof. "Where's your...oh."

"Yeah," I agreed glumly. "Oh, indeed."

"Did any of it survive?"

"Bugger all." I sighed. "I'd been half expecting the shit to hit the fan at some point and I'd been fully dressed, with my gear in place, ready to rock and roll. I even had my damn sword on my back!"

"And it was all destroyed?"

I nodded. "What was left was basically a lump of melted metal and alloys."

"Was it worth it?"

"It was," I admitted. "Or I think so, anyway."

As I said it, I pulled up my core, staring at it again and feeling that self-same sense of awe as I did when I'd been naked earlier and I'd seen it.

The core had transformed from a sort of neutron star-looking thing from farther out, and a collection of high spires from closer in, to a globe—one that was studded with protrusions and yet glowed and spun, flaring with a sort of golden light that mimicked my heartbeat and made me feel…weird.

I knew that it was my Divine core and that now that I'd created it, it was generating a small amount of Divine power, each and every second, from those who… I stopped, trying to figure this shit out as I described it aloud to Kelly.

"It's not like the power comes from me, and yet it does." I scratched at the side of my chin. "Gods, I'd kill for a goddamn wiki. But the core seems to gather in power from those around me, and at the minute? I'm full and there's more coming in than I think I could use."

"Don't tell Robin that," Kelly muttered, and I snorted.

"You're still salty over her?"

"No." She sighed, before cuddling in closer to my side. "I'm not, not really. Just a little worried that she might bite off more than she can chew and start draining you again."

"If it's any consolation, I can stop it," I told her, staring into the distance as I examined the core. "Or I think I can now. Robin could store five points of Divine essence at a maximum, and as it is right now, I can generate that in an hour. So as long as I keep her on short rations, that's fine. With the core in place, I can control it a lot better."

"But?" Kelly asked shrewdly, and I shrugged.

"Honestly, I don't know. I can store up to twenty points myself currently, while before I was essentially radiating everything I generated, I think. If Robin has a need, I can grant her more power, and she can go to town on someone. But unless I want to let her draw all of it like before, I can now cut her off as well. This whole religion and Divine system is really weird, but as near as I can tell, there's tiers. The stronger I get, the more power I'll generate and be able to hand out, just as the stronger my followers become, the more they'll be able to do."

"But where does the power come from?" Kelly frowned.

"I don't know," I said, but I chewed my lip as I thought about it, and she noticed.

"You know something," she said.

"I *think* I do," I admitted. "It's not the same as knowing it."

"Go on."

"I think—again, fuckin' *think*, I don't know…it just sorta feels right—but it's down to belief." I shrugged, holding one hand out and summoned my lightning to my palm, bathing us both in its incredible radiance.

"If people are believing in me, there's a prompt that the system said I could use, the power of organized religion. And that got me thinking…what if it's like a tithe system?"

I glanced at her as I snuffed the light out. "What if it's like everyone is giving a fragment of their mana to me, and I'm just somehow using it, converting it into Divine essence, and then parceling it back out?"

"You want to start a church?" she asked me slowly. "An organized religion?"

"No!" I said firmly, then shrugged. "I mean, maybe? Dammit, Kelly, I don't know. All I know is that the system said that you can essentially go the 'trainer wheels' route with that, that it provides safer methods of working through it, and I can get both priests and paladins.

"If I have people giving a little bit of belief and their mana to me every day already, if that's where the power is coming from, then maybe they can get something back? You know, like the priests were supposed to be, not chasing the choirboys around but instead having proper warrior priests. Knights who can call down lightning and smite the shit outta our enemies, who can turn undead and make use of the situation."

"This all sounds very weird."

I nodded. "Believe me, I know…I *know*. But if we're looking at this as a path of organized religion, maybe we can twist it a bit, so it's not me they're worshiping…"

"Oh?"

"Maybe…it could be us?" I said softly, reaching a hand out and focusing, as the Divine shard flickered to light in my hand, bathing the room in its glory.

"Matt, what is that?" Her eyes went wide.

"The system called it 'Zeus's Master Bolt,'" I said. "But regardless of what it might be calling it, it's a shard of Divine energy, something that I managed to make when I formed my core, and something that I can either use to improve my affinity to Lightning, or…"

"Or?" she asked when I said nothing else.

"Or, I can use it to raise another to the Pantheon of the Storm," I said. "We're in the lead for now, but I don't know for how long. And this? This is a chance for us to pull ahead even further. If each time we form our cores, we can do this, then we could raise our pantheon even higher. Three more Divine core shards are going to be granted by the system. They're basically cheat codes, a way to boost our faction higher and further, and…"

"No," she said quietly.

I kept going.

"When you reach the same stage I'm at, I can guide you to remake your core so that…"

"No," she repeated, and something about how she said it got through this time.

"What?" I asked, confused. "Kelly, this is…it could make you a goddess!"

"Do I need to be?"

I frowned at her, confused as I absorbed it back into myself.

"For us to be together, and for me to continue in this role, in the dungeon and as your partner, do I need to become a goddess, even a baby one?"

"No!" I said quickly, shaking my head. "No, Kelly, I want you. I just—"

"Then this is too important a bargaining chip for us to give up."

"A bargaining chip?" I mumbled, frowning. "What the hell…"

"Think, Matt!" she snapped. "What do we need?"

"Mana?" I guessed. "Time?"

"People we can trust!" she corrected. "Everything else can come from that. But the alliance against us is growing, and although as far as we know, none of the Dungeon Lords you met have joined the fight against us, none of them have come forward and offered to form an alliance with us either."

"Right," I agreed.

"Well, they have access to a dungeon fairy, they have information we don't, they have their own territories and their own focuses and technologies, so eventually we're going to have to deal with them, right?"

"Yeah."

"Why not start as you mean to go on?" she said quickly, moving around to stare up at me, reaching out to lay her hands on my hips, as I rested mine on her shoulders. "Matt, what if instead you used the bolt and promise of godhood—under you—to bind one or more of them to you? What if we formed our own alliances? How many do you think will rush to side with our enemies when it's not just you and your dungeon alone, but when you're killing them off and you have allies who can come to help at a moment's notice? We have the nexus gates, almost nobody else does—and they probably don't even know they exist yet!"

"So you're saying…" I whispered, the potential making fireworks pop in my mind.

"We form an alliance with one of the other dungeons; we give them the Divine shard and bind them to your pantheon, and they'll have to share anything we need to know, because they're stuck with us. And we'll have a backup army that we basically don't have to feed or house, one that can come streaming out of the nexus gate, ready to fight by our side!"

We stared at each other for several seconds, the possibilities spinning and dancing in each other's eyes.

"This could change everything," I said slowly. "*Everything.*"

"It really could. But before we do it, I think you need to talk to Aly, and to the council, and definitely to Chris."

"Chris?"

"You know, the big guy?" she joked. "Smells a bit, gets in the way but…"

"Oh, him. Yeah, I vaguely remember him, but why…?"

"Because as much as he jokes and acts the fool, he's your best friend and he's always there for you. He's your right hand in the field and in almost every battle. You need to make sure he understands why you're not giving it to him."

"I will." I sighed, before snorting. "Besides, can you see him as a god? He'd be writing 'That's what she said' jokes in the stars."

"Don't make me cry," she said. "That's the only realistic response to the thought of him as a god."

"So…what do we do first?" I asked her, trying to get my head back in the game.

"First, you kiss me some more, and then we head out and grab breakfast where everyone can see us. We get a report from the others and see what's happened while we were…busy. Then we deal with whatever has been going on, and we have a meeting with the council. We make sure everyone's on the same page, and we start negotiations, I guess. Can you arrange a meeting through the nexus?"

"On the platform?" I scratched my chin as I thought. "Yeah, I think so."

"I think that'd be wise," she said. "And this time, no Ashley. I'll be with you, if that's okay with you?"

"Definitely," I said firmly. "I'd rather have you there. You'll see things I'll miss, and then after, you'll be able to interact with the other lords and ladies as their equal, so they're more likely to answer if you ask."

"And we can get a feel for the situation, and who might be a better partner." She nodded. "That being said, I think we'll need to move quickly, and you'll need to start teaching a few of us as well."

"Teaching?"

"If others have made it to the lower levels of godhood already without the shard—and you did, too, don't forget—then you can teach some of our people, and…"

"And?"

"And it's more likely that the others will be working toward it already as well. If we let them achieve it without us and then we offer it, either we set them up to pass us or we're definitely, at the very least, in a weaker position."

"So, let's go get breakfast." I sighed, before smiling slyly. "Just in case you weren't aware, though, you're walking a little funny this morning. Might want to hide that…"

She smiled sunnily at me, walked over to the bed, then proceeded to snatch up a pillow and start beating me with it as I burst out laughing, trying to scooch out of range.

Later in the canteen, I did the rounds, mainly walking around and letting myself be seen, letting people on the chow line serve me—even though I could have summoned the food much easier—and generally doing the whole "I'm a benevolent godling, honest" routine.

Once I'd spoken to a few dozen people, accepted Jenn and Emma's apologies for trying to game the system and sneak into meetings, and I'd answered a million questions—or so it seemed—we eventually left the main dungeon building and marched across the short distance to the Parthenon.

169

Once inside, and out of the cold, which was once again getting blustery and grim, the sky—where it could be seen—was iron grey, and the promise of rain or snow was already beginning to be fulfilled.

I followed Kelly up the stairs, waving to a small band of children and their guardian who'd lined them all up and had them chorus "Good morning, Dungeon Lord and Mistress" as I passed. I couldn't help but frown at Kelly as she glared at me.

"What?" I asked her in a low voice as we moved quickly up to the top landing.

"All those little innocent kids, and Shelly, who I know is a bloody gossip, and all I could think was that they've got to see I can't bloody walk straight! Do you know how sore I am?!" she hissed, and I snorted.

"Haven't you thought about healing?"

"Oh yeah, that's going to avoid the rumor mill, isn't it? The Dungeon Lady comes in and tells the healer that she'd been fucked to within an inch of her life and needs *down there* healed!" She glared at me again.

I fought to contain my laughter, before swallowing hard and speaking in as understanding a tone as possible. "So why not heal yourself?"

"I can't!" she snapped. "My class doesn't work like that, and you know it! And what's the alternative? I summon a healing potion, do a handstand, and ask you to pour it in?!"

"Oh gods!" I burst out laughing, then choked it down and made a "locking and throwing the key away" motion over my mouth, before taking a deep breath, and speaking as normally as I could. "What about one of the spells in the focal orbs? I mean, you've got access, and you know where they are, right? Ten seconds' effort, find somewhere slightly private, and boom. All done."

She stumbled to a halt, staring at me wide-eyed, then nodded. "Go. Go now and get one of those damn things. This is your fault—you can fix it!"

"And you're going into there?" I gestured at the command room, and she nodded. "Oh, okay, and how do you want me to explain to Aly what I'm doing when I come in and press that to your—"

"You know what?" She cut me off, glaring at me. "I think I'm just going to get on with my day. I'll be fine soon enough, and I damn well know not to let you near me again for a while, so this'll remind me!"

With that, and with me trying not to grin while following along behind her, she stalked ahead to the command room.

Once inside, I gave Aly a hug, then dropped into a seat and relaxed, doing my best to ignore the way Kelly sat so carefully and glared at me from time to time.

She also, however, reached out a hand to take mine under the table and squeezed it, making it clear as much as she was playing at being all grumpy, that she'd really loved every second, and that even the aches were good ones.

The first hour was catch-up details again, an explanation for Aly and an expansion on the latest stages of my ascension, as well as explaining a bit more about what it meant, what we knew, and then discussing the plans that Kelly and I had come up with.

There were some details raised, some suggestions, and finally, a handful of points made about preferred allies. The unknown partner of the American dungeon, for example, was the least favorite at the minute because we literally knew nothing about them. But on the other hand, if they'd not been picked yet, there was a chance to insert our own pick into that dungeon, and we'd essentially gain control.

Also, there was the added bonus of getting access to the American continent, and I noticed the way the other two were looking at me as I got talking about the potential for gaining control there...and snorted as I realized what I sounded like.

"And we'll tax them all!" I finished. "Tax them for Good King James and—"

"And that's enough maniacal planning for you." Kelly reached out, miming turning me off with a switch. "Go on, back in your box!"

I opened my mouth to reply to that and got a groan as she realized the innuendo coming, and then struggled to stop me, pressing her hand over my mouth.

"BEHAVE!" she scolded me, her eyes dancing with a mix of outrage and outright laughter. "Just behave, all right? You monster!"

"I'll try," I offered, smiling back at her.

"Fuck's sake, you two, are you going to be okay to work today or do you need to go find a corner to hump in? I mean, I get it...you're young, younger than me anyway, and you've been apart a few weeks, but come on!" Aly groaned. "Do I need a bucket of cold water?"

"Kinky." I shrugged. "I've heard about people who pour hot and cold water on others while they're fucking. Makes the experience more intense, apparently..."

"Cold water," Aly warned. "Very, very cold!"

"I'll be good," I promised, laughing and holding both hands up in surrender. "Okay, so to get back onto topic, and please stop distracting me, you two, but what's happening with the dungeon generally?"

"I'll get you," Kelly warned me, before sighing, reaching up and fixing her ponytail and gathering her thoughts. "Okay, so the core is complete. A load of new data systems unlocked and we're basically drowning in data now. Dante said he knows a couple of computer nerds who can read all that kind of thing and draw them into a comprehensive report that'll help us, but it'd mean giving them advanced access, a lot more advanced than the usual."

"Hard pass on giving people we don't know, command system level access to the dungeon," I said.

"Exactly," Aly agreed. "For now, I think we learn what we can, and get on with things. We'll learn more and more as we go, but for now, this is the level we need to build on. The Glass core is analogous to the Information Age as near as I can tell, so that's basically as suspected. We've got the potential to replace any of the lost tech we'd had back before the fall, but with one major difference.

Electricity still doesn't function. How that works with the electrical impulses of the brain, the heart, and more, I don't know, but it does.

"That means that the systems will always need to be based on mana, and mana can be far more powerful and variable. With that in mind, I'm tentatively grouping things into ten new categories, as the system allows me to change the layout now, and the research options have massively expanded."

CHAPTER SIXTEEN

The table before us dimmed, as did all the lights around the room. Aly and Kelly laid back, closing their eyes, so I took the hint, sliding into the dungeon sense and blinking as I found the image that was forming before me.

The research screen had been redone into a tiered system, with several sections marked up as in progress. On the left-hand side of the screen were ten subjects; by clicking on any one of them, I could find out more details.

As always, there was a hell of a lot of crossover, but it was impressive.

1) Mana Manipulation

- Basic: Simple mana channeling
- Artifact: Reality manipulation through mana

2) Crafting Systems

- Basic: Rudimentary workbenches
- Artifact: Automated mana-driven fabrication chambers

3) Materials Development

- Basic: Basic single-stage materials
- Artifact: Programmable mana-matter

4) Agriculture and Food Production

- Basic: Farming and basic growth
- Artifact: Matter-to-food conversion systems

5) Defense and Weaponry

- Basic: Crude weaponry
- Artifact: Dimensional weaponry

6) Health and Medicine

- Basic: Basic medical facilities
- Artifact: Cellular regeneration and life extension

7) Energy Generation and Storage

- Basic: Mana Converters
- Artifact: Infinite mana loop generators

8) Transportation and Logistics

- Basic: Carts, transport materials, and muscle-powered devices
- Artifact: Teleportation networks

9) Structures and Environmental Controls

- Basic: Structural development, walls, defensive berms
- Artifact: Terraforming capabilities

10) Research, Knowledge Preservation and Education

- Basic: Basic research
- Artifact: Direct knowledge transfer via mana

All in all, it was a mouthful. Some of it, such as the materials sciences, once you clicked on it, offered a load of sections that had already been unlocked. Stone, bronze, and iron as well as all derivative versions of each, including steels, basic alloys, and more were there.

There were dozens of other materials that were shown as possible to research but greyed out. And when I realized I'd never even heard of most of them and clicked on one mentally to examine it, only to find that it was beyond us until we had access to direct mana-meta conversion?

I got the hint. As far as I was concerned, that was what we had already. I mean, we could convert mana into matter, right? Apparently, it was a case of without a certain variation of this, though, the materials science that was based on matter we didn't have on Earth would remain beyond us.

That was fine, though, because the sheer number of random-ass things I could see here? Insane.

Most of the lowest level of things were already done, of course—basic medical facilities up to advanced had been unlocked. But now, as I saw them in this layout, the trees just kept multiplying. Looking at the advanced medical facility, I could see all the possible add-ons, each unlockable through technology research, followed by more that needed specific items.

Lastly, there were dozens, if not thousands, of options that linked onward. Where the scanners, for example, had needed several subsidiary sections of research to be completed to unlock, after them rolled still more options, greyed out and invisible beyond the first two levels. But what I could see was incredible.

Fire mana-based systems that could be used in surgical applications. An entire section on blood and related technologies that were only available if you'd unlocked the research into blood magic, and that required...

I broke off before I lost myself and turned to the other two, who'd apparently been watching me again.

I'd just done exactly what I'd told them to be careful with yesterday, and by their smiles, they knew it.

"So...now what?" I cleared my throat uncomfortably.

"This becomes part of the deal we offer through the alliance," Kelly said. "Not just the information we can see here, because I'm betting the dungeon fairies have access to some, if not all of this, more probably, but the different options."

"Exactly!" Aly agreed, sitting forward excitedly. "We know we can trade technologies, so we plan that out. We find out what the focuses of the other dungeons are and we set up research alliances as much as military ones. Where we focus on, say, expansion and reclamation, as well as war, one of them might be heavily focused on farming, or nanotechnology. Space access might be something that the Chinese or African dungeons are working on already, while the American one might be focused on livestock, breeding, or crafting.

"If they're working on those areas, we don't need to. We set a schedule to share the data—daily, weekly, whatever—and then we focus on what we need. We multiply what we get by the number of allies we have, and none of us get overwhelmed!" Aly practically vibrated with suppressed desire to start the ball rolling, and I nodded my agreement.

"Okay, so let's say they're interested—they might not be, remember...they might be pissed that we managed to make Glass first—but if they *are* interested, how do we do this?" I asked.

"You take Ashley and you go schmooze them and—" Aly started, only to be cut off by Kelly.

"No, this time I'm going," she said resolutely.

"Kell?" Aly blinked. "Are you sure?"

"I know I'm not as pretty as Ashley, but I think I've got a better handle on things. And if Matt's going to continue focusing on the whole godhood thing—" She broke off as I struck a heroic pose, then sighed and deliberately shuffled herself around to present her back to me. "Then we need to be able to directly deal with them ourselves. Matt's going to be elsewhere, and Ashley, with the best will

175

in the world, is a diplomat for us. She's not the Dungeon Lord, or Mistress, and I am. They're always going to be conscious that they're dealing with someone who can only say or agree to so much."

Aly glanced from Kelly to me and back again, before smiling widely. "Girl, I'm so proud of you." She stood and stepped in close to Kelly, who blinked, then stood to get a hug from her sister-in-law.

"What brought that on?" Kelly asked, confused.

"You're standing up and claiming things, rather than just doing what you're told." Aly stepped back and curled one leg under herself as she sat down; Kelly did much the same but with both legs. "You know, when you and Matt first got together, I wasn't sure, because…"

They started chatting, the pair of them grinning, while I was apparently supposed to keep my ass silent here and just be a good boy.

"So…" I interrupted after a few minutes, "you, uh, fancy getting some work done?"

That was apparently not the thing to say. The next half hour was a bit uncomfortable as they asked my permission to do things, to check details and more.

At the end of it all, though, the main details for the dungeon and the future had been hammered out, and we were ready.

First, we were back to a new dungeon setup, but this was going to be a dungeon with a massive difference. The three options that had come about when I'd set up the original northern dungeon were easily brought up on the original prompt.

Seed Core Stabilized. Please select from the following options:

1. **Form symbiotic link with parent dungeon.**

2. **Form secondary associated/unassociated dungeon.**

3. **Specialize dungeon core for subsidiary action.**

First was what I'd chosen, forming a symbiotic link with the first dungeon, allowing control on my side as a subsidiary dungeon. The second option was to form an associated or unassociated dungeon core. That one was tempting, as in theory—we'd need to spend a million mana to be sure, so it was a hell of a risk; maybe I'd ask the dungeon fairies if we ever got an alliance sorted—we could start a new core up from Stone.

The advantages were massive. We could set up a fuckload of little things— mana crystals, for example—and start the new core off with a massive bonus.

We power-level it through the lower end doing research, unlocking things like the mana converters from basic to artifact, then storage and more. We do that at each level, and move up in a faster, more coordinated arc.

Then we share that level of technology with the main dungeon, and booyah. We were fixing the lower-level technologies we'd missed—in theory.

In reality, I knew it wasn't going to be that easy. The cores were the way they were because they were built one atop the other. If I spent a billion mana making this new core perfect, and then tried to slap the same data into the original core?

Chances were that core would just explode. There were dozens of possible and probable issues with it, and they included that the core would need to be set up, leveled through each stage, and then and only then, upgraded.

Stone, for example, even with almost unlimited mana, would take weeks to complete, simply because without the dungeon being able to reach out and do anything, what use was it?

We'd have to step it up, push the manafield out, establish each stage, and take that time to do it right.

While it was doing that, because it was associated but not symbiotic, it wouldn't have access to everything the way the northern dungeon did.

My super-sneaky plan was to make a mobile dungeon. That was it; it was out and I'd said it. It was the best way that I could see to make it both as hard as possible to fight us, and as safe as possible for the dungeon's inhabitants.

We'd make a mobile dungeon, and one that had a nexus gate as part of the design, meaning that we would have a massive advantage in the field, as our forces could be at home and then step through when they were needed.

The benefit of this plan was that we could move on. If the worst happened, that dungeon could be destroyed, and the others would be fine. We'd be making the next level of warship or tank or whatever, and the dungeon battleship would be an incredible weapon. But if anything happened?

People would be chasing the weapon, not our people's home.

That was my hope.

It also meant that we could continue to grow, and to develop our home without being tied in place or being as panicked about draining an area dry of mana. If we did that with the battleship... Fuck it.

If we did that with the dreadnought, then we moved on and let nature refill the void.

The issue?

If we did that with an unassociated dungeon, then yes, we could get a shitload of the tech we'd missed, and it could be game changing. *But*...if we did that, the new dungeon was limited to the level it was at. No summoning healing potions, or rail gun weaponry, no ammunition replenishment, or whatever else we needed. If it was a Stone dungeon, we were back to crude spears and so on.

That meant that the dungeon we were going to develop needed to be modular, able to be increased and improved upon at every opportunity. It needed to be strong, and most of all, it needed to be secure.

That was also why I was back to symbiotic.

If we did option two instead and something went wrong? We could be handing a mobile dungeon to our enemies.

It was a logical progression, I felt, to build the dungeon in this way, as otherwise I didn't see how the hell we'd be taking this fight to the enemy.

I mean, at the very least, we needed to hold the orbitals, right? If they took them, they didn't have to fight us; they could just decide that Honolulu looked great and they were going to keep that as a game reserve, set up shields around it, and then burn the rest of the planet to ash, never having set foot on any of it.

If we had a dungeon or three in space, though? I couldn't get my head around spaceflight, and I frankly couldn't see myself getting involved in it no matter what, but what I did foresee was that the Orcan were mad for fighting.

They were going to want to go toe-to-toe to prove themselves or whatever. When they did that? I'd be there.

Set up targets they needed, like a mobile friggin' dungeon, and let them come to me.

That was why our focus now, at the northern dungeon and with the engineers' help, was to produce a solid option for transportation.

Three different vehicles were decided on as the minimum.

The boxers would do for the first: fast-moving, long-ranged, and solid as hell, they could take a hit and keep going. They'd be the scouts and fast attack.

The second would be the main transportation vehicle—think truck but made up of equal parts RV, tank, and military transport. It'd be fast-ish, but more importantly, it'd be a solid, safe way for our people to travel. And when we needed to, it'd be a platform to fight from.

The third vehicle would be the core—the dreadnought in seed form, and this would be how we managed everything we needed. Not only would it be a bigger one, with room inside to work, but it'd grant us access to the dungeon and all its facilities on the go. It would be a dungeon in its own right, but it'd also allow us to set up—I hoped—a nexus gate, which would mean that if the shit hit the fan, all we had to do was park, hunker down, and activate the gate.

This had been my idea for a while, though I'd been planning to build a transport, and then set up a dungeon at strategic points, then cede control over them to loyal members of the dungeon, until I realized that I didn't need to yet.

The risk that was running wasn't great, and admittedly, sooner or later, we'd need to do it...but right now, fuck it. I didn't have people I wanted to put in a position of that kind of power. I trusted Mike and so on, and I trusted Griffiths with the northern dungeon, but at this point, that was all we needed.

They were close to home, but when we went south, we were either going to end up fighting and destroying a dungeon or two, and then hopefully taking their territory into our own, or we'd have to establish control over areas to block their expansion.

Either way, we'd need to be able to react on the fly, and travelling hundreds of miles, sneaking into the backyard of our enemies, and then trying to set up the new dungeon, one that might take days again to be big enough to activate, before we could even consider defenses and summons?

Not a risk I was willing to take.

No, if we could make this work, then this was by far the best option. We build a transport for the dungeon, secure it inside, and then we drive it down with us. Even if the dungeon couldn't claim land as we went—I wasn't expecting it'd be able to if we were travelling at any real speed, but I could hope—then it'd be able to claim the limited space around it on the truck bed or whatever.

We could do this, and when we managed to unlock higher levels of technology—well, the Empire had those triangular spaceships, and damn, they always looked cool as fuck on the outside.

Sure, there was the "falcon" design as well, but realistically that was just too small for what we needed. It barely had a handful of rooms inside, when you took the actual tech needs into account, and then, having space to transport anything besides smuggling?

Nope.

I'd have to adjust the design too heavily, and that meant I might as well build something from scratch.

A long triangular base, engines at the end, and a fuckload of weapons meant that it could be used in atmosphere and out, and there'd always be space to increase its size.

Realistically, I was trying to go from a horse and cart to a starship, so there was a lot more to consider, but fuck it. Best to have high hopes.

Shoot for the moon, and if you miss? Well, that fucker was huge and you were clearly a shit shot. Not sure where that comparison was going when I started it in my head, but to hell with it. The thought was what mattered.

The park was going to continue with its upgrades. The walls were going to be increased in size, with towers being set out evenly along their length. The central accommodation block would be raised higher, and it'd be lit, so that even for miles around people would see that there was safety to be had.

The walls would also be pushed out farther, giving us a lot more space to expand, and a new factory would be built. That was going to take a while, but the various basic facilities could be built fairly rapidly.

Then a new research facility would be built, and an even larger outdoor pool. Or hell, the original plan was for an outdoor one like the one we had here, but after a little discussion, the new plan was that the entire thing would be under a dome, one that would be at least six inches thick, with the best glass we could manage.

That way, if some crazy-ass flying monster tried to attack, everyone got to see it splat into the glass like a goddamn pigeon.

It was the simple pleasures in life that mattered the most, I found.

The main dungeon would get some upgrades as well, but there'd be a lot less of them: mainly a little improvement in the living quarters, upgrades to the converters and various technology, but that was it.

The northern dungeon was going well. Under the twin leadership of Griffiths and Arend-Jan, the place was apparently booming.

A few hundred people had already volunteered, and they were working with Arend-Jan to clear huge tracks of land as the skeleton teams claimed them, digging down multiple meters. They then leveled the fields, adding in drainage and control points, layers of sand, soil, and more…rocks and loads of random stuff that made no sense to me, but I was assured was what was necessary.

Then the outer edge was being enclosed by a high wall to act as a windbreak, as well as to defend the area.

Jack had been requested back there, and I'd almost refused. I would, in fact, be bringing him when it was time to head south, but for now he was proving invaluable.

After the fight in the Galleries, we'd found him solidly encased in a section of melted wall, apparently sunk into it by magic. I'd had to detail a group to break him free with hammers. As soon as he was free, he'd been sent on patrol again.

For living units, be they Scepiniir, kobold, soldier, or other, they needed to deal with the weather and take regular rest breaks; he didn't. He roamed for hour after hour, day after day, hunting down any threat. Although I had so many uses for him day by day that I constantly nearly recalled him, in truth he was where he needed to be.

We'd estimated that he was at least as valuable as a party of twenty warriors, and as he didn't need rest or to recover from the sapping effect of the weather, replacing him was going to be a massive problem when I eventually did pull him off that job.

For now, though, he roamed and eliminated the enemies that appeared around the base, and Arend-Jan continued to work.

The newly lowered and refreshed soil of the area was to be heated slightly—again, this was part of his plan that made a little sense, but that was it—and overhead, there were to be, eventually, more domes.

They'd cover individual fields and have their own Nature and Life converters dotted around, with Light generators to help boost the plants' photosynthesis, sprinklers to simulate rain, and more.

Basically, he was determined within another month he'd have the northern dungeon ringed by self-sustaining, fully defensible massive farms.

That they'd each be producing food that could then be provided to the dungeon, or sold to our allies—or better yet, evolved to be more beneficial—was a bonus.

The main point for me, beyond redundancy just in case, was that the farms gave a lot of people somewhere to be. Arend-Jan had quickly become a community leader in more than name. Every time I turned around, I heard his name passed around as the guy who had arranged a cookout or who had set up a community area and more.

Griffiths loved working with him as well. The soldier had a wealth of experience in leading soldiers, training them and keeping them on task. But outside of that?

He had an entire army camp that was filled by people who had been worked to the point of death, and who had lost their loved ones while they stood on, uncaring.

The trauma coming to the surface there was horrific. Although a lot of those memories had been lost on awakening, some had started to resurface now, apparently.

The solution was something like the twelve steps for drug addiction, I was told. You accepted it, you made your peace, and you took each day as it came.

For some, they accepted that there was nothing that needed nor could be done, and they just...healed. I was told again and again that at some point, some of them would see how much they were suppressing and have a full-on breakdown, but that some would be okay. It depended on the person.

Others would need this support daily. They needed to break away from their old life, and that included from the camp entirely. They'd agreed to wait until the tests were complete, and then they'd be brought through the nexus gate in batches. They'd be examined, assessed, and then they could either visit the park and stay a while and then return, or they could move there permanently.

My hope was that most of them would be fine with returning to army life—we desperately needed them, after all. But the reality was that we were better off losing those people from the army than having them collapse and break down when we needed them the most.

That covered most of the areas we needed to be caught up on. But it did bring up a single, wonderful new addition as well, when we finished the assessment.

I'd not just gained one race to my available dungeon creatures—I'd gained *two*.

CHAPTER SEVENTEEN

Neither of the creatures would be hugely effective in what was to come, or at least so I first thought, but the one thing they were, was utilitarian and *useful*.

Reading over the system descriptions, and the lists, I could see a handful of different uses straightaway.

Monsters

Fey: The Fey, or Tuatha De Danann, are an unusual group, sub-divided into many species. The Fey as a group are often misunderstood. From the playful sprites to the solemn dryads, to the capricious Daoine Sidhe and the thousands of variations in between, the Fey are as likely to hinder as to help, usually anyway.

Beware, Dungeon Lord:

Although the Fey have donated their essences to be included in the core, they may yet take issue with your use of this…no two Fey regard their inclusion in the dungeon core program the same way. Some "wild" or "free" Fey may ignore your dungeon-born variants, others may include them joyfully…while some may declare war on you for your effrontery in summoning such as they.

You have been warned.

Fey: The most common of the Fey is the **Fairy**, and while the common variant is somewhat unreliable in many ways, they grow more advanced and powerful with each evolutionary level.

Cost: Fairy (Common): 100 Nature, 400 Pure Mana, 5 Control points. Maintenance is 5 mana point per day, per individual.
Current Level: Common.

Already existing research boost detected!

The Fey "Fairy" class has already been absorbed into the dungeon with integrated cybernetics and nanite upgrades. Although cybernetic and nanite upgrades still require numerous prior technologies to be researched to make them available for general production, the original variant is available now.

Dungeon Fairy: [Enhanced] This specifically augmented dungeon variant of the fey designated [fairy] can greatly improve on the dungeon's reliability, production, and expansion rates.

Cost: Dungeon Fairies spawn individually for 250,000 pure mana each. Maintenance is 500 mana points per day, per individual; control points are not required.
Current Level: Advanced.

Fey: Dryads are less common than the fairy folk, but are still plentiful in the universe. A literal Nature elemental, the dryad is uninterested in anything beyond land entrusted to its care, but it will defend said land with its life should any seek to despoil it.

Note: Be wary in harvesting land cared for by a Dryad.

Cost: *Dryad (Common):* 400 Nature, 1600 Pure Mana, 10 Control points. Maintenance is 15 mana points per day, per individual.
Current Level: Common.

Fey: The Daoine Sidhe, or "people of the mounds," as many refer to them due to their preference for underground halls and homes, are often also referred to as the "lords and ladies." A graceful and glamorous creature, the Daoine Sidhe live for their revels, their pranks and parties, but this is not to say that they are useless to a Dungeon. The Daoine Sidhe are rogues and infiltrators without compare. Their natural affinity with glamours and mind-altering magics have firmly established them as some of the most powerful—and hated—rogues in the cosmos.

Cost: *Daoine Sidhe (Common):* 300 Light, 1200 Pure Mana, 15 Control points. Maintenance is 40 mana points per day, per individual.
Current Level: Common.

Elemental: The Primordials are rarely seen, and ancient beings composed of pure elemental energy, capable of shifting between different elemental forms. Once they reach adulthood, however, they are locked to the elemental makeup they have accepted.

Cost: *Primordial (Uncommon)*: 1500 each of Fire, Water, Earth, and Air (6000 total), 15000 Pure Mana, 200 Control points. Maintenance is 500 mana points per day, per individual. Current Level: Rare.

Note: This species may be summoned as infants, and are unbound to their element, or as adults, bound to a specific element, and are then considered Advanced Elementals.

Note: As Primordials advance, they gain the ability to combine elemental forms, creating powerful hybrid states. At higher levels, they can even influence the elemental makeup of the dungeon itself, potentially altering entire sections to suit their elemental nature.

Fungal: Mycomorph are a race of sentient fungi that thrive in dark, damp environments. They possess a collective consciousness and excel at decomposition and rapid growth.

Cost: *Mycomorph (Uncommon):* 200 Nature, 800 Pure Mana, 8 Control points. Maintenance is 20 mana points per day, per individual. Current Level: Uncommon.

Special Traits:

Note: Higher-level Mycomorphs can develop potent biochemical abilities, including healing spores and hallucinogenic defenses. They are particularly useful for resource management and area control within the dungeon.

Mammal: The Dvorks, Dvorkian or People of the Deep, are the ancient enemies of the Orcan, a people that were recently disabused of their final world by the Orcan expansion.

The Dvork are shipbuilders and engineers beyond compare, but suffer from two significant situational modifiers.

1. The Dvorkian race is now formally acknowledged as extinct, and those summoned through the dungeon and given artificial life are unavoidably aware of this. As such, they suffer from significant emotional and physical issues, including uncontrolled aggression and a desire to render themselves insensate through external means. Commonly alcohol.

2. Dvorks as a race evolved on high-gravity, mineral- and ore-rich worlds, resulting in physical differences from most races. They are shorter of stature, broad and enormously strong. These are all minor issues compared to the fact that no Dvork can successfully

mate outside of such a location. This results in an extremely high likelihood of Dvorkian breeding programs failing.

Cost: *Dvork (Common):* 500 Earth, 1500 Pure Mana, 20 Control points. Maintenance is 45 mana points per day, per individual.
Included Level: Common.

Mammal: Goblins as a species have multiple variations, ranging from the lowest caste, who are barely sentient, to the High Grenai, a race that suffers little interaction with "lesser" species, due to the enormous gulf of grace and beauty between those races and their own. The most basic can be spawned as Dungeon Monsters. Utilizing their species' polymorphic tendencies results in greater enhancements than are commonly available.

Cost: Goblins spawn individually for 5-30 mana each. Maintenance is 2-25 mana points per day, per individual.
Current Level: Common.

Mammal: Orcan, or as they are more commonly known, orcs, are a muscular, thick-skinned race. Similar to the goblinoid races in that they share a highly polymorphic tendency, resulting in as many versions of the Orcan as there are worlds, the gift of life to Orcans is a costly and highly risky decision that few Dungeons are willing to make lightly.

Note: The Orakai sub-species is blocked from reproduction by any and all Dungeons due to treaties and enforced by magical interference.

Cost: Orcan spawn individually for 25 mana each. Maintenance is 25 mana points per day, per individual.
Current Level: Common.

Mammal: Scepiniir are rarely seen, and are proud warriors. Only through a life debt were the Scepiniir convinced to permit their essence to be given to the dungeon core program. The conditions were made clear, and are passed onto you here as well:

- No Scepiniir may be forced into a bonded pairing against its will.
- No Scepiniir may be sacrificed to another species, nor consumed by any through any bond or partnership with the Dungeon.
- No Scepiniir can be forced into servitude, nor arenas for the purpose of entertainment.

Any breaking of the Three Edicts will constitute a declaration of war by the Scepiniir Empire.

Jez Cajiao

Cost: *Scepiniir (Common):* 400 Nature, 1600 Pure Mana, 10 Control points. Maintenance is 15 mana points per day, per individual.
Max Number of Scepiniir you can summon: 4 per hut.
Current Level: Common.

Monster: The Lesser Ghast is a misnomer, considering the reality of the breed. Whereas most "monsters" are simply scared or confused members of races other than the one observing and identifying—example, goblins—certain species are quite rightly defined as monsters through their excessive bloodlust and violent natures.

Cost: Lesser Ghasts spawn individually for 100 Shadow mana, 400 Pure Mana each. Maintenance is 40 mana points per day, per individual, and requires 7 points of control.
Current Level: Uncommon.

Monster: Harpies are rarely used in dungeon settings, mainly due to their unpredictable and violent natures. Harpies will happily feast on their fellow dungeon-born unless forced to leave them be and are one of the most aggressive and antagonistic of the dungeon's innate catalog.

Cost: Harpies are 100 Storm mana, or 400 Pure Mana each. Maintenance is 40 mana points per day, per individual, and requires 7 points of control.
Current Level: Common.

Reptilian: Kobolds are a common, highly structured, caste-driven species. Semi-sentient kobolds are a standard sight in Dungeons, due to their advanced trap-making skills and low cost.

Cost: Advanced Kobolds spawn individually for 2,500 mana each, 25 control points. Maintenance is 100 mana points per day, per individual.
Current Level: Advanced.

Dinosauria: The Triceratops Horridus is an ancient herbivore, specifically evolved to be as unpalatable and difficult to consume as possible. Where many herbivores are peaceful, and even cowardly creatures, the Triceratops evolved with a slightly distinctive design. Be this through nature or nurture, the Triceratops, through its many variations, became a highly feared sight in the late Cretaceous era.

Cost: Triceratops spawn individually for 12,500 mana each, 50 control points. Maintenance is 150 mana points per day, per individual.
Current Level: Common.

Avian: Impai are simple creatures, easily distracted by their own hungers and difficult to control, but they excel in two areas: randomized destruction and threat detection. The Impai as a species are widely viewed as unreliable and unstable, resulting in repeated attempts to eradicate their species.

Despite this, they remain a popular choice for lower-level Dungeons and lower-scale conflicts.

Cost: Impai spawn in packs of three for 25 mana each. Maintenance is 10 mana points per day, per individual.
Current Level: Common.

Undead: The various forms of the undead are as numerous as grains of sand or stars in the sky; they are matched only by their antithesis, the forces of Life. Undead can be split into two simple categories, Sentient and Non-Sentient, with the simple Skeletons, Zombies, Ghouls, and so on beginning with non-sentient forms, while the average Wraith, Vampyr, or Banshee begins with a form of rudimentary intelligence and awareness.

Cost: Variable.

Skeletons (Uncommon): 10 Unlife, 40 Pure Mana, 1 Control point.

Maintenance is 1 mana point per day, per individual.

Zombies (Basic): 20 Unlife, 70 Pure Mana, 1 Control point.

Maintenance is 2 mana points per day, per individual.

Wraiths (Basic): 100 Unlife, 400 Pure Mana, 5 Control points.

Maintenance is 5 mana points per day, per individual.

Corpse Lord (Uncommon): 500 Unlife, 2,000 Pure Mana, 10 Control points.

Maintenance is 250 mana points per day, per individual.

Special: Due to your Lightning affinity and the effect that your species change has on your Dungeon, you may summon a single Raiju at a time. Raiju are exceedingly rare beasts, and as such cannot be summoned in large numbers. Their playful nature means that many underestimate them, to their peril.

Cost: 150 mana per summon, 50 mana per day, 10 control points.
Current Level: N/A.

Vermin*:* Rats are a common pest that are ubiquitous across the universe. Vermin of this type vary in size and limb count, but often conform to similar local design.

Note: Flying variants have now been unlocked…cost remains identical.

Cost: Vermin spawn in packs of three for 5 mana each. Maintenance is 1 mana point per day, per individual.
Current Level: Common.

The elemental, as near as I could tell, could be bloody incredible for mages—or, dammit, *mancers*. For Dante especially, I could see him wanting a Fire elemental for his floor of the tower, though the risk of the fucker melting its way through the walls or floor couldn't be overstated.

There was also the minor detail that they could be used for war, as I had to think that a pair of Earth elementals would fuck up practically anyone's Tuesday.

The mycomorphs, on the other hand, might not be as generally useful. But as living mushrooms, I had to guess they'd be incredible farmers? Maybe?

Fuck it. Rereading the species options made something else jump out to me as well. Dryads.

"Just as a side note…" I said slowly, having brought up the new species options to discuss with the ladies. "What do you think about these races as helpers for Arend-Jan and Starr?"

"Starr?" Kelly asked, confused, then she shook her head, waving the comment away. "Sorry, I know who you mean. I just forgot for a second that as a shaman, he's been helping with growing things there. Yeah, thinking about it, they could be useful, but you did read the description, right?"

"Note: Be wary in harvesting land cared for by a Dryad," I quoted, and she nodded.

"So if you summon one, you probably need to be really clear on the details, like this is land that it's to help care for, but no slaughtering of the other dungeon-born or humans as they come to harvest it!" Kelly said carefully. "This is one of those 'don't fuck it up' situations."

"I can take a hint," I assured her. "Oh, wait a minute, you're the one who's really worried about this, and you're the Mistress of Minions, so you know, you get to do it!" I winked at her, and she glared back. "I'm going to pay for that in all sorts of subtle ways later, aren't I?"

"No, of course not. I'm not going to be subtle," she assured me flatly.

I winced, before turning back to work.

In the end, it was agreed that we should have a meeting with the other dungeons as soon as possible on the Nexus platform. First because there was a lot of information to share with them about the way things were going and the battles to come. Then because we needed to lay the groundwork for any alliances that we were going to work toward, and it was the best place to set up such a meeting.

I asked Aly for them, and she retrieved the portal tokens that she'd been using, passing them over.

I glanced at them, mentally sorting them into three piles. There was the glossy black token that came from Onyx first. It was an easy one to recognize, as she'd been the fairy who looked humanoid but with long gossamer wings, and yet everything about her seemed to suck in the light. Like that ultra-black paint, at certain angles you couldn't make out anything about her, beyond that her eyes were bright white and glowed.

She'd been bonded to the African pair, Kaatachi and Akuba, and she'd been pretty unsubtle when she'd questioned me, thinking I'd been responsible for the death of my dungeon fairy. But once I'd explained my situation, she'd been fine.

Next came the Chinese dragon's scale. It, like her, was brilliantly glossy, red, and shimmered gently as I turned the triangular token over, looking closer at it. The tokens were about a third the size of my pinkie nail, and yet they were perfectly formed and distinctly beautiful.

She'd been called…I paused a second, trying to remember, then nodded to myself. Lysander. Lysander was the dragon, and she'd been with the Chinese pair, Kai and Leilani from the Hainan Province.

That had been the pair from the first and third dungeons; the fourth had been that Bryan guy, and he'd been ejected out of the station. That scale was golden, and I bit my lip, trying to remember the name of the fairy… nope, it was gone. I'd have to ask when I met her again.

We were the second dungeon, in the order they'd named us, and one of the dungeons had sent a pair of big frog-looking motherfuckers. They'd been aggressive as hell, and when none of us had taken the bait, and I'd blown one a kiss, it'd attacked me.

Before it'd gotten close enough, the overmind that ran the station had booted them off, literally ripping them through the floor and ejecting them into space, same as it did when Bryan had assaulted Ashley by trying to make a finger puppet of her.

That had resulted in that dungeon being booted to the back of the line. Apparently, the access rights to the station were highly limited; the first six had been granted nexus gates as a congratulations for getting this far.

There was a new dungeon granted access in place of that pair, but the nexus gates took a few days to activate, and there'd been no sign of anyone else arriving in their place. Nor had the sixth dungeon sent anyone at all.

We were also granted exclusive rights for the first six of us to have access to the "first stratum" of the platform. Basically, it was the main floor, and we got that access free. From then on, as any of the other dungeons unlocked the nexus gate technology, they could link to the station and visit it, but they'd be charged a fee for each transportal linked and used.

I pulled up the old notifications and quickly read them over, double-checking and finding that we were currently set to have "trading hub access" in two more cycles.

I had no clue what a cycle was, and on checking, found that we had been due to have a turn four cycles before, so either the cycles were something I had no frame of reference for…or we got one regularly, and had missed our last.

That would sort of make sense, I realized. The prompt said "solar cycle" and I didn't see any reason they'd use a different planet's solar cycle, so it was most likely on a daily cycle. Using that logic, we were getting a turn regularly, but no clue just how regularly that was.

It might be monthly; it might be more or less. Fuck it.

"Looking at this, we might have an opportunity here, but we'd need to move fast…" I said aloud, staring at the "trading hub access" notification and grinning.

Note: Trading hubs may be constructed and offered for 1 premium grade Mana crystal per solar cycle, discounted per your position as a member of the Primary Six. Current position in random rotation: 2nd.

"Oh," Kelly said after a few seconds as I explained my plan to her, before she grinned. "Okay, now *that* works. And if we've got a trading hub set up, then we can talk to anyone who comes. Matt? It's time to prepare some samples for sale. Aly, we're going to need some…"

CHAPTER EIGHTEEN

"As you can see, the rifles are in perfect condition, and each comes with one hundred rounds of ammunition." Ashley smiled prettily at the pair who stared, goggle-eyed at her demonstration.

She'd been pulled into the meeting along with most of the council. After an hour, she'd dragged off Rhodes, the pair of them going on side plans, as we'd decided that she and Chris were going to be our salespeople.

Ashley, because as well as her being beautiful and therefore distracting to anyone whose tastes ran that way, was a Courtesan and had an entire skillset that was built around manipulating her target, and Chris, because not only was he good-looking, great with people, and a fast learner, but because he was a hell of a fighter as well.

The terms for selling from your trading hub on the Nexus platform were clear: no weapons were to be brought aboard generally, but the exception was when you were there for trade. Selling weapons required showing them, after all, so we'd had the perfect opportunity to go loaded for bear.

Ashley was particularly impressive right now. Not because she was wearing anything revealing—she really wasn't…plain black pants and a pristine white top, exactly the same as Chris—but because she'd had Rhodes spend almost six hours training her to strip, prep, and rebuild the SA80 rifle.

She'd invested in Dexterity a lot anyway—far easier to be a spy if you could sneak something into or out of somewhere unseen, after all—which meant that she was terrifying when it came to something like this.

Ashley had an audience of two. Neither were Dungeon Lords or Ladies. Instead, they were the advance party from a dungeon that we neither knew the location of, nor anything else about. They'd looked terrified when they'd been pushed through. Their clothing was clean, but threadbare, which made no sense considering how easy it was to create. And the only thing they'd say was that they were here to examine and to report to their lady.

That was it.

We didn't even get their names.

Beyond them, there'd been two others. One was a hulking brute of a man, literally someone who had put almost every point he'd ever gotten into

Constitution and Strength, without ever considering that he was probably unable to wipe his own arse now thanks to the overdeveloped muscles.

The other…I was fairly sure she'd been an assassin. She'd arrived on one of the lower levels, and had made it up to the primary floor easily enough. But once there, she kept her face hidden, moved around us all slowly, staring and unspeaking, then had left the room, her backpack clutched tightly to her. Thirty seconds later, we were told that an individual visitor had breached the peace of the station and had been removed.

We'd rushed to the window and got to see her frantically thrashing around in space as blocks that looked like chemical explosives drifted out of her reach.

That'd been it so far, and we'd made the effort to send out a message to any nexus gate-capable dungeon that we had opened a trading stall for the day.

Paying for the stall was done by handing over a three-inch block of highly compressed and polished mana crystal. It'd been a pain in the arse to make, getting it as pure and perfect as could be. And still it wasn't high grade enough, so we'd had to pay with two, but I'd expected more.

Thankfully, after nearly five hours on site, by which time I was thoroughly ready to call it a day, Leilani arrived with another man, stepping out of her dedicated portal on one wall.

The six of us each had a specific portal set in the wall on one side, a silvery-grey liquid metal-looking thing that shimmered energetically when they were in use, and seemed to revert to a wall when not.

When Leilani stepped out of the portal, and her companion with her, I felt a wave of relief that at least one of the others had responded to our invitation.

"Matt." She greeted me, smiling and inclining her head. "This is my companion, Engineer Zheng."

"Welcome. It's good to see you again, Dungeon Lady Leilani, and to meet you, Zheng. I'm Matt, Dungeon Lord of Newcastle, and this is Kelly, Mistress of Minions, and Lady of our dungeon."

"Thank you, and greetings." Leilani smiled at Kelly.

"It is an honor to meet you both," Zheng said as well.

"So, you have set up a trading post?" Leilani asked after a few seconds.

I gestured across the floor, showing her what we'd brought.

When I'd reached out to the overmind through the nexus gate, it'd offered to provide everything that we would need for the trading post. But, as we'd found out on arrival, its idea of what was needed and our own was very fuckin' different.

According to Kelly, who'd once dated a guy from the convention circuits, this was basically the way things were done, which was why she'd been ready with the backup plan.

When we arrived, we had a single table ready for us, and that was it.

Literally, we could summon chairs, and we could alter the table's length, but not so much as a cloth was available to tart the place up and make it pretty.

There were malleability advantages, such as the ability to stick things to the walls and to raise or lower the tables, but bugger all else.

That meant that we had samples of guns on the wall behind Ashley, swords and various melee weapons behind Chris, a box of assorted potions, samples of several different foods, piles of mana crystals, and everything from technical manuals to porn stacked to one side.

I'd actually been the prudish one who didn't think that porn was appropriate, but Kelly had pointed out that for certain cultures, most even, it might not be, but if you were stuck in a dungeon as the only human around? You might be willing to pay an incredible amount for some of that, making it highly valuable.

She had, however, put it with magazines that hid the cover as much as possible, while making it clear what it was.

I wasn't going to judge...much.

We showed Leilani and Zheng around, and I made absolutely no comment on the minor detail that Zheng deflected every question about his engineering background and moved like a well-muscled dancer. Constantly standing between Leilani and anyone who moved too close.

He was a bodyguard, and we all knew it.

"So..." Leilani said after a brief look around. "Is this all you are selling, or are there more items for the discerning client?"

"Such as?" I asked, and she hesitated.

"Leilani, the old world is gone, and none of us are interested in its laws," Kelly said. "If something was illegal then, as long as it doesn't hurt people now, we don't care. What do you need?"

"Sentients," she admitted after a few seconds of mulling over how to say it. "Non-human, and skilled."

"Slaves?" I blinked, totally thrown. I thought she was asking whether there were more guns that were maybe cooler or something.

"No," she said flatly. "But we have access to certain species, and would be willing to trade species to unlock them for your dungeon, should we both have ones that the other desired."

"Sample sentients," I muttered. "That sounds so wrong."

"It does," she agreed. "It is highly wrong, and yet it is needed. All the dungeons have access to such creatures. Genetic codes that have been gifted or obtained by our alien 'benefactors' and made available to us."

She said "benefactors" with a curl of the lip that said she believed they were anything but, and I damn well agreed.

"We have a few species," I admitted. "What are you looking for?"

"What do you have?" She smiled widely.

In the end, it turned out that we both had the same main species: goblins, kobolds, orcs, and more. They didn't have the Dvork, but she also had no interest in a race that were basically depressive alcoholics. Beyond that, she had access to a few sub-races that we didn't, and I loved the descriptions that her system offered them with:

Jez Cajiao

Mammal: Mutated Canines, often referred to as *Houndborn*, are magically enhanced versions of common dogs. These creatures retain the loyal nature of their ancestors but possess heightened intelligence and various magical abilities depending on their specific mutation.

Cost: *Houndborn* spawn individually for 150 mana each, 5 control points. Maintenance is 15 mana points per day, per individual. Current Level: Uncommon. Note: Houndborn make excellent companions for dungeon inhabitants, particularly rangers and Druids. Higher-level mutations may develop elemental affinities or enhanced sensory abilities.

Mammal: Arcane Felines, colloquially known as *Magewhiskers*, are magically altered panthers with increased size, intelligence, and mystical prowess. They retain feline grace and independence while developing a stronger bond with compatible humanoids.

Cost: *Magewhiskers* spawn individually for 200 mana each, 7 control points. Maintenance is 20 mana points per day, per individual. Current Level: Uncommon. Note: Magewhiskers are particularly attuned to magical energies and can assist spellcasters in rituals or act as familiars. Advanced mutations may develop the ability to manipulate small amounts of mana directly.

Mammal: Ethereal Equines, or *Phantomsteeds*, are mystically enhanced horses capable of feats beyond normal equines. They possess increased stamina, intelligence, and often develop unique abilities based on their specific mutation.

Cost: *Phantomsteeds* spawn individually for 300 mana each, 10 control points. Maintenance is 30 mana points per day, per individual. Current Level: Uncommon. Note: Phantomsteeds make exceptional mounts for dungeon defenders or adventurers. Higher-level mutations may develop the ability to gallop across water, phase through solid objects, or even fly short distances.

We had dogs, though they were much closer to normal dogs and simply bigger or stronger, some with variations that meant they were never going to be successful in life's lottery beyond this generation.

When I pressed, it turned out that Leilani's brother Kai had a particular love of animals, and had made use of the breeding huts to create the three variants.

In exchange, we gave them trikes. The triceratops that we'd managed to unlock were incredible, but they were also slow as shit and low leveled. Leilani acknowledged that she and her brother had sent out raiding parties to the nearby museums in search of dinosaur bones; they had only retrieved replicas, but would continue looking.

I got all three in trade for the one species from me, because as Leilani readily admitted, we could easily replicate their breeding efforts to produce similar animals ourselves. Horses, cats, and dogs were plentiful; triceratops weren't.

I left off that we'd found sod all use for the massive creatures beyond as a source of wonder, and simply smiled. A handover was agreed, and a crystal chip the agreed-upon exchange.

Basically, the dungeon, now that we'd reached Glass and had unlocked basic crystals, could be commanded to produce the data in a sharable format.

Leilani, as her dungeon had a genuine dungeon fairy as part of it, could have produced the same thing at Stone level.

That was annoying, but it was life.

We avoided discussions about how we'd leapfrogged our way to Glass first, beating all others, but we did admit that it was down to the fact we were constantly at war.

Apparently, the reason that Akuba and Kaatachi hadn't come—again, according to Leilani—was because they were currently involved in a war themselves. They'd spoken several days ago, when Kaatachi had purchased ammunition from Leilani, but contact had been cut off when the area around the nexus gate had fallen.

That left few others as viable trading partners, and the unconcerned way that Leilani spoke of the African pair's likely demise meant that I just didn't feel comfortable dealing with them for more than we'd already agreed.

The conversation changed to more mundane matters, and half an hour later, she was gone.

An hour after that, we were getting ready to pack up…when the sixth portal flared to life, and a new visitor arrived. One that I almost shot in the face and got us all ejected from the Nexus platform for attacking.

"Well, this *is* interesting." The lich smiled, staring down at me as Kelly grabbed my arm. "I had no idea that your kind were here as well."

"Our kind?" Ashley moved out from behind the table and strode forward.

"Please, my dear, my tastes are not to be trifled with, and your use of a glamor, while amusing, is not needed." The lich sighed, waving a hand negligently. "While I yet lived, you would not have been to my tastes, and now, with the pleasures of the flesh so far behind me, you have nothing to offer me."

"How did you get here?" Kelly asked him coldly.

"Through the nexus gate," he replied calmly. "The same as you have."

"You're a Dungeon Lord?" I asked incredulously, feeling the icy prickle of horror that the fucking undead would be using our one advantage against us.

"No, I am my lord's right hand. My lord is a summoner, and has no desire to expose himself to risks such as this," the lich explained. "I am Dorne, and yes, the dungeon I hail from is an undead aspected and focused dungeon, one that has been able to reach Steel only recently. We are, however, not aligned with the various pantheons."

"You're not with the Pantheon of Unlife?" I asked dumbly, and he sighed, the sound like crumpling chip packets.

"I see this is going to require more of an explanation. First, do you wish to do this, or shall I leave? I have no desire to waste my time further than is necessary."

"You don't want to be here," Ashley said softly.

"No, my dear, I do not," Dorne admitted. "My master ordered me to attend and see what was being offered for trade, then I shall return and continue my experiments."

"And what experiments are those?" I glared at him.

"None of your business," he replied coldly. "But I was an astrophysicist before my untimely death, so I assure you my experiments are unlikely to be whatever your puerile brain is imagining. Now, do you wish to discuss this in a civilized manner, or not?"

"We'll talk." Kelly squeezed my arm in warning, but it wasn't needed.

As much as I was instantly on alert, expecting that this Dorne was a plant and about to try to kill us or something, I also had to admit that we made constant use of the undead, and so if there was another dungeon out there that had figured out the possibilities we had, I could hardly blame them for doing the same.

"Perhaps a seat?" Dorne suggested, before smiling and nodding as a collection of seats rose from the floor on one side. "Ah, how convenient. Now, I have introduced myself…what should I call you?"

I forced down my annoyance and my instinctive desire to punch him in his stupid undead face, and started introductions.

Dorne was a tall man, or he had been in life, thin, and well dressed—possibly still in the suit he was buried in, judging from the formal style—and although he was clearly dead, he was also a lot less, well, less than the other undead I'd met.

For a start, he wasn't visibly rotting, and his eyes had a solid blue glow that came from within them. He moved more like a living man. When he sat, he undid his formal jacket and adjusted his trousers, making himself comfortable in a series of gestures that were clearly solidly embedded over a long life.

He raised one leg over the other and folded his hands atop that knee, waiting as we all sat, having murmured things like "Charmed" and "An honor" as each of the group were named.

He'd twitched as if about to offer his hand to shake as well, but had apparently thought better of that instinct.

Now, as we all sat, Kelly summoned drinks and offered one to him, only to get a polite and clearly amused smile.

"Alas, I think not. My *condition* means that such things disagree with me now."

"Of course," she agreed. "So, you wanted to talk?"

"As I said, I was sent here to make contact and to possibly purchase items, technology or weapons. What have you to offer?"

"Information, technology and weapons, food and more," Ashley said when Kelly looked at her in question. The experienced, if young diplomat smiled. "In your dungeon, you will have a clearly different focus from one that's peopled by the living. Perhaps you could tell us more so that we can offer more appropriate things?"

"An excellent segue into an interrogation." He smiled. "You…" he glanced at me, "…could learn much from this one."

I smiled and stayed silent as he glanced upward, clearly gathering his thoughts, then started to speak.

"I will share some details, then you will reciprocate. That way, we both get what we need, without either side feeling that we've been slighted. Is it agreed?"

We all agreed or nodded, and he smiled.

"Capital. Very well. My master's dungeon is in a neutral location—we will not be discussing exactly where, nor will I ask you for yours—but the area when the dungeon permitted entry had highly limited living options. My master was already a summoner, having only the dead to work with to protect himself.

"When the dungeon accepted him as a partner, he decided that the theme would continue, as the dead have far fewer needs than the living, including ongoing maintenance and rest requirements. Due to this, the dungeon has thrived. But it has meant that now that he has permitted living guests, he finds himself unable to offer much in the way of hospitality.

"Thus, the point of my visit: should a middle ground be established, then perhaps trade for certain basic foodstuffs and other staples for the living would be appropriate." He paused, then sat waiting as Ashley and the others glanced at me.

"I established our dungeon myself. Your master had a fairy allow him entry and work with him, is that right?"

"It is," Dorne admitted.

"Well, we didn't have that. It means that we had to learn a lot of things the hard way, and we've been essentially at war since the beginning. A lot of those fights have been against the undead, so if we seem a little prickly…"

"Understandable." He sighed. "There are many variations of my new kind, it seems. Although I'd never imagined that I could be satisfied with such a prosaic existence, in truth there was little change from my first life to my second. I lived for my research then, and now I find it much the same."

"Well. We set up the dungeon, and a nearby secondary area for refugees. We've been working to secure and expand it, all the while fighting for what feels like every inch of ground."

"But your dungeon is one based around the living?" he pressed, and I nodded.

"Excellent." He sighed. "Then not only do you have things to offer, but you are also, and let's be frank about this, not competing for resources."

"What resources?" I blinked.

"Why, isn't it obvious?" He frowned. "The dead."

Jez Cajiao

CHAPTER NINETEEN

"You can't be seriously considering this!" the priest asked me, aghast. I glared at him.

The silence went on until he remembered that he and his fellows were here on sufferance after he'd gotten them all kicked out last time.

"I think what my learned friend means to say, is that to offer up the bodies of the honored dead would be met with resistance," the imam said diplomatically.

"I don't like the idea," I admitted, settling back in my chair, and tapped one finger on the table as I sorted through my thoughts. "Seriously, I don't. *But*...the one point here is that the lich we met was...well, he was conscious."

"An abomination!" the priest snapped.

"Yeah, he was. I don't like the undead much, and the conscious undead I like even less," I said. "But we make use of them, like any resource, and the difference here is that they can apparently do so after death. They bring people back, their memories and mind intact, and then..."

"An abomination!" the priest snarled again, standing and shaking his head. "When we die, our souls travel to—"

"Thank you and goodnight," I snapped, flicking my hand in a dismissing gesture as I banned him from the council chamber. "To be very clear, people..." I waved a finger in the direction of the now suddenly empty seat as he vanished.

"*That* was one of the reasons some of you were invited to attend through the dungeon *sense* instead of physically. This way, I don't need to grab you by the scruff of the neck and drag you out. Now, is it wrong? I don't know. I feel that it is. I don't like it *at all*, but that's why you're here. You're advisors and my council, so fuckin' advise me. Don't just scream and froth. Or boom, you're out."

"I fear that I offer little to this discussion then." The imam sat firmly upright, his hands clasped on the table before him. "For I too agree that the bodies of the fallen are not a resource to be traded and exploited."

"And I agree on that." I nodded. "I don't like it. I don't want to do the trade. But to be clear, wherever they are, they're searching for graveyards. They're far off the beaten track. I'm guessing they're a long ass way from the nearest settlement, and Dorne admitted he was where he was until his death, because it was to ensure there was no light pollution to ruin his observations when he still lived.

"That being said, they're going to reach civilization eventually. If we leave them to it, we delay them access to the undead here—literally, we prevent them from touching these corpses for now. Beyond that? There's nothing much we can say. Unless we go out and start clearing and stripping the cemeteries, absorbing the dead into the dungeon and destroying their remains, there's nothing that I can see will prevent them from eventually being resurrected by these guys."

"We would be less than sanguine about the cemeteries being despoiled by yourself as well," the imam admitted. "But if it was done in a respectful manner, and with the intention that the dead are being protected, then it would be preferred to the current…request."

"Dorne said they're looking for those who had been preserved, that if they've rotted away then there's nothing they can do. In his case, he was preserved by ice…wouldn't that mean that most of the cemeteries are safe?" Chris asked.

"I think so, and that he was preserved in ice means that they're somewhere that's either really cold or high up," I agreed. "If it was a cryo facility in some city, then the bodies would be toast by now, I think. Which, when you come to think about it, is annoying because one of those mad-ass cryo facilities would actually be full of people who would probably desperately want to be brought back as an undead." I shrugged, before glancing to the side as Kelly sat forward.

"Well, if there's anything we know, it's that as they level and explore their abilities, they're likely to be able to do more and more with less. So, anything that they get now, even if they're skeletons, are likely to be more useful to *them* than they are to us," she said.

She went on. "Look, I'll be honest—I'm against it. If our people fall in battle, they get burned to make sure they don't come back as undead and attack us. I don't see this as any different. And knowing that one of the cemeteries that'd be open for consideration—the one next to the park—holds our mum? I'm against it even more."

"Shit, yes," Mike muttered, before raising a hand in apology. "Sorry for the language." He directed his comment over at Clarissa and the imam. "I'm on Kelly's side there. The thought of our mum being raised as an undead and then put to work doing…*whatever* for some loony isn't one I'm willing to consider."

"Anyone in favor of it?" I asked, cutting to the heart of the matter. "I'm not either. But it could mean a powerful ally, and they're going to get bodies somehow anyway. We need to accept that either that's going to happen, or we need to go to war with them as well."

"I don't want to start another war," Kelly said, and I nodded.

"Me neither, but do you see another way to stop them? I think for now we say no, and offer other trade goods. Otherwise, we smile and nod and keep the fuckers away from us."

"One point in favor of the deal," Markus said suddenly, raising one hand. "I don't like it, to be fair…but should the recently dead, one of our people, for example, have volunteered before death, then they would be given a chance at a second life. Is it up to us to refuse them that? Can we do this ethically?"

"We have to," I said after a few seconds scratching my chin in thought. "I don't like it, but we have to assume that anyone who is raised by them is going to have a degree of loyalty to their dungeon, right? What if it's a magical thing? Or not. Hell, there's enough who have joined us because it's their best option for now, nothing more. What if they then spill everything they know to their new master?"

"And there we have it," Griffiths said. "It's both an operational and physical security risk. Anyone you hand over to them, if they retain any memories at all, is going to tell them enough that they could probably find us and any weaknesses. Best to say a firm no."

"Works for me," I agreed when nobody else spoke up. "Okay, so they also want to purchase grains, foodstuffs and similar, but not things like living quarters. The food—well, once we've handed it over, they'll not be buying any more, so we have a limited opportunity to buy tech with this. They offered four different techs to choose from, so tell me what you think."

The table in the middle of the room lit suddenly and four different screens appeared, floating there equally spaced out. The left of the screen showed an image, and the right showed the text and breakdown.

The first was a box within the box—quite literally—and was marked as "Minion Material Transportation."

It was something that had been made out of what I was guessing was a horse— probably several, in fact—and a cart.

It was basic as all hell, as it was a cart and that was it, something like an ore cart from an old mine—though clearly built to handle a much lower weight limit—and it had six legs.

There was no front or back, and it apparently simply stomped along and did as it was told. It could be used to carry small to medium loads over uneven ground, but was both slow and probably dumb as shit.

Think "donkey" without the lovable repartee and the need for breaks. I could see the uses, but also that we could probably make something very similar—hell, we could make something *better* in about an hour.

The second technology was a marked improvement on how basic the first was.

The "Necrotic Regeneration Chamber" was an enclosed pod filled with what looked to be a glowing green gloop. Reading the attached details, I found that it was a specialized "necromantic energy field." Designed for repairing and rejuvenating undead minions, it could also accelerate natural healing in living creatures.

However, the additional text gave some concerns: "Prolonged or frequent use by the living may have unforeseen side effects." I could see dozens of uses for the technology for both undead and living-focused dungeons. But would I trust it? Fuck no. If it was obvious enough that you felt you had to give the warning on a sales pitch, then there were a *lot* of side effects and you damn well knew it. Hard pass.

Next came the "Ectoplasmic Communication Network."

It was a system of spectral "nodes" created to transmit messages and images across long distances within a dungeon. It apparently used bound spirits to carry information, allowing for "instant communication between different dungeon levels or even to surface outposts." The last line made it a bit more interesting, and yet still freaky: "Although primarily designed for undead use, living beings can interact with the network through specially crafted focus crystals."

We had the crystals being researched in several areas already, so I didn't see the expense being a big thing here, though I also saw ways that we could simply recreate the same thing using the crystal pads or whatever, like tablet computers to make calls before the fall.

Lastly, came the "Osseous Fortification Ritual." It was a magical ritual designed to reinforce existing structures or create new barriers using bones. The ritual enhanced the strength and durability of bone-based constructions, making them "rival steel in terms of defensive capabilities. Although thematically tied to undead dungeons, this technology could be adapted by living dungeons to create strong, lightweight fortifications using animal bones or other organic materials."

It was cool and all, but again, I had so many questions that I wasn't sure where to begin.

Did we need bones from some other fucker? Did they have to be once-living ones, or were dungeon-summoned bones viable?

Was this something that we needed to bother with at all, considering the cost difference from say, titanium to bone wasn't that huge? And frankly, when I had the option to build a wall out of spooky bones and shit, or titanium, I knew which I'd prefer.

I was all set to refuse them all, when Kelly pointed out that we had the food to spare; if we just refused outright, it was likely to mean that the people who were being "protected" by the dungeon—we still didn't know whether they were prisoners or slaves or genuine refugees as they claimed—well, those people would be left to starve or eat only the same old shit every day.

If we looked at it as more of a charity thing, that we were supplying food and anything else we got was a bonus? Well then, it changed the situation a lot.

As did Mike's comment.

"If we look at the last option as the best, then we can take a load of bones with us, random ones that are prepped by the dungeon, and look at them as a repair tool. Think of it like one of the boxers gets hit by an RPG at just the worst spot or whatever—we chuck the bones on and reinforce that area, rather than having to return or waste a load of time working to repair it.

"I know you're talking about taking a seed with us, but it saves us having to set up somewhere else and waste it," he pointed out, before rolling back to the other three. "The others…they've all got a load of issues. I mean, the dungeon communications network. That'd be awesome, we *need* one, but are all communications being intercepted by the undead then? We only have a lich's word that they're not aligned with the Unlife Pantheon. And let's face it...it's not like when he's there on his own, he was going to risk it all and attack you, as well as admit that he's actually the high priest of muckety-muck or whatever."

"Yeah." I sighed. "I agree with the comm network. We need it, we want it—but we can't let a potential enemy have a backdoor into our system. That also means that we can't trust the others. The first option, that walking box? Weirdly, that's probably the most useful, and hardest for them to turn against us. The communication one? I totally agree. Can't trust it—screw it.

"The necrotic regeneration chamber? Tempting, as we could repair our damaged units instead of scrapping them, because honestly, with the undead, that's the only realistic option. But no. For all we know, they'll also let the other side take control of the undead we put in.

"Lastly, the ossification... If all we need are some bones, then it's not a massive ask, *BUT*..." I paused, looking around. "Did anyone else pick up on the phrasing?"

"It's a ritual." Dante, predictably, had spotted it.

"Exactly. It's not a spell, it's not a tech that we just use—it's a ritual. This could open the door to ritual magic, and the only spell I have that's even close to that is the Summon Demon one, and that's incredibly powerful."

I leaned forward, resting my chin on one hand and stared from one of the details to the next, my mind working over the options steadily.

"I think, realistically, that's the best option. What do you all think?" I asked, before blinking at the look I was getting from at least half of them. "What?" I asked, confused.

"You have a *demon* summoning spell?" the imam asked me carefully.

"Crap." I groaned. "Yeah, it's something that came as a reward for a quest. Believe me, it's not something that is all religious-based. It opens a portal to somewhere else and forces a demon to obey a simple command. In my case, I used it to fight a bunch of assholes while Chris, Patrick, and I ran like our arses were on fire."

"I remember that." Chris shook his head, glancing at Patrick. "Do you?"

"Oh no, not really," Patrick deadpanned, rolling his eyes. "I mean, it was such a minor thing, and so small. I mean, it wasn't like something that I'd been told my *entire fucking life was going to punish me for my sexual choices just appeared*!"

"Really?" Kelly asked.

"Really did the demon appear or was I threatened with hell because I'm gay?" Patrick quirked an eyebrow.

"Both," Kelly said.

"Definitely both," he replied sagely, nodding. "Believe me, the damn thing was terrifying. It was huge, and I was in no way prepared to see that."

"That's what..." Chris started to say it before I could, and received a clip across the back of the head from Becky.

"Thank you," Clarissa murmured to Becky, before turning back to me. "Matt, on behalf of those who are generally the most likely to be put in the ground soonest—beyond those who risk their lives to protect us all, of course—I'd like to be firm in refusing this," she said, having glanced over and inclined her head to Griffiths as she accepted the risk that the soldiers faced every day.

"Refusing any deal with them, or selling them bodies?" I asked.

She hesitated, then sighed. "I don't like it, but the bodies only," she admitted. "I know you said that you agreed, and we wouldn't be selling them corpses, but I wanted to be clear, and I'm going to start this as a separate discussion, one that I think the entire dungeon needs to get in on. I believe we should start destroying the bodies of those we lose as a matter of course.

"I know we do—as you say—burn the bodies after a fight or whatever, but I think we should address that formally, and begin to destroy the graveyards around us as we move on. This seems like a minor issue right now. But the living have never outnumbered the dead, and the one massive advantage the undead have over us is time. If it takes them ten years to convert a country, the next, due to the size of them at that stage, will take a quarter of that. Once the undead have taken all of Europe, the world will have no chance. They have no need of ships, when they're in no rush and can simply decide to walk across the bottom of the ocean to America.

"I accept that until now we've had a great many more pressing concerns, but I don't believe we can allow this Patheon of Unlife to continue. Should their leader be anything like a true Napoleon or Hitler, then we would have no chance. And worse yet, should they be able to resurrect the greatest military minds of history, what do you think would happen?

"For that matter, what happens when they reach the beaches at Normandy or any of the great battlefields?" She paused, seemingly overcome for long seconds with horror. "Matt, you said once you could sense them, the leaders of your enemies in the pantheon?"

"Yeah..." I paused, thinking and reaching out to see what I could sense.

The map that showed up in my mind was centered over me and the dungeon. But the farther out I drew, I could sense a much greater distance, and more accurately. The limit was still the horizon, though.

I could sense that—as before—there were several of them—three, in fact—and that two of them were to the southeast, roughly. The sense I got from them was that they were still a good distance away. I didn't know exactly how far, but "that way" and "a good distance" was about as much as I could tell.

"They're..." I paused, then brought up a map of the country, grinning as I realized I could do it. The damn thing wasn't a real-time display, like the local area was, but I'd finally remembered that part of what we'd done when we were expanding into the area was to take over the nearby library and strip out everything we could get.

All that information was made available to the dungeon, but it wasn't magic.

What I meant was that if I scanned and absorbed a book of explosives, the dungeon didn't magically have access to everything; it just had access to the book, and then that book could be reproduced and read at leisure.

The maps, though? They were easier to find and mentally open, then integrate into the dungeon.

The result was an "Ordnance Survey map of Great Britain" that could be zoomed in and out, and showed all the way up to the nautical border eight miles offshore.

That wasn't hugely beneficial, as I really needed to be able to see the world beyond as well. But in this case, it was enough so that I could say they were definitely not on the island, as near as I could tell.

Scouring across it to the edge, I could still sense them "that way." Although the feeling wasn't exact, I felt confident in passing that on.

"Okay, and the other one is in America somewhere?" Clarissa asked, and I nodded again.

"Any idea how many there are or what they're doing?" Mike asked me, and I stared at him.

"They're hairy, not crystal," I said flatly.

"They're...?" He frowned, then snorted out a laugh. "Your balls...sorry."

"Yup." I sighed, before wincing at what I'd just said in a formal council meeting. "Okay, people, so moving on, we've also got this..." I tapped the map and a point flared, starting to pulse slowly and steadily with a red light.

"What's that?" Dante leaned forward eagerly.

"That's the only dungeon in the UK that I know of," I admitted grimly. "There might be five more or a hundred, no clue, but there probably aren't many. The reason I know about this fucker? They declared for the undead."

"It's the undead dungeon?" Clarissa asked, and I shook my head.

"No, no clue where they are, but if there's bodies preserved in ice and it's in the UK, there are very few places that could be. No, this is the dungeon that's—" I broke off to double-check the prompt, only to have two new quests pop up in my vision. "Crap." I groaned, before reading them out.

Congratulations! You have discovered a new Quest!

Quest: *Mechanist Menace*

Simon, Lord of the Mechanists, has allied his dungeon with the Lord of Unlife, threatening to give our enemies an insurmountable advantage. His dungeon, now identified in the city of Oxford, UK, must be neutralized before it becomes a foothold for the forces of Unlife.

Jez Cajiao

Infiltrate the Mechanist Dungeon, defeat Simon, and either claim or destroy his dungeon core to complete this quest and receive the following bonuses:

- **+5 to top three Attributes**
- **+2 Class Skill Points to allocate**
- **Access to Mechanist technology and blueprints**
- **50,000 XP**
- **Increased influence over UK territory**

Warning! Failure to complete this quest within 96 hours will result in severe consequences for your dungeon and the UK.

Congratulations! You have discovered a new Quest!

Class Quest!

As an Arcane Dungeon Lord, you have the unique ability to absorb and adapt enemy technologies. Successfully claiming the Mechanist Dungeon's core will unlock new research paths and evolution options for your own dungeon.

Complete this quest to receive a boost to your Artificer and Magical Researcher skills, as well as unlock the "Techno-Arcane Fusion" creature summon path.

- **Infiltrate Mechanist Dungeon: 0/1**
- **Defeat Simon, Lord of the Mechanists: 0/1**
- **Claim or destroy dungeon core: 0/1**

Remember, First Lord of the Storm, only you can prevent the spread of Unlife in the UK. The clock is ticking…

"What's the problem?" Chris asked after a few seconds. "We needed to do this anyway, and it gives good loot."

"Chris, it's a good thing you're handsome." Becky groaned, putting her head in her hands, as Aly started to speak.

"For anyone else who's wondering as well, the issue I see is that this quest gives us four days. That's it. If we were to set off right now, and we started running with as many of our creatures as we could muster, we'd be very lucky to make it there in that time. Not to mention that Oxford is in the south, sure, but if we were heading to the south coast to set up to try to defeat the incoming army, then we really needed to be heading to the southeast coast. Oxford is around the middle, possibly even off to the west. Hell, draw a direct line here…"

She did just that; a direct line from where we were in the northeast all the way down to the southeastern coast suddenly appeared, and I let out a low whistle.

That meant that even if we followed the best and widest of the roads, we'd still be heading around a hundred miles out of our way to go to Oxford. If we didn't? We'd be letting an unknown dungeon that was publicly against us and had declared war, sit there at our back.

That wasn't going to end well for anyone.

"And just to make it worse, every hour we spend fighting or even travelling to the dungeon here, is an hour we're not spending travelling, setting up, nor getting the battleground ready for the fight with the undead." I groaned. "And four days?" I checked the clock and found it was actively counting down. "What the hell is that counting down to?"

"To the enemy landing at Dover?" Kelly suggested, and I shook my head.

"Who knows. I doubt they were waiting and decided to set off at exactly the time that we were talking about it, but fuck's sake!" I snarled.

"Well, regardless of why the timer is the way it is, you need to look at the details," Griffiths said. "The Glass core is active now, right?"

"It is," I agreed glumly, still staring at the map before me.

"So, we have access to better tech. What do we need to get the planned vehicles up and running?" he shot at Aly.

She opened her mouth to respond, then paused and sat back, a thoughtful look on her face as she clearly checked the details.

"What do you need?" she asked after a few minutes. "To run the vehicles, I mean?"

"The engines would be a good start." Mike smiled at his wife.

"No, I mean seriously." She smiled back at him. "Is it just the engines? What else?"

"What are you thinking?" I asked her.

"Mana crystals." She shrugged. "We've got access to them, and it might be better to think of the vehicles as electric now, rather than fuel-based."

"Why?" I frowned, stifling my immediate "there's no electricity" response.

"Well, the main expense in the electric vehicles was the battery, right?" Her eyes appeared unfocused as she clearly looked at something nobody else could see. "What if…" She paused, checking something, and then nodded and blinked, seeming to come back to the room mentally. "What if we replaced the engines with a crystal and a mana converter?"

"Go on," I said.

"What I'm thinking is we scrap the entire engine. I mean, it's there to convert the pumping fuel and the burning part, so we just take all of that out, and then we build in a new transmission, one that has only three settings: off, forward, and backward. That means that the crystal is there all the time, ready to go. Maybe make two, so that one can be a battery for the other, and the converter is plugged into one. With that charging from the converter, and then charging the driving battery in turn..." She was speaking quickly now, obviously excited as her vision ran away with her, until Mike reached out and took her hands in his.

"Aly..." he said slowly. "We've got four days, three, at most if it's going to take, say, a day to do whatever you're thinking, to take on an enemy dungeon and then travel across the country to fight the enemy. Stop and think. Can you build this in a day?"

"I..." She hesitated. "I need to speak to the engineer, and the mechanics!"

"Go," I said. "Go, and if you can, then that's how long you've got—a single day. Then we're leaving."

Aly settled back, closing her eyes. She was physically in the command room, but she clearly went elsewhere mentally.

I turned back to the rest of the room.

"Okay, people, what I'd expected would be a planning and trade meeting just became a war council. Those who shouldn't be here for this, you can leave. But before you do: first, we're agreed that we won't be giving up the dead. You can spread that around. Clarissa's point has merit as well. Spread the word that she'll be having a general meeting in the coming days, once she's talked it out and gotten the community leaders' agreement. The bodies of our dead and *all* those we can reach are to be absorbed into the dungeon. That's not to use them for mana— that's to prevent the enemy from raising them and attacking us with our own loved one's remains.

"Clarissa will come up with a plan for doing it, and hold a town hall-style meeting to discuss, take any advice on doing it respectfully and when we're to begin. But it *will* be happening." I paused, then went on.

"Secondly, we'll be taking a regular position on the Nexus platform selling technology, and we'll be looking for allies. As such, we're going to need brave souls who are willing to join Ashley, to serve and learn under her..." I paused and pointed a finger at Chris. "*Not one fucking word,*" I warned him before going on. "Ashley will be setting up outreach plans and will be travelling to the other neutral dungeons to see what they need, what we can trade, and then how we can best work out the middle ground."

She nodded and made notes. "I'll be asking for volunteers, and I'll need trainee courtesans, diplomats, and bodyguards, as well as merchants."

"That's fine, that's your side of things," I agreed. "Kelly will be introduced to the other Dungeon Lord and Ladies by me when I'm available and they are, or will be reaching out on her own. Yes, I know that it'd be more effective if I was there for these meetings, and it'd carry more weight—sorry, my love—but frankly, if we're leaving tomorrow? I need to focus entirely on my spells and personal development."

More and more people were nodding and making notes now.

"Griffiths, we're going to be hitting this dungeon, clearing the fucker out and taking it either as our own, or destroying it and taking the core as a prize. Then we'll be heading to London—passing through, not staying." I held my hand up and looked around as a few mouths opened to speak. "I know we have a lot of people with family to the south. We *will* try to reach them all, one way or another, but this is going to be a hard, fast hit. It could take a much longer time than we can spare to take the dungeon, and we need to be on the southeast coast, ready to take out the enemy…"

Griffiths raised a hand and I glared, before waving generally around.

"If you're not needed here for the war side, you can go now. Dante, Ashley, Clarissa, Kelly, Finn, and Patrick, you all stay, as well as the military people. Everyone else, go get busy please."

Most of the room vanished, with Barry quirking an eyebrow at me in question, and I waved at him and smiled.

"Dude, you don't need an invite," I said quickly. "I think of you as both the leader of the park and military, so you've got two seats here."

"Thanks." He smiled.

"On that note, I should have invited Arend-Jan." Griffiths groaned. "He's out in the fields and it didn't occur to me. I'll apologize to him for that later."

"Fair enough," I agreed. "Though I should have asked where he was as well." I summoned a drink—a can of energy drink—and then settled back. "What's up, Griffiths?"

"The plan for the south," he said. "I think we need to split up, and possibly into three."

"Three?" I blinked, surprised. "I could see two, though I don't like it. What's the third?"

"The best place to fight the enemy is where they least expect you, and are naturally constrained." He slipped into lecture mode as he gestured to the map and started to twist and shift it. "Here…" He spun it around and slid the map all the way to the southeast coast. "Is Dover. This is what's always been accepted as the closest point between the two land masses."

"Right." I nodded.

"Well, they *could* march across the bottom of the sea," he said, but the look on his face said it was unlikely. "The issues are strong tides, the depth of the water, and the actual topography. I've got no clue what it's like under there, but I'm betting it's not just flat and smooth. And there's going to be sea creatures. Yeah, they can probably kill anything, like a giant shark or whatever, and resurrect it, but the shark is going to be fuck all use once they get out of the water, so any losses they suffer will be hard ones.

"The tides are going to seriously fuck up the weaker undead, and the depth will do a number on them as well. They could walk across the bottom of the ocean or the sea, but I don't see them doing it once they have a good think about it as I really consider the implications. It's just impractical."

"Makes sense, I guess," I agreed. "Good news there at least. So where will they land?"

"My guess is here." He tapped a town called Folkestone on the map. "It's the exit for the Channel Tunnel, and that's both the fastest and easiest access to us."

"Why not ships?" Dante asked, before facepalming as he answered his own question. "Because they'd need thousands of small ones to move an army, and without electricity, they'd need it to be sailboats, which would need experienced sailors. Damn, of course, sorry."

"And the big ones won't work without electricity." Griffiths nodded. "So, it has to be the Channel Tunnel. *But...*" He looked around to make sure we were paying attention. "If it was me, I'd send a smaller but strong force across the seabed, as you suggested, or aboard a handful of larger sailboats. Maybe summon some giant tuna or something and have it drag them across the sea. Then I'd have them make landfall somewhere out of sight. While we're all fighting the main army, all the individual and weak but numerous undead, the real elites are moving around us, collecting up all the dead in the mass graves down there. Then they hit us from behind."

"So we think we're fighting the main army, and we're nowhere near." I nodded. "Makes sense. What about these mass graves? I didn't know we had any."

"There's a lot," Kelly said quietly, clearly working her way through the plan. "Think of any of the older historical events—the Black Death, various other plagues, the Battle of Hastings. Hundreds of years—no, *thousands* of years of conquest and back and forth raids and wars with Europe. Then there's the Roman legions, the Roman invasion, the..." She shook her head and sighed. "A lot of the old battlegrounds will be buried under cities now. A lot of the places, like the plague pits, were deliberately concreted over, but if the leader of them is powerful enough, he's going to be able to sense them, I bet."

"Okay, so I get why you want to split our forces—one to the dungeon, one to set up at the Channel Tunnel area. That gives us as long as possible to set up there while the other group fights and hopefully takes out the mechanist dungeon. That's two places, though, and the third? I mean, what? You want to take the entire south coast just in case they decide to land somewhere?" I asked skeptically.

"No, I'm thinking we set up another dungeon, and this one is in the center of London." Griffiths grinned evilly.

CHAPTER TWENTY

In the end, the meeting broke up quite quickly after that. People were being sent off in all directions as each job was finalized, and I felt almost ridiculous in that I was going off to navel-gaze and consider the deeper aspects of magic, while the others were all going to be running around like headless chickens.

Aly had come back briefly to report that there was a way to sort the vehicles with the mana crystals. It would be expensive and take the majority of the mana we had, and all the rest of the mana we'd have coming in tomorrow until we left to accomplish it, but that it fortunately included the basic cost of building and updating the vehicles as well.

I wasn't going to be getting anywhere near the dedicated massive rig that I'd wanted for the mobile dungeon, but I would be getting a seed *and* the mobile dungeon, as well as a few minor bonuses. So I could either be huffed or chuffed, because that was the best I was going to get either way.

Otherwise, we'd need to build the vehicles in a very different way, because there was no way that what we currently had, supplemented by a transport or two, was going to cut it.

We expected a lot of impassable points on the roads between here and there, not to mention the need to fill up the tank and hopefully carry people and gear.

That meant we needed some vehicles that could bully their way through multiple cars. When the shit hit the fan, we could hopefully move the mobile dungeon up and absorb whatever was causing the blockage, without risking losing it or us, but there were going to be situations where that wasn't possible.

We were taking forty human soldiers, and another forty dungeon-born that were going to be split between twenty kobolds, ten goblins, and ten Scepiniir. They'd all be provided with mounts, eventually, if all went to plan. We'd hopefully be starting with ten of the dogs…sorry, houndborn. They'd be the fast-moving and more vicious of the cavalry, with ten of the magewhiskers as farther-ranging scouts, and twenty of the phantomsteeds as general mounts.

The animals were going to be summoned as we went, with more mana coming in all the time, hopefully. But until then, the vehicles were going to be loaded up to a ridiculous degree.

Jez Cajiao

The kobolds were happy with the ten dogs and ten of the horses. The Scepiniir wanted the cats. And the goblins…well, we hadn't summoned them yet, but they'd be getting what they were given, which was the other ten horses.

Finn was focusing on the armor and armaments, including a new suit of armor for me, as I'd accidentally totaled my newest upgraded suit in my last breakthrough.

Then there was the last party to arrange. That was another group of ten, but we—as that was my party—were going to have a boxer vehicle to ourselves, thank you very much.

I'd looked at the designs for the horses, cats, and the dogs and I'd just said "fuck no." I didn't need my balls smashing up around my ears while I rode that spine. The only spine I wanted pressed against my nether regions was Kelly's, and even then, I could think of much better things I did want there.

Also, after a single disastrous horse-riding experience with an ex in Egypt, I had no intention of ever doing that again.

Dante and his people were getting everyone ready; he'd been given lists of equipment and had Ashley watching over him. I'd agreed to let Mike run lead on putting together our party, knowing that he'd arrange the best we could have for what was to come.

Also, hopefully, this was all we'd need for the trip, given that we'd be building another nexus gate as soon as we could afford it, and then reinforcements could come pouring through that.

Instead, as everyone else ran around like lunatics, I went to the mage's tower—*fuck it, it was my tower and I'd call it whatever I wanted to*—and wound my way through the random people standing around talking shit instead of studying.

This was the best place for me to work on a single quest that I had a highly limited time to cover. I quickly read it over again, getting it all sorted and ready in my mind.

Crafting the signature spells of the Apprentice [Arcanist] is a hurdle that many sapiens fail to clear, as each spell completed not only limits the paths available to the mage for their future growth, but is also correspondingly more difficult.

Choose to create three separate spells of any two of the following categories to reach Apprentice Rank as an [Arcanist]. Alternatively, create a single spell in each category to receive an increased boost to your selected affinities and a bonus magical item:

- **Animation: 0/1**
- **Blood: 0/1**
- **Divination: 0/1**
- **Elemental: 0/1**
- **Enchantment: 0/1**

- **Mental: 0/1**
- **Rune: 0/1**
- **Temporal: 0/1**
- **Spatial: 0/1**
- **Summoning: 0/1**

I needed to work on the spells that I used regularly, sure, but I also desperately needed to learn some new ones, and get my affinities boosted up as far as I could manage.

So, given the relatively little amount of time I had, I'd also pulled privilege and I'd spent the fifty thousand mana I needed to, to summon the "basic" knowledge on the magic of Light.

I wanted the others, *desperately*, but I needed to know whether it was worth spending the mana first, considering the literal six hundred thousand plus mana cost to get the damn thing to the point that we needed to be able to produce the damn things.

If I went all out and started producing, say, a lightning tome so that I could learn more and others could study it as well, and then we found out that it was just some general advice and no actual use? Yeah, that was going to go down like a lead balloon.

So, as we'd needed to unlock a load of the Light research first anyway, it just made sense to go the extra fifty thousand down the road to summon that information.

When I did, though?

It was both incredible and utterly, completely shite at once.

Opening the book—which was marked as a magical tome—offered me a single simple option.

Congratulations! You have discovered [Tome of Light]. Do you wish to access this tome?

I was about to press it, when I realized what it meant and groaned. The damn thing was like a *spellbook*. That was cool, in that hey, using it meant you got all the information magically downloaded to your brain in one fast hit, or so I thought. But the downside?

It was fifty thousand for the most basic information. Information which might or might not come with a spell, or might just be general "look around, if you can see, that's light" shitty levels of information.

Moreover, it was almost certainly single-bloody-use! I stifled my cursing and turned, glancing over the people all around me. Nope, nope, nope… I didn't want

213

to give this to a human; there might be side effects, and we already... I finally spotted Dante as he entered with the small group of goblins, apparently intent on summoning them one at a time, and waved him over.

I wanted to learn it, I really did, but I already had a Lighting focus , and my fucking Light affinity was shit. I wasn't sure what was going on here, but I had a pretty good idea. "Dante!" I called as he approached. "Have any of the goblins got much of a Light affinity?"

As I asked him, I hefted the tome in my hands, and his eyes locked on it like a laser range finder.

"I have a..." he started, licking his lips nervously.

"Not gonna happen," I said firmly. "I want a dungeon-born, just in case."

"But..." he whined.

"It might erase your current class, so you'd lose access to Fire," I said warningly, completely lying through my teeth. I had no clue, really.

He gasped, moving back and putting his hands behind his back like a naughty child at that thought.

"Yeah, I thought that might be the case," I noted dryly. "So, the goblins?"

There did turn out to be one with a slightly higher Light level. It was forty-seven, and although that was fairly crap, all things considered, we didn't have the luxury of summoning a hundred until we found one with better stats.

The goblin—well, all the four summoned so far, in fact—were advanced goblins. They weren't the standard issue, lobotomized at birth and then beaten around the face and body for sixteen hours a day version.

All the goblins were apparently planned to be summoned here, by Dante, so that he could examine them with the intention of picking out any that were naturally gifted to become mages, while the rest would be guided to fighters and more.

Unlike with the lower levels of evolutions, I'd basically sworn off on evolutionary meddling with the higher and self-aware versions, mainly because...because...

"Fuck!" I swore, eyes widening as I remembered something. "STOP!" I ordered, shouting it at the goblin that was just about to read the book I'd handed over.

It, or more accurately, *she*, flinched and dropped the tome with a clatter, staring at me wide-eyed.

I grinned, my evil mind working at a blur as I spoke up. "It's okay. I just realized something," I assured her. "Okay, do you *want* to be a mage?"

Silence as they stared at one another, then back at me, then one another. "Do you have a name?" I asked, and she shook her head, making me blow out a long breath and think. "Okay, Dante, which of the goblins has the very best affinities for magic—all of them, I mean?"

"The most natural mage?" he asked, and I nodded impatiently. "Probably her," he admitted, gesturing to the female that stood before me.

"Okay, well, this is either going to be messy as all hell and traumatizing for everyone involved, or...well, let's not dwell on the 'or,' shall we?" I grinned, settling back down, and stared into her eyes. "No need to waste time on a name yet either, I guess... Uh, Dante?" I said absently. "If the others have no chance as mages, then you can take them to the kobolds and Finn; get five of them outfitted as warriors, then leave it at that and come back here."

"You want me to keep summoning them?" he asked, clearly enjoying that he'd been granted the ability for this, and his face fell when I shook my head.

"No, I'm going to see what the new ability to guide an evolution actually does here," I said distractedly, pulling up the text and reading through it as I had done so many times before.

Imbue: You may choose to give freely of your own manapool to imbue an item or creature of the Dungeon with magic. This ability can fail, and spectacularly so; however, creations of wondrous might can also be brought into being. Be wary. (Selected)

Evolution: Foresight: No longer are your creations the chance things they were...now see the true potential of a creature! (Selected)

Basically, it was almost a cheat code...if it worked. I'd been so busy so many times that when I'd tried to do this most recently with the kobolds, it'd been a hit-and-miss effect, though, and I'd basically sworn off it. I'd also sworn off it for another reason besides exploding and screaming kobolds, and that was the bone golem.

I'd created that when I'd been trying to make a stronger warrior variant for the dungeon, and I'd almost killed myself fucking around. But I had to be fair to the system: the golem *had* been impressive. Right up until I'd had to destroy it to prevent it draining me dry and killing me to keep itself powered.

Now, though, I was doing it with a lot more experience with the dungeon, with a shitload more mana, and with, yeah, a lot riding on it, but more understanding at my base.

When I'd created different versions of the goblins before, I'd had massively varying degrees of success, and I thought I knew why as well, now that I'd had a little time to think.

It'd not come in a particular flash of inspiration as it did in the movies; it was more of a collection of little things...hints, tips, and details that when you looked at them all at once, just gave me a solid suspicion.

The most success I'd had with the goblins—and the other creatures, to be fair—wasn't when I'd been playing with the various elemental forms.

Some of them had grown massive. They'd been turned into things like the smasher, a seriously overpowered, but dumb as a rock version of the standard-issue gobbo.

That'd come from infusing loads of Earth mana into it. Although I could in theory infuse them with pretty much any mana I wanted, I guessed the detail I'd been missing until now was the affinity one.

Some of them had basically exploded, melted, or died in screaming agony, while another would survive, or evolve even. It'd felt like I was doing what I was supposed to do, but the last bit for me had slid into place when I'd been thinking earlier that I needed to resummon my weapons and that as part of that, I was going to be experimenting with infusing my mana into them again.

The issue with blindly infusing something, as I had done with the longsword that then became the basis for all our magic swords, was that you ended up with a weapon that was partly "you" and partly down to the item itself.

If you awakened it with blood and mana that were basically Lightning infused, like my own, you could grant it Lightning powers.

The void blade had been awakened by someone else, and I'd damn well loved that thing. I'd have had him awaken another for me if I could, but he'd died.

So, if the skill I was using was the same for imbuing the weapons and creations of the dungeon, and the ability of Foresight that should have been letting me see what the creature could become had been failing, maybe the issue was that I'd not been considering the subject matter.

I was Lightning-aspected. I bet that if I poured Lightning mana into a goblin that had a very low Lightning affinity, what I'd get was a cooked goblin. If, however, I poured in *pure* mana, that'd make all the difference.

Looking at it, I couldn't help but grin.

Inside myself, I had generally unaspected mana—not Lightning, not Fire, not…whatever. It was all the broken-up bits that weren't entirely pure, but that weren't all the way into anything either.

It was converted into the various forms as I tried to use it, and as I personally was Lightning-aspected, I could flood my body with that mana easiest of all, sure.

It started as general mana and could be changed, though. It was all a little complicated, but that was life in the fucking apocalypse, after all.

Looking at the goblin before me, I suspected that if I tried to give her the wrong type of mana, but in the combinations that had worked before, I'd kill her, and that was where I'd been going wrong.

To put it another way, I'd been picking things and deciding that this was what I wanted. Say, more Fire mana, or more Earth to build bigger muscles, etc.

That worked in theory, but where it failed was that it might work today, if the goblin I tried it on was gifted with a high Fire and Earth affinity…or at least not a shit one.

If I did the exact same thing on the next goblin that I summoned, though, they might explode.

My affinities were so high for Storm and Lightning mana now that when I was attacked with them, it actively healed me. Water, though? Not so long ago, that'd have fucked me right up.

Now, as I directed the goblin before me to share her affinities, I searched quickly.

Most of them were crap. Literally, she was gifted in certain areas, but nothing I could see being of any use. I mean, Korean cooking? Kelly had the same, and yeah, I was always up for trying that, but I didn't see anything with a high enough level to be an advantage.

I didn't, that was, until I came back to Light.

I decided to try imbuing her with a fifty-fifty mixture of general and Light mana, mainly because I'd be able to start with more or less pure and see what happened, and then hopefully dial it back if I made a fuck-up.

As near as I could tell, pure mana poured into something through this ability made it more…well, it made it *more*.

More *real*, more generally like it already was. If it was predisposed to be a mage? That'd hopefully activate whatever was missing and give it a boost.

For this goblin, as I poured the first five hundred mana in, I expected to hit a limit, one that her body refused to go past. When that didn't happen, and I felt nothing like the "filling" sensation I remembered from before, I knew I'd found the edges of a truth.

At five hundred, I could sense changes on the very edge of being…so close and yet not quite there.

That was when I switched to Light, and damn, did that make a difference.

For a start, she hissed, clearly discomforted, and I slowed the input, dialing it back to half the speed of the pure, but still going. She settled back, yet looked…different as I continued.

I didn't know how else to put it, but she and her companions—who'd now left with Dante—were a very different breed from the earlier stupider gobbos.

Where the lower tiers were bald, primarily, with sharply pointed, wilting ears that appeared too large for their heads, comically lengthened feet and hands that could double as paddles, a thin chest and a protruding belly, finished with a weak chin and an overall expression that said *I'm too dumb to live, but I'd still shank you if I thought I'd get away with it,* the new versions were clearly more evolved.

They had sharper features, higher cheekbones and brighter eyes, a clear awareness behind the eyes and softer skin. Her ears were pointed still, and yet less than the long, flappy ears of the lower castes. They stood around five to five and a half feet tall, with long but more dexterous fingers, rather than the bestial claw-tipped ones that others had.

They were—and I was well aware of how much of a dick it made me sound, even to myself—but they were a load more human in their overall outlook.

Less beast and monster, and much more human, with…well, I was trying not to look as she was clearly filling out the basic garb that had been summoned on her.

She could have had an average chance in modeling contracts, not particularly because she was beautiful, but because she was exotic and unusual-looking.

She still had no hair, but—there wasn't a chance I'd be chasing her personally—she was clearly female, and massively more aware than the average goblin on summoning.

Now, as I dialed back the mana I'd been pouring in, noting the glow that was steadily building in her eyes, with her nails, teeth, and eyes starting to change to a brilliant white, I shifted back to pure mana, increasing it until I felt that I'd gone as far as I could.

The system had given me some vague senses and blandly generalized pointers, but it still wasn't saying "put this in and you'll get a mage," which I guessed meant I was still missing something.

At eight hundred pure and two hundred Light, I stopped and watched as she breathed fast and hard, her eyes wide open and yet unseeing as the changes continued to cascade through her even without any more mana being added.

Ten seconds passed. Although she was still alive, I was feeling that I'd been wrong in the guesses I'd made. Twenty seconds, and I was mentally berating myself, swearing that I wasn't going to try this shit again.

Thirty seconds and I reached out, trying to see whether I could dial it back still, but found a change in her connection through the dungeon.

She no longer appeared as a simple goblin—they often had a sort of identifier above them in the dungeon sense, that could be changed to show their name or description—but instead registered as a collection of symbols. They moved slowly, shifting from one point to another, adjusting constantly on the fly, as the dungeon registered the evolution that was being forced upon her.

A dozen different symbols flared and vanished as I watched, until in the end, two stayed, before fading away. The prompt, though, when it came, made me want to leap up and cheer.

Congratulations! You have successfully Imbued a creature of your Dungeon: "Advanced Goblin" with your mana! "Advanced Goblin" has been altered at a fundamental level. Two paths are now available to the Advanced Goblin:

Luminary: Goblin Luminaries are masters of light and radiance. They harness the power of illumination to both protect and purify, standing as beacons of hope among their kind.

Spells:

Radiant Burst: Releases a blinding flash of light that damages and disorients enemies while invigorating allies. Damage: 10 points of Light damage to

enemies within 5 meters. Allies within range gain +2 Dexterity for 1 minute.
Cost: 100 mana

__Light Shield:__ Creates a barrier of pure light that absorbs incoming damage
and reflects a portion back to the attacker. Effect: Absorbs up to 50 points of
damage. 20% of absorbed damage is reflected. Cost: 150 mana, lasts for 5
minutes or until depleted

Summoning Cost: 2,000 mana to summon, 80 mana per day, 20 control
points.

OR

__Illusionist:__ Goblin Illusionists are masters of deception and misdirection. They
bend reality to their will, creating intricate illusions to confuse and misdirect
their enemies.

Spells:

__Phantasmal Image:__ Creates a perfect illusory duplicate of the caster that can
move independently and even appear to cast spells. Effect: Creates one
duplicate that lasts for 5 minutes or until dispelled. Cost: 25 mana

__Mirage Veil:__ Cloaks an area in illusory magic, altering its appearance or
hiding it completely from view. Effect: Can alter or conceal an area up to 10
meters in diameter. Cost: 30 mana, lasts for 10 minutes

Summoning Cost: 1,800 mana to summon, 75 mana per day, 18 control
points.

Current Level: __Advanced.__

It'd worked! Holy shit, it'd actually fucking worked!

I couldn't believe it. Staring into her eyes, I knew instantly that not only was she fully aware and seeing the same information that I had, but that she was aware that I might have killed her if that had gone wrong.

The flinty stare I was getting made that *very* clear, and then the dungeon-enforced obedience would kick in. A reverent stare would start to glaze her face, before the memory kicked in and...

"I'm sorry," I said to her. "I felt that I knew enough to raise you from a generic goblin to gift you your class, but I didn't know for sure. I decided it was worth the risk, but I should have asked you to volunteer first. Do you want to choose your evolution?"

She stared at me for a few seconds, then nodded, once.

"I... I am... Luminary," she said haltingly, clearing her throat and trying again. "I bring hope."

"You do," I agreed, staring at her spells. She was essentially a crowd-control build, one that would be perfect against any creatures of the night. Although the undead might not be too affected by the light—they tended not to have eyeballs, after all—I was betting others would be. "Okay, what's your name?" I asked her.

"Lumi... Lumos." She changed it, and I nodded.

"Welcome then, Lumos. I'm hoping to awaken several others to join you now, but either way, why don't you go find the Light converters, settle down there and talk to Dante about your class? He can give some advice." Then I raised my voice, realizing that there were a lot of people watching me currently.

"Okay, everyone, this is Lumos. She's a Luminary, a form of Light mage or, as Dante likes to call them, luxomancer. We've just discovered that there are two distinct paths that can be offered to Light mages—there are probably more, but we know about these—one is Luminary, and that's for Lumos to share any information about. The other is Illusionist!"

I quickly covered the basics of the class to the room at large, then settled back down, cracked my knuckles, and got to work. The four additional goblins I summoned were each different, none of which had anywhere near the natural ability that she'd had with Light. They were, in order of summoning, an umbramancer, a ferromancer, and a golemancer, with the last one...well, enough said about that. I decided that an additional goblin construct artificer was a better idea than replicating that experiment again.

It'd also probably make everyone feel a lot better about things when the remains were scraped off the ceiling, and everyone around.

I quickly read over the prompts and advised people on the meanings, explaining that these were possible paths that were linked to shadow, metal, and summoning.

Congratulations! You have successfully Imbued a creature of your Dungeon: "Advanced Goblin" with your mana! "Advanced Goblin" has been altered at a fundamental level. Two paths are now available to the Advanced Goblin:

Umbramancer: Goblin Umbramancers are masters of shadow manipulation. They can bend darkness to their will, using it for stealth, attack, and defense.

Spells:

Shadow Bolt: Launches a concentrated bolt of darkness at a target, dealing damage and temporarily blinding them. Damage: 20 points of Shadow damage. Target has a chance to be blinded for 3 seconds. Cost: 100 mana

Veil of Shadows: Wraps the caster in shadows, granting near-invisibility and protection from Light-based attacks. Effect: 90% invisibility in shadowed areas, 50% in lit areas. 50% resistance to Light damage for 5 minutes. Cost: 350 mana

Summoning Cost: 2,300 mana to summon, 95 mana per day, 23 control points.

OR

Nightweaver: Goblin Nightweavers focus on manipulating shadows to create illusions, control minds, and sap the strength of their enemies.

Spells:

Shadow Puppet: Allows the caster to control the actions of a target by manipulating their shadow. Effect: Can control one target for up to 30 seconds. Cost: 500 mana

Life Drain: Saps the life force of a target through their shadow, healing the caster. Effect: Drains 5 HP per second from the target, healing the caster for the same amount. Cost: 100 mana per second, can be maintained for up to 10 seconds.

Summoning Cost: 2,100 mana to summon, 90 mana per day, 21 control points.

Current Level: Advanced.

***

Congratulations! You have successfully Imbued a creature of your Dungeon: "Advanced Goblin" with your mana! "Advanced Goblin" has been altered at a fundamental level. Two paths are now available to the Advanced Goblin:

Ferromancer: Goblin Ferromancers are masters of metal manipulation. They can shape, control, and even liquefy metal at will, making them formidable allies in both combat and crafting.

Spells:

Metal Spike: Launches a sharp projectile of manipulated metal at high velocity toward a target. Damage: 15 points of piercing damage. Can penetrate light armor. Cost: 25 mana

Iron Skin: Temporarily hardens the caster's skin to a metal-like consistency, providing significant protection against physical attacks. Effect: Increases physical defense by 50% for 5 minutes. Cost: 30 mana

Summoning Cost: 2,200 mana to summon, 90 mana per day, 22 control points.

OR

Metallurgist: Goblin Metallurgists focus on the alchemical and crafting aspects of metal manipulation. They excel at enhancing weapons and armor, and can transmute lesser metals into more valuable ones.

Spells:

Weapon Enhance: Temporarily imbues a weapon with increased sharpness, durability, or elemental properties. Effect: +5 to weapon damage and adds a chosen elemental effect for 10 minutes. Cost: 35 mana

Metal Transmutation: Allows the caster to change one type of metal into another, or purify ore. Effect: Can transmute up to 1 kg of metal per casting. Cost: 40 mana

Summoning Cost: 2,000 mana to summon, 85 mana per day, 20 control points.

Current Level: Advanced.

***

Congratulations! You have successfully Imbued a creature of your Dungeon: "Advanced Goblin" with your mana! "Advanced Goblin" has been altered at a fundamental level. Two paths are now available to the Advanced Goblin:

Golemancer: Goblin Golemancers are masters of creating and controlling animated constructs. They can bring inanimate matter to life, creating powerful allies and servants.

Spells:

Summon Minor Golem: Creates a small golem from nearby materials to serve the caster. Effect: Summons a golem with 100 HP and 15 attack power. Lasts for 30 minutes or until destroyed. Cost: 500 mana

Golem Enhancement: Temporarily boosts the strength, durability, or speed of an existing golem. Effect: Increases chosen stat of a golem by 50% for 5 minutes. Cost: 300 mana

Summoning Cost: 2,400 mana to summon, 100 mana per day, 24 control points.

OR

Construct Artificer: *Goblin Construct Artificers specialize in creating more intricate and specialized golems, often imbuing them with elemental properties or unique abilities.*

Spells:

Autonomous Programming: *Grants a golem increased intelligence and the ability to carry out complex tasks independently. Effect: Golem can understand and execute complicated instructions without direct control for up to 1 hour. Cost: 550 mana*

Modular Construction: *Allows the caster to quickly assemble or modify golems using interchangeable parts. Effect: Can create a customized golem in half the usual time, or modify an existing golem's abilities mid-battle. Cost: 300 mana*

Summoning Cost: 2,200 mana to summon, 95 mana per day, 22 control points.

Current Level: Advanced.

It'd kinda derailed the point of me being there, again, but only for an hour or so. I now had an eighty percent success rate with the new method, which was a hell of an improvement.

I also had several goblin mancers, which was awesome. But as much as the golemancer and construct artificer were cool, they had very limited use for the trip.

I resigned myself to being able to summon them on the fly if I needed them. Instead of planning to take them with me, I sent them to the crafting area, where Finn was over the moon to receive the pair.

Then I summoned another Luminary and another Umbramancer, figuring they'd be useful.

With that done, and after a long conversation with the golemancer about his abilities that was very frustrating, I started to play with my spells again.

CHAPTER TWENTY-ONE

"I just do it," I mimicked in a high-pitched voice, glaring at the ground in front of me, where a pile of random iron ore and rock lay doing absolutely fuck all.

The golemancer had been incredibly unhelpful, and although, yeah, okay, he was like half an hour old at that point, and hadn't even cast the spell more than the single time I made him do it so I could watch…that wasn't the point.

It was still a dick move to not teach me what I needed to know straight off.

"Sooo…" A voice came from the side, interrupting me, and I glared over at the grinning face of Dante. "Any chance I could get that book now?"

"I already told you…" I started, and he shook his head.

"I know what you said. I don't think that's right, but there's a great way we can test it."

"Oh?"

"One of the kobold mage trainees is level four and has been using the healing orb. But he's got a high Light affinity, so we could give it to him and…"

"Tell me what he learns." I simply passed the tome over, before sighing and getting back to work. We'd need to test whether giving one of those things to an already established Light mage did anything as well, but fuck it. Limited time for experimentation meant limited experiments done.

I didn't have enough time to keep playing now.

I'd gotten fairly skilled at projecting my mana outside of myself by this point. Although I knew more or less what I was doing, that came with its own specific problems. What I needed to do for summoning was use that mana in a way that matched that particular feat.

To cast a summoning spell, I needed to use summoning forms of mana. Diving into my affinity lists, I scrolled through them, before wincing as I found it. Twenty percent.

I had twenty percent affinity for summoning magic, although, there'd been a useful change to the system that I'd missed since I reached apprentice tier with my Arcanist skill.

I could now see the breakdown of specific mana forms.

So…summoning mana was a mix of…Conjuration and Life mana. Fair enough, Life was one of the base eight elemental forms of mana, so that was okay; I had a thirty-eight in that. But Conjuration… I went looking for that, and found to my annoyance that it was in turn made from Arcane and Space.

Space was Darkness and Aether. Darkness was another base element but the Aether, I'd need to study. And Arcane…fuck's sake!

Arcane was a mix of Energy, Aether, and Void, which further broke down into Light and Air for Aether, Darkness and Death for Void, and…and Fire and Lightning for Energy.

Now I had a pretty low mix for Void…hell, that was an understatement. Minus two was that affinity, meaning if I saw anyone tossing that kinda magic around, the best thing I could do was shoot them in the face instead of saying hello. But Energy? That I had a reasonably high number in: thirty-eight. Sure, not great, but not bad.

Mind you… how the hell was I so comfortable with a blade that was using void energy, when I was also made to feel sick around running water before all of this, and my level with water was higher? Maybe something to do with the void magic being constrained in the blade?

An enchantment? I made a mental note to look into that when we got someone that was studying enchantments.

I was starting to get why some people were just naturals in a specific area, and why it could be so damn hard to replicate those abilities and spells for another.

It could take me months to teach myself enough to raise my level to be able to cast even the most basic Void-based spells, but…if I could? No wonder there were so few apprentice mages, and those would be fucking nightmares to face.

If they could figure out your affinities, they'd be able to counter you with the most damaging spell you were susceptible to.

I paused, seriously tempted to go for the quick and easy method then, and forced myself to reread the text and work through it, seeing what was hinted to, as much as what was outright said.

Crafting the signature spells of the Apprentice [Arcanist] is a hurdle that many sapiens fail to clear, as each spell completed not only limits the paths available to the mage for their future growth, but is also correspondingly more difficult.

Choose to create three separate spells of any two of the following categories to reach Apprentice Rank as an [Arcanist]. Alternatively, create a single spell in each category to receive an increased boost to your selected affinities and a bonus magical item:

- **Animation: 0/1**
- **Blood: 0/1**
- **Divination: 0/1**
- **Elemental: 0/1**
- **Enchantment: 0/1**

Jez Cajiao

- **Mental: 0/1**
- **Rune: 0/1**
- **Temporal: 0/1**
- **Spatial: 0/1**
- **Summoning: 0/1**

Okay. Knowing that if I learned three separate spells in any two categories, I'd hit apprentice and get whatever boost that regular apprentices got was great and all, but the text that caught my eye was "as each spell completed not only limits the paths available to the mage for their future growth, but is also correspondingly more difficult."

So what I was seeing was that if I wanted to be able to do all sorts of magic, and use them all to be more powerful, I needed to do all sorts of magic *now*.

If I didn't, then in the future I was going to be stuck.

Sure, as a Lightning god, I was thinking that Lightning was going to be my bread-and-butter spells. But knowing that I might be unable to learn or use any kind of healing magic, or no longer be able to learn Incinerate or something similar?

No, I wanted to learn as much as I could. Although this little experiment had shown that summoning might be beyond me if I was going for the obvious path, summoning *mana* might yet be achievable.

Energy was something I could access, and fairly easily. It didn't flow as easily as either Fire or Lightning did, certainly, but it was achievable. Now, creating Energy mana, and then trying to bring that form of mana into the rocks and ore…

I started playing—it was *experimenting*, really…officially, anyway—and it was totally valid, considering what I was trying to do. But it really felt like playing, because as much as it was for a real goal, it also was fascinating.

An hour passed as I examined the way that the ores sucked up the energy, starting to sparkle with it, and at one point vibrating enough that they started to shudder across the floor. But as soon as I stopped, they'd vent the energy, second by second until it was all gone.

I didn't get it. If I imbued something with the mana…

Imbue.

When I imbued it, I got a sense of things, like how much it could hold. Shifting to thinking in those terms, I found that the rocks and ore could hold almost no Energy mana at all, which, when I thought about it, sort of made sense. It wasn't like they were moving around or alive.

Alive.

Life mana, on the other hand, that was fairly easy to work with. And if I fed that into the mass, it felt…it had so much more space! There was loads of space for Life mana!

Well, not *loads,* but certainly far, far more than there had been for Energy. And when I fed in a little Energy? That got a reaction. The rocks started to shiver. And after a few seconds, I was finally hit with inspiration.

Directing both Life and Energy mana into the rocks, I pushed them mentally together, built a picture of them shifting, and then ordered them to stand.

It failed, the first time anyway—and the second, and the third. The fifth time, they held together for several seconds, then slid apart. But on the seventh try, I noticed that the iron ore seemed to keep the parts closest to it that also had trace elements of iron, and I focused on just the iron ore.

It didn't work, not fully. But it was going in the right direction, so I added a little Earth mana, getting a surge of movement and stability that lasted almost three seconds.

Emboldened by that, I tried again, adding a little less Earth, and some Metal mana to work with the ore. Finally, as the tiny creation clambered laboriously to its feet, shuffled around in a crude circle, then collapsed again as the infused mana ran out, I received a prompt.

Congratulations! You have created your first signature animation spell:

Iron Shambler

Congratulations! You have created another signature class spell! Through what is assuredly a questionable series of experiments, you managed to infuse raw iron ore with a spark of Life and Energy, Earth and Metal mana!

Congratulations! You are now one of an extremely small number of beings that have created a golem, however crude and temporary, with neither proper training nor resources!

You have gained the following spell:

Iron Shambler: At a cost of 200 mana, as well as a minimum of 10 health per casting due to the strain, you can bring a crude iron golem to life! Now you too can create a staggering, barely functional construct that will confuse and potentially mildly inconvenience your friends and enemies for a few brief seconds!

Note: This ability requires a mix of Earth, Metal, Life, and Energy mana, and will leave you with a splitting headache and possibly iron dust in uncomfortable places if cast repeatedly.

Effect: **Animates a basic iron golem that lasts for 11 seconds. The golem can move up to half a meter per second but cannot take any actions beyond basic movement.**

Cost: **200 mana**

Cooldown: **1 minute**

Note: **Although rudimentary, this spell forms the foundation for more advanced golem creation. With practice and increased understanding of the involved mana types, you may be able to create more stable and capable constructs in the future.**

This spell counts toward your Animation category for the Apprentice [Arcanist] Class Quest.

Current Progress:

Animation: 1/1

It'd worked! I couldn't help but thrust one arm into the air and let out a whoop of triumph, before wincing and looking around.

Only Kilo sat nearby, in a heavily plush chair, watching me curiously.

"It is good?" He glanced from me to the settling pile of rubble on the floor, and I opened my mouth to say that of course it was...then sighed and told the truth.

"Well, it's shit, actually, mate, but it worked, and that's all I needed, I guess." I settled back, shifting and rolling my shoulders; I was stiff from uncounted hours sitting there. "It's a summoning spell, though, and I needed one to reach my apprentice tier as an Arcanist."

"It is? Where did you summon from, an elemental plane?"

"Uh..." I checked the details and cursed. "Okay, it's my first *animation* spell, for the apprentice tier."

"You have reached it?"

"No..." I admitted, before sighing. "I'm working on it, though. So, what're you doing here?"

"Meditating."

"Really?" I asked him skeptically. "Because I know you're a Cryomancer, and surely that'd be done by the Water converters, or Ice, if we have any?"

"We don't. So yes, it would, but without a dedicated Ice converter, here is fine." He shrugged, then grinned. "I wanted to talk to you anyway."

"And here it goes." I grinned back. "What do you want, you bugger?"

"An Ice converter." He shrugged. "And another Cryomancer."

"I'd not say no to one," I admitted. "And the Ice converter should be easy enough to arrange..." I checked the system and snorted. Sixty thousand mana— that was all it'd cost, as some of the research had been done in the supplementary paths and the converters had been levelled up heavily already.

We had that available, but I didn't know whether that was needed, so I held off.

"We can get it on the way." I scratched my chin in thought. "I mean, I think we can. As cold as it is right now, it'll generate extra anyway, so it should work. You're coming with me, right?"

"Yes." He nodded sharply in the kobold fashion, a single deep, fast angle down and up, almost like a velociraptor taking a bite and ripping it free. "Captain Mike came to me. I have been asked, along with Beta." He grinned at that.

I paused, then realized that the strange expression…he was trying to raise nonexistent eyebrows suggestively!

"No!" I gasped, then burst out laughing at the hurt look he gave me. "No, no, it's okay," I tried to reassure him. "I was just surprised! You like Beta?"

"Of course!" he replied, as if surprised. "Is it not obvious? I have had much advice from friend Chris and—"

"Oh gods." I groaned. "Please, Kilo, fucking please tell me you're not taking cross-species dating advice from that idiot?"

"He is not a master of this?" he asked, shocked. "He assured me that he was a master?"

"A master-bator." I grunted. "Okay, mate, first rule with Chris is…" I settled into what I hoped would be a quick conversation, which, predictably, turned out to last more than an hour. It was only when I changed the subject to elemental magic that I managed to get him off the subject of Beta and her magnificent flanks.

I guess males *are* all the same, no matter the species.

The next hour was spent with him going over the details of his Ice-based spells, focusing primarily on area of effect as my Storm spell was awesome and I already had both Lightning and Incinerate as single-target ones.

By the end of the hour, and thanks to the use of several props, including a bathtub full of water, some ice, and a lot of plunging myself into the damn thing to "feel winter's touch," I got another prompt.

Congratulations! You have created your first signature area of effect spell:

Frostbite Flurry

Congratulations! You have created another signature class spell! Through what is undoubtedly a series of ill-advised magical experiments involving your bathtub, several bags of ice, and a poorly understood weather manipulation ritual, you've managed to harness the power of winter itself!

Congratulations! You are now one of an extremely small number of beings that can create their own personal blizzard, and haven't frozen themselves solid in the process!

You have gained the following spell:

Frostbite Flurry: At a cost of 500 mana, as well as the temporary loss of feeling in your extremities, you can unleash a localized ice storm! Now you too can turn any space into a winter wonderland of pain and regret, slowly freezing your friends and enemies into artisanal ice sculptures!

229

Jez Cajiao

Note: This ability requires a combination of Water and Air mana, chilled to perfection. Prolonged use may result in an unshakeable craving for hot cocoa and a newfound appreciation for thermal underwear.

Effect: Creates a swirling vortex of ice and snow in a 10-meter radius around the caster. Targets within the area take 5 cold damage per second and have their movement speed reduced by 50%. The storm lasts for 30 seconds.

Cost: 300 mana

Cooldown: 5 minutes

Note: Although chilling, this spell forms the foundation for more advanced crowd control and area denial tactics. With practice and increased understanding of the involved mana types, you may be able to create more potent and larger-scale winter effects in the future.

This spell counts toward your Elemental category for the Apprentice [Arcanist] Class Quest.

Current Progress:

Animation: 1/1

Elemental: 1/1

The snark levels were starting to piss me off, but not anywhere near as much as the stunned look on Kilo's face. Mainly because when he spoke, I realized what the fucker had been doing.

"I didn't think that would work!" he whispered, clearly to himself and not realizing he'd said it aloud.

That was when I realized that, yes, the fucker had indeed been spending too much time with that ass-wipe Chris, and he'd been damn well fucking me over! I'd been clambering in and out of the fucking bathtub, chilling my bollocks to damn near absolute zero, while he'd been secretly laughing his arse off!

I glared at him, before forcibly smoothing my face and painting a smile on. I'd get him, but if we were playing those games, I wasn't going to warn him.

Thankfully, everyone else had left the room ages ago, leaving the two of us to experiment, so I'd taken to stripping off before clambering in and out, and had towels and more ready.

It was still Baltic, though, and it was with that firmly in mind that I spoke up.

"So, about Chris's advice..." I started, and he nodded excitedly as I set about evening the score.

By the time I'd finally remembered that we had someone with Phantom as their primary affinity and therefore maybe an inside line on summoning, I was almost ready to give up for the day. My brain was melted from the constant mental and magical experimentation, but when I did finally remember…damn, it was a relief.

I left Kilo planning what he should provide Beta as an example of his interest—my vote was a sculpture of her made entirely from flowers, and the look he gave me at that meant it was either going to be hilarious or a downright disaster—and I headed on up.

When I finally strode on out onto the Death floor, I found Catherine in a chair on the far side, and as usual, she was alone, staring into the distance.

"Dungeon Lord!" she gasped, leaping to her feet and dropping to her knees before me. "I'm sorry. I didn't mean to—" She broke off, swallowing hard as I paused, then continued toward her.

"You didn't mean to do what?" I asked her quietly as I reached her.

She lifted her head, staring at me in surprise, before clearing her throat and ducking her head again. "I didn't mean to…disturb you?" she tried.

I snorted, looking around and sighing. "Seriously, there's only a single chair here?" I asked rhetorically, before summoning a mirror to the one she'd leapt out of. "Come on, let's get this over with first. What did you do?" I sat back in the tall, winged-back leather chair.

"I…"

The look of fear on her face said it all. I winced, realizing just how much she was panicking.

"Seriously, I've not heard anything, so it can't be that bad, okay? Just explain it."

She nodded. Instead of sitting, though, she remained standing, dry-washing her hands and clearly petrified.

"Catherine, please," I said softly. "Just talk to me. What's up?"

"I didn't mean to do it," she whispered.

Instead of pushing her this time, I stayed silent.

The seconds ran to minutes, and eventually, barely ahead of me asking her again, she started to speak.

"I just knew he missed her, you know? And I figured my gift was for Phantom, so maybe?" She shrugged, waving one hand in a sort of "who knew" gesture.

"Go on," I said patiently.

"I didn't know how to do it. I mean, it's not like there's anyone to teach me."

That came out almost as an accusation, and I quirked an eyebrow at her, before she swallowed hard and went on.

"I mean, there's no others like me," she clarified.

"Like you?" I asked gently.

"You know," she whispered. "No other Nethermancers."

I sat up straight at that. I'd had absolutely no clue she'd even unlocked her class, let alone been given one I'd never heard of.

"Okay," I prompted, waiting and hoping she'd take the bait.

"I saw how upset he was, okay? And I thought maybe that's what I'm supposed to do! Maybe I'm supposed to help people. Maybe it's like you said—it's a gift!"

"But?"

"But it wasn't!" she almost wailed. "It wasn't at all! And now he's blaming me. He says I did it deliberately, and they think I don't hear them, but I do!"

"Who?"

"All of them, when they talk about me…the whispers, the names! I know what I am, okay? I'm not pretty like the other girls. I'm not strong and I'm sure as hell not smart. And the only place I've ever been happy was when I was around the dead! I used to hide in the graveyard to get away from bullies. And when I got older? I just—well, it was just where I was happiest, okay?"

That came out as a very defensive accusation, and I looked at her.

"That's fine," I assured her, thinking that she wasn't that bad… Sure, she usually looked a bit haggard and a bit… "Catherine, how old are you?" I asked her suddenly, as I noticed a few more details that rang wrong in her overall appearance.

"Twenty-three," she muttered, picking at her nails sullenly.

"Twenty—!" I strangled off my gasp and stared at her.

"I know," she whispered, looking down at her feet. "It's genetic."

"Genetic?"

"My condition. My mother was the same."

She ignored me when I asked what the condition was.

It wasn't like the name would have meant anything to me, but knowing that she was in her early twenties? I'd have bet around mid-forties, if not older at the very least. And as Mama Aurelia would have said: *Tha' girl done had a hard paper-round, fo' sure.*

I just nodded when she started talking and waited to hear more.

"So, you know, I liked being there, and I like it here. It's quiet and nobody comes here. And those who do? They tend to just, you know, leave you be?"

"Uh-huh," I said noncommittally.

"So, when he came, and he knew who I was, I wasn't sure. It was nice that someone wanted to talk to me, and to ask me things, but… I mean, I didn't even know that people knew that much about me. And that someone knew my class? I'd not told anyone! Nobody! So, when he came, and he said he knew what I could do? It's just…he asked me, and I thought it'd help him."

She paused, then sighed and sat back in the chair, massaging her knees and thighs as if uncertain how to explain it.

"She died when those soldiers attacked us, and he said he missed her—they were supposed to get married and she'd been pregnant—he wanted to talk to her about, *I don't know*…he just said that he needed closure, and he wanted to talk to her one last time!"

"And you helped him to do that?" I asked, impressed.

"It's my class," she repeated sadly. "I can reach through the veil and help them reach back, but it…well, it hurts, and I'm not very good at it."

"What happened?"

"He told me what happened, and where she died, and we went there. I thought it'd help, maybe I'd be able to sense her more, and he gave me some of her things…her hairbrush and some clothes. I reached out and…and I was really surprised, you know? I could feel her almost straightaway. But then I realized that I'd never done it for someone else before. When I tried it, it was just for me, and when I do it, it's my class, so I can see them, I can hear them, and I don't need to pass it on to anyone else."

She looked really uncomfortable at that, and was talking faster now, as if all the words had been held behind a dam, one that had now burst.

"I asked her to talk to him, and I asked him to tell me what he wanted to ask her, but she couldn't make him hear *her*, and he was getting really upset, so…so I let her touch me. I let her talk to him through me. It started out good, but then he kept asking her things, and she kept wanting more, and to keep talking." She'd wrapped her arms around herself now and was sunken down in the chair, almost as if she were cold or afraid.

"The more she tried to do, to touch him, and the longer they talked, the more it *hurt*. She needed my mana to do anything, though, and I could feel it, all right? It's so cold there. They need *us*—they can't do anything from that side, and they need our strength to reach out. But as soon as she'd had a little, a taste of life and mana again, she just kept wanting more!

"He asked her about the baby, and…and she kept asking him to help her, to bring her back. He started telling me to, to let her through, and I tried explaining that it doesn't work like that. But she cut me off. I didn't know they could do that, but when I'd pulled her to me, when I'd let her in, it was suddenly so hard to stop her. To push her out again. When I tried, she started hurting me, trying to stop me, and because I felt it, she did too. It gave her more feelings—she felt the pain, and she… I don't know. She *liked* it."

"She liked hurting you?"

"Not just me," she whispered. "I don't think she was like that before—not into pain, I mean—just not a very nice person, maybe? And feeling something, anything, was better for her than the grave. When I kept trying to push her back, to stop her from hurting me, she panicked and fought me. Then he kept trying to ask her things. He didn't understand what was happening, and he was crying…

"We were *all* crying suddenly. She wanted to come back, and he was mourning losing her *and* their child. I was… I could feel all her emotions. She wanted to come back, she wanted to be alive again, and she got so angry! She screamed at me to let her through, and made me shout at him, telling him that he failed her, and that it was his fault that she died, that their baby died, and then…"

She was sobbing now, tears rolling down her cheeks.

233

"She started lying to him. She said that he could have it all back, that he could have her back and their baby. That was when it got worse. She was saying through me that I was a nobody, that nobody cared about me. Then he started agreeing and saying that I should let her through, and I realized that was what she'd been after all along!

"She'd not moved on; she'd not left, because she was desperate to return! She was so afraid of what came next, she didn't know if she'd be judged or not, but she'd done so much. And when she was saying all of that, I saw the things she'd done.

"Most of them weren't much…just, you know, low-grade petty stuff, but loads of it. Like complaining about people to their managers because it was funny, and eating in restaurants and running away instead of paying. But the thing she was most worried about? That he'd find out about? It was that the baby wasn't his."

I winced, and she went on, rushing to get it all out to someone, anyone, willing to listen.

"When I saw that, when I saw that was what she was most afraid of, and he had me—he was shaking me and shouting at me to let her through, and she was hurting me—and it just…it just came out. I couldn't help it. I tried telling him to stop, and I was pushing at her, but it was all getting too much…and I just, I just screamed it at him."

"What happened?" I asked quietly, my mind full of the vivid image of the confrontation.

"He didn't believe me." Her head hung low. "He slapped me, and the shock…she nearly got through. I could feel her in me, all the hate and all the hope. I could feel her as she was settling into me. For a few seconds, I could see it all. I saw who it was, and when I saw how many there were, and that she'd had to lie to him before when one of their friends had told him she was having an affair…

"I knew what she'd said to convince him, and I told him. I blurted it all out, told him about her nickname, the places she went, that when she'd gone away 'with the girls' last year it wasn't, and who she'd gone with. And all the time I was telling him that, she was cutting me up!"

She shook her head. "It was too much. He let go of me. He backed up, and I managed to get out the names he'd called her, the little fun names that nobody else knew, and when he left me alone, without him hitting me and shaking me, I…" She cleared her throat. "I managed to push her out. And when I looked around, he was gone."

"Are you okay?" I asked her first. "When was it?"

"All of this?" she asked, and I nodded. "Three days ago."

"Are you okay?" I repeated.

She sniffed and nodded.

"Okay, I don't believe you, but that's fine. I'm not going to make you talk to me about this if you don't want to, but you *are* going to talk to John."

"Who?"

"John, the judge."

"I... I don't think I need to..." she whispered. "It's okay."

"No, it really fucking isn't, because as the Dungeon Lord in these parts, even if you decide you don't want to press charges, I'm looking at this in a coldly fucking logical way. He nearly helped his mad ex-girlfriend to possess you. That might have kept you as a slave in your own body, or it might have erased you, or fuck knows what. But attacking you and beating you to try to help her come through isn't going to help the *dungeon* one bit. At the very least, we'd end up out one potentially highly powerful Phantom mage. I don't know how you're going to help, but it might be that in a goddamn fight with the undead to come, you'd be goddamn pivotal!"

She sniffed and nodded, clearly afraid but unwilling to push back when I was so firm on this.

"Now, before we talk about anything else, and we deal with this shit, you were apologizing and claiming it was all a mistake. But as near as I can tell here, you're the victim, so what haven't you told me?" I tried to soften my glare as I said this, but fuck me. At times I felt like the goddamn maid. I just cleaned up here, and now look at it.

"He...he must have told people."

"Why?"

"I went to try to get some food, to try to be around people earlier, and they all knew." She closed her eyes. "I got...some of them said things."

"Like what?"

"Like that I was trying to seduce him, and that I threw myself at him, and told him stuff about his ex to hurt him when he wouldn't fuck me."

"You...?" I took a deep breath, seeing the bright red of her cheeks and having a flashback to people I'd known like this in school.

She was average in looks at best, and physically, she both looked much older and was more haggard than most. Fair enough—life beats us all down one way or another, and her looks were her business; she didn't need to go around with makeup on and her tits pushed up to her chin if she didn't want to. Didn't matter to me in the slightest. But I remembered the way the girls who did look like that at school had treated those that were...plainer, less self-assured or confident, less experienced.

And when I added that basic "mean girls" diatribe to the situation that was the aftermath of the fall and that she already looked like she was at death's door, and was all alone—yeah, she had a class that was going to push people away from her, at best.

None of the situation was right. I didn't think, personally, that she was right to have done what she did, to go to somewhere away from everyone else, to try to contact the dead and to basically try to be a bridge—but that was me, and I was an untrusting bastard.

It sounded like she really just had been trying to help. And the grieving boyfriend? I didn't like what he'd done, and yeah, if John judged he needed his balls in a vise for the assault, I'd do it personally. But I *understood* it.

Even the dead girl wanting to be back? That made sense. Fuck, who wouldn't want to? And if I was entirely honest with myself? If it was me, and Kelly had been taken from me? I knew myself enough to know that I couldn't ever allow myself to be in a position where I had the choice, because I didn't know I could say no.

No, the issue here was a shitty one, and I was damn glad that we had John, because this fucker was right in his wheelhouse.

"Okay, well, we—that's you and me—are going to have a discussion with John about this, and possibly Kelly as well. She's going to be able to give him and us advice on it. But for now, while there's an investigation going on, and under the strict understanding that I have only your side of it, you've got nothing to worry about."

"If you've embellished the truth a bit, or you think you've phrased things poorly, then now—or when we meet John definitely, if not before—is when you need to make sure you're a hundred percent accurate." I watched her to make sure she understood. "He'll know if you're lying, and it'll go badly for you, so please, tell him the truth."

"I will, and I have," she whispered.

"Then that's fine," I assured her. My automatic instinct with seeing someone hurt was to touch them—even Covid hadn't beaten that out of me—give them a hug, a squeeze of the shoulder, whatever. I'd been raised to believe that touch was massively important. It certainly was to my parents, who'd always hugged me and told me they loved me, and it had been for Mama Aurelia as well.

I started to reach forward on instinct; when she flinched back, I realized what I was doing and cursed. Of *course* she wasn't going to want me touching her.

"It's going to be okay." I stood, and she nodded, unable, or unwilling to look at me. "Is there anything you need?" I asked her, and she shook her head, reluctant to speak.

"Okay, I'm going to go, and we'll talk again soon, okay?"

She nodded, and I sighed, before heading for the door. I was furious that this poor woman had experienced this essentially under my roof, and also that I just…didn't know how to make it better.

I knew people that would be furious that I felt the need to "fix" it, saying that I was a misogynist, that I was wrong, that I was "stealing her agency" and a hell of a lot of other things. Society never seemed sure whether what I was feeling was "allowed" this week or not, and I hated that.

All I knew was that it was wrong to leave her in pain, and to not at least try to help.

It wasn't until I stepped out into the cool air outside, watching as my breath misted in the cold evening air, and the distant sound of splashing came to me from the nearby pool, that I remembered that I'd gone to her for a goddamn reason. But by no means was I going to try to pressure her into a magic lesson right now.

Glancing up at the stars that broke through the occasional foggy patch, I shook my head.

It was a lot later than I'd thought it was, though, and there was no way I was going to complete the magic experimentation I needed today.

With that thought making me even less cheerful, I set off, heading in the direction of the Parthenon, ready to have a very weird conversation with John and Kelly.

CHAPTER TWENTY-TWO

The morning of our departure dawned bright and clear. The air was cold and crisp, and despite the warmth of the pool in the middle of the dungeon, more than half of the enclosed area was covered in a glittering skein of frost.

"I wish you weren't going," Kelly whispered to me as we made our way out of the Parthenon building, headed over to where the others were gathering.

"So do I," I admitted. "There's so much to do here, there really is, and I feel like I've made no progress. It's like running in tar, and yet…" I blew out a long breath. "I was really hoping for a few days, you know? Just some time to relax, to learn and practice, and yeah…" I grinned at her and nudged her with my shoulder.

"Some time for us?"

I nodded. "Not just the sex, though that was fantastic." I lowered my voice so those we were approaching couldn't hear me. "More that I wanted to make use of the aerie again and to just have some private time to have a nice dinner, to talk and to live a little. As much as I love the sex, just to have another date, and to spend time with our friends when I'm not in a firefight, would be incredible."

"I know," she said softly. "I think it's really getting to the point where unless we can find that, and soon, for us all? We're going to have more and more breakdowns."

"Have we lost many people to that?" I asked, suddenly concerned that I'd missed it.

"No. But as much as we all joke about it, and about never having five minutes to do anything, it's…it's starting to get a lot."

"I hoped it was getting better."

"For most people, it is," she assured me. "The problem is us. Those of us who are dealing with everything at the top of the chain, I mean. The more we get hit over and over in short succession, without having that downtime, the more burnt-out we get. It's getting a lot better for other people, but they don't see all that we do." She paused, then smiled sadly.

"They presume that we're not working that hard, because they don't see it. They don't know what we do, so they assume it's nothing and think they could do our jobs better than us. It's annoying, but there's two choices. Either we invite them in to see exactly what it's like, and those who have insight into their own capabilities would be horrified, and would leave us all be and support us more. The majority, though? Those who shout the loudest are almost always those who are the most lacking in insight. Think of all the Karens out there who go ballistic at the slightest annoyance, but happily ruin things for everyone else without a care.

"Those people would still assume they could do our jobs better. And honestly? For the toxic people, it's better just to ignore them. All of that, well, it was to say that burnout is happening more and more, and it's to those of us at the top. The best way to combat it is to *live*. To enjoy our lives, as much as we can, and to embrace positive things as much as we can. We all need to be aware of the situations, and to deal with them as much as can be. That's why..." She paused, taking a deep breath, then went on.

"This plan that you've got for the mobile dungeon?" she asked, and I nodded. "Well, you're going to have to start planning for a two-shift system for it, two crews that can run and operate it, because when you've finished this mission? When the undead threat is no more and all the country is in progress, converting over to us? That's when you and I, and at least half of the leadership cadre, are taking a week off, solid."

"A *week?!*" I gasped, loving the idea and being horrified at the same time. "Kelly, I—"

"You don't see how we can do it and you're thinking of everything that's going to go wrong when we do it." She cut me off. "That's why Aly and I, as soon as you're gone, are going to start recruiting, and training. The plan is that we'll begin to operate in two shifts, one that'll work days for a month, and one that'll work nights.

"The two teams will work around the clock. If the shit hits the fan, then both teams come online together to sort it, but for the day-to-day running, this means we can hopefully sort twice as much, and we'll have cover so that we..." She paused, gripping my armor by the pauldrons and shook me slightly, or tried to.

"Are. Going. To. Have. A. Break," she growled. "A few days to a week—no more, and sure as shit no less. We're stopping and refreshing, before we burn out and break."

"I agree," I said when she stopped, and the look she gave me made me snort a laugh. "I mean it, I agree," I repeated.

"That was too easy," she said suspiciously. "You agreed too quickly."

"You think I don't want to take that time off?" I asked her. "Hell, I know I need to take the time off. I really desperately want to be somewhere away from all of this with you. Knowing that it's not just an excuse that I'm wanting to try to get away on a bloody holiday, but that we actually all understand that we need to take some time out and get ready for the fight to come by getting a little rest and a bit of recuperation?" I shook my head, grinning, then leaned down and kissed her. "Believe me, you're not going to have to work hard to sell that to me."

"We're getting a holiday?" Chris stepped up, cocking one eyebrow at us both in question.

239

"All of us are," Kelly said resolutely. "And no, I don't mean we're all off to a Greek island to party and get drunk. I mean a solid, relaxing few days to a week. And as soon as we can, we're going to start sending people away in relays to somewhere we know is safe. There'll be booze, and hopefully even a little sun, but it's still the end of days, so we need to all be ready for the shit to hit the fan at any point."

"I can still fight better than him, even drunk," Chris said. "Hell, at least I can find my goddamn hammer and hold onto it for more than five minutes…"

"I hate you," I said to him conversationally. "With every ounce of my soul, I hate you."

"I get that a lot." He grinned. "So, you ready?"

"I am." I sighed. "How far out are they?"

"Just passed the Jesmond turnoff," he told me. "They should be here in a few minutes. It's not like they're going to run into traffic, after all."

"Best thing that could have happened to the roads around here, the end of the world," I quipped. "So, Mike," I said in greeting to him as he and Aly walked up. Kelly, by my side, smiled up at her big brother. "What's the plan then?"

"The transports are almost here. You and your team are split between the heavy transport that's going to become the mobile dungeon and your personal boxer. The rest are to be loaded wherever they can fit until you get the dungeon up and running enough to provide them with mounts. Then the teams will be split between mounted reconnaissance and transport. The boxers and mounts will be roaming ahead and back; the transports will be taking the routes that they suggest."

"Makes sense," I agreed. "And my team?"

"Our team," he corrected. "Griffiths is going to lead his soldiers and take the mobile dungeon once we split off, as we agreed. That means I've been stuck with you, and just in case you forgot…" He tapped a magazine on his battle rattle and quirked an eyebrow. "What's this called?"

"A dickhead," I said with a straight face.

"Don't test me, Matt," he said slowly.

"A clip?" I tried again, stifling a grin, as his expression got darker by the second. "A potato?"

"Fine, I'm going to shoot you and leave you by the side of the road. I give up," he sighed before going on. "Now, remember, the plan is that we head straight from here to the A1 highway. We head south to Catterick Garrison. Once there, we check on the condition of the garrison, and if possible, recruit—send people back to the dungeon or take them with us, in the best case. Worst case, we avoid a fight if we can, and eliminate the threat if we can't. Most likely, we trade for information, offer advice, and fuck off.

"Then we head south. The trip from here to Catterick should take about two hours. It was just over an hour before the fall, but I don't doubt there's going to be damaged vehicles and fuck knows what along the route.

"Most likely, if we account for double the time needed, that'll be enough. The fall, when it came, was in the early hours, around zero-three-hundred in the morning. That meant that the roads were quiet, but not deserted. We should be good to wind our way around most of the remaining traffic on those roads. Where we can't, we'll use the new dungeon to absorb all that we can. If that fails? Good old muscle power and a pair of corpse lords are loaded aboard.

"Yes, we could use the bars on the vehicles, and that would be safer in the short term, no need to pause and so on, but the damage will mount up and we need to get there in one piece, not break down and have to walk from halfway." He paused, checking to see whether I was going to disagree. When I didn't, he nodded.

"Moving along, when we approach Oxford, we're going to send out scouts, see what we can see, and then hopefully, we will divert and take out the mechanist dungeon, along with any troops we need, and the others will move to secure the Channel Tunnel. If we have time, as discussed, we'll split off another team and set up a secondary dungeon in the heart of London. That's most likely the best bet to ensure we can hold the country. As much as I hate the damn place—too many southerners, for a start—there's going to be a hell of a lot of potential matter to scrap and gain right there." Again he paused, and I nodded.

"I agree. And yeah, it makes a lot more sense to have one there than in Folkestone or anywhere else. The shit we could strip from the heart of London and the sheer number of survivors we can hope to rescue and recruit there would be worth it alone. But it's all down to time," I said.

"We'll do our best to make sure you've got the mana," Kelly added in, and I reached out, pulling her in close giving her a one-armed hug.

"You can count on it being ready," Aly agreed grimly. "And forces here when you get the nexus up and running. One last point—we've also noticed that there's a significant loss when we've tried to 'feed' the other mana through a portal, that means that the most efficient method is to produce crystals here and ship them through once you have the nexus gate up and running. The distance from here to say, London, or Folkestone? We're not going to be able to help you with anything beyond advice if we don't get the gate opened, so remember that."

"Thank you, and I will," I said.

"If we can secure the Channel Tunnel, hold them off there for as long as possible, and then use that time to start stripping London? It should turn the tide," Mike agreed. "Okay, so enough of the overall plan. You ready to approve the team?"

"Who's coming?" I nodded as he led us over to where the others were waiting. Not for the first time, there were some surprises.

"I kept it to a small team, as we need to be able to get in and out, and not strip this dungeon of its defenders—and yeah, limited space in the transports. So, our team has Chris and me, as usual. Beta and Kilo both wanted in, and frankly Beta is getting so terrifying that I couldn't say no," he quipped.

But seeing the way that Beta nodded proudly and stared around with a flat threat clear in her eyes, I wasn't entirely sure it *was* a joke.

Beta had evolved from the lower-leveled uncommon kobold that she'd been summoned as. Her draconid lineage was becoming more and more pronounced.

She'd started out much as the others had, large lizardman—or woman, obviously—in appearance, with a look that was halfway between velociraptor and human, definitely lizard-like and kick-ass in all sorts of ways.

When the advanced kobolds were unlocked and summoned, they had wings. Sure, they weren't going to be launching themselves off to tame the skies anytime soon—they were more of a short-distance glide than a full-on flight capability—but they were bigger and better in every way than the standard uncommon grade kobolds. They were smarter, stronger, less animalistic, and more refined and humanoid, and less…

Well, closer to dragon and human, than lizard and human, I guess.

Beta had been incredibly loyal to me, all the way from when I'd summoned her in the dungeon when we'd been locked into Bronze. Since then, she'd backed me to the hilt every time I'd needed her.

Her loyalty had taken her from a dusty grey and black to a golden sheen for her scales, and a host of new abilities that I was fairly sure she didn't understand yet. But more than that, to a position of absolute authority over her kind.

She'd been, well, less than the others. She'd always been my intended leader for them, but as newer and smarter kobolds were being summoned, it'd become clear she was getting out-classed. I'd worried that she would be "put out to pasture" or kept as a mascot, if she survived at all. When I had the option to unlock the improvements that her loyalty then brought her? I'd been over the moon.

Then she'd shown that loyalty and had kicked the shit out of the asuras' avatars. Yeah, it'd come down to me in the end with the Soul Beam, but that was literally only possible because of the time she'd given me.

That she'd given *all* of us.

Now she stood as tall as any of us, seven feet of rippling muscle. I realized in shock that although Robin was a Paladin in style and class, Beta was fast becoming the same.

Her signature stealthy style that she'd been so good with as a younger kobold had been put aside in favor of the weapons that she'd evolved to wield, a mace and shield, with a hammer on her hip now, I noted.

She also carried a trio of short stabbing spears, six foot or so in length on her back between her wings. And the wings themselves?

They were significantly larger than they had been.

All in all, she was a badass, and she'd clearly been the recipient of some of Finn's hard work. The latest generation of body armor was nowhere near what he could eventually craft, I was sure. What it was, though, was a big step up from the last generation. As well as the armor itself being lighter and smaller, it was also stronger.

Finn had assured me that it should take short-range fire and ignore it from smaller caliber weapons, allowing at least two hits in an area before it failed, and possibly more.

Higher caliber weapons, such as a .308 or worse, would still be lethal, of course, or if the wearer was hit in an unshielded area with a lower caliber, but what was, was.

Beta looked like the queen of her kind already, and in this gleaming black and silver armoring, it just made her more badass.

Kilo had been given the same makeover. Although Beta had grown even larger since we last fought side by side, he remained the same. Yet between his armor and his own blue-tinted scales, he looked awesome as well.

He held the SA80 assault rifle comfortably. He was armed with secondaries—a handgun and several daggers—but his main lethality came from his spells.

The Cryomancer was levelling quickly, and the way that Beta studiously ignored him—and he her—despite them standing side by side, meant that either they were destined for true love, or hate.

These things were always fifty-fifty, really.

Lastly, they wore helmets that were open at the front to accommodate their extended muzzles, and to allow them to use their teeth should they need.

Finn had also—he was a wonderful guy, really—replaced my armor, provided a new hammer, shield and sword, and a handful of little touches, like a new dagger, a set of brass knuckles—made of steel, but still shiny—and a few other bits and bobs.

I'd thanked him, glad to be equipped again, and he'd just grinned, before going on about the new bags he was working on for everyone.

Most were utilitarian, but now and then there was something that'd make a fashion designer weep. Probably from the eye-searing combinations.

"As well as those three reprobates and me, I figured we needed a dedicated healer. We're going to be far enough away that if the shit hits the fan, it's going to really go badly, and well, loyalty means a lot to me." Mike went on, and I tore my attention back to him. "The things we bring, as a team, are a hell of a lot of slaughter potential, but little depth. That's why I asked Rhodes, and she agreed to lend me these two reprobates." He nodded at Jimmy and Andre, who grinned at me.

"And the ladies?" I asked, noting the way that both Emma and Jenn looked nervous.

"Well, Jenn is shaping up to be a decent healer, and she's dedicated, while Emma…" He paused and looked at Emma, who stared back challengingly. "As you can see, she doesn't give ground and she's determined." He shrugged.

"She's also using the thunderbolt orb, and hasn't reached level five yet. No class," I said calmly.

"You're saying I'm common?" she snapped at me, only to be shushed by her sister, who quickly grabbed her wrist in a death grip.

"No, I'm saying you haven't been awarded your class yet," I said more clearly. "So that means that at level five you might be offered a usable class, or you might not."

"I will," she swore.

"Emma…" I paused, waiting until I was sure she wasn't just going to talk over me and bite back, but actually listen. "You've thought the worst of me since we met. If you come along on this, you're going to have to do as you're told. If you get a healing class, or something that I decide is going to be more useful elsewhere, like with Griffiths? I'll send you there. This is the time to say if you can drop that chip on your shoulder and do as I tell you or if you can't. Because, believe me…"

Silence fell between us all as I made my position very clear. Kelly and Aly stepped closer to me, making it subtlety clear that although it was my decision, they'd back me, and there'd be no salvation coming from elsewhere.

"If you decide in the heat of battle that you know better than me, and you disobey an order, you'll get people killed. If you do that? Now, after I've given you a warning? You'll not be coming back here. Stop and think about it. I'll respect you a hell of a lot more if you just tell me the truth. But if you lie to me, I'll boot you. And you damn well know that your sister and the boys will follow you.

"You'd be condemning them to a life outside the dungeon. I need to know that I can rely on you, and that if I tell you to hold your damn mana, to stay where you are, when your husband is at risk, I need to know you'll do it. I would never put any of you at risk without reason, and I'll never ask you to do something I wouldn't. You all need to think about this, and think hard."

I saw the concern on her face, and I nodded.

"Take a few minutes and think about it," I offered, gesturing to the side.

She nodded, moving off with the other three in tow.

"You really have to push her like that?" Chris asked. "Don't get me wrong, I know she's a hard bitch at times, but…"

"He was right to." Mike nodded to me. "I was going to push the confrontation if you didn't, but you're growing up, Matt. She needs to understand her place, and that if she does this, she and her sister and their husbands are soldiers. Better that they decide not to go, than can't be relied on."

"Yeah, but then we're out a healer, a mage, and two soldiers," Chris pointed out.

"You'll take a focal orb each, as well as summoning healing potions on the move," Kelly said. "And anyway, I know Mike…he's got a plan."

"Well, yeah," Mike admitted with a grin. "I'm betting they'll come, but just in case, I've also got Patrick, Catherine, Robin, and Saros."

I paused, glaring at him and the way he grinned at me. "Mike…" I said slowly. "I know soldiers aren't the brightest generally, but you can count, right?"

"Me and Chris, Beta and Kilo, Jimmy, Andre, Emma, Jenn, Patrick, Robin, Catherine, and Saros." He counted them off on his fingers, then pretended to look shocked. "Well, what do you know, there's twelve!" he said, all wide-eyed.

I stared at him.

"Seriously though, was there a magical, mystical reason you said ten people?" he asked. "Because this gives us plenty of options. It gives us a dedicated healer. Sure, she's new to it, and so's the thunderbolt, but in this mission, they'll either get the hell up to speed, or they'll die. I'm hoping the former, but if it's the latter, then that's the risk they take."

"And the others?"

"I'll bring ranged with my sniper rifle, as well as tactical know-how and assassination techniques. Chris brings comic relief and the occasional furry to the party, but now and then he can help with plants and shit."

"Go on," I agreed, deliberately not responding to the fake hurt noise Chris gave as he tried to explain that he'd given up on the plants.

"Beta is, as I said, lethal these days, and she's only growing more so. Kilo brings ranged and magic to the mix. Being a Cryomancer and it being winter, he's going to be useful, I'd imagine. Jimmy and Andre? Basic firepower, and I'll teach them. They'll also work their arses off. They're loyal, specifically to you for some reason, though I'm fucked if I know why.

"The girls? They're desperate to keep their men alive and to prove they deserve to be here. They're both sharp as tacks and yeah, prickly as fuck. But a mission like this will either rub the edges off Emma, or she'll not be a problem ever again. I'm betting on the first, or I'd not have picked her, but still. She's got real potential.

"Patrick? Well, maybe we need someone seduced and you know, he might as well earn his keep." He raised his voice at that and grinned at the tall martial artist monk.

Patrick rolled his eyes, then turned back to Finn, who was going through the bag he'd made for him.

"Then we've got Robin, who, yeah, is a bit of a fruit loop." Mike made sure to say this in a lower tone and have his back to the nervous Paladin. "But, if you're getting a handle on your side of it, she's going to grow to be a hell of a handful if she does go all Paladin for us. And I have to think, a Paladin to face the undead down there? It just makes sense. Add in that the mechanist dungeon offers a hint that it's going to be a mechanical one—"

"No shit, really?" Chris stared at him, mouth open.

"And so blunt weapons might be the way forward. You know, like his head. It's solid and there's nothing in there to damage," Mike finished dryly, nodding at Chris, who grinned.

"Oh, good one." Chris nodded.

"Thanks, I liked it." Mike returned the look and winked.

"And Saros?" I asked, not discounting her, but curious.

"She's a scout. They're never a bad idea to have around. Yeah, she's not the brightest—I heard about the stream incident—but she's learning and could be useful."

"Catherine?" I glanced from him to her, where she stood at the edge of the group, clearly believing this was some kind of punishment for speaking up, and dwarfed in her gear.

"She's the wild card," he admitted. "John came to me after he'd spoken to her, and yeah, he's going to have a word before we leave, but he pointed out that if she's good with the dead and we're facing them, she might be able to bring something to the table. No clue what, seriously, but hey. If she can speak to the dead, maybe the locals can tell us more about that dungeon? I don't know. Let's call it intuition and a need to add to the mages. If she survives the mission, she's going to level a *lot*."

He finished quiet enough that I was sure she'd not be able to hear.

"Also..." Chris glanced over at me, "we taking Jack with us? Can't help but think he'd be damn useful."

"We are," I said. "He's already roaming the road to the south, checking the route out. As soon as we pass him, he'll fall in with us."

"Glad to hear it." Mike grunted. "So, lucky thirteen then?"

"Shit," I muttered, having never heard anything good about a group of thirteen people trying to accomplish something. "You know this is going to go wrong, right?"

"Of course it is." Mike snorted, clapping me on the shoulder. "But then, you're in charge, so that was inevitable. Might as well lean into it!"

"Incoming," Chris muttered.

I turned, glancing over as Jenn and Emma walked over, flanked by their partners.

"We're in," Emma said without preamble. "And...I'm sorry for being a bitch."

"Don't worry about it." I smiled. "Emma, I genuinely respect you because you never give ground and you're always the one the rest of your little group looks to. That's testament to your strength and your mind. But in this situation, it can be a weakness if you're not going to listen, and it'll be one that gets us all killed. So, you're in? Glad to hear it. It'll be good to have someone I can talk Lightning with as well, and I'll try to teach you a little as we go. Just remember that as you're not 'there' yet for the thunderbolt orb, it's going to hurt. But if we need you, you'll have to push through it and—"

"I know." She interrupted, holding a hand up and wincing. "It really hurts."

"You've been trying it?" I asked, curiously.

"Every two hours," Emma confirmed.

"What?" I asked, not sure I'd heard right.

"I cast it every two hours. It's all I've got the mana for at the moment, two castings every two hours, and then Jenn gets to heal me."

"It's why I've hit level five, and I got my Healer class," Jenn said quickly. "We think that Emma's not getting the experience because she's not killing anything with the spell, so it's just a waste, as the system sees it, but I'm actively healing her, so it's helping to level me."

"Holy...shit," I said slowly.

"And you weren't sure about her." Kelly nodded and smiled at Emma. "Well, *I'm* glad you're going, believe me."

"Yeah," I murmured, eyeing the pair, and their massive husbands who bookended them. "You know what? Me too."

The nearby gates that led from the main dungeon into the smaller holding area of the castle began to creak and rumble just then, opening slowly. I nodded to the group, then spoke to Mike as we turned to face the incoming group.

"You think we're good for this?" I asked him, and he shrugged.

"Honestly, I don't know," he admitted. "It all depends massively on the mechanist's dungeon. It might be a mess and we can stroll through, or it might be a horrific meat grinder. In which case, we fall back, we prepare and assault it with everything we've got.

"I'm not looking forward to fighting a place that's got a designator like that, but it's also one of the reasons I wanted Emma. Thunderbolt and any Lightning attacks you make are likely to be a lot more effective against mechanical foes, but fuck it—what do I know? Might supercharge them. All we can do is check it out and make an assessment based on what we find."

The vehicles that drove in were a slight change from what I'd been expecting. There were three boxers, one in the lead, two at the rear; three mastiffs that had been upgraded and had outside handholds, rails, and more for people to hang onto; and last of all?

"What the absolute fuckery is that?" I gasped, staring wide-eyed at the massive vehicle. "I thought we were tapped out! Using a bloody truck?"

"We were." Mike grinned, before pulling Aly in close and kissing the top of her head proudly. "That, my son, is the Oshkosh M1070. There was one bought and used for maneuvers nearby. Tank transports and the like. The mechanics went out and dragged it in close enough for the dungeon to get hold of it. Barely managed it in time, but damn, it was worth it."

"I agree," I breathed, staring up in wonder. "Damn good job, Aly!"

"Thank you." She smiled, while the rest of us looked on in awe.

Trucks and transports in the UK were generally a lot smaller than in the US, mainly because we were hampered by much less space and tighter, winding roads. Where in the US there were a lot of larger roads, here in the UK, there were sections in the country where the roads were literally one lane, and cars had to pull over at passing points to let their opposite past.

247

That caused no end of annoyance to both sides at the best of times. When the transport was as wide, if not wider than the road? There was just no way that any transport company was going to be buying one of those.

That meant that when we did see the "big rig" US monsters, it was always a sobering experience.

This one had been clearly flown in for tank transportation duties. The fucker was enormous, but instead of a Challenger Mk2 or Mk3 on the back in the truck bed, there were two shipping containers, and they looked to have been lightly armored.

I squinted, then revised that estimate. The shipping containers were already made of bloody steel, and then, with the slanted sides, the extra inches of armoring that looked to be a mixture of stone and titanium?

Damn.

"That's...that's a lot of armor." I left unsaid that if I'd been doing it, I'd have gone for a lot less armor on here, and the damn mounts for the party.

"It's not," Aly assured me. "The top layer is; then it's rubber beneath and then another layer of titanium. It's titanium and stone layered in strips running along the outside of the structure—that's the striping pattern. I know it looks like a lot, but trust me, it should work and be a lot more efficient."

"If we could have reproduced this without magic, we'd have taken a lot less casualties in the sandbox," Mike added.

"The strips are designed to fall away once they take too much damage, exposing the rubber beneath, and then a layer of titanium. It's a lot of weight, but that weight is on the back of something that moved tanks, so it's a lot less than it's used to." Aly gestured to the patterns.

"It also means that it'll take serious effort to do any lasting damage to the dungeon core, which means even if the shit really hits the fan, you can either escape and repair it, or if need be, the escorts can retreat and you can turtle up, working on getting a viable counter in place."

"Fair enough," I said. "Damn, I hope this works."

"Me too, or we've spent a hell of a lot on nothing." Aly nodded. "The two seeds are ready, although it means we're on the bones of our arse for mana production at the minute."

"Thank you." I nodded to her, before turning to Griffiths as he swung down from one of the nearby transports and grinned. These were the last change. I'd been expecting basically an armored version of the normal transport truck, and instead, they'd fixed up three of the mastiff transports.

They were clearly the nuclear, biological, and chemical secure ones that had been damaged and left in the coronaught queen's nest. But aside from some scuffing and dirt, they looked fine now, most of the mess cleaned off.

"Griffiths," I greeted him, staring at the long convoy filling the inside of the dungeon currently. "Wow."

"That's been said before." He smiled. "They're impressive, aren't they? Most civilians will never see machines like this up close, just on TV, and the difference is surprising, I know."

"We all set?" Then, unable to help myself, I asked the real question. "Is this really a good idea to take you, the leader of our military, him, the leader of our special teams, and me out of the dungeon all at once again?"

"That's why we've got Rhodes here, Captain Sanderson at the northern dungeon, and why we're going to be pushing out patrols as soon as the mana is there to pay for them." He nodded. "I can understand the concern, Matt. Truth be told, I share it, but the risk we face from the south means that it's not really something we can ignore.

"If they manage to make landfall and take the south of the country, we might as well start work on methods of running, instead of fighting. There's that many dead that they can recruit down there. And it doesn't even start to consider the damn dinos and more. Just the human dead in and around London will be enough to form a significant army that we'd have serious issues facing.

"Should we defeat him, but let him escape? He'd be able to replenish and drown us in a sea of the dead. We *have* to stop him at the Tunnel, or the shore, before he manages to take a foothold. Then, with the potential of London as either a place of recruitment and harvesting for us, or a, well…recruitment spot for him? One side needs to hold it.

"Lastly, if we leave the mechanist dungeon to grow, to attack us from behind or whatever they've got planned? No. If I could, I'd be taking ten times what we are. But to strip this place would be insanity after all that's happened. Instead, we have the dungeon secure, and a hell of a lot more troops available than we've ever had before."

"And a nexus gate," Kelly pointed out. "Now that the concerns we had about the coronaught vurms have been proved unfounded, we've got the nexus gate under construction at the northern dungeon. We paused it while we got everything else in place. They're expensive, after all, but at three million mana, we can do it today without bottoming us out. That means that unless there's a massively coordinated attack on both the northern dungeon and here, we can pull reinforcements and hammer any attacker into paste. We've got this, Matt."

"I hope so." I sighed, then forced a smile. "I mean, I know you do, don't worry. I'm just, you know…" I finished lamely.

"I know," Kelly assured me. "So, before you go, there's two last things, if you've got a minute?" She inclined her head to one side.

CHAPTER TWENTY-THREE

I frowned and nodded, following her as the others started gathering their packs and climbing aboard the vehicles, even as several dozen more disembarked. Rhodes directed the reinforcements she'd apparently requested into their new homes.

"What's up?" I asked Kelly.

She hesitated. "I heard from John this morning, and there's two issues we need you to rule on."

She said that while waving him over, and I nodded, waiting as he jogged over from speaking to Rhodes.

"Sorry, Matt," he apologized, coming to a halt. "I know you asked me to deal with the Catherine issue, but when I spoke to her—well, there's a lot more going on here, and a lot of additional potential."

"Go on, mate…no stress," I said to him, before glancing to Kelly. "You're aware of this?"

She nodded. "After you told me about it last night, I reached out to John when you were asleep. It just kept rolling around in my mind. He agreed, then took it to Mike."

"Right?"

"Well, after a little investigation, yeah, it's pretty much as she said. She might have left out a few minor details, such as how she had a little history with the woman—she was another of the crowd responsible for her being ostracized in the past—the majority is on point. That leaves me with two options, as surprisingly there wasn't a law about helping your dead ex to come back and possess another woman's body," he said dryly.

"First, we can introduce the law, and make it public why. That doesn't give us a realistic way to deal with the guy, but that's not the point. In this situation, I've questioned him and he's genuinely broken. I don't recommend punishment. If anything, I want him under watch to make sure he doesn't do anything stupid and hurt himself.

"That solution would be more aimed at dealing with the rumor mill, and stopping the persecution of Catherine. The group making her life miserable…again, I've investigated and they refuse to accept what she's said, as it means that their friend was in the wrong, and after her death…they're not ready to do that. No matter what we say, they'll nod and agree, then they'll keep on doing what they're doing." John paused.

"Unless we take away free speech and start going down that route, we don't see how we can fix that," Kelly clarified, and he nodded his agreement.

"Fuck." I grunted.

"Think of it as the worst of social media trolls. They think they're doing nothing wrong, just like any Karen. The difference is that these have been made to do it face-to-face, rather than behind a screen," Kelly added.

"So, the solution is she comes with us?" I cocked an eyebrow.

"In part," Kelly agreed. "This is another 'hearts and minds' as much as it is a military choice, but let's go over it. First, from a military point of view, as Mike said, she can question the dead for us, and as a Nethermancer, it might be that her class skills grow powerful. Either way, though, her spells are going to help a lot. Did you ask about them?"

"I...no," I growled. "I got so caught up in everything that happened I totally blanked on it."

"I made notes, but essentially, as a Nethermancer," John pulled out a small notebook, reading off it, "she has the ability to question the dead, and in exchange she shares mana and life force with them. It's not much, but she basically bargains to get them to share what they know. The more mana and Life energy, the more she's fucked up and needs to rest, so go careful on asking her to do that.

"Second, she has a ranged destructive spell, called Soul Eater, apparently. It reads about as you'd think, but she can charge it up as well as fire it in a single burst. She's used it on a few rats, but never had a reason to use it on anything else. They all just collapsed, dead, but obviously I'm wary of trusting that for anything bigger. Might be powerful, might be crap. Rely on her for that with caution."

"Okay, makes sense," I agreed.

"Then there's Echoes of the Grave. Essentially, she can sense things. Take her to a place where there's been a death, and she can sense it...gets flashes of insight and information. And if the spirit is still there? She can contact it and make use of the first spell. If not, using things like a hairbrush and clothing can help, a bit like the way a dog tracks by scent, but this is by 'sympathetic resonance,' whatever that is."

"So that's the potential uses for her." I nodded. "And if she levels, she could get a hell of a lot of extra skills. Might actually be useful for you, John," I suggested, and he nodded.

"Believe me, if we could have had her before the fall? I'd have had her in a heartbeat. As it is now? Knowing we could take her to a murder scene and have her tell us who, what, and how? It'll be incredible for law enforcement and security. We can tell what kind of monster did it and so on. But that doesn't solve the trolling issue."

"That's where you, the girls and Ashley come in," Kelly said with an evil smile. "First and foremost, one of those girls has reached a class, and she'd kept it from us. Well, when she was asked, she pointed out that she didn't hide it; she simply chose not to come forward and tell us. That's not something that I like, and we really need to bring in the oath from the colonel as soon as possible to prevent this kind of thing, but I digress.

"She's an Etheric Chronicler. Her name is Xanthia, though I'm damn sure that's not the name she was born with. She can tell your class by looking at you, as well as hints of your future. She was the one who outed Catherine to the others and told them all what she can do."

"Okay, not happy about that, I'm not gonna lie. Yeah, we didn't say they *had* to tell us, but I thought that was kinda implied by the whole 'we're training you to help the dungeon' thing!" I ground out.

"Yeah, she's had this ability for a while and didn't bother to tell us. That's not sitting well with Kelly, and frankly, I'm not too pleased about it either." John agreed.

"Now, abilities-wise, we've got Mana Resonance. Basically, she can tune into someone's mana signature just by looking at them. This lets her see their class, how powerful they are, and any significant magical abilities they've got.

"Then we've got Temporal Echo. She can focus on a person and see echoes of what they've been up to in the past few hours. It's not perfect—more like snippets and fragments—but it could be damn useful.

"Potential Insight is next, and this is where it gets interesting. She can analyze someone's mana flow and get an idea of how they might grow or what abilities they could unlock. It's not set in stone, mind you…more like educated guesses.

"Lastly, we've got Aura Transcription. This one's neat. She can make a visible representation of someone's mana aura. Others can study this, so she can effectively share what she sees with the rest of us, but it's basically her writing down what she thinks. But with her actions so far, I'm not exactly feeling overly trusting of her, are you?

"You'll note she's got four abilities or spells as well, and she claims to be level eleven. That she's even passed five is a hell of a jump, considering she's been living in the dungeon and a month ago wasn't even a mage. In that time, she's learned enough to gain a class—somehow—and then she's hammered the living shit out of it, mainly, as near as I can tell, for the amusement of her and her friends.

"Now, there are limitations. The information she gets can be abstract, needs interpretation. And if someone's got a high enough level or has abilities, I'm betting they might be able to hide from her perception.

"Also, again, this 'Xanthia' was the one who outed Catherine to the others. She told them what she could do, but kept pretending in the magic lessons that she was still learning. That's partly why we're in this mess now.

"So, that's what we're dealing with. A potentially very useful ability in the wrong hands, causing trouble. We need to decide how to handle this, and that brings us back to Ashley."

"Oh gods," I muttered. "Why do I feel like this is going to give me a headache?"

"Well, she also apparently was the source of the rumors about Ashley being your personal courtesan, and why she gets to do 'whatever she wants,' so Ashley paid her a visit. Turns out that although this girl and her friends are a group of vipers, Ashley is a damn mongoose. They had no chance against her. And when it all started coming out, she started wrapping them around her little finger. She's going to be making use of them, heavily, as part of her team. She's asked that before you go—and yes, I know we're short on mana—but she's asked that you use the oath stone and bind them to you, and her." Kelly grinned.

"Now, what Ashley suggests and intends you do, provided you agree—and I already have, just so you know, so if you want me to deal with this shit, then back me—is to take Catherine with you and power-level her. She's going to reintroduce her into the groups with the help of Emma, Jenn, and the boys as our resident Nethermancer, and a damn powerful mage they don't want to fuck with. Then she's going to have Emma and Jenn publicly back her. They've apparently already agreed to adopt her, and Emma lives for this kind of shit."

"So, basically, I keep my mouth shut, we've got a mage who might be damn useful, might not, but who will be damn useful to the dungeon for investigations if nothing else, and probably against the undead. I just need to back you and give her a chance to prove herself, and I don't have to fuck around with any of this manipulative clandestine shit?" I asked, and both Kelly and John nodded. "Hell yes. I agree."

"Glad to hear it. The usefulness of the girls and Ashley's burgeoning spy network lessens if people know that they're yours, though, so you need to go inside there…" She pointed at the entrance to the training dungeon. "And you'll find them waiting with Ashley and the oath stone. Go have fun."

With that, she shooed me off, turning back to the others.

"Uh, you said there were two things?" I prompted her, and she blinked, surprised, then winced.

"Dammit, Drak!" She groaned. "I forgot about him. Hell, I keep forgetting about him. He's got a gift for that! Okay, between his hiding in the pool around the clock, trying to rent out the use of his scale-cleaning services to every kobold female that crosses his path, and the fact I've had to restrict his access to stop him spending a fortune in mana on healing potions, we need to do something with him."

"He's summoning potions?" I pressed my lips together.

She nodded. "When we made sure he understood that he could only summon minor potions, and only those that he could 'afford' after helping to absorb enough mana to offset it, he went out and found Starr. He and Ashley are our main source of potions, and they're still weak as hell, but he's started making himself indispensable."

"That sounds like a good thing," I questioned curiously.

"It would be, except he's basically gaming the system. It's much cheaper for us to produce the healing potions by harvesting or summoning the ingredients and then processing them into healing potions, than it is to summon them. Again, it's the way the dungeon is set—to force us to learn the skills, not just use it as a crutch."

"I understand." I nodded.

"Well, Drak helped to make the potions, then started making his own. He's essentially cutting corners to put in a token amount of effort, less than an hour a day, and as soon as he could make his potions without Starr and Ashley, he cut back to the absolute bare minimum of helping. Instead, he started creating his own gear—paid for by breaking down and getting the dungeon mana—and has set up a supply situation where he came to me yesterday and offered to sell us more potions that he'd produced for himself, provided we give him more powerful potions in return."

"That sneaky bastard," I muttered, unable to help but be impressed.

"He's essentially finding the loopholes and making the most of them, screwing us over, and yet...doing nothing 'wrong,'" Kelly growled. "He even made the point that you gave him permission to do whatever he needed to, as long as he helps, and he sees *this* as helping!"

"So the question becomes, what do you want to do about him?" John asked grimly.

I thought for a minute, then shrugged. "Fuck it. Put him in charge of potion production."

"*What?!*" Kelly gasped.

"He's motivated," I pointed out. "He's literally drugging himself, but instead of making himself ill, he's basically making himself as healthy as can be. All right, well, we've got Sierra working on the glass, Alison on the sand, and we're constantly running trying to keep everything going.

"We've got someone who's addicted to the potions, so he's got a serious drive to make sure they're as powerful and concentrated as possible. I bet he's been experimenting to increase their efficiency as well. Put him in charge and make it his problem to get the potions out. Set him solid targets, and make it his job. If he wants the highest strength potions? He needs to figure out how to make them, and that means we all get the benefit of that."

"That feels wrong as hell," John muttered. "We're enabling an addict."

"One who will continue until he gets his fix, and if we try to cut off will only find a way or be driven to do something we can't prevent," I observed. "He's doing the literal opposite of hurting himself or others right now, and isn't that the only reason we regulate drugs and shit anyway? So that people don't hurt themselves?"

"And they don't hurt others in trying to get their fix," John said, before nodding. "It's a pragmatic approach, and not one I particularly like, but...I can't deny the elegance."

"You're welcome." I grinned. "Now, was there anything else?"

Kelly sighed, smiled despite herself, and then kissed me deeply.

"Be careful, be faithful, and when you're home, I'll give you a treat?" she suggested.

I couldn't help but laugh. "I'll be good," I assured her, kissing her back.

"Good boy." She winked. "Seriously, Matt, I love you, so, you know, be careful, okay?"

That last was said seriously, and I nodded, gave her one final kiss, then headed in the direction of the training dungeon, determined to get this last step out of the way.

It was almost an hour later by the time everything was done and we were rolling out of the dungeon. But damn, the rumble of the convoy made me grin.

I had the main dungeon, overall, as set up and safely running as much as could be. We had a pair of dungeon seeds—one ready to be turned into the mobile dungeon and one ready to be deployed to the south—with a third to be summoned if we managed to gather enough mana, and we were off, finally!

Rumbling across the bridge into Gateshead, I was instantly glad we'd taken the time already to claim and repair it. The thought of driving so much weight over it could have been a nightmare, but it was solid, and we made it without issue.

As the convoy maneuvered on, we'd spread out a little, with my smaller team inside the dungeon transport and the boxer that had been put aside for us, currently filled with kobolds.

It was a bit of a squash for the massive creatures, but it was infinitely better for them, as cold-blooded creatures, to be inside rather than hanging onto the outside.

I needed to be inside the bouncing and swaying transport to work on the new dungeon core I was about to bring to life, so it just made sense for the others to be with me.

Before we left, we'd entered the core area, the inside of the two shipping containers, joined end to end, and I'd winced. I knew that everything had been produced on a budget, and that as we went, I'd be able to add to the dungeon, but damn.

We had several mana crystals set in place, ready to go, to assist the start of the new dungeon. That was going to really help, because until the new dungeon was up and running, we were stuck on cold steel floors, without so much as a goddamn cushion.

I'd opened my mouth to say something, then shook my head and climbed in, moving to the far end and getting started.

Do you wish to activate this Dungeon Seed at this location?

You will have 36 seconds to place the Seed and activate it before it becomes unstable and detonates.

Dungeon Lord detected. You have a sufficiently high enough level of Control to be able to assume full command privileges over this Dungeon Seed. Do you wish to assume control?

Yes/No

Estimated area consumed by Dungeon Seed detonation: 0.473sq miles.

Same as the last seed I'd activated, I noted, before approving it and moving on.

Current Level of Seed Activation: 0%

Dungeon Core Seed has been placed and is absorbing mana. Full control privileges will be released at 100% charge. It is recommended the Core is not disturbed until primary activation has occurred at 10%.

Current Charge: 1%

Estimated time to full charge: *calculating...* **367 minutes**

Basic functions will be made available to Dungeon Master in 18 minutes.

I winced at the timescale, but accepted that the original time for the northern dungeon had been so much shorter because it was in a high mana area. This...well, it wasn't.

As we bumped along the road, the broken asphalt making its presence known, I held the seed, watching as it started to change.

The outer shell of the seed cracked and split down its length. A gritty, barely visible mass like overlapping spiderwebs in their tens of thousands poured free. I underhand tossed the seed toward the farthest point from the others, sitting myself between them and it.

It wasn't because I didn't trust them. Instead, it was to make damn sure the thing didn't attempt to drain them!

Instead, we watched it. The distant sounds occasionally made it through the walls, along with the jolts and, now and then, a crash of one of the vehicles pushing a parked or dead car out of the way.

The seed continued to break apart, lifting slowly into the air atop a spike that...well, it was like watching goddamn paint dry, to be fair, or watching ants make a sandcastle.

Grain by grain, they appeared, stacking one atop the others, with the lower ones smoothing together and sliding higher and higher.

It was mesmerizing...and after a few minutes, boring as all hell.

"This was what it was like last time?" Mike asked, clearly looking to start a conversation.

"More or less," I admitted.

"Worse," Chris corrected. "He'd chucked it into this old man's toilet, right? Here we all are, the passage is full of smoke, we're all dying of inhalation, and he's chucked the seed in the crapper!"

"Seriously?" Mike asked, surprised. "Why?"

"Well, it all started with the snow…" Chris said, getting more comfortable and playing storyteller.

Seventeen minutes later, the dungeon eventually began the final countdown to unlocking for me. I let loose a sigh of relief and braced myself against the wall, closing my eyes and settling back, escaping the magical tale Chris was spinning. I was fairly sure there'd be a dragon in it by the time he was finished.

Five seconds.

Four… three… two… one…

Zero.

As the counter ran out, the world around me slowed, shifting from reality into a wire-frame outline of everything nearby, harsh lines and angles granting strange structures to my companions.

With a thought, I slid through the wall nearby and saw the slowed reality of the world beyond as it crawled by.

Dungeon Seed Activated — Permeate area? — Yes/No

Nope! No, no, no! I made that choice very clear, as the fucker would have stripped everything nearby to fuel its activation. I'd be fine, but the rest of the team? They'd be rendered to mana and used to feed the new dungeon's growth.

Instead, I chose the manual option.

Confirm: Manual Permeation and expansion selection.

Yup, that was the badger, I decided.

As soon as the selection was made, a new bubble was forced outward from the core, five meters on a side and circular. Everything inside it that I selected became part of the new dungeon.

Obviously, again, I didn't select the others—I made sure they were safe—but the four small mana crystals that were all we'd had time to make were fair game, I decided. I selected them, but prevented them from being broken down just yet. I needed to wait and boost the next stage of the dungeon's early growth.

Seed Core Stabilized. Please select from the following options:

1. **Form symbiotic link with parent dungeon.**

2. **Form secondary associated/unassociated dungeon.**

3. **Specialize dungeon core for subsidiary action.**

257

Again, I chose the same as the northern dungeon—option one—and I made a symbiotic link to the main dungeon.

The reason was simple. I could have started this one from scratch, starting it at the Stone level and working its way through the lower options until we managed to research and claim all the various forms of tech. Yeah, it was probably something we'd need to do, eventually, but I had neither the time nor the resources to do it now.

Instead, as soon as my choice was made, the next screen popped up.

Symbiotic link selected: Estimated time to full activation: 58 days, 4 hours, 2 minutes, 57 seconds.

Nope! Next screen, please.

Activated and fully charged Dungeon Seed housing detected. Please select from the following options:

1. **Break down and absorb Dungeon Seed housing, providing an immediate mana boost to the new core — Time limited.**

2. **Store Dungeon Seed housing and begin growth of secondary Seed.**

3. **Consume Dungeon Seed housing for a one-time boost to this dungeon.**

Option three was taken, unsurprisingly, and the core surged with light and life as not only the seed, but now the mana crystals were absorbed, boosting the early establishment by a massive degree.

Clearly this was how the dungeons were *supposed* to be established, as the prompt changed again.

Symbiotic link selected: Use available mana?

Yes/No

The changes cascaded through the dungeon, and I groaned as the new prompt popped up again.

Symbiotic link boosted: Estimated time to full activation: 1 day, 11 hours, 16 minutes, 58 seconds.

"Dammit." I opened my eyes. Time around us had resumed, and I sighed, reminding myself that it was some kind of sped-up hyper-focus I was experiencing. There was no way the galaxy just slowed right down for me to do that shit—it was insane. "Okay, people, good news/bad news situation!" I called out, while mentally designating everyone in the small area and upgrading their access level.

"What's up?" Chris and Mike asked at almost the same time.

"The area's too low on mana. As much as it's absorbing all it could from the seed housing and the mana crystals that we brought, that was all we could get produced in the time we had. So…we're all on expansion and claiming duty."

"Damn, I hate this shit." Chris winced. "Sorry, Matt, everyone, that came out louder than I intended. Let's get to it, I guess, then."

"Let's." I totally understood what he meant. "I'll summon a single undead to push out as well. Fortunately, we already had to do this once, but…the range might get fucked up. Remember, we're moving, so this is going to be a learning curve for us all."

As soon as the link was fully established, the dungeon would be able to access the full list of available designs. But just like last time, for now all I had were a limited number of options, fortunately, they again included the skeleton.

As soon as the skeleton appeared—the small amount of mana that I'd reserved from the mana crystals that was specifically for this was a kick in the tits, compared to the levels of mana we had available these days—and I dragged it into the dungeon sense, designating its areas and setting it to work.

Then I turned to Mike and shook his shoulder, making his eyes pop open.

"What's up?" He blinked in confusion.

"We should be past the park already, but we're still surrounded by parked cars as we head for the highway. Can you get up there and get the driver to stay close enough to the parked cars for the next hour so we can absorb them?"

He paused, then grinned. "I can, but you know what might be a better idea?"

"Go on."

"Think we can manage a two-hour diversion, to get enough mana to unlock the access and anything else we need?"

"Oh gods." I closed my eyes. "I hate it when you come up with plans."

"Weird, that…Kelly says the same…"

"For a good reason!" I snorted.

"About you," he finished, before winking. "Seriously, I know we're short of time, I know that, and two hours is a lot. But, if we loop around and head north on the highway, instead of south, forty minutes' drive from here? Newcastle Airport." He said it and left it like that, waiting.

"The airport…" I muttered, brain rushing ahead and back to holidays, and trying to remember why I'd wanted to go there recently.

Jez Cajiao

"Come on, you can do it," he prompted, and I glared at him, trying to work my way through, until…

"Goddamn," I whispered as my eyes shot open. "The planes!"

"The planes." He smiled widely. "Fancy a little diversion?"

"Do it."

CHAPTER TWENTY-FOUR

In the end, it took more than an hour to get there, not the forty minutes he'd suggested. But along the way, we absorbed several dozen vehicles and a load of random shit as frequently as it came within range.

All told, trying to claim things from the mobile dungeon was…weird.

As we travelled, we pushed the mana field out farther and farther, but every inch cost mana. And the more we pushed, the more of us who were pushing, the faster we used up the little we had.

By the time we rolled up to the airport, or as close as we could get, it was down to us all taking turns to absorb, while the others relaxed and talked.

Also, minor point, the light we'd had internally when we moved in? It'd been from the mana crystals. So, once they were used and the dungeon core stopped glowing as madly as it had at first? The darker the storage container became.

By the time the transport rolled to a stop, we were all more than ready to get out and stretch our legs, if nothing else.

When my turn through the doorway and into the cold mid-morning air came, though? Damn.

A plane had clearly been on approach to the airport when everything had happened. Judging from the devastation that had cut across the highway that led up to the airport like a knife, it'd ended very badly.

The highway—it was a minor one; the main highway that ran north–south was about ten minutes behind us by this point—was a two-lane one, with two lanes heading west and two east, more or less.

Then, from there, as you drove along, there were numerous overpasses, where other roads led up and joined or ran off.

All of that was pretty normal, and certainly not of much concern normally.

What *was* of concern, though, was the massive trail of devastation, the broken and burned seating, the mangled wreckage, and the million and one sections of devastated human detritus that covered the road.

Standing there on the trailer bed and staring out, seeing the destroyed road as the crisp frost covered everything, hiding little but softening the edges and evidence with a blanket of frozen snow, I cursed the fucking Cinthians all over again.

We all did.

Hundreds had died just in this crash. And considering the flights that had probably been in progress all over the world at that stage? Millions probably died in those first minutes.

"What do we do?" Griffiths grabbed a handhold and hauled himself up to stand alongside me, staring out across the ruined road. "I don't see us making our way through that. And even with the wreckage absorbed by the dungeon…unless you can get all of the scrap, we're going to fuck the tires up."

"We go around," I said after a brief pause to consider, nodding to myself as I said it. "We roll back, head up there…" I pointed to the raised area that bordered the road on either side and that hid the airport in the distance.

"The dungeon leads, and we'll absorb anything here we can get. Then we'll eat our way through the barriers and the hedges, solidify as much as we can, and we drive through the field on the far side."

"The weight of this thing…that's not going to be easy," he pointed out.

I nodded. "That's life, mate. Looks like we're on track for the new normal, though, as it should have been fuckin' easier than this."

That was more or less the way it went as well, apart from us running out of mana about two hundred meters from the edge of the airport and being unable to solidify the field between us and the airport into a solid road.

That left us all trooping out, and the entire lot of us all working together to strip everything nearby of any tech that we could. We dragged everything from laptops to car batteries to goddamn coffee machines back into range of the dungeon. After another hour had passed, we were slowly rolling through the deserted airport.

In the end, it was worth it, undoubtably.

We pulled eight hundred thousand mana from the first three planes, and that was incredible, considering that it was a single large commercial jet and two smaller ones. That was enough to unlock the link to the main dungeon, and it came as a hell of a shock to Kelly and Aly when I popped back into the command center and shouted "Surprise!"

The explanation was met with a mixture of reactions. They were glad that we'd managed to get so much done so quickly, and pissed that we were so far behind schedule.

Once the additional mana started pouring in, though, they had to admit it was worth it.

I gave everyone a solid hour to strip as much as possible, while the dungeon slowly rolled through the silent airport. Although we lost a lot of the mana we could have received—the dungeon could only hold so much at a time still, and the conversion to crystals to help kick-start the new dungeon was slow—it was still worth it.

By the time we rumbled back onto the nearby highway, the vehicles had been heavily upgraded, and the additional mounts were summoned.

The inside of the dungeon transport—now officially known as the dreadnought—had changed a lot as well. Considering that we were going to be stuck in here for the next few hours at the very least, most likely the day, I didn't have any problem making a few more luxurious changes as well.

Hammocks, for a start, weren't that expensive in mana. But spreading them along the length of the shipping containers, and extending those containers in length slightly, made a massive difference.

It was also hilarious watching everyone trying to get into them.

Then there was the food. With a little effort, we'd managed to extend the dungeon's influence from the transport around ten meters to the front and back, with a lot more on the right extended out than the left. That wasn't for a big reason, just because on the route we'd taken, the planes had been on the right.

The advantage for this, as we headed south, was that the other vehicles could pull in close to the right, in front and behind, and summon anything they wanted to eat and drink.

Again, minor things, but it made the passage of time more bearable.

By the time we caught up to Jack—he'd stopped and waited for us, in the end—we were less than ten miles from the main infantry base for the north. It was the center of all the basic infantry training for all of the British Army, and we'd still not run into any sign of the army, or the group that had been sent from our local garrison to here to report in.

That, as it turned out, was *not* a good sign as we drew close to the target.

"Contact!" I heard screamed distantly, roughly at the same time as heavy fire opened up, pounding the advance boxer into absolute scrap.

Judging from the arcs of fire, they'd presumably tried to avoid hitting the engine, most likely in preference for capturing the vehicle intact. But whoever was in control of the .50cal that they'd set up by the side of the road was, frankly, shit with it.

They shredded the driver's side of the vehicle—the right-hand side, as we were a civilized country—and then as it swerved out of control, they apparently pursued it and kept firing at it, right up until Jack broke free of the truck and started racing toward them.

They tried to track onto him, missing with at least three-quarters of the fire. And what did hit him was scarcely more than glancing damage.

The boxer that had been hit careened into the barrier in the middle of the road. Although the body of the vehicle had held up to the incoming fire—more or less— the windshield hadn't, and the driver had taken several direct hits.

He, we found later, was killed almost instantly, and Griffiths, who'd been in the passenger seat, grabbed the wheel, trying to get control.

It was too little too late, though, and the barrier buckled; the vehicle rolled. A second heavy machine gun opened up at that point. The gunners shouted and panicked as the incoming fire tracked across to the base of the boxer. Someone was either freaking out or clueless, as they were wasting their ammo on the more armored part.

263

That was when the other boxers, the mastiff, and the riders all returned fire with their heavy caliber mounted weapons. Brakes squealed and everyone tried to avoid adding to our own casualties by rear-ending each other.

The ambushers' camp, less than a mile from the army base we'd been heading for, was shredded. The sprinting figures that broke and ran were outlined by explosions as someone opened up with a rotary grenade launcher, but the damage was done.

Jack roared and tore into the few figures that stood their ground. The minor damage he'd taken did little more than piss him off at this stage.

"Push out the scouts!" Mike roared, already sprinting from the transport.

Although my instinct was to follow him, I didn't.

He took Andre and Jenn with him, left Jimmy and Emma out on the transport, and gave Chris a single nod as he took over the close protection of the dungeon.

I stayed in the dungeon sense, already pushing out and searching, sensing the little that was clear, but able to rise up fifty meters and stare around in shock at the area.

We'd been hit by a small outpost, that was obvious. After some four hours of travel and running around with nothing beyond snow and ice to be seen, we'd let our guard down, and now we were paying for it.

By the side of the road, some twenty meters ahead on the left here, hidden on the other side of a collection of shrubs and hedges, was what had once been a police trap.

It was somewhere that the police could park and wait, essentially out of sight until you were almost on top of them, perfect to catch you if you were speeding, or if they were waiting for a specific vehicle.

Between a load of added bushes and the snow, the old police trap had been hidden and upgraded into an outpost. Whoever had been manning it had clearly panicked when they saw the vehicles. Now, as our troops flowed out to encircle the outpost, its former inhabitants ran like their arses were on fire.

I scanned the area as best I could. Another post was up ahead, hidden on the right, and with a little movement around it still. But because of the bend in the road, we were currently sheltered from its view.

"Chris," I called, blinking awake and out of the dungeon sense to pass the word on. "Right-hand side of the road, just around the bend, about a hundred meters, there's another outpost. That's all I can see."

"I'll pass it on." He moved out of sight, shouting orders to spread the word.

Ten minutes later, it was all over. Both sites were cleared out, and the vehicles repaired, though a good soldier, an old friend of Griffiths' named Duke, was dead.

We absorbed him into the dungeon, using his essence to help to repair the damage the assault had brought, and then did the same with the attackers, though with markedly less respect and reverence.

It was the first time that Catherine had the chance to truly use her gift for the betterment of the dungeon. Although she was clearly nervous as all hell, allowing his close friends to say goodbye, and then allowing Griffiths to question one of the attackers, it made her use very apparent to the rest of the party.

It was still a case of unless she invited the dead "in," then it was only her who could see and interact with them. But as Griffiths asked the questions, she repeated them, then repeated the answers, and we found out all we needed to know.

When the fall came, the base here was split. First and foremost came the belief—from a commanding officer from the south—that the army would be needed to secure London. As it was the capital, the rest of the country was far less important.

Anyone from outside London would disagree with that, but he was the commander, and his word, especially in this situation, was law.

Martial law, in fact.

Of a little less than eight thousand serving personnel on site at the time, some eleven hundred had apparently been left, and that had been at the main base. I'd never served, though I knew plenty who had, so when I'd seen "Catterick Garrison" off to the east of the main road, heading south, and the odd times I'd driven through the main town of Catterick, perhaps three miles to the west of the road, I'd just assumed it was all part of the same base.

Now, as the dead man answered Griffiths' questions, I realized how wrong I'd been. This section, that these idiots had been set up close to, had apparently been an old RAF—Royal Air Force—base, one in the process of being decommissioned and reused as a heavy vehicle depot for the army.

This didn't sound like much of a difference—certainly, it'd never occurred to me that it was. But clearly, when most of the base had moved off, marching south, they'd left the now unusable heavy transports, tracked vehicles, and more securely locked up.

The remaining eleven hundred people on site, primarily spread across areas of the main base three miles away, had understandably pulled back when the monsters started prowling. They'd also taken most of the locals, who came to them for protection, with them.

Again, totally understandable.

That had, however, left this base that was neither really theirs, nor part of the RAF anymore, completely open. The dead man Catherine interrogated admitted that he and a small number of others who also lived locally had realized the opportunity that this brought, and had started to hit the passing caravans of people headed south in search of safety.

They'd basically dressed up in army gear and had jumped them, robbed them, and taken various liberties with them and their goods, before sending the survivors on their way, celebrating the "new world order" and their new place in it as "robber barons."

The base had already gone silent when they came, and they only knew as much as they did because they were native to the area.

Jez Cajiao

Whatever had happened to the base, they'd sent a small group over, looking to try to get food when their own supplies ran low. They'd found it locked up, but apparently deserted.

A group had run inside to loot the place, and almost immediately they vanished in screams, with spraying blood coating the inside of windows, panicked gunfire, and flying limbs.

Something had slaughtered every single member of the first group to go in. And when, bare minutes later, one of the horrified watchers realized that the windows that had been coated in blood seconds before were now spotlessly clean again...they'd turned tail and ran.

Nobody had entered the base since, as far as this idiot knew. Or, at least, if they had, they'd never been heard from again.

That prompted a leadership meeting, and Catherine was sent to rest with my thanks.

"So what do we do?" Mike scratched one bearded cheek. "Damn, I wish I'd shaved this fucker off before this," he muttered.

"That's why you need to be clean-shaven, soldier." Griffiths grunted. "Beards and helmets add up to ingrown hairs, and annoyed soldiers who get distracted."

"Bollocks, we just don't look as pretty, that's all," Mike rejoined, before sighing. "Seriously, though, what do we do now?"

"Under any other circumstances, I'd say you need to explore it." Kelly joined us in the dungeon sense, as the five of us hovered above the dreadnought, staring out to the distant towns and barracks over the hills.

"Yeah, but we're already on a time constraint," Mike replied. "If we didn't have that? Sure."

"I don't like it," Griffiths said. "Whatever happened there, it's right in the route of resupply for us as the dungeon, and that means its unwise to leave a potential threat here. As a soldier?" He shook his head and glared around. "We know as soldiers that it's not always practical to live by the axiom 'leave no one behind.' No matter what you want to do, sometimes in war, that's just the way it is. Otherwise, every single retreat would fail, every assault would be ten times as bloody, and well...anyway."

He was clearly struggling as he went on.

"We know that someday we might be asked to make that ultimate sacrifice so that our brothers and sisters, and our family back home, can live. We *know* that, and we accept it. That's part of what being a soldier is. What sucks ass here right now is that this is their home. People die, and these days they die all the time and for stupid fucking reasons. When you join up, you accept that you might have to give your life, but knowing that something happened here? Right here in the goddamn middle of the main goddamn base for the north? We need to check it out."

"Griffiths..." I started, and he shook his head, raising one hand.

"Matt, I mean it. You trust me to lead our forces?"

"Yeah," I agreed, frowning.

"Then trust me on this. We need to know what happened here. If we don't, then we could all be fucked. Catherine said that he saw nothing at all, and that the base was spotless afterward? That means that others will see the same. If nothing else, we're allowing free experience to march into a meat grinder, leveling up something until it gets to the point that it could slaughter us all."

"I massively disagree," Aly said. "Yes, we need to know what happened, of course we do, but we're already on a time crunch. Repair the boxer, mourn your loss, and move on."

Even Mike looked at his wife in surprise with the hard tones.

"It sucks," she agreed. "But we need to be realistic. If we stop at every point we need to investigate, it'll take a month to get to the south coast, and there'll either be none of you left alive, or there'll be an army of refugees with you."

"Exactly! We have a duty—" Griffiths started.

"You have a duty to protect the dungeon and those you need to save outside of it." Aly cut him off. "The king, the royal family, your own family, and any civilians you can reach. I know you want to look after your fellow soldiers. That's what your oath and heart is telling you, right? Can you do all of that and reach the south coast in time? If you get mauled here, or worse, all wiped out, what happens when the undead get here?"

"Fuck."

"And…" Kelly sighed. "Let's say you save them all here—you find the monster or whatever and you kill it. You free them and everyone celebrates. Then you're too late to stop the undead making landfall and they start raising every single grave they come across? You'd have saved people to have them *all* die a week later."

"I know that, dammit, but—" Griffiths growled, and this time it was me who cut him off.

"But you need to do your job," I said. "We'll dispatch a squad from the team here, the goblin riders and the Scepiniir, along with…" I paused, thinking it through and staring into the distance. "I'd have said to leave them with Beta. But that's not gonna fly," I grumbled, thinking fast.

"Beta?" Mike asked, confused.

"She's the most experienced dungeon-born we have. She's lethal and a survivor, not to mention can kick the shit outta any ten regular monsters. But, she's a kobold and it's goddamn cold here. We send her out there, and she'll be unconscious when they need her."

"Add to that, if any human who's not used to their kind sees her, they'll fire on her or panic." Griffiths snorted. "No, that's not going to work."

"No, and that's why I stopped," I admitted. "Okay, Griffiths, five people, and you and Mike aren't one of them."

"What?"

"You heard me," I said sadly. "We can't afford to stop. That diversion we already had gave us a massive boost, but we couldn't afford that either. Now? We need to make up the time and we've already been hit once. You can have the two teams of ten dungeon-born and a squad of five soldiers. That's the maximum. No more. You leave them here to scout and try to make contact. And it's a volunteers-only mission. We're out of here in fifteen minutes."

"If there are soldiers still in there, the Scepiniir and goblins will be seen as monsters." He shook his head. "They add to the threat, not lower it."

"And if they die, we can resummon them," I said flatly. "You lose your soldiers, they're gone forever. You willing to take that chance?"

"You think I don't know that?" he asked angrily, gesturing to the torn-up vehicle.

"No, I know you do, but sometimes you need reminding," I said. "Griffiths, you know *you* can't stay. I know you want to. I know that and I understand it, and I damn well feel the exact same goddamn way. But if we do? We risk the deaths of everyone else in the damn country."

I shook my head, exasperated. "It's literally that serious, mate—that's the level we're at. If it doesn't advance this exact mission, we mark it up and leave it. You don't want the dungeon-born to be the point of contact, and I agree it's probably not the wisest idea, then we leave it the hell alone and we move on."

"Matt…" Griffiths ground out, gesturing over in the direction of the main base. "I get what you're saying, *sir,* but—"

"Then you understand why I'm saying no," I said. "I agree with your point about the dungeon-born. And considering what we're headed into, we cannot risk the human soldiers here as well. Get them back on the road, Griffiths. That's an order."

"I…yes, sir." Griffiths snapped a smart salute, then vanished from the meeting.

The sudden exit left us all in silence for a few seconds.

"Well," Kelly said softly.

"Yeah," Aly agreed.

"You disagree?" I asked, already second-guessing myself.

"No." Mike was the one who spoke up this time. "No, it was the right call to make, and he'll know that too. We *all* know it. It's just refreshing to see this side of you, that's all."

"What?" I asked, confused.

"The commander and Dungeon Lord," Kelly said.

"Eh?"

"Matt, you're a nice guy, all right?" Aly said, trying to explain it. "You remember back when we first met?"

I nodded, and she went on.

"You remember when Kelly and Mike arrived, and they, like I had, helped themselves to your guns?"

"Yeah, fuckers," I muttered.

"Why'd you let us do that, Matt?" she asked. "I mean it—why?"

"Because I needed backup, you needed a weapon, and..."

"And?" She prompted when I paused, trying to figure out how to say it.

"And I didn't need them," I admitted. "I was more lethal without the weapons, with my magic and more, so if I gave up the guns, it meant we've got more strength and depth."

"Exactly," Aly said. "Most people would have never considered that. It's the smart way to do it, and it was a lot of kindness to scared people, especially when you barely knew us all. But it was the beginning of the end of the world, Matt. Most people would have never even considered it. You could have killed any of us at any time with a thought, though. Not just in summoning creatures to do it, but with your magic. You could have done that, and easily. So, instead, you deliberately made it so that you were at more risk because you knew it was the wisest plan overall, and it was the safest for the rest of us."

"So?" I asked.

"So, you did it without a pause. You were annoyed, and you didn't hide that, but when you could have demanded the weapons back, and forced us to give them up if we didn't want to, you didn't. Most of the time you've been asking people to do things, and even when the shit hits the fan, you try to do that. It doesn't always work, and yeah, there's times where you need to listen. Not hanging those assholes Gerald and Sharon, for example, when they first got kicked out."

"I still think that was the right thing to do," I muttered.

"And all things considered, in hindsight, it probably was," Kelly agreed. "But at that point, it would have made you look like a dictator. Look, I'm not saying this very well, but what I meant was that there's times when you listen to advice and that's good, but when you need to, like just now, it's also right to remind people that you're the Dungeon Lord. If you give an order, they can damn well follow it."

"And..." Mike added, "with the other dungeons that are going to be set up, they're subservient to yours. That means that their leaders are too, and you need to make that clear. We don't need a dozen different dungeons deciding that this direction is better than that one. Ask, and take advice, yes. When push comes to shove, though, you rule."

"You do," Aly agreed.

I looked from one of them to the next, before letting out a long breath. "Thank you," I said. "Sometimes it just feels wrong, you know? I was raised to listen, and that running something—a shop, a house, a government, whatever—it should be a democracy where everyone has a say."

"It *should* be. But it's never a good idea." Mike snorted. "Why do you think businesses are run by a single person at the top? Say what you will, capitalism gets shit done. Democracy doesn't. You're doing good, kid."

"Thank you."

"Okay, looks like things are getting sorted out." Aly pointed at the way that people were clambering back into vehicles, the damaged one already repaired thanks to the wonders of the dungeon, as Griffiths barked orders.

"Okay, come on then. Time to get back to work." Mike gave Aly a ghostly peck on the cheek, a nod to his sister and a wink, and then vanished.

I did much the same, kissing Kelly, waving to Aly, and then exiting the dungeon sense as they, too, faded.

CHAPTER TWENTY-FIVE

Jack's repairs weren't that bad, but the big automaton needed enough of them that I seriously considered bringing his remodel forward, before deciding not to.

I *wanted* to, but the cost, the parts, and, more to the point, the time meant that I couldn't. Also, I had very definite plans for the big lad, and until we had more tech unlocked, I wasn't going to be able to bring him to his full potential yet.

Not that I'd been using him to that potential, I'd be the first to admit. He was mindless, mainly: there were no needs, nor wants from him, so I treated him as the automata he was. That meant that, unfortunately, as he wasn't in front of me, and with everything else that was always going on, I tended to forget about him entirely.

Also, when I needed the area scoured of any threat, and generally patrolled? He was incredible at it.

If I took the time to replay his memories, I got a nonstop, sped-up blur of him battling, shredding random creatures and moving on. That was actually awesome to watch, but he'd started hunting down the attached monster nests since his last upgrade, rather than just killing whatever he encountered and moving on, and that...

It underscored just how useful he was at doing his job, frankly. If I took him off that, I'd need to double or possibly even triple the patrols we had out there.

Yes, they'd all get more experience, which was an idle argument I'd had more than once with Chris—right up until I asked him whether he wanted to be the one who replaced Jack out there, slogging through the snow and melting crap of winter.

He usually promptly summoned a large drink, often something either hot chocolate or fruity based, winked, and generally made up some story about how he'd love to, but couldn't possibly because of...

And that was it. We were back to Jack roaming and being the incredible bear-shaped slaughter machine he was.

I actually felt guilty about taking him away from the dungeon, along with so many of our forces. But considering what we were likely to be facing in the mechanist's dungeon, it just made sense.

So, Jack's upgrades got kicked down the line until we were finished with the next battle.

I fully expected that the work would take at least a day, possibly two, and until we were in place, we couldn't afford to take what was probably our heaviest weapon out of the field.

That meant that he spent the next four hours lying atop the shipping containers of the dreadnought, being repaired, while we rolled steadily southward.

While he did that, and considering there was little else for us to do besides be good little boys and girls, push out the dungeon's area of control and try to absorb anything we could…I spent a lot of it working on my magic again.

Not spells—definitely not the spells. Mainly because if I tried it and made a mistake, then everyone inside with me was toast.

No, I worked on *enchanting*.

Or, in my case, imbuing. Imbuing an item, a weapon, or a being with magic was a toss-up between blind luck and science in my eyes, in that I was getting a much more solid expectation of "do this; get this."

Where it changed was the minutiae of the details. As I'd said before, if I added in Lightning to a creature or creation that wasn't able to handle it? Well, that was where I got screaming, collapsing minions and exploding items from.

If instead I added something that the item or minion was aligned with? That was where the magic happened.

Now, thanks to my little ascent into godhood—something I was still fairly goddamn confused about and fairly sure I was only at the baby-steps stage of— I'd lost all my old gear.

Fortunately, I'd given Finn the bag of holding beforehand to study, so that'd survived and he'd made a sort of "man-bag of holding" as a replica to provide the others, but that was a different story.

This meant, though, that I was down to standard issue for most of my weapons, and I really wanted some good shit, dammit! Plus, giant metal monsters and all were out there, and I felt like I was going to need to even the score a little.

That was why I was now in a much smaller, enclosed section at the back of the containers, just in case anything went wrong.

I had both my sword and hammer to hand, and a large kite shield that I was planning to wear strapped to my back—but that might be a bit much, even for me.

I set that aside, along with my helmet, gauntlets, and more, planning to work on enchanting everything, once I got the chance. For now, they would just have to remain "normal."

I decided to start with the hammer, mainly because I genuinely had no clue what I was going to do with any of them, beyond the usual, and I'd never had the spare mana nor the time to work on the hammer before.

First things first—I examined it.

Hammer	Item

A dungeon-summoned war hammer. This item can be used for war or peace, and yet has been given a hint of its future in its naming.	
Durability 250/250	Special Abilities: 0/0

Well, yeah, fairly obvious, I had to admit. The newest generation of hammers had come out of Finn's crafting teams. Although it wasn't markedly different in any ways that stood out, the durability was a little higher than the average hammers, and they looked pretty good.

It was a cross between a sledgehammer and a war hammer from the movies, in that one side was a flared then flattened head, large and meant for crushing your enemies' skulls. The other side was a spike, slightly hooked and ready to be driven into enemy armor, probably so that you could shuck the unlucky fucker out of it like an oyster from its shell.

The haft was an experimental, specially treated mixture of wood, metal, and rubber. I had no clue how it worked, not at all, nor how they'd made it, but Finn had been telling everyone that it'd be used to replace tires on the vehicles next.

It was as strong as steel, had the vibrational dampening properties of rubber, and the flexibility of wood. That alone would have been worth a king's ransom in the old world.

It was darkened as well. Some aspect of the overall crafting process left the surface less reflective, apart from a small collection of marks that ran the length of the head.

I'd asked what they meant, and one of the crafters, apparently an old world fantasy buff, had shyly admitted that it was a form of elvish—the kind we used to make stories about, not the kind that presumably existed out there somewhere—and it said "Speak, friend, or be entered." She'd added that it was a play on the code to enter Moria, and I'd just nodded.

It sounded vaguely familiar, but I didn't have time at that point to fuck about with it.

Now, with absolutely no hint as to what the hammer's affinities were, and a fairly good understanding of what would happen if I tried to force too much into the fucker, I was being very careful.

First of all, to my mind, the head of the hammer and the haft were very different. They *felt* different and they *looked* slightly different.

They'd been made separately and then combined. That meant, to my admittedly stupid mind, they probably had two different capabilities.

It also might result in the fucker exploding the first time I used it. But to hell with it...what was life without a little risk?

I started with as pure and unaspected mana as I could manage, resting the hammer across my knees, with one hand on either end, and mentally selecting just the haft.

It poured in easily. More and more was accepted by the second. As I watched, cycling my mana up from my core and along my arms, pouring from my palms into the solid matter that lay beneath them, first a hundred, then two, then three hundred mana slid out of me, and into it.

At nearly four hundred, I started to feel the strain. At four hundred and fifty, I could sense I was definitely approaching the limit.

I also got the feeling that with numbers like this, and as little as I understood, stopping and starting would be a massive mistake.

I switched from pure, sliding a little Lightning into the haft, then quickly reversed course as from the very first drops the shuddering grew worse.

Lightning was clearly not what the haft wanted. Neither was Air when I tried that. I didn't try Fire, having gotten the hint. Instead, I tried Life and Earth, shifting through to Nature as the feedback lessened and more mana was accepted.

Another fifty was all that I managed to pour in. But I also felt that the haft was the focus of the magic, not the head, and hopefully that'd help.

Now, as I slowed and stopped the mana, I nodded to myself.

There was a sense of "is that it" as I lifted my hands. I shifted the hammer around, this time letting the base of the haft rest on the floor, with the head on my knees, and I placed my hands on either side of that.

The first touches of pure were accepted, no question, but this time it was clear before I'd even reached a hundred that I'd done something wrong. The head felt weirdly malleable, almost like I could squeeze it as hard as possible and leave fingerprints in it.

Being me, I tried and found that I couldn't. But still, it felt like it should have worked.

I tried Earth, and the feedback got worse. Air? Much the same. Fire came next, and the shaking intensified. In a moment of panic, thinking it was about to explode, I tried Water.

Much to my amazement, the Water bloody worked! I couldn't see how, nor why, but the hammer soaked up another two hundred and fifty mana like parched earth, before I finally decided that was all that I could afford to spend.

Finishing and settling back to look at the hammer, I found that the head's feeling of softness, while also being apparently solid enough I couldn't damage it, had only increased.

I stared at it for long seconds, before examining it again. It'd been granted two special abilities, but absolutely no details on what they were.

With a definite sense of annoyance, I swept the notification aside and focused back on the hammer, trying everything to awaken it, including cutting my palm and smearing blood on the head and shaft—which sounded all kinds of wrong now that I thought about it—before giving up when still nothing happened.

Considering a little blood had been what was needed to awaken the imbued weapons before, that was even more confusing and annoying, but fine. I dumped it on the floor and brought up the sword instead.

The sword was larger than the original bronze longswords we'd all been armed with in the early days. Although it wasn't a great deal heavier, that it was at all was a point, I'd noticed. Bronze was a heavy metal, and when I'd upgraded to steel, it'd felt a little weird that it was so much lighter.

Now, whatever the changes that had been made to the latest generation of weapons, the sword felt heavier and more…solid, I guessed. I didn't have the words for it. I just knew that it seemed different, with an almost comforting weight to it as I'd accepted it from Finn earlier on.

Now, as it lay across my knees and I stared into its depths, fingers tracing the damascene patterns, I felt a definite resonance that I recognized instantly.

Almost before I'd thought or realized what I was doing, I was pouring a little Lightning into the blade, and *damn*. It drank it in like the ocean accepting a cup of water!

I poured in more, and more. The blade warmed slightly under my palms, but beyond that? Nothing. After five hundred and it still felt like I wasn't achieving anything, I continued, frowning. At seven hundred and fifty, I shook my head and kept going. At a thousand? I cut the stream there. It could take more—I wanted to give it more—but I wasn't confident enough in what was to come that I dared waste so much of my mana now.

On stopping, though, the entire blade pulsed once. The swirling patterns of the rippled metal beneath my fingers seemed to dance and shift, before solidifying once more.

Examining it, I got nothing beyond that it was a sword and imbued with a dungeon lord's gifts. It had only a single ability as well, but I set it aside, staring in wonder as the patterns shifted slowly, drawing my eye back repeatedly.

Again, I tried giving it a little blood, and yet there was no feeling of strumming power as there usually was at this.

The final work I decided to do was the shield. This one, thankfully, came with a very clear reaction to the mana: Earth and Metal, both solid forms of their own. The shield took five hundred of each, before I stopped.

It was clear that although weapons and shield were blooded and bonded to me, they weren't going to reveal their secrets just yet. But on seeing that there were two abilities again with the shield, it was enough for me to guess that if there were two large and distinct forms of mana in an enchanted—or imbued—item, then they would each have an ability to grant.

Setting it aside, I moved back through to let the others know of my little triumph, before sinking back into my hammock and starting to meditate, replenishing my mana as much as possible as the hours passed.

Griffiths had most definitely learned from that attack that the holiday was over and had pushed out a boxer into the lead as a scout.

The Scepiniir riders, now with their mounts, were ranging out to the sides. Their magewhiskers added to the sheer weirdness of humanoid friggin' cats that were sapient, riding massive cats that weren't.

Whatever they were, though, they were damn fast-moving, and as scouts, if they were slightly faster, they'd have become the primary scouts for all our forces pretty much straightaway.

They were almost as fast as the boxers, though, and they were certainly fast enough that they were useful in the fields, racing up and over the overpasses, roaming to the sides of the advance.

Truth be told, due to the issues the boxers had with the parked and abandoned vehicles by the sides and across the roads, they'd have probably become the primary scouts there as well, if not for the fact that Griffiths came up with the plan to load a pair of corpse lords atop the lead boxer and the secondary, and he moved his ass to the third in line, now a mastiff.

What happened was that the lead boxer would roam until it encountered a blockage. It'd pull up, drop off the corpse lords, and provided they could clear it, then it'd load up again and roam ahead.

If they couldn't clear it immediately, they'd leave the pair working and drive back, taking up the next spot in the convoy, and the former second in line would roam ahead in their place.

They'd then add their pair to the blockage, and when they cleared it, they'd take their two and roll ahead. The second in line would stop and reload its corpse lords as we reached the former blockage, and boom. Everyone kept rocking with minimal interruption.

In theory, once we hit a blockage we couldn't deal with in this way, then we'd roll up and absorb whatever it was. But so far, that hadn't happened.

We continued to clear as much as we could, absorbing it into the dungeon as we went. And thanks to a pair of converters we summoned on the dreadnought and then connected up to the conduits, we were constantly harvesting as well.

As the hours passed, again and again I checked our progress, only to curse and grumble. Thanks to the limitations of the tech, the joys of the weather, and the damage done to the roads, we were essentially relegated to twenty miles an hour.

All told, it was another nine hours after we'd set off from the airport, in the dead of night, when we encountered the first of the mechanist's creations. And fuck me sideways with a live salmon and chili lube, it wasn't the happiest of experiences.

Like us, he'd clearly decided that a scout or guard was a good idea. When we were introduced to the fucker, it was right as Mike, Griffiths, and I were in the middle of a conversation in the dungeon sense.

"So, we reach this turn off here, we head for Leighton Buzzard, and you continue on," I agreed. "We'll continue straight off to the dungeon, do some scouting with the dungeon-born, and you head on. You bypass London and the surrounding area entirely, and straight on to Folkestone."

"While you hit the dungeon, assess it and see if you can crack it. If you can't, you take the second dungeon seed and head straight for London, hole up, begin the conversion and creation of the new dungeon," Griffiths agreed. "As much as I hate splitting our forces, I don't see another choice."

"Two missions, two teams," Mike concurred, sitting back. "No need to try to split us all again...just makes sense. So what do we—"

That was when the entire conversation was derailed. Three huge forms activated within our supposedly secure perimeter, startling us all with a combination of the dungeon's sudden burgeoning warning sense, the exterior echoing shouts, and the roars of challenge they issued.

We were in the dungeon sense at the time, and as such, I led the way and flitted through the wall and into open air. The other two followed me a heartbeat later.

The scene before us was one of instant chagrin, mayhem, and devastation, all at once.

The three creations had seemingly been laid dormant at the top of the nearby hill. Judging from the positions of the tracks and the current stunned looks on the faces of nearby Scepiniir? They'd had no clue that the mounds were anything at all.

That was the joy of our lives—we got to experience every fucking day anew.

What had looked like mounds of abandoned farmyard equipment, almost entirely buried by snow and ice, had apparently stood up, shaking off their concealing cover, and let lose a bellow of challenge, before sprinting down the side of the hill right at our convoy.

What made it worse? They looked like mechanical bulls. Giant mad-ass mechanical goddamn bulls!

Why was that worse, some lunatic observer might ask? Well, my answer would have to do with the friggin' size of a giant mechanical bull, the horns, and as the lead bull raced ahead, the way its eyes and body started to radiate brilliant yellow-red light.

Mike barked orders to our people inside the dreadnought, and Griffiths did the same outside. But the three bulls were coming damn fast, and there was no way that we were going to take this well.

Time from them appearing at the top of a nearby hill, to them punching their way into the convoy and hammering full-on into their targets was measured in seconds. But still, in that time, all the boxers had opened up with their mounted guns, two of the Scepiniir had managed to get off a rail gun shotgun's shot at their targets, and Jack had leapt from the top of the dreadnought to challenge the trespassers.

Unfortunately, the .50cal on the top of the boxers did minor damage, and although by concentrating fire on the left-most one of them, the soldiers managed to take that fucker to the ground with its front legs reduced to scrap...it did nothing to the others.

A grenade hit the lead bull full-on in the face. The bull tossed its head and bellowed, but it barely slowed.

"Brace yourselves!" I heard Mike shout.

I cursed, realizing what the hell I'd missed in a moment of detached observation. They were moving hellishly fast, and the farthest right-hand bull was aiming directly for the dreadnought.

The new lead bull, who had also started glowing with brilliant reds and yellows that shone from within its frame, plowed headlong into a boxer, dipping its head at the last second. Two gleaming horns drove through the side of the vehicle's armoring, and into the occupants.

The vehicle skidded sideways, bouncing on its wheels. The side dented inward and screams filled the air as the bull ripped its now bloody horns free.

Worse was yet to come, though, as it planted its hooves, drove its face forward into one of the ripped holes in the door, and then, the mouth locked on.

Lamprey-like, clamps extended down from the sides of its face to latch onto the vehicle. The bull froze in place, almost as if it were sniffing—or kissing—the side of the boxer.

Then it vomited flaming napalm into the vehicle's interior.

As that was happening, the last bull was closing on us. Although Jack had been repaired and was even larger than these fuckers—if not by much—it had the advantage of momentum.

It wasn't glowing, but damn, it hit him like a truck, lifting him and slamming him back into the side of the dreadnought.

Considering at this point it was basically a pair of armored shipping containers with hammocks inside…it didn't go well for us.

I was hurled from the dungeon sense as the shipping container suddenly rocked back. A massive dent appeared in the wall nearby and sent me from my previously comfortable hammock, and into the one next to me.

Shouts and screams sounded from all directions, as well as roars. I could hear distant heavy fire being poured into the fuckers.

"Stop!" I barked at Chris as he reached for the door, about to open it into that bedlam. "Ricochets!" I fought to untangle myself from the hammock and snarled, then viciously wrenched it apart.

"What?" Chris barked, his blood clearly up. "That's our people out there!"

"And if we open that fucking door, they're firing a .50 right outside!" I snarled. "One of those things crashes in here and we're all fucked up!"

"Dammit!" he shouted, glaring at the door and then back at me. "What do we do?"

"We make another door!" I snapped, bracing myself against the wall and focusing. I started to change the armoring into an openable door to let us out the far side from the fight even as I spoke quickly.

"Those without much experience, I want you to shoot the fucking bulls *once* with whatever you have, then get back out of sight and stay down!"

"Are you crazy!" Emma shrieked. "What bulls?"

"Fuck's sake!" I snapped back. "Check the dungeon sense. Then fire at them *once*, and then get back inside! Use the rifles!" With that done, I wrenched the new door open and jumped down, bending my knees at the drop. I launched myself into the air, twisting and staring down as I lifted higher.

The scene was a mess. One of the bulls was down, the first one, and though its forelegs were shredded, it was still glowing and pulsing with bright light.

Considering the head was more or less facing toward the main fight right now, I growled and cycled my mana, drawing in and up as much Lightning as I could.

The second bull had released the clamps that had held its mouth over the holes in the side of the boxer. It staggered backward, presumably intending to get a run up at something else, and as it turned, the flexing panels on the sides of the beast had apparently uncovered something. The incoming .50cal fire must have managed to find a gap, because it suddenly coughed, let lose a gout of smoke, and with a sound like stripping gears, it jerked from side to side, its back legs locking up.

That was all the break that was needed. Everyone concentrated their fire on it. An insanely brave advanced goblin sprinted at it, then threw himself down on his back and skidded underneath, just as he unloaded a double blast from the rail gun shotgun into its head at point-blank range.

It would have been incredibly cool and impressive, I had no doubt, if the snowy ground under the beast hadn't just been both melted by the backlash of heat, and scratched clear by the pounding, kicking hooves.

Instead, the sticky asphalt slowed him, the blast ricocheted, and the bull, now missing half its head, toppled forward.

The brave goblin disappeared under his kill with a crunching of bones and a brief, despairing shriek.

The bull toppled sideways and somehow managed to lift what was left of its head. It unleashed another bright and horrifically hot gout of flaming liquid, coating the side of another boxer, before a burst of .50cal to the side of the head, where much of the armoring had been blasted free, took it out.

That left two: the crippled one and the one that Jack was fighting. Jack was in bear form, and a giant automata bear fighting a giant mechanical bull was just incredible to watch.

Jack had been partly gored; great torn and scratched panels ran his length, both down his side and half of his face. His right arm was damaged, and barely able to lift with a dented and broken panel on the shoulder.

The bull, though—the "Colchis Bull" as I examined it—was clearly coming off worse. Its face was torn and dented; one horn was entirely missing, torn free by Jack. And as I glanced over, he was twisting the head sideways.

Colchis Bull	Mechanical Creation

279

These massive mechanical constructs are designed to resemble the mythical Colchis Bulls. Created by a rival mechanical dungeon, these formidable war machines combine ancient legend with advanced technology. Their ability to camouflage as mundane objects makes them perfect for ambushes and surprise attacks.

Each bull is a masterpiece of engineering, with a frame built to withstand significant damage while delivering devastating attacks. Their unpredictable nature and raw power make them a terror on the battlefield.

Ability: *Flame Core Overdrive!* The bull's internal core heats up to extreme temperatures, causing its body to glow as the power builds to a crescendo, destroying the tempering of its body, but providing an overdrive ability that allows for high speeds and devastating damage.

Ability: *Thermal Detonation!* When damaged, the Colchis bull can overcharge its mana core, building to a highly destructive self-detonation.

Ability: *Adaptive Camouflage!* When stationary, the bull can alter its external appearance to blend in with its surroundings, making it nearly indistinguishable from mundane objects.

Ability: *Reinforced Frame!* The bull's mechanical body is highly resistant to small arms fire and explosives. Only concentrated fire from heavy weapons or precise strikes to weak points can significantly damage it.

Weaknesses: Overwhelming force, unknown

HP 1387/2500	**Special Abilities**: 4/4

I glanced back at it, then snarled. It was starting to glow. I turned back to my target. "Take them down!" I roared, as I unleashed my overpowered Lightning Bolt into the bull's head.

It hit, filling the air with a brief radiance before dying away.

I cursed. A mere double-strength blast had done little more than char it; the metal warped, and secondary crackling discharges danced away from the point of impact.

"Fine, you want to play?!" I snarled. This time, I went up to five hundred mana invested in the blast. Behind me, more fire rang out, followed by a smaller, yet clearly powerful thunderbolt blast that rocked the other bull as Jack grappled with it.

He yanked the head suddenly sideways hard enough to send the bull to the ground on its side. The crash of so much steel landing rang out. With his enemy downed, Jack gave it no chance to recover, instead pinning the face down with one paw and all his weight, as the others started to tear and gouge at the neck reinforcing.

Both bulls were pulsing madly now. The light grew brighter and brighter; I shouted for everyone to fall back, glorying in the feeling of my lightning as it ran up and down my arms...the dancing, crackling light caressing me, as I built it up...then unleashed it.

It hit, a bar of thick blue-white light that rocketed out from my hands, the wrists clenched together and my teeth bared in challenge. All around me, people flinched back from the sudden overpoweringly painful bright light.

It hit the bull's forehead. The bolt punched in and left both a burned hole in it and a far more powerful secondary discharge that caused the glass of both of its eyes to explode free.

The Colchis bull's pulsing suddenly faltered. The light staggered like a drunken dog, then failed, with smoke and a smell of burnt plastic rising from the massive creation.

I twisted in place, summoning my mana again, hanging over the battlefield...only to let it die away, as Jack lifted his maw free and roared his triumph to the night sky.

He'd bitten clear through the neck and torn the fucker's head free.

CHAPTER TWENTY-SIX

"We can't afford to let them react." I looked around at our small team, as Griffiths and his people continued to triage and fix what could be fixed, or absorb what couldn't.

The design for the Colchis bull had refused to unlock. Unfortunately, it required a mechanical aligned core, or several more tech unlocks. I understood it, really; the mechanist dungeon would be impossible to face if this was its standard-issue minions. But looking them over?

I suspected it wasn't.

They were big, for a start. And the mana cores that were the beating hearts of the bulls? They were...inelegant, to say the least.

I'd looked at them—the one that I'd had Jack rip free of the most damage, at least—and it was clearly on its last legs even before it was killed. The overdrive and planned explosion left sections heated and warped out of place. But the main issue?

They required a truly massive amount of mana to operate.

I examined them as carefully as I could, waiting on the others gathering their gear, with Jenn doing as much healing as she could for the most badly injured.

What I found was that the bulls might be incredibly deadly foes if they took you by surprise, but they weren't particularly agile. And if you gave them the runaround for maybe ten minutes? They'd have to stop.

Their storage was that limited; once they'd done that, they'd be collapsing and waiting while their core refilled from the ambient mana.

Examining the local hill had shown me that it was right on the edge of a high mana area as well—Coal mana, which was a little weird. But basically it looked like the enemy had set these up here, on low-power mode, waiting and refilling with the intention of killing anything that came past.

If they were set to watch out for us or someone else, I didn't know, but I did know that the dungeon-born required mana to keep going. They could eat and drink as normal creatures, but they still needed a little mana. Although they could survive on just mana, without one or the other, they'd die, just as surely as the rest of us would.

These had been set here, on the edge of a high mana zone, to watch the road, and to be ready, just in case.

Now we had a choice: we could wait, get everyone together and we could assault the dungeon as a group, now that we knew how dangerous some of the creations were, or we kept going.

We decided that the best course was that we attacked as soon as Griffiths and the others were ready to move out, because we couldn't risk the fuckers getting their hands on the dreadnought.

"I know," Griffiths said to me grimly as I walked up. "You need to go, and so do we. Five minutes, people!" he shouted, even as Patrick, Jimmy, and Andre finished tying the gear onto our new transport.

"We're almost ready," Chris told me, jogging up. "Jenn's on her knees...totally drained herself, but nobody else is going to die. And you can summon more healing potions on the way." He directed that at Griffiths, who nodded his thanks.

"Jo says she's good." Griffiths sighed. "There's a lot of burns that would have been a lot worse if not for her," he admitted before offering a hand to me. "You sure about this?" he asked, as I took it.

"I am. You need control over the dungeon to be able to do what you need to do, and the choices are that you either all come with me to attack this fucker and this is left undefended, or we leave a load of our people here to defend it and we attack with basically what we have anyway. The only difference is, by the time you reach the Channel Tunnel, you might be too late." I shrugged, as we let go, and he nodded.

"It's shit, but that's life," he said. "Fair enough. I'll fuck off and go take over the world." He grinned at the joke, before sighing. "Seriously, Matt, take care of yourself and your people. Get this shit sorted out and then get yourself down to join us. We're going to need the help."

"We'll do what we can," I promised. "The London dungeon seed might not have time to fully establish, but if I can set it up somewhere and get it started even, it might be enough to turn the tide."

"Do what you can, but if it's not going to work, abandon the plan and head for us." Griffiths nodded. "No plan survives contact with the enemy. The undead are the priority for now."

"I will," I assured him. "Good luck."

"And to you." He turned back to the bedlam behind him. "All right, people!" he roared. "Let's get moving!"

I stepped up and pulled myself into the rear of the boxer that had been put aside for our use. The loss of one of the boxers and an entire team from it, plus the damage done to another, would have been crippling in more normal circumstances. In this case, as horrible as it was to admit, we'd lost two human soldiers, which was terrible, I know, but the rest of the boxer's contingent had been kobolds.

It felt wrong to be relieved that it was "only" the dungeon-born that had died instead of "real" people. But as much as I tried to hide it, it was a relief.

The damaged boxer was being repaired by the magic of the dungeon, and the injured were being treated and healed.

Jo, I was willing to bet, could have healed them all. But one glance into the back of my transport to see Jenn as she rested her head against her husband's shoulder, fairly glowing with pride as she talked about her level-up, showed it'd been worth her sharing the task.

She'd gained practice, the experience, and most definitely the real-world experience of the situation, not just the awarded stuff from inside the safety of the dungeon.

"You look like shit," Emma was saying to her sister, who grinned back at her and waved her off.

"Mana fatigue," she admitted as Chris started the engine up. "I pushed a little too hard, that's all. But I'll be back to full in just over an hour."

"Until then, we've got health potions if we need them," I reminded everyone over my shoulder, looking around. "How many did we manage to summon on the way?"

"A medium each," Robin said quickly. "And three weak."

"That'll keep us going," I assured the group, before turning back to Chris and staring out of the front of the windshield "I fuckin' hope," I finished under my breath, before wincing, remembering that we had Saros and the kobolds in the vehicle as well. Knowing those buggers, they'd have heard that perfectly.

Actually, I reflected, anyone who had upgraded their Perception would have as well. Double fuck.

The remaining trip wouldn't have taken that long, not normally. But now, with a small contingent of Scepiniir, five of them on their cats, and with Chris driving, Mike in the front passenger seat, and everyone else inside the vehicle pinned to the limited windows to watch out into the darkness for any kind of sign of more enemies, it seemed to take forever.

The one advantage I had was that we knew exactly where the fuckers were. The link that had been created when war was declared allowed me to pinpoint the enemy and...

I paused, trying to figure out why that was giving me the willies suddenly. I knew where the enemy were. That was an incredible advantage, and yet...something about this was wrong. A little voice at the back of my mind shrieked at me there was danger, but I couldn't figure out what the hell was wrong with it.

It was a damn useful thing, being able to spot the location. And it wasn't like it'd moved at all. He and his dungeon were still in the same rough area it'd shown me originally.

I knew that the undead leadership weren't in the UK yet, because I could feel them over that way still, and the distance was too great. Hell, I couldn't even see them on my mental map yet. And that was great news because...that meant...that meant that they weren't here.

I kept worrying at it, knowing that there was something wrong here, something that was so incredibly, utterly alarming and yet...I couldn't tell what it was!

They weren't in the short-range access I could see from this little baby dungeon. That was both great because they weren't about to hit us and fuck us up, but it was fucking terrible, because...

I froze as it all suddenly came together. My mind screamed as a thousand little hints and details just twisted a fraction of an inch to the lefty, and the cogs, instead of spinning, finally connected.

"*Shit!*" I bellowed it aloud, startling Chris and making him almost crash before quickly turning to the others as everyone scrambled to see what had gotten such a reaction. "Dammit, just get ready," I said. "We're about to be hit again."

"What's going on, boss?" asked Andre.

"I don't see anything," Chris warned me.

I shook my head, too angry at myself to form coherent sentences right then.

"Just pull over, fuck's sake!" I snarled. It was obvious now. Might as well call myself Captain Goddamn Hindsight, I realized. If I could see the dungeon, thanks to that declaration of war? Well, that thing had two sides, and that meant that fucker could see us!

"Which way?" Chris asked grimly, staring first out the front, then to all sides.

"What's going on?" Mike checked his weapon, getting ready.

The others had started getting ready as well. They'd already been keeping watch, but now with a warning that we might be attacked at any second, the atmosphere changed drastically.

"What's going on, boss?" repeated Andre. The big man leaned forward, and like the others, checked his weapons again, getting ready for the fight.

"Yeah, seriously, what the hell, man?" added Chris. "I don't see shit."

"How could I be so stupid?" I raged at myself as my mind ran back and forth over the obviousness of it. As soon as the tires skidded near enough to a halt, I leapt free. The door behind my own jerked open almost as quickly as Andre and Mike jumped out into the night as well.

Mike dropped to one knee, rifle raised, scanning the silent frosty night, as the bigger man stood over him. Andre spun in place, looking to the left, the right— hell, up and goddamn down in confusion.

I couldn't see anything, but that didn't mean they weren't out there, I knew. Given something as obvious as a way to watch your enemy coming directly to you, though, there was no way I wasn't going to be setting up an ambush if I were him.

Cursing, I bit my lip, before turning back to Chris and the others as they stared at me through the windows and started to climb out.

"No," I said quickly. "You guys need to keep going..." I paused and then forced myself to speak as calmly as possible as I realized the little issue with sending them off into the night without explaining anything.

"Okay...listen up, and then you need to leave. I'll explain it all, but we don't have much time! I just realized if I could tell where *they* are, then they can tell where *we* are. Or more accurately, they can tell where *I* am!"

"Are you sure?" Chris glanced around but accepted what I said.

"No, I'm not, but I should have thought about this." I cursed myself.

"How?" Chris asked. "Seriously, dude, how the hell does this work? What should we be looking out for?"

"Chris...I just don't know. I'm making this shit up as I go along." I rubbed at my face and swore in frustration. "When I accepted the declaration of war, I got a link...a way to see where the enemy was," I explained. "It's not as simple as that sounds, but it's not far off. I don't get to see them down to the exact street. And it's not like I somehow fly above an interactive map of the world and just jet across to look down and see them. Instead, it's more of a static map, all right? In this case, I knew the dungeon was in Oxford.

"I don't know *where* in Oxford... like, I don't get a postal and an address I could give to a taxi. I just know roughly it's over there, and around this area, in general." I paused, sucking down a breath and fighting an urge to shout. "Jesus, I'm a fucking idiot! I got so tied up in having advantages that nobody else does that I forgot I'm facing another Dungeon Lord."

"Okay, so what do we do now?" Chris asked.

"You fuckers get back in the van," I decided. "You get back inside, turn around, then loop back up the highway to the last turnoff. Then, when they're not going to be watching you anymore, come back down. Take another route to Oxford. Head west, then change direction a bit and then come around from the north. I'll fly south from here as well. If we're lucky, this Dungeon Lord Simon is as much of a fucking idiot as I am."

"Yeah, I mean we can hope but let's face it, you're like the Olympic standard, mate," Chris quipped, trying to make me feel better with a little brotherly abuse I knew, but I didn't have the time for it.

"Yeah, well, we can hope he's silver at least, okay? So, I'll head south. Hopefully he'll keep watching me and we can drive some of his support out of position. You guys come from the north... Mike, have you still got that flare?"

"Are you for real? Flares have been out since the '70s." Chris grinned. I glared at him and he winced, taking the hint.

"Yeah, I've got it," Mike assured me. "What's the plan?"

"I'll make it nice and simple. I'll head south, see if I can get their attention and if they follow me. I can start going all god of lightning then, and trash the place...pick a fight with them and pretend I'm all alone. Once that happens, you come in from the north, start searching and hopefully kick some ass and take some names. If you get in the shit or you decide that it's time for me to come back, then you fire that flare."

"So, we're winging it then?" Chris grinned at me.

I nodded. "Dude, when are we not winging it?" I asked rhetorically, before sighing. "Seriously though, just once I'd like a plan to go the way we want...you know, just for the sake of variety?"

"Okay, everyone, you heard the boss." Mike grunted. "Back in the van!"

"I thought it was a boxer?" Jenn asked in a low whisper that carried, and Mike, Chris, and I shared a long look.

"Can you take one of us with you?" Chris asked, and I snorted, shaking my head.

"Seriously, mate, I appreciate the thought. You know I'd always rather have you at my back, but right now? It's going to be really obvious if I start fucking around." I paused. "Plus, I mean, what the hell, dude, how would I take you with me?"

"Easy, we head back to the mobile dungeon—"

"The dreadnought," I corrected.

"The goddamn trailer," he countered with a grin. "We go back there, and I fit you for a saddle. Seems simple to me."

"Head back and loop around," I growled. "Chris, you know that this is incredibly important, right?"

"Yeah."

"You know that we can't afford any fuckups, that people will die, and that only someone I trust with everything could ever be the person I'd leave in charge with this, right?"

"Oh yeah." He straightened up, nodding.

"Well, if we had that fucking furry bastard Thor with us, I'd sooner leave him in charge than you. And we all know he'd wander off in a fight to go lick his balls. Mike, you're in charge, mate."

"Thank God." Patrick sighed. "I nearly defected to the other side there."

"I'd have come with you," I said. "If Chris is ever truly in charge of anything, then we know the world has gone to shit."

"Don't you leave me behind, you bunch of bastards," Chris added. "You think I'd want to be in charge? Believe me, I know it'd be a clusterfuck. Matt?"

"Yeah?" I asked.

He paused as the others were locking seat belts and racking weapons quickly. "Be careful, brother."

I nodded, sighing. "I will. And you do the same."

"Here." Mike quickly pulled the map he'd brought with him out of a pocket and showed it to me. "You're sure this is where he is?"

"No," I growled. "That's where I *think* he is. That could be massively different. For all I know, it's locked onto him personally and his dungeon is ten miles away, or the other way around. My goddamn kingdom for a wiki!"

"Head south slowly," Mike said seriously. "Give us time to get back and turn around. The smaller roads are less likely to be watched, but they're also more likely to be blocked. Give us an hour. Then, even if you've not seen the flare, start coming back."

"You sure?" I asked, and he nodded.

"We can't afford the time, or the distraction," he said. "This is a sideshow, meaningless beyond making sure they can't hammer us from behind when the real fight is going on. We need to remember that and take them down hard and fast."

I nodded, stepping back.

He leaned a hand down, bumping a fist against my own, before smacking his palm on the side of the boxer.

Chris took the hint and started to move, even as I lifted gradually into the air, hanging a few meters off the ground as I turned slowly.

"Time to make some noise," I muttered, mentally prodding Jack, who stood off to one side by the side of the road, and sent him into the lead, as we searched for a new road, heading south.

It didn't take long to find one, fortunately. Yeah, I didn't have to follow a road—I mean, Jack could probably plow through houses, so hedges weren't an issue—and I was flying; if they were tracking me somehow, then me following a road would make a lot more sense and raise less questions, I was betting.

As I went, I wondered at the sheer madness of coming out and supporting a lord of the undead...*Unlife*, yeah, but come on...in a battle against another Dungeon Lord at all.

He was apparently a human—the name of Simon was a hint at least—and he was already dumb enough to have joined a war against the one Dungeon Lord who was consistently winning.

Then he'd joined it on the side of the friggin' undead? It wasn't like deciding to support Celtic or Rangers for the cup! It was a seriously long-term decision...although, if I was honest, if you came out as a Celtic supporter around a bunch of Rangers supporters, it might be equally as long-lasting and probably terminal for your health as signing up to support the undead.

I flew along long-abandoned streets as I passed through the old towns that surrounded Oxford, arcing to the south by southwest. Minutes turned, one by one, as I stared, searching for any hint of risk, of a threat to me, and then, to any sign of life.

There were depressingly few.

A couple of gang types, a looter, a pair of what I thought were kids at first, and then I realized were feral goblins...

As the minutes climbed, and I started to feel like it was time to turn around, I came across the first sign of "normal" life in the distance. I checked that Jack was still with me and that he wasn't sensing anything else. We drifted through the silent night in the direction of a collection of lights.

CHAPTER TWENTY-SEVEN

The houses I saw in the distance were set atop a small hill and were cheerfully lit, the golden light of candles and possibly a fire shining out at the night from a collection of windows.

As I drew closer, I climbed slightly higher, staring in bemused wonder. The houses were inside a small compound. A high fence ringed it, in turn set atop a solid stone wall, and yet...the collection of a half dozen houses stood within the protective fences, walls, and—yeah, I did a double take and then nodded to myself—a damn frozen moat as well.

Everything there screamed "keep out!" But then, inside? The houses were red-bricked and tall, looking like they should be straight out of a lifestyle catalog in the nineties.

The fucking place was an absolute collection of madness. They were a single step from announcing that Santa was inside and ringing bells, hot chocolate on arrival and the best of the girls from his 'naughty' list, and then, on the other side of the coin, they were doing everything they could to keep people out.

Frankly, I loved it.

It was either an absolutely blatant trap, or I'd found somewhere that people were actually holed up and were trying to live out the apocalypse. My money was on the former, especially as close as it was to Oxford and that I'd seen hardly anyone else anywhere.

That was concerning. No, that was downright terrifying, as was—

My running thoughts broke off with a suddenness that was impressive as a figure wandered into view upstairs, then just as quickly vanished.

She—because it was *very* clearly a she—hadn't slowed nor looked out of the window. But when I looked at the next window in line, expecting to see her there a few seconds later, I frowned.

No sign of her.

No sign, and she'd walked from one side to the next, and...and again, she suddenly showed walking in the opposite direction, with an almost supernatural smoothness to her gait as well.

It might not have been obvious from down in the street, but from here? Where I floated, above and to the side of the compound, I could see in the window clearly.

Although I could barely see her head, I could see that her left arm ended at the wrist—just *stopped*—and the right was the same.

Between that little difference and me wondering why the hell a woman—apparently on her own—in the goddamn apocalypse would choose to wander around the house, in front of the windows, fully naked?

That was enough of a weirdness to finish the image for me. *Definite* trap.

But, when you know it's a trap, and you've got both a little time to kill and a need to make sure the enemy is paying you attention, and not your friends?

Well. It just made sense, right?

That's what I told myself, anyway, as I directed Jack to stay back and remain as hidden as possible, on the very slight chance that whoever or whatever was maintaining this trap wasn't paying attention.

I didn't think it was likely, but then I also thought I'd figured out what this was.

I was betting it was a man-trap.

Not just in the sense that "here's an apparently naked woman, all alone and defenseless…come on in, any scummy men in the area" but also that there was more hidden to stop any victims getting loose.

Plus, frankly, I really wanted to kick someone's arse.

I was feeling really stupid about forgetting the local Dungeon Lord almost certainly could sense me as easily as I could them.

I didn't get why the outside was so well protected around a trap, but I figured I'd get an explanation or not, so fuck it.

I descended smoothly, landing just inside the perimeter and lifted both hands up. My rifle rested against my chest, with my sword hilt over one shoulder, shotgun over the other, hammer on one hip and handgun on the opposite, and shield hanging from the hook on my back.

All in all, it felt a bit ridiculous, both pretending not to be a threat when I was armed enough for a squad and when I knew, just knew, the fucker was a trap. But hey, that's life.

A shriek echoed from inside the house. A second later, the door creaked open, accompanied by a distant scream of "Help, please help."

I snorted, glad my helmet covered my face.

It was all I could do not to burst out laughing, but I decided to keep playing along and struck a heroic pose, fists on hips and head thrown back.

"I shall save you!" I called out, doing my best space ranger impression.

It was probably ruined at least a little by the fact I was giggling to myself as I ran forward. But it gave me an excuse to slide my hammer free and secure my shield, which I suspected was all that I was going to need inside. I did mentally make a secondary all-lightning shield ready as well though, just in case.

I hit the slightly ajar door with my shoulder. The red paint contrasted sharply with the carefully wallpapered passage beyond. I slowed, glancing to the left and right, seeing immaculate rooms that awaited their inhabitants.

"Where are you, oh fair maiden!" I shouted, trying not to laugh, while paying more attention to the surroundings.

The passage had a strange line that ran its length and down the middle of the floor. Every what I'd guess were roughly two meters, a similar line ran up from the floor to the walls and looped around. Clearly each section of the house was individually decorated, with paper following those lines perfectly.

The grain of the wood that ran along the floor was a burnished oak. Though, as I looked, I noted the perfectly repeating pattern of the whorls and knots in that wood.

The staircase that led up to the second floor took up half the hallway. The passage ahead of me led back into what I guessed was the kitchen, with the main living room on the left and a study on the right.

A scream echoed down from above along with, "Upstairs!" being shouted in a strangely tinny voice.

"Downstairs?" I bellowed back. "Okay!"

Then, grinning, I started forward. There was no way this wasn't a trap now, I knew. The same exact scream and shout repeated again, and then when I shouted back that I heard them and I was going *downstairs*, it cut off abruptly.

The sudden cut-off of the scream, and then the exact repetition made me snort to myself with its obviousness.

Mechanist, indeed!

The voice quality was shitty.

I reached the kitchen, totally ignoring the steady "scream, beg, scream, direction" layout of recording from overhead. Although the kitchen looked fantastic—a cross between an old country house manor and one of those housekeeping magazines you always saw in dentist's waiting rooms—the differences, when you looked for them, were evident.

Everything was perfectly in place. The kitchen was spotless, like they were ready for a photographer and the state's assessors—or worse, their mother-in-law—to arrive.

Not a single dish in the sink, nor a knife out of place. The table was set for four people, even though I'd just seen what looked to be a young woman in her twenties wandering the house upstairs naked. And last of all? The refrigerator.

There were candles everywhere in the house, lending it an atmosphere of cheer and warmth, and a single glance at them dispelled even that illusion. They shone with a perfectly flickering—and timed—light.

As I looked from them to the fridge, I couldn't help but start to laugh.

The fridge would have been perfectly at home in an American household advert from the sixties. All the white polished, lead-based paint, the silvery brand mark on the face, the rounded edges…the whole show.

The thing was, that was what made it even clearer that this dungeon was bullshit. Nobody had made fridges like that in *years*. And even if they had? A house this size was big enough for at least a family of four—just like the table had been set for. That wasn't a big family, sure, but that fridge?

It had enough room inside for maybe a single shelf's worth of a modern refrigerator.

In the sixties, there were pantries and foods that either didn't need keeping cold or that people didn't know they should be looking after in that way, so it'd have been fine for then. But if that was fake, and the candles and the screaming naked woman…

I could go on, but instead I turned and called out, shaking my head as I did, and ready for the attack I knew was coming.

"Hello?" I tried.

The "Help me!" scream echoed out, plus begging, directions…

I shook my head and tried again. "It's a nice fake, but come on, we both know it's not working!" I called out conversationally.

"Help! Please help!" immediately echoed from upstairs, and I snorted, shaking my head as a second recording, once more complete with a shriek, rang out, "Upstairs!"

"If whoever that's supposed to be was really in danger? It'd be all over by now," I pointed out. "You want me up there instead of down here, and I'm betting that it's because that's where the traps are. Down here's the honeypot, am I right?" Getting no answer again, I went on.

"Now, there's the candles—fake; the fridge—fake; the woman upstairs and the… well, let's be honest here, the whole place is fake. So how about you come out and we talk?"

This time, there was a break before the recorded voice rang out again, begging for help.

If it hadn't been so perfect a repetition, I'd probably have fallen for it, especially if I'd not been on my guard already. There was a load of real pain in that voice, and as I hesitated, I cursed under my breath.

I wasn't doubting my assessment of the situation.

The repeating recording was literally identical. It was down to the millisecond, I'd bet, if I'd been capable of recording it. That meant that whoever had been shrieking originally had probably been recorded doing that, to provide the recording.

"So, you going to come out and talk to me then…Simon?" I asked, making an educated guess.

Silence fell, and I paused, thinking through it all.

Yes, I was a good ten plus miles to the south of where I was thinking that the dungeon was, and where this Simon was showing on the war map as being. But the way this place was laid out?

Maybe it was a subsidiary dungeon. But that I doubted very much, considering that—I quickly pulled it up and checked, then nodded to myself—I was in a low mana density area.

There was no reason to set up a dungeon here, none at all that I could see. But the perfect replication of the passage? That was a dungeon's doing, I was sure. The flickering "candles," the figure that glided back and forth upstairs…it was all a trap and yet…

The first attack was one that, for all my suspicion, I still didn't see coming until it was almost too late. It was the click of the latch that saved my life. The fridge door suddenly swung open, and a creation that could have only come from a mind as twisted as the one that came up with a clockwork orange, launched itself at me.

I spun, bringing my physical shield around, and triggered the Lightning shield at the same time.

It didn't have time to establish to catch the first blows, and my shield juddered and twisted in my grasp as hands latched onto it and tried to wrench it sideways.

The figure doing the wrenching, though, although mechanical in nature, was far too small. On seeing its attack had failed, it instead ducked down, braced its feet, then launched itself up and at me, aiming for my face.

It was a roughly humanoid creation, all bare cogs and iron, with a collection of small lights that lit and danced across its chest and limbs in confusing patterns.

Its feet were simple panels, laid out equidistantly around the central circular base. The hands? Much the same: four individual "fingers" that closed around the base. There was a magnetic clang as they clamped onto my shield.

I just knew they were going to be a fucker to remove.

The head, though? That was the fucked-up bit.

Where the trunk was a simple cylinder, clearly designed more to hold a power unit and to give a little length to the fucker, the head was on a swivel with a joint of the neck that allowed three-hundred-and-sixty-degree rotation.

Atop that was a collection of three discs, each with serrated, cog-like teeth like something out of a horror movie, or a mining show.

They rolled inward, all meeting in the middle in a mash of cogs that I mentally marked as a crushing and tearing design meant to render anything fed into it into dust.

Possibly red, mushy dust.

It threw itself at my helmet, and I yanked my head back, cursing. It lifted its feet; the clangs as they hit the shield and locked on echoed around the room as it swarmed up and over, reaching for me.

That was when two things happened.

First, my shield finally established itself all around us—typically late and with a minimum range that was on the far side of the fucker. And the second was that I brought my hammer up and forward, slamming it into that nightmare maw.

The hammer head might feel like it was almost soft metal, but the reality was anything but.

It rocketed forward into the head. The cog-like teeth clattered against the hammer and dragged it into the middle, and then they bounced and ground against it in a cascade of sparks.

Then I started pushing and altered my Lightning shield, pulling it in tighter.

The first hit of the head of the hammer against the cogs had been up from over the top of my kite shield and hadn't had a huge amount of force behind it. It was more of a "get that fucking pit of hell away from my face."

It'd still done a little damage, though, and as I started to shove it back, the little mechanical monster discovered a massive design flaw it'd been bequeathed.

Basically, once something was in that mouth, it wasn't coming back out the same way. Not without the cogs being smashed out.

I rammed the head backward into the Lightning shield and grinned evilly as the lightning both began to fry the monkey-like fucker, and through it, it connected back to me, where I absorbed the mana all over again.

That was when the second creation hit me from behind.

Or, more accurately, it hit the shield.

I turned, stepping forward and angling to the left as I looked to my right. I shoved the one trapped between my shields against the wall as well, as I glanced back at the sparking and thrashing creation on the floor.

"Well, you fuckers really are shit with lightning, aren't you?" I offered conversationally, before pulling back from the wall and then ramming the first attacker into it, again and again.

It only took three blows before it started to spark and jerk. That was when I noticed the damn chest area had started to pulse and glow a cherry red. I cursed, rolling the head of the hammer and cutting the flow of mana to my Lightning shield.

I peeled the twitching machine off my shield with a little difficulty, then pressed it to the floor and leaned hard on the hammer, trying to break it free of the hammer's head or hold it in place, before growling and kicking a flailing arm away from the shield again.

The feet were apparently magnets. Although they weren't hugely strong, they did latch on easily and that was annoying.

The second one leapt onto my back again then; I cursed and twisted, yanking my head aside as the maw tried to close over my helmet. Instead, all it managed to do was send a cascade of sparks in all directions and fill my ears with a sound like two chainsaws humping.

I lifted the shield and brought the lower edge down, hard, on the neck of the damaged one beneath me, hitting it twice. On the third attempt, the head came free.

I lifted my hammer and rammed it back over my shoulder as I took three quick steps back from the ticking-down timebomb on the floor. I reactivated my Lightning shield, grunting as it barely had time to activate; the explosion picked me up and threw me backward into the fridge.

Fortunately for me, the fucker over my shoulder took most of that impact. And as I had the Lightning active again, it was also heavily shocked by it.

I cut the mana *again* and stepped out of the wreckage, twisting and cursing as the magnets on this one's feet kept it attached to my back.

"Jack!" I bellowed, getting more and more annoyed with the little bastard. If it started to take more damage than it could deal with, it was likely to blow itself up. "Where the hell are you?!" I snarled, before making a monumentally bad decision.

I dropped the hammer and reached up over my shoulder—the other one's head was still attached to the head of the hammer, after all, so it was practically useless except for prodding something—and I grabbed one of the stunned creation's "hands."

It twitched.

A split second ahead, my brain caught up with how bloody stupid a move that had been on my part, and I yanked my hand back.

Even in my gauntlet, I felt the brush and scrape of the construct's cog-jaws as it lunged at my hand, missing by about a quarter of a second's movement, but instead clamping onto the back of its own hand.

Again, the cogs spun, and a cascade of sparks flew as it tore and chewed up its own hand. This time, snarling to myself, I triggered Lightning Bolt, right to the fucker's head.

The head practically detonated, followed a second later by its torso, and although my armor held—more or less—I was hurled from my feet, across the kitchen and into the far wall.

The table that had been between that wall and me exploded into splinters. And as for the counters that ran along the wall?

They turned out to be full of crockery to maintain the illusion. For a long collection of seconds, I was in a world of heat, pain, concussion, and shattering crockery.

Then I hit the floor and all of it fell atop me, just as Jack barreled in the front door.

"What a clusterfuck," I groaned to myself. My head spun as I tried to focus, only to see, as my eyes finally cleared, Jack standing protectively over me. And on the far side?

Another half dozen of the creations, all arranged around a single, half-broken one in the shape of a nude woman.

"So... I don't suppose I could convince you to never tell anyone how badly this went then?" I asked the question, getting only a cold, triumphant smile in return from her.

"Can you afford the cost... dungeon lord?" She asked, and I frowned, staring around Jack at her.

"Depends what you want." I grunted, struggling to my feet. "Fucks sake you knew I was a dungeon lord? Why the hell attack me?"

"Call me Marchioness, and I need a service from you dungeon lord, one I had to be sure you were capable of surviving…"

MIKE

"Keep your eyes open," Mike said for perhaps the fifth time.

Chris snorted. "Mike, mate, if they're not by now, they never will," he pointed out quietly.

Mike grunted in return, staring out into the darkness as the boxer edged around a long-abandoned car, bumping up onto a curb and driving half on and half off the sidewalk as they rolled past.

"If I don't remind them, they'll start arguing again," he said.

It was Chris's turn to grunt.

Since they'd left Matt, nearly an hour ago, Emma and Saros had quarreled constantly. If it wasn't over whether it should be Andre or Jimmy on the mounted .50cal, or whether they should stay inside, it was over whether Saros herself should be inside the vehicle.

She was bound and determined to be off on her own, leading the advance and making sure that the path ahead was clear.

That she'd not suggested this when Matt was still with them—or, more to the point, when they were back at the mobile dungeon, where a mount for her could have actually been summoned—was something that Emma hadn't wasted any time in throwing in her face. The two women of such radically different species had done nothing but argue over anything and everything since then.

What had started the argument in the first place was when Chris had misjudged a corner and scraped the side of the vehicle along a parked car.

That it was a mistake anyone could have made was a fair comment. That it was goddamn pitch black and the lights on this thing were crap? That had only added to it.

That the noise hadn't alerted seemingly anything nor prompted an attack was probably the reason they were all increasingly on edge.

But it'd been clear when Emma made a muttered comment about Chris's driving and Saros bit instantly, that the two women weren't destined to work together for long.

The roads had grown progressively worse over the last twenty minutes, cars parked here and there as if to deliberately be as difficult to get around as possible.

Now, as Chris cursed and twisted, trying to get just a little more of an angle to get around, swearing at all the gods that whoever thought parking a truck here was a moron, it all came to a head.

The first impact hit the front passenger's side of the car. The left-hand bumper dented as the entire vehicle clanged like a struck bell.

A split second later, the second and third impacts landed. One hit the hood slightly farther up the vehicle and bounced off, whiffling and vanishing into the darkness. The other hit the front left side again, this time ricocheting downward, hitting the curb, then bounced back up to hit the inside of the wheel. It snapped the axle as the wheel jerked out at perfectly the wrong time.

The vehicle, already bouncing and rocking, lurched sideways and dropped. The severed end of the axle crashed into the cobbles, even as Chris slammed it into reverse, frantically trying to back it up.

"What the hell!?" he roared, as bright lights came on all around, with more fire crashing into the vehicle from the sides—mostly hitting and glancing off, fortunately. The houses on either side of the road, literally close enough to reach out and touch, were filling the air with crunches, cracks, and booms as most of the shots that missed slammed into them.

"Andre!" Mike bellowed. "On the mount!"

"On it!" Andre shouted back, shoving the hatch back and wriggling himself up, trying to reach the gun.

He'd barely managed to lock it into readiness, when he screamed, jerking back and falling inside, his right hand mangled, and blood and bone clearly showing.

Whatever had hit him, it'd practically pulped his right hand. As he fell back into the well of the seats, Jenn was already reaching for him, as his brother Jimmy roared and lunged up to take his place.

The shots were still coming in, hitting the heavy armoring of the vehicle and bouncing off, as Mike cursed, seeing the truth suddenly.

"Chris, can you get us back?" he snapped.

"Trying!" the big man ground out, having realized that the reason that truck he'd been edging around was placed just so? It was to make it as difficult as possible to retreat. With a broken front axle, it was a nightmare.

"They're cannonballs!" Patrick shouted over the din inside the vehicle. "They need a damn lucky shot to do damage to us!"

"Well then, they're goddamn lucky!" Emma shouted back, before snarling "Fuck this!" to herself and yanking the back door open.

"Get back here!" Mike bellowed after her.

But she was already gone, landing in the darkness behind the vehicle, and sprinting around the nearby abandoned cars, vanishing around the corner and out of sight.

"Saros, get out there and damn well kill something!" Mike snarled. "Chris, get this POS back out of the line of fire, then fall back to that building!" He pointed to a large one that ran alongside the left-hand side of the vehicle, and the door that was swinging open behind them.

"Everyone else, move!" he yelled, clambering over the seats and into the back. "Up and at 'em, soldier!" he shouted at Andre, who had his teeth clenched as Jenn desperately tried to repair his hand. "Stabilize it," he growled at Jenn. "Do that and no more. Then move!"

"Sir!" She nodded, her eyes wide, before from somewhere overhead, to the drumbeat of cannonballs hitting and bouncing off the armored transport, a new sound entered the fight.

One of a thunderbolt being unleashed.

"Goddammit!" Chris cried as the vehicle bounced and jostled. "They took out the axle. I can't get onto the curb! I'm jammed!"

"Then abandon it and move!" Mike ordered him, before slapping Jimmy's leg, a half second before the .50cal opened up, returning fire in a barrage. "Patrick!" he bellowed.

The martial arts monk spun around, making eye contact and nodding.

"Get them inside and secure!"

Glancing forward as he directed people out of the stuck vehicle, Mike tried to make sense of what he was seeing as Beta hissed and shoved Kilo and the others out ahead of her.

The dungeon was here; he had no doubt about that.

The plaza that had been revealed ahead was right in the heart of Oxford. It was surrounded by ancient buildings, but once past the section they'd just come into, dozens of them had been stripped to the ground of anything and everything. Mere frozen dirt was left, presumably what was left of the original ground the city had been built upon.

A circular space had been cleared just ahead. Here and there, there were hints of buried lower floor structures—old cellars and more—but for half a mile in all directions, it'd been cleared to provide this killing field.

No buildings aboveground remained. Torches glowed with a weird monotonous flicker, illuminating the dead ground. Each stood atop a pillar grown in position, and there, beyond them all, at the heart of the new plaza, stood a single, tall building.

A rotunda stood atop it, gleaming in white marble and black glass. But the building below it had clearly never been designed by a human mind.

It was roughly circular, with vents that belched flame and billowed smoke. The sound of hammers and complex pounding machinery echoed from inside as something had clearly decided that the time for secrecy was long past.

The lights that ringed the plaza were suddenly joined by brightly billowing flames that shot skyward from exhausts that ran along the wall.

That wall, in turn, was clearly rusting iron, and extended a good five meters into the air, hiding whatever else was beyond it.

299

What the rocketing flames did show, though—and which were quickly obscured by drifting clouds of gun smoke and gunpowder as they fired again and again—were the cannoneers.

They were squat creatures, almost turtle-like, two meters across with stumpy legs at each corner, and a stubby cannon on their back that, after each shot, was raised to point to the sky, as an apparently internal mechanical system reloaded them.

Then they'd swing forward, lock on, and fire, vanishing behind a cloud of sooty powder smoke like something from the age of sailing ships and piracy.

The wall drifted into sight and vanished again and again behind the cover, as cannonballs boomed and cracked, more than half still whiffling past to crash into the buildings on either side.

"Get your arse down here!" Mike bellowed up at Jimmy, who, though he could feel the big captain slapping his leg, had no clue what he was saying, over the booming chatter of the .50cal as he returned fire.

The fire chewed up the top of the wall, then slammed into a turtle, tearing it apart in a cascade of gears and light, before it exploded as its magazine charge went off.

"Get some!" Jimmy bellowed, walking the fire along the wall and into the next in line. "Fucking yeah!" he screamed as that, too, died.

Cannonballs tore through the air on all sides. One impacted and ricocheted off the roof of the boxer less than an inch from him and made the gun jerk and bounce, but he was lost in the sheer manic joy of returning fire, and Mike knew it.

He clambered out the back door, dropping to the cobblestones and twisting, bringing his own .50cal sniper rifle around and resting it atop a nearby vehicle that had helped to cause them so much trouble.

From here, he lined up the first shot, aiming for the center of the creature's head. It was blank-faced, simply a circular bulge with three eyes that glowed a malevolent red. He rested the aiming reticule on the middle point of the three, let out a breath, held it, stilled his heart as much as possible, and then stroked the trigger.

He was adjusting his aim before the massive bullet had even landed. As the cannoneer was hurled backward in a welter of shattered parts, he was already servicing the rifle, in preparation for the next.

Before he could fire, though, a thunderous detonation rang out. The night was briefly lit up by the incredible power of Emma's thunderbolt as it lashed out from overhead.

"All right, maybe she's worth bringing after all," he muttered, adjusting his aim as a section of the rotunda collapsed, falling almost in slow motion to take out a pair of cannoneers on the right-hand side. "She better have planned that," he mumbled, even as he lined up again, paused and then fired.

From inside the building to his left, he heard screams and gunfire, and he cursed, before the crash of metal on metal and the roar of Chris in full fury rang out.

Then came more sounds—sounds he recognized as Beta and Kilo's characteristic hissing and roaring, as well as complicated destruction.

He swore and fired one last time. Then, as the .50cal machine gun mounted on the boxer ran dry, he bellowed at Jimmy, "Down! Get down!"

Jimmy dropped, vanishing from sight almost a full second before a cannonball impacted right behind him, ricocheting off into the darkness.

Mike stared, wide-eyed, realizing that one had had Jimmy's name on it.

"Get your sorry arse out here and in there!" Mike yelled, waving at the building, before twisting and lifting the rifle on instinct, firing up at a shape dimly seen as it rocketed past.

He snarled, the pain of firing such a large rifle "offhand" more than made up for as something crashed into the cobbles, in a detonation of parts.

"Shit!" Jimmy shouted, diving aside as soon as he left from the back door, landing just as something slightly larger than a seagull crashed into the ground where he'd just stood.

"Get inside!" Mike roared, already running, then cried out. Something hit his helmet, half tearing it free, rotating it around and staggering him.

He was blind, his helmet turned around to the point he could only see out of the very corner-most section.

Hands grabbed him as he tried to wrench the helmet around, to free up his vision; he almost fought it on instinct. Then he realized what was going on as those same hands dragged him inside, out of the fire as more cannonballs crashed into the building and occasionally smashed through the walls.

"Move, move, move!"

Someone was screaming in his ear, and he snarled, finally yanking the helmet off and cursing as it took a load of skin with it.

For a few seconds, the ground seemed to tilt and sway. Someone was shouting something at him, but he just couldn't make sense of it.

The next thing he knew, as the world flashed in and out of focus, Chris was there.

"Damn, man, you look like I feel!" Chris grunted, helping to hold him up and looking at the blood that ran down Mike's face, and the heavily bleeding left ear.

"Stings…" Mike slurred, reaching up and touching the dangling flap of skin.

"Hold up a minute, damn it," Chris muttered as they followed the others, moving deeper into the old building. "Hold up, man!" he snapped, finally managing to yank the focal orb out of his pouch and grabbing Mike by the shoulder.

"There's no time for that," Mike mumbled.

"You can barely hear, and half your ear's off. Damn well hold up." Chris grabbed him again, dragging the older soldier to a halt, and pressed the flap of skin into place, while triggering the focal orb with his mana.

301

Mike hissed for a second, then squeezed his nose shut, snorted, and blew to equalize the pressure. He released and blinked as his injuries were healed in a stinging, fast-knitting growth of flesh.

"Damn," he admitted. "Yeah, that's a lot better. Thanks, Chris."

"No worries." Chris grunted.

"Where is everyone?"

"Other side of the building," Chris answered quickly. "When I dragged you in, you were concussed as well. Thought you might not know it…your eyes were all weird and your head…well, you were still ugly. Jimmy tried talking to you, and you blatantly didn't see him."

"Shit, really?" Mike grunted. "Okay, fill me in."

"The others are running through the building. We're headed for the far side. Plan is we're going to try to loop around, or at least hold up for a few minutes to figure out what the hell we do next." Chris shrugged.

"Andre is fighting one-handed, though that won't be for long—I saw him chugging a potion before. Jimmy, Jenn, and Emma are fine. Saros is scouting, Beta and Kilo are up ahead. Robin as well, though she's basically just trying not to shoot any of our side and to stay out of the way at this point. And Catherine is…well, she's fucking terrified and cursing us all."

"She's new to this…best thing she can do," Mike agreed. "Emma?"

"On the roof, last I heard, hammering the dungeon with thunderbolts, and drawing attention and fire away from the rest of us." He paused, then sighed. "You know, she pisses me off no end, then she fucking does this and I can't help but like her."

"She's braver than a lion, with the social control of a diseased goat," Mike growled. "But yeah, we'll need to get her trained up and the rest of the team broken in."

As they entered the next room, it was to stumble over the remains of a humanoid machine that lay shattered on the floor. Its legs had been frozen to the ground in a block of ice. It looked like Beta had gone to town, because besides the obvious claw marks, there were entire sections that appeared to have been ripped free by strength of arms alone.

"Scary," Chris muttered, before pointing at a handful more scattered around the room in various shattered states.

"Your work?" Mike asked, and Chris shook his head.

"Patrick's, I'm betting." He pointed to the clear punch and kick dents on several of them. "They're fast, though, so when they come after you, back it up. Look at the head."

Mike did, pausing as they passed and he shook his own, whistling in recognition. "That'd hurt," he admitted as the pair ran up the stairs, chasing the sounds of the others.

The machines were fast and as happy on two legs as they were on four. The central trunk was basically a cylinder, and one had already blown itself up, so clearly there was something dangerous inside them.

"No clue what they were intended for originally, but as fighters, they're a bit shit," Chris pointed out. "As long as you don't let your guard down, no stress at all with them."

"Damn, you had to say that, didn't you," Mike snapped as they took the final staircase, exiting onto the second floor from the roof, and finding the others in a pitched battle with waves of the humanoid machines.

"Fall back!" Chris roared. "Fall back on us!"

"We need to kill them all," Mike countered, slinging his sniper rifle and pulling out a regular SA80.

"We need to regroup—" Chris started, only for Mike to cut him off.

"It's a dungeon!" he snapped. "That means they can summon reinforcements around us easily, from any room!"

"So we need to run!" Chris repeated, firing a three-round burst into the chest of a new figure that raced through from an adjoining room.

"No!" Mike bit out. "As soon as we do, we leave all this scrap to be reabsorbed into the dungeon. We need to kill them as efficiently as possible, then plan in here, where he's locked out. Think of the way it is from the other side! Either way, the next step we take needs to be to get to the roof."

"To rescue Emma?" Jenn asked, as the others fell back to stand with Chris and Mike.

"Yeah," Mike agreed, glancing over at Chris and tapping his hip, where the flare gun hung. "And to get us all out of here."

They were essentially in a huge gathering area. For whatever design reason, the architect had set things up so that the stairs they'd just come from led up to a large open-plan area. It had multiple doors that led off in different directions.

The more Mike stared, the more he saw that as much as they needed it to be…it just wasn't defensible, drawing a curse from him.

"I hate it when you're right," he said quietly to Chris as the other man grinned to him, then fired a three-round burst at the incoming humanoid enemies.

"Well, look on the bright side." Chris shrugged. "If it helps at all, it weirds me the fuck out when I'm right as well, and…" He paused firing again, then grinned. "Whatever the plan this guy had, it sure as shit didn't include us having modern weapons."

That was true, Mike reflected, aiming and taking down another target with a fast burst. The swarming creations looked terrifying, but the one thing they weren't was robust. Their chests—hell, the entire design—was metal. But they were iron at best, and it was only a thin covering.

A single shot through the center of mass, and they tended to go down, either dead or leaking mana and light before exploding. As it was, they had to be responsible for at least half of the deaths of their own side.

It wasn't long before they'd taken down the group. As soon as they had, the others gathered around Mike, and he called out, "Everyone okay? Any injuries?"

"All minor," Jenn assured him, and he let out a long breath.

"Okay, Andre, you shooting again?"

"Aye," the big man growled, flexing his right hand in demonstration, wincing as he did so.

"How bad is it?" Chris asked him.

"More like I overdid it or pulled a muscle…little creaking, but it works," he guessed.

"Good. Okay, people, we need to get to the roof. Emma's up there, and we need a clear spot to fire from…" He paused as a thought came to him. "Anyone think to check what's powering these fuckers?"

"Mana," Jenn said. "I can feel it every time one of them dies. The air in here gets thicker with it."

"And have we tried opening them up?" he asked, only to have the others look at him in confusion, before Chris started to laugh.

The big Druid took two quick steps to the nearest corpse, then dropped, dragging a knife from its sheath, and started to cut.

"Cover him," Mike ordered, as the others maintained their intermittent fire.

Thirty seconds later, it was done, and Chris stood, looking at the dimly glowing thing in his hand.

"Here." Jenn grabbed it and focused, then grinned. "It works!"

The core, which looked like nothing but a single finger of crystal wrapped in a bunch of gleaming copper wires, shattered. She flinched, before dropping it to the floor, then reached out to Andre.

He gasped; his formerly damaged and still rebuilding hand popped and clicked. His next shots went well awry, before he grinned as he shifted his grip and took aim again.

"Well?" Mike snapped at her, and she nodded quickly.

"We can draw from them. That one only held a hundred or so, but it was already damaged. I'd bet that's the most expensive part of the machines for the dungeon to produce."

"Then we've got another plan, people!" Mike called out, seeing Saros coming back in looking battered. "Take them down with minimal damage to the core. Then, if there's no sign of explosion or whatever, Chris gets to loot them, and we fall back. I want this room stripped in three minutes. Catherine, keep an eye out for any dead—we're going to need some directions. Patrick, Saros, I want you leading the way, unless there's news?" Mike asked and Saros shrugged and shook her head. "Fine, Andre, Jimmy, you're with me on overwatch. Here's the sectors…"

CHAPTER TWENTY-EIGHT

"Fuck, my life just gets weirder and goddamn weirder," I muttered, angling out a bit more to avoid the section Marchioness had warned me over. I squinted, seeing the lumbering movement as the turtles streamed back toward the under-siege dungeon in the distance.

I grinned and adjusted my angle slightly, taking aim…then opened fire with a long blast of lightning, taking the rearmost in the back of the head and rolling along, taking them out one at a time as I continued on.

The turtles were, as she'd assured me, lethal opponents only if they could hit you. From my position high in the sky and flashing past overhead, they were virtually bloody useless. Their cannonball ammunition was highly limited—there was room for precisely three shots internally—and they used gunpowder magazines that went up easily when hit by lightning.

Combine that with their slow movement and unless they were defending a fixed point, they were basically ineffective. At least in the bell tower that she'd warned me to look out for, they'd had additional ammunition laid in and gunpowder bagged charges.

Here, running back to the dungeon, they had none of those things, and the dungeon's range was highly limited as well.

Marchioness had explained a lot of it, and for a brief time, I'd actually started to have a little hope that this could be resolved with minimal bloodshed—right up until the distant booms had sounded, and shortly after, the bright red of the flare had lit the abandoned city.

I'd paused only long enough to get a final lay of the land from her, and a warning about what was where. Then I'd launched myself into the air and headed north.

As fast as I was, though, time passed even faster in a fight. As I approached the main entrance to the dungeon, the one place that I'd been told to ensure we avoided at all costs, I could track a path of destruction leading straight to it.

Mike and the others appeared to have charged straight into the dungeon's entrance and the doors had sealed after them, trapping them in a full-on dungeon dive.

I twisted and rolled on instinct as soon as the sooty white flash of a launch caught my eye. Then I snorted, lashing out with a blast of lightning that scoured the top of the wall clear in retaliation.

The cannonball passed me at least three meters to my right—it'd been nowhere near me—while my own blast had cut off, then aimed for the far side of the wall, on the inside, for the easy target I'd been told would be there.

The top of the wall exploded in a sudden detonation, followed by a rolling one that started out slow, then picked up to a terrible speed. I shook my head in disbelief.

Simon was apparently an idiot.

He was also that special kind of idiot who came with a degree and a doctorate, and a double-barreled surname that had commanded troops since the Battle of Waterloo and still had never had to learn from their actions.

This particular brand of idiocy had helped to set up the explosive broom that was currently sweeping the wall clear, thanks to him providing a specially designed trench that held the bagged charges for the turtles to rearm easier.

It'd been set up, Marchioness had explained, to allow faster reloading, and to keep the powder dry.

It had a lovely section that kept the little baggies off the ground, and a half tube that protected them from incoming fire from the top as well, or even from inclement weather.

In fact, the only weakness was the area that the turtles had to reach into in order to pull the bag out.

That someone might fire into that and set the bags off with a blast of lightning? Well, that had apparently never occurred to him.

Now the entire wall was vanishing behind the rolling, concussive blast. Stone fragments, metal shards, and unrecognizable bits flew out of the cloud of smoke that quickly enveloped the wall, followed by the occasional detonation of the turtles' mana cores as well.

All in all, it'd have been a fantastic distraction, if not for the fact that I needed to get the fuck inside, not provide one of those.

The others had managed to make it inside through the large gates in one wall. The devastation that had been unleashed on them, I was betting, had been Emma in a fit of rage, using her thunderbolt orb. But if that was the case, she apparently had access to a fuckload more mana than I thought, because the gates had been half blasted, half melted free.

Then, on the far side of those gates, stood a massive set of iron doors, set into an impressive stone wall, leading angled downward.

They'd already been closed as I came into sight, but the bodies that lay strewn around were clearly dissolving into the dungeon even as I arrived.

The fucker had lured them straight into the dungeon entrance, just as Marchioness had suggested he would. From there, they'd have to do a full dive to reach the exit on the far side.

The trick was, though, that exit? It led to the other side of the wall. Literally, there was no way into the "real" dungeon from it—just a place to fight your way through and traps to face before you found an exit that would leave you on the far side.

The dilemma I had?

If I ignored them and left them to fight their way through there, and they died? I knew what they were facing. As a Dungeon Lord, I could claim any structure that was an enemy one. Provided I could hold it? I could start a claim on their dungeon.

I didn't think to ask her whether that included the dungeon run itself or not, and I genuinely didn't know.

What I did know, though, was that the dungeon came with strict rules. They had to have a way out of there, and if they completed the dungeon, they had to be given a reward. It couldn't just be a case of you enter a room, the way out seals up and all the oxygen is pumped out or lava is poured in.

The dungeon system enforced a strict "play fair" policy, even if it layered the advantages a lot.

I hesitated. Then, cursing, I did what I knew I had to do regardless.

If I could claim the dungeon myself, then I could free them of any traps they faced.

Besides, Jack was coming as well, racing through the streets only a few dozen meters behind me. With a mental flick of the wrist, I directed him to tear the gates from their hinges and follow me in.

Having a giant automata in the shape of a bear had to be a help in there, right? Either way, that left me with a new fun task: find the goddamn entrance.

Marchioness had told me that the dungeon had three actual entrances. One was in the rotunda…

A glance at that made me shake my head unthinkingly. Something had hit it and shattered half the columns on one side. The entire thing had collapsed inward. If there was still an entrance there at all, it was buried under multiple tons of stonework and shattered, fluted columns.

The second entrance was hidden inside the city, half a mile or so to the north, and was set up as a bolt point. Apparently, Simon thought it was completely secure, and that not even Marchioness knew about it.

It came out into the basement of an old zoo, long closed. Although I could probably find it, it might take me an hour or more, and there was nothing stopping the dickhead from causing a tunnel collapse when I was coming along it to fight him.

No, that left number three—or blind luck that I drag him out through some form of trickery. Although I might be a cunning bastard at times, it was more likely I'd be compared to Baldrick with my plans than Blackadder the Fourth.

Jez Cajiao

The inside of the rotunda had a single passage that led from the ground up, with the top level currently buried under a mass of stone.

When he'd taken over the main building, he'd decided to go all in on the steampunk Gothic design. The bottom floor had originally been something like the surrounding buildings, I'd have assumed—what was left of them anyway—and surely more like the remains of the rotunda: all white marble and ornate fluting, posh statues, and so on.

Here now, though? Flaring fires, the sound of trip hammers pounding away mercilessly and the corresponding flash of sparks, the whoosh of flames, and of course, billowing black smoke that smelled like the devil's arsehole all combined to suggest I was looking at an entrance to hell.

One that was clearly envisaged by a goddamn lunatic fringe that viewed the Victorian era as the height of design aesthetic.

Literally, it was all battered columns, rusting iron, flashes, smoke, and booms.

It looked the part, but it just underscored what Marchioness had told me about Simon: he was single, had always been single, and unless he paid for it, he was never going to be anything but single.

There was no way anyone who wasn't single and desperate was going to come up with the Victorian-era version of the Dark Tower, fill it with manic death-dealing mechanical monsters and think it was the look that was going to win them friends.

That wasn't because I was against the whole goth style, either. There were plenty of cool and even insanely hot goths. It was that this place just fairly screamed, "I've got a tiny dick and I want you to look up to me."

I twisted around, flipped and dove, pulling up at the last second and landing, already in a run. I covered the last dozen meters on foot, watching out for the markers I'd been told about. At the last second, I jumped, just as I unleashed a second lightning bolt.

This was a longer, more powerful one, and it tore through the wall ahead, easily melting it in a roughly circular pattern, even as the ground beneath me dropped, exposing a pit trap that was filled with rusty spikes.

Landing on the far side, I flooded both hands with my Storm-Strike ability. Instead of lashing out with them, I clamped my hands on the still incredibly hot metal and ripped the hole wider.

With a scream of tortured metal and a popping of rivets, the inside of the building was revealed. Inside, it looked more like an S&M crowd's dungeon than anything else.

I ripped the right-most panel free, allowing me to fully see inside. I shook my hands, reaching for the clasps that held the gauntlets to my armor.

My hands hurt like a bitch, and I bit down on a scream, already circulating my mana through my body. The lightning flared up and caressed my hands as the accelerated healing began.

My gauntlets were burned and melted; the molten iron had turned the damn things to slag. I quickly stripped them free, dropping them to the floor as I kicked at the left side panel, before ducking into the room and stepping over a battered and broken body laid on the floor.

A single glance at its face showed me that Marchioness was right.

Obsessed wasn't even close to the word for the fucking lunatic.

It looked like he'd made a perfect replica of her, then he'd peeled her, inch by inch.

What did that achieve—not even considering the obvious issues of morality? But to do it to a mechanical creation that you had complete control over? Nope.

He was a fucking nutjob, all right.

I crossed the room quickly. A flare of light reflected from under the door, and I picked up speed, yanking the hammer from my belt and reaching back for the shield.

I'd almost reached the door, shield coming back around, when it opened, and before me wasn't, as I'd expected, a dozen of his humanoid creations.

Instead, it was a single one, and it held in its arms a fucking *cannon*.

It vanished in a cloud of dirty white smoke.

I was hurtled backward, crashing straight into the wall, and then dropped to the floor, coughing. My head rung and my left arm proclaimed quite loudly that it was broken.

I blinked, spat, and pushed myself back up shakily. It was difficult to do one-armed, considering the goddamn panel of the wall had apparently fallen on me while I was on the floor and I'd not noticed.

That said to me that I'd been either knocked out, or stunned by the impact. I looked at the little bastard in the doorway. He was trying to reload the cannon. Had I been out for more than a second, that fucker would have no doubt shot me in the head and ended all my concerns.

No, I bit down on my pain and forced myself upright and to my knees, then fired off a lightning bolt straight across and into the mouth of the cannon as it lowered it for a second shot.

The resultant explosion destroyed the cannon and sent the little mechanical monster hurtling from view, giving me the time I needed to push myself fully to my feet. I cursed as I looked over my shield.

It was bent inward in the middle; the dent was basically right between the straps that I put my hand through. One was a loop that went around my left forearm, and the other a grip that I held in that hand.

The issue was that the straps were tight, and I snarled in pain as I dragged my broken wrist back through the loop, before fumbling a healing potion one-handed from my bag of holding.

I managed to angle it up under the bottom of my helmet. I bit down on the cork, dragged it free and spat it onto the floor, before chugging the potion—it was a weak one—and I immediately started to circulate my mana as well.

The combination of the two should be enough that I'd be able to heal it up fast, with a minimal loss of mana. But the shield?

I laid it facedown, then tried hitting it with my hammer, and cursing when all it did was bounce.

I wasn't getting that dent back out without a machine shop.

I left the shield, something I'd just bloody enchanted as well, on the floor. With the dent where it was, any hard hit to it would only break my wrist again.

Instead, I moved out into the passage beyond. The mechanical monster crawled away with one arm and leg functional, and its chest emitted a pulsing blue glow.

"You're not catching me with that fucker again," I snapped, stepping forward and bringing the hammer around and down, crushing its head. I looked up and got ready as the clattering sound of more enemies incoming grew louder.

"Let's fucking go!" I roared, running forward. My left hand conjured lightning as the bones flexed and shifted, and my hammer was at the ready in my right.

CHRIS

Chris took the lead, running at the mechanical monster and hunching down behind his shield as it opened fire.

This was the third volley these fuckers had managed as the small group worked their way around the cavernous area. Between the slowly flowing molten rock that fell down the left wall, the steam that rose from the pool it fell into, and the narrow walkway to cross that pool, as well as these bastards constantly reloading and firing?

He was just about done with taking this dungeon's shit.

It was only that they'd fired in volleys that had saved him and the others so far. The impacts against his shield? They were bad. Twice, he'd nearly fallen into the boiling water below. But had they timed their shots one after the other, the group would have been stuck.

As it was, the enemy were down to just one group of riflemen left.

The fight had been going on for half an hour now, with them moving in relays: Chris took point or Kilo, who could create a short-lived ice shield that melted almost as soon as he summoned it.

Weirdly, although Beta was fully embracing her draconic heritage and had already launched herself into the air, soaring over to take out one of the groups, Kilo was hunched down and looked like he was in real trouble.

"Fire!" Mike roared.

Chris threw himself to the ground. A half second later, a return volley, fired by Mike, Andre, Jimmy, and Emma tore into the remaining riflemen, and they fell almost as one.

"Shield!" boomed Mike.

Kilo hissed, extending his right hand, a hand that was visibly shaking, as he summoned a shield between Chris and the downed mechanoids.

A second later, one of their cores exploded, followed quickly by two more.

Chris let out a long breath. "Cheers, mate!" he called in the kobold's general direction, before cursing as Saros bounded over him, landing and rolling, then coming back to her feet and firing at something he couldn't see around the next bend in the cavern.

"Three more clankers!" she called. "Incoming!"

Her rifle barked again, then she leapt back. A burst of fire hurtled through the air in reply.

The mechanoids were presumably a much more expensive or advanced version of the dungeon defenders, as they not only were more humanoid, but they carried actual rifles this time.

Sure, they fired lead bullets, which were both heavy and inaccurate. But what they lacked in easy lethality or technological prowess, they made up with quantity.

Chris pushed himself wearily to his feet, blinking away sweat that ran down his face, and once again forced himself not to rip off his helmet and strip.

His armor was hot and heavy. It always was, despite the more advanced versions that they kept being upgraded to and his impressive size.

The problem now was that in this place, with all the smoke and as close as it was, and with the steam, the sheer heat, and the constant exertion, he was getting dangerously close to dehydration.

The others couldn't be any better. And poor Kilo?

Glancing back at him as Saros stepped out and fired again, declaring the passage ahead to be clear, Chris couldn't help but feel for the guy.

Suffering was an understatement, considering that it took Jenn and Beta to get him back on his feet. Seeing that, Chris winced. Clearly the shield that he'd put together to protect him from the explosion had taken the last of his strength, not to mention mana.

Beta dragged him across the narrow bridge, then pinned him to the nearby wall and proceeded to have a conversation with Kilo in some variant of a language that Chris had never heard, all hisses and growls. Although Kilo started out barely being able to speak, he ended it with a vicious snap of his teeth and a glare, before Beta nodded firmly to him and strode off.

"You all right, mate?" Chris stepped up as the kobold waved Jenn on again as well, refusing her offered healing.

"Am fine," Kilo snarled.

"And I look great in a dress," Chris replied without pause. "Come on, man, we both know that's bullshit. Is there anything I can do? You want one of my healing potions?"

"No." Kilo scowled, before he sighed and shook his head, stepping away from the wall and following the others.

Chris fell in by his side.

"I am…just tired," he lied.

"Fucking baked alive is more like it." Chris grunted. "What color are your scales normally? I know it's not fuckin' pink!"

"Pink?" He gasped, looking down and letting out a groan of dismay.

The kobold Cryomancer, a highly respected warrior in his own right, a mage who frequently held his own in technical discussions and helped to teach the next generation, and who was pretty damn clearly trying to chase Beta for her affections, was currently the color of a lobster having a very bad day.

And it was only getting worse.

"What can I do?" Chris asked as the pair hurried to catch up with the others.

"Cover me in a blanket and hide my shame," Kilo spat, before shaking his head and patting his friend on the shoulder. "Nothing. Just...let's just get through this and back outside where I can breathe. I have known nothing like this terrible heat!"

"Ah, man, just you wait." Chris forced a smile to hide his genuine concern. "A month, two at most, and we'll have all this shite sorted out. Then it's you, me, and Matt—we'll have a lads'..." He looked at the kobold and then shrugged and went on. "A *males*-only holiday in the Greek islands. Just sun, sea, and fucking drinking 'til we puke. You'll love it."

"This 'Greeks islands'...it is cold?"

"Nah, mate—hot!"

"I will stay here," Kilo said firmly. "At our home, in the snow and darkness, I will stay."

"Trust me," Chris said. "We'll get air conditioning sorted out and a pool, you'll love it."

"If he will not go, I will," Saros offered, popping up at Chris's elbow and damn near making the Druid shit himself. "If you change your form, anyway."

"Fuck's sake!" He cursed. "Will you stop that! I'm not interested. I've already got a girlfriend!"

"So?" Saros shrugged. "If she cannot fight beside you, then she does not concern me. I shall fight her, and when I prove myself then you can mate with me. *When* you change your form." That was added as just a minor thing, something that was already obvious and agreed.

"Will you fuck right off!" Chris snapped.

The Scepiniir laughed, then bounded ahead to catch up with the others as Chris and Kilo continued after them.

"You know, you're only encouraging her." Patrick snorted, and Chris growled in frustration. "Don't worry. When the time comes, I'll be a witness, and I'll explain it all to Becky...probably."

"Oh, screw you!" Chris glowered, and the big monk laughed, before jogging ahead.

"What's the plan?" Chris asked Mike as they caught up in the stone passage a minute or so later.

"We rest and recover. Saros is scouting. No more traps found yet, thankfully, but that's a mixed blessing," Mike said quietly.

"Because you wish our companion ill?" Kilo slumped down to sit on the floor.

"No, though she's determined to get on my last fuckin' nerve," Mike growled. "Because usually the clankers trigger the traps before we can. Either they're finally wising up—or the Dungeon Lord is—or they want us hurrying along."

"What was that?" Chris asked suddenly, looking upward.

The others turned to him, then cocked their heads, listening.

"I don't hear anything," Mike admitted, with most of the others shaking their heads as well.

"Impressive." Beta nodded as she said it, with a click of her teeth. "I hear. Explosion?" she suggested.

"Probably," Chris agreed, relieved that at least today his truncated bond, all that he had left over from Simo, was working in his favor again. "You think it's Matt?"

"Perhaps." She shrugged. "Either way, he is up there, and we are down here. We must fight on."

"Well, with that cheerful comment, what's waiting for us ahead?" Mike asked Saros as she jogged back around the corner, the dust and dirt that made up most of the ground barely stirring as she passed over it.

"Two groups ahead of clankers, each with the smoking rifles. They protect a door, and beside them, a taller, strange-looking creature waits."

"Describe it," Chris ordered.

"Tall, at least twice the size of the others, and more ornate, decorated with carvings and inlays. It has two arms and legs, a barrel chest, and a small head. But the shoulders have holes in them, as do the hands."

"So probably something that can shoot at us." Mike grunted. "What about the clankers?"

"The same design as before. They carry the smoking rifles, and they stand behind a row of stone, a wall with a pattern like missing teeth."

"Crenelations." Mike nodded. "The wall...it goes along, down, along, up, along, down, like this?" He drew a line in the air, moving up and down, and she nodded.

"So he's set it up like a medieval wall, so they can hide behind it. Is it high?"

"Like so." She shook her head, indicating chest height.

"Weird."

"What if this is like the dungeon back home?" Jimmy asked, and Mike looked at him inquiringly. "You know, so you can only build so much—like, it's done before we came, so the Dungeon Lord had no clue what he'd need and he set it up to cover all the bases?"

"Might explain the enemies we're facing," Chris said.

"We're seeing the same stuff mainly, none of the turtles that'd have been a nightmare in the enclosed spaces, and none of those fliers again—" Mike agreed, before they all broke off, looking upward as dust and dirt cascaded from the ceiling.

"Well, that was a lot closer," Chris said softly. "Anyone else want to run like fuck just in case?"

CHAPTER TWENTY-NINE

"I know you're in here!" I roared, unleashing a fresh blast of lightning down the passage. I summoned a surge of power to my right fist and punched the nearest door, shattering it down the middle. "Come out, come out, wherever you are!"

There'd been no sign of Simon yet. I'd found rooms full of weird-ass shit to no end, as well as empty food wrappers, abandoned cans of lager, bottles of wine and even champagne. But what I'd not found in at least ten minutes now was a single thing to fight, despite sending Jack climbing up into the rotunda to see whether the sneaky fucker had ended up moving everything up that way instead.

The place was a mad mix of warping passages, sometimes so tight I could barely squeeze through, then much wider, grander ones. There were areas where the lights were reduced to smoldering flames in sooty lamps, where rust ran in slow rivers from hammer holes and rivets driven into iron plates...

Then the next section would be all marble and stonework from the 1800s and oak loungers, rows of over-filled bookshelves and oil paintings of people who had been dead for five hundred years or more.

The passage I'd gone along before had, as Marchioness had suggested, led to a stairwell that in turn led down to a lower floor. When she'd lived in the dungeon, she'd assured me that there were three levels to it: the main ground floor one, the first level below that housed the living quarters and experimentation chambers, and below that, the core and Simon's quarters.

Like me, he'd felt the need to be as close as possible to the core. Unlike me, when he'd opened the dungeon to outsiders, it'd been with a very simple purpose in mind.

He let them in, let them eat and drink, recover a little, and then, in twos and threes, he'd shown the dungeon to them, taking great pleasure in showing them a choice of weapons and telling them about a prize at the end. Then he sealed them in, and watched while they panicked and died, facing his creations.

In time, as she tried again and again to make him accept that their joint purpose was not to rule the local area and settle his own old and festering scores, but to save enough of humanity to fight the Orcan and to protect the Cinthian Empire, she'd began to regret that she had such a limited pool to harvest samples from.

With that in mind, and her limited experience and understanding of humans, when she later discovered him making a strange cage in secret, she'd introduced a few flaws into the system, and had planned to turn the tables on him, should she need to—up to and including creating a pair of specialist mechanical creations. One that looked similar to all the others that wandered around the dungeon on their various tasks, but which would respond only to her directly, and a second, a constructor that she hid nearby...again, just in case. Then she'd gotten on with her primary duty.

Marchioness had admitted that even she had no clue he was so mad, but by her nature, she was a paranoid planner, so had made those contingency plans. Plans that were there just in case he did *exactly* what he had.

She, like all of her sisters, had been forced by their programming and training to hunt out a compatible local to bond with to enable the dungeon to reach the next stage of their mission. When she'd scoured the local area clean in the first day, feeding all those she needed to, to boost her dungeon's growth, she'd clearly missed that although this potential partner had been a survivor, and therefore a bonus to her, he was also certifiably insane.

When he'd been given the option, just like I had, to create the automata, he'd selected humanoid from the list of options. Among them was, unfortunately, the facility to make something that was far more lifelike than anything I'd realized was possible.

I'd built Jack originally from a literal collection of scrap and waste metals, abandoned computers, wood, old mechanical parts—everything that had been long abandoned in a basement of a public semi-governmental building.

He'd gone in entirely the other direction.

Using a collection of high-tech prostheses from a nearby research lab, mannequins, silicone, and a hundred other parts, as well as inspiration from a nearby plastic surgery and their modelling devices, he'd created an automata that could indeed pass as a human, one that appeared fully real—provided you didn't get too close. But under the plastic and silicone surface, it was all mechanical.

She'd agreed to help him when he explained that the body was there as a design *example*, and although he understood the possible bonuses for him to have it there dedicated solely to serve him, he'd rather dedicate it to the dungeon. She'd been overjoyed and had assisted him as he copied it into the dungeon, then began dissecting it and assessing the various parts.

The dungeon couldn't fully replicate it, unfortunately. Not yet anyway. It was far too complex for that, and would require much higher levels of core technology to be researched and unlocked. But the dungeon could take what was already there and repair it.

So, with that in mind, and with the clear understanding that doing this would enable their shared dungeon to grow significantly more powerful, and quickly, she'd gone along with the experiments.

They'd removed and examined limbs, rebuilt and reverse engineered mana cores, and more. Mana crystal circuitry was examined, understood, and unlocked, all while the dungeon was barely Iron.

They'd done all of this together, and when it was done, when they agreed there was nothing more for them to learn from the automata, it was reassembled, repaired, and made use of.

She'd even agreed when he expressed his fear that something might happen to her, and that the perfect location for her was in the hibernation chamber that had transported her to this world, with it stored in the automata's chest cavity, being used to directly power it.

She'd begun to suspect that something was wrong with him at this point, but she'd gone along. Partly, that had been because she also knew that as a dungeon fairy, she was vulnerable, if an enemy could catch her. But inside the automata, with its core and higher functions ripped out and replaced with her own, she was far more powerful.

The only issue was, he'd known and understood far more about the system than he'd been letting on. As the Dungeon Lord, the automata was bonded directly to him and his mind, not to her. He was careful not to let on, as she adjusted to her new form, that he knew that.

Apparently, the final turning point had been when he'd declared her new form to be perfect, but when she refused to help him attack and capture fairies of the other dungeons, to provide an army of such upgraded bodies for him, and that the dungeon's capacity was currently too low to support any more, he'd flown into a rage.

That had coincided with an announcement that I had achieved something—I didn't catch what, but probably us reaching Steel or maybe even the religious one, I guessed—and hoo-boy had it tipped him over the edge.

Turns out that the kind of people who were happy to tie themselves to dungeons and set up as overlords to lead humanity, probably weren't the ones any of us needed to be in a position of such power.

He'd accused her of trying to sabotage him, that he was the only hope for humanity, and that if she wasn't helping him, then she was "just like all the others."

Then he'd stormed off and had focused on what he assured her was "going to change the game."

Instead, as the days passed and she focused on the day-to-day running of the dungeon, he'd devoted himself to the design and construction of a special cage, telling her it was there as a last resort, in case the enemy dungeons—which she was pushing him to ally with—instead attacked them.

The cage was designed to block any signals that came in or went out, a magical and modern mix of the Faraday cage, with the addition of a rack and pinion system that attached to the walls to secure the victim.

This would enable them to latch onto the limbs of the enemy and drag them back into recesses in the walls, keeping them stretched out and immobilized as far as possible. And once the loops were locked on? They were designed to never be opened.

There was no latch to be flicked, no lock to be picked. Instead, the only way to get them off was to cut them free, and that would result in the enemy being dropped to the floor.

That meant that they were free of the chains, sure, but it also meant that they'd have no hands or feet. That would stop them escaping, should anything happen.

That the little fucker had planned this all so meticulously was a hell of a sign that he had issues by the truckload already. But, oh wait…it got *worse*.

Fortunately, it wasn't as though rape were a threat. Although she looked female, there was apparently a marked lack of the main parts required for that to be a danger. But for a dungeon-bonded fairy, there were far worse fates.

That was when she discovered that built into the body that she now inhabited was a *reboot* facility, one that shut the entire body down for a few minutes before it rebooted and she regained control. Only, when she could see and sense again, it was to find herself already dangling in the chained grips, and the field powered and in place to cut off her access to the greater dungeon.

She'd been furious, raging against him for days as he tortured and damaged her shell, starving her of mana and weakening her. That was when she found the real reason he'd been so adamant about installing her in the strange form.

It wasn't—as she'd half expected—something to do with his peculiar sexual urges. Instead, while he wasted valuable time ignoring the outside world, he focused only on breaking her control over the dungeon.

It was because her new outer form was something he'd created directly, and because she was linked *through* it…that in the end he'd been able to break her link to the wider dungeon using it.

She'd been fairly sparse on the other details, once she'd made sure I knew that the fucker was both mad and a danger, and simply said that she waited until he was distracted and had escaped.

She'd fled as mechanical creations that she'd help make, that she'd established *her* dungeon with, were suddenly deployed to hunt her. Using her limited access, she'd stolen parts from her deployment vessel, and ran.

It'd taken her three weeks to find the house, delayed heavily by her lack of unmutilated limbs, but she'd managed it. She'd taken over the old residence, then fed the original residents and any passing travelers to the replication core she was using her creations to build.

As soon as the basic systems were in place, she'd set her physical form onto an auto routine—wandering around the house, showing itself at the windows to attract prey, then using the mana released from their deaths to create more and more machines. Her only plan: to retake her dungeon and continue her mission.

She'd been straightforward and as honest as I could expect, offering an alliance with me provided I retook the dungeon and handed it over to her.

I'd agreed straightaway.

After all, I was a Dungeon Lord, and this was a dungeon. Of course I understood the worth of having another allied dungeon under my control as a dubious ally of uncertain worth.

I mean, it wasn't like she was going to try to backstab me at all, or that she'd already admitted to using the setup to lure in other humans and kill them.

Nooooo, of *course* I wanted to just accept what she said at face value.

Fucking lunatic fairies.

She'd given me what I needed, though. Between the three mana cores she'd had left—each held nearly a thousand mana—and the details on what I could expect and the layout, the fight had been going well.

Right up until the point I discovered the additional floor.

This new one didn't correspond at all to the things I'd been told to expect from the other floors. And the bodies I'd found? Marchioness was the identity that the fairy had used when we met, and almost every room I went into was filled with at least one of her bodies, identical in every way to her. Identical, that was, save that where her arms ended in stumps and she ran around the inside of the house on a railing that lifted from below the floor, these had once apparently been perfect.

More or less.

They'd all been destroyed, though, killed in a variety of ways—from hammer blows under an automated trip-hammer, to acid, to lava, the rack, blowtorches...

The list was endless. I stared in disgust as I passed yet another of her bodies, this one carefully dressed in a formal suit, or what remained of one.

Jack was seeing the same, room after room of just...waste. He must have been dedicating the entirety of the dungeon's resources to creating copies of her, and then smashing them up!

I shook my head at the kind of a mind that would do that. I mean, even if you were really fucked up in the noggin and were into that kinda shit, the fact that this wasn't her? I mean, it was part of the dungeon that he was creating each time, so he'd be seeing and sensing it? None of it made sense to me.

But as I kicked a pile of debris out of the way, seeing an elegant hand roll free of a container, I froze, as a collection of booms from overhead rang out.

"Jack!" I grunted, then shook my head grimly. The sensation that was the giant automata in the back of my head suddenly vanished. I glanced upward in the general direction he'd been in.

He'd literally been cut off like a snuffed-out candle, and although he wasn't alive, per se, that still pissed me right off.

"GET OUT!" a voice boomed, seeming to shake the walls all around me with its volume. "Flee! You'll not be warned again!"

"Seriously? Fuck's sake, Simon...she was right. You're about as imaginative as a puppy with piles!" I called back, still reaching out and trying to contact Jack.

But he was literally just…gone. How? How could he have vanished? I mean, it wasn't like he ran out of range, or someone turned off the Wi-Fi!

The seconds passed as the voice boomed again, ordering me to leave, to abandon my foolish attacks, or that I'd suffer.

"Simon, you attacked my people. You declared war against me and you're helping my enemies," I called absently, taking a few steps back toward the nearest stairwell. Jack had been up there somewhere, so maybe…

"How about you quit this shit and try talking to me? We can still sort this out without more bloodshed…"

I managed a single step more, before a section of the roof slid down and crashed into the floor, closing off the way back up and outside, before laughter rang out.

"Now you die!" he snarled.

I jerked back as a pair of spears lanced out of the walls at chest and ankle height.

"Oh, that's just sad," I called out. The trap had triggered a good six inches ahead of me. I got a long silence before he finally answered.

"That was a warning!" he bluffed.

"Bullshit," I shot back, turning slowly as I searched the walls, ceiling, and floor for any signs of further traps. Or, you know, the damn speakers.

I smashed my hammer into the spears and broke them, leaving shattered sections jutting out of the walls as I examined the slab of metal that had cut off the way back upstairs.

It was solid; grooves had been sliced into the walls to make it possible for the metal slab to fall smoothly. But I bet chocks or something similar were in place to stop me levering it back up.

It was academic, though, because I didn't have anything to use as a lever besides my sword, and that'd render it useless.

No, Jack hadn't registered any damage before he'd vanished; he'd just…gone. Probably a suppression field or something that Simon had come up with, much like the place he'd used to hold Marchioness.

"Well?" I asked after a few seconds. "If that was a warning, what the hell happens now? I mean, what the hell did you think? That I'd see it and go, 'Oh, all right then, no worries, I'll just fuck off, shall I'?" I spat at him, before shaking my head. "If that's the case, where would I fuck off *to*? The door is sealed, dickhead! So all this shows me is that you're incompetent and stupid!"

Silence.

"I mean, come on, Simon!" I shouted. "That's you, right?"

More silence.

"Simon…Marchioness sent me!" I called out, trying a new tack. "You remember her, right? She said that she'd change sides. She said she never wanted to threaten me, and that it was all you. That I should kill you and put her back in charge, and then the dungeon would serve me. She said you were too dumb to see the truth… Was she right?"

After a long minute or so of silence, I tried one more time.

"I mean, you do know that Balthazar is just going to kill you, right? Marchioness does. She's just set herself up to wait for it. As soon as the undead slaughter you, she gets control back…you have to know that, right?"

"WHERE IS SHE!" a voice roared from all around me, echoing up and down the passage. "GIVE HER BACK!"

"What, you don't know?" I played for time and a hint of where this mad fucker was, now that I had him talking. "Shit, man, she's practically under your nose!"

"LIES!"

"Do you want her back?" I called out. "I mean, she wants to come home…"

"YOU WILL TELL ME EVERYTHING!" he bellowed.

I nodded, gesturing in patting downward motions. "Simon, she wants to come back, and I want this dungeon not to be a threat to me, right? That's all we want. How about you? What do *you* want?"

There was a pause, then: "SURRENDER! DROP YOUR WEAPONS!"

"Not gonna happen, Simon!" I retorted. "You know that's not gonna happen. You've got my friends trapped somewhere inside. You want to sort this out? I need you to stand down…to calm your creations and we can sort this out…"

I paused, as I heard a distant boom from below. A section of the wall nearby suddenly swung inward.

I glanced inside, then back at the corridor around me, then stifled a curse. This "invitation" was the best chance I was going to get to find Simon.

The aesthetic of the dungeon changed again as I stepped through, no longer cold rusting iron, the orange and red seeping stains that ran down the walls to pool on the floor. Flickering lights made me think of a mine, but with too little light.

Out in the main areas, the lights hid as much as they illuminated, but as I stepped through into the new section, I shook my head in disbelief.

The lights were bright and welcoming. The walls were covered in a kind of faun-colored fabric. The ground was metal, I could tell that as I stepped on it, but there was a carpet laid inexpertly atop it.

Low-level lighting ran along the ground and ceiling, making it look like the entire place was a ship out of some nineties TV show about exploring the universe. The only difference?

The walls held precious paintings spaced along regularly.

"What the absolute fuckery is this?" I asked, unthinking.

"A distraction," a new, clearly manic voice admitted from behind me.

I spun in place, lightning flaring to my hands, but I was too late. While I'd been looking in all the directions but the one I'd needed to, the bastard had sprung his trap.

The ceiling and walls shattered, revealing they were literally no more than ceramic and millimeters thick, as three new forms smashed their way free and lunged at me.

321

The first, to my right, smashed its way free of the wall and received a hammer blow on instinct to the face. It crashed backward, staggering into the wall, then surged back at me, its head torn apart.

The one that crashed through the wall ahead of me took a lightning bolt to its head as well. The chest looked like far too thick a section of armoring, and that was when it clicked for me.

Unfortunately, that was just as the third, seemingly made entirely of links and hands, landed atop me, crashing through the roof.

Hands clamped on my wrists, pinning me down, even as another grabbed the back of my head, crashing my helmeted head into the floor over and over again, stunning me as the last seconds played back and I struggled.

The two to either side had four legs, two arms, and a wide chest, but a small head with a round target painted atop it.

I'd seen them for a split second and I'd attacked, aiming for the target in trained reflex from decades as a gamer.

That, of course, was a trap. The head, I saw as I replayed the blow and the lightning blast landing, was hollow and only a target! Fucker!

Hands tore my weapons free. My head was slammed into the floor every time I struggled. And even though I tried to get off a lightning blast, a spell or a Storm-Strike, they were ready for me. With each attempt, I was stunned and beaten, the spell interrupted and the backlash leaving me drooling. I was hauled to my feet, then chained in place. As the world reeled and spun around me, clamps attached onto me from above, yanking my arms out to the left and right.

My legs were fixed into place and some kind of a box locked onto my helmet, sealing me inside as I jerked and twisted. In a matter of seconds, I'd been immobilized, blinded, and trapped. Now, as I frantically tried and failed to unleash so much as a single lightning bolt at random, the one thought that rose in me was that I might have made a massive mistake.

That, of course, was when the impacts started.

The first blow was a bit of a pathetic one. Even through the seal over my helmet and the muffling, I heard a pained grunt at almost the same time.

Then there was some cursing, as I tried to talk to him, trying to get him to respond to me, before a sudden, much heavier hit slammed into my side.

I grunted as my armor rang like a bell. The clamps on my arms and legs held me securely in place as the blows began to rain down on me.

I grunted and hissed in pain as the pounding continued. None of them were particularly savage, but they were constant. I closed my eyes, trying to make sense of exactly what had just happened.

The clamps on my wrists and ankles were tight and locked into place. This was probably some last line of defense, something to capture a fucking idiot if they got this far or... I swore internally again as I guessed what I was trapped inside of.

I seemed to be doing that a hell of a lot these days, but the simple truth was that a lot kept going wrong, and the more I raced to respond to events, the more often it happened.

The cage she'd mentioned? I suddenly knew damn well that I'd found it. And fuck me sideways, that wasn't happy making, considering she'd had to wait until he'd gotten bored and drunk before she'd made use of one of the tiny faults she'd introduced into his design, and a heavy reworking of the automata's internals to enable her to summon help.

There was no way that I could make use of her trick to escape, either, considering she'd grown conduits, similar to the ones that the dungeon core extruded, and she'd spent hours burrowing them through a weak spot to reach just the right machine that was paused in a preprogrammed location, ready for her.

She'd told me that it'd come inside, hacked her hands and feet free, and had escaped with her. The pair had looted the remains of her ship for usable technology on the way.

That was when she made her second major mistake, in that she stopped to attempt to break back into the dungeon and wrest control from him, while intending that the other mechanoid continue on to the reserve location.

She'd been convinced that she knew the dungeon better, that there was no way that she would be caught, and that she was being overly paranoid in even using the other machines.

That was apparently when Simon had sobered up, or at least had awoken. The various systems of the dungeon were sent into manic overdrive, and as she realized that she was slowly becoming more and more surrounded, and without any real options, she'd hidden herself in a house and had sent the single unit she'd had with her, with her severed—and still not reattached—hands and feet, to make a break for it.

As soon as it was spotted, as she knew it would be, it triggered an overload of its power core. The detonation deliberately flung parts of it, and bits of her hands and feet, in all directions.

Now, I was stuck in the same trap. And from the grunts of effort, the screams, and the words that just made absolutely fuck all sense, I guessed that Simon had me caught, and was venting his frustration on me. The kinky fucker.

At first, the blows were harder. He clearly tired easily, and thanks to the combination of my highly upgraded body and my armor, whatever he was using wasn't doing a great deal of damage.

Although the repeated blows had been painful, they'd been ignorable as well, as I tried to figure a way out of the restraints. Unfortunately, he apparently realized this.

The first blow that came from what I guessed was one of his mechanoids was a different story.

For a start, the bat broke, shattered almost instantly. And not only was the breath knocked out of me, but the side of my armor also felt dented.

A minute later, a second blow landed, and I cried out in shock.

Clearly the fucker had taken the time to make a bat that was either clad in iron or was *entirely* iron. My armor was protecting me at least partly—there was a lot to be said for higher-tech materials—but the one thing that nobody had apparently considered was if the person wearing the armor was having their limbs ripped out, as it was doing fuck all to counter the sudden yanks and the force on my arms and legs.

I hissed in pain and tried to haul the chains inward, bunching my muscles and straining for all I was worth.

If I could just get a little slack, I could then use that to unleash a Storm-Strike and... *WHAM!*

The world spun and danced, my head rang, and by the time I came back to myself, it was to find my head hanging low, brain feeling like it'd been entirely rattled and what felt like blood encrusting my mouth and lips.

My head, I realized groggily—the fucker must have hit me in the goddamn head!

I checked my mana bar. It was at a little over fourteen hundred. I stared balefully at it, before grinning through bloody lips.

"All right, you want to play?" I muttered inside my helmet and the sealed container that covered it. "We can play."

I'd not realized that the container over my head was only attached to the front; I'd recognized that something was on my helmet and that I was blind. Something on my neck as well, and yeah, I'd taken it as a solid square or whatever. But instead, judging from the pain in my head and the dent I could roughly feel pressing in on the back of my skull, it was a semi-circular thing. Presumably for exactly the opportunity to do that.

I pulled my lightning up from my core, spreading it along my limbs—then *WHAM!*

The world rocked back and forth. My head pounded, and the sense of wrongness, like I'd just arrived and someone else had been hanging here in my body right before but had just popped out for a coffee, was back again.

Concussion I guess...that, or brain damage.

WHAM!

This time, it came from my left-hand side. I cried out as my armor was hit with incredible force. Before I'd even managed to make sense of the blow, another came again, then again! One came from behind, cracking into the base of my spine and sending a coldness, a numbness through my legs, that flared and vanished. Then as I was hit again from the side, it came back, even worse.

He was breaking my fucking spine, I realized!

"STOP!" I bellowed. The world spun again, as a last impact came in hard. "Stop...!" I tried again. The world bounced, then surged into primacy, before washing away with a sound like the tide retreating. Then a voice was by the side of my helmeted head.

"You're a terrible actor, Matt. But do you know what you are good for?"

I shook my head slowly. The blood filling my helmet stuck my hair and face to the inside.

"Wha...?" I muttered, trying to focus on the voice.

"You're a great bargaining chip," he admitted. "The Lord of Unlife is coming, and when I told him I had you? He agreed that England is *mine* in exchange. No undead, no wars, no fucking foreigners getting in the way. Just me and those I decide are worthy! There'll be no more filthy..."

I stopped listening to what he said then. But I didn't need to hear it. The venom in the voice, the hoarse-throated exhilaration that he was going to be free of "them" ...he started a tirade, one that, from the bits I heard, ranged from people of different races, to his mother, his stepsisters and women in general, to "all of them, those filthy scum." I just hung my head, trying to focus as I summoned my mana and started to circulate it, flooding myself with Lightning to heal me and...

"ARGH!"

The scream of pain shocked me out of my numbness, as I realized, with a distant kind of savage glee, that he'd apparently tried touching me.

Normally that wasn't an issue. But when I was flooding my body with Lightning? Apparently some rose to the surface.

The scream of rage was high-pitched and furious, and exactly the kind of noise a frustrated child would be told off for. Instead, though, it was me who received the punishment, and it wasn't a fun one.

I still couldn't see shit, but I could feel it as at least two more bats came into play, hammering into my body over and over. Bones broke, tendons were pushed past the breaking point... Then another blow to the side of my head, and the world spun away from me entirely.

Jez Cajiao

ROBIN

Robin had been staying as quiet as possible for the last few hours, feeling that more and more, she was just out of her depth entirely.

Matt was a god. *Literally.*

He'd not only been identified as a god by the system that seemed to be integrated with everything all around her now, but had proved it again and again. This was the guy who she'd seen all those notifications about for weeks as she plodded on. When she had no hope and believed that she might as well give up, he was establishing a safe haven. When she'd been worried about fighting a few thugs with their powers just starting, he'd been declaring war on behalf of all living things, against the lord of the dead, and he'd been planning to do it all with just him and his people!

While she…she'd read them; she'd seen it all, and she'd wondered, dreamed even, of what it'd be like to be *that* kind of a person.

The kind of people who went out and took the world by the throat and made people sit up straight and pay attention. And then to find out that not only was he not a slaving asshole like so many, but he was actively trying to rescue people?

He fed them, he clothed them, and all he asked in return was that they helped each other and did the same for others that he did for them.

When she'd realized who and what he was, she'd been hard pressed to even *talk* to him. But she'd forced herself to do it, to do anything he said, because it was the only chance for her friends.

He'd apologized that he needed to ask her to fight, like it was his fault that he needed her help to win a fight he wasn't even responsible for? And yet he'd still gone out and done it.

When the system had offered her the class of her dreams, a chance that she felt with every fiber of her being was *her*, and then it offered her the chance to pledge to a god to receive extra powers? She'd not hesitated.

She could have pledged herself to some asshole she'd never heard of, some undead thing, or to the man—no, the *god* who was achieving all of this. No, there was no way she hesitated.

Then, as she always did, she absolutely fucked it up!

She nearly killed him, draining his powers into her so that she could win a fight that they'd been winning by that point anyway. And then? When she'd literally fucked up the only person who could keep everything all going, she'd been hauled in front of his *girlfriend* to explain herself.

That she, the Dungeon *Mistress*, was stunningly beautiful, a figure of crackling rage and authority, and was clearly trying to be patient with her had only made it even worse.

She'd been told to basically stay quiet and out of the way, and above all, safe as she'd just created a situation where her fucking up, as the lowest-leveled person there, might end up killing their one true chance at survival.

She spent the next few hours bouncing from building anger at how she'd been treated—it wasn't like she'd damn well tried to fuck it all up, after all—and utter terror and panic.

Then, out of it all, he strides back in and gives her not only a chance, but puts her in charge of a small team to see what she can do.

She's out to fight monsters, to protect people, and yeah, he has to step in time and time again as it all goes badly.

Sure, some of that is his fault—he's not perfect—but *seriously*?

She'd always felt that if there were two forks in the road, and they led to the place she was supposed to be, to the easier and right path for her? She'd been a mile down the other path before she'd realized.

Always.

It was like she was cursed. So this time around, she'd been determined, she'd been absolutely goddamn determined that she'd not fuck this up! She was on an insanely important mission, and she had a real chance to prove that she was someone the others could count on.

She was a Paladin, a Paladin with a shield and a fucking mace, and the enemy were basically robots.

They ran at her, and the few times they survived long enough to get into range, yeah, she finally did some good. But the rest of the time? She was too weak to lead the way through the doors, she'd been told, because if the enemy got a hold of her, they'd kill her. And she had only two spells still, thanks to her quests being to basically kill any threat to peace and spread the word of her god!

She had an area healing spell that was great, but it wasn't cheap. And her Smite? She could either use it to boost her healing spell, or she could use it to smite her enemies.

The thing was, though, it required a blow! She needed to hit the enemy to unleash that power. If she was kept back, basically on crowd control, then she was never going to get enough XP to reach her next level.

Last, and worst of all, Matt *hated* being the focus of a religion! That was really obvious, and she felt terrible about it. She'd taken to hanging back at the back of the group. And when she did try to do her job and to spread the word of his powers to complete her quest? The looks she got from everyone was like she was trying to gargle with his dick in public.

She *hated* it. The whole situation was utterly stupid. It brought her to the edge of tears constantly, with only her helmet keeping the others from realizing just how shitty she felt. Now, as the group ran forward, the sounds of battle distantly echoing down from overhead, she desperately tried to bury the feeling that everyone would be better off if she just died in this fight.

That, as she ran forward, seeing the massive form of what had to be the dungeon boss, was how she felt, right up until her Divine link to Matt surged.

A white-hot searing pain burst passed through her. She gasped, almost falling as she tried to make sense of it all, slowing and ignoring the contemptuous snort of Saros as she bounded past her.

Only Catherine, the one person who was even less use in the dungeon than she was, even noticed she was having issues. And what was she supposed to say to her? No, she just waved her on, frantically trying to figure out what had just happened.

A second wave of pain flared and vanished. Her eyes were drawn upward, to latch onto a patch of rock overhead, where she knew, she just *knew* that Matt was fighting for his life.

She snapped her head around, seeing the huge doors that lay sealed tightly shut on the far side of the cavern, the two rows of clankers that were reloading and firing in constant, unchanging waves, and the giant construction that stomped its way forward.

She took it all in, in a split second. Righteous rage filled her for the second time in her life.

Five points of Divine essence she could hold. Five points. Ten seconds a point, and for every blow that she landed, the damage doubled.

Fifty seconds…yeah, she could do this. She *WOULD* do it!

She screamed out her war cry. A distant part of her cringed at doing something so stupid, something that would draw attention to her. But the greater part, the part that was rising into ascendency right now, was the same part that had driven her to act to protect people on the march from Sunderland. It was the part that had made her stand up for Jonnie, to fight in his memory, and to lead a damn rebellion and an escape.

It was the part that drove her, despite her fear, to fight to free the others, and then to become a Paladin in truth, no longer just in her dreams.

It was the part that was who Robin *could* be, and the tiny voice was the shrinking voice that was left from the abused, bullied, and ignored woman she had been.

Robin the Paladin roared in fury and leapt into the fight.

CHAPTER THIRTY

Impact.
Pain.
Confusion.
Impact.
Pain.

The world was shrinking as I tried time and again to summon my mana, to heal myself, to stop the attacks!

Something surged in me now. Over and over, it rose—it screamed, it roared, and it sank.

As each impact drove me further from my sanity, further from thinking things through and instead deeper into my core, the core of myself, of who I was, it surged again and again.

The power was there, filling me and then vanishing each time I tried to clutch at it. I felt it.

I needed it.

The minutes came and went; tens of them blurred past as I hung there, being beaten and battered. The world receded; my grasp on things weakened, until the golden light flared again.

I lost it over and over. Every time it flooded me and every time I grabbed at it and tried to feed it through my channels to accomplish *anything*, it failed!

I'd come back to myself. A sudden surge of power stripped away the pain and confusion, the bleariness and fear, and I'd have a tiny fragment of time in which I was aware… Then I'd reach for it all, and it'd slip away again.

I was blind. The helmet and its covering kept any light from getting through. The clamp around my neck kept me in place as blow after blow mercilessly rained down. And inside, that bright-white golden power surged repeatedly!

I felt the crackle of it, even as my mana bottomed out, the last of it drained long since to keep healing me, even as the points ticked back upward again and again.

The mana migraine made everything harder. The broken bones, the grinding of them together and apart. The ache. The spreading heat. The feeling of internal bleeding. The sight of my HP plummeting second by second: all of it rolled together into one long barrage of pain and punishment until finally I cracked.

What use was it!

What fucking use was the goddamn Divine core and its essence if, when I needed it the most, it never responded!

I stared at it, desperately furious with it. Then, checking my Divine core more carefully, I was filled with even more anger. It wasn't…it wasn't full!

It was down to half! I panicked, a sudden fear that Robin was about to drain me all over again, until the pulse washed through me instead.

It was healing *me*.

My Divine core was flooding my body *reactively*; it was healing me. It was…that was why it was…

My mind spun, and for the first time, I stopped grabbing at the golden blue-white stream of power that flooded me.

Instead, I let it come and go. And the difference? I was getting low on it…I could feel that. I was down to six points, and it'd take forever to refill. Well, about four hours, actually, but as things stood right now, that was longer than I was going to live unless something changed, and right goddamn now.

The light poured through me and without me fighting, desperately trying to grab and direct it, it filled my body. The pain smoothed away. I distantly heard shouts and felt…something.

It felt like the next impact was by a cushion rather than a bat, or even one of those foam-padded things.

My Divine essence bar was draining still, but I suddenly knew what the difference was…or so I thought. Either this was going to work, or this was going to go very, very badly wrong.

I didn't try to guide it. I didn't try, as I had been doing, to drag and shove it into a form that I wanted. Instead, I let my mind sink into myself, surrounded by the golden glow, and I relaxed.

The shield that I was betting was surrounding me right now wasn't something I'd summoned.

It was something I *needed*.

The healing? Again, it was need.

Now, as I opened my eyes in the deep blackness of my helmet, I knew exactly what I needed. I envisaged it, the ring of force that would wash out from me, destroying anything that was within an arm's reach of me with purifying lightning.

I didn't guide it, or ask for it. I simply released it: no curbs, no pushing…just utter *destruction*.

I felt the release as the power erupted from me. The last, single point of Divine essence that I'd forced myself to keep back still filled me, binding my bones and sealing my latest injuries closed. But all around me?

The ground beneath my feet slammed into my boots as the clamps and chains that had been holding me in place were annihilated a mere six inches from me.

Everything on all sides, out to three meters in every direction, was utterly devastated, including the arms that had been holding me, the mechanical creations that had been beating me, the walls, the floor, and one of Simon's hands, where he'd been apparently gesturing languidly, directing his creations to beat me to death.

I saw all of this, as I reached up and dragged the covering that had been clamped onto my helmet around, the clamp still latched onto my neck. But the space between it and my helmet allowed me to twist it enough that I could now see.

I could also hear—and that little fucker was screeching in fury and panic, disbelief and horror.

It was a noise that changed and warbled, right up until I grabbed him by the wrist and yanked him forward, straight into my other fist, as it lashed out and into his face.

As soon as my fist hit his face, a new notification flared. It was suppressed instantly. But it, and many others, were simply added to the pile at this point. With a shift of my feet, I bit down on the grinding pain that filled me with the movement. Then, as he slumped back in the chair he'd been sitting in, I stomped on his crotch.

His mouth had been open with the scream, and the sudden change of volume and pitch would have been music to my ears at any other point. But I knew what he'd been attempting to do to me.

He'd been trying to keep me too off-balance and in pain to use my spells or abilities, and damn if that wasn't exactly what I needed to do.

Either he died, here and now, *hard*, or he needed to be neutralized as a threat.

As a Dungeon Lord, one whose dungeon was actively surrounding me right now, the only way he wasn't a threat was if he was unconscious or dead.

I ground my foot on his balls, then moved it off, grabbed the back of his head and, fully understanding that Simon had picked a totally different path than me— he was about as un-martial looking as it was possible to be—I grabbed the back of his head and drove the bridge of his nose into the edge of the table he'd been sitting at.

There was a crunch of bone, a loud one, and when I lifted my hand away, he stayed where he was.

"Maybe..." I panted, staring at the way he was pinned in place, the edge of the table literally driven into the front of his smashed skull. "Just maybe...I used a...*little* more...force than...I meant to."

The dungeon immediately shook around me. Another notification dinged, flashing to get my attention. This time, after glancing around sharply and shifting the metal box as it slid so that I could make sure I was indeed alone, I opened it and quickly read.

331

There were a dozen or so notifications. I had no goddamn time for most of it. I dismissed a kill counter, the experience I'd received, and paused as the dungeon one showed up, then quickly flicked through them.

Congratulations, Adventurer!

You have discovered an actively hostile Dungeon! As the latest adventuring party to enter the Dungeon, in knowledge of its potential and your own capability, you have received a Quest!

Whoever rules the Dungeon, rules the land!

As a rival Dungeon Lord, you have entered a hostile dungeon, triggering a maximum-level response…

The Hostile Dungeon, identified as Dungeon 047, and its Dungeon Lord are now fully aware of you and your identity—and will stop at nothing to terminate you. Should you make it through the Dungeon to the Core, however, and claim control, you would receive the following rewards!

- **1x Satellite Dungeon Facility**

  OR

- **1x Dungeon Core Shard**
- **1x Additional Dungeon Core Upgrade Path**
- **1x Dungeon Perk**
- **1x Tech Upgrade (Random)**
- **1x Class Skill Point**
- **10,000 XP**

Next…fucking *next*!

Congratulations, Dungeon Lord!

**You have found a: [Torture Chamber].
Do you wish to claim the [Torture Chamber] for your Dungeon?**

Yes/No

I selected yes, even seeing the thousand mana it was asking for and knowing I didn't have anywhere near that. Currently, I had a grand total of four points—four goddamn points—but it was better to claim it than to let the opportunity pass me by.

The next screen was better.

WARNING

Personal Combat between Dungeon Lord 112: Matt, Lord of the Storm, and Dungeon Lord 047: Simon, Mechanist, has been initiated!

As this is a personal combat between two Dungeon Lords, please select from the following possible prizes:

- *Total control of the Dungeon*
- *Territorial Claim (to be specified)*
- *Resource Claim: (to be specified)*
- *Subjugation!*

To the winner go the spoils!

That was the latest one, and apparently it'd triggered when the bastard had hit me with whatever he'd been using. I'd been too out of it and he'd apparently been too consumed with madness, bile, and hatred, so we'd both missed the chance there.

Congratulations!

Dungeon Lord 112: Matt, Lord of the Storm, has defeated Dungeon Lord 047: Simon, Mechanist, in personal combat.

WARNING:

Another claimant has been declared for control of Dungeon 047; Unaligned fairy #047, identification "Marchioness" has initiated a claim on this dungeon.

Do you wish to relinquish your claim as conqueror?

Yes/No

"Fuck no." I snorted, and the "no" section flashed as my decision was accepted.

As this dungeon is currently [Contested], please access the core, or provide sufficient mana to claim the immediate location around the core and hold it for one solar cycle.

333

I read it, then grinned evilly as a new thought occurred to me. I didn't know where the fucker had hidden the core, but I damn well knew it'd not be far from his quarters. This was apparently his personal torture chamber and seeing the slovenly shitehawk, I was betting he'd not be moving around much.

I glanced over at him, noting the filthy clothing, the grim and greasy coating on the multiple rings on each finger, the potbelly and lack of anything even remotely related to hygiene or sunlight. I forced myself to move around the room, looking at the rest of it.

The nicely designed room was completely trashed. Clearly, it'd been laid out to achieve exactly what it had: a totally different ambiance that distracted you as soon as you stepped in.

The area now looked like someone had blown up a big balloon, then everything that it'd touched or pressed against had been reduced to dust. A circular mass around where I'd stood culminated in a shallow bowl that had been directly under and above me.

Just beyond it, in the far end of the room—behind me as I'd stepped in—had been the table, and apparently a recess in the wall where Simon himself had hidden. Sod's Law, I'd chosen to look in entirely the wrong bloody direction on entry.

The pain as I moved was...well, it was significant. A big part of it came from the condition of my armor, as it was dented inward in places that were applying pressure that was more than uncomfortable.

I was still finding myself easily distracted and woolgathering. And the dent in the back of my head where the helmet pushed in? That wasn't going to be good when I eventually removed it.

At best, I was betting bleed on the brain, and that was being held at bay only by my Divine essence healing me.

That ticked up to two points, then back down to one as it infused my body again. I sighed as some of the pain was washed free.

Okay, the core... I'd brought three cores with me, mana cores that were used to power the mechanoids. I'd used them on smashing my way in and killing the fuckers outside, but that just meant that I needed to kill another and free the core from it. I'd absorb that, then power that mana into the torture chamber—not something I really wanted to claim, but that was life—and then I should be able to start pushing outward.

I staggered out into the corridor I'd come from. It was silent and abandoned; the lights had failed, and only a little reflected light from something in the distance burning gave me enough for my own augmented vision to help with.

I moved back and snatched up a candelabra that had been on the table, hefting it; then I searched the room.

After two laps, I spotted the hilt of my sword poking out from under some debris. I ripped it loose, flipped it around, and promptly beheaded that fucker Simon, just in case.

With that done, and ignoring the remaining flashing of notifications, I started to search.

The corridor beyond was empty and soundless. Even heading in the other direction, I passed nothing of any use. Reaching a stairwell that led downward, I took it, bracing myself on one wall...before getting ready as sounds ahead caught my attention.

They filtered through weirdly; I couldn't make much out. But focusing, I took the turn in the stairs, and kept listening, trying to determine whether they were the rest of my party or that crazy dungeon fairy or...

I took the corner again and yelped. I threw myself back, arms flailing, as I came face-to-face with one of the machinist's creations.

My sword—of course—chose that moment to get caught up on the handrail that ran down the wall, twisting itself painfully around before the tip, now robbed of any real force or speed, gouged a thin line across the metal of its left leg.

Then I fell down.

That, *of course*, was when the noises I'd been hearing finally resolved with meaning, as Saros slipped out of the darkness to stare down at me.

"Dungeon Lord?" She frowned, clearly taking the overall position, the damage, and the blood-stained armor, and the silent and still figure that stood over me all into account, before she spoke. "You are afraid?" she asked. "Or have drunk too much of the fermented juices?"

"Ferment... No!" I finally forced out. "I'm not fucking drunk *or* afraid!" That last one had clearly been a lie, considering the shock of coming face-to-face with the damn thing, but that wasn't the point. "The others...are they okay?"

"They are, though somewhat tired and damaged. Armor and fur mainly, nothing a good rest will not fix," she said. "There was much fighting, and even some honor to be found for the kittens."

"Kittens?" I asked, then shook my head. "The younger ones." I nodded that I understood, even if it was a case of she was the youngest by a significant margin. Clearly, she didn't agree.

"Open that bastard's chest," I ordered her, before calling into the darkness. The flickering candelabra by my feet now offered less and less illumination as the candles guttered out.

"All clear!" I called in the direction of the incoming sounds, wincing at the internal echoing of my own voice, before picking up a candle and forcing myself to my feet.

Saros scraped and battered at the creation's chest. "You wish to fight me, eh?" she muttered to it. She lost her temper, beating on it harder and harder, even as the noise of her claws catching the metal rang out.

"Matt?" Chris's voice called from the darkness.

But Beta reached me first. The big kobold, loyal as ever, bounded out of the distance and ran to grab me, taking my weight as I nodded to her, my helmet barely allowing me to turn my head thanks to everything.

The others appeared soon after, gathering up and standing around. Their questions filled the air until I held a hand up in exhaustion.

"We need the mana core out of this, then we need to get back to the section I was in above us…unless any of you have found the dungeon core?" I asked to a general shaking of heads.

"Let's move." Mike came to help, and got growled at by Beta, then backed up with a smile. "You help him then. Saros, you not got that out yet?"

"It is metal!" she snapped. "I try to remove it, without the damage, yes? You want me to damage it?"

"Here!" Kilo growled, stepping in close and dragging his claws down the side of the housing. The air filled with even worse squealing noises that lasted until Chris could shove them all back.

"Fuck's sake, get him up there and leave me a candle. I'll sort it," he growled, taking my offered sword from me with a nod.

I didn't need all the help that Beta was offering—I'd managed to get down there on my own, after all—but the sheer level of damage, the exhaustion, and the nigh-on total lack of mana meant that I was physically dropping now.

It had to be because I knew that the others were there—that was all that I could attribute it to. The wave of relief that swept over me, knowing that each and every one of them had my back, was incredible enough that I felt light-headed.

Well, that or the dent in the back of my skull.

Either way, the world was definitely a little wibbly-wobbly. That was the only reason I could put it down to, as some time later, Chris clicked his fingers before my eyes, breaking me out of the reverie I'd fallen into.

"Shit." I mumbled, "How long was I out?"

"If by out you mean catatonic and unresponsive?" Mike asked worriedly. "About ten minutes."

"I'm here," I muttered, checking my mana and nodding to myself, relieved that I had just over two hundred mana in my pool and two Divine essence points. "The core," I murmured after a few seconds of hard thought. "I need to get the core and…"

"Here," Chris said worriedly, pushing it into my hands.

"Oh, thank fuck." I squinted at it with one eye shut. It seemed to be getting harder to think, definitely harder to stay focused. I spoke as I quickly drained the mana core.

"Okay, people, I'm going to claim this…" I waved generally in the direction of the overall room as I went on. "Once it's part of the dungeon, I'm going to assign some rights, and then try to absorb this…" I tapped at the collar and shifted around the torture and blinding mask that still covered half my head.

"Yeah, it's a bit of a weird fashion accessory," Mike noted.

"As soon as I've done that, I need this helmet off. It's against my flesh, so I can't just absorb it the way I can this thing..." I tapped the box thingy. "And that dent in the back? It's pressing into my skull, so it's not going to come off easily. Do it fast, then use this..." I pulled the highest strength potion I had from my pocket and pushed it at Chris.

"You sure about this?" He exchanged an uneasy look with Mike.

"Not really, no," I admitted, tossing the depleted core aside and blinking, sucking down a deep breath. "Whoa, when you're not in a mad panic, that hits like a line of the best Colombian marching powder," I muttered, checking my mana, before shoving the needed nine hundred and ninety-six mana into claiming the torture chamber.

Congratulations, Dungeon Lord!

You have claimed an enemy Dungeon's [Torture Chamber] and have imbued it with 1000 points of your own mana!

Are you ready to establish your Foothold here?

Yes/No...

That really wasn't a hard decision to make. I selected the *yes* as soon as the option appeared. The world shuddered slightly, before the comforting presence of my own dungeon appeared all around me.

The torture chamber was converted into a tall obelisk that acted as the foothold on the enemy dungeon for me, just like last time the breeders' hut had been changed the same way.

The difference was that this time as it did it, the room had been badly damaged and recessed into the ground. As the light faded, we were suddenly surrounded by bare stone walls on two sides, the corridor we'd entered from on another, and then finally, a small room that reeked of unwashed bodies—or, specifically, a single unwashed body and a load of rotting food.

The dungeon's influence reached out for five meters in all directions. I sagged backward in relief as I sank into the dungeon sense, mentally tagging Chris and Mike and assigning them full authority alongside myself over this section of the dungeon.

Then I selected the metal that still half covered my head, and almost wept in frustration at the refusal from the dungeon. It was seeing the metal just as it did

337

my armor or clothing. It was in contact with me, with my flesh or something, and as such, it couldn't affect it.

I sat there for long seconds in silence, before finally nodding. It was only iron, I reminded myself; just untreated iron. Sure, it was hard and strong, but it wasn't like it was a fucking diamond or something.

It was going to suck monkey balls getting the damn thing off, but the rest of the job still had to be done. As I turned to Mike and Chris, I could see that they understood it too.

"So how do we do it?" Mike asked me, and I hesitated, then shrugged.

"We start with the sharpest, strongest snips we can come up with, maybe a saw, and then we look to add heat when we need to," Chris said. "Matt, mate, this is going to…"

"It's gonna suck." I agreed, amused despite everything that we'd both thought the exact same thing there.

"So, no time like the present." He nodded, focusing and summoning a small hacksaw, before grinning at me nervously. "Shall we?"

"There's a fairy out there still," I said as he moved around to stand behind me, one hand braced on the metal and looking for a position to start sawing. "She's sealed into a…well, into a humanoid automata, and I just remembered that Jack is as well!"

"Jack's human?" Chris paused and looked at me.

"No, dammit." I fought to think straight and to explain. "Jack vanished. He's somewhere overhead, though I think he's just in a trap. Marchioness said…"

That led into a ten- or fifteen-minute conversation, while they worked—one that ended with the others being spread out throughout this underground hellhole, searching, and finding precisely fuck all of use.

A further fifteen minutes after that—with a crowbar, two kobolds, and a lot of swearing—finally, the clamps around my neck, wrists, and ankles were off, and I could start stripping out of my armor.

That took a little longer than normal, mainly due to the sheer levels of damage done to it. And now that I no longer had the bits that had been covering some sections and people could clearly see all of it?

There was a general acceptance that I'd had the living shit kicked out of me.

The helmet was the first thing to go. Jenn sat by my side, Kilo on the other. Apparently, if I went into shock, he was going to try to drop my temperature to help deal with that, and to slow any bleeding on the brain. And Chris was ready with both his own healing spell and a spare healing potion.

Jenn had her healing spell and a potion, and Robin was ready with her area of effect heal, while Mike was prepared with his own basic rough-and-ready special forces medical training.

All in all, it was a shitty thing to do, but as Beta gripped my helmet, and I spoke the words, I knew I had my best chance for survival.

"Do it." Then I hissed in pain.

The dent in the back of the helmet was the main issue. But it'd also twisted the helmet slightly to the side, meaning that much in the way that there was only one way to wear a helmet due to its shape, removing it was going to be a painful experience.

I'd told Beta before this that she couldn't stop, that when the time came to pull the helmet off, it was going to really fucking hurt, and she needed to keep doing it.

She'd nodded and accepted that. I'd understood what I was asking, but I still wasn't prepared for the reality of it.

The helmet was dragged upward, even as Jimmy braced my shoulders to keep me straight and down. What I'd expected to be a bit damn painful, and maybe draw a hiss or a manly grunt at the pain, instead drew a shriek, before the pressure on the back of my head that had been kept in more or less check by the constant low-level cycling of my Divine essence was suddenly made oh, so much worse.

The crackling of the widest and rearmost part of my skull as she dragged the dented section upward, as well as the immediate hot wash of bleeding into my brain, only compounded that damage.

Her claws, to maintain her grip and allow her to literally pull metal across and up over bone, breaking it, had to be latched under the rim. That meant that as the helmet passed up from my chin all the way over my entire goddamn head, her claws tore furrows as they went.

I lost my left eye.

Quite literally, I felt it as one of her claws dragged across the cheek, the twanging of the muscles and tendons, and that unforgettable sensation as the tip got caught under my eyelid, ripping it and the front of the bulging eye to shreds.

I *shrieked*.

The pain was horrific and made only worse by the fact that I was prepared and knew it was going to be bad. In a fight? When things like this had happened in the past, I was filled with adrenaline and they were over almost before I knew about it.

Right now, I was ready, aware, and damn well knew what was happening—and that made it all the more awful.

The helmet came free with a sickening, final crunch. Before I knew it, I was being doused in healing potions, magic was washing over me, and as soon as the others had moved back, a sudden crash of Lightning joined the rest, as even Emma unleashed a thunderbolt into my face.

It wasn't the first time that woman had wanted to do that, I bet, but the healing power of the storm was incredible for me.

The pain was horrible still. Sections of my sodden cranium snapped, crackled, and popped back into their correct place, and finally, finally, as the last vestiges of my agony and fear receded, I felt a touch of relief.

That had been awful, terrible in such a way that I just knew I was going to be having nightmares over it.

I was alive still, though, and the enemy weren't—and that made all the difference. Or at least it did, right up until I was stripped down to my under armor layer—the armor was laid out to be repaired—and Saros bounded into the room with the good news.

Marchioness was here, and she'd brought friends.

CHAPTER THIRTY-ONE

"**M**att!" the fairy greeted me, as I reached the hole we'd torn in the floor to allow Saros to clamber up and go on watch. "You survived! I was pleased to note your success, right up until you claimed my dungeon as your own. Perhaps this is a misunderstanding?" she called down.

I looked from her to the figures that ringed her, all looking down at us.

"No," I shouted back. "I think *this* is a misunderstanding. You, here, with armed people I don't know, thinking you're a threat. Back up, get rid of them, and come back tomorrow. This was a hard fight, and we'll talk then," I offered, gesturing to them to back off.

"Alas, I think not." She shook her head, waving one damaged arm like the elegant noblewoman she was pretending to be. "I think that would only compound the error, Matt. Surrender my dungeon back to me *now*, and I'll permit you to leave. We can discuss the terms of any future alliances when I've had time to settle and pacify the area again."

"And leave your weapons," the thug to her left called out as well, pointing a handgun at my face as I peered up at him. "Leave them, and anything else you've got. *Then* you leave."

"And our women as well, I take it?" I suggested. "Kiss your boots and beg your forgiveness as well?"

He stared down at me, a smug, self-satisfied smile on his face. Marchioness smiled coldly by his side, braced in a seat carried by two other automatons.

"Matt, there's no need for this to be any more unpleasant than it has to be. Your betrayal of our deal meant I had to seek alliances elsewhere. These gentlemen have already agreed to help me settle the area and develop my dungeon. While you betrayed me once already. What did you think was going to happen?"

"I think you had no intention of dealing with me fairly at all, and you expected me to capture and hand over the dungeon to you in exchange for a little advice and background I didn't need. I think me leaving you alive was a mistake and a kindness I'm coming to regret. But we both know where we stand now." I glared at her.

She sighed and then nodded. "It's a shame, but then, this was always how it was going to end," she admitted. "You'd never have given up the dungeon willingly and I knew that. So do you want to see what I spent my time doing,

Matt? While you fought and bled, like the good little blunt weapons your kind are, I made an *alliance*. I broke my home and many of my creations down, making these in their place."

As she spoke, the first barrel was rolled into sight, swiftly joined by others. I nodded as I realized that she had indeed come up with a plan, and fuck me, was it a doozy.

"That what I think it is?" I called up, while gesturing to the others to back up.

"You called it diesel, I believe," she responded. "I found the original components in one of the internal combustion engines that dotted the area. While there are more efficient and powerful compounds that I could have created, there was simply no need. I require minimal structural damage to be done before rebuilding can begin. It will, however, be more than powerful enough to either burn you all alive, or ensure you remain trapped in there, while I reach my core and reintegrate. Goodbye, Matt, and again, thank you for your service."

With that, the first of the thugs stepped up and pulled a bung free, then tipped the barrel over. The liquid sloshed and poured down the wall toward us, as I bellowed at the others to run.

Then, being the utter bastard that I was, as I started to run, I did the only thing I could. Rather than wait for them to throw in a torch and set light to the fuel, I instead spent all the available mana I had, and a bunch of my health as well through my blood magic, and triggered a lightning storm behind me and up on the level above, focused in tight around the area they'd been standing.

Mutually assured destruction, baby.

I grinned evilly as I ran, as the sudden pressure change occurred and the first rumbles of storm clouds filled the area. Shouts and screams rang out. I damn well knew that not all the storm would activate, nor be of any use…but that area she'd been in?

The area that they'd all been standing in? That'd been open to the sky, letting my spell make itself known. I imagined the thugs' and her faces as they realized that we still had teeth. Then, as the clangs of falling barrels rang out, the scuffing of running feet and panicked cries echoed back, I banished their soon-to-be lesson from my mind. I needed to ensure we fucking survived.

The others ran grouped around me, and, stumbling as I went, I summoned small walls as soon as we hit the outer edge of the dungeon's control area, staggered behind us, each of them slowing more and more of the racing liquid.

There wasn't time to summon a full wall and seal before some of the liquid made it through, disrupting the summon. So instead, they were more like water breaks, or walls in a harbor.

Each served to delay the water—or fuel—and the amount that made it over and into the next area was lessened and slowed.

The first bolt of lightning that hit a barrel above was obvious. The muffled boom that shook the entire building made me nod, as I imagined the look on those fucker's faces, right before it was melted off.

Then the tempo increased as a second, a third, then five and more bolts echoed. The mixture of fuel and air-born particles behind me—already filling the areas we'd left behind—now exploded with a solid *whump* that I felt in my chest.

Fortunately, I was far enough ahead at that point that the wave front, when it hit, did little more than stagger me. Ahead of me, I saw that one of the others had already had the same plan as I had, but more time to carry it out. I dove over the low wall that appeared, landing with a clatter of gear as the last of the others joined me.

"Now!" someone shouted.

The glittering fireflies of the dungeon's summoning slid upward as soon as I was through. Another section was added atop it, then another, and the billowing flames that sucked the air from the room died away.

I rolled, coming to my feet, and beat the few flaming spots on my clothes out, knowing that this was only the first round.

"Everyone okay?" Mike called out. A chorus of nods and affirmative responses rang out, before Chris added his own.

"Well, my fucking pride took a hit, but that's it," he admitted. "What the hell did they hit us with?"

"Diesel," I said shortly, glancing over the under armor outfit I'd been wearing. It was scuffed, filthy, and bloody before, and the fire really hadn't improved it.

It felt...well, crispy was probably the best description.

"Seriously?" Chris shook his head. "What the hell was that? It went up more like friggin' napalm!"

"The fire?" I asked, confused, then I winced as I realized that he'd missed my little gift; they all probably had. "Ah, that explosion was me," I admitted. "I saw what they were doing, and thought fuck it. I didn't have enough mana for a full-on powerful lightning storm, so it was just a little one, but it got the job done."

"Nice!" He laughed. "Ah, no stress then. So now that they're all dead, what's the next step?"

I checked the notifications, then growled under my breath. "I killed some of them, but not her."

"So you just trapped us inside in a burning building for nothing?" Mike frowned at me.

I shook my head. "She was going to light it to keep us contained, either way. This way, she lost some of her forces as well. Even if she's got more, they're going to be a lot less happy to attack us now, and they know we've got teeth. Time to get to work on claiming the area, expanding the dungeon, then fucking them all over."

"You say that like there's a plan?" Emma noted, and I nodded.

"There's always a plan. We're trapped in here at the minute, and we don't know where the core is, only that it's here, somewhere. Marchioness wouldn't have bothered to try to kill us or trap us if it wasn't. She'd have just gone straight for it and have sealed us all in.

"The one thing she doesn't realize is that Simon, that wonderfully sneaky dickhead, created a trap for Jack. I'm betting that big, beautiful bastard is still up there somewhere, just sealed away inside it."

"How does that help us?" she asked.

I smiled. "Well, he's on one of the levels above, right where she's licking her wounds right now."

The smiles that broke out from the others were evil, as we all imagined the damage that Jack would be able to do to them, especially unprepared as they were going to be for a giant bear-shaped automata with a bad attitude.

Even more so considering that she was housed in an Iron core version and he was in a Steel one, as well as being intact and heavily designed for war, while she was…well, I didn't want to think about what she'd been designed for, now that I thought about it. But I was fairly sure that a sex doll had been involved in her ancestry somewhere, and that was just nasty.

"All we have to do is keep her locked out, expand to him, then let him wreak havoc," I said. "And while we do that? Griffiths and his team are going to be setting up, ready for the main event, so we need to be getting our fingers out to move ahead with the plan."

"What do you need?" Mike asked.

I hesitated for a minute, then shook myself clear of the thought. "It's back to basics time," I said. "Instead of going all out making this dungeon into a massive bonus for us all, I think it's time to make field expedient decisions instead. First of all, we're all pushing the dungeon out as fast as possible. We repair what we can, and we make sure the structure is solid, but beyond that, anything here that doesn't get us to the core is unneeded.

"We've got hardly any mana. Until the dungeon has additional parts, like a full-on core to generate its own mana, we're limited to whatever mana we put into the local system, or whatever we get from absorbing things in the immediate area. As such, I want two teams. One is on cleanup—anything and everything, absorb it and move on. Second team—any spare mana goes into expansion of our control area, and searching the fucking place.

"I don't think the core can be far away, or she'd not have been so desperate to stop and kill us. But we need to find it, and before she does. As soon as that's done, we claim the core, and we'll make a decision then. Most likely, we break it and learn a new skill or bonus for the dungeon."

"It seems a waste to break it and abandon it," Emma said softly, and I nodded to her.

"It is," I agreed. "Hell, if we had the time, I'd much rather set up a colony or city-state system here, turn this dungeon over to an ally and move on, leaving them to grow it and bring more of the country under our control. The issue is that we don't know what the area is like. For all we know, we're right in the middle of a bunch of gangs and we'd need to entirely pacify the area again before we could move on. We've not got the time to fuck around with that, and we can't risk handing a fully functional dungeon over to the gangs."

"One point," she said suddenly after a few seconds' thought. "You said that if you die, the dungeon dies—is that not right then? I mean, you just killed this guy and now you're going to claim his dungeon, and you're deciding what to do with it. Surely it should be dead...right?"

"And there it is." Mike snorted. "I knew if anyone figured that out, it'd be you."

Emma glanced from him to me and back suspiciously. "So it was all a lie?" she asked me shrewdly.

"No." I sighed. "We weren't entirely sure is the honest truth. When we fought the dungeon that was presumably supposed to be set up in our area at home, the one that was built in the Tesco supermarket in Gateshead? As soon as the dungeon fairy died, things started going to pieces. And we know that the dungeon is linked to living creatures. There's a lot of warnings in the system about dungeons that do things that are highly destructive to their surrounding areas, and these ones are manufactured, as near as we can tell, to primarily uplift the human race.

"From what we know, the dungeon can massively fail and even go feral, breaking down or killing everyone...maybe even going nuclear if it's left unmanaged. And to integrate with the dungeon properly, you need the prerequisite classes. Like Dungeon Lord." I tapped my chest.

"Will it all fall apart if it doesn't have a Dungeon Lord? Probably not, so long as it still has a fairy. We don't have a fairy, and this one doesn't have an attached lord either. As near as we know, it's a symbiotic relationship. Take one away and the dungeon is weaker but survives; take away both and the shit hits the fan. Long-term, I think the dungeon would go feral and create stronger and stronger monsters until it was defeated and someone claimed it, or it went nuclear.

"Short-term, if someone managed to get to the core, they'd probably be able to take over—again, providing they could get the class."

"And how would they get the class?" Emma watched me carefully.

"Thinking of assassinating me?" I asked her calmly, and she snorted.

"Hardly. It's far too much work right now, and I don't deal well with people. If I was in charge? There'd have been a lot less niceties with the idiots you kicked out and a lot less *please* and *thank you* with the general running."

I lifted an eyebrow, and she shrugged.

"I'm not good with people, you know that," she admitted. "I try, but I'd end up burning it all down or going to war in a week."

"We're at war," I pointed out.

"Yeah, but I mean for no good reason." She sighed. "Honestly, do I want a dungeon? Yeah, I do, because everyone always wants to be in charge. I know there's a lot of things you've done that I'd have done differently...sure there is." She paused and took a deep breath before going on. "*But,* I'm not the best person

345

for something like this. I know myself too well. I was just curious, and yeah, thinking for a second that it'd be worth it if we could get our own family dungeon."

"Well, that's a step in the right direction," I said after a few seconds. "Knowing that you're not the right person is half the battle. It means that you try harder, and that's also why you have a partner, or in my case, a partner and a council of friends to tell me when I fuck up or to convince me when I might be making a mistake. Right now's not the time to talk about the future, though. That *would* be a mistake, and one that'd cost us everything. So…"

I looked around. Most of our small group was in the room with me as I gestured with one hand in a chopping motion down the center. "If you're on this side…" I indicated Mike, Beta, Kilo, Jenn, and Andre. "Then you're on cleanup. If you're on this side…" I indicated the remainder of the group. "Then you're on expansion. Come on, people, find somewhere as comfortable as possible to settle down, and then we get to it!"

And that, more or less, was that for the next two hours.

The outside of the building from ground level upward was on fire, and although the flames didn't last forever, they got hot enough that pretty much everything in there that could burn, now was.

That meant that the entire building aboveground was a no-go area for anything living. For Marchioness and her machines…although it'd be survivable for them, it might not be for her.

Regardless, if the core was underground, somewhere down here with us, she needed to get down here and past before she could do anything.

That was easily dealt with by sealing up the passages where we could, and pushing out.

The rooms were stripped to the bare stone and metal; everything that we could absorb was steadily taken in and destroyed. Room after room fell to our people as they worked in relay, side by side: one absorbed, the other pushed and shoved out the wall of the dungeon's control, pressing it into the actual walls and searched, checking for hidden doors, tricks, or spaces under the floor or whatever.

Hours passed as the search grew more and more desperate. More than once I switched, flitting from the section I was searching to get up and walk, trying to find a hint, a goddamn sign, somewhere that the fucking thing was here.

Without fail, though, I soon settled back down into the dungeon sense and got back to methodical searching.

By the end of two damn hours, I was increasingly frantic, second-guessing my decision to have everyone focus down here on expansion to reach the core, when instead I could have had everyone work on expanding our area of influence upward, burrowing through marble floors and through smoldering, smoke-filled corridors, in search of Jack.

Once we'd found and released him, we could search at our leisure, knowing that he'd rip her head off and shit down her neck…and then I'd reconsider.

Maybe as a dungeon fairy and an automata herself, she'd be able to stop him, to redirect him, to claim him or even be marked up as officially verboten as a target?

I didn't know whether it was possible, nor whether I'd be inches or meters away from finding him when she finally broke through to the core. So I'd searched for that instead, but with every second that passed, I second-guessed myself more and more.

Finally, when the doubt reached an absolute goddamn crescendo, Jenn let out a gasp of horror and ordered everyone back from the former lord's quarters in a panic.

"You've found it?" I demanded, flitting across the dungeon from where I'd been looking. "What's wrong!"

"The core?" she asked, stunned and barely able to tear her eyes from the pack rat's warren beyond, even seemingly standing next to me in the dungeon sense. "No, but I found so much more!"

"What?" I asked, confused, peering in. "Like what?"

"All of this!" She gestured to the room beyond, and I stared, totally bewildered.

The room she'd uncovered was buried in an entirely different section of the dungeon from the area I'd been searching, one that had apparently been hollowed out from the bedrock behind the dungeon's "kitchen."

Why the fuck it even had a kitchen when, as a dungeon inhabitant and the Dungeon Lord, he could just summon food was beyond me, but there you go.

On the far side of the kitchen, hidden behind a false wall—that I had to admit was damn well concealed—was the entrance to his quarters apparently, and yeah.

It was a fucking mess.

Even looking in, I was struck by the chaos and clutter that filled the place from wall to wall. It was a mess of haphazard but possibly brilliant innovation and utter filth.

In the dungeon sense, I couldn't smell it, but even at a glance I knew the air was thick with the smell of old paper, the stink of machine oil, and stale, rotting food.

Everywhere I looked, there were piles of discarded food wrappers and half-eaten meals, some moldering in corners with flies breeding on them. Fucking maggots literally fell to roll across the floor from a stack of discarded pizza boxes.

In the center of the room was a massive workbench. The top was barely visible under a sea of tools, gears, springs, and half-assembled contraptions.

Salvaged and rebuilt old and new mechanical marvels in various stages covered the area, piled like rubbish in some places, and stacked atop each other alongside drawings in others.

I even spotted one of those intricate orreries—or I thought that was what they were called, the planetarium things—with planets made of gemstones. In one case, as I drifted forward, I saw a plaque that identified something called a difference engine in a glass case with brass cogs glinting in the dim light, alongside a complex clockwork automaton with its covers removed and the interior half built.

Bookshelves lined the walls, although some of the shelves had collapsed under the weight of massive books. I paused, staring hard at a weird collection of books. It was literally what had to be a complete set of the *Oxford English Dictionary.* Then I let out a low whistle as I realized that for it to be here, stashed rather than left as a bloody dictionary and therefore not exactly night-time reading material should have been...it was probably the first one.

Its leather bindings were certainly cracked and worn enough. Nearby, a glass case housed what looked like an original manuscript, and Jenn, in a wondering voice, told me that its yellowed pages were covered in Lewis Carroll's distinctive handwriting.

I recognized the name, but little more than that, and was impressed that she knew it, frankly, given that of all of them, she often seemed the least aware of the world around her.

In one corner, a sign identified a "Vintage Marconi" radio set, atop a stack of scientific journals. Next to it, weirdly, was a modern laptop computer, its screen dark and covered in a layer of dust.

Glancing up, I saw that even hanging from the ceiling was an assortment of mechanical models—everything from steam engines to clocks and what, according to the plaque that stood next to it on a stand clearly looted from a museum, was proudly named as Charles Babbage's Difference Engine, suspended by chains, and much larger than the other one.

On another wall, I saw a cluttered desk, and a tarnished brass telescope peeking out from a stack of papers covered in complex mathematical equations. Strangely, there, next to all of this, was a blackboard nearby with clearly old and faded chalk markings on it. No clue whose they were, but someone thought them important enough to rescue the damn blackboard.

The room was an absolute clusterfuck of inspiration and madness, a testament to its former occupant's batshit and chaotic mind. It was probably a treasure trove of historical artifacts and mechanical wonders, and everything was buried under layers of neglect and disorder. The only thing that looking around here made clear was that in his obsession with his creations, Simon had no understanding of organization or cleanliness.

On the far side, tucked into a corner, was a ratty collection of magazines and a rumpled bed, and I just knew I didn't want to see what those magazines were.

I hesitated, chewing on a lip, then glanced at Jenn, only to find her staring at me.

"We can't," she said very firmly. "We can't absorb this—none of it!"

"Some of it we have to," I said just as firmly, determined that I didn't want to go anywhere near that corner.

"We don't know what could be in here!" she countered. "Do you realize what some of these things are? They're artifacts of our past, some of the greatest treasures of the age. These are things that I thought were all destroyed in museums, and they're things that we should be recovering anyway. This is our past, and we have to preserve it."

"She's right, dude," Chris said from the door, drifting in. "She's totally right about saving this place, but that's not why I'm here. Buckle up, buttercup—we found it!"

I hesitated, looking from her pleading expression to the mass of possible mana in the room, and the piles of moldering food, maggots, and worse.

"Seal it up," I told her after a brief pause. "Absorb anything and everything that you can in there—the pizza boxes, the trash—but leave the artifacts. Then seal the place up and we'll come back. But this is your responsibility, all right? I'm not interested and too fucking busy. You want to loot museums as we go? Claim everything and take it all home for safekeeping? Well, I guess it proves we're British. You want it, you come up with a plan to get it home. For now, just seal it up and get rid of the trash."

With that, and ignoring her effusive thanks and the relief, I turned to Chris. "Show me."

He reached out, grabbing my arm, and blurred us both across the dungeon to a location I'd passed over twice already.

CHAPTER THIRTY-TWO

"I noticed the floor," Chris admitted as I looked at him in question. "Everywhere else in this mess is either gleaming marble or really expensive carpets, right?"

I nodded at the comment, then let out a groan.

There was a massive difference. When I looked at this, even at a casual glance, it stood out like a sore thumb.

I'd been so focused on all the possible really sneaky hiding places that it'd never occurred to me to look at the really obvious difference.

The carpet that ran the length of this corridor was ill-fitted—too short for the actual full length, ending a good three feet from one end—and looked like something an elderly relative would have had forever, complete with the stains from an incontinent small dog. Possibly one of those yappy fuckers that was always savaging people, and was inevitably called Muffy or Princess.

It was stained, the pattern was faded to fuck, and unless this had come from the literal hallway of Einstein's house or someone like him, it had no business being here at all. That also made me think that if it had, it'd probably be mounted on a wall for students to stare at in search of inspiration, not realizing that the X mark was actually where the great man had once spilled his curry, drunk or high as fuck.

All in all, it was a really shitty hiding place, and that Chris was beaming the way he was, I couldn't help but groan.

I drifted down, passing through the layers of carpet, unidentifiable mess, and then the polished marble, the stone, some more general building materials, then a metal trap door, into a narrow section of the room that had been claimed, with Mike and Andre already working to claim more.

The room was roughly square, about two meters on a side, with a chair set to one side and a ladder that led back up to the floor overhead. The trap door indicated that it'd been awhile since it was last opened, presumably due to Simon's ability to access the core through the dungeon sense, just like mine.

The issue for me, and I saw it straightaway, was that the room was obviously custom grown for the core, and it looked like it'd been here months.

That meant that the damn fairy knew where the core was, and that bloody idiot Simon—possibly a genius in other ways, sure, looking at the evidence of his quarters—totally lacked any common sense.

The first thing I'd have done in his place was shift the core, no matter how much effort it was, and put a fucking trap in here.

That made me freeze, wondering whether this was an elaborate trap...then I shook that off. I could feel the core, now that I was through whatever shielding the walls and floor had been built with.

No, this was the real thing, and I knew it. Unfortunately, I also goddamn knew, as I reached out in the dungeon sense, that I couldn't just claim it from here.

I needed to physically touch it, and the effect... Well. It was going to suck monkey balls.

I looked up, outlining the trap door in my mental vision and clicking to absorb it all, just eating it into the dungeon, and then the carpet above, before blinking out of the dungeon and back into my own flesh.

Thirty seconds later, I sprinted down the corridor, leapt down stairs, bounced off walls and hurdled fallen debris and random shite that filled the corridors.

By the time I dropped to a sliding tackle that would have done my old footy coach proud, I was filled with a low level of panic that the enemy was still going to somehow beat me to this. So when I dropped through the roof to land on the floor, bouncing off the wall and slapping both hands directly onto the core, it was with a thundering heart. One that wasn't comforted at all by the crackle and zip of power that flooded my fingers.

Congratulations, Dungeon Lord!

You have found an unguarded Dungeon Core and have completed your Quest!

Now is the time of choice. Do you wish to raise up another Dungeon Lord and cede control of this Dungeon to them, thereby creating another dungeon in your Vassal Empire? Or do you wish to fracture the Core, claiming its treasures as bonuses for your own Dungeon?

Rewards:
- *A Satellite Dungeon*

OR

- *1x Dungeon Core Shard*
- *1x Additional Dungeon Core Bonus Research*
- *1x Dungeon Perk*
- *1x Tech Upgrade (Random)*
- *1x Class Skill Point*
- *10,000 XP*

This time, I did hesitate. I should claim the dungeon as a full dungeon, bringing it under our control. It was a mechanist dungeon, after all! There was so much we could learn from it. And the potential for another already established dungeon here?

It could be huge. All I had to do was…all I had to do was stay here myself and leave the others to fight against the undead, which I'd never do.

Or I could leave one of them here, to establish the dungeon and see what they made of it. Although I trusted most of them even to that level, that still felt all kinds of wrong. Or…or I could seal it up and just hope. Leave it running and just hope that nobody found it and managed to take it over.

If I'd killed Marchioness already and she'd not involved all her friendly neighborhood thugs, I might have done that. But as it was, for all I knew, she'd sent a copy body along, and she was hiding, waiting until we left to take over.

Or maybe I'd succeeded in killing her and all those she brought with her. Unlikely in the extreme, but it could have happened and I'd missed the notification. In which case…*well.*

There was no way I could know for sure that we'd gotten all of those that knew about the dungeon, and I couldn't see any gang leader with bodies to burn leaving the destruction of the dungeon down to a *maybe.*

I stared, still cursing internally, then picked a spot on the exterior of the dungeon and marked it as the fracture point.

I was going to have to kill the dungeon and escape with the others. Whatever artifacts and random museum-worthy goodies and general tech would have to be left.

We had places to go and undead to kill.

Nucleus point F-2 selected.

Core Fracture is beginning.

Please select from the following:

- *Dungeon Shard 4:*
  Grants +5 Constitution, +1 Endurance to all Dungeon Creatures
- *Dungeon Shard 23:*
  Grants +1 Ability/Spell depending on Dungeon Creature's proclivities
- *Dungeon Shard 37:*
  Grants +1 Creation Blueprint

I read and reread it. The tingle of the core's power flowed through my fingers. I was incredibly glad that it was reduced to a similar flow that I'd faced when I'd done this with the Gateshead dungeon at Bronze instead of the horrifically powerful backlash of power that'd nearly fried me from my own core when it was Steel, and damaged.

Clearly that'd been an effect of facing a damaged core, which was a massive relief.

Looking over my options, and seeing that the others, now visible to me in the dungeon sense through the glow of the core, were moving at a fraction of their normal speed, I decided to take a few minutes to make sure of things.

The Constitution and Endurance bonus was fairly big, or it was for a new dungeon.

When I'd first started out, that was a massive difference, granting my creatures the equivalent of several levels of points all in one go to start from.

Now, with the advanced creatures I was summoning, it wasn't even a full level.

Dismissing that option, it took me down to either all my dungeon-born getting an additional ability or spell—depending on whether they were magic users or martial or whatever, I guessed—or a single creation blueprint.

The creation blueprint was tempting—genuinely, it was. I wanted it. Just wondering what kind of a creation it could be rolled through my mind like it was Christmas coming early, considering the potential of the mechanist dungeon.

The mana cores? Massive bloody upgrade on my mana crystals, just as a single example... But, if I went out and searched, found one of the dead mechanist's creations and ripped it out? I could absorb it into the dungeon and, if not produce them straightaway, Aly would be able to reverse engineer it, I had no doubt.

I debated for a handful of seconds, then made the choice I knew I had to. I selected the additional skill or ability for all of my dungeon-born.

That was massive, after all. Granting all my mages—sorry, *mancers*—an extra spell? Sure, it was just the dungeon-born, not the humans, but still. It had to be done. Moving onto the next screen, I let out a breath as I searched the text. I wanted *everything*!

Additional Dungeon Core Bonus Research Unlocked! Please select from the following Structures:

Dungeon Specialist Structures are sub-divided into the following forms, with each area being further researchable and gaining improvable bonuses.

1. **Advanced Production:** *Currently available: Precision Engineering Facility (1)* **This facility allows for the creation of complex mechanical devices and intricate components, enhancing overall production capabilities.**

2. **Sustainable Agriculture:** *Currently available: Hydroponics Bay (1)* An efficient, space-saving method of growing crops using mineral-nutrient solutions in a mana-enriched water solvent.

3. **Enhanced Detection:** *Currently available: Mana Resonance Scanner (1)* A sophisticated detection system that uses mana fluctuations to create detailed 3D maps of surrounding areas, including hidden spaces.

4. **Information Processing:** *Currently available: Analytical Engine Hub (1)* A mana-powered computation center, capable of processing vast amounts of data and assisting in research and development.

5. **Energy Manipulation:** *Currently available: Mana Conversion Array (1)* A structure that allows for more efficient conversion between different types of mana, opening up new possibilities for spell creation and enchantment.

6. **Advanced Materials:** *Currently available: Alchemical Foundry (1)* A facility for creating and manipulating advanced materials, including mana-infused alloys and composites.

This was…well, frankly it was annoying. Why the hell couldn't they offer me some shit and really obvious "no" options?! I sighed, then started reading again.

Moving through them one by one, I had to force myself not to just select and be done, mainly because there were so many options. And I knew that conquering other dungeons wasn't going to be something I could do regularly.

Advanced production was tempting. If I set up one of these in the middle of the crafter areas, I was betting those lunatics could come up with incredible upgrades. Link it to the research facilities, and boom. There was no end to the possibilities.

Sustainable agriculture sounded like the least useful so far, but thinking about it? There would be ways to stack the growing sections over one another, and mana-enriched solvent? That'd probably bring bonuses to the damn herbs and so on. Forget using it for crops, or at least not just for crops. The healing potions, the mana points—hell, the goddamn beers we could create from this?

It'd be like dwarves in all those games, where they could drink and get buffed up rather than hammered. Literally! We'd be able to have a shot of vodka before a fight and get a bonus to our stats rather than a minus.

Admittedly, that came with its own issues as well, but fuck it, there'd be solutions. And the cocktails? We'd be taking warfare to a whole new level as the entire army started sipping Singapore Slings or whatever and then steamed through the opposing forces.

Not only would we be stronger, but we'd have an image that would be incredible. And the photo opportunities? Just imagine the cocktail bars that would be set up behind the main army.

"No, let's not be uncivilized about this... We'll fight after happy hour..."

Damn, I could just see it now.

Recruitment would be a dream.

Enhanced detection? That was a no-brainer. If we could set up with that and just know, constantly in real time, what was going on around us? That would be a hell of a bonus. If nothing else, we'd be able to finally catch those goddamn fliers that were always buzzing the park.

More to the point, though, with those in place, the soldiers who had crept up weeks ago wouldn't have stood a chance of surprising us.

Streaming through to the next option, I paused, mulling it over. Information processing was basically IT, which I'd spent most of my working life in. But in this case, instead of being in a digital electrical engine, based on binary coding, it was a mana-based analytical engine.

My IT background screamed at me twice over at that. First of all, it was the instinctive tech enthusiast's response: I see it; it's new and shiny; I want it.

The knowledge that the Information Age's upgrades in terms of technology were driven massively by computational power made me want it like little else, imagining the vast leaps and bounds that could come from such a thing, especially if it was linked to and worked well in the research facilities.

The second, equally strident internal screaming, however, also came from my IT background: nine times out of ten, until one of the team had solid months to devote to a totally new form of tech in IT, it was more of a hinderance than a help.

Just consider all the goddamn video calls and their loss of sound, the live broadcasts I'd been involved in, and yeah, the goddamn Windows upgrades that always installed at the worst times and borked the system.

Fuck, thinking about it, it had to be a literal case of for every single system a hacker had taken down a major system maliciously, Windows and similar systems rolling out an upgrade that wasn't ready yet, had taken down three more.

I'd lost track of the nights I spent sweating blood and tears over an upgrade that should have taken half an hour, and that had borked entire company's systems.

Not that they ever knew, of course. All but once I'd managed to fix the fuckers before people came on-site the next day. It'd just cost me years of my life, that was all.

No, that was a pass, and I shuddered as I moved onto the next option. Energy manipulation was another cool one, but less so than the others. Basically, it was an upgrade to the current converters, so it'd allow us to flood a particular area with a load of different forms of mana.

I suddenly realized at that point that I'd not seen any of the "you have discovered a new form of mana" notifications in ages, and checking, found them in the list of hidden ones. I'd still been getting them, it seemed, but once I hit Iron for the core, they stopped granting improvements to the dungeon's storage options.

Meh, the twenty-five extra points of storage optimization had stopped being noticeable a long time ago anyway.

It was cool, but not "oh my God, I must have it" levels of cool, that was for sure.

The last one was advanced materials, and that…that was a strange one.

The alchemical foundry was marked as "*a facility for creating and manipulating advanced materials, including mana-infused alloys and composites.*" That just tweaked something in the back of my mind as I stared at it. I mean, we could create any kind of metals or composites that the dungeon came across by absorbing them into the dungeon anyway, so surely that wasn't that much of a biggie, right? I mean, it sounded like it was a facility to basically make, say, titanium, but *mana-impregnated* titanium.

That seemed cool and all, but it wasn't game changing, and it didn't really make that much sense, because I could literally have an ingot of titanium or whatever we needed printed up, then I impregnate it myself—with mana, I'll stress, not just me getting freaky with a slab of metal—and boom, reabsorb it and the crafters had that as an option to work with, right?

To work with…

That was the phrase here, I suddenly realized. The alchemical foundry enabled them to *work* the metals, not just create them, and I groaned as I got it.

If I created a bar of impregnated titanium, the mana would most likely not give it a special magical power, like enable it to absorb fireballs or whatever, until it was completed and tweaked to do that.

It admittedly raised the question of how many things that were intended as amazing magical artifacts ended up as cog wheels or shower curtains or whatever out in the greater galaxy. They probably kept randomly adding Earth enhancements, or improvements to the user's Charisma or whatever to things by accident and then cursing as their new coffee table started making everyone uncontrollably horny. The sheer number of really fucked-up enchantments out there had to be mind-blowing.

This was the answer to that, I bet: a facility to work and guide the metals into the proper lanes, that could then later on have the appropriate enchantments added.

I, and my dungeon as a whole, needed to figure out the exact enchantment process instead of just me pouring mana in and going "Whelp, I hope that doesn't explode" and this was, I guessed, a step along that line.

That meant that, as always for this kind of bonus, I needed to break this down. I needed to think about not what would it do for me, but what would it do for the dungeon overall.

It was down to the hydroponics, the sensors, the foundry, and the precision engineering facility. When I looked at them like that, I knew straightaway that the hydroponics were out. As much as I wanted it, I could probably figure that out myself.

The sensors...maybe. The precision facility, maybe. And the alchemical foundry...

I cursed and made my decision. As much as I really wanted them all, I could only have one of them, and as such, the best option, I decided, knowing that I'd regret it no matter which I chose, was the alchemical foundry option.

It had come down to that or the precision engineering system. And the only reason it was the foundry instead was that the precision system was taking away a step, rather than bringing an overall improvement.

We could already design things in the research facilities, and yeah, once we had that blueprint, we could create whatever we needed. That basically meant that the facility was good, and interesting, but that was it.

It was the first level of the facility, though, and I damn well knew that with a few levels done, it'd be incredible.

The alchemical foundry was awesome *now*, though. And, more to the point, it would enable us to bring about upgrades in most of our technologies almost as soon as it was finished.

That had to be the decider.

With that done, I moved onto the next option.

The dungeon *perk*.

Now, these things in the past had been incredible—huge differences if you got lucky—but some of the options I'd been offered? Well. They must have a pool of all available options to choose from, that was all I was assuming. Random pull of the cards and see what you got, rather than "this is appropriate to you."

That or the system hated me.

Even odds, really.

I pulled up the perks and read, growing more and more aware by the second that I had places to be and shit to do.

Dungeon Perk!

As the conqueror of an Iron-level Dungeon, you have gained access to more advanced perks. Please choose from the following:

1. ***Mana Resonance Network:*** *Establish a network of advanced mana conduits that resonate with each other, increasing overall mana production by 5% and allowing for faster mana distribution throughout the dungeon.*

2. *Adaptive Defense Matrix: Your dungeon's defenders learn from each encounter and are provided additional training facilities, becoming 10% more effective against previously encountered threats. This bonus stacks up to 5 times for each specific type of threat. Note: This perk unlocks additional research and creation options.*

3. *Synergistic Crafting: When two or more crafters work together on a project, they gain a cumulative 5% boost to their crafting speed and quality for each additional crafter, up to a maximum of 25%.*

4. *Dimensional Pocket Rooms: Unlock the ability to create small pocket dimensions within your dungeon, increasing your effective space by 10% without expanding your external footprint. Note: Storage of inanimate items only. See dungeon reference 2.967.312 for removal solutions.*

5. *Mana-Infused Evolution: Dungeon creatures have a 5% chance of spontaneously evolving beneficial traits when exposed to high concentrations of mana for extended periods.*

6. *Harmonic Resonance Traps: Traps within your dungeon can now be linked, creating chain reactions that are 20% more effective and difficult to disarm than individual traps.*

7. *Empathic Dungeon Core: Your dungeon core gains a limited ability to sense the emotions and intentions of those within its influence, providing a 15% boost to reaction time for dungeon defenses.*

8. *Resource Transmutation: Gain the ability to transmute excess resources into other needed resources at a 75% efficiency rate, reducing waste and improving resource management.*

Okay, now this could be good too. The perks were potentially massive improvements, but again, it really depended on the situation. Like, the conduits sounded great, and if we had all the time in the world, that would probably be the way to go. Except that when I had real needs and a war to fight, a five percent improvement right now wasn't going to be really noticeable.

The adaptive defensive matrix was interesting. I guessed it was designed in addition to the usual training facilities…the usual training facilities that *I didn't have.*

Dammit, we'd built the training dungeon and we'd set up the army training core, but beyond that, we didn't really have anything but the trainers giving general advice and then people learning by fighting.

That…that was a real option then. If I was reading this right, all the dungeon-born would gain ten percent additional effectiveness in facing set creatures. So, if, for example, I set it up for orcs, and kept summoning more orcs in the training dungeon for them to face, then as they got more experience, they'd also grow up to fifty percent more effective against any orcs.

That sounded really obvious, until you looked at the real killer detail there. I wasn't sure, but it didn't say that you needed to face full-on higher-leveled ones. If this was the loophole it looked like, then I could have, say, Beta fight a load of lower-leveled orcs, then do whatever training she needed, then fight the same low-level idiots again and again; when she came to face the Orakai at full strength, she'd have basically been power-levelling against their smaller, dumber cousins.

I didn't know whether that would work, but no way was the training going to be entirely ineffective.

That was a consideration, at the very least.

Moving on to the next: the synergistic crafting option. It was tempting, sure, but yeah, a lot less so than the training. Right up until I considered that if we got four people working together in the production of potions—from herbalism all the way to the glassmaking and alchemy we probably had already—then the potion would be twenty-five percent stronger.

Damn.

That could be a life saved right there.

Moving on to the pocket dimensions…that sounded pretty damn good. Basically bags of holding, but stationary. It'd make a hell of a difference in our bedroom, I knew that, considering we could get rid of wardrobes and drawers, etc., but…

It didn't say anything about how much it cost to use them, to establish or run them, and although I couldn't access the warning, clearly if you put living tissue in there, it was a big no-no.

That didn't sound like much of a dealbreaker, until you asked yourself about the idiots I surrounded myself with. Usually, to get anything out of a bag of holding, and in all the movies, you just stuck your hand in and focused; then, hey presto, boom! The item was in your hand. This might work like that, or it might not and any living tissue that entered the space was killed.

That'd mean that it was essentially a garbage disposal for us, and we absorbed the garbage back into the dungeon currently. Pass.

Mana-infused evolution was also a pass. It might make our people stronger, and it did say beneficial, but two issues were there straightaway.

First, if you only had a five percent chance of it working, I'd basically need to create entire rooms that were saturated all the time. That was fine, as it was a method for improving your affinity to a certain strain of mana already.

But that meant that those who had a high affinity to that strain would be happy, and everyone else who entered that room would at the least feel uncomfortable and probably sick constantly. That didn't even consider that there were hundreds of forms of mana out there, and that meant we needed hundreds of different rooms created for basically nothing beyond sitting around in.

It just reeked of creating cliques to me. The Lightning users are better than the Water mages and all that. It'd be three weeks at most before some fucker was writing an angsty teen romance about the fucking place, I just knew it, and I wasn't having that.

Also, minor additional detail: who decided if something was beneficial? For a race that loved the water, growing gills might be beneficial, or webbed toes.

I shuddered at even the thought and quickly moved on. I *hated* feet. Not one of my admittedly many kinks at all. I'd leave that to my old friends Richey and Matt D, I decided. Weirdos.

Harmonic resonance traps were interesting, but genuinely we didn't really bother with traps. So although it was intriguing, it was little more than that for now. Pass.

Empathic dungeon core? It sounded a little like it was going to help the core become sentient or warn people of danger. In theory, that could be great. But if the core then evolved further and decided it didn't like something, like say, the French—although that was entirely understandable—we'd all be woken by feelings of uncontrollable rage whenever a Frenchman came near.

Too complicated for me.

Then there was the resource option, to convert a resource into another, with the loss of the original mass at 'only' 25%. That could be good, but... it felt wrong. It felt like a waste to me, when I could already summon any material we needed. I considered it, then moved on.

That basically took us down to the crafting bonus or the training one. When I looked at it like that, a fifty percent bonus beat a twenty-five every time.

I took the adaptive defense matrix, and made a mental note to get the training systems up and running as soon as possible. You know, once the current war was over and the million other jobs were dealt with.

That was when I opened the notification about the new tech upgrade blueprint, and promptly started to swear.

Mana-Infused Potato Peeler	Item
This Mana-Infused Potato Peeler is a Bronze Age tool enhanced with magical properties. It effortlessly removes potato skins with a precision that would make master chefs weep. The mana infusion allows it to automatically sharpen itself and repel food debris, making it virtually maintenance-free.	

Peeling Speed: 6-20 potatoes per minute (Skill level dependent)	
Special Features: Self-sharpening, Debris-repelling	
Durability 100/100	**Special Features**: 2/2

I read the goddamn thing three times, then closed it, took a deep breath and moved on. Just my luck, really. Not only did we not need a goddamn potato peeler, but a magically enhanced one that would keep itself clean? I'd have made a fortune in the old world...

Or not, as most chefs would have still used a "rumbler" anyway. Bastards.

A class skill point, though—that was the next bonus, along with ten thousand points of experience, and... I pulled up my character sheet and scanned it quickly. I'd hit my next level. I grinned and moved back to the quest notifications I'd been checking over.

Congratulations! You have completed a Quest!

Quest: Mechanist Menace

Simon, Lord of the Mechanists, had allied his dungeon with the Lord of Unlife, threatening to give your enemies an insurmountable advantage. His dungeon, now identified in the city of Oxford, UK, had to be neutralized before it became a foothold for the forces of Unlife.

Unfortunately for him, he also proved to be wholly unsuitable to the role of Dungeon Lord, and although his fairy could have held off your attack with a small team of highly lethal creations, she was unfortunately exiled, leaving the dungeon open to assault.
You receive the following bonuses:

- **+5 to top three Attributes**
- **+2 Class Skill Points to allocate**
- **Access to Mechanist technology and blueprints**
- **50,000 XP**
- **Increased influence over UK territory**

***

Congratulations! You have completed another Quest!

Class Quest!

As an Arcane Dungeon Lord, you have the rare ability to absorb and adapt enemy technologies. Successfully claiming the Mechanist Dungeon's core will unlock new research paths and evolution options for your own dungeon.

Complete this quest to receive a boost to your Artificer and Magical Researcher skills, as well as unlock the "Techno-Arcane Fusion" creature summon path.

- **Infiltrate Mechanist Dungeon: 1/1**
- **Defeat Simon, Lord of the Mechanists: 1/1**
- **Claim or destroy dungeon core: 1/1**

That was when I got a notification that practically made my eyes bleed from the complex and mind-buggering data dump I received.

Apparently I wasn't getting all the mechanist's secrets—probably because I chose to destroy the dungeon instead of keeping it. And yeah, I also wasn't getting anything like his last creations. Instead, I got something very, *very* different.

Congratulations!

Due to your rare circumstances—unlocking the techno-arcane fusion path at a relatively high level of dungeon—you have received access to higher-form beings.

Beware: mistreatment of the Glassine Race is considered a crime across much of the galaxy!

You have gained access to a new race!

Glassine	Dungeon-born
Techno-Arcane Construct: The Glassine are a primarily peaceful race, one that evolved through harmonious development of their technology, biology, and minds. They are a solvent-based species that have fully integrated the ability to build their own bodies, resulting in long-lived beings of exquisite beauty. Glassine reside within intricately carved and often embossed bodies crafted by master artisans.	
Cost: Glassine (Advanced): 1000 Crystal, 4000 Pure Mana, 50 Control points. Maintenance is 200 mana points per day, per individual. Current level: Advanced	

Note: *Glassine are highly adaptable and can attune themselves to various energy types within the dungeon. At higher levels, they can manipulate and redirect energy flows, potentially enhancing the dungeon's overall efficiency.*

Special Traits:

Self-Sculpting: Can alter their own form for aesthetic or practical purposes.

Energy Harmonization: Can attune to and manipulate various energy types within the dungeon.

Tech-Magic Interface: Can create seamless connections between magical and technological systems.

Warning: While generally peaceful, Glassine may take offense to crude attempts at replication or forced evolution. Respect for their craftsmanship and autonomy is advised to maintain positive relations.

Durability: 250/250	Abilities: ?/?

There was also a more "standard" construct that I guessed was how the other dungeon had actually started out, and that was, well, pretty shit in comparison.

Clockwork Crawler	Construct
A small, insect-like automaton powered by a combination of basic clockwork mechanics and minimal mana. Abilities:	
• Basic Scouting: Can explore and report on simple environmental details.	
• Rudimentary Repair: Can perform very basic maintenance tasks on mechanical objects.	
Summoning Cost: 20 mana to summon, 2 mana per day, 2 control points.	
Durability 5/5	Abilities: 2/2

As soon as the final dungeon-linked notification finished flashing before me, time seemed to stagger, stutter—and then, with a pop or releasing pressure, everything was moving again.

"Everything good?" I called out absently. A minute or so later, as I continued to read the screens, I got a distant response from Chris.

"No, you're a wanker," he called down.

I snorted, banishing him from my mind as I worked through the multitude of notifications.

The stat sheet, when I pulled it back up, made me smile, though. I'd managed to increase so many sections over the last few hours. The plus five to the top three used attributes was nice, as was the level-up.

I'd scrapped the kill notifications too many times when I'd been busy, and now when it'd tried to jump up again, I'd closed it. There were several for constructs and one for Simon earlier; then there were several dozen thugs and some more constructs, but no dungeon fairy still.

What was there, though, was that I'd reached the grand total of seventeen thousand and change in experience from kills. Then, adding on my ten thousand for the quest and my fifty thousand for the second quest, I had a very nice little notification waiting for me.

Congratulations!

You have reached Level 30!

Current XP to next level stands at 961/90,000

You have 18 unspent Stat Points, 2 Class Skill Points & 5 Skill Points

***

"Who will you be? (4)"

You have reached your Fourth Choice! Your path so far has been unique, blending the powers of a Dungeon Lord with the knowledge of an Arcanist. Now, new possibilities unfold before you. Choose wisely, as this Choice cannot be undone.

Due to your actions and previous choices, two Standard paths, two Advanced paths, and one Rare path have been unlocked:

Standard Classes:

Scavenger:
Scavengers are experts at finding and repurposing resources in the wasteland, essential for survival in a post-apocalyptic world.
They gain the following one-off bonuses:
- + 2 to Perception
- + 1 to Constitution
- + 1 Salvaging Skill
- + 1 Class Skill Point

Survivalist:

Survivalists excel at enduring harsh environments and making the most of limited resources.
They gain the following one-off bonuses:

- + 2 to Endurance
- + 1 to Wisdom
- + 1 Wilderness Survival Skill
- + 1 Class Skill Point

Advanced Classes:

Warmancer:

Warmancers combine tactical prowess with arcane knowledge, excelling in wide-ranged magical combat. They gain the following one-off bonuses:

- + 2 to Intelligence
- + 1 to Wisdom
- + 2 Class Spell Points
- + 1 Class Skill Point

Urban Planner:

Urban Planners specialize in efficiently organizing and developing settlements, crucial for rebuilding civilization. They gain the following one-off bonuses:

- + 2 to Intelligence
- + 1 to Charisma
- + 1 City Design Skill
- + 1 Class Skill Point

Rare Classes:

Dungeon Lord (3):

Dungeon Lords control the vitally important Dungeons of the Multiverse, capable of uplifting civilizations or becoming dreaded overlords. They gain the following one-off bonuses:

- + 2 Spells
- + 2 Class Skill Points
- + 1 Random Dungeon Blueprint (Level Appropriate)

As much as I could see the utility of investing again in the Dungeon Lord class, and yeah, it was great, there was just no goddamn way I was passing up on my Warmancer class!

The spells that Ramnik had access to when she'd taken it had made it clear that it was a hell of a path, and opening up the evolutions that would come from that just made sense.

I selected that without a second thought, dismissing the Scavenger and Survivalist classes out of hand. And Urban Planner? What the hell was the system thinking in offering me that? In comparison to Warmancer! I mean, it was like you ordering a drink from the bar, the barman takes the order, takes your money, makes the drink, then pours it down the drain.

Then acts all surprised when you ask what the hell is going on. I mean, how was he supposed to know that you wanted to drink the drink, as well as order it, right?

Goddamn madness!

Congratulations!

As a new Warmancer, you have gained a boost of 40% that can be divided out into up to four of your elemental affinities.

Choose wisely...

Congratulations, Dungeon Warmancer! You have received an upgraded spell list to choose from and may select two new spells, or invest in those that have already been unlocked.

Spells:

Class selection: Dungeon Warmancer

Summon Demon: Summon a Demon. Formed entirely of your power and imbued with terrible purpose, the Demon exists to see your will achieved, and will allow nothing to stand between it and its goal. (Selected)

Evolution: Demonic War-Host: Select a location and summon ten lesser demons to the battlefield to unleash the horrors of various hellscapes upon your enemies for so long as they survive. (N/A)

Incinerate: Cast a blast of terrible heat at a target, achieving up to 1000 degrees of heat in a single location. Note: This spell has lessening effects, depending on the area covered, and ranks from 0 (10cm) to 5 (1000cm). (1)

Evolution: Atomic Furnace: Select a location and summon the power of the sun to turn all inside that area to glass! Note: This spell has lessening effects, depending on the area covered, and ranks from 0 (1m) to 5 (1000m). (0)

Evolution: Thermal Lance: Summon a short-lived lance of incredible, terrible heat. The plasma lance can turn steel to liquid, so imagine what it can do to those who annoy you! Note: This spell has lessening effects, depending on the area covered, and ranks from 0 (5cm) to 5 (500m). (N/A)

Cold of the Grave: Where lesser spells injure, this spell simply reduces all inside its AOE to absolute zero, snuffing out the chemical fires so necessary to continued life. Note: This spell has lessening effects, depending on the area covered, and ranks from 0 (10cm) to 5 (5m). (N/A)

Tame: Tame a creature, adding it to your Dungeon lists. (Selected) (1)

Evolution: Affinity Boost! As you "Tame" a creature, you can now choose to imbue it with an elemental affinity. The higher your own affinity, the higher the chance the gift will result in a successful union. (Selected)

Evolution: Forced Enslavement: Now you too have a chance to rip your enemies' mounts from their control, unleashing formerly treasured pets upon their masters to wreak havoc! (N/A)

Sapient Enslavement: Why should your enemies have a choice in which side they're on? Force the heretic to embrace the true power of the dungeon! This spell ranks in levels from 0 (Unfriendly) to 5 (Sworn Nemesis). (N/A)

Examine: This spell allows the nascent Dungeon Lord to divine details about a target that are hidden from the eyes of most mortals. This skill ranks in levels from 0 (Curious) to 5 (All-Knowing). (1)

Evolution: Secret Knowledge! Those you encounter frequently have their own agendas; why not make them share that information? This skill ranks in levels from 0 (Fears) to 5 (Darkest Secret). (N/A)

Evolution: Arcane Assimilation: Too many spells out there exist only in the arsenals of your enemies—why not change that? This skill ranks in levels from 0 (Idle Curiosity) to 5 (Spell Thief). (N/A)

Summon War Elemental: Summon an Elemental designed for war to do your bidding. Note: This spell will summon a creature of the Elemental Planes, depending on your ability, to serve you for a short period of time, and ranks from 0 (Lesser) to 5 (Elemental Lord). (N/A)

Lightning Bolt: Cast a blast of Lightning at your target, stunning and possibly frying them with the power of electricity. Note: This spell has lessening effects, depending on the area traveled, and ranks from 0 (50,000V) to 5 (150,000MV). (1)

Evolution: Lightning Storm! Select a location and unleash the true power of the Storm! Note: This spell has lessening effects, depending on the area covered, and ranks from 0 (10m) to 5 (10km). (1)

Evolution: Emperor's Hatred: When the enemy, or even friends refuse to obey your reasonable requests, why not treat them to a wonderful surprise? Each finger unleashes a branching lightning stream that has a chance to spawn repeating streams of their own. Note: This spell has lessening effects, depending on the target, their affinities and the mana dedicated, and randomly produces from 1 repeating burst to 10. (N/A)

Wrath of the Heavens: Call down a meteor shower upon a designated target area, dealing horrific devastation upon your enemies for a limited time. Note, this spell has alterable effects, starting at a maximum distance of 20m from the caster, and a maximum of 10 meteors, before increasing in both range and bombardment numbers with ranks from 0 (20m/10M) to 5 (5km/100M). (N/A)

I read and reread the spells, grinning at the sight of Ramnik's old favorite, Wrath of the Heavens. On the other hand, some of the choices really suggested that as a dungeon Warmancer, I was expected to be a bit of a dick. Enslavement? Hell to the no. But, I had five spells to select! As much as I didn't like some of the new versions, there was no way I was passing up on the massive improvements that they could bring.

I had five spell points to spend, and damn if I wasn't getting my money's worth out of this one now, the three points I'd had to spend before joining the two from the level up.

The first spell I unlocked was Wrath of the Heavens, because in what world would I _not_ get that? But with that unlocked, I hesitated. Not because I didn't want anything else, but because a question had just occurred to me.

I'd been getting my ass handed to me a lot in the lower levels because those I faced had often gone "glass cannon" in their builds, whereas I'd always gone for strength and depth.

Now, as I'd reached what was arguably a plateau that I was standing atop beyond most others, I had the opportunity to continue with this strategy, or go all out in the other direction.

I had four points left, four spell points that could unlock a hell of a different level of devastation, and I needed to think about it.

If instead of unlocking anything else, I went all in on, say, Wrath of the Heavens, then I could designate a space that was half a kilometer—or much more—across and rain down eighty or so meteors atop it.

Now, it might just be me, but I couldn't see much walking away from that. Unleash that on the undead and there was going to be a fuckload of bone dust left behind. Very little in the way of intact enemies were going to be coming out of that to try to face me, and yet…

If I did that, and we ended up fighting in the Channel Tunnel itself? The spell was useless…unless I wanted to smash the tunnel and drown myself, of course.

Alternatively, if I went all in on Lightning Bolt, that could be fantastic…provided the enemy were right there and I could see them, or they were small in number.

I bit my lip, chewing as I thought. I'd held off on spending the spell points, knowing that I'd be able to do this sooner or later, and now that I actually had the chance before me, I genuinely didn't know what to do for the best.

It took a few minutes, but in the end, I decided to go with my heart, and invest in Lightning Storm for two more points, taking it from level one to three, and wincing as soon as I did. I suddenly knew exactly where I was investing a load of my available stat points.

Something about the path I'd followed to this point meant that I now had additional details on the spells as I unlocked them. Rather than just having to try to cast them and then work out how much it cost, the Lightning Storm came with a simple breakdown of cost, and damn was it expensive.

The range had now leapt to four hundred meters that I could spread the storm over. And the cost? Seven and a half thousand points.

That was more mana than I had, to cast it at its full strength. I grimaced, selecting my final spell and spending two points in it. There was only one I could choose, all things considered, and that was Arcane Assimilation.

It gave me a chance to learn any spell that I saw cast. Although it wasn't a great chance—ten percent…that was it at the second level—it meant that when we weren't busy, which I knew was rare, I could have my friends cast their spells and I could try to learn them all.

It was a bit of a ballache that the mana cost for the second level, per casting, when I'd only have a ten percent chance of learning the spell, was five hundred goddamn mana. But that was life, I guessed.

Fortunately, there weren't many more screens to deal with. I pulled up my skills next, double-checking and nodding to myself. I had three class skills and five regular skills to assign. Well, given all we'd learned of late with the skills, the regular skills were the easiest to assign.

All five points dropped into the Advanced Dungeon Management skill, taking it from level four to nine, and boosting the efficiency of the dungeon-born workers' efforts by a further twenty-five percent, all the way up to forty-five.

That sounded like a lot, and seriously it was, but when you considered that I had been saving those skills to boost my individual crafting skill, maybe leveling something like enchanting through the roof, it really wasn't that much of an outrageous bonus.

If instead I'd been saving them all for that, I'd be a craftsman apprentice, if not a journeyman by now, and my creations would be things people fought wars over on Earth.

Instead, my undead cleaned the bricks away a little quicker. It sounded crap when I put it like that, but that was what it was, really. The end result of an extra twenty-five percent on the mana production was just another way of saying it.

With that out of the way, I reached for the dungeon skill list, and pored over it, reading the new options.

Class Skills:

Class selection: Dungeon Warmancer

Imbue: You may choose to give freely of your own manapool to imbue an item or creature of the Dungeon with magic. This ability can fail, and spectacularly so; however, creations of wondrous might can also be brought into being. Be wary. (Selected)

Evolution: Foresight: No longer are your creations the chance things they were…now see the true potential of a creature! (Selected)

Evolution: Arcane Fusion: Combine multiple magical essences or items to create more powerful and complex enchantments. This skill ranks from 0 (Basic Fusion) to 5 (Legendary Amalgamation). (Current Level: N/A)

Evolution: Warmancer's Imprint: You can now imbue creatures and items with specific combat-oriented magical abilities. These imprints can grant offensive spells, defensive capabilities, or tactical advantages. The higher the rank, the more powerful and complex the imprinted abilities can be. This skill ranks from 0 (Minor Combat Boost) to 5 (Legendary War Magic). (Current Level: N/A)

Monster Master: No longer do the creatures of the Dungeon view you with apathy or irritation when you pass by. Now they are devoted to you! This skill ranks in levels from 0 (Interested) to 5 (Worshipful). (Current level: 2, Revered)

Evolution: Lord of All! The creatures of your Dungeon know their true master, and those who follow willingly can now receive arcane gifts that match their level of devotion! (Selected)

Evolution: Arcane Symbiosis: Form a deeper magical connection with your creatures, allowing you to temporarily inhabit their bodies or share their senses. Ranks from 0 (Surface Link) to 5 (Perfect Synchronization). (Current Level: N/A)

Evolution: Battle Commander: The creatures of your Dungeon now form organized military units. You can issue complex battle strategies that they will follow with precision. This skill ranks from 0 (Squad) to 5 (Army). (Current Level: N/A)

Arcane Breeder: Some Dungeon Lords wish for only the purest strains to survive, while others enjoy the randomness of evolution…select the genes you wish to see and promote them!

Evolution: Elemental Infusion: Introduce elemental traits into your creatures' genetic makeup, creating hybrid beings with unique abilities. Ranks from 0 (Minor Traits) to 5 (Elemental Lords). (Current Level: N/A)

Evolution: War-Forged Lineage: Create specialized breeds of creatures designed for warfare. These creatures have enhanced combat abilities and can be quickly produced in times of conflict. Ranks from 0 (Foot Soldiers) to 5 (Elite War Beasts). (Current Level: N/A)

Artificer: You may gift magical artifacts to your creations, and when combined with Foresight, these creatures will gain significant bonuses to magical item creation and replication. This skill ranks in levels from 0 (Curiosity) to 5 (Legendary). (Current level: 0, Curiosity)

Evolution: Living Artifacts: Create semi-sentient magical items that can grow and evolve alongside their wielders. Ranks from 0 (Awakening) to 5 (Artifact Ecosystem). (Current Level: N/A)

Evolution: Armory of Power: Create magical weapons and armor that adapt to the user's needs in battle. These items can store and release combat spells. Ranks from 0 (Minor Enchantments) to 5 (Legendary Artifacts). (Current Level: N/A)

Jez Cajiao

Arcane Pets: Your sentient Dungeon inhabitants can gather and breed pets, but where before there was an element of random chance, now you may lure those you wish into the range of your tamers. This skill ranks in levels from 0 (Magical) to 5 (Legendary Creatures) (Current level: 0, Magical).

Evolution: Familiar Bond: Forge deep magical connections between your dungeon inhabitants and their pets, granting shared abilities and enhanced communication. Ranks from 0 (Empathic Link) to 5 (Spiritual Fusion). (Current Level: N/A)

Evolution: Battle Companions: Summon and bond with powerful magical creatures that fight alongside you. These companions can merge with those with the relevant gifts temporarily, granting enhanced abilities. Ranks from 0 (Minor Familiar) to 5 (Legendary Beast). (Current Level: N/A)

Insatiable Curiosity: Random Sentient Dungeon Creatures will now have the chance to be spawned with an Insatiable Curiosity. These creatures can be put to work in your Research Nodes to increase Research by a staggering degree. This skill ranks in levels from 0 (Incompetent) to 5 (Genius). (Current level: 5, Genius)

Evolution: Magical Researcher! Before, your researchers were generalists, plodding along at their task, be that a better toilet seat or a converter; now they stand a chance at developing true magical gifts, and at learning the secrets of creation! This skill ranks in levels from 0 (Novice) to 5 (Master). (Current level: 1, Apprentice)

Evolution: Eureka Cascade: Researchers' breakthroughs can trigger chain reactions of inspiration across your entire dungeon, temporarily boosting all research efforts. Ranks from 0 (Minor Ripple) to 5 (Innovation Tsunami). (Current Level: 0, Minor Ripple)

Evolution: Tactical Insight: Your curious creatures now focus on combat strategy and magical warfare. They can analyze enemy tactics and develop countermeasures. Ranks from 0 (Basic Tactics) to 5 (Grandmaster Strategist). (Current Level: N/A)

Manafield: Your Dungeon's Manafield will now passively expand at 10% more than the previous rate, enabling greater growth in a shorter period of time. This skill ranks in levels from 0 (Restricted) to 5 (Expansive). (Current Level: 1, Limited)

Evolution: Tides of Mana! All life creates mana, as do elemental interactions. Now through the wonders of gravitational magic, you can start to draw more mana into the area of your Dungeon. This skill ranks in levels from 0 (Gentle) to 5 (Vortex). (Current Level: 1, Steady)

Evolution: Mana Crystallization: Convert excess mana into physical crystals that can be used to power artifacts, enhance creatures, or traded as valuable resources. Ranks from 0 (Crude Crystals) to 5 (Perfect Lattice). (Current Level: 0, Crude Crystals)

Evolution: Mana Fortification: Your expanding manafield now reinforces your dungeon's defenses. Create mana shields, traps, and automated defensive spells. Ranks from 0 (Minor Barriers) to 5 (Impenetrable Fortress). (Current Level: N/A)

Reach Out and Touch Me: Your Dungeon is no longer only controllable when you are within its own environs. Now you can interact with it at increasing distances. This skill ranks in levels from 0 (Local) to 5 (Interstellar). (Current level: 1, Regional)

Evolution: Gates! No longer is the Dungeon a distant creation. This skill unlocks the creation of the Gates, transportals that can be built inside the Dungeon and activated at a remote location to provide a stable link between the two points.

This skill ranks in levels from 0 (Single Gate) to 5 (Unlimited) (Current level: 0, Single).

Evolution: Multidimensional Anchor: Establish your dungeon as a fixed point across multiple dimensions, allowing for easier interdimensional travel and resource gathering. Ranks from 0 (Dimensional Echo) to 5 (Nexus of Realities). (Current Level: N/A)

Evolution: Battlefield Projection: Project your presence onto any battlefield within your influence. Observe and communicate as if you were physically present. Ranks from 0 (Local Projection) to 5 (Global Presence). (Current Level: N/A)

I had three options, three points to spend, and there were plenty of things I wanted. But to make sure we could win this damn war, I knew what I had to choose first. The next nexus gate that I invested in unlocking took me to an additional two gates available, which although I'd been hoping for five, was all that I needed. Bit of a relief there.

The next point, as much as I'd have liked to spend it elsewhere, needed to enable communication, both for me and those I chose to unlock it for.

Jez Cajiao

Tagging Reach Out and Touch Me for a second time, this time I unlocked the increased distance interactions, taking it from around a hundred miles to a thousand. No clue why that was identified as "Archon's Domain" but okay, thanks very much, you weird alien bastards.

The last point was the hardest because there were so many that could offer huge improvements with multiple points, and yet pretty pathetic improvements with single layers.

Taking Battle Companions as a perfect example: it was basically summoning a familiar. Sounds cool, right up until you realize that for the early levels, instead of a dragon you've basically got a lizard with intestinal issues that presumably wants to sit on your shoulder and shit down your back.

I had friends before all of this with goddamn pet birds. Their houses were permanently covered in crap. No thank you.

But...that was basically closing the door to awesome familiars as well. What if I got Chris a lion familiar, or a bear? Something he could summon, merge with, and fight in his augmented form for a short while, then chill out and he had a companion again when he unlocked from it?

That also raised the goddamn question: if you got one at the first level, could you get another if I upgraded it? Did you end up stuck with just a little annoying bastard when everyone else had full-on dragons? Or did you end up with up to six of them? Swap them in and out depending on your need?

Were they there all the time? Did you summon them at will or was it a one-time deal?

So *many* goddamn questions, and that was just this skill. But as much as I hated it, I knew that I needed to take it seriously as well. Humans were evolving, sure, but we were at a fundamentally lower level when it came to competing on the galactic scale.

We were average to start getting our points. The advanced kobolds, for example? Not even the rare...just the advanced and self-aware ones? They were *far* more powerful at a base level.

That meant that for the future, we needed a force leveler. Something to even the deck. Maybe this could be it? The worst part was that it was probably awesome, further down the line.

I shook my head and went back to the beginning, forcing myself to consider each of the options, not just toss it off.

Warmancer's Imprint meant I could share my abilities with my creatures. That could be cool. Share my Lightning spells with a dozen kobolds and have them march out and unleash hell—right up until one of them didn't have a high enough affinity and they exploded or whatever. Again, weak to start with, but looked like it'd be cool in the end. Pass.

Battle Commander was next. That was much more useful, I'd bet, once I could put a few levels into it. I mean, for the lower levels, it was only a squad I could command. In the fights that were going on all the time these days? Not much use, but a possibility, as a few levels invested in it and it'd be good.

War-Forged Lineage was another cool one. It'd let me summon specifically war-like versions of creatures. So, if I was reading this right, we could summon say, the magewhiskers and get battle tiger versions instead of the usual. It also made it look like they were cheaper and easier to summon than they'd be normally. That was tempting.

Armory of Power was literally what it said on the tin: a way to enhance the armory we were all pulling from, including helping with enchantments for people's weapons... I sighed and took it at that point, dismissing the rest of the options.

Yeah, I knew there were other things I needed, and that this—again—wasn't a straightforward winning strategy. It'd need time investment and effort, but I had enchanting as part of the shit I needed to study anyway. And well, if I could make everyone magic daggers or whatever, that'd help no end.

I took it, and let out a long sigh as I received a notification that "due to the size of the information required," I basically wouldn't just be taught what was to come.

Instead, I needed to build an Arcane Forge, set up a runic tome, and finally a fucking ethereal anvil. Great. On the upside, that meant there was hope that I could learn that shit soon and teach others as well. Now that it was done, I finally pulled up my stat sheet, reading it over, and snorting at the damn easy choice.

Name: Matt, First Lord of the Storm				
Host Powers: 1 (Enhanced Regeneration)				
Species: Thunderstorm			Bonus: None	
Level: 30			Progress to next level: 961/90,000	
Stat	Current Points	Description	Effect	Progress to Next Level
Agility	60	Governs dodge and movement	Heightened chance to dodge attacks 120%+24%= 144%	23/100
Charisma	43	Governs likely success to charm, seduce, or threaten	72% more likely to succeed in events that require seduction, persuasion, or threats (10%+ (33x2) = 72)	14/100
Constitution	58	Governs Health and Health Regeneration	HP: 58x60 = 3,480	88/100

Dexterity	45	Governs ability with weapons and crafting	+45% Increased chance of improved result +17 to melee damage	76/100
Endurance	47	Governs Stamina and Stamina Regeneration	Stamina: 47x50 = 2,350	52/100
Intelligence	93	Governs base manapool, standard intellectual capacity	Mana: 93x100=9,300	81/100
Luck	51	Governs overall chance of bonuses and critical hits	+82% increased chance of positive outcome	91/100
Perception	44	Governs ranged damage and chance to spot hidden items/traps	+34 to all ranged attacks	33/100
Strength	41	Governs damage with melee weapons and carrying capacity	+62 to all damage with Melee weapons	27/100
Wisdom	60	Governs mana regeneration	1200 mana regenerated per hour *(Arcanist class 2 boost)*	49/100

I'd put all eighteen points into Intelligence, boosting my mana pool all the way to nine thousand three hundred, and giving me essentially enough of a pool that I could go swimming in it and still battle demons if I needed to.

Once, I'd have totally imagined this as out of hand. Now, knowing that I needed to take on literally entire armies, it was starting to just barely reach respectable levels.

That left me with two jobs as far as I was concerned, in the area at least. They also needed to be done before the unstable and fracturing dungeon entirely broke down.

First, push out the limited range I had, because I'd just realized that the goddamn boxer that was practically wrecked in the local area was our only transport, and there was no way we were fixing that by hand.

Second? Fuck up the locals and make sure they knew not to get in our way, and kill Marchioness.

Then we could go on our merry way and take over London.

Or, you know, because it was such a shithole of corruption and the home of most of our politicians...raze it to the ground. Either or, really.

CHAPTER THIRTY-THREE

I closed the last of the notifications, sighing as the changes rippled through me. What had originally been painful was now barely worth noticing.

Instead, as I blinked, the world seemed to sharpen ever so slightly, and tasks were suddenly somewhat less complex. I knew, in myself, that at least some of that was purely down to believing that they were easier now that I was marginally more intelligent, but fuck it.

The dungeon core here was changing, drastically so. As I watched, the lines that flooded its surface shifted like water. Points rose and fell, segments appearing as more of the core adjusted.

Through my link to both this dungeon and my own at home, I could feel the changes that this core was undergoing in ways that I hadn't the first time around, as inexperienced as I was.

Although, to be fair, I was surrounded by evidence that the dungeon fairy had been torturing families at that point as well, so my attention had been a little redirected.

Now though, as I watched, the core made internal adjustments, splintering off a fragment of itself, impregnating it with saved information.

That was where the majority of the upgrades were coming from, the access to the new species and more. When I attached this to my main core, though, that would then upgrade it again, essentially cannibalizing the old fragment to improve on the new core.

The core itself was a little larger than a tennis ball currently, and solid as a rock. The presumable fragment that I was getting to take with me rose; the blunt end of a wedge slowly slid up from the greater depths as the core itself focused all its energy on creating a fragment.

"Shit," I muttered, then slid into the dungeon sense and summoned everyone who was still in it here. "Everyone, back to work!" I ordered.

"What?" Mike asked. "You found it, right?"

"I did, and the fragmentation is beginning. But that means the core has only a few hours left before it fails entirely, if I'm reading this right," I finished in a mutter, scratching at my chin as I double-checked.

"So?"

"So, if you want us to be able to free Jack, or repair the goddamn boxer, we need to get them both inside the dungeon's radius ASAP," I said quickly. "Once the core finishes the fracture, it then begins to break down. That means all its functions fail. And I'm thinking we don't want to be an inch away from freeing Jack or from fixing the vehicle when it shuts off. We need to get to London, and this fucker being damaged means that's gonna be a long run on foot, all right?"

"Back to work, everyone!" Mike cursed. "Come on, let's do it!"

"I'll round up those who already left it," Chris offered, and I nodded to him, then grinned as a thought occurred.

I slid free of the conversation with the others. Now that I'd unlocked another level of the Reach Out and Touch Me skill, I slid straight to the main dungeon, finding that there, and outside here, actually, it was late at night.

Fortunately, knowing that we were fighting, the girls had stayed up late, hoping for contact, and were just reaching out in turn, having noticed the change in the dungeon there.

"You did it?" Kelly asked. "Is everyone okay?"

"Mike?" Aly asked almost as quickly, glancing from me and then to the illuminated wall monitor, where a section showed a map of the UK, and on it, four flashing dots.

"He's alive. We all are," I assured them, frowning and stifling a curse as I tried to set the dungeon a task and the system refused. "We won, but Marchioness—the dungeon fairy—is still on the loose and she's rallied the local thugs to support her. I dropped a lightning storm on them in an enclosed space, so that had to have fucked her up—" I shook my head.

"We've got no time to explain," I said instead. "We desperately need to increase the dungeon's range. The core is fracturing and our vehicle is toast. As soon as the core finishes with the fragment for us, it's going to start shutting down. At that point, we're fucked because we can't do anything about repairs—"

I broke off again as Griffiths suddenly appeared.

"You said to tell you as soon as he made contact," Kelly said to him by way of an explanation, and Griffiths nodded.

"Any casualties?" he asked.

I took a deep breath and gave them all a very fast overview, before pausing and exiting the core to speak to Mike.

"I thought you were expanding the dungeon's field?" I asked him quickly.

"I was. There's little room, though. And with whatever changes you made, the mana is faltering almost as soon as we put it in. It's up to five of us on absorption for one increasing the range. At this rate, we're not going to make it to the boxer," he said flatly. "As much as I want to tell you we can do it, I've ordered the others to push for the area you said Jack was in. If we can recover him, that's something at least."

"Yeah." I bit my lip, instantly furious at myself. I should have waited to claim and fracture the core...but, at the same time, had I done so, if I'd waited? For all I knew, Marchioness was literally on the other side of the nearest wall with a jackhammer right now.

379

"Two minutes," I told Mike, then slid into the dungeon sense again, flitting back to join the others, as they couldn't reach out to here.

"So, what do we do now?" Griffiths asked when I'd filled them in.

I hesitated, then straightened, turning to him. "I need a car," I said. "And I need it as fast as you can."

"When did I get a fully grown kid?" He snorted. "Son, you have to *earn* a car. You know that, right?"

"I don't love you anymore," I said, playing my part in the drama and getting a grin from him.

"I know. All right, you need transport. Give me a few minutes. We can move people around and have them sitting on the roof or whatever... Is the way going to be clear?"

"Probably not," I admitted. "The gangs had to have come from somewhere. I didn't see any trace of them on the way in, but there might be more out roaming...maybe I just missed them."

"So I need to send it with an escort," he muttered. "Squad strength at the very least, just in case."

"And that weakens you," I growled. "Dammit. I'm sorry, mate."

"It is what it is," he said with grim practicality. "I'll get to it now. We're maybe five hours from you, setting up at Folkestone. No sign of anything major yet, but the undead are definitely in the area. We had to clear them out as soon as we arrived, so I'm expecting a hard push to come soon. If they have any sense, they'll want to hit us before we can get established."

"Fuck."

"No time for one, and you're not my type." He winked, a bit of manic cheerfulness clear in his tone. "Just do me a favor—if this all goes pear shaped, make sure you seal off the south and find our people."

"I will," I assured him. "I'll sort a meeting point with Mike. Set up a rendezvous point for them, and I'll fly out and escort them—"

I broke off, left the dungeon and explained the current plan to Mike, who nodded and grabbed his map, poring over it.

"We can sort a position," Mike assured me. "It looks like the dungeon isn't going to be viable as a hidey-hole for much longer, anyway. We'll sort out a point to meet up, and we can set off running from here in, what? Half an hour?"

"It's that bad?" I asked, grimly, and he nodded.

"We're going to do our best to get to Jack, but if we can't, then we can't. I've got Chris working on making sure we've got an exit we can use. It's *that* bad."

"Dammit." I cursed, then made a mental note as he named a meeting spot and time, then thanked him and dove back to the others. "Griffiths, Mike said to meet up here..." The map on the wall flashed and updated, and he nodded. "Okay, thanks. Now, I came here hoping to fill you in..." I nodded to Kelly and Griffiths. "But also to borrow undead to speed up the process."

"Okay, we can…" Aly paused, looking at something, as she sensed the same reaction to her from the dungeon that I'd experienced as soon as I'd reached them, and mentally marked that as a task.

"You can't do it," I told her, and she nodded.

"Why is the…oh." She trailed off. "You're outside of the dungeon."

"Yeah," I agreed. "Had I claimed the core here as a full-on core, we could have linked it to you, and then had full access, but it'd have needed the mana investment to form the link, and then I don't know how I could have unlocked the core to fracture it again. With it not being linked to the main dungeon, we have only the most basic access, and that was only through the local core."

"So you can create things at an Iron level that you have personal knowledge of, repair any damaged, already-constructed items, and summon minions that you have access to, but beyond that…"

"Nothing," I finished for her. "And if we had the mana, we could have summoned mounts, but we need to use the mana to get as high in the building to free Jack instead."

"I'll arrange it," Griffiths said simply. "Matt, good luck. And if you can, expedite getting me those men and vehicles back as fast as possible. Keep our people alive. And ladies, I don't envy you having to wait on the information as things change so rapidly. Good luck to us all."

With that he was gone, and I sighed, nodded to Aly, gave Kelly the ghost of a kiss, and then slid back into our own little pocket of the dungeon.

I slid through the walls to find the others working with frenzied efficiency. I joined them. Emma was in the lead, forming the single path upward that was still narrowing by the second.

I didn't distract her, instead drifting upward behind her, letting myself relax and reaching out, staring through the solid walls, and searching.

With the local area not being unlocked as part of "my" dungeon, unlike normally, where I could pass through the walls and floor like a ghost, flying upward to a significantly higher position than the dungeon's physical reach could manage, here I was limited to the exact radius of the dungeon, and damn it was a pain.

We could have found the core in minutes otherwise, and we sure as shit wouldn't be stuck trying to reach out toward the upper floors blindly, either.

Chris was here as well, close by, following along a dozen meters below, absorbing everything as he went and unlocking an escape route for us all.

I knew Jack had been mainly in *that* direction—or so I thought, looking to the northeast. But I could be wrong. I'd been searching at the time and desperate, and I'd barely noticed Jack at all before he'd vanished.

Even worse was that right now we were lifting up through a section of stonework that joined onto a stairwell. That meant that as well as absorbing the section of solid rock, building materials, and structural supports leading from the lower levels up to here, Chris was working to form rungs in the wall. That little detail made sure that we'd actually be able to reach the next level when we popped out...though there was one last issue.

It still looked like a war zone.

Parts of the building were smoking; still others were on fire. As I reached out, smoothing out a section and starting to absorb that, making sure that as soon as Chris reached it, we could join it up, I also saw the way the smoke rolled in and started to fill the section.

I slid downward, getting Chris's attention, and warned him, making him curse. As long as he left a tiny, thin layer that we could easily punch through when the time came—literally "punch" in case the core had entirely failed—then at least the smoke wouldn't pour in and start choking us all.

It was a pain in the ass, but he got it, and quickly moved on, working right up to the edge of the section I was absorbing, before leaving it and moving through. The pair of us took turns leapfrogging ahead and absorbing the next and next sections.

We managed nearly another full minute, the corridor finally coming entirely into view as we worked, before Emma called out.

"I think I've found him!"

I flitted up, leaving Chris to keep working, even as Emma angled across and forward, rather than just straight up. And as soon as I did? Yeah. I totally understood why she thought that.

There was an entire section of the corridor that cut off abruptly. What looked to be solid iron or possibly low-grade steel blocked our view, with exterior bracing clearly in evidence.

Most telling of all were the sections that showed something anchored to it, presumably to hold the weight of something on the inside.

Arms, I was betting—the same as the ones that had held me in place, though I thought that whatever was in here was designed to hold automata as well.

I frantically absorbed everything within reach, knowing damn well that no matter how much I wanted to, I could expand the limited dungeon's range no faster myself than she was doing currently.

Glancing at her, I was sure that her physical body was bathed in sweat right now, as she pushed and shoved deliberately as hard as she could, working to expand the reach before we lost the chance.

We were all working our asses off, I knew, pushing as hard as possible, even as second by second the dungeon's functions grew more and more distant. The connection faltered. I cursed, reaching out and tagging literally anything that came in range, absorbing it for a single point here and there to fuel the failing expansion.

Feeling the dungeon waver, I glanced over at where Emma strained. She pushed forward, inch by inch, arms outstretched, kneeling as to not force the bubble high—instead working simply to get it forward, pushing as the last few meters became a meter, became half, became...

The dungeon connection was dropping in and out now. Things we absorbed started to collapse into mana, then just…vanished, the mana not absorbed as the connection was lost. Nearby converters that had been used by the original dungeon here vented their mana: clouds of darkness and light, flame and water poured out.

Thirty centimeters, twenty-five, twenty-four…

It dropped as Emma grunted and sobbed with frustration and the effort, unwilling to take the time to step aside, when we might lose by a fraction of a centimeter yet. She heaved and fought, even as from somewhere nearby shrieks of rage, hatred, and madness resolved from the crackling and smoke-filled ruins.

I paused, twisting around and tried to figure out what and where, then cursed, knowing what it meant.

In following her up through the most direct line I could, I'd bypassed the sections that we'd been in before, and she'd pushed through the lower floors and into the rotunda above.

Then, she'd pushed onward, ever onward, hitting the second floor above, and finally she'd spotted him.

That meant that the cries I heard could well be from the floor between us and Jack…and I knew who that was. I didn't hesitate. Either I trusted her to do it or I didn't. I slid out, pausing only by Jenn's form in the dungeon sense, as I ordered her to stay with her sister and make damn sure that there was a hole in the trap around Jack as soon as possible.

Then, I left the dungeon sense, looked up, then back at the core. The fragment had literally a few millimeters of connection left, if that—a thin wedge that extended practically free of the core.

The core itself was blackened now, no longer gleaming and glowing, spinning or seemingly alive. Now the core was an inert rock, one that was splintering off a glowing fragment that in turn contained all the life the dungeon had left.

I reached out and touched it, thinking to see whether I could hold it off for a few seconds, to slow it, or…

It broke off. A sudden pulse of power flashed out and passed through me, making me gasp.

I felt different as it passed—sadder, like I'd just watched something die. And then a second pulse flashed out, one that came this time from the core fragment in my hand. Above me, a fresh shriek sounded, going from rage and loss, to a terrible hunger.

"Motherfucker!" Chris muttered above me, blinking awake as he was presumably ejected from the now fully shut-down dungeon.

I glanced up, then gestured for him to move back from the edge. As soon as he was away from the trap door, I crouched and then leapt up, not even bothering to fly, just grabbing the sides and pulling myself through, then stood as the dim light on all sides started to fail entirely.

In seconds, we were left with candles, and above, I still couldn't feel Jack's presence. Cursing, I set off down the corridor. Chris jogged alongside. The candelabra clutched in one of his hands streamed guttering light as we went, serving to illuminate practically nothing.

It didn't matter, though. In a matter of seconds, we'd reached the passage he'd carved upward in the dungeon sense. Most of the others gathered there as well. The shouts of rage and fury echoing distantly down filtered through the thin seal between the levels, and we knew it as soon as the first enemy found it.

The crunch and falling stone that was designed to stop the smoke and flames from incoming barely beat the first figure down: a massive man in firefighting gear. He bent his knees on landing, looked up, and roared.

I could see his eyes through the mask he wore, literally a firefighting full setup, axe included, with a jury-rigged air system on his back.

He glared around, then swung the axe wildly, right to left, driving everyone back a step, before Mike shot him.

It was a three-round burst. The guy staggered back, left hand rising to his chest as the blood suddenly spurted. The look of horror and shock on his face was mainly hidden by the mask.

Then the axe fell to the ground and he collapsed, even as another figure dropped down.

This one landed atop his friend. He stumbled forward, barely catching himself as he tried not to stand on him. Then he promptly forgot all about his friend as he saw the enemy all around.

More screams, more shouting and rage, and three more shots.

Cue the body falling, and we backed up slightly, getting ready as more and more leaped down, most coughing and hacking now, as the firefighting gear apparently ran out. By the fifth body, we were about to drag them out of the way, until an entirely new form landed.

This was clearly one of Marchioness's things. It hit the ground on three legs, then leapt forward before anyone had managed to get a bead on it. And damn, it was fast.

We'd fallen into a rhythm of taking turns to conserve ammunition, but in the heartbeat's hesitation as it landed, it was already screaming forward.

Chris fired. His bullets hit the shoulder of the thing, and it dodged to the side. Then, before he could adjust, it dove, hitting the floor, rolling and coming back to its feet.

The overall image was similar to the humanoid things we'd faced earlier: two arms and two legs, along with a head full of grinders and a torso that was almost a cylinder.

The difference was…this time, the fucker was *armored*.

Mike and I opened fire as well. The brothers joined in a second later. But it was Kilo who brought it down, the floor before it as it tried to run forward suddenly becoming an ice rink.

"Cease fire!" Mike roared.

I did, cursing. The bullets flew in all directions, the armoring heavy enough that all we were doing was endangering each other. As soon as we cut the fire, Robin and Beta were there.

I'd not seen much of the Paladin of late, but between her shield and mace, and the evolving kobold's claws and fury, I gave them their space.

The first impact was Robin's shield. Her shoulder tucked behind it, she took the sliding, skidding creation full-on and heaved it back, crashing it to the floor. Then Beta pounced on it, grabbed both its arms at the wrists, planted a foot on the ground in a patch that suddenly cleared of ice in a split second—Kilo, clearly keeping his love interest in mind—and the other foot was planted on its chest.

She braced and then heaved. The arms creaked as she literally started to rip them off, before Robin stepped up and ended it with a single blow from her mace into the creation's upper chest.

Ten seconds later, Beta ripped the core free, hefting it...right before it exploded.

She was hurled back, crashing into the wall and then sliding down it. Robin, clad in her more modern armor and partly shielded, standing on the far side of Kilo as she had been, was smashed from her feet and bounced off the wall as well, hitting headfirst and slumping to her knees.

That was when the next landed, and then two more behind it, barely pausing before leaping into the fray. Kilo threw up a wall of ice, staggering the first as it crashed through it, and I unleashed a blast of lightning, taking the fucker through the chest and taking no chances.

Chris had the second; a low blow by his hammer turned one leg to mangled metal. Then his shield battered it from its feet, into the third in line.

Then Mike finished it off. A single round from the sniper rifle tore through its chest and destroyed the one behind's left arm at the elbow as it continued on.

Then it was Andre's turn, hitting it full in the head with a mace, one that I recognized as being Robin's. The mechanical creation flipped arse over teakettle. As it landed with a crash, Chris lunged in as well, hammer falling to crush its mana core.

There was a detonation again, but a much reduced one. It became clear that the reason the last one had gone nuclear wasn't that it'd been damaged; it was that it'd been turned into a bomb.

One more figure appeared, a much younger, smaller, and skinnier man. As he landed, he broke his left ankle with a loud snap, screamed, and fell to the floor. The knife he'd been brandishing skittered away on the floor as Chris stepped in close and booted it.

Then he was frantically pleading to surrender, as the big man stared down, hammer rising, ready to end it all.

"Please!" he begged desperately. "I didn't want to fight you!"

"Then you should have run," Mike growled, and the boy shook his head.

"She said she'd kill us all!" he explained. "She said she'd eat our souls, make us into them, if we didn't help her. And if we did? We'd get food!"

"Bullshit." I grunted.

"Please!" Tears tracked lines down his filthy cheeks.

As much as I wanted to end the threat, looking at him, it was clear he really wasn't about to attack us. If anything, in dealing with him the only risk we were at, was us dying of boredom.

"How many are left up there?" I asked instead.

"Four!" he admitted quickly. "Three of the gang, and one more of the machines."

"Marchioness?" I asked.

He shook his head. "She was making something." He wiped ineffectually at his nose with one hand while clutching his ankle with the other; the red of blood seeped through the filthy remnants of his jeans. "Oh gods...help!" he begged again.

I snorted. "You want to live?" I asked, and he nodded, sniveling. "Tell me what she's doing, and we'll leave you here," I promised.

"I'll *die*!" He wept. "You know that!"

"Probably," I agreed, uncaring. "You jumped down here to fucking murder me and my friends, though, so you'll forgive me if I don't give two shits."

"I didn't want to!" he cried again. "I didn't want to, but we needed the food, and she was going to kill us all!" He drew back suddenly, hissing in fear and fright.

I looked over, not seeing the issue, until I finally got it. Kilo was helping Beta up, and from somewhere Jenn had appeared. She was using a spell to heal the big kobold.

Twin streams of blood dripped from her draconic nostrils, and as the spell took hold, she hawked and spat, trembling, but quickly recovering.

It had been the light of the spell that had done it, I realized. The kid, being under-leveled and inexperienced—coupled with the darkness of the passages down here and the flickering lights of the candelabra—had meant that he'd not gotten a look at them before now. As he did, his eyes flared wide, before he doubled over with a fresh wave of coughs.

Smoke was thinner than it had been before. The whoosh and crackle of distant fire extinguishers echoed down to me, but the combination of the fire suppressant, the fumes, and the smoke was doing a number on him.

"Should I heal him?" Jenn asked me uncertainly, and I shook my head, seeing that she'd already checked on Robin as well.

"You might need the mana," I said coldly. "What happened? Did you find Jack?"

"We did," Emma said tonelessly. "It's not good news."

"He's still trapped?" I shook my head. "Dammit. Fine, we'll find a way to—"

"He's dead," Emma clarified, cutting me off. "I'm sorry, Matt. Whatever happened in the box? When we cut our way in, we found the far side was already open. He was trapped inside…then probably, as you thought, shielded."

"And then?" I asked woodenly.

"And then the arms in there cut him up," she said. "I'm sorry, Matt."

"It was a trap, one built to contain her," I muttered. A mix of emotions roiled through me. Rage that he'd been killed. Grief, at his death. A touch of relief in knowing that I could always rebuild him—he was an automata, after all. Then came more anger that a trap meant for her had gotten Jack and thanks to whatever shielding Simon had designed, I'd not even known it. He must have spent forever building that trap, making it as perfect to kill her as he could, and then Jack had wandered into it, sent by me.

"Goddamn it!" I roared, slamming a fist into the wall nearby, even as Mike stepped up and helped Robin to her feet.

"Are you okay?" he asked her.

The Paladin nodded. "Thank you." She gestured gratefully to Jenn, who smiled at her, even as the others prepared themselves.

"Four more you said, but not Marchioness?" Mike asked the thoroughly terrified kid, and he nodded. "So where is she?"

"She's above," Emma answered him. "Using Jack's body to rebuild her own."

"MOTHERFUCKER!" I bellowed into the darkness, not caring who heard it.

CHAPTER THIRTY-FOUR

Mike was ahead of me this time, reaching the narrow passage that led upward, grabbing the rungs Chris had provided and starting to drag himself up even as Emma continued to explain.

"The far end of the container, or trap or whatever it was, it was open. Marchioness was there." She reached out uncertainly to touch my arm, clearly trying to offer comfort and having no real clue just how furious I was.

Nor how afraid.

If Marchioness could take over Jack's body...

"He's in bits." She continued, "A *lot* of bits. And the sections that were intact were separated out. It looked like he fought at first, then...I don't know," she admitted. "Maybe he gave up?"

"That's not something he *could* do," I forced myself to explain, striding across to the rungs and taking my place behind Chris, who had followed Mike. "He'd fight to the end, so it was probably something they did to him."

"Well, she's there. And just before I lost the connection, I saw her climbing into the box," Emma added, making me grind my teeth.

"We need to get up there." I glanced up at the others already in the tunnel before me.

"I'm not just hanging around here because I like the view!" Chris called back down at me, and I grunted a response.

"Be ready for a fight," I ordered the others, checking my weapons. But almost before I'd finished saying it, with the smoke and fumes already starting to tickle my chest, I heard a shout from above. I cursed, grabbing the rung before me.

Mike was at the top and almost out already. He'd switched to a handgun as he climbed, and he was firing almost as soon as his head and gun were out. Rounds cracked into the unseen distance; shouts echoed back. Mike grunted, adjusting and then firing again.

He'd paused at the top of the narrow tube, feet braced on the rungs and back braced against the far side, handgun ready. As soon as he'd popped up, he'd clearly found someone he didn't like. Shortly after, he was moving again, clambering up and out of sight.

Chris followed, muttering swearwords all the way. As soon as he was out of the way, it was my turn.

The area beyond, when it finally came into sight, was a mess.

In all the confusion of twisted corridors, traps, and searching, the levels had ended up blurring together. And now, looking around, it made one thing very obvious. These corridors had clearly been close by in the building to the area I'd set off the lightning storm. Between it and having ignited the barrels of diesel, the devastation was almost total.

Walls, where they weren't solid stone, were either burnt if they'd been plasterboard or shattered where they'd been coated in marble. Finally, if it wasn't one of those, it was charred to buggery where they'd been covered in polished wood paneling.

Probably the wooden panels alone had been worth more than my old apartment.

The decorations, seats, pictures, and random collections of posh crap scattered around from Oxford's insanely rich past were all just rendered down to scrap. Scrap that had then been covered in the flame-retardant foam.

That foam was then, in turn, churned to a muddy mess. That mess was then added to by the dead, with three bodies laid bleeding, and a fourth, clearly mechanical creation standing solidly in the distance, apparently uninterested.

The image lasted all of two seconds longer, before a single shot rang out, punching a hole into the creation's chest, which detonated a brief pause later.

"Got the fucker," Mike muttered.

"Upstairs," I growled. "She's up there somewhere, tearing Jack apart. We need to find her, stop her, and salvage whatever we can of him."

"How bad is this likely to be?" Mike asked me, following as I started to climb the stairs, the tube we'd just crawled up having exited into the bottom of them. "I mean, can you fix him?"

"You want to fight Jack?" I asked him, and he shook his head. "Well, that's how bad this could get. I seriously doubt I can 'fix him' if she's rebuilt him into her body!" I snapped.

He swore under his breath.

The vision in the dungeon sense—as it had been a mixture of my own dungeon abilities, the local under-leveled dungeon and the limitations it gave, and the whole "passing through the floor and walls"—had made me think that the trap was on the floor above, not the one that we were approaching. But as soon as the passage came to view, I knew I'd been wrong.

The metal that had been at one end, that Emma had been frantically working toward reaching was still mainly there, covering a serious section of the corridor, floor to ceiling, wall to wall. The hole she'd managed to eat away in the middle of it wasn't big—a matter of centimeters, that was all. I had a massively enhanced Perception, which was both a relief and a curse.

That was all I needed to make out the movement on the far side. As soon as we reached the floor and ran toward it, a fresh burst of movement on the far side made it clear we'd been spotted, and were too fucking late.

With a shriek of rending metal, a sound like the bellows of an enraged dinosaur, and a crash of metal on stone, the far end of the box, the end closest to us, suddenly sprouted claws I recognized.

They punched and tore through, enlarging the hole.

Then they dug into the edges of the metal and gripped, before they proceeded to tear the hole bigger—inches at first, then more and more—until the hands rearranged and gripped again, bending back an entire panel.

"That's not Jack, right?" Mike asked me as we slowed to a halt, staring and cursing.

"No," I said clearly. "That's *definitely* not Jack."

"Then let's kill it," Emma snarled from behind me. She pushed a hand through to the front and unleashed a thunderbolt as thick as my thigh from literally between Chris and me.

The sound of the blast was ear-battering; even I flinched away from that. But Mike and Chris, who'd been standing by my side, cried out in pain. It definitely didn't help them that weak but still irritating and painful crackles of lightning discharge danced across their armor and skin from the close-range casting. For me, though, it was a different story.

The lightning crackled and danced across my skin, bringing a feeling of rightness, an enervation that just made me want to shout, fly, and kick my enemies' asses all day.

The bolt certainly didn't have that effect on the amalgamation that was Marchioness, though neither did it have the usual—and extremely terminal one— as it screamed across the distance and slammed into the emerging figure.

She took the impact on one claw-tipped hand, shoving it forward into the beam. Instead of it burrowing through, it dug in, sure, but only did a small amount of damage before it dispersed across the paw, doing a fraction of the usual damage.

"What the hell!" Emma gasped weakly, staggering back. She'd clearly poured a hell of a lot, if not all, of her mana into that, only to have it have such a pathetic response.

"Resistance!" Jenn shouted suddenly over the heads of the others from somewhere at the back. "Matt, he was yours, and you're literally a lightning god. Did you give him a resistance to your spells?"

"Not intentionally," I said grimly. "But it looks like he has one. Get ready, people!"

"Let's see if it's resistant to a fucking bullet." Mike dropped to one knee and lifted the sniper rifle to his shoulder, sighting along it, then fired. The boom as the round was launched was barely heard before the equally loud boom of impact rang out. That same paw was smashed backward, though more mangled, before three more latched onto the panel and tore it all the way free.

Marchioness stepped free of the containment box, ducking under it and into the corridor, clearly enjoying the shock that her new form brought. She smiled and gestured at Mike to try again.

"Oh, this is bad," Chris muttered by my side.

As much as I tried not to on general principles, I had to agree with him this time.

Marchioness hadn't had a great deal of time to work, literally minutes, but whatever the design of her body, it was clearly supposed to be upgraded, much like Jack's form had been.

Jack had been in the form of a giant short-faced bear, something that had gone extinct centuries before on Earth. She'd taken what she wanted from the overall structure of him, added armoring to her chest, where I knew she'd said "she" was housed. Then she'd added on all four additional arms, and she was apparently in the middle of attaching the head over her own, making it look like a horrifically burned woman was trying to wear a badly fitted bear outfit.

The issue was that the head and other parts were still integrating.

Lots of the torso was in torn sections behind her, some of which were still flashing and sparking. Others shuddered or lay still. But the way she'd wrapped some of it onto herself, pressing her front into the belly, meant that the legs were shifting around and bending almost back upon themselves.

More and more of the twisted and torn metal was folding in upon itself. Wires burst free, like a thousand tiny spiders trailing butt-ropes being launched out over sections, then burrowed into them and connected the systems up.

The head? Her face was seriously fucked up and partially subsumed into Jack's neck. The metal of the neck flexed in and around, locking onto her and resealing. Eyes flared with life again. The jaws creaked, juddered and then moved in mindless mechanical chewing of the air as more and more sections came online.

The result was a short, stubby, eight-limbed, upright monstrosity that lurched and staggered forward.

I swallowed hard at seeing it.

Jack... Jack was dead.

"Matt?" Mike grabbed my arm as she straightened to her full height, now free of the obstructing metal panels. "What do we do?"

"You give it to me!" she hissed. "Surrender the dungeon—the fragment and your own! Give me back what you stole, *thief*!"

"Kill her." My voice cracked before I tried again, raising it and shouting. "Kill her!"

I'd seen the result of the lightning spell on her, but fuck it, I didn't just have lightning. Although I'd not intended to give Jack any kind of lightning resistance, I guessed he—and now she—must have developed it thanks to the nature of the dungeon.

Well, I knew what she'd not like: fucking Incinerate!

I cast it. The usual cost was a hundred mana, and I poured five hundred into it, aiming for the middle of her new body, planning to cook her core.

With one hand thrust forward, I probably looked ridiculous as the others hefted weapons and fired, and I waved, but fuck it.

I frowned, then pushed harder, sinking more mana into it, then cut it, stunned.

"What the hell?" I muttered, gaping as she continued to lumber forward, staring down at us all with her bear-head brushing the ceiling.

"FIRE!" roared Mike, suiting actions to words as he fired again and again. The high-powered sniper rounds slammed into the stomach, but to little effect.

The others opened fire as well. SA80 assault rifles chattered, the reflected sound of the gunfire hammering us from all sides.

Kilo hissed something, gesturing in a sweeping up motion from the ground to mid-thigh, like he was directing the tide. Despite the heat that still filled the corridor, a sparkling frosty-blue expanse of ice surged up from the ground. Tendrils reached out like tentacles from the deep to wrap around the hulking monstrosity's legs…only to explode into steam as soon as they touched the belly.

The steam and ice as it touched and shattered made it clear that my Incinerate had an effect. Hell, it must have had but…

But the containment unit that she, the fairy, had arrived in and that had been used as her home and interface, had been designed to withstand reentry and the trials of space!

That mine had been punctured to kill the fairy, must have been a design flaw, because as that clicked into place, I cursed. It was common sense. If you built something that was this important, of course you bloody installed protections for your goddamn people!

That meant that Incinerate was out. I'd planned to use it to cook her in there, but okay. And lightning was out because the damn body had some kind of resistance.

She clearly didn't… I glanced at her face, once so beautiful, now a mess of melted plastics and rubbers, silicone and fuck knew what.

Sections of metal shone through, gleaming from beneath charred and burnt plastics, lights that seared with eye-watering brightness and others that flickered, barely functional.

The arms, the legs…

"Aim for the human parts!" I shouted before I'd realized I'd said it. "Weaken her there!"

I didn't know whether it was a viable strategy, certainly not long-term, but it'd gain us time, I hoped.

She was almost as wide as the corridor here, and as she swiped claws in our direction, the entire group backed up instinctively.

We needed room to spread out. To maneuver and to dart in and land blows, to use our smaller size and faster speed to our advantage.

As it was, the corridor massively played in her favor. She was all strength and mass here, and we had neither of those advantages against her.

She'd been mauled before all of this. Even now, she only had one hand that worked, clearly taken from another machine. Both legs were awkward as well: one ended on a spike and the other a three-tipped claw.

As the fire shifted from the more monstrously powerful areas to the less, the effect was immediate. She twisted around; the bear form crashed down onto all four of its limbs. The head rotated around to point directly at us, as the other limbs folded in, drawing as far from sight as possible.

"Well, at least we know she can hear us!" Chris shouted, before taking a deep breath and casting a left-handed handful of something at a shattered planter on that side.

As soon as what I guessed were seeds hit the soil, they burst to writhing, green-coated life, burrowing from sight, making the toasted soil in there look like it was hiding a nest of snakes.

Mike ripped a grenade free, pulled the tab, and bounced it off the wall, banking it to land under her—only to have the hand lash out and catch it.

"Don't!" I shouted in warning, frantically casting a shield and shoving it forward, even as Kilo did the same. Neither had the time to fully establish, and although Mike had paused before he threw it, he'd not done so long enough.

Instead, it went off almost as soon as it left her hand, travelling back toward us.

The explosion slammed into and through our shields. Fragments from the literal fragmentation grenade tore into us…some being deflected by armor, some not.

Jenn, of course, was one of those who cried out. The damn healer was taken down, and worse, she fell back with blood spraying from a neck wound.

"Here!" Chris barked, shoving back her husband, Jimmy, who abandoned his post and dropped back to help his wife, even as Emma did the same. Andre held his position, but he was basically spraying and praying before the explosion went off and was now hissing in pain, a fragment driven into a gap in the armor over his knee.

It wasn't good.

The shock wave from the explosion so close had been bad enough. The fragments added to it, but worse was that before we could get over it, she bounded through the smoke and sparking, failing shields.

She leapt through, trailing smoke. The side of her neck was damaged, the head cracked and sparking on the right.

I was shoved aside a second before she could crush me. A shield rose and took the face head-on, battering it back, even as Robin's feet scraped and skidded backward, no match for the might of the armored bear.

Then Beta was there, lunging in. A hammer arced around and crashed down atop the flattened, smoking crown of what had been Jack's head.

The metal dented inward slightly, but that was it.

Marchioness ducked and then tossed her head up, nose under the shield, and shoved it aside, lunging forward to snap her jaws shut an inch away from Robin's face as she in turn desperately leapt back.

I bounced off the wall and triggered Storm-Strike, lunging forward and punching into the side of the head. It snapped sideways; sparking lightning cascaded across the surface, and a fresh dent appeared…but the damage was minor to her, and the damage to my hand wasn't.

I cursed, shaking my hand in pain. The bruised bones healed as I flooded them with Lightning mana, desperately thinking, my mind racing.

Behind me, Emma popped back up, screaming and striding forward. Her bursts of furious gunfire were more dangerous to us, considering the close-quarters battle and the ricochets, than they were to the enemy.

She was also screaming in fury as Chris worked to seal the wound on her sister's neck.

"Robin!" I barked, and she looked at me in question. "Smite that fucker!" I ordered, stepping back and focusing. I currently had a handful of Divine essence, and I just hoped I could choke it off before she used too much.

"I've got five points!" she shouted to me, clearly knowing what I was thinking, and I nodded.

"AOE Heal, then Smite!" I roared and she nodded, stepping back from the fight as Kilo darted forward.

The bear head lunged at Beta, opening wide, only to find a sudden burst of ice, formed into a triangular block, hurtling forward to crash into the mouth. Beta drove the hammer—one I recognized in all the madness as being Chris's—into the chin, crushing the underside and actually managing to lift its head, before a massive, clawed hand crashed into her hastily up-raised shield.

Beta was shoved back. The squeal of claws damaging the shield filled the air. Then she lunged forward, bringing the hammer around to crash into the shoulder joint from an overhead blow with enough force to crack the housing, bend the hammer's haft, and drive the bear-shaped monstrosity to the floor.

Kilo was moving already—we all were—but he was a blur. Ice formed up and over limbs, cold-welding it to the ground, only for the horrific heat of the earlier fire to already be playing a part in breaking the seal.

Stone shattered, exposed to too many rapid heating and cooling cycles. As Robin roared something unintelligible in all the madness, slamming her mace against her shield and then pointing it at me, a bright burst of blue-white and then golden light flared from her, arcing out in a bubble that passed over and through us all.

She'd said before that it was good for a one-meter radius, that was it, but this was at least five. While I drew down a breath of invigorating air that seemed to bring a little relief to the pain and cacophony of battle, it hit the trapped automata with crackling sparks.

Clearly, she'd leveled up since telling me of its capabilities.

I cursed momentarily as I hefted my hammer, lunging forward to shield bash the head from the side, then crash my hammer down on the armored foreleg on my side.

All that was going through my mind was how ridiculous it was that we were going to be killed by my own fucking familiar, and how much I really wished I'd taken that goddamn Thermal Lance spell right now!

"She's stable!" Chris barked from behind me. "Falling back!"

I didn't have time to look. The melee here was fast and dirty; we were in too close for real thought, and the fight was mainly carried by Beta with her enhanced strength and Kilo, who kept freezing jaws or sealing a limb to the floor at an opportune time.

I added what I could, but the space, the size of everyone else in it, and that there was literally barely enough area for four of us to walk abreast here, never mind three to fight side by side with a giant bear, meant it wasn't much.

"Kilo!" I barked as thought occurred. "Ice spike in its mouth!"

He nodded and did it, as Robin started chanting again, clearly working up to her Smite.

"Everyone else, back it up! We need more room!" I ordered.

Mike helped to half-carry Jimmy, still firing the rifle offhand when he got the chance. It had to be nearly breaking his wrist to fire the damn thing. The jerking made that clear, but with his investment in his stats, he was managing it…even if only just.

I cast Incinerate again, though this time I focused on the ice spike in its mouth. It detonated, doing minor damage, essentially boiling the ice away and cleaning the mouth. It made it slightly less likely we'd get an infection from the bites, provided we survived one. But in my haste and seeing a possible target, I didn't consider that it was a mechanical mouth. There was nothing to damage: no tissues to scald, no throat to clog up, or lungs to sear.

It'd have worked great on a living enemy, though.

I made a mental note to try that in the future.

The now-ursine Marchioness lunged forward, jaws snapping shut on my recently repaired shield and yanking her head sideways. I cried out as my wrist was nearly broken again, and I rammed my hammer's head forward, getting it into the jaws just in time to prevent the second bite closing on me.

That was when Robin joined in. The first blow that landed barely scratched. The second did little more. But the third? That got a dent.

The fourth through sixth were really starting to do damage, but just as she started to get up to real damage, she cried out and sagged backward, staggering.

Beta was there in a heartbeat, shield coming around and blocking the swipe of a massive paw. Then Robin was back up again, swinging wildly at the air as something tiny flashed past the kobold, focused on the Paladin.

I turned, getting a last-second blur of warning as something dove at me. I ducked my helmet, feeling the impact as something about the size of a mouse crashed into me at speed.

It exploded in a collection of cogs and springs, bronze and mechanical parts. But the distraction was enough that I nearly lost my arm.

The jaws snapped as far shut as they could as I tried to back up, the head of my hammer still stuck in there. I yanked hard on it, buckling out two front teeth as the hammer came free.

I brought the shield around hard, slamming the tipped base into the bridge of the nose and making my shield and arm ring with the reverberation, leaving a small dent on it.

Then I left a larger dent as I brought the hammer around again.

Kilo grunted something and a collection of spikes lanced up from beneath, spearing into and shattering against the body, before he called out.

"The bear form!" he barked. "We're damaging it, not her!"

"Fucker's right," Chris called from somewhere behind us. "Get ready to run!"

"Break on three!" I called to the others. Then I cursed, seeing the way that the automata shifted, clearly hearing and getting ready as well.

Well, I wasn't having that.

"One…" I called.

Robin stepped up, swinging a single blow that dented in a significant section of the nearest leg. Then she cursed, backing away again at the veritable swarm of smaller fliers trying to attack her.

"Kilo, clear them off her!" I heard Mike bark.

"Two!" I shouted.

Then, just before I shouted *three*, two things happened. First, Marchioness lunged forward, clearly expecting us to start to try to run, and to be able to catch at least one of us and probably crush us.

The second thing was that I slammed my hammer down atop the bear head with all the strength I could muster, and triggered Storm-Strike through the weapon.

The weapon unleashed a much-magnified version of the blast. It literally shocked and staggered the bigger, at least partly resistant creature.

It was enough that instead of the bear lunging forward and up, it was slammed downward. The shoulder hit me and slammed me into the wall. As I bounced off, I suddenly found myself pinned in place by that same shoulder, as the head jerked and shook.

"Matt!" came the shout.

But before I could figure out who it'd been, I was slammed against the wall again.

The bear recoiled as a new impact rang out, then another.

I dimly saw the handful of Divine essence points I'd managed to regenerate start to dip. I looked up. My armor held me together for now, but only just.

Beta roared in fury, lunging forward, grabbing its opposite leg and yanking it up and dragging the massive creation free of me through sheer muscle power alone.

I sagged.

Robin, instead of fleeing, brought her mace down hard, over and over like she was beating a drum, atop the bear and it fell.

I saw my chance and launched myself up and over. The narrow gap between its back and the ceiling flashed past as I twisted around to land with a grunt and gasp, now behind Marchioness.

"Hey, bitch!" I gasped, my ribs and gut where I'd been pinned aching. "Looking for this?" I dragged the core fragment free.

As soon as the fragment left my bag of holding and entered the normal world, she clearly sensed it, going absolutely apeshit trying to get turned around, shoving the others back but ignoring them beyond that.

That was when I powered another Storm-Strike and brought the hammer down on her rear right leg, right on the knee.

It crumpled, the bearings and more crushed beyond repair. The leg now useless, she fell.

The shouts from the other side let me know that they were making equal use of the opportunity. I couldn't see much of what was happening, but as I switched to the other side, I heard Kilo shouting.

"The legs!" he cried. "Take out her legs!"

"No shit, Sherlock!" I grunted under my breath. I took aim and powered it again, the last of my available mana going into another blow.

The second leg buckled, and from there, I knew we'd won.

Obviously, she knew it as well, because Marchioness suddenly started speaking.

"Matt, you have no fairy!" she called. "You know this! You know what a fairy can bring to the dungeon. And with this, with your dedication, you've proved yourself—you're worth allying with!"

"Oh, you have no idea," I hissed, swinging again, smashing another blow into the nearest limb, the spiked one that she'd walked with before.

That had no such armored resistance as its friends did, and it broke with a single blow.

"She's my SISTER!" roared a voice.

I tiredly shifted to the side.

Emma, her hair wild-looking, shoved Chris aside. "That fucker is *mine*!"

"Emma…" Andre and Jimmy spoke up at almost the same time, but they fell silent fast enough as well. Chris and the others backed away too, as Emma suddenly lifted into the air.

It wasn't far, only a few inches, but her feet clearly weren't touching the floor as she flung out her arms, and her eyes suddenly were flooded with reddish-black liquid.

Veins across her face, neck, and arms throbbed, livid and black against her pale skin. Her mouth and eyes seemed to develop deeper shadows, creating the impression her eyes were holes in the fabric of reality.

"You NEVER hurt my sister!" Bloody spittle flew, as blood-red and black lightning flared from Emma's fingers. Her hair fanned out behind her, lifting on waves of static.

She looked down at her hands, seeing the lightning that grew there, then arced around, suddenly seeming to flow over the surface of an invisible ball.

Blood flowed from her eyes and mouth, streaming into the empty gap, even as the lightning danced and spun around it. Black, blue-white, and red combined, until she lifted her head with a hiss and threw out her hands.

Thankfully, everyone had backed off, seeing the otherworldly spectacle— even Beta and Kilo.

The ball—thumb-sized if that—streaked forward and punched into the middle of Marchioness's bear form's back.

The explosion was incredible. The sound was all kinds of wrong, like a bar of noise, almost a pulse of electrical energy—and that was the weakest and least impressive part of the effect. The hole it created as the leading edge of its containment failed and impacted the bear's back was beach ball-sized.

Even that might not have been that much, if not for the fact that it wasn't vaporized. It wasn't blasted out...oh no, it was *crushed* out.

That beach ball-sized radius of force cratered the back of Jack inward to his body. Those parts shifted others. He wasn't fucking hollow, after all—well, he was in a few places to store items, but this wasn't apparently part of that section— and entire sections were suddenly buckled bodily outward from their original placement.

The sound of the shifting metal was a screech and a boom. Marchioness howled in agony, even as Emma collapsed, Jimmy catching her.

"Kill her!" I heard Mike roar.

The others resumed their attack, while I stared in shock. My mind raced, wondering what the hell new class that had been.

The one thing I knew, as I shifted and looked at where I could strike to do the most damage now, was that if Marchioness hadn't managed to wedge herself against the wall, trying to turn to get at me, I'd have probably been crushed by the impact of the giant body.

What the hell had that been?!

It took only a minute of us all attacking before the shrieks turned to pleas, and to begging.

"Disengage!" I ordered her. "Disengage from Jack, *now!*" I held a hand up. A last few blows landed, then she gasped out an answer.

"I surrender!" she screeched. "I will serve!"

"Disengage!" I roared back at her. "I won't say it again!"

"I am!" she promised. The creaking sound from underneath made it clear that it wasn't an easy process.

It took a few minutes, long minutes that I spent watching my Divine essence climbing by a single point, and my mana creeping up slowly as well.

"What state's she in?" I called to Mike as he stumbled closer, grim-faced, coming from checking Emma.

"Unconscious. I'm betting whatever that was, it took a hell of a lot of mana out of her." He shrugged. "Chris had the healing focal orb. That did it for Jenn, though she lost a lot of blood and is going to be out for the count for a while."

"Everyone else okay?" I asked, and he nodded slowly.

"We're as good as we can be, anyway. A week's rest and a fuckload of beer and bottles are needed, but we're all right."

He looked at Marchioness and cocked an eyebrow in question. I just shook my head, my face flat, and he nodded.

"I will serve," she called out again from underneath. The broken leg shifted around as she struggled to extract herself. The main bulk of what had been Jack scooched slightly as she inched closer. "I will...serve!"

I stared down at her, my face emotionless as she finally dragged herself free.

"Can Jack be recovered?" I asked her, and her melted and broken face stared up at me in confusion. "My automata you butchered."

"I did not." She shook her head. The neck servos glitched, making her head judder suddenly sideways and back several times. "I simply made use of the available parts."

"Can he be rebuilt!" I snapped.

"As a new automata?" she asked. "Yes, of course. Your former selection will have been erased, and the dungeon will accept a new one. I will ensure it..."

She reached out a battered and broken limb, and I stared at her coldly.

"All you have to do is accept my bond," she whispered. "I will serve you now, my master. I know my place. I can serve, however you wish!"

Instantly, my mind rebelled at the clear insinuation of how she expected to be used, and the sex doll form made even more terrible sense.

"Jack can't be repaired?" I asked again, wanting it very clear.

"This automata is erased." She shook her head. "The core was already deactivated. Clearly, my former master believed I was inside and wanted to be sure."

"Disengage," I ordered her bluntly.

"I...have?" she tried, her head jerking sideways again.

"From the automata!" I snapped. "Remove your core!"

"You will protect it?" She hesitated before sounding hopeful. "You will free me?"

"Disengage," I repeated. "Or I'll destroy you right now."

399

"I surrendered," she reminded me, not moving.

I lifted my hammer. The cracking lightning of my Storm-Strike rose in my eyes and flowed along my arms and hammer.

"I will obey!" she hissed. Clicks sounded as sections released, and the already damaged body suddenly sagged.

"Matt?" Chris called over from the far side of Jack's body. "Everything okay?"

"It's getting sorted," I assured him grimly, as the central cylinder of her torso, now scratched and dented in a dozen places, let loose a sudden blast of gasses.

They swirled and dissipated; then the cover clicked and started to open, before jamming.

I lost the little patience I had left, dropping the hammer to the floor, reaching out and slipping fingers in the crack, then grunting and heaving. The latch held for a second; then, with a creak and a pop, it broke. The cylinder jerked open, exposing an identical little capsule to the one that my own fairy had been inside.

The difference was, although this one was now cracked and battered, its occupant was very much alive.

"I swear my life to your dungeon!" the tiny fairy, barely decent in an outfit that was clearly designed to appeal, proclaimed, dipping to her knees and staring down, hesitant to meet my eyes. Her wings were short and stubby, but glittered with multiple colors. She quickly shifted her appearance further, apparently taking cues from the women of my party as to my tastes. Clearly she thought she was being clever, in that she was swearing not to me, but to my *dungeon*.

"Do you like the sunrise?" I asked her as calmly as I could. A nearby window made it clear that dawn was indeed breaking.

"If my master does." She nodded, smiling suddenly, obviously thinking the danger was past.

I looked down at her and then turned, calling over my shoulder to the others to rest, and that I'd be right back.

The nearest window wasn't far. She'd presumably broken it when she entered. The shattered glass was everywhere, and I paused as I clambered through the holes torn in the trap and passed the remains of Jack.

She, or Simon, had clearly torn his literal heart out. A shattered creation on the floor nearby looked a lot like the mana cores I'd seen in the other mechanical creations. I gritted my teeth, moving on, and stepped up to the window ledge. I leapt out, flying upward, ignoring the few confused and terrified gang members who ran as soon as I did.

The dome of the building had a little cupola, and as I landed in it, stepping up to rest one arm and the cylinder on the ledge that ran around it, ready, I spoke aloud what I'd been wondering since I found the place.

"Why here?" I asked, unthinking.

"It was the center of your learning in the area," she replied, clearly unimpressed. "A library...the Radcliffe Camera, my previous master had called it. He taught here, or nearby."

"Whatever," I said coldly, dismissing what had probably been a stunningly beautiful sight once and now was a shattered ruin. "Do you see the sunrise?" I asked with brittle patience, and she nodded.

She'd shifted her appearance, apparently deciding I wasn't a sick fuck like Simon. She had a humanoid form still, but she now wore a small dress, black, with her skin pale as cream. She noted me looking at her, and her wings vanished. Other changes came as the dress shortened, and she smiled more, pointed feral teeth glinting as she stared, adjusting her form to whatever she decided would enable her to manipulate me easiest.

"I see it," she agreed, seeing that I was waiting for a response.

I nodded. "Good. Because it's the last you'll ever fucking see."

And with that, I lifted the capsule, and as she screamed, beat her and it into the stone balustrade until the case was leaking bloody fluids and the entire thing was broken.

When it was done, and I was sure she was dead, I scooped her out of the remains of the capsule, and cast Incinerate on her, making goddamn sure.

Then, as her ashes floated away on the rising breeze, I lifted into the air and returned to the others.

CHAPTER THIRTY-FIVE

"So, how you feeling?" I asked Emma, turning to her.

We'd been picked up only a few minutes before. As soon as I'd seen that everyone was settled, I'd checked in with the team that had come to collect us, and at last, I'd ordered Andre to move, swapping seats to sit next to her.

"I'm fine," she whispered, still looking wan and tired.

"You look like shit," I said bluntly. "That was blood magic."

"It...maybe?" She winced. "Is that bad?"

"It's...dangerous," I admitted. "I've done it before myself. It's dangerous as fuck, but sometimes, you need to do it. Given the choice between dying from not doing it, and using it, yeah, I've used it, but it's not a good choice. It's addictive, I know that much."

"Yeah..." she whispered.

"You feeling a need to use it?" I asked, and she hesitated.

"No..." She hedged. "But I keep thinking of ways I could. And it felt good to be able to make a difference."

"The power?"

"Yeah. Being a Storm Mage didn't do anywhere near as much."

"A Storm Mage?"

"That was my first choice, my first class. Storm Mage."

"Sounds cool," I offered. "Is it?"

"I get bonuses to weather manipulation, so I can help control the storms. But I've got no clue what I'm doing with it. And when I've tried to help or to do anything, I'm nowhere near powerful enough to do anything with real weather. I can basically make a tiny cloud...maybe enough to make a garden wet from it, that's it."

"Radius?" I asked, thinking about it.

"Ten meters by ten."

"That's pretty fucking powerful." I shook my head, and saw the disbelief on her face. "Okay, let's look at this instead. You can make a localized rainstorm, say it's over ten meters by ten, and you cast that on an area our enemies need to travel through...you know, like a street."

"And we get wet enemies." She snorted. "Hooray. Well, that's won the war, lads. Everyone can go home."

"And then I cast Lightning Storm in the same area," I continued, grinning evilly. "The lightning is conducted through the standing water. It fries everyone equally instead of just those who would be directly hit each time. It's a spell combination that could make an area totally impassible, and for a much lower cost than if I went all in on my Lightning Storm. How much does that cost?"

"To do the ten-by-ten? It's dependent on the area. If there's much Water mana about already and so on...but three to five hundred."

"So, call it four. And I could then use the lower end of my Lightning Storm, at a thousand, rather than the higher end to ensure I got as many as possible at several thousand more. Do you see the utility? Against the mechanist's stuff, that would have been seriously useful...if we'd had a position we could have used it from, anyway."

"Yeah, a narrow corridor didn't work out so well." She ducked her head again, seemingly happy to leave the conversation there.

"You said it was your 'first class,'" I pointed out. "What was your second?"

"Ummmm." She paused, glancing around at the others.

They were all listening, although many were pretending not to. The inside of the boxer wasn't really set up for private conversations. The configuration was apparently modular, and this one had been set up for transport, with four seats on a side, with the floors and walls all being metal. Besides the gear we had dumped on the floor when we climbed in and the food that people were eating, there was nothing besides one another to stifle the sound of conversation.

Usually, that wasn't the case. Any military vehicle's interior seemed to be designed specifically to magnify the engine noise, I'd been told, but between the mana engines and the lack of electrical activity, it was far quieter than normal.

"They're going to see you fight," I said. "They're all going to see what spells you have, and they know you. You're not going to be less of a person because you don't like your class. Remember Ashley's?"

She nodded, remembering how upset Ashley had been when she told her about the Courtesan class.

"I'm...a Bloodwytch," she admitted quietly, before taking a deep breath and repeating it louder so that those who were listening, knew.

"Okay, so what's a Bloodwytch?" I asked her.

She opened her mouth, then hesitated, seeing that nobody gave a shit, and if anything, Catherine looked interested and excited for her.

"Uh, two seconds, I'm getting the details," she admitted, clearly pulling up the description and reading it over again. "Okay, so I basically still have the same storm powers, but now that my mana pool is practically wiped out, I've had it drop to half, but my health increase by the same.

"All my class spells require blood, and they do various amounts of damage. The one that I used back there, Bloodwytch's Fury, is the most powerful and

403

devastating of them. It cost me all my mana and three-quarters of my health to cast."

"What other spells do you have?" I asked curiously as I tried to think about how little she was going to be able to cast her spells now if she wanted to remain unaddicted to bloody blood magic.

"Thunderbolt and Summon Storm are the same as before, but Crimson Spark is a sort of weak version of Lightning Bolt I think, except it can inflict bleeding. It says it's got a chance to, anyway. Then there's Curse of Vulnerability; I can make them weaker to my spells over time."

She took a deep breath, clearly reading as she continued on. "Then there's Hemomancy Missile. I cut myself and throw the blood; it shifts into a crystal structure and acts like a heat-seeking missile. Low damage per missile, but the more blood, the more missiles. When they impact and shatter, literally fragments of crystal-like sharpened glass explode into the wound. So, if it's just one, and it hits somewhere that's not major, it'd be painful but little else..." She looked at me.

"But if you got two or more on the same spot, or took out an eye or a major vein, that's fatal," I agreed. "That could be nasty. Anything else?"

"One more." She shrugged. "It's Blood Ward. Basically, I bleed on the ground and it creates a shield, but it takes my life force to use it. So if a truck hits it, it might stop the truck, but I still die as it takes all my life force to do it."

"And that's the kicker with blood magic." I nodded. "It'd be interesting to see if you could cast these spells with an outside source. You know, if I gave you mana or blood, I mean."

"But then it might take your life force," she said, eyes wider.

"Maybe. Or, if you stabbed an enemy, could you use theirs?"

"I... I don't know." She suddenly looked thoughtful and not a little scary as she seriously considered basically using an enemy as a battery.

"Well, regardless, I'm more interested in the Summon Storm. Can you use mana from external for that? And does it still cost you blood as well?"

"I don't think so." She shrugged. "Not to needing the blood, I mean. It's not like I can cast it now, though. Like I said, my mana got nerfed, and I only had six hundred to start with."

"Now you're down to what?"

"Three hundred." She looked annoyed. "I know math isn't everyone's strong suit, Matt, but come on, you can take half away from six hundred, right?"

"I didn't know if you'd used some common sense and invested in your Intelligence again," I said mildly. "You know, when you hit level ten, you had all those points, after all. I mean, you are level ten, right?"

"I am." She looked surprised that I knew, then nodded. "Your Examine skill, right?"

"Spell," I corrected. "And no, but it's pretty obvious. Hey, Jenn." I leaned out and looked around the abrasive thorn in the side that was Emma. "You feeling any better?" I asked her, and she nodded, smiling wanly.

"Much, thanks. I just got a bit hurt."

"More than a bit. You need to rest," I told her. "You lost a lot of blood."

"Oh, we both do," she assured me, nodding. "Emma rigged an IV and gave me a pint of hers back before we set off."

"Did she now?" I sighed, before nodding and getting up, moving back over and giving Andre his seat back. "What am I saying—of course she did. Well done, Emma."

The other woman just nodded, and I sat back, closing my eyes and reflecting on the fact that no matter what happened, every time I spoke to Emma, it was a challenge...and every single goddamn time, there was more to the story than I thought.

She was a pain in the arse at every chance, and yet...setting up an IV drip and sharing her blood with her sister and then helping her as we ran—that was just her. As was not asking for a break or drawing anyone's attention to it.

We'd run from the dead dungeon in Oxford for a few hours to the rendezvous point, reaching it barely ahead of the driving team, and I was bloody glad we had. They rocked up, turned around, and literally changed over—the spread-out squad that had brought both boxers consolidated into one vehicle—and we got on the road as fast as we could.

They broke off again thirty minutes later to head south around the mess that was the outskirts of London. We continued due east, planning to approach from the north and head for its heart.

As it was, the entire group was close to exhaustion, and I was damn well hoping that nobody was going to get in the way.

I wanted there to be survivors in there—of course I did. And thanks to the mentality of the military and humans, it was most likely that if there was law and order anywhere in the country, it'd be in London—ha, first time *that's* been said with a straight face—because so many of the military and governmental groups would automatically fall back on the capital.

Add to that, apart from the rural communities that were used to growing their own food, people would instinctively head for the largest population center to try to get answers.

In the north, that hadn't happened, mainly because we were much more spread out, and Newcastle wasn't viewed as the "leader" of the local area; it was just that there were more people than elsewhere.

Down here? London was the be-all and end-all of things. Or, at least that's how they liked to portray it. And as such, everyone had run there.

For me, before the fall, it was loud, far too expensive, and too many unfriendly types. But most of all? There were just too many people. *Far* too many. Everywhere you went, it was like that—from bars to shops, clubs to the rail system.

I was honest enough with myself at least to admit that was one of the reasons I disliked the place, that there were just too many people for *me*, and my wages that enabled me to live a good life up in the north would have me living in poverty there.

Now, though, as we bounced and jostled along, the boxer occasionally slowing to nose into parked vehicles and then the engine surging to shove them aside, we were seeing more and more weirdness.

Some roads, although apparently silent and abandoned, were entirely cleared, we realized. It happened now and then, seemingly without rhyme or reason. After the third such, with the surrounding areas choked up by the shifted vehicles, Mike called back to get everyone's attention, before backing up to go around to the last road we'd been on.

"What's up?" I climbed from my jump seat along one wall and moved forward to lean against the side of Chris's seat and stare out of the front window.

"These roads are clear again," Mike said

I nodded; that much was obvious. Normally, every house in the area had a car or two out in front of it, and due to the difference in the population density, there'd been a hell of a lot of people apparently out and about, clogging up the roads when the fall had come down here.

"He means the roads ahead are a nightmare and these have been specifically cleared," Chris explained for him. "We were following the signs for the bypass but that road back there?" He gestured distractedly ahead, out of the windshield, even as he was backing up, using the mirrors. "There's been vehicles pushed and shoved off the road here and onto that one. Either they're looking to block it off, or they're making this clear. Either way, someone's done it, and with a plan in mind."

"So…?"

"So let's find out who our neighbors are going to be and why they're clearing the area." Mike sighed. "I mean, if there's a fucking battalion here or a slave camp or whatever, do we really want to set up next door?"

"Point," I muttered.

Chris got us back onto the road and clear of the route we'd been taking, then shifted through the gears as we rolled back to a decent speed.

We passed the houses on either side quickly, most simply abandoned and long silent. Occasionally, there was one with the windows or doors smashed in—or once out—and here and there were sections of burned-out houses. Fortunately, between apparent firebreaks—houses and buildings that had been pulled down deliberately—and what I guessed had been serious efforts, the fires had seemingly been stopped before the conflagration could really take hold.

Clearly either in this area the community spirit had been better than in the north, or more likely, they'd realized sooner the consequences of letting the houses burn, and the population at that point was large enough to stop the spread.

We drove for only a few minutes, climbing a long hill at the end that let us look back along the route we'd come from. It was from there that we got the first real hint why the road had probably been cleared through.

The route we'd taken had come in from the west and then turned south. As such, we'd missed that just to the north, past where we'd joined the cleared section, was a section of what I guessed was farmland or grassland, right on the far side of a shopping center.

"Somewhere that could be used to grow more food, and somewhere to loot," Mike guessed as we pulled over, staring into the distance through his binoculars from near the top of the hill. "Looks like it's a teaching farm, maybe? Or maybe one of those smaller ones that was absorbed into the city as people moved farther out? Probably worth a damn fortune before the end, all that land that could be converted into housing…"

I nodded, satisfied that we'd found why they'd clear a path, just not who was doing the clearing.

Between the snow—which hadn't been as heavy here, but was still fairly solidly falling—and the distance, we couldn't be sure, but it damn well looked like there were flat sections of clear land under all that white from here.

One part of the mystery solved, we all clambered back in—after a very brief pause for the necessary ablutions. Then we continued up toward the crest of the hill.

"There," Mike said suddenly, seconds after we'd reached the top and before we could descend. "Stop—stop, dammit!"

Chris slammed the brakes and we all braced as the slow-moving juggernaut skidded in the snow, then came to a full halt.

"What?" I squinted out across the city.

"Fuck's sake, man—what's wrong with your eyes?" Mike snapped. "There! Between the towers…"

I looked where he was pointing and grunted in shock.

As much as I'd looked out over the city, my natural reaction—I guessed that was what it was, anyway—was to look for the sights I recognized and remembered from my visits. As such, and given that we'd just come over a rise and could see a fair distance from here, I'd been searching for any sights in the London skyline that I'd known from TV or whatever.

I'd therefore totally missed the small walled-in area that was about half a mile away farther down the hill and to the left. Even as I stared at it, I saw both a handful of small vehicles moving around inside it, and horses being ridden in the distance, presumably on patrol from it.

There were what I guessed were soldiers atop the walls and the horses, but at this distance I couldn't be sure.

"Head for it," I said after a few seconds' thought. "It's too small to be a settlement. It has to be an outpost."

"No fields and nothing else," Mike agreed, nodding, then offered me his pair of binoculars.

I tried them, then handed them back, disgusted. I had no clue how people used them. For me, it was always a crappy blur. And bouncing as we were, the only thing that me staring through these would bring was a goddamn headache.

"Listen up, people!" I called back to the others. "There's what looks to be an outpost up ahead. We're heading for it, and we're going to try to make friendly contact with the locals."

I paused and predictably, it was Chris who called back over his shoulder from the driver's seat.

"That means we try not to *shoot* them in the face, but *stabbing* is fine. It's London."

"It means we try not to get into a fight," I corrected. "Down here, there might be a big enough force that they can cause us issues. Or it might be that we've found actual civilization after all."

"Or more likely, more gangs and warlords," Emma groused.

"It looked like the army," I told her, trying to be reassuring.

"That just means it's the biggest gang around, right?" Andre asked, and I snorted.

"Yeah, well, check your weapons, make sure you're ready, and when it comes to it, I'll try to make contact. If the shit hits the fan? Hold your fire until you have to. I'd rather they think we're defenseless until they're out of their fortification."

"It's not like small arms fire is a threat to this," Mike agreed, rapping his knuckles on one wall of the boxer. "So, you want me to make contact?"

"Not sure," I admitted. "Maybe I should do it. All thunder and lightning and shit."

"Save that for the main event," he advised as we drove down off the hill and the outpost vanished from view again. "This is too small to be much of anything...I'm betting a recon setup. It'll be a jumping-off point for people heading out into the surrounding areas, support and medical, an FOB." He glanced around again and then sighed. "An FOB is a forward operating base," he clarified. "The barracks farther out will be taken next so that they can expand control."

"You think this is an official setup then?" I stared out of the front of the boxer as we rolled along, passing the boarded-up, abandoned, and burnt-out buildings on either side.

"Possibly." Mike shrugged. "There were enough forces down here that unless the shit hit the fan in a far worse way than it did for us, they should have survived with some form of a command structure intact. Who's at the top of it, I don't know, but a lot of the officer corps is drawn from the area. They'd have kept control of their forces if possible, and then it'd be logical for them to fall in on the capital. We might actually be able to get some backup here."

"Don't tease me like that," I muttered.

"Heads up," Chris said suddenly, and I looked back to the road ahead.

"There," Mike agreed. "I see them."

"What?" I asked, still not seeing it.

"The tower on the left. Snipers, probably. I'd guess on overwatch," Mike said grimly. "I don't blame them. And I'd have set up the same. But that means they know we're coming, and I hate being under sniper's eyes."

The road ahead dipped down to a low point about three hundred meters ahead of us, then it flattened out for a good two miles, before finally climbing again.

On the far side of that was the outpost. About two-thirds of the way up, one of the two towers that were set farther on, off to the left from the small secure area, was apparently flashing a light at others.

I'd have not seen anything, but the morning was dull and heavily overcast with drifting snow, and the light was being shined out from a darkened section of the tower already.

I couldn't see anyone responding, but then a flag lifted at the outpost, and I grunted.

It was the British flag, so yeah, go us, but that didn't mean much. It could mean, "Hey, this is who we are." It could mean, "This is all they had at the shop when we looted it." Or even "Kill anyone in sight and come back; it's time for cake and sandwiches."

You never really knew with flags.

I was a firm believer that every year when cars started driving around with them on and proclaiming their support of a particular football team, that it was actually down to a legal thing that men with extremely small penises were required to show a flag in breeding season. Just so women didn't waste their time.

My evidence for this slightly outlandish theory? Well, I'd never gotten a letter, so clearly I wasn't classed as one of them. I'd explained this logic once in the pub and a few people had tried to point out issues with it, but they also drove those cars, so I guessed they were just embarrassed I knew their secret.

Flashy lights...yeah, okay, they were the same, I guessed. They were meaningless unless you knew the code, and even Mike was shaking his head.

"I think they moved it," he said after a second, his binoculars in hand. "I can see movement, but not the signal anymore. Probably they fucked up and realized we might be able to see it, so moved it back. Regardless, there's someone in the towers and they're in contact with the outpost; the outpost passed a message back, and boom."

"Well, let's hope not 'boom.'" I sighed. "Okay, if it's a military outfit, you're up, Mike. If it's not, I'll deal with it."

"Everyone else to stay inside?" he asked.

I nodded. "If the shit hits the fan and I can't get inside, I'll take off on my own. You all get out of here, then set up somewhere and pound the fuckers when they chase you. Kill anyone you can, then run again. I'll reach you as quick as I can."

"And if the shit hits the fan and I'm outside, wait the fuck for me to get in." Mike snorted. "I can't fly like Twinkle-Toes, so I'll be running like fuck."

"Point." I grinned at him, then moved back and checked my gear.

Trying to do this kind of thing in a moving vehicle was hard enough; that it was all weapons like swords and rifles, shields and hammers made it even harder. Pointy bits really got in the way, and I checked my armor over as much as anything else.

It looked terrible, I had to admit, even if I was only admitting it to myself. I'd done some very rough-and-ready repairs back in the dungeon, but when the choice was spend the mana on fixing my armor so it was prettier, or put the mana into the expansion project that got us back outside and—I'd hoped at the time—Jack back on our side, it was no contest.

It still took us ten minutes longer to reach the outpost, making it even more impressive that they'd cleared such a long run of the main roads here. But by the time we pulled up at the end of the road, coming to a halt to one side, already ready to floor it and about-turn, the wall was filled by heavily armed soldiers.

"Halt!" one of them roared through a cone, making damn sure we heard them. "Hands where we can see them. No weapons. Exit the vehicle slowly. Make no sudden moves!"

"Wish me luck, as I think that's my cue." Mike grunted, before opening his door slowly, then sliding out, leaving his rifle behind.

He stepped to the side, hands out, then reached across, making sure they could see him, and that what he was doing wasn't a threat, and slid the handgun out, before passing that to me where I stayed in the vehicle.

Then he stepped back out farther from the door. But as he started to speak, the soldier on the wall shouted over him.

"*All* of you!" he shouted. "All out—all weapons left behind!"

"Not going to happen," Mike called up, almost conversationally. "I'm Captain Mike Jefferson, formerly based out of Credenhill, Herefordshire. I've been based in the north since the fall, and I've brought important people to meet with whoever is in charge."

"Out of the vehicle!" the soldier screamed again. "Last warning, soldier!"

"If you try shooting me, I guarantee, not only will you personally regret it, though probably not as much as me, but every single soldier on that wall will as well. This is an FOB, so where's the commander?" Mike called back, as calmly as he could manage.

Another soldier came into view as the shouter grew more red-faced, and he called something to him, before running forward. There was a quick muttered conversation, including a lot of glares from the mouthy one, and we all waited.

"What's the betting they want to know how and why this works?" Chris suggested, drumming his fingers on the steering wheel.

"That's a point," I agreed. The vehicles I'd spotted in the distance had been too far away to see clearly, but the one thing they were obviously not was armored transports. They looked to have been trucks and old cars.

"Hold one," the first soldier suddenly called down.

Mike nodded, settling to stand at parade rest.

They clearly didn't like that. The look on the soldier's face suggested he was about to scream at him again, but the soldier next to him instead took the megaphone and set it aside.

"You're SF?" he shouted down to Mike, who nodded. "Your commander would have been..." He called a name I missed; Mike laughed and then called back up at him.

"Nice try, but he retired last year. My commander was..."

That started the ball rolling as they both questioned each other, basically making sure the other side had actually been serving military at the point of the fall, regardless of whether they were wearing the uniform now.

It took less than a minute from that point for a new person to reach the wall. He took one look over the side, then shook his head and picked up the megaphone.

"What the hell are you doing here, Mike?" he called down. "You run out of things to kill in the north?"

"Josh?" Mike called back up, suddenly grinning. "Damn, I can't see...is that you? The glare from your bald head's too bright."

"Dammit, it is him," the soldier—Josh apparently—said loudly. The pair ignored that he was indeed wearing a helmet, and so they clearly did know each other. "All right, you lot, back to work. Sergeant, with me. And you...you wait right there. I'll be down."

He waved at Mike, then vanished from sight. About half of the soldiers apparently left the wall, but that was it. Those who stayed suddenly started acting a lot more nonchalant, but they also kept their rifles ready.

Mike dropped his voice, angling his head as he spoke to me so it was harder for any of them to hear him. "I know him. He's SF as well. We served together, but that doesn't mean we can trust him. He's playing nice, but don't expect the soldiers on the wall to have gone far. If he thinks he needs to, he'll shoot first."

I nodded, looking back up at the wall and asked the question. "Do I get out, or stay out of it?"

"Best you stay out of it. You're the leader here—so's he. But you're a Dungeon Lord and he's commanding a piss-poor FOB, with soldiers who look like shit. If I introduce you, sure, say hi. Otherwise, you're too important for the likes of this."

"Gotcha." I nodded, squinting at the wall. "Still, it's damn impressive they built that."

The wall was literally that: a wall that ran from one side of the street to the other, perhaps fifteen to twenty meters wide. Concrete, if I was to guess, and perhaps five meters high.

There was a parapet for the soldiers to walk along, with a raised barrier to shelter behind, a single tower in the middle for a very obvious sniper team, and a shitload of barbed wire. Considering it had to have been built entirely with muscle power, it was hellishly impressive.

411

Brick, I could have understood: tear a bunch of houses down, mix up the concrete, and boom, you can make a load of options. But this…

"It's shit." Mike shook his head. "There's cracks in the walls, and they took the bracing down."

"Bracing?"

"It'll be poured concrete, probably into a mold with rebar to give it extra strength. The metal bracings give it shape while it sets. Here, they took the bracing off—probably to use them on another project the same way—and from the look of the walls, it was done recently. They should have left it on. It's metal generally, and that'd have given them more protection."

"Still looks impressive," I pointed out, and he snorted.

"Sure, but it's not hard to dig a hole in concrete. Have someone run up, hammer it with a pickaxe or hammer and chisel, then pack in explosives and set it off—that'll fuck this right up. Leave the metal on? That's not gonna work."

"You complaining about my wall?" a new voice called.

Mike turned and nodded, as a party of five came out of the base. The large gate was drawn open only far enough that they could move past it, and a grating sound echoing back suggested the gate had then been braced, "just in case."

"You've been investing in Perception," Mike called to him, clearly annoyed that he'd been overheard from there.

"Had to. You'd be surprised at the shit that's been going on since the end. The fall, you called it?" The same NCO he'd spoken to before walked out in the middle of the party, three obvious riflemen and a sergeant bracketing him.

"Good to see you, Josh." Mike sighed as the man approached.

Josh nodded to him, peering at the rest of us before offering Mike a casual fist bump. "And you, Mike. What about your friends? They stepping out to join us?"

"Not until we know where we stand," Mike said. "How about this? You're here because you need to find out who we are and what's going on. Then you're going to report it up to the higher-ups, along with anything I tell you. You're hoping you don't have to get into a firefight, but if you have to, you accept that. It's shit, but that's life. That sound about right?"

"You know the drill," Josh responded with a nod. "Except that we need to add that we've been told to ensure that any working vehicles that come this way are sent on to London for use by the army as well, and that"—he nodded in the direction of the boxer—"is one of ours already."

"It was." Mike nodded. "Of course, it stopped being one of the British Army's vehicles when we had to kill to recover it, then rebuild it to work again."

"*Some* people might not agree," Josh said carefully.

"*Some* people also lied about nuclear and biological fucking weapons testing areas," Mike said clearly. "*Some* people claimed that we weren't researching them and that minor things like international fucking law mattered."

"You sure about that?" Josh asked after a second, looking a bit unsettled.

"I am. The research facility was under Otterburn Camp," Mike said. "I was there, and I fucking saw them, and the monsters that we had to clear out to rescue the people there. I know what I saw, and I know that a single real fuck-up there, as close to a major population center as it was, would have utterly fucked the north into the ground."

"You've been on an active site that had biological weapons, that wasn't maintained?" Josh asked cautiously.

"Yeah," Mike agreed. "And I'm healthier than you have ever been, mate. We have healers. We have magic, and we have a dungeon. How about you?"

"A dungeon?" He cocked his head to one side. "You want to explain that?"

"Not around ears." He shook his head. "This is a cut-your-throat-after-hearing situation. I don't know what needs to be shared and what doesn't at what level. But there's a war on, mate, and that I was willing to share that we know where one of the *four* nuclear weapon research sites in the country is, and I'm not willing to talk about that, with you, out here, should give you a fucking idea just how much of a game changer this is."

"All right. Well, color me intrigued." Josh nodded. "I still need your weapons before you're to be allowed in the base, though."

"Then we won't be coming in." Mike smiled. "We keep our weapons, Josh. And this is our vehicle, and it's staying that way."

"You know we need to take it," Josh said, glaring.

"You know that I'm not going to let you." Mike's smile stayed firmly on his face. "Josh, you know me. You know there's a reason I was where I was in the service. You know who I was in service—and you know what I'm capable of. Do you really think, in a world where we've all gained additional abilities, that if I'm happy as I am to leave my weapon behind, it's because that makes me less dangerous?"

"Is that a threat, Mike?" Josh tensed.

"Not at all," Mike said. "If you try to take me and my group, we'll be forced to kill you all and tear down your pissy little walls, probably without so much as breaking a sweat. *Then* we'll roll on to the nearest base, and we'll do what we came here for—namely, speaking to command and negotiating. And when they see what we're bringing to the table, they're not going to give two shits about you, or any of this. In fact, they'll probably apologize that we had to waste time on slaughtering you all. *That's* a threat."

Mike smiled at Josh, and then ostentatiously looked over at his escort before apparently dismissing them.

"Mate, you and your people are here, running a shitty little FOB on the outskirts of London. A mile, maybe two or three is probably as far as you've explored of this new world. And I seriously doubt you're more than level twenty. We've travelled all the way from the north, killing everything that tried to face us. We're at war with the undead, we have training facilities like you'd not believe, and actually…"

413

He held up a hand. "This is a demonstration, not a threat, so keep your people under control, all right?" He reached in and, guessing what he wanted, I passed him out a rail gun shotgun, getting a grin from him.

"This," he said to the soldiers as he hefted and turned, being careful to keep the barrels pointed away from them, "isn't even the peak of our technology, but it'll do as an example." He lifted the tri-barreled shotgun and shifted it from side to side so that everyone could see it.

"What's that?" Josh asked in a hard voice. "I'll be honest, Mike, it's not that impressive."

"It isn't, right?" Mike smirked. "Of course, for the first portable rail gun—and I mean *man* portable, not on a fucking battleship—does it really have to be polished up? Watch."

He turned and pointed the barrels at a nearby house, then paused. "Tell me that you've not got anyone inside there, right?"

"We don't," Josh said slowly.

Mike fired.

The sound of the firing wasn't that impressive. The hum of the building charge wasn't even really that noticeable. But the launch? The tiny fléchettes that screamed across the distance and punched a hole through the front wall, then expanded inside the house, tearing through wall after wall and then out the far side, taking the rear wall with it, was probably overkill.

Especially as most of that was conjecture, because as the primary impact occurred, the transfer of kinetic energy into another form became explosive. We had to guess at the rest, because what was left of the house was utterly trashed.

The roar and crash as the entire house proceeded to collapse at that point showed to those who knew it—us only, basically—that Mike had overcharged it and used the full power pack in a single shot.

He grinned and handed the weapon in to me before turning back to face Josh and going on in a friendly tone.

"So, I'm going to suggest that all the conversation up to this point was just dick-beating, and now we're starting again. Hi Josh, great to see you. We need to speak to the higher-ups, so you're going to give us an escort, and pass us through, because you really want us gone. Am I right?"

"You're not wrong," Josh said after a few seconds. "How many of those do you have? And anything more powerful?"

"Again, not something to discuss here," Mike said. "You waving us on or starting a fight, Josh? We've got no time to fuck around."

There was a long pause, where I felt it could have gone either way, before Josh spat on the ground.

"Better that you're someone else's fucking problem," Josh decided, nodding. "Back it up and get ready. I'll sort out an escort, but I'm warning you—you'll be under eyes the entire time. Try using something like that offensively and you'll be taken down."

"Not what we're here for," Mike said calmly, before nodding. "Thanks, mate. And believe it or not, I didn't come here to fuck your Tuesday up."

"Not gonna change what comes, though, is it?" the other man said sourly. "Just stay in your vehicle and don't start shit."

Mike said nothing more, but clambered back inside and tugged the door shut, speaking to Chris first. "Pull us over to the other side of the road, park against that curb, and be ready."

Chris nodded, and we all waited, watching as Josh headed back inside with his escort, and the gates were closed.

"Now what then?" I asked. "And it might just be me, but I don't think he likes you?"

"He doesn't." Mike shrugged. "There were a few incidents in the sandbox, and he was a part of most of them. He's the kind of a guy who's perfect for this role— out on the shitty end, and willing to do what needs to be done. That's not saying that as a bad thing—we do what needs to be done all the time. But let's say, *hypothetically*, that you needed some people moved from an area. Maybe you needed to set a base up, and it turned out that a family owned that land, or claimed they did, and it'd already been purchased from the local warlord..."

He paused and looked over at me, and I nodded.

"He's the guy who'd be sent in to move them on?" I guessed, and he nodded.

"To be clear, he wasn't the kind of a guy you send to shoot them and bury the bodies," Mike added with a sigh a few seconds later. "He's not a bastard or one of the wet-workers used for the real off-the-books actions. But if you need to do something that's morally grey, and you want it carried out no matter what? That's seen by the public as the SF line, that we'd do anything that's needed, and sometimes, yeah."

He shrugged. "Sometimes it's the job of SF to kill one so that we can save a hundred, and that one...well, there's a reason a lot of us don't sleep well at night. Mainly, though, we're sent in for totally honorable jobs. We're not the ones sent to do morally wrong shit. We're sent in when the job has to be done, no matter the odds and that's it." He waved over his shoulder in a general direction of the now closed gates.

"You don't send us to turf a family out so that you can bulldoze the area to build a parade ground. That's the kind of a job that the local bully boys do, or...Josh. He's the kind that would just march his people over at the first sign of an issue and he'd deal with it personally. It made him popular with some of the brass, but unpopular with his unit and the rest of the operators."

"So what happened?" Chris asked, and Mike shrugged.

"Nothing. He just sort of got sidelined. Word got around that nobody wanted him in their teams. There's always a couple of problem children in the units...a little quiet backroom dealing, and all our problem children got shifted into his squad. Once that was done? All the other units were a lot happier, and he was

415

pissed. He'd finally realized that he was getting the shit detail, but with nobody willing to help him and back him to move to another team, he just put up with it, and moved on.

"Like I say, he's not a bad guy, just a bit of a knob and perfect for this kind of positioning. Imagine you have a normal commander seeing the shit that's been going on these days, and they have some soldiers who just refuse. They've seen too much and won't go back out? You know, in the past, with the Roman army? You know where the term 'to decimate' comes from?"

"Vaguely," I admitted.

"It was when a unit was fucked. They'd been cowardly; they'd failed again and again...insubordination, whatever. They'd be split into units of ten, then they'd draw straws. Whoever got the short one was beaten to death by his friends. One in ten, that's the meaning, roughly. Well, he's the guy who'd be ordering it, or who'd take part without a pause. Just drag one out of the pack and kill him on the spot for mutiny."

"Sounds like a dick." Chris shook his head.

"Not really," I disagreed. "I mean, let's face it, we lost a fuckload of our people in the big battle with Dickless and his minions. Imagine if a group of our people just decided 'nah, fuck it' and buggered off?"

"We'd not beat them all to death," Chris said. "Matt, I fucking know you—you wouldn't."

"No, I wouldn't," I agreed. "But they'd have caused the deaths of hundreds of others. And if we'd won at all then, we'd have booted them all out, after stripping them of their weapons. Thinking about it, and the way the world is right now, that'd have resulted in them all dying, and pretty quick."

"And so you see why I say he's not a bad guy—he just does the shit that needs to be done." Mike sighed, shifting around in his seat and looking out of the window. "Damn, that was a shitty conversation."

"Made it clear who and what he is, though, and it's best we understand that," I offered. "Seriously, in the stories, it's all black and white. Do this, rescue the princess, slay the dragon...all that shit. In reality? It's always fuckin' grey."

"Princess rescuing is grey?" Chris shifted around to face me as we waited on the others coming out. "Matt, who pissed in your porridge this morning?"

"Nah, you know what I mean. Like, if we roll it back to when we first opened the doors to people in Newcastle, the group we brought down from Hillsong. They were mainly great people, Clarissa and Markus. Hell, Ashley was one of them." I looked over at Emma, Jenn, and the twins, getting a nod that they were listening.

"Then we found that a bunch of those people tried to rob me, literally," I explained. "We found them in my bedroom, looting weapons off my stands, my grandfather's watch...loads of shit. I booted them all out of the room and stripped them of my gear. Then, when one of the same assholes started getting demanding, I kicked him out." I paused then went on.

"I killed him—actually, three of them, I think—which is terrible that I'm having an issue remembering. They were acting up. They were thieves, and then they proved it to me, talking about the abuse they'd inflicted on others since the fall."

"I don't see that as grey," Robin said softly, and I looked over at her and nodded.

"Said like that, it doesn't sound like it," I agreed. "But, then when we took the Galleries and freed you all, we had that group that we took out with us." I looked from her to Saros, Andre, and Jimmy. "We took them out because they beat and attacked other refugees—they abused them—and we gave them a chance, because we heard their side of the story. It's shit—it really is and I hate it every time I have to think like this—but nobody gets up in the morning and decides they're the bad guy. They all have a reason for what they're doing."

"Except sometimes the reason is that they're a dick," Chris pointed out. "Or, you know, French."

"Okay, yeah, all right, I'll give you that one. There's always the cheese-eating surrender monkeys to consider," I agreed, pretending to be serious.

Then, the mood broken, the conversation shifted to other, less grim topics.

I sat there for a few minutes, watching out the window at the slowly falling snow, barely enough to notice at the minute, but enough that the cold of the outside was more than noticeable.

Glancing over at Beta, I saw the tired look on her face as she shifted irritably. She, and many of the others, sat with blankets around them. Noticeably, she also had Kilo's, who by nature of his Cryomancer class, was pretty immune to the cold's detrimental effect on his species.

Beta wasn't, and although she was less affected than most kobolds, she was also still cold-blooded and hard as nails. That meant that it'd taken some serious effort to get her to accept the blankets when others didn't need them.

Saros was, as always, apparently totally unconcerned. She seemed to have gotten the message that Chris wasn't interested in going all tiger-man and setting his girlfriend aside for her. And as there was nothing else to do right now, she'd curled up and was braced against Jimmy, trying to get some sleep.

Jimmy ignored her, while Jenn and Emma talked to Catherine and were clearly starting to reach the end of their tethers with the Scepiniir scout.

Beyond that, the others were generally engaged in a low conversation, one that petered out after another twenty minutes. I turned to Mike, opening my mouth just as the gates were finally cracked again.

A pair of riders moved out on motorbikes that looked to have been dug out of a museum. The puttering of their engines filled the air as they passed, heads hidden inside featureless motorbike helmets.

Then the gates closed again, and I glanced at Mike.

"Probably been sent on ahead to warn whoever is in charge about us," he guessed. "They're probably going to make us cool our heels here for another hour or two, until they're ready for us and a detachment is sent this way."

"Well, fuck that." I grunted. "Chris, follow them."

"Let's piss off the special forces types and make them look incompetent, aye!" He laughed, pressing the starter, and grinned evilly as the shouts from the wall suddenly rang out behind us.

I watched in the mirrors as the soldiers atop the wall waved and shouted, trying to get our attention. But I bet someone was about to get an ass chewing for not putting guards all around us.

"You think this was a bad idea?" I asked Mike, who'd stayed silent as we set off.

"Not saying that." He sighed, then shrugged. "I mean, maybe? I don't know, honestly. There's times that it's best to just slide into the chain of command and climb it, playing by the rules, and then there's times to skip it. If we stay inside? We're going to have real issues further down the line because they'll expect us to be under their command. On the upside? They'll treat us as allies a lot easier if we slide in nice."

He looked out of the side window, then back to the base that was falling behind us in the mirror. His fingers drummed on the empty mana crystal that he'd replaced in the shotgun as he went on.

"The other side is, we really don't have the time to pander to these fuckers. Admittedly, we didn't tell them that, but let's be clear, we don't have time to fuck around. Any news on the fight?"

I shook my head. "I'll need to check…have I got time?"

He nodded. "The FOB will be a few miles out from anything else. No point in building it otherwise."

"Point." I sighed. "All right, I'll shout when I have something, I guess."

With that, I shifted around, braced myself as best I could against some of our gear, and closed my eyes, sliding into the dungeon sense.

CHAPTER THIRTY-SIX

It took literal seconds to reach Griffiths. And when I did, it was made very clear that we didn't have a great deal of time to fuck around.

The dreadnought dungeon was in full production, the surrounding area looking like it was being assaulted by thousands of burrowing, invisible earth-eaters.

The ground, the poured tarmac, sidewalks, roads—all of it was being consumed to fuel the dungeon's expansion, and damn, was it all balls to the wall.

There were already fights being held in the area. As soon as I reached the command center—the heart of the dungeon and the core, anyway—I'd zipped straight up into the air. Griffiths was already there, a few dozen meters up, giving directions.

"You made it safely then," I said to him, coming to a halt.

He nodded, but continued his conversation with another soldier. "There, okay? We need to ensure they don't just dig their way out and attack from another side."

The soldier nodded, and Griffiths dismissed him, before turning to me. "Matt, good to see you. Give me good news."

"Your people are on their way back to you," I said. "We've discovered an FOB on the outskirts of London, and we're heading in deeper, following a pair on motorbikes."

"I note you say that you're following them. Are they an escort, and do they know you're following? For that matter, are you being allowed entry or not?"

"Meh." I shrugged. "Details, details."

"Matt." He groaned. "Please tell me this is going well!"

"Nobody is shooting at us, and there's an operations command structure and army," I said instead. "Mike knew the commander of the FOB and said he was a dick. We were clearly supposed to sit here and wait for orders from higher before coming in, but we weren't officially told that. And they also thought they were confiscating both the vehicle and our gear."

"So you're making it clear you don't fit into their command structure." Griffiths sighed, then nodded. "Okay, that's understandable. But we need support, Matt. If there's a way of getting it, you need to do it. And remember, you promised—"

"To try to find your family, to make peaceful contact with people if I could, and to rescue the king and his family." I nodded. "Believe me, I know. I remember my oaths…not just the ones that I swore to the colonel but all of them. If I can, I'll make an alliance. I know we need them, and desperately."

"Good man." He sighed.

"So, what's the plan?" I asked, and he gestured out before us.

Folkestone was a weird place to look at from above, and thanks to the mobile nature of the dreadnought dungeon, it was even weirder.

It was a town close to the south coast of the country, surrounded to the north and west by fields. The main roads for the area came in from the west and then flowed along to the east, where most of the town was laid out.

The actual tunnel and all the infrastructure that was associated with it was in the north of the town, on the outskirts, with the main highway, the M20, flowing through and separating the tunnel from the town.

To the south and east of the tunnel and its areas was the main town, the surrounding villages, and eventually, the sea. Long, sandy beaches and rolling surf were somewhere down that way, as were, a little farther along and to the east, the White Cliffs of Dover.

Little of that was noticeable from here, though, as I watched the dungeon sitting in the middle of a rapidly expanding area of cleared muddy ground.

The tunnel itself was at the eastern-most point of the area below me, and it could be seen sliding up out of a hill. Leading directly from that hill were a dozen rail lines; the original four that exited the tunnel split into more and more. Those lines in turn then led up to disembarkation points, places where the cars or vehicles that were loaded aboard could drive up and get on, or drive off and bugger off from.

There were roads that led up and around then back onto the highways and gentle rolling hills that had been landscaped to make the area as pleasant as possible. Where they could, they'd hidden the actual stations and so on from the public, and I had to admit that they'd done a good job.

Then the undead had come.

The area was, by necessity, fully enclosed. At some point, I was guessing by the shattered gates and crushed fences I could just make out to the west, the gates had been sealing the compound off.

It was an entry point for the country, after all. There'd been heavy security at some point, and even if they'd all fucked off eventually, there'd still been high fences, walls, and more.

"When we got here, the place was lousy with them," Griffiths said grimly. "Only a few hundred, but as we rolled in and started exterminating them, more and more escaped into the tunnels."

"That your doing?" I asked, referring to the metal barriers that sealed the entrance of the tunnel, and he nodded.

"They won't hold forever. Sure, we could manage it if we had the time, and could keep the undead back long enough. But all that would achieve is forcing them to go back and dig their way out somewhere else."

"Somewhere we won't have control of," I agreed. "So you gave them a barrier they'd be able to break eventually. Then what?"

"We started the dungeon off by the barriers." He gestured. "That was the only way to get it all inside the radius. Then, as soon as it was sealed and we could all start work, instead of just fighting, we started rolling it back and absorbing. We've got the undead resource team eating the area inch by inch."

"Getting mana to use." I nodded.

"That and it gets us embedded into the area." He shook his head. "The whole point is to make sure we have control over it. As soon as we need it, and we've got both the mana to do it and the space, we'll be laying pitfall traps and more, ready to collapse when we need them."

"Okay. And the reason that you're eating everything, if it's not to get the mana?" I asked. "I mean, it'd be quicker to just push out and claim than absorb, right?" I asked, making sure he knew that.

"Yeah, it would, but this way, we remove any cover for the other side. At first, the ground was solid. Once we've eaten it down to the earth, we can add in water and it becomes a swamp—less traction…it becomes an easy and cheap way to slow the undead. It's not going to make a huge difference, I know, but every one of their number that falls and gets trampled back to death is one that we don't have to waste a bullet or a spell on."

"Point," I admitted.

"Now, the plan is that once we've got all the valley absorbed, or claimed, we get back to the far side. You'll note that there's a team already pushing out in that direction, just heading straight?"

I nodded. The dungeon was about a third of the way across the small valley now, moving from east to west, and teams were pushing out in all directions. But one was noticeable by the advanced distance they'd covered.

They were at least a dozen meters beyond anyone else and pushing hard.

"They heading for the main building?" I asked.

He nodded. "We'll set up the keep, or that citadel, at that end, as far along as we can get it. We'll give it the best walls, structure, and bracing we can. It'll become our refuge, both as somewhere we can bleed the undead against, and somewhere if the shit hits the fan, we can hunker down in."

"You building from scratch or making use of the existing buildings?"

"A bit of both," he admitted. "The main hub there is the largest building, and it's got fairly solid walls. The plan is to permeate that, and drive the dungeon in, then raise the walls around it. Yes, I know it limits the dungeon's mobility, but frankly it's the best way to secure it and provide a fallback location."

"Here's hoping then," I said softly. "So, moving forward, we're setting up a valley that's a kill zone, an old-style keep at one end, and we're going to basically try to fucking slaughter them as they breach the tunnel, right?" I shook my head. "Sounds a little…"

"A little like we're just hoping and praying but it's a bit uninspired?" Griffiths asked, sounding caught between amusement and disgust.

"Yeah, basically."

"Well, that's where we are. If you've got a better plan? I'm all ears. But the thing is, we're going to be facing tens of thousands, possibly hundreds of thousands if it all goes to shit here, I bet. And so far, they're almost all trash mobs."

"What?"

"Trash mobs," he repeated. "Fuck's sake, I thought you said you were a gamer?"

"I did," I agreed sourly. "I also know what a trash mob is…generally, anyway. It's someone that's shite—no challenge to fight, no experience, and no loot basically, but…"

"That's exactly right." He sighed. "You see them?" He gestured to the hundreds of walking, destroyed, or currently being faced undead, and I nodded.

There were literally hundreds in sight—*hundreds.* Although the sight of that many enemies behind our lines, basically surrounding our forces and right while the dungeon was this close to the tunnel and ready to be captured, should have filled me with serious butt-clenching fear, the condition of them dispelled that.

They stumbled out of the surrounding area in ones and twos—broken, limbs missing. Half of them were barely ambulatory. And the few actually capable of putting up a fight? They were taken down in seconds.

We had a handful of roaming teams—human, kobold, Scepiniir and goblin—and they were using them for target practice. They used everything from bows and arrows to rocks, to the occasional spell, and it was obvious that our people were loving the opportunity to train with almost no risk.

"What's the problem?" I asked. "I mean, I can see your face, so I know there is one, just not what it is."

"They're *trash* mobs," he repeated. "That means that I've already had to order that nobody lets their stamina, health, or mana get below seventy-five percent in facing them. They grant a single point of experience, that's it, and there's a hundred or so of them here. My concern is that the majority of the enemy will be like this as well." He shook his head, clearly disgusted.

"A moving wall of shit, that instead of any kind of skilled and dangerous enemies, will essentially wear us down to the point that we can't so much as lift a hand to defend ourselves when the real threat arrives."

"I…never considered that," I admitted lamely.

"Neither did I," he said. "I guessed that they'd have some, of course, but that's the real strength of the undead. It doesn't matter how many of them we kill, because there's always going to be more dead than living, especially these days."

He gestured out generally over the hills and away. "We talked about not letting them get an advantage over us by getting access to the great battlefields, but honestly? Right now, my main fear is that they swamp us in waves of the weakest undead, and then walk over their own dead to face us."

"So what's the counter?" I asked.

"Besides a few of our highest-leveled people who can crush entire armies?" he asked, with a wry grin, before pointing off to one side. "Well, Matt, I'm glad you asked, because that's where a friend of yours comes in."

"Oh gods," I muttered, seeing the kobold in the distance that he was indicating. "Is that Drak?"

"Certainly is!" He grinned. "Turns out the miserable bugger doesn't just spend all his days hammering the potions after all. He used to be an adventurer…"

"'Til he took an arrow to the knee," we both quoted, grinning at each other.

"Well, once he escaped that for a life of idle luxury in the dungeon—he's really pissing Aly and Kelly off with that, by the way, just in case you didn't realize…it's a nightmare to make him help."

"I know," I admitted. "What's he doing and what's it costing us?"

"He's training a handful of the advanced kobolds in trap-making." Griffiths shrugged. "Apparently it's sort of a national pastime, and back home—wherever the kobolds originate from—they hold annual competitions."

"And he was a winner?" I asked, a sudden hope surging.

"Nope, never even placed. Makes it sound like he came oh so close and was robbed of the medal and awards. But he also admits that the winners and all the major runners-up have massive sponsorship deals and live a life of luxury. *So*, despite what he says, by any stretch of logic, if he was any good at it, he'd not have been an adventurer on his own."

"So, as usual, he was lying through his teeth?" I guessed, and Griffiths nodded.

"Regardless, though, he's going to be useful here. He's already suggested a handful of changes, including constructing barriers that are pushed out along rollers. We can use them to crush anything in the way. It pushes the enemy back from the walls. Mount one end in the outer wall, the rollers on lines that extend from the walls, and we let them come and try to fight us.

"When we need a break, we push out the rollers; they crush everything in their path and push the enemy back. Then we can repair and resummon in the cleared area."

"Sounds surprisingly simple," I said slowly.

"There's still a lot that can go wrong, believe me," he said grimly. "As much as I'd like it to be different, if they get caught on anything—and they will—they'll break. And if the press is too strong, they'll be a bugger to use. They'll operate on cogs and we'll be turning cranks that magnify the effort, sure, but they're likely to break after only one or two uses."

"So they're limited use." I nodded. "But it means that we can push them back and absorb everything nearby."

"Exactly. Between them and the other traps we're working on, that should account for a lot of the trash mobs. Beyond that, we're going to be down to fighting, literally using the weapons we have and killing them, until they kill us."

He paused then shook his head. "If there's a way to get us reinforcements from London, Matt, we really need them. If I'd realized just how bad it was, and that we're as limited as we are, I'd have brought more troops."

"Summon more." I shrugged. "That was always the plan, right?"

"It was," he agreed. "But they're appearing as level one, and that's limited fucking use when they get a single point of experience for killing their enemies. Even worse is when they fight as a unit, they get that experience split between the unit—so we've got teams of kobolds that are tired out, and they've earned a single level each. That's it."

"Well, they'll get that experience in the fight to come." I shook my head. "I'll do my best to bring us reinforcements, but act as if we won't be able to get any help."

"Help in the fight?" he asked sharply. "Matt, we need you."

"I know," I said quickly. "Don't worry—I meant beyond me and my team fighting alongside."

"The dungeon?"

I grimaced, my mind reaching the same point at the same time as my mouth did.

"It's looking uncertain," I admitted. "We can't set up the dungeon and just strip the area if there's people here. They'll see what we're doing and stop us, or hell, they'll attack."

"We need those reinforcements, Matt!" Griffiths growled. "Both the ones from the people living there and the damn ones you were to send from stripping London!"

"You think I don't know?" I snapped. "What do we do, Griffiths? You're the Commander of the Guard. Tell me what we should do, if we set the dungeon up in the middle of an area secured by uncertain allies."

"You'll need to guard it," he started, then fell silent.

"We'd need to guard it, to strip the area of everything we can build; then we need to build a nexus gate, so that we can send you the reinforcements you need. A gate that would lead into the middle of our other dungeons, a point of entry that we don't really understand and that I'm betting could be circumvented by a particular skill."

"And if you do that, you need to stay there, or you need to keep enough forces there to protect it," he added. "Those reinforcements that we desperately need would be trapped there, protecting the dungeon."

"And then if the locals figure it out, and what it's capable of, what's the chances they'll just leave it alone and want to be respectful allies?" I asked.

"Zero," he said sadly. "That sounds like I distrust my own people, but it's not like that. I'm a realist," he admitted.

"So am I," I agreed. "They'd *have* to try to take control of the dungeon, because they need to protect their people, their loved ones. And if they have the dungeon? They can produce medicines, reinforcements, food, and eventually everything they need. Sure, they'd have to take it from us, but when the fate of the nation, of however many hundreds, thousands or even millions are resting on their shoulders?"

"It's not a choice," Griffiths finished for me. "They'd do it in a heartbeat. And as much as this would absolutely suck for us, the call 'for the greater good' is one that's hard to resist. If I'm being honest, and we'd met down here, with no prior knowledge of who you are, and what you were capable of, just that you had a dungeon that could produce all of that, and frankly, that there were only a handful of you to guard it?"

"You'd have attacked," I said, a sinking feeling in my stomach. "Even with those shitehawks in charge?"

"The government?" he asked me, and I nodded. "Yeah, and I'd have hated every minute, believing that they are as useless as we all agree. But the difference would be that my side, and the side that would protect my family if something happened to me, would be the side that would have control of it then."

"So we're fucked." I grunted. "You're a damn good man, and you'd have still attacked me with any opportunity."

"That's life, mate. If the situation was that I was on my own, I'd never consider it. But to protect women and children? To make sure my family and those of all the people I'm responsible for had that chance? I'd have no choice."

"So we can't let them know what we have," I whispered. "We can't set up in London at all, and hell, we can't even stay here long."

"No, because I damn well need you back and as quickly as possible." He sighed. "If you fuck around in there, you might be able to bring some reinforcements, but..." He paused, then went on. "But is it worth it?"

"What?"

"Matt, you need to be careful," he said. "Shit, I can't believe I didn't think of this before, but if the government and the army or whatever are holding London? You need to get the hell out. If you can get them to send reinforcements? Great. Make sure you have damn tight control over them if they come, though."

"Why?" A reason occurred to me as I spoke, but I hoped I was wrong.

"Because if they realize what we have? As soon as the fight is won with the dead, we'll be looking at a fight with the goddamn living." He cursed. "Any soldiers inside our walls at the end, if they have any doubt that they might be able to take command of the dungeon from us? That'll be in their orders to damn well do it."

"Shit," I muttered, then nodded. "All right, I'll be in touch. You do…you do what you can and get as much ready as possible. What's your priority in terms of a build list?"

"Secure the area, create a redoubt, forces to defend the position, and a nexus gate. Then additional bonuses like traps and higher walls, a castle-style fortification, all that shit," he said. "The worst part is that I can't even go all out. As much as I'd like to make an impregnable castle and keep all my people safe, if I do that, the undead will just flow around us and ignore us. We need to make it so that the only way they can get past us is if they fight their way through. That means we need points that they can overrun, as much as I hate it."

"I need to make two changes to the plan then. I'm gonna need a shitload of Storm and Lightning converters. They're going to be on the roof of the castle, and what I'm going to need is…"

A handful of minutes later, after pulling Kelly and Aly in, and starting the conversation practically from scratch, then going over solutions, my plan, and yeah, all the mad shit that could go wrong with it, I finally sat up, blinking and back in the real world.

"Okay, everyone, it's time to get serious," I called out.

Those around me stopped what they were doing and perked up, ready to listen.

"There's a change of plan," I started, and I ignored the snort from Mike at that oh so unusual of situations. "We've learned too much to stick to the old one. Some of this was foreseeable, but that so much of London had survived? It wasn't. We need to get in there, figure out what's going on, and then get the hell out. We're giving a couple of hours to this, at most, and then we move out."

"That's not a lot of time," Mike said, the concern in his voice clear.

"No, it really isn't," I agreed. "The problem is that we can't risk getting drawn in too deep here. I'm seriously wondering if now that we know they're here, we should just turn the fuck around and…"

I grunted then. A sudden warning flare of pain started deep in my chest, making me gasp. It constricted my heart, seizing up, feeling like someone had stepped up behind me, someone incredibly strong. They'd wrapped their arms around my chest and squeezed as hard as they could, and were continuing to do so even as I struggled for a breath.

The pain was…it was… I let out a relieved breath as it passed. Blinking, I realized that I was braced, one arm against the wall, and the other around Kilo's shoulders as he held me upright.

Jenn examined me, her eyes bright as she used her mana to search for issues. For several long seconds, it was all I could do to blink and catch my breath.

Then I stared in horror as I realized what it had been. The pain that had come and gone clearly was intended as a warning—a warning that I'd been about to cross a line.

It was the oath. The oath I'd sworn to the colonel and his people, and to all my people that bound me to try to rescue the royal family, and to find the soldiers' families as well.

"Motherfuckers!" I groaned, then shook my head. "You can't find anything, can you?" I asked Jenn.

She hesitated, then shook her head. "Not really. There was a sense of something when I first touched you, but it wasn't enough to identify and then it was gone."

"It's because it's not a physical damage." I sighed, scrubbing at my face, then forcing myself back upright and gripping Kilo's shoulder in thanks. "It's okay, both of you...don't worry," I assured them. "Okay, so I was about to suggest we turn the fuck around, see if we can get out of here without getting any deeper. Clearly the oath I swore means that's not an option. And as much as I don't like it, that's life."

"Explain that," Mike said grimly.

"We've already seen that the locals were planning to take whatever we had 'for the greater good' with the boxer," I pointed out, rapping my knuckles on the roof overhead. "Once we're inside their walls, somewhere that they fully control, I don't think it's going to be as easy to get back out. This vehicle, these weapons? Hell, I'm so used to not giving a shit about the different species around us that I'd not even considered how they might react to Beta, Kilo, and Saros. If London is held still, the heart at least, then we might be right up shit creek. As soon as we roll in there, they're going to strip us for anything they can get, and that's not the worst bit."

"The dungeon." Mike grunted. "You think that once they know you've got a dungeon seed, they'll take it."

"They will." I nodded. "That gives us two options, neither of which are good."

"Go on," Mike said slowly.

"First, we give them the dungeon seed," I said, not liking it in the slightest. "If they think they're getting a chance at capturing a dungeon, then they're likely to do whatever they have to, to take it. If instead we make it a condition of them helping us, then we gift it to them? Maybe, just maybe, we walk out of this."

"I...are you serious?" Mike asked after a few shocked seconds of thought.

"I am," I admitted. "Though I don't fucking like it at all."

"Okay, and what's the other option?" Chris asked over his shoulder, focused on the road ahead, following the tire tracks through the snow.

"Well, either we turn and burn, see if we can get out of here and leave them to make their own decisions..." Pain flared warningly in my chest again, and I forced the words out, feeling the chest contractions lessen as I did. "Or..." I gasped. "Dammit, or I go into the center and I do the whole god of lightning arrival. I fly in over the wall, summon lightning to me and make a big show, while you all head straight for the battlefield to the south. I find out what the hell the situation is inside, and then I address it on the fly."

"Make shit up and see what you can get out of it. Damn, that sounds familiar," Chris quipped. "Last time I tried that, I ended up getting kneed in the 'one-shot yogurt rifle,' though."

"Yeah, well, we're not interested in your sex life," Mike snapped at him, before turning back to me. "Matt, those options are shit," he said grimly.

"I know," I agreed in annoyance. "You think I don't know?"

"Then we change the game," he suggested. "You all drop me at the gates. Then you drive off, leave me to make a deal, and if the shit hits the fan, you can come get me after this."

"That's not going to work." I sighed. "We both know it. Sorry, man, but—"

"But I'm not important enough to negotiate on behalf of the dungeon?" he asked, one eyebrow raised.

I shook my head. "You know I didn't mean that," I countered. "I mean that…"

"Matt, you had two things right in all of this. If you walk in there with a dungeon seed, they'll take it from you if they can, and we need them. That's it. As much as I hate ever admitting you're right on general principles, *you're right*. The thing you're wrong about is in offering yourself up. The general doesn't go into enemy territory to discuss a deal; he sends his subordinates.

"In this situation, if we all roll into the base with this…" He banged one hand on the frame of the boxer as he spoke. "Then they're going to take it. First, they're the army—or at least a lot of them are. They have the legal and moral responsibility to defend the country against any and all threats. To do that, yeah, they're going to see taking this vehicle as a necessary step. Second, as much as you and I won't like it, they have the fact that these are military vehicles to back them up. We made changes to them, and we recovered them, but they own them."

"Bullshit," I said, and he waved a hand, going on.

"Lastly, we're going to be inside their walls, surrounded by their troops and under a massive amount of their control. They won't think twice about taking it, and that's because of the balance of power. We're here, a small group in a vehicle they need, asking them to come and help us in a war that they've got a vested interest in, sure, but that they know they might not have to fight. If there's any way they can get out of this, they will. That's not me bashing the government or anyone else. That's being realistic."

"If we were here with an army passing through, they'd treat us with respect and consider their options," I translated. "But as it's only a handful of us, they're not going to show that."

"Not unless we go all out. And in doing that, we start a fight that we might not be able to win, not to mention weakening us right before the battle with the real enemy."

"So what do we do?" I asked. That same phantom pain started to clench in warning again.

"First, you order me to find out what I can about the royal family and the families of the soldiers down here…" he said pointedly, and I did, before letting out a relieved sigh as the constricting pain vanished.

"Thank you," I said softly.

"De nada." He shrugged. "Now, as soon as we reach the outer perimeter of the base or whatever, you drop me off, and you all fuck off, sharpish," he said. "You leave me to talk to them, and…" He paused. "Here, give me that…"

He reached down and lifted Chris's shotgun, checking its charge and nodding to himself that it was in good condition. "You all head straight to the battlefield from here. You get your arses in gear and you hold out.

"I'll take one of these as a gift." He patted Chris's shotgun, and then patted his own, grinning. "And I'll keep mine, thank you very much. I give them that one as a free sample. It's a demonstration of the benefits of working with us, and why they need to play nice. The other stays with me, and I make it clear that trying to take it from me is an act that changes the dynamic. I'm here to recruit some help, and I'm an emissary of the dungeon. If they play nice, then we'll consider supplying them with arms and equipment that they literally can't get anywhere else. If they're dicks, they get nothing."

"And the dungeon?" I asked.

"Trump card only. I'll make a deal that agrees to us producing a single core for them, but only if they bring their entire army and fight for us. They try any half measures…they fuck around? We do this without them, and they lose the chance."

"I don't like it," I said. "And not just that I'm basically abandoning you here."

"You don't like leaving me behind or you don't like the idea of handing a core over?"

"Both," I admitted. "That's what I fuckin' said, wasn't it?"

"Meh. Well, let's be realistic. If they think they can get us onside with this, then it's worth a core, especially as it'll be one that's a fresh core and not linked to the dungeon. That's how this works, right?"

"It'd be a third-party unaffiliated dungeon," I said. "We'd then negotiate for examples of tech and tech advances themselves, make them give us large amounts of high-tech equipment to boost us—" I broke off, thinking.

"What?" he asked after a few seconds.

"The only thing we really need from them are allies," I said. "Now that we're mobile, we can hit places they can't. Heathrow Airport, for example, is going to be a major area we… Holy shit." I stared at them as it finally clicked, before I went on hurriedly.

"Shit, we need to get moving. All right, Mike, you're up. Get to work here and damn well make sure that you get us allies who are actually worth a damn. They need to bring an army, *their entire fucking army*, and they get a new dungeon core. It'll be a Stone one. They'll have to navigate it, but we'll be their only point of contact for a while and we'll trade with them. They agree to focus their research on certain tech upgrades, and we use them to fill in any areas we're missing, as much as we can."

429

"And if they refuse?" he asked.

"Then you escape. You go to ground, head straight to Heathrow Airport and wait there. We're going to be heading to the battlefield from here, and we're going to set up. Then the rest of the team, along with an escort from Griffiths, will take the dreadnought to Heathrow. They're to strip anything and everything."

"And what's Griffiths going to do without a dungeon?" Chris asked.

"He's getting one—*this* one," I clarified, patting the core in my bag of holding. "We're jump-starting it, and we're going to damn well make the most of the limited time we have in control down here."

"That sounds like we're running a risk," Mike suggested.

"We're all running a risk, Mike." I shook my head. "All of us, all the time. But this means that nothing that Griffiths is doing is a waste. He was already focused on turning the valley into a closed system first, so all we need to do is get there fast to be able to get the next stage rolling."

"Okay, so I'm a go?" Mike asked, as clearly my change of direction had him off-balance.

"Do you think this is the best way to handle this?" I asked him instead. "You going to them instead of me and you negotiating? I knew there was always the chance that there were others here, but..." I shook my head and went on. "Mike, I never gave it much of a chance that there were many people here, and I should have. I'm sorry; this is on me. We should have been negotiating from a position of strength but we are where we are. Between the snow and vehicles available to both sides, we're going to be able to get away from them without much difficulty, but it's still a risk."

"I think you need to drop me off, and I can do it." He nodded. "And if the shit hits the fan and they decide I'm a deserter, and arrest me?" He grinned wryly. "Well, worst case, I get a cot while they decide how to hang me, or they force me back to work and take my dungeon gear. I'll break free soon enough, and I'll be waiting at Heathrow."

"And best case, we get allies and an army." I nodded. "Okay, Mike, that sounds like a plan. Thank you."

"Not an issue." He squinted through the snow into the distance, then nodded. "I think I know where they're going..." he muttered, gesturing ahead. "This and the last road weren't cleared. Most likely they clear a single road out from each spot, and then it's out to a bypass enabling quick transport and communication. That means that the next road that will be clear is this..."

He pulled his map out and marked possible routes through the area, and the best way to get out, heading to Griffiths.

Ten minutes later, after losing the bikes twice, we finally pulled up at the foot of a hill, staring up at a freshly built massive wall at the top that just screamed "fuck off" in multiple languages.

"I think that's my cue." Mike snorted, gesturing as the first shouts rang out. "Any last orders, boss?"

"Don't die, don't take any shit, and get me an army," I said. "Priority in that order."

"I think the army should be a higher priority," Chris suggested. "We all hear how much shit Aly gives him…you know he's going to be doing the dishes inside an hour."

"You're an idiot, but keep them on the straight and narrow," Mike said to Chris. Then he looked over his shoulder to the rest of us. "Good luck, everyone, and 'may the odds be ever in your favor!'" he quoted, before stepping out of the boxer's side door. Then, as he picked up the rail gun shotguns, he spoke to Chris seriously.

"Just you wait until the kid's born… You're in for a treat. I know I wasn't supposed to say anything, but just in case we don't see each other again…congratulations!" Then he grinned and slammed the door, turning and walking away.

"Wait, what?" Chris went pale. "That was a joke, right?" he shouted after Mike, who started whistling as he went.

CHAPTER THIRTY-SEVEN

A s soon as we set off, about-facing and heading away with a reasonable turn of speed, there were a hell of a lot more shouts ringing out from the walls ahead. As we reached the end of the road and picked up speed, now driving out from this point toward the cleared roads ahead, we saw a dozen horses and riders approaching from the side route we'd just used. All of whom started shouting and spurring faster as soon as they saw Mike left behind, marching resolutely forward to their walls.

"I fucking hate this," I muttered, staring at the small mirror and watching as they moved to surround him, horses stamping and riders shouting. "I feel like we're sacrificing him."

"We are," Chris said, then he shook his head as I glared at him, moving up from the back into the passenger seat that Mike had vacated.

"Hey, don't get me wrong." He looked over at me, then shrugged. "I don't like it at all, and I agree with what we're doing. If we drove this..." He lifted his fingers from the steering wheel and flicked them, then patted it again as he went on. "Into the base? Now that we know that they're the army and not a gang we can intimidate or fight our way clear of, we'd never have seen it again.

"That means we'd have no goddamn chance of getting to the battle in time. The dungeon? If you hand that over, they'll promise anything you want to hear. Then they'll break that promise so fast you'll not know if it's bum or breakfast time. The only way you can make this stick is with that oath orb. You use that, and they'll have to stick to the deal. Otherwise?" He shook his head.

"And leaving him behind?" I asked.

"He'll be stripped, examined, and anal-probed within an hour. They'll question him, realize that the rail guns are a level of tech they didn't have before the fall, and that he's either genuine, or he's a setup. Then...they'll decide what they decide. Matt, I'm not gonna blow sunshine up your arse, mate. It's shit leaving him behind."

I swallowed hard, my mind racing.

"But..." He went on. "It's the right play to make. Worst case, I think they'll hold him and try to use him to negotiate with you. I don't see any reason to execute him...seriously, I don't. Even if they're utter cockwombles who are in charge and they're pretending to be the army or government or whatever. If they do that, all they do is lose their leverage and make a definite enemy. Hold him, threaten him or whatever? Yeah, there's a chance of that. But as he said, I think the best chance is that as a soldier and one who can prove his position, he'll be respected. Questioned, pumped for information on you and us, sure…but he should be safe. Then it means they evaluate the chances that he's telling the truth.

"Are there armies of undead coming? Maybe. If they send their army though, they'll have scouts; then they'll see the evidence. Once that's in place, then they get to choose. Ally with us, the side that's offering an insane advantage, but only if they fucking help, or they stay out of it and risk that the dungeon dies with you. Last of all, they could always join the other side, but with the undead marching, I don't see even the most self-centered wanker of a politician having the time to set up a back-alley deal."

"How would you even start it?" Emma chimed in from the back. "I mean, realistically, if they wanted to make a deal, they'd have to get close enough to the undead and hope that this one is what, aware? If not, it's going to chew your face off. And if it is? How do you start that conversation? 'Oh hi, I wondered what you'd offer me to be a traitor to all of life…you got any deals going?'"

She shook her head in disbelief, and there was a low round of chuckles, until Chris spoke up.

"You'd be surprised," he said flatly. "We've already faced vampyres and liches that did just that. The only consolation is that at this point they're coming in from outside, rather than building up a power base in the area and making alliances first. Humans are shitty creatures, and we'll basically jump into bed with anyone."

"And I don't know if I should be disgusted or ask a question…" Emma said after a few seconds.

"Ask," I suggested, sighing as I sat back. Mike and the group around him were lost to the twists and turns of the road. I tried to banish the feeling I'd just let my friend, my girlfriend's brother, and husband to my right hand in the dungeon, walk to his death.

"Well, is it true you fucked the vampyr?" she asked, and I cursed even as Chris burst out laughing.

"Seriously?!" I snapped. "Fuck's sake, how the hell is that rumor still going!?"

"I heard it from Chris."

I twisted to glare at him, as he grinned unrepentantly at me.

"I'm going to stab you in the face," I promised him as calmly as I could.

"We're in London…that's practically a proposal of marriage here," Patrick added with a wide smile.

"Not with the level of violence I'm going to use."

"Oh, kinky!" Chris blew me a kiss, and I shook my head in disgust before turning back to Emma and the others.

"In case you haven't got it yet—no, I didn't fuck the vamp. She had an ability that made everyone around her horny as fuck and practically start humping her leg. So I pretended that it was working, and got her to send everyone else away.

433

Then I killed her. That's where the rumor came from. But thanks to this utter wankstain, every so often I have to repeat myself. No, I've never fucked a vampyr."

"Ah, what about your ex?" Chris countered.

I stared at him, then snorted. "You mean…?" I asked, leaving the name unsaid, and he nodded.

"Drained you of everything, that one…money, your will to live. If she wasn't also so good at draining your balls, you'd have gotten rid of her a lot sooner."

"True." I sighed. "Probably a lucky thing that she was off draining half the town the rest of the time as well." I saw the look on Emma's face, and I shook my head. "Sorry, old joke, but she actually was. I know we all complain about our exes at times, but that one actually was sleeping with half the town."

"I know of four she'd been with since she got remarried just over a year back," Chris chimed in, glancing over his shoulder at the others in the back and shaking his head disgustedly and nodding to me. "Genuinely, she was an animal. You're better off out of that. I dread to think what she'd be doing now."

"Or who, by the sounds of it…" Patrick muttered.

"Point right there." I grunted.

"Well, thanks for the lovely direction of this chat," Jenn said with a forced smile. "Come on then, how far is it to Folkestone?"

"About three hours," Chris replied, accepting the change of topic. "Or so I'm guessing, anyway. In better times, it'd be about an hour and a half from here. The road here is clear, but I doubt it will be for long. Then we're back to pushing our way through the traffic."

"That's my cue then." I sighed. "Might as well get the first phase over, as soon as I've updated the others on Mike's actions and the shit to come."

With that, I settled back, closing my eyes and taking a deep breath, working up the courage to go and face Aly.

When I did it, zipping straight to her, and finding that she and Kelly were hard at work helping Griffiths in the dreadnought, it was both as bad and better than I feared.

"That goddamn idiot." Aly swore. "That's…that's Mike to a T—off to risk his own neck before anyone else!"

"You let him do that?" Kelly asked, clearly worried and disappointed in me.

"It was the right thing to do," Griffiths said. "As soon as you'd gone, I realized the potential issues and tried to reach you, but it's one-way only. When you reach out, you can join the dungeon anywhere—provided you're in range—and it seems you can access it with those around you, but it doesn't work in reverse. You have to initiate it."

"The right thing…?" Aly snapped.

"As much as it sucks, it was the right thing to do, and I should have suggested it beforehand," Griffiths repeated. "If the army deal with you openly and honestly, as much as the vast, vast majority of people I've served with would do, then all will work out fine. If not, though? If there's a few bad faith actors involved, and as much as we all joke about it, not all politicians are, but a few, then it could go horrifically wrong."

"And at what point is that supposed to make me feel better about my husband being left behind in that situation?" Aly asked as calmly as she could, nostrils flaring.

"None of it," Griffiths admitted. "The point, though, isn't to make you feel better, Aly. I'm sorry, but Mike was right to go. He's the least likely to be threatened for anything here, the most likely to succeed if he has to escape, and the only one they're likely to deal with openly." He sighed. "It's a shit situation, but they gain nothing by punishing him, save the loss of what could be a powerful ally, and gaining a definite enemy."

"And if Matt had stayed?" she asked tightly.

"Then it's much more likely it would have led to bloodshed. If they believed that he was the Dungeon Lord without some kind of proof, then he's a possible existential threat that has fallen into their hands at the moment he's weakest. If they don't believe he's who he says he is, they'd at the very least strip him of his weapons, vehicles, and gear. At that point, I don't see things ending well, not when they're trying that shit."

"That was our concern as well," I admitted.

"Okay, so you said that there were changes. What else is there?" Griffiths asked.

"First of all, just to add to the list, as soon as I started saying I'd not go to London and I'd put it off, I basically started to have a heart attack," I said. "Mike is going to check out the situation with the royal family and the soldiers' families while he's there as well, but it seems like the oath didn't like me trying to deal with things later. That's a point to remember," I added.

"Damn." Griffiths shook his head. "Fine. So what else?"

"Well, that's where we have a little gamble to make…" I sighed and laid out the plan, offering it up and asking for suggestions and if they could change my mind.

"I don't like it," Griffiths said gruffly. "There's far too much of a risk with this."

"There is," I agreed. "If we don't, though, do you see anywhere else we can raid for a fuckload of high-tech items to render down for mana?"

"I don't like it," he repeated.

"And neither do I," I said. "I can set up the dungeon in the surrounding areas here, and that'll get us some of the mana we desperately need, but…"

"But if you're discovered, you'll be stuck wasting that mana to defend it, and we lose out on you as well."

"Yeah." I nodded. "If we lose the dungeon, we have two options. One, we try to retake it. Two, we abandon it. That's it. We can't afford to allow an enemy to have control over the dungeon. Even an infant dungeon is a hell of a danger to us.

But if we're going to allow another force to have one, it's best that we do it with a situation that leaves us as a senior partner, not an enemy."

"You're talking about trading it?" he asked, aghast.

"I'm saying we produce another core. One that's totally unconnected and unlinked. It'd be Stone, and we can give advice, but leave them to make their own minds up with it. It'd mean that, most likely, we'd have an ally who'd have no real reason to fuck with us. It'd also mean that we could set the price, rather than giving them a reason to view us as an enemy. They've got an army and need the support that only a dungeon can give, and we need their army…" I left it hanging.

"So we sell them a dungeon core, one that's a baby essentially, and we make the price that we get the use of their army?" Kelly asked slowly, and I nodded.

"Basically," I agreed. "But as Mike pointed out, if we're within reach, they're more likely to take the core and make vague promises, or not at all."

"Because even with the best will in the world, they're going to look after themselves first," Kelly said. "God, I hate thinking like this. I wish…"

"I hate to break it to you all, but as much as people try to pretend it's only been like this since the fall, it was exactly the same before it as well," Griffiths said. "Fine. So, we're all agreed that the Mike situation is shitty but it's the best solution we had, and now we need to deal with it and move forward. So?" He prompted, and I nodded, gathering my thoughts.

"So, we're on our way to you now. When we reach you, I want to send the dreadnought off on its way to Heathrow Airport. I know it's a long way. I know it's a hell of a trek that'll take at least five hours, and that's being optimistic with the traffic around there…" I held a hand up as they started to voice objections.

"*But…*" I said loudly enough they all paused. "But, once the core is there, it can strip the planes, the traffic control systems, everything. The massive amount of mana that it can gain will first be used to build an on-board nexus gate. And then, when it can link directly to here, it'll be funneling through incredible amounts of mana.

"Also, and this is important, people—the converters? We need more of them, and on the roof. Because although the airport plan is a risk, and I know it is, we can offset it by stripping the storms that are coming."

"What storm?" Kelly asked.

Fortunately, instead of cutting me down, Griffiths spoke up.

"There's basically one every few days down here at this time of the year," he said. "The hot air rising from the Sahara and northern Africa meets the cold air blowing in off the Atlantic and the wetter…just trust me. Down here for the next month, it's going to be a procession of storms."

"And you're thinking strip them?" Kelly asked me, and I nodded, grinning evilly.

"That might work, except that we'd need two more gates," Aly said. "One on the dreadnought and one at Folkestone, and we've not got the mana at either point for them…yet."

"We don't," I agreed. "But we've got the additional gates unlocked, I made sure of that already, and what I need you to do now, until then..." I looked at Griffiths. "Is to start to convert anything and everything you can loot, absorb, and eat into the dungeon into mana crystals."

"They can be used to leapfrog the growth of the new dungeon." Aly grunted, clearly seeing the potential despite her annoyance and anger.

"Exactly," I agreed. "The mobile core can do the same when it reaches the airport. Then, as soon as the southern gate is online..."

"Southern?" Griffiths asked. "Folkestone?"

"Yeah." I waved the interruption aside. "As soon as that one is up and running, Kelly, you start marching any of the forces you've got ready through, and have them carry as many mana crystals as you can produce."

"I can do that." She sighed. "Griffiths, with regard to the forces, are they the same as we already discussed? Mainly kobolds, armor improved to lessen the effect of the cold..." She paused to glance at me. "Drak came through there as well. Turns out that the kobolds basically make use of a form of mana crystal-powered hot water bottle built into their gear. In times when they need it, they can drink from it, and when it's too cold, they simply heat it. It took Finn less than an hour to make an improvement to the uniforms."

"That's great," I said, massively relieved.

"Yeah, mainly kobold rank and file," Griffiths said. "As much as the corpse lords and so on would be great, I don't see how we can risk them, knowing that the literal lord of the dead is going to be their enemy."

"So," I said, "just one question, and I'll start with setting up the new core..."

"Yeah?" Aly asked, seeing the way I looked at her. "Matt, what have you done?"

"Nothing!" I said quickly, possibly *too* quickly, judging from the disbelieving stares I was getting. "I just need a little research doing, that's all," I said innocently.

"Oh, for fuck's sake!" Aly snarled.

As much as I knew she was worried, as much as I knew it genuinely did piss her off when I pulled this kinda shit, I also saw the twinkle of curiosity in her eye.

"Well, this should be nice and straightforward..." I lied through my teeth. And the entire time? She glared at me as I kept going.

Ten minutes later, my ears well and truly chewed off and a very clear "you are not popular here" impression having been left with me, I sat up and looked around, blinking. I was in the boxer with only Jenn and Catherine, while everyone else was outside.

"What did I miss?" I stifled a yawn as I looked out through what had turned—thankfully—into a fairly steady rain.

"Not much, just an enterprising group of slavers." Jenn rolled her eyes as she said it, looking offended.

437

"Slavers?" I frowned, squinting out the window.

"You missed most of it. The others didn't want to wake you, so they did it mainly without guns," she assured me.

"I wasn't asleep," I corrected unthinkingly.

"Really?"

"Yeah, I was talking to Griffiths, Kelly, and Aly. Why?"

"You...ummm, you snored?" She looked embarrassed, and I blinked, shocked.

"Seriously?" I looked at her, then winced, having finally spotted the fight that was apparently all that was left of the "ambush."

"How did that happen?" I asked, and she snorted.

"They tried to surround us, with four of them. Chris just drove straight through their little blockade—it was only brush and scrap, after all—and then pulled up on the far side around this corner. Saros and Kilo went out and flanked them, Jimmy and Andre set up waiting, and Patrick climbed upstairs into that building there." She pointed to the house on the corner, and I nodded, seeing how it must have gone down.

"Then they ran around the corner after us?" I asked, and she nodded disgustedly.

"Wow." I shook my head, amazed.

First of all, we were in a little side street, one that had only a single car parked, and clearly long abandoned. The buildings on either side were old, probably houses that had once been converted into a mixture of shops and small storage areas. The end of the street had a pair of houses still, but to the left, behind us, was the burnt-out remains of a garage.

Across the street from that was what had presumably been a local "extra" type of super store that had become so popular the last few years. Basically, it was a small supermarket but that only carried a third of the stock of the bigger ones. The kind of "I'll just pop to the shop for some milk and bread" kind of store, rather than a "I'll do my monthly shop now."

The store had been looted—probably multiple times—and the garage opposite it, when it'd been burnt out, had taken some of the houses to either side with it.

I could see the scuff marks on the side of the brickwork that indicated where someone had climbed the side of the house, and then I guessed that they'd dropped down behind the idiots who had chased us.

That someone had was pretty clear—my money was on Patrick, because he stood in the upper floor window, watching as Chris currently had a guy by the back of the head and was smashing his face into the wall.

Another was frozen into a basic block of ice, with Kilo going through his bag—it'd fallen on the ground—and the others...

Yeah, they weren't a threat.

The only thing they had in common was that they were filthy, terrified, and were all able to be described by the moniker "pissy-pants."

I shook my head and stepped out of the boxer, looking over as Chris asked the one he held by the back of the head something, then smashed his face into the brickwork again.

"I think he's had enough," I called.

"I think he deserves a lot more," Chris disagreed.

"Chris?" I asked, surprised.

"He was wearing this." He tossed a collection of sticks through the air, and I caught it, before dropping it in revulsion.

"What the fuck is that?" I wiped my hand on my battered armor.

"Cats' legs," he growled.

"Protection!" Pissy-Pants One gasped, before flinching away.

I winced as Beta picked him up by the throat and hissed into his face, her sharp teeth clacking bare centimeters from his nose.

"Please! We needed them!" he screamed.

"Fucking animals." Chris shoved the one he held down to his knees, and drew a knife. One quick blow and it'd all be over I saw, as Chris raised the knife.

"Wait!" I shouted. "Fuck's sake, Chris—wait."

"What?" He looked surprised.

"Why's he wearing that?" I asked him, and he shrugged.

"They all say it's for protection, though what the fuck they think it's going to protect them from I don't know."

"From us," came a new voice.

I spun, staring at the figure that sat atop the boxer, having arrived so silently that Jenn, leaning out of the passenger door as she was, squeaked and threw herself back in, having been totally unaware.

The figure sat there, seemingly patiently, clad all in black, head to toe. They had additional swathes of fabric wrapped around them, alternating in direction and color, though mainly whites and creams.

The effect, as they waved one arm, was that sections of the black, the white, and the other colors showed through or vanished. Some trailed tattered streamers, and overall created a winter version of a ghillie suit that worked surprisingly well, right up until the rain currently coming down had started sloughing the snow off everything.

"And who the fuck are you that they think slaughtering cats and wearing their legs is going to help them?" I asked grimly.

"They're idiots." The newcomer reached up and tugged their mask down, showing...a Scepiniir face!

"What the hell?" I muttered, as she—the face and voice now that I had it as confirmation was clearly female—finished dragging the mask down, then tapped the edge of one knife on the top of the boxer's armoring.

"I like this...you want to trade for it?" she offered.

"Not really," I said. "Too many places I need it to get to."

439

"Maybe you should reconsider?" She smiled at me, and on the rooftops around us, figures suddenly moved, standing and making their presence known.

"No," I said. "Jenn, lock the doors."

There was a click from below as Jenn did as she was told.

The figure on the roof of the boxer let out a little sigh of annoyance. "You think you have a choice?" She tapped the blade again, seemingly growing bored. "You have those pretty rifles, sure, but we have our own."

I looked up. Sure enough, here and there were a handful with rifles held nonchalantly.

"Okay, first off, before this all goes sideways..." Chris called out suddenly. "Seriously, what's with the cats' paws here? This is freaking me out."

"They see our little cousins, and they think that slaughtering them will ward us off for some reason," the woman said languidly, before rising to her feet and tapping the tip of a blade against her chin in thought. "It is foolish, and yet still they do it. The last of their kind we caught, we returned to their group with all his friend's fingers on a nice little line around his neck as a response. They still do this. Why, I do not know."

"Perhaps they're just arseholes," Chris suggested, and she nodded, seriously.

"Perhaps!" she agreed, smiling. "Now, we have decided they are not of your group. This is good, yes?"

"Yeah?" I agreed slowly. "I mean, they're definitely not."

"Good!" Her smile widened. "Then what are your plans for them?"

"This." Chris then snapped the neck of the man he'd been holding pinned.

"And this." Emma blasted another, short range with a lightning bolt that practically blew his head apart.

"That one can wait until he thaws," I suggested, pointing at the one that was half encased in a block of ice, and she nodded in agreement. The last of the four I'd apparently missed being killed, and I shrugged, then turned back to her. "So, you're Scepiniir."

"Impressive." She nodded slowly. "You know of our kind?"

"We do." The voice of Saros came from the roof as she stepped up, resting a handgun against the shoulder of one of the figures nearby.

He didn't react, and she shifted, making it even more clear that she'd snuck up on him...until two more appeared at her shoulders and rested their weapons on hers.

"Ah." She sighed. "Sneaky..."

"You're clumsy, young one." One of the figures pulled his mask down. "But you are new and have potential. Which clan are you from?"

"Clan?" she asked. "Dungeon, you mean?"

"No..." He cast a glance down at the woman atop the boxer, then back at Saros. "I mean clan."

"She's dungeon-born," I called out. "As are several hundred others of your kind." My first thought was to make it clear that we were a larger force than they saw here, and that there were more like her. Then I remembered that they might react very badly to their race being forced into servitude in the dungeon, and I winced internally.

"Several hundred?" the woman replied slowly. "A large clan then."

"Yeah," I agreed. "Look, no offense, but we've got somewhere to be, and we need the vehicle. Would we be interested in trade? Sure. Later, though. We need it now."

"Perhaps this is not the kind of offer you say no to." She smiled, and low laughter rose all around us.

"Perhaps I'm not the kind of person you try to jack," I growled, holding my hands to either side, empty, and then lifted into the air, as lightning crackled and danced across my fingers.

"Interesting," she drawled. "But we still have you under our eyes. You cannot kill us all, yes?"

"I can," I corrected.

"Your armor says it is unlikely," she pointed out.

I smiled. The battered and broken state of it meant that I knew exactly what she implied.

"My armor shows that a lot of others took that gamble, and I'm still here," I said loudly, lifting higher. The lightning started to grow and crackle brightly, until a voice rang out that I didn't expect.

"Whoa, boss," Chris called out. "Maybe this is a good time to calm the fuck down and see if we can all be friends, eh?"

"Seriously?" I shifted around, disregarding the group in my shock even as my lightning died away. "Dude, this is the first time I've *ever* heard you be the voice of reason."

"Well, we failed to get any friends to help with the war in London. Maybe here we can make some." He shrugged. "Besides, they're stealthy as fuck. It'd be nice not to keep getting surprised by shit."

"Point." I sighed, before turning back. I drifted forward, before twisting again and rising twenty meters or so into the air, ignoring the weapons that tracked me.

From up here, I could see that there were indeed around fifteen of them: ten that were clearly visible and wanted to be seen, and another five staying as hidden as possible on the bare roofs.

Knowing that now, I slid back down and landed with a few quick steps forward, before looking at the woman in question. "What do you want?" I asked her.

She paused, regarding me, and then tapped a foot on the boxer's roof. "This."

"Why?"

"It is quiet, it is quick, and it is strong." She shrugged. "With this, we could move our people easily, expand our hunting grounds, and be safer. Why would we not?"

"Well, you're all going to die if you try to take it by force," I said without preamble. "You say you want it to bring a little safety—all right, I can get that. But we're at war. That's why we need this. And in case you don't know, the army back there want it as well."

"They are not here." She smiled. "We are."

"My point is that they couldn't take it." I sighed. "They want it; they're not getting it. And neither are you, not by force. If you want it, you buy it, and we've not got the time to dick around and trade. So, how many of you are there?"

"Enough."

"Enough to die here trying to take it...sure, I get that." I nodded. "Listen, you know it and we know it. I just showed you that I can control the storms, that I can fly and control lightning. Others of my party can. We're in better armor than you, and we're better armed. Sure, if you kick this fight off, some of us will be hurt, maybe even die, but you?" I shook my head. "If we hit you, you die. If you hit us, you need to hit us in just the right place."

"You have no helmet. You will die first," she pointed out, showing a lot of teeth.

"No. You'll *try* to kill me first, and I'll unleash a lightning storm. That'll kill most of your group. And if you do manage to kill me, then my people pick up the pieces and move on."

"So what do you offer?" she asked. "And you do not plead for the lives of more like these?" She gestured at the others we'd killed as she stepped forward, walking to the end of the bonnet and dropping off, landing lightly, then proceeding to circle me.

"Oh fuck no." I shook my head. "Why would I?"

"They are your kind." She said it as if that meant something.

"They're slaving bastards who kill cats and wear their limbs as trophies," I countered. "I like animals more than people, and I'd have killed them for that happily. That they also are apparently carjackers and slavers?" I shrugged. "We'd kill them all if we had time."

Then, as that just occurred to me, I turned back to the others, and specifically Chris, who'd been the driver. "Why the hell did you stop?" I asked. "I mean, we could have just kept driving, and we're in a fucking rush!"

"Needed a piss," he admitted, a little shame-facedly. "I'd needed one before they tried to stop us, and I saw that they had a few slaves tied up off to the side. Figured we'd be stopped for like five minutes—we kill them all, do a good deed, get some free XP, and then I get a piss. We roll on, and it's a few minutes to really improve the world."

"Great, your child-sized bladder caused all of this then." I sighed. "Did you rescue the slaves?"

"I was busy!" he said defensively.

I shook my head again, disgustedly. "Get your arse in gear and rescue them then," I called back, before turning to the woman. "Listen, we need scouts, and we need soldiers. How many of you are there and how do you fare against the undead?"

"The undead..." She paused, then looked at another of the cloth-wrapped figures. "You are trying to hire us?"

"Yeah." I grinned. "Look, we're leaving in a minute, and that's happening no matter what. You can try to fight us, and some of us die, but all of you do. You know that you're outclassed, and so do we. Attack and you *all* die...while we have a healer. So, you know, we've got a reasonable chance of walking away from this with just an ouchy. That's how this works. You came here, I think, planning to kill those fuckers." I pointed at the bodies on the ground. "If that was your aim? It's a win. Congratulations."

"Go on."

"We need more help. The army is hopefully coming in exchange for an item, and now that you show up, they might come...they might not. You might come...you might not. But if you want this?" I gestured at the boxer. "All good by me. You come fight for us, and at the end, once the fight is done, you drive this away." I pointed at the vehicle.

She nodded slowly. "How do we know you will hold up your side of the deal?"

I smiled. "You don't," I said. "I'll say I will, and I know I'm being serious, but you don't know me. Hell, for all I know, you're the entirety of your clan, and you're not going to be much use to us."

"Why not?" she asked.

"Not enough of you. We need an area of at least fifty miles to be scouted and checked regularly while we fight to make sure we're not attacked from behind. How many of you are there?"

"Enough."

"Yeah, that's not going to cut it," I said. "We're facing a fuckload of undead. Possibly tens of thousands, maybe hundreds. And if we fail? You're going to get to meet them in a few days. They'll kill you all, and then go on their way. So let's make this clear. If you want to live 'til the weekend? Get your troops, your scouts and whatever, and come with us. If you don't, and we get flanked, you're all fucked."

"This is all you have to fight thousands?" she asked with a snort of derision.

"This?" I looked around. "No, though, personally I'd not count us out of a fight against a thousand undead too easily. We have our own army, and it's already in place. We're passing through, looking to make friends, though we're now out of time. Let's do this nice and simple."

I stepped forward and slapped a hand on the bonnet of the boxer. "Do you want this?"

"Yes." She bared her teeth.

"Do you have access to maps?"

"What are…?" she asked before another of her group let out a low chuff and nodded. "The pictures?" she asked him, and he nodded again. "We have these things." She shrugged.

"Okay, well, can you read?" I asked.

She looked offended at the suggestion that she couldn't, her ears going flat as she glared at me.

"Hey, I don't know you," I pointed out. "Chris… Fuck's sake," I muttered as I saw that he and Andre were gone. "Rescuing the slaves?" I asked Jimmy, who nodded. "Fine. Find Folkestone. It's a good few hours run from here, maybe as much as a day, depending on how you travel. We'll be at the Eurotunnel entrance."

"And you expect us to come and fight for you? You said there are hundreds of thousands. Perhaps we simply move on, head away from them, hide."

"They're undead. They don't get bored of looking for you, and they'll just keep coming," I pointed out.

"We cannot face hundreds of thousands. We are a small clan," she said instead, grimly.

"And I'm not asking you to," I repeated. "We need scouts. You do that for us, and at the end of the fight, once we've won, you can have this."

"I thought the army wanted it?" she said.

"They do." I smiled. "And they can keep wanting it."

"You are seeking to trade the item they are coming for, to us instead?"

"No, they want something else."

"What?"

"Nothing I can trade twice," I said. "Look, we're going. The next few days are going to be fucking hard on all of us, so if you want to help and have a chance at this? Get your arse in gear and come help. Even a handful of you would be enough to make a difference. But the more of you there are? The better a chance we all survive. If we win? You get the vehicle."

"We take the vehicle," she said, and I glared at her. "We come, we help…we take this. We do not wait until the end."

"And what's to stop you fucking off and leaving us to it?" I asked her.

"Honor."

"I don't know you," I pointed out again.

Her ears went entirely flat this time, the growl rising. She and her group apparently found that highly offensive.

"Hey, honor is fine, but trust is earned. You come and you fight with us? Then I'll trust you. Until then, I don't know you."

"You seek to provoke me?!"

I snorted. "No, I just don't give two shits if you like me or not. You want this? You bring fifty of your people and you fight with us."

"Ten," she countered.

"Forty."

"Twenty."

"Let's cut the shit and agree on thirty," I said.

She growled, then offered me a hand, speaking just as I took it. "Twenty-five."

"Fuck's sake, whatever." I grunted. "Just get your arse to the Eurotunnel terminal at Folkestone in the next eighteen hours, or there's no fucking point in having scouts."

"We stay and scout for you, but this…" She slapped a hand on the bonnet again. "This leaves with our people."

"Can you drive it?"

She glared at me, as if daring me to ask more stupid questions.

"Seriously, it's not easy."

"We are the people. We can make it work," she said.

"Whatever. Folkestone. The Eurotunnel. Find it on a map, and then get your arse there. You want this without bloodshed? That's how you get it."

"We want two," she suddenly declared, clearly trying her luck.

I laughed, turning my back on her as I headed for the driver's seat. "You want two—bring fifty people to fight and scout. Otherwise, you're getting one!"

And with that, the deal was done, I guessed, considering they all backed off. I clambered into the driver's seat—helpfully unlocked by Jenn—and the others moved over and started boarding as well, the drop-down ramp at the back apparently meeting with the watching Scepiniir's approval.

Less than a minute later, as we edged to the end of the street, the Scepiniir stepped aside and watched as we rolled past, Chris, Patrick, and Andre came running…

"Oh, for fuck's sake, *really*?!" I cursed.

"What?" Emma asked, before she started to laugh.

"You idiot! What the hell are we going to do with them?!" I snapped at Chris as he jogged up to the passenger side of the boxer, the three former prisoners or slaves of the idiots we'd just killed looking terrified behind him.

"Take them with us," he said with a confused look.

"To a fucking *battle*?" I asked acidly.

"We're activating a nexus gate, right? They can go straight through?" he countered, and I paused, then nodded.

"Yeah, all right, but surely they'd rather be here?"

"They've been taken prisoner twice, escaped once, and one of them had all her fingers on her left hand cut off for running away last time. They want to be as far away from here as they can goddamn get. When I freed them, they kept crying and begged me to be gentle with them. That's what their life is like here, so yeah, when I asked them if they wanted a new life, in the north and to be free, they jumped at the chance."

"They know that we're going to war?" I asked after a brief pause.

"Still better than being here. And either this works and they can go through the gate and be safe, or the undead come this way in a day or two and they're all dead anyway."

"Fuck's sake. All right, get them in the back," I grumbled, before speaking over my shoulder. "Jenn…"

"I heard," she said. "Get them in here."

Chris waved them around, and Andre went with them, all climbing in the back and making do with the small space. They started, seeing the massive kobolds, but beyond that and a brief pause, they simply clambered in.

"That's weird," I muttered to Chris, as I started us rolling out.

"What is?" He settled his rifle and gear into place, then put his seat belt on.

"They didn't seem bothered by the kobolds."

"Dude, we just met a goddamn clan of ninja Scepiniir. As much as I hate to say it, maybe we're a bit provincial up north."

"Bite your tongue," I replied absently. "Okay, which way?"

"Uh…." He grabbed the map, turned it one way, then the other, then cursed as he turned it around again, then nodded. "No fucking clue. I'm still lost."

"Still…" I took a deep breath. "How long have we been lost for, Chris?"

"Oh, twenty minutes?" He shrugged. "There were a few roads that were blocked by burned-out cars and with fights going on, so I bypassed them while you were having your beauty sleep."

"I was…you know what? I don't even care." I gave up, squinting at the signs as I passed them. "Is that…"

"Take a left ahead." Jimmy reached over, taking the map from Chris. "You missed a sign back there. It was pulled down, but it said there was a bypass and 'the south' that way."

"Can you read a map?" I asked him.

"Sure."

"Chris, fuck off into the back and keep our passengers entertained. Find out what they know, and let him up here."

I drove for about fifteen minutes, making sure we were well clear of the immediate area, then pulled over, activated the dungeon, and set it up the same as the dreadnought and then left it to slowly expand, the others working in it to claim anything they could as we inched past battered and burned-out vehicles.

It tried to form the usual spires for it to sit atop, but with the vehicle as it was, that wasn't possible. Instead, and with a little focus and a lot of ongoing, low-level, grim-faced repeating of commands to it, it eventually seemed to understand that it was a mobile core that couldn't establish fully yet. Instead, it formed atop a spike of silvery metal, one that Chris confirmed he could touch.

That part wasn't intentional; the mad bastard just grabbed it, then nodded that he was still alive. Asshole.

That, as weird as it seemed, was the last interesting thing to happen for several hours, right up until we topped a rise about four miles from the Eurotunnel and the site of what was to be the southern dungeon.

"Well, that's not happy making." Chris peered forward from behind us, and frankly, I had to agree.

CHAPTER THIRTY-EIGHT

"Tell me that's not what I think it is." I braked gently, drawing us to a slow halt at the top of a hill.

"That's not what you think it is," Chris said.

"What is it then?"

"Well, it looks like the mother of all cock-blocks to me, but you know, I'm just helping out by doing as you asked."

"I hate you."

"I know."

The object of my ire, and Chris's shitty joking, was scattered about on the road before us, spread over about half a mile. And damn.

They were dead, or undead—that much was very clear from up here—and that they were between us and our target was the first bad news.

Then came the minor detail that they were marching merrily along—admittedly, every so often a limb fell off, but still—headed to hit our people from behind.

Lastly? The goddamn detail that there were at least a thousand of them, and a pair of wraiths drifted at their head, all of which seemed completely unaware that we were here.

We'd been passing the undead for the last hour or so, mainly seeing them in the side streets or the distance, and occasionally detouring to run them over just because we could.

Emma and Kilo had gotten a little free experience with their ranged magic, and once, Catherine had managed to cast an area of effect spell that she'd gotten at her last level-up, trapping a trio in the middle of the road for me to drive over.

There'd been little else though, just a few here and there. And now? Hundreds.

"Okay, where's Mike's rifle?" Chris said suddenly, grinning. "I've got to try this shit."

"Mike's…" I frowned, then realized what he meant. "Oh, hell no! You're a shit shot!"

"Better than you," Chris countered, drawing the rifle up and out from the back with a nod of thanks to Andre. "I'll be right back," he promised, before clambering out of the boxer's passenger door and then onto the roof.

"I hate him," I repeated.

"On the upside, boss, he's getting wet and we're not," Andre suggested, making me nod.

"There is that," I agreed, before squinting at the group in the distance. "The question, though, is how did they get here?"

"Walked?" Jimmy suggested.

"I mean the undead in general," I explained, shaking my head. "If they're headed this way, they have to be coming for Folkestone, right? How did they know we were there?"

"Maybe the undead god can talk to them?" Jenn suggested, and I nodded slowly.

"Maybe."

"Does it matter?" Emma asked. "It might be as simple as the undead just like grouping together. We've seen them do it before. Maybe it's like a general thing, like magnets."

"That they just decided to head together?" I asked, toying with the idea.

"More like the more there are in one place, all the others start heading that way," she suggested. "You said there were a fuckload of them all gathering...maybe that's making the undead here want to join them. Not a conscious thing. Just like the way that people flock to the beach or whatever."

"You think the undead like beaches?" I snorted. "Damn, there's a mental image." The conversation, which was admittedly going nowhere, was broken off by the sudden firing of the rifle on the roof of the vehicle.

Mike had done some heavy modifications to the rifle, including fitting a suppressor, but it was still clear that Chris had fired. And by the cursing and second shot, then the third as the wraiths spun around, it was made even more clear that he was, indeed, shit with it.

The fourth round hit the wraith on the left, hovering over the now milling crowd of undead on the road, in the head.

It practically disintegrated, falling to the ground in a silent—thanks to the distance—clatter of bones.

"Got it. Now I know how to do it!" Chris called, before managing to miss the next three shots as the remaining wraith headed straight for us. His fourth shout nicked its arm. The near miss that would have dragged the blood from a living human did little more than rearrange the undead's tattered clothing, and it screeched in outrage.

That was when the undead between us and it started to run.

"Get in here!" I shouted up at him out of the window.

Cursing, Chris fired three more rounds, then clambered down.

I backed the vehicle up, swung to the left to avoid a ball of necrotic fire, then gunned the engine. "Someone get on the fifty," I ordered. "Everyone else, get as ready as you can. I'm gonna try to get through them."

"I'll..." Chris started to say, before cursing as Andre finished clambering through the roof and settled into place.

"I told you, you're shit," I shot at Chris, as we started to pick up speed. "Get ready, everyone!" I called back, as Andre charged the fifty and then started to fire.

Where the rifle was undoubtably more powerful, the fifty had the advantage of tracers and a high rate of fire. Andre made the most of it, squeezing it in short bursts that he adjusted, tracking in on the flier as it threw more handfuls of necrotic fire at us.

The wraith was torn apart in a sudden burst, but by then the air was full, and swerving to try to avoid a barrage, I nearly tipped us into a roadside ditch.

"Get him in here!" Chris shouted back to the others, and Jimmy nodded, grabbing his brother's leg.

The next few seconds were harried ones. I skidded and twisted. The boxer went sideways in the half-frozen rain at one point, even as Andre ducked back inside, pulling the hatch closed behind him.

"Hold on!" I growled, straightening up and flooring the gas. The boxer crashed through the undead as they reached for us, their limbs and bodies getting pulverized.

At first, it looked like we were going to make it—the boxer was made of strong stuff, after all. But as the press got tighter and tighter, we started bouncing more and more.

"I could fire…" Andre started, and I shook my head.

"Get ready!" I ordered instead, seeing a space and going for it, twisting off to the left of the road and onto the grass. The road was now almost shoulder-to-shoulder packed with undead.

Hitting the grass wasn't a problem. This was an army vehicle, after all. It was designed for off-road, and if anything, was probably more stable there than on the water-laden, occasionally blocked roads.

Or, it would have been, if that wasn't right where, hidden by that shambling mass, there was a car parked and abandoned.

We hit it hard. The entire vehicle, already bouncing from side to side, with me attempting to get it on an even keel, suddenly hit the sloping back of an old sports car, the low slope that climbed in a graceful arc crumpling like so much tissue paper under the impact.

We drove up and over, the entire boxer tilting crazily. Shouts and screams filled the air from behind me, as I desperately tried to get control…

Then we hit the overgrown ditch.

It was filled to near the brim with muddy, icy-cold water, that was itself all that was left of only slightly warmer rain, dissolving snow.

It exploded up, covering the windshield. Another undead hit at just the wrong time and we were rolling and bouncing. For long seconds, gear and weapons ricocheted and screams rang out.

Then, eventually, mercifully, we finally came to a halt, upside down, the rear of the boxer slanted upward, and the nose buried in an overgrown farmer's field by the side of the road.

"That's it, no more letting you drive." Chris groaned.

I ignored him, bracing one hand on the roof and taking my weight, before flicking the latch on the seat restraint and letting myself fall sideways.

"Ow. Everyone okay?" I called out, hearing snarls, grumbling, and swearing, as well as one bout of sobbing from the back. "We need to move!" I shouted. "ARE YOU OKAY?!"

That got a chorus of "Yes" and "Sort of" and more, apart from one of the rescued former slaves.

He was a middle-aged man, balding, with filthy clothes. He was laid on what had been the roof, atop a pile of gear, cradling a broken arm and weeping.

"Get him moving," I ordered, managing to force my door open, then cursing as the first thing I saw was a stumbling set of legs. "Move, people!"

I regained my feet, punched out with a left hook, and sent the undead human crashing to the ground. It started to reach for me; I stepped in close, batted its hands aside, and grabbed the head, then ripped it free, tossing it to the side, uncaring.

The animating force was apparently still contained in the head, and the rest of the body collapsed at that, giving me the space to grab Emma's hand and help her out.

The others streamed out of both sides, all apart from the same man, who was sobbing and now curled up in a fetal position, refusing to interact.

"Head across the fields!" Patrick called out, pointing in the general direction of our destination, before twisting and snapping out a kick that took a skull off like a party popper.

"We got all our gear?" I asked Chris, waving the others to start moving.

He nodded, before gesturing at the figure in the back.

"I'll try." I passed the gleaming core to him. "Go. Take the fucking dungeon core. I can fly."

"Good luck, Sparkles." He grunted, clapping me on the shoulder, then started off after the others. They were jogging out into the abandoned field, sucking mud and streaming rain slowing them as they tried to go cross-country off to the left.

We'd passed a sign only a few hundred meters back warning of delays with the Eurotunnel, and clearly someone had made the decision that through the fields was a better bet than through the undead.

I nodded to him, put my hammer into place, then reached back in and gripped my sword, drawing that out and unsheathing it.

"Come on then!" I called to the figure in the back of the boxer, before stabbing the next undead that approached through the skull.

A quick glance before dismissing the kill notification showed that yeah, they were trash mobs. One point of experience, that was it.

Clearly the disparity of me fighting one of these when they were such low level was just insane.

"Oi," I called to him. "Listen, mate, I don't know your name, but I'm Matt. No time like the present to get moving, eh?" I suggested, before cursing and stabbing at another. I missed the lunge, the grinning skull swaying at just the right time, but took the head off on the back draw. I quickly stepped out, hacking the blade sideways at head height.

Three more fell, and I did a little spin, reaching out for another, then a quick overhead swing, riposte, and return.

More of the undead fell, but they were climbing through the torn and smashed sections of the farmer's former hedges. There was clearly about to be too many for me to fight unless I was willing to dedicate serious effort to it.

"Hey…" I called. "Shit, man, you in there!" I kicked the side of the boxer, then banged my sword on it. The clang only served to make him draw even more in on himself as his only response.

"We're getting surrounded!" I called to him. "Look, if you want to stay here? Fine, just lock the doors and stay in there. I don't know how long the fight will take, but we can come back in a few days. But last chance, all right? You need to come, *now,* or lock up!"

I stepped forward, slashing left and right. Then, hearing a scream from inside, I darted back and stabbed in from my door, at the undead clambering in through the far side, reaching for him.

More were following it. I cursed, taking down another, then another with a spin and a cut, lopping off a head here and there.

"Fuck's sake, man, fight!" I roared, killing another and then grabbing the door and shoving it hard, forcing it to close.

As soon as it clicked, I leapt into the air, arcing over and landing, stabbed at another and grabbed a third, yanking it back.

Hands reached for me from all sides now. I kicked and punched, swung and slammed the hilt into skulls, before throwing my left hand out and unleashing a bar of lightning that I dragged left to right at head height.

A dozen fell, but behind them were hundreds more. I realized what that meant as another wraith screamed nearby.

I darted upward, spun, then grunted, before dropping again, slashing down and then hacking from side to side, opening up as much room as I could.

The ones we'd seen, the hundreds? They were only part of the nearest group.

There were more on the road that had been out of sight, and the group here were now being reinforced as, hearing the sounds of battle and presumably scenting fresh meat, they started to run in our direction.

"Move, man!" I roared, kicking another back and unleashing a blast of lightning across the gap, from the open door by my side, out of the door on the far side, working to keep both sides clear.

It was hopeless, though, and he wasn't responding at all.

Another figure lunged for me, this time getting inside my guard as I stabbed a different one. I knew what I had to do, as much as I hated it.

"I'm sorry!" I shouted to the catatonic figure inside, grabbing the door and shouldering it closed. "Lock the fucking doors!" I roared, kicking another back and lopping off a head before launching myself into the air, barely dodging a wash of necrotic energy that blasted past.

I returned fire with a lightning bolt. The freshly arrived wraith detonated, but even as I climbed higher, I could see another undead on the far side of the vehicle pawing at the door I'd just sealed.

I hesitated, then cursed. I had no choice. I couldn't save those who wouldn't save themselves.

I turned my back and streaked to face the incoming wraiths. If I didn't, they'd only follow and guide in more and more of the undead.

I'd barely covered half the distance, weaving and bobbing, returning fire with a Lightning Bolt here, an Incinerate there, taking them down, when the horrified, pleading scream rose behind me.

Shaking my head and gritting my teeth, I unleashed blast after blast, then landed, hard and fast, spinning and carving a hole in the middle of the undead before launching and streaking at another flier.

The road we'd been coming down had been over hilly territory, all up and down. And as such, there wasn't much of a distance that we'd been able to see ahead from road level. Now, as I saw it from the air, I had a rising sense of dread.

The core was the most important thing right now. It was vital to us surviving this, and although I'd needed to start it off—even the few hundred mana it'd managed to collect on the way passively and the few cars the others had got had helped—but it needed time to establish.

The systems were incredibly complex, and it'd really not liked being forced onto a spike. But damn, I was glad that I'd forced it not to just establish in the vehicle as it'd tried to.

We'd have been stuck in there.

Of course, I really wished I'd not crashed the fucker as well, so there was that.

That came with its own issues now, because as I killed the last of the wraiths, then paused and slid higher, I realized that yeah, I could see three other columns of undead heading inward toward the Eurotunnel. *Streaming* might actually be more accurate, in fact.

I leaned forward, giving up on trying to clear a space here, and instead streaked through the air toward the others, flashing past overhead, then looping slightly to the right and waving.

Emma got the message, shouting to the others, and they shifted their headlong rush. They'd already fallen in around her. Chris had passed Jenn the core and was running with his rifle ready; the twins, Andre and Jimmy, were doing the same.

Jenn was in the middle and Emma by her side, with Beta coming last, Kilo close by her side, with Patrick and Robin helping Catherine and Saros... I blinked, seeing a flash as she vanished, then appeared in mid-leap across a ditch ahead, before she opened fire into a staggering mass of undead.

I passed over her head in a blur, realized that she had to have unlocked some kind of fast movement perk or ability, the way she was crossing the intervening distances, and I made a mental note to ask her about it at some point.

Then the thought was banished as I landed, blade flashing as I frantically started to clear the road. Ten seconds of hack and slash and then I was airborne again, darting across the field and hovering, seeing the distant signs of fighting around our target.

It took us an hour in the end, with me landing, fighting, launching, and zipping back and forth, trying to conserve my mana by just using my sword as much as possible, instead of spells. But in the end, we climbed the final hill, and peered down at the trees that ringed the Channel Tunnel compound.

From higher, I'd been able to see the entire area. But from here, as low as I was on the ground with the others, slogging through sometimes knee-deep mud, I was cursing, filthy, and desperate to get back onto solid ground.

"I'm… sorry…" Emma called for what had to have been the fifteenth time, as she took my hand, and I pulled her up onto a less soaked, though still muddy track that ran along the side of the field.

"Don't be," I assured her. "I'd have told you to come this way," I admitted, before quirking a smile. "And when you level next, don't put everything into your Intelligence, or your Wisdom. If you get too far ahead with the mental stats, your body will freak, and believe me, the effect isn't good."

"I hate this shit," she whispered, bracing her hands on her knees as Jimmy and Andre helped her sister to stand with us.

The undead had been in three distinct columns heading for the dungeon site. Where the rest of the world might have changed drastically, Murphy was still hanging around and going strong, because we'd practically plowed into their point of convergence on the run.

The field behind us was now scattered knee-deep in places in the bones of the re-dead, and we were all sick of fighting the fuckers at close range.

Magic was so much better suited to this crap, but, we were all going to need all the magic we could raise in the coming days.

The last few hundred meters didn't take long to cross. The field that we'd just left was now revealed, by a wonderful sign that we passed on the way out, as a drainage site for the area. That someone had thought to put up a sign with "Danger – do not attempt to cross in wet weather" made it abundantly clear that our day was just getting shittier.

Five more minutes, and we were through the small set of houses, past the trees and stumbling up to a chain link fence. I ferried everyone over the top of it and past its razor wire, to drop them inside the outer edge of the tunnel's land.

Then it was another few minutes, this time running across poured and cracked concrete and through wide-open areas that had once been teaming with huge lines of trucks, before we finally saw the walls that Griffiths had been working on.

They'd not seen us coming until then. But as we stumbled, staggered, ran, and generally cursed the perverse world, the god's evil sense of humor and their prophet Murphy's name, we were finally spotted by one of our own, though how they'd missed the sporadic gunfire, magic, and so on was beyond me.

Then, *of course*, they shot at us, which fortunately missed. Next came a shouted apology, which was responded to with promises to rip out the shooter's balls via their throat. A few more shouts were exchanged, and finally, gloriously finally, as the fucking freezing cold rain practically reduced us all—especially Beta—to numbed zombies, we were guided around to the doors and permitted inside.

We'd made it to Folkestone, and the new site of the southern dungeon.

CHAPTER THIRTY-NINE

"Well," Griffiths said slowly, sliding into a seat across from me and looking me up and down. "Don't you look like shit? And, I heard you lost my damn APC as well!"

"APC?" I asked tiredly, setting my, by now de rigueur, can of energy drink down and looking at him.

"Armored personnel carrier," he translated. "The boxer."

"Oh, I didn't lose it," I assured him balefully. "I know where it is. It's about three or four miles over in that direction." I waved generally back the way we'd come.

"Well, it ain't here," Griffiths said grimly. "We could have done with the transport capability and the fifty cal."

"Yeah, well, leaving it wasn't something I was happy about either. Sorry, man," I admitted.

"Well, what's the breakage then?" He gestured at the way I came from. "I see you and your squad, plus two random civilians—though why you thought bringing them *here* was a good idea, I don't know. What I don't see are *my* people."

"Yours?" I blinked tiredly, only just realizing that we'd been on the go now for at least two days straight, maybe three. It'd all blurred that much. "They're not here?"

"No," he said. "I sent out a full squad and two boxers to get you as you asked, and we got you back, which believe me, I'm glad about. But the squad and both vehicles are still missing."

"Fuck." I groaned. "Dammit, man, I'm sorry. They were a few hours ahead of us, arcing around to the southwest to pass around London, while we headed for the north and through."

"Great." He sighed. "How shitty is this—normally I'd be raising heaven and earth to get out there and find our missing people, and yet all I can damn well do now is just hope they somehow find their way here through whatever mess they found." He rubbed his face and let out a long-suffering sigh. "Gods, I'm tired, Matt."

"Me too, mate...me too." I sighed. "What's the situation here?"

"FUBAR," he said. "Or actually, the way things are these days, maybe SNAFU is more accurate."

"I've heard both of those..." I muttered, trying to remember and he explained.

"FUBAR is fucked up beyond all recognition, and SNAFU is situation normal; all fucked up."

"Yeah, well, they both fit, I guess." I sighed. "How bad?"

"We've got twenty small crystals ready, but as you're replacing the core here, I've not begun work on the nexus gate. The basic walls are up, and we've done some strengthening of the ground under us, but that's it." He gestured vaguely around the room, meaning the area outside the little office we were currently sitting in.

That much I'd seen as we'd been escorted into the makeshift headquarters. The area that ringed the tunnel exit had been entirely surrounded by the kind of walls a medieval king would have married a Frenchwoman for.

They were tall, well built, and were definitely beyond the average undead's ability to climb. There was that, but unfortunately, beyond turning the area between the walls into mainly a pit—and a very muddy one at that—there was little else done.

They ringed the compound, designed to keep the undead from outside the area out and the undead coming through the tunnel in, and that was about as far as he'd gotten, it seemed.

The tunnel was at the farthest point east, and the building that we were in was at the westernmost point of the oval claimed area. A narrow ring of roads surrounded it, and a steadily building undead presence roamed slowly around the outer side of the walls.

At the tunnel end, there was also a wonderfully rhythmic banging that, despite the possibility, wasn't a hooker working on overtime.

Instead, it was apparently several thousand undead working steadily to batter down the gates that had been made to seal them in.

"No sign of the big bad yet," Griffiths said after a few seconds of silence. "So far, the whole 'drown them with bodies' thing seems to be the way it's going, though there's a lot more undead showing up and wandering around moaning than I was expecting. Showing up from the UK side, I mean," he corrected.

"We've got a theory on that." I nodded. "We, by which I mean there's been a vague conversation and it seemed plausible, but we think that the undead try to congregate with others of their kind. Like a kind of mindless peer pressure."

"Explain that," Griffiths said. "Do we need to play them Thomas the Tank Engine music and give them eyeliner or are we talking real undead?"

"Heh, I remember that video," I admitted, thinking about the goths in the underpass in America that someone had dubbed to make it look like they were all dancing to Thomas instead of whatever mad shit they'd been listening to.

"Matt?"

"Yeah?" I blinked, and he nodded.

"I need you to focus. Give me a plan, then get some sleep. We've got at least a few hours, and Aly and Kelly will be back online soon. They can help me. You look like shit."

"So do you."

"I'm a soldier. I'm used to it."

I snorted. "Mate, I'll bet dollars to donuts my Constitution is higher than yours. I'll be fine. I just need to stop for five minutes."

"Matt, I've had three of your people speak to me since you arrived. They're worried that the long-term effects of too little sleep and trying to work through the dungeon too much are affecting you. Your body has started falling asleep while you work. And if you've got no clue it's doing that, and you're this fucked up? You've got to be missing shit. Tell me what you need me to do, then you grab a few hours of shut-eye. That's an order from the Dungeon Commander."

That last bit was said with a smile, but I nodded, seeing his point.

The fight that was to come might not be a little one, most likely, considering we were fighting the undead, whose greatest advantage was always going to be that they didn't need rest. They could simply put solid pressure on, and keep going until our arms dropped off from exhaustion.

Or that they didn't have concerns like time, or cold, or food... Fuck me, the undead had too many advantages.

"We think the undead are naturally drawn to each other to congregate. Not for comfort or anything, but just because we've seen it so many times in graveyards and more. The bigger the number of undead, the more they collect together. No matter where they are, you see them move closer and closer until they seem to stand a few meters at most apart." I scratched at my cheek and sighed. Then rubbed my eyes.

"It's mad, but I don't think it's a conscious thing. I think they feed off the Unlife mana. And the more of them there are in an area, the more is generated, so the more they want to be close, maybe?"

"Sounds like there's a lot of 'I think' and 'maybe' shit in there."

"Yeah, well, my kingdom for a wiki," I muttered, staring at the tabletop before me as I wondered about the weirdness of the undead. Was it a case of the Unlife mana of a location produced them, and then they needed it to survive? If we found a way to drain the Unlife mana out, would that then wipe out the undead? Or stop them being created in the first place?

Unlife was a form of mana after all, one that... I pulled up my affinities and started looking, vaguely remembering that Unlife was a mix of Life and Death, but in specific quantities...

"So, the plan?" he prompted.

I sighed and nodded, banishing the screens. "Sorry, man. Okay, I'll fly up high, make sure the route is clear and we send the others off with the dreadnought. As they go, they'll be harvesting things that they see along the way, and basically plowing everything they can into their nexus gate and the production of mana crystals. Nothing else matters—as much of the crystals as possible, so they can be transported through and used to feed and jump-start this dungeon, and the nexus gate to get them through."

"They're to harvest along the way?" he asked, and I hesitated and then nodded.

"Only specific opportunities," I corrected. "Look, I don't know the area, not at all. I passed through once, that's it. But I know that the place I was sent to was in a town called..." I racked my brain, before grunting and going on. "It was Maidstone. Fuck me, we passed it."

"What was there?"

I grinned. "You know I used to work in IT, before all of this, right?"

"Yeah?"

"Well, the highest concentration of data and high-tech devices that the old world had was in data centers. There are dozens, hell, hundreds, up and down the country. But there's about a dozen major ones, and they're not on any maps you can buy. We'll need to hit the records centers for the army and more to get them, because they *always* have armed guards on sight. If they can hit one of those on the way to the airport? It'll be like they spent a week harvesting normal places."

"Okay, so the Maidstone center on the way back up to Heathrow...that's going to take, let's be conservative about this, six to twelve hours. They do that, and they harvest as much as they can—that's the very earliest we can expect to see a link from them here. I don't think we're going to get a connection here ready in that time."

"Nope," I agreed grimly. "Here, the focus is going to have to be the citadel. Make as much as we can, have the other sites harvesting as well, and we build. We build as heavily as we can. And as soon as we can open that gate and get reinforcements through, that's when we can take a break."

"Until then, we're on cleanup and kill duty?"

I nodded. "Massively so. The biggest issue is the core. I know it's a risk, sending the dreadnought core away, but if we don't?" I shook my head.

"We could keep it here. Your other core is mobile now as well, right?" he suggested.

"It is," I agreed. "But it's *small*. We'd have to rip the dreadnought core out of the vehicle we'd used to transport it, and plug the new one in. That starts the whole process off of setting up the dungeon anyway. It might give us a hairsbreadth of an advantage here, but it sets us back further along. Believe me, we need this.

"We need a dungeon down here to face them, and we need to grow it anyway. If we had the mana and the equipment to set up another transport, a large truck again and a full convoy to do it, that'd be ideal, but we don't. We need the truck to make it mobile; the core is barely established because it can't 'fix' onto its surroundings.

"We sink it into the ground here and let it go full bore. Then we feed it with the crystals you've been making, and it'll grow damn fast. If I'm right, we leapfrog the time it should take to establish, and we use some of the additional mana to cheat in pushing out our influence."

"How do we do that?" he asked.

I grinned evilly. "Well, you know me. I've got a plan," I assured him, much to his groans.

Ten minutes later, I blew out a long breath as I stared out, hovering some five hundred meters up in the air, at the swarming undead starting to build up around us.

There were more to the south—hell, there were a *lot* more moving past when I went higher and higher up. I stared in shock at just how many of what I was guessing were the naturally occurring undead from the south.

They'd started to move—be that they were summoned, or that they were just mindlessly swarming—but they were headed south in a general "we must go this way," like moths being drawn to a flame.

Beware! Area Event Discovered!

Due to the large numbers of undead in the area, a naturally occurring event has begun! Can you survive it?

The Lord of Unlife is drawing closer to his fated battle with the Lord of Storms. His arrival upon this formerly tranquil isle has been long awaited.

Along the way, he has invested heavily in drawing and raising all the undead available to his banner but in doing so, he has crossed a threshold!

The undead are now being drawn to him like a lodestone, and for the remainder of this event, he will receive continuous reinforcements.

Escape the area/survive the event to receive the following rewards:

- **+3 to top three Attributes**
- **+1 Class Skill Point to allocate**
- **25,000 XP**

I read the new notification, then reread it and sighed. "Well, nice to have a little confirmation for a change, but fuck, not what I was really hoping for."

Now that I knew that the undead were indeed being drawn to him, it meant that the grouping up of them all around the walls was probably due to the presence of the advance party in the tunnels.

If they were being drawn to the main force, they weren't going to be drawn to here; they'd be drawn to it, where…

I turned slowly, focusing and thinking, and then nodded.

He was still on the far side of the Channel. I didn't know why, but the undead asshole was still over there, and I had to guess that most of his army was still in transit.

What was hammering its way out of the tunnel currently was serving to draw the undead of the area, who were then seeing us, hearing the responses and doing the whole "it's a reaction" and attacking, much like all undead did. Or toddlers, for that matter.

Searching from even higher, with the undead below me reduced to ants, noticeable only due to their swarming, I could now see that they were staggering into the sea to the south, and I couldn't help but grin.

If I could get rid of the local presence and those surrounding the walls currently, and do it as quietly as possible, then there was still hope.

We could reseal the tunnel, then build and hide, basically just get as ready as we could, until the main thrust came.

The event that we were seeing wasn't endless, so all we had to do was outlast it. And the best way we could do that was to let the undead of the area wander into the ocean and get pulled apart and broken by the denizens of the deep.

The only hiccup in that plan was, of course, that we needed to get the dreadnought core out first.

I nodded to myself, seeing the streaming lines of undead in the distance to all sides. They clearly had no clue that there were so many here, nor that there was a tunnel that would lead them straight where they wanted to go. Instead, provided they were out of whatever passed for their sensing range, they were marching south-by-southeast and into the ocean, headed for the Lord of Unlife's armies.

Provided we could clear out whatever was drawing them in this direction— the undead and motion already detected, I was betting—then they'd just continue to stream past instead. Simple.

I landed quickly, Chris waiting where I'd asked, ready, and talking to Griffiths as I did.

"You ready for a little drive?" I asked him, and he snorted.

"A little drive, he calls it. I drove most of the way here; he took over, and the fucker crashed. Coincidence? I think not," he said to Griffiths.

I sighed and turned to the older soldier, then started to explain. "If we alter the front of the dreadnought and make it into a Mad Max-style road clearer with a cattle catcher on the front, then we make some basic changes to the overall structure, we should be able to get the truck out of here in about three hours," I said. "We'll need that long, because we've got what might be a solution to our low mana in the area situation and a way to deal with the undead, and sort that at the same time."

"I'll take that gold now." Chris smiled, holding his hand out to Griffiths, who cursed and slid a fat coin from his pocket.

"What's this?" I frowned.

"He bet me you'd have a cunning plan." Griffiths sighed. "I bet it'd take a few more hours."

"Nah, he's at his best when sleep-deprived. The rest of the time he's too depraved and thinking about Kelly's arse too much to focus," Chris said, before biting the coin. "Why do they always bite these things?" He asked curiously after he took it out of his mouth and peered at it. "Always wondered."

"Because it's soft enough a metal that if you leave teeth marks you can see it's real." Griffiths sighed again. "Okay, hit me."

"We establish the new core and use a couple of the crystals to send out two lines—one to the tunnel and one to the gates. Both are taken under the new dungeon's control as we modify the dreadnought to plow through anything in its path. I spend the next few hours sleeping. Then, when we've got both areas under the new dungeon's control, we go all out." I grinned.

"The majority of the undead are still in the tunnel, or across the Channel. The undead in the local area are being drawn in that direction, so we know that much."

"Okay…" Griffiths nodded.

"So if the majority aren't here, and by here I mean on the other side of that fucking tunnel gate, then we make a line that'll slow them down, and we let them loose."

"What?" he asked. "Matt, we barely managed to seal the fucker once already."

"I know." I grinned maniacally. "That's where the genius of my plan comes in. The tunnel is straight, right?"

"Mostly. It means they can go faster, but it winds. There's a lot of chalk in the area and they needed to follow it."

"But it's *mainly* straight, right?" I asked. "I mean, no sharp bends. It keeps going in more or less a straight line and weaves slowly in whatever direction, right?"

"Yeah…" He nodded.

"Great. So what we do is we reach out to the end of the tunnel. We create a block-braced system that we can drop down over the exit if there's too much coming out, so we've got that safety net—you know, like a few massive blocks of concrete set atop braces. Then, if we start getting fucked up, we simply smash the braces and the concrete falls down. Then we create a tunnel through it slowly back up to the edge, and let them out again…bleed them in batches."

"Okay." Chris nodded. "Like we did in the training dungeon, back in the day."

"Yeah, exactly, like we did with the first undead forces we were surrounded by. Man, it's like they just don't take a fucking hint, right?"

"Exactly," he agreed. "No imagination."

"It's a failing of the undead."

"Okay, so I know what you're going to do with the emergency measures." Griffiths sighed, rubbing the bridge of his nose. "Can you tell me the actual plan without all the witty repartee, please?"

"He thinks we're witty." I grinned at Chris.

"He's half right," he agreed.

"So, now we have a way to deal with it if it gets out of hand. What we do is unleash absolute fucking hell on the undead in the tunnel. They're stuck in a small space. I can't summon a full-on lightning storm in there—I need room for the clouds and shit—but I can summon Lightning Bolts, and a shitload of it," I said.

"Emma and I step up. We gave you a few focal orbs before we set off, so what we do is I replace the spell inside with Thunderbolt—it's the upgraded form of Lightning Bolt and that's how the focal orbs work, for whatever reason. We blast everything in sight...me on one side, Emma on the other, and we basically fry it all. Then she hands it over to your soldiers. They take turns, any of them who have any kind of affinity that's high enough, and Jenn is there for healing any who need it.

"We slaughter anything and everything there. Then we wait until we've cleared the absolute maximum we can out of the tunnel, while we have others pushing into it in the dungeon sense. As soon as they reach as far as we judge the maximum reasonable point, say fifty meters, but it'll depend on the thickness of the undead, they start making new doors.

"Once they're in place, we seal the tunnel again, and we start absorbing all the bodies. That provides the dungeon with mana we need, and we move to the front gate."

"The gate that leads out?" Griffiths asked, and I nodded.

"Try and keep up, dude," I said. "Man, it's hard to find good help. Anyway, I set off a full-on lightning storm, and anyone who can, helps with magic only to kill as many of the undead out there as possible.

"Once we've cleared the immediate area—and understand, this is going to be very loud and messy; it'll draw the undead from all around toward this—then we open the gates. Chris and his team drive the dungeon out, plowing through the remaining undead.

"He drives all out, honking the horn, whatever, gets their attention and draws them away from our walls. Then he goes dark, say, three miles or so out.

"As soon as he leaves, we close the gates and seal up, go silent. With him making so much noise and the undead being basically brainless, they follow him. That clears the immediate area..." I explained.

"What about the wraiths?" Griffiths asked. "They're the brains for the undead, right?"

"Yeah, glad you reminded me." I nodded. "*Snipers*. We use any snipers we've got and get as many as we possibly can. And as soon as Chris goes, like I said, we all get inside and go silent if there's any left. We want them to believe that we all left with Chris, so from that point, the only movement they see if any survive and fly over is chip packets in the wind, all right?"

"You think that once the living—that sounds so wrong—*active* undead are destroyed, there'll be nothing to hold them to the area, so they'll wander off?" Chris asked.

I nodded. "That means that if they do like the others I can see in the distance are, then they'll just head straight into the sea and be lost. Probably one in a

463

hundred, maybe less will make it to the far side. And when they do, that's not our problem." I shrugged. "This way, we can claim the bodies all around and absorb them in. That should hopefully be enough to give us the mana we need to build the nexus gate. If not, then we start on another plan. But it gives us a start, all right?"

"And while you're doing this, you're betting I can drive through the undead with a cattle catcher on the front of the rig?" Chris asked.

"Yup," I admitted. "Might not sound fancy, but a little additional armoring, some more fixes...I think you've got a real chance. Plus it means that, provided you're careful on the route, you should be able to smash through more on the road, and possibly even through cars and shit if they're in the way."

"So I get to smash and crash, while you beat the shit outta the undead." Chris nodded. "That could work. One point, though."

"Yeah?"

"Who goes and who stays? I mean, we all know I'm incredible, but I can't do a whole airport alone, or the data center," he asked.

"You take Jenn—"

"You're more likely to need another healer here," he interrupted.

I shook my head. "We'll all need a healer, but your mission has to succeed. If it doesn't, we've got no chance. If this all goes to hell, if the shit totally hits the fan, as long as we can get the nexus gate up and running with you here, I can evacuate people to you. I can kill the dungeon and fly my ever-lovin' ass up into the stratosphere, if need be...flip around and rejoin you. The one thing we need most of all is that mana, because with that, everything else becomes possible.

"Even if the army doesn't come, if the Scepiniir don't come, if Kelly's plans for diplomacy and the reinforcements from home all fall through...if you claim Heathrow, we can set up and create our own more traditional armies from there. You have to succeed."

I paused, looking at him and making sure he agreed and understood before I went on.

"If the worst happens, and the dungeon here..." I shook my head. "If we can't get enough mana together to build the nexus gate, then we're fucked. But if that happens, we'll lock down the building and basically try to fight our way through. If you hit the airport, you strip it, and we're still not operational? Start heading north. I'll contact you, and we'll arrange a point for me to reach you. I'll fly out, grab as many crystals as possible, then fly back. If we have to shuttle the fuckers over while you summon an army? That's what we'll do. But here? There's nowhere near the mana we need, unless we can harvest everything in the area."

"You won't be able to make the gate with what you have?" Chris asked.

I shook my head again. "Three million mana to activate the gate, mate. We've got a couple of hundred thousand at most. We'll do what we can, but for us to win, we need you to strip that airport."

"I don't like leaving you all—" Chris started.

I nodded. "I know, brother, but I need someone I know will do this, no matter the fucking cost."

"Bastard," he muttered, and I nodded soberly.

"So you're taking Jenn, Andre and Jimmy, Saros—"

"Saros is a scout—we're better with her here." Griffiths cut in.

I thought, then accepted it. "Fair enough. I suppose it's not like she can scout ahead from the truck."

"So I take Andre, Jimmy, and Jenn, is that it?" Chris asked.

"Beta and Patrick as well. That pair are the most lethal of us all in close quarters. Then, if anything happens, if you're hit by someone who knows too much, who senses something or whatever, you've got her. That's how important this is. Then, two more would help him," I suggested, glancing at Griffiths, and he shook his head.

"We're on the bones of our arse here. I'd recommend the first summons he does when he reaches the data center are a small contingent of Scepiniir or goblins—full loadout. Then use them as additional security."

"That makes sense." I sighed. "Chris, can you do it with that?"

"As long as the roads aren't on fire and hell hasn't arrived, I'll make it inside of three hours to the data center, and six to Heathrow," he assured me, then grinned and shrugged. "If it does arrive? Then it might take an extra hour or two."

"Good man." I took a breath. "Right. Griffiths, can you sort the changes needed if I plant the core?"

"I can, and then you get some rest," he ordered. "Real rest, not sliding into the dungeon sense and working instead of resting. Seriously, don't make me wake Jo up and have her chase you."

"Hell no, she's a spicy one." I snorted. "I'm not crossing Jo."

"Then that's it. Get some rest. Chris, gather your people. And Matt, you get to break it to Emma that you're separating her from her twin and husband." He snorted, and I laughed.

"Yeah, fair point," I agreed. "We're going to need her here, though."

"Then let's do it." Griffiths stood, offering us both a hand to shake. "Good luck, gentlemen!" he boomed, before striding off.

Chris and I stared after him for a few seconds in silence, before looking at each other.

"He's really that gung ho." He sighed. "Damn, the army really corrupted him, didn't they?"

"Nah, might be he was always the hero type, and they broke him back down to human...you never know," I replied. "Okay, so, you gonna be okay?"

"Fuck no. Can I get a cuddle and a pacifier, maybe a blankie as well?"

"Nope, you're big enough and ugly enough that there's nothing out there you can't handle, brother," I said seriously. "Chris, we need this. I don't have anyone I'd trust more to get it done, and who I know will manage it, but if...if there's no

465

way to do it, you need to accept that and turn around, all right? If there's no way to accomplish it, you need to go north, back to the girls and our people, and you need to get them the fuck out of there."

"Sink the dungeon and make it a solid hiding place." He nodded. "I know we've talked about what we'd do to weather the storm if it all goes wrong—dig the core right down deep, move everything and everyone—but we're not there yet, brother. We can do this."

"I hope you're right." I gave my oldest friend a hug, before breaking loose after a few seconds and straightening my shoulders. "Let's do it."

CHAPTER FORTY

I strode across the muddy ground a handful of hours later with Emma at my side, as well as three others, including a kobold, who had all tested high enough for Lightning affinity.

Kilo was there as well, just in case the shit hit the fan. Beta was firmly ensconced in the dreadnought, in the core chamber. Her job: to be the last line of defense for it.

We'd gotten the new core up and running, spiked into the ground in the new core-room, set in the heart of the main building here. It was as far from any form of contact as we could make it. And just for good measure, I'd removed the door and sealed it over with stone to make it look like part of the corridor. But it still felt terribly bloody weak back there, considering how little mana there was in the area to feed it.

It was a problem that Kelly and Aly were working on, though. They said they had a plan, just not what it was yet. Apparently I'd get the details once they'd figured out a few more minor kinks. So, rather than waste time, I was off to kill something.

The ground underfoot crunched as we walked across it again. The temperature had dropped massively in the last few hours, as the sun dropped as well. The clouds in the distance suggested another heavy snowfall was coming. As much as I tried to banish the thought, the very real concern that we might be getting a fucking ice age at this rate was starting to raise its head a lot.

I knew it was just the winter, really. I knew that sometimes you have weeks of storms and sometimes they just all hit at once, sure.

It was that the weather had gone so badly wrong, so fast that was getting me. Practically overnight, it felt like it'd gone from the tail end of autumn, into a full-on "depths of winter" shit. And if this lasted six months, there'd be no chance for the majority of the Northern Hemisphere.

I banished the thought again, marching across the dirt and frozen mud, to stand at the entrance of the tunnels. The massive concrete blocks we'd summoned were now directly over our heads, making me feel incredibly at risk.

"We could stand farther back," Emma suggested for the third time, getting a nod from a clearly worried Catherine and I snorted.

"We need to be close enough that the dungeon's area of control isn't pushed back," I pointed out. "If we're too far back, the enemy might swarm the sides and pour loose. They need to see us, they need to come, and I need to be close enough to do this."

"I… I think I might be able to get their attention, if they do that?" Catherine said hesitantly. "I mean, I can talk to them, I don't know if it'll work, but it might?"

"If you need to, then do it." I agreed. "Might be it'll give me time to get on top of shit, but for now, until we've trained you up a bit, you're still very new to this, so run if you need to."

"Can I run too?" Emma asked in what was probably supposed to be a joke, but came out as a fervent wish.

"We can do this!" Robin called out, and I stifled a groan, before speaking up. Even as the small band of nutjobs she'd gathered up from somewhere cheered as well.

"You'll damn well stay out of the way and only kill anything that gets past the secure area!" I shouted at them, before feeling—once again—like I'd just punted a fucking puppy.

With that, I reached out, selecting the braces for the massive bar that crossed the door, keeping it closed…then ordered the dungeon to absorb the connections holding the post in place.

It didn't want to at first. The undead were in contact with the far side of the doors, and their area of influence prevented me from making changes to the doors themselves. But as I moved closer and closer, my own level of control, as the lord of the dungeon, pushed theirs back. And as I wasn't actively trying to affect something they were in direct contact with…it finally worked.

"Get ready!" I called to the others.

The doors, gates—whatever they were—were shoved open by the press of undead that were unleashed…and fuck me with a running chainsaw attached to a dildo conveyor belt.

That was not a nice sight.

The undead burst forth, just as the snipers behind me on the small building, where we'd crammed everyone else into, opened fire. Wraiths were smashed from the air on all sides around the walls, even as skeletons and zombies, corpse lords and weird amalgamations of bones stumbled and crashed free of the tunnel.

They came in a wave. Dozens fell in the first seconds, not due to any action of ours, but instead to the incredibly poor luck of tripping over that massive oaken bar.

The undead behind them swarmed forward, clambering up and over, crushing their former compatriots.

Hundreds of skeletons rushed at us, forced by the lack of space into a tightly packed mob, one made up of individuals that had long since succumbed to the touch of the grave.

Bones were broken and shattered. Scores were toppled and trampled underfoot, their skulls smashed by the uncareful steps of their companions.

They came in a vast tsunami, missing limbs, or with arms that had been broken in repeated banging attempts to break through the portal. And now that they were through, I swallowed hard.

There were a hell of a lot of them, and I started to wonder whether I'd just made a literally terminal mistake.

"Matt?" Emma hissed. "What do we do?!"

"Fire!" I barked, shocked into motion. "Lightning!" I corrected, thrusting both hands forward and unleashing a pair of blasts, one from either hand, aimed at roughly head height.

The Lightning, with little to attenuate it, punched through the skulls of the first in line, then vanished into the creaking, silent morass of bodies behind, destroying more and more.

I fired again, then again. Emma, by my side, did the same. Her Thunderbolts did more damage individually than my Lightning—it was a totally different spell, after all—but after five casts, she was done, panting, and I'd barely begun.

"Catherine, no time like the present to try out that spell!" I shouted, and as I looked back at her, I found her staring at me like a rabbit caught in the headlights. "Your spell?" I tried again. "That distraction for fucks sake!"

She nodded frantically, before stepping up, then pressing her hands together and focusing. She stood next to me, as purple light flared, and a handful of the incoming undead staggered, staring, slack jawed at her.

Then she apparently dug deeper and tried again, staggering almost half.

That was great, very impressive, right up until she collapsed. "Dammit, Robin get her out of here!" I shouted over my shoulder, wading forwards again.

Kilo sent waves of frigid ice lapping up from the ground to clutch at the legs of those that strode forward, tugging them off-balance and to the ground. The others rotated in, using the focal orbs, firing their blasts and then running out of mana.

"Get them back to the building," I ordered Emma. As stubborn as she was, she'd stay with me otherwise, and there was little point.

They started to back away, and I unleashed another blast, then another. The bright blue-white blasts of Lightning barely seemed to illuminate anything before they died away again.

I checked my mana and cursed.

I'd used ten Lightning blasts already. I still had another thirty-nine hundred and fourteen points left, but I needed a thousand of those points for the Lightning Storm I was going to be casting out by the front gate, and…

"Ah, fuck it." I swore, before focusing in. I had enough for a single Lightning Storm, and then nearly three thousand points more. That gave me plenty to have a little fun, considering just how many of these bastards needed sorting out.

469

I'd been worn out before, when I'd crashed the boxer. Chased, standing in ankle-deep mud, and, I rather suspected considering how hard it'd been to concentrate at that point, either dealing with literal exhaustion, or a minor concussion.

Now I wasn't, and I'd come on in leaps and bounds since that day literally weeks ago when I'd stood outside of our walls with the corpse lords and I'd beaten the undead army like a red-headed stepchild.

It was time to demonstrate just what I was capable of, and besides…with another twenty-nine Lightning Bolts available to me, if I got in the shit, and against literally level one and two undead? I didn't deserve to be where I was.

No, it was time for a *demonstration.*

I was grinning, I realized, as I stopped casting spells and instead ripped the blade from my back and strode forward. The idiot brigade behind me with Robin started to cheer, before someone apparently ordered them back again.

They were coming for me ten abreast, in a staggered line. Fuck me, they really wanted a mouthful of man-meat—and they weren't even willing to buy me a drink first.

I couldn't help but smile.

Striding forward, I heard Emma shout out from behind me. I called over my shoulder to Kilo instead.

"Kilo, get them all back, then do crowd control. Keep the undead in close to me but stagger them. I need to thin the herd."

"On it!" came the sibilant voice, and I swung my sword through a few quick arcs back and forth as I closed on them, loosening up and getting ready.

A single last blast of lightning from my left hand held and channeled rather than simply unleashed tracked from right to left; heads exploded, taking at least twenty more down. And then I was there, a horizontal cut from right to left, a loop, and then left to right.

I did it at head height on a short-arse, meaning that for most of the undead that I caught next, they lost their heads at the neck.

Two were taller than average, meaning that they got hacked apart at around the shoulder. That slowed the blade a hell of a lot, but a spin kick and another blast of channeled lightning into the onrushing pack took a dozen more down.

A handful of minutes, I battled, moving back and forth, alternating between being able to hold the line—admittedly thanks to Kilo's excellent crowd control—and having to take a step back, and then another.

The fight came in waves. The occasional burst of stumbling and falling undead skeletons took down others and enabled me to face "only" a half dozen at a time, before ten or fifteen would come at once.

For a regular human, this would have been impossible. The stream of reaching hands and clacking teeth would have done for them in seconds. But the undead were *weak*, and I wasn't a regular human anymore.

Every so often, I'd flood myself with Lightning. It banished the exhaustion, and then I'd hold it, enjoying the feeling, before unleashing it in a sideways blasting bar of blue-white light that carved through to the tunnel.

As the minutes passed, the press lessened, and for the first time, I started to head back toward the tunnel's mouth. I kept going, aiming to clear a little of the tunnel and then retreat, right up until the frantic rush of undead slowed, only a few dozen in sight before a gap opened. I pushed harder, hacking them down, and grunting at what I saw next.

The undead weren't limited to humans—I'd known that, though the majority were—and the next line, rolling out of the darkness in a veritable wave of undulating backs, tails, and gleaming empty eye sockets, came the dogs.

That was enough for me. I focused, backing up, then sensed Kelly by my side. "We need that wall," I said grimly, hacking a few more apart, and getting a distantly sensed message from her that it wasn't going to happen so long as I was in contact.

I checked my mana, then grunted.

Clearly I'd been fighting longer than I thought. My mana was back up to just under three thousand. I focused, aiming a dozen meters ahead of me, and cast Atomic Furnace.

It wasn't a spell I used a lot, but considering the onrushing force, it was perfect.

Fifteen hundred mana vanished in a heartbeat, and I turned and burned, shouting to Kilo, who, predictably, had followed me farther in than he should have. I held it as long as possible before releasing it.

"Seal it!" I shouted. "Wall to fucking wall, right fuckin'…" I ran past a section and then gestured at the floor as I crossed it. "There!"

The passage was huge, ten meters plus high and round, three tunnels across, and it was only bloody luck that we'd managed to keep it to just the one tunnel that was open currently.

The effect of a sudden wall of ice that rocked out from one wall to the other, when a dozen meters beyond it I activated a spell that was rated to literally turn steel to gasses, was impressive.

The center of the impact, considering the spell only covered an area a meter across, was probably the least impressive.

The rolling wave of dogs, seven of which were roughly inside the circle, simply ceased to be. They were reduced to impurities floating in the wind.

The closest to the blast were incinerated, literally turning to ash; those in the next few meters out from that point burst into flame and collapsed into burning, charred fragments that bounced and rolled along the ground.

Bones exploded, scything down their compatriots. Clothing and flesh ignited on the few humanoid bodies in there. Fur atop the animal remains flash-burned to ash.

The walls glowed cherry red, and later on, we'd realize that using such an incredibly powerful spell in such an enclosed area was one of the stupidest things I'd ever done.

If I'd channeled it, instead of cast and release? The walls of the tunnel would have melted, and most likely the air would have caught fire, possibly leading to the extinction of all local life.

That was the power of the spell, and I'd used it out in the open before, not even realizing!

The issue here, though, was that where the thermal dissipation before had been more than space enough thanks to the outdoor nature and the burst of the spell, and then it vanished, now, instead there were both bountiful fuels available and a tightly enclosed space.

The thermal bloom rocketed out in both directions along the tunnel from the point of release. One side hit the icy wall within a few meters when headed in my direction, and the other continued down the tunnel to fry and disintegrate the oncoming undead.

In my direction, the combination of the ice, the wall that Kelly was frantically summoning into being, and the curvature of the walls of the tunnel meant that the majority of the force was then redirected back into the other tunnels.

They opened into each other about a hundred meters deeper in, and the overlapping blast fronts tore the undead apart in a great wave.

Kilo had, fortunately, learned not to link the fucking shield to his life force. As such, he and I were merely picked up and flung unceremoniously about a dozen meters from the tunnel in a blast of smoke, fire, steam and disintegrating ice that probably looked like a rocket's exhaust.

I managed to grab onto him and carry him, flooding my flight ability with a little too much mana that resulted in us screaming across the open area and barely coming to a halt without catapulting into the building on the far side.

I'd scarcely avoided crashing into Robin and her merry band of lunatics on the way past.

The tunnel continued to vomit flames for a few seconds before guttering out. Judging from the distant glow of molten stone and flames inside it, I'd definitely gone a little too far with the overkill.

Americans would probably be saying it was excessive, and I'd been across the pond for 'Ungrateful Colonial Day' before.

I knew how mad those bastards were.

I picked myself up and dusted myself off, looked Kilo over, who was slightly dazed but grinning from ear to ear, and nodded in satisfaction.

Glancing around, I saw the others wore a mix of horrified amazement, dismay and outright terror, Catherine especially, with Emma glaring at me as if she'd shank me given half a chance.

A job well done, I decided, right up until I sensed the furious presence of Kelly nearby. I did the only reasonable thing in the situation. "Kilo, get the others inside and tell anyone who might be waiting for me in the dungeon sense that we need to seal the tunnels and grab any bones we can. I'll get Chris and the others moving," I declared cheerfully, before launching myself into the air.

I was so going to get *such* an earful later. But as I landed on the wall and looked down at the milling undead, I decided it was worth it. Then, cracking my knuckles, checking my mana, and grinning for all I was worth, I designated a ten-meter radius right outside of the gates and unleashed a literal storm of lightning, washing away anything that thought it was a threat to us.

There were only ten bolts in the flurry, but the ten-meter designated target area and the four seconds that the spell was compressed into meant that there wasn't anything in there that was going to be surviving for long enough to care.

The bolts thundered down, the air rent apart by the horrifically powerful discharge. And then, like magic, it was over. The silence rung in my ears as bits of bone and old clothes, many smoking or shattered, drifted and fell through the air.

That done, I turned. Grinning maniacally, I bowed, and waved Chris forward through the already opening gates. It was all going to plan, more or less.

With hindsight, I should have known that was a bad sign.

I watched him as he drove through the devastation, then I hopped back out of sight, catching myself with a little flight magic as I neared the ground to land softly, bending the knees and taking a few steps to stop, before I saw the gates closing.

They slid to an almost silent stop. The latches on either side, like opposing claws, slid across into their housing and locked with a faint *snick* that was lost in the sudden roar of the massive truck's horn.

It wasn't the piddly little "excuse me, please" of a normal truck's horn. Oh no, this was a full-on "I'm military, bitch...*move*" and damn, did it make that clear.

The truck, now hidden from me by the high and silent walls of the base here, had been transformed from the admittedly impressive transport it'd already been, into a real Mad Max version, complete with the cattle catcher that you sometimes saw on the front of trains in the US.

It was still only early days in the monstrous machine's list of transformations, but I just knew Chris was going to be loving every minute of the drive.

I turned and hurried from sight, or at least, I did my best. The building that was all that we had for cover was going to be boring to be hiding inside of for the next few hours, but still, it was there, and it had actual walls, a floor, and a roof.

Hell, there were lots of rooms, really. The building was a massive square thing. It was just that we couldn't use the outer goddamn rooms because so much of it was glass, and it towered over the nearby walls, being as big as it was.

The plan was that as we expanded the core, we'd claim the rest of the building, and we'd replace its walls gradually with something more appropriate. Meter-thick titanium was probably a bit excessive, but you know, I like a little security when I can get it.

The issue here currently was that there was precious little available mana, and we were in an area that seriously needed it.

We had, thanks to a last-minute surge of effort before we moved the dreadnought, a grand total of twenty-three crystals.

They each held about ten thousand mana, giving us a wonderful total of two hundred and thirty-ish thousand mana. That sounds like a lot—and in some ways it was—but the nexus gate was a solid three million in cost, and we weren't going to be earning much else around here.

That meant we were down to consuming the undead bodies that I'd just terminated with extreme prejudice and the remaining vehicles in the area.

There were still a lot of them on the outer ring of the territory, which was lucky. But they weren't exactly high-density electronics, and they weren't going to be bringing in a huge amount more than pushing the dungeon sense out that far was going to cost us.

That meant that we needed to pull in as much as possible, as quickly as possible, and yeah, of course, Griffiths had already torn out everything high-tech in the surrounding buildings.

That left cheating and investment as our only options.

Cheating in that there were accepted ways to earn mana in a dungeon, and there were...*less* accepted ways.

As far as I knew, the first main way was through dungeon mana converters, sucking mana in and then converting it to the kind we wanted. They then stored that form of mana, and pushed the rest, now purified, into the dungeon's core.

Second was through absorbing the mana that was released as creatures in and around the dungeon died. That meant we could create a dungeon that the undead could unthinkingly run into, and we could kill them, releasing their mana and powering the dungeon that way.

Third was in the absorption of mana from items or solid matter. Everything from bricks to balls, stone to skulls—it all had a mana value if we absorbed it into the core.

The vast majority was a very small value, but there were advantages to it still. We didn't need all the pavement that had once been roads here, for example, and absorbing it all in had served two purposes. First, it gave a small amount of mana to the core, and second, it created a boggy field that would slow down attackers.

All well and good.

The thing was these three options all had issues.

Primarily, we were fucked because this was a shitty area. Had we set up ten miles or so to the east, there was an area of high mana right there, I could damn well sense it, and if we were there, we'd have a fuckload more mana coming in.

We weren't, though, because the tunnel was here. So...that's life.

Second, besides the undead, there was fuck all left here to kill, and we'd just done our best to make the undead from outside believe we weren't here anymore, because we really wanted them going into the sea, not helping the undead dickhead when he came.

Third? There was fuck all of value in the area still besides trucks, cars, and stonework.

That meant it was time to cheat. Just a little.

"So, tell me again about the mana," I said to Kelly and Aly in the dungeon sense a few minutes later, though mentally now sitting around a table in Newcastle, rather than squatting on the floor as I had been.

"When you killed them, they released Unlife mana," Kelly said grimly. "If you'd not killed so many, I'd have missed it. But there's so much of it, I'd have to be an idiot to not see it."

"I didn't see it," I pointed out, trying to make her feel better, and she and Aly stared at me, until I realized what I'd just said. "And moving on." I colored slightly and gestured to Kelly.

"Thank you." She glared, still clearly pissed at me for some reason. "So, there's Unlife mana coming off the undead, and we're getting about ten to fifteen mana from each of them…from absorbing them, I mean." She paused, checking I was following and then nodded. "Now, we never bothered building any of the Unlife converters, because although we use the undead in support roles, they've not been a real important part of the dungeon. Or at least they weren't, until now."

"I hate when you say things like that." I sighed. "Go on."

"The amount of Unlife mana released when they died is impressive, but our theory is that there's a lot of it coming off the undead all the time."

"Uh-huh."

"So…Aly diverted some of her research to unlocking the basic details for Unlife, and we're going to take some of the ideas from the healing towers, and the setup we used to rescue people back up in Otterburn Camp."

She gestured and the reason for the meeting being here instead of at the southern dungeon was immediately clear as a wire-form diagram of the dungeon suddenly appeared, complete with the section of the tunnel I'd just pretty much trashed.

"Now, fortunately, we only unsealed one of the doors into the tunnel, and although we managed to smash the place up a lot, there's still plenty of the undead to go around."

"So?" I prompted.

"So instead of wasting our time in grubbing for a handful of points here and there from the trucks and just hoping we find something worth the effort in the backs of them—we might…I mean it's unlikely, but we might—we want to build a new dungeon."

"I thought we were going for the storm option," I said carefully. "I mean, that's why we kept Emma here as well, right? We use her ability, boosted by crystals to help build a more powerful storm, then I charge my own and drag down a lightning bolt into the roof here. We use that to channel into the core, and you two get ready to party."

"To party?" Aly asked, one eyebrow raised.

"Fuck's sake, I mean you spend it all as fast as you can. You summon everything you can and simultaneously build the nexus gate. We know that the average storm has millions of mana—we're just draining it all in one go."

"One issue," Kelly said carefully. "Well, no, actually, several, but the main one is that what if we don't get enough mana?"

"From the storm?" I asked, and she nodded. "Well, that's when we start reaching out. We try to strip the trucks, send scouting parties into the town to strip out basketloads of high-tech phones from the stores or whatever."

"And if they've all been looted already?" she asked again. "If you can't get to the town for the undead that are passing, or that the storm fizzles out and is only maybe a quarter of the mana we need?"

"Then we're fucked, and we do it all old school," I said grimly. "If need be, we start building a goddamn mineshaft and absorb all the way down to the center of the fucking earth. We need that mana and we're going to get it." I hesitated. "Maybe I could fly to the server center that Chris and the others are headed for. Have them split it down the middle—they hand over half the crystals they produce and I carry them back here. We could use that to—"

"Matt." Kelly stopped me. "We need to be sure, and this gives us a better chance."

"What does?" I asked. "We don't have the hundreds of thousands of mana it'd take to build a new dungeon—not a raid dungeon, if that's what you mean!"

"It is, and we do," Kelly corrected, realizing that I wasn't arguing because it wasn't my idea; I was arguing because I didn't understand. "If instead we create a long, snaking route from a central point, maybe we dig down, say, ten meters with the dungeon. Then we make an entrance there from here, a vertical tunnel with rungs that we can remove easy enough for safety. That's our starting point from here, and then we wind it back and forth, snaking it all the way. Make sure the dungeon is no wider than two people abreast.

"We give it maybe another two meters of stone between the winding tunnels, think like an S and here…" The image showed a section of rock that looked like an incredibly industrious badger had been at it, digging meandering tunnels that folded back on themselves. For every ten meters from here to the east, there'd have been a hundred meters travelled in back-and-forth weaving lines.

It reminded me of the lines in the airport, where they wove in and out with those elasticated belts making lines.

Then, in the sections of "solid" stone that remained between the tunnels, new glowing dots appeared, every few meters.

"These are the Unlife converters," Aly said quickly. "If we build them with small holes in the walls, then we ensure the mana can be dragged in through to them. That gives us a small take from the still moving and 'living' undead"—she held her hands up for that, making air quotes—"and every time we kill them, we gain more."

"But we just drove them all off or killed them," I growled.

"The tunnels are already filling up, slowly," she corrected. "The heat is too much for most of them in the one you attacked. They're just crumbling still, which is impressive as all hell. But the other two tunnels still have some in, and there's more coming. Plus there's the undead that are still around the walls. Around half were drawn off with Chris. That's it. With this in place, we could essentially 'farm' the undead, and use them to provide us with the mana we're needing. The overlapping fields of Unlife converters would drag in the mana they give off and provide us with significant power. Yeah, there's problems, though."

"Go on." I sighed.

"Hey, there's no such thing as a free lunch." Aly quirked a little smile. "We'd need the higher level of converters...and they cost fifty thousand each. The mana we'd get from them passively would be, we think, around fifty points per unit per hour."

"Well, that's a net loss." I grunted. "Fifty thousand for what, twelve hundred a day? We need a much, much faster solution than that, and we need the goddamn things to not be scrap after this."

"Scrap?"

"Say we win—which we're going to," I corrected myself. "Then there's no more undead here to power the converters and they're a net loss."

"Ah, no, but I understand where you're coming from." Aly shook her head. "So, they bring in twelve hundred mana each, per day, that's correct, but that's the passive earn."

"Uh-huh."

"The active earning is the mana released on death." She went on quickly. "There's about three times as much released on death as we'd get by absorbing the undead. So here's the basic math—get ready and brace those eyelids open. It's important."

"The average undead is worth around forty points of mana to summon in the first place, and that's for the advanced. The cheaper and weaker are correspondingly less. But to be clear, we're looking at about ten points of regular pure mana as the cost of those around us currently for us to summon. That's the *summoning* cost," Kelly said, and the figures appeared in the air.

"Right," I agreed.

"Well, that's the cost to make them out of mana. But the average living creature generates mana all the time—sentient life especially, but all life does. That means that for a creature to live, all the while producing a tiny amount of mana, it's either far cheaper to create one, or the 'real,' naturally occurring undead are different from the ones we generate," Kelly went on. "That's logic, right?"

"Yeah."

"Wrong!" she said. "The mana value of the average-sized human is ten points once we absorb them into the dungeon. The larger the human, the more the value."

"How the hell does that work?" I asked, confused.

"The naturally occurring undead have come from years, decades of life," she theorized. "We think that mana was always here. It was just that before whatever those dickhead aliens did, it was a tiny amount, that's all. We know life generates it, so as we live, we basically soak our bones with it. That's one of the reasons we think the undead come about. Their bones are impregnated with Life mana already, then they die, releasing Death mana, and that surrounds the corpse. The corpse is buried, burned, whatever, but that mana is left seeping around the area. In graveyards, it builds up until a body is given Unlife. Once they start to generate Unlife of their own, it grows, spreading and reawakening more and more of the dead."

"Okay...so we've got a theory about the undead, that's great." I sighed. "But it doesn't change the math." I paused, seeing the smiles, and I nodded. "Sorry. I'll stop interrupting. You go on."

"Three times as much Unlife mana is released as the undead die, making them worth about thirty mana each per kill, and ten for absorbing the body, so..." Kelly gestured to Aly to take over.

"So what we do is make this winding path, and we let our people fight and kill all they like in there. We destroy the undead in literal droves, and we do it steadily, like around the clock. If you can kill a hundred an hour...does that seem reasonable?" she asked, and I snorted.

"I think I can do better than that." I scoffed.

"But can the average fighter?"

I nodded. "I don't see why not. Depends on the gear, but a hundred an hour should be easy."

"Okay, so that increases our take to three to three and a half thousand mana, per fighter, per hour. We create say five paths, each with a dedicated Unlife converter next to the fighter but buried in the wall where it's safe. That gives us fifteen thousand per hour, or three hundred and sixty thousand mana a day." She smiled. "It's not enough for a nexus, sure, but as a start? It's great."

"Okay, but the cost?" I asked, and she nodded.

"That's the risk. But to make the tunnels, all we have to do is eat away and absorb the rock, which gets us some mana anyway. What I'm suggesting is that you get ready for the lightning plan, we build a network of tunnels, and then when you activate it, we slam in the converters as fast as we can. You said that the undead leader is still on the other side of the Channel. If he travels at the speed he's been travelling, how long to reach here?"

"Honestly, I don't know," I admitted after a brief thought. "It's like he stays still for a while, then moves fast. Might be an ability...?"

"Or he doesn't like exposing himself to any risk and will stay out of the way until the undead have cleared an area?" Kelly suggested.

"Possible, certainly," I agreed, nodding.

"Okay, so what we've got is two hundred and thirty thousand mana or so. It's nowhere near enough to make the nexus gate, but between it and the undead that you destroyed—by the way, less destruction is better. We're getting three and four units of mana from each, that's it, because you smashed them into such tiny pieces." She stopped to look at me, and I stared back.

"Really," I said after a few seconds flatly. "I'm terribly sorry that I'm too efficient at killing our enemies."

"Well, you should be." Kelly smiled. "Look, you need to recover your mana, and we need to get things in position, so what we're suggesting is that we push out the last few meters from the core now to reach the roof. We set up a Storm and a Lightning converter on there as you wanted.

"From there, we guide our people in eating out rows and paths that are like snaking lines. That brings in a little mana. And once you get the storm really going and feed the power in, we'll add the converters as fast as we can."

"That's the part I don't like," I said. "What if we don't have enough because of this? I mean, you're spending a hundred thousand on the converters, and a few hundred mana will be the cost from the expansion—no stress there. The winding routes make sense if we need to bleed the enemy, but the converters there?" I shook my head. "I don't like it."

"I know," Kelly said as Aly fell silent. "We both do, and we get it. The cost is too high with the risk, but Matt, we can't build enough mana storage devices, nor the crystal converters to store any of the mana you're going to drain from the storm to make a difference.

"All that power is going to come tearing down, and if you remember, the first nexus gate took a few *days* to make. Now, sure, that was probably because the damn thing was being grown out of whatever fucked-up shit they use in the back system to award bonuses, but it wasn't instant. That means that when we try to make one, it's not likely to be instant either. The one we made for the northern dungeon to here took nine hours. Do you think that the dungeon can store three million mana to dole it out over nine hours?"

She had me there. And when she put it like that, I knew it was unlikely. The converters produced the crystals now thanks to that upgrade, and additional mana was being saved from being lost like that, but it, too, was a slow process.

That meant that either we use the mana or we lose the mana, and I seriously doubted we could store enough to get the nexus gate done in one.

"Okay, so you use a hundred thousand to make the Storm and Lightning converters on the roof, then you use thirty to start the nexus gate off," I said. "You leave the last hundred thousand in the crystals in case we need it, and everything else we get..." I nodded. "You risk it for a biscuit, and build both the Unlife converters and shove any and all the mana into the gate that you can. To be clear, though—the converters only get the overspill from the gate, not the other way around!"

"Thank you," Kelly said softly, knowing that I would have done very differently, but that I was trusting them instead of working as I felt we should.

"*But...*" I said with an evil grin. "You get to explain it to Griffiths."

CHAPTER FORTY-ONE

"**Y**ou know," Griffiths said to me several hours later as I stood on the roof with him and Emma, watching the building clouds and the incoming snow. "Just once, literally *once*, I'd like to make a plan with you that didn't get fucked in the ass within a few hours."

"Nah, you'd just get bored." I shot him a smile as I adjusted my armor, the battered and broken links getting more than a little annoying now. "You ready for this?" I asked him, and he shook his head.

"No, I'm not. And neither are my people." He sighed. "Good luck, both of you."

"Thanks, mate." I straightened and returned his salute, before watching him hurry to leave the rooftop, grabbing the rungs we'd created in the wall and swinging himself over and around the edge and then down out of sight.

Once I was sure he was gone, I turned to Emma. I paused then, seeing the way that she was standing: one arm resting on the Storm converter, clearly working on building the courage she needed for this.

"Emma? You ready?" I asked her after a few seconds.

She shook her head, silently.

Unlike when I'd said it to Griffiths and he'd been more or less joking, I damn well knew that Emma was deadly serious. I opened my mouth, thinking to say something soothing, then shut it with a click. I just didn't know her well enough to really help. So after a few banal comments, I left her to her own devices, striding to the edge of the roof and looking down.

The plastic coating on the roof tiles creaked underfoot, and I tried not to imagine just how likely it was that I'd go crashing through at any second, instead staring out at the walls and seeing the undead as they drifted mindlessly past.

The numbers had kept growing until it was obvious that whatever the rotten dicked bastard was doing in France, it was waking every corpse that was even slightly intact for hundreds of miles in every direction.

I had a few minutes while she got herself ready, and so, knowing that it was important and I might as well see what I could figure out, I started examining the undead.

The first thing that I noticed when the boxes popped up was that they were all marked as naturally occurring. That was a bit weird, as at first I'd thought he must be raising them all, but okay...

What else could I tell from them all, considering that the undead I could currently see were plainly just the shambling type?

There had to be some kind of an effect, I decided, that increased the chances of the long-term dead to rise again over the more recent. Although zombies had a chance to spread their infection, and the various wraiths and corpse lords or whatever could do much the same, the "normal" dead seemed to rise in much greater numbers when they were old, rather than when they were fresh corpses.

That meant that for every ambulatory body out there that could have passed— at a distance and with your nose stoppered up and maybe a little fog—as living people, there were thirty or forty that would have had no chance.

As such, the sheer number of rotting parts that were falling in the path left by them meant that plagues were going to become a very real concern.

It was bloody lucky that the limbs, when they fell, seemed to lose their animating power, because the crawling of ten thousand hands along the road would be bloody awful to watch.

There didn't seem to be many naturally occurring dogs or cats or whatever for some reason, nor farm animals, which again made the argument for awareness and mana creation being more or less linked hand in hand.

Pausing I noted that little oddity, the fucker must have raised all those dogs I fought before deliberately and sent them through the tunnel then. Bastard.

I shrugged, ignoring the few undead that had spotted me, and returned to the top, striding up the gently sloping side of the roof to come to a halt near Emma. Then I sighed and turned around again, trying not to rush her.

The groans were starting, and the cries, as more and more of the zombies saw us. The regular undead occasionally managed a hiss or a shriek, but generally it was just the clacking of teeth. Zombies? They were much more vocal motherfuckers.

As more and more saw us, the "word" spread, and the slowly drifting lines that snaked around our walls contracted and grew deeper.

The handful became dozens; the dozens became hundreds. And glancing to see that Emma still wasn't ready, I lifted from the roof to fly into the swirling snow. As far out as I could now see—which was dropping in distance by the second as the storm closed in—more stumbled in our direction.

I turned and flew back, slowing to land next to Emma and speaking in as reassuring a voice as I could.

"Emma, you've got this, okay? You don't need to worry. It's literally a low-level class ability. That means it's as intrinsic to you as Lightning is to me. Are you ready?" I frowned as I saw just how grey-faced and trembling she actually was.

"I'm really not," she admitted, her eyes screwed tight shut and her head resting against the side of the Storm converter.

481

I bit my lip, wishing I was better at this shit. "Emma, we've got the undead able to see us and we're drawing them in. The storm is almost upon us, and I can feel the potential in the air. So we either need to move, now, or we're going to miss the chance."

"You think that helps?" she snapped. "Fuck's sake, Matt—it's the goddamn storm that's scaring the shit out of me!"

"The storm?" I asked, confused. I looked up, staring into the rising winds, and seeing the iron-grey clouds overhead. "Why is the storm…" I paused, then turned. "Emma, describe the feeling you've got." A horrible thought reared its head.

She hesitated a second. "I feel sick. I'm fucking more scared than I've ever been in my life, and I just want to curl up and hide." The words almost tumbled over themselves as she blurted it all out through chattering teeth.

"Sick?" I cursed as my fears were confirmed. "Your affinities—what are the main ones?"

"What?"

"No time to explain. Fuck's sake, Emma, what are your main affinities?"

"Main?" she asked, confused.

"Earth, Air, Water, and Fire?" I said quickly. "What's the lowest?"

"Uh, Earth. Twenty-seven."

"Not that then…" I muttered. "Okay, read them out to me, all four."

"Earth, twenty-seven," she repeated. "Fire is seventy-eight, Air is sixty-four, and Water is fifty-eight."

"Nothing that should be causing you an issue…" I muttered. "Okay, the primary elements are those four, plus Light, Darkness, Life, and Death. What's the lowest?"

"Death, minus four."

"And we're surrounded by the dead, so yeah that's not a good combination, but it shouldn't be affecting you up here…" I racked my brains for an answer as she spoke up.

"Why? What were you looking for?"

"I thought you might have had a component of the storm that was fighting you," I said absently. "Like I used to hate water—don't laugh, and I wasn't unclean…I just hated the sea and water generally—when it's in a storm, though? All good."

"And that would make me feel like shit?" she croaked, and I nodded. "What about the snow?"

"Snow? No clue," I admitted. "It's like if there's something that you just hate being around, something that triggers that automatic feeling like a lump in your throat, where you feel just wrong at every level? That's…"

"Ice," she said, forcing the words out. "My ice is at fourteen percent."

"Ice?" I grunted in shock. "We're facing an incoming fucking blizzard!"

"I KNOW!" she practically screamed at me, before sucking in a breath and going on in a brittlely calm tone. "It's one of my lowest." Her voice dropped, and for the first time I realized that her lips were blue and her trembles had gone to the point that she was shaking like a shitting dog.

"Fuck! Emma, relax and let go. Trust me," I ordered her, trying to hide the frustration as I took the quick steps to her side and grabbed her. I pulled her from the Storm converter and took her in my arms, then lifted us both into the air, carrying her over the side and around to the nearest door.

It was unlocked; hell, Griffiths could have only passed through it a minute or two ago, and we'd planned to use it again soon enough anyway. But to keep people safe, there was nobody in these outer rooms, just in case.

I carried her as quickly as I could through the first two, before finding some of our forces sitting, quietly talking. They jerked to their feet, stunned, as I crashed in.

"Get her to Jo!" I ordered the pair of Scepiniir and the human. "Right bloody now! She's half frozen!"

They jumped, and Emma tried to protest weakly, only to have me cut her off.

"Don't," I said grimly. "Fucking talk to Jo. Get warmed up and damn well tell me next time if there's something that I ask you to do that scares you fucking shitless!"

Then I stormed back out, heading for the doors and cursing myself, her, and everyone in earshot.

I couldn't believe it. I just couldn't goddamn believe it! Why the hell wouldn't she have thought to...why not tell me! Was I such a bastard that she was that scared of me that she couldn't do it? No, not Emma...so what the hell had she been thinking? I worried at it as I slammed the last door open and stepped out into the cold air.

I launched myself from the ground, arcing up and around to land on the roof, then slapped a hand down on either converter. The two mushroom-like tops to the pillars were set just close enough I could do that. I sucked down deep breaths and tried to focus. The anger that filled me was only made worse by the fact I knew, I *knew* I should have asked her what was wrong sooner.

"What's up?" Kelly asked me as I paused and slid into the dungeon sense.

"How much of that did you see?"

"All of it, though I think I'm missing something."

"She's terrified of ice, and it's a fucking snowstorm. She was building the courage to open herself to the storm and suck its power down, for me, because I told her we needed this and didn't think to ask her about it."

"And..." she asked, confused.

"And it's not goddamn fear—it's her affinities being shit for this!" I thundered, my anger roiling in me. "If she'd done it, she'd have died in seconds. And the storm would have gone nuts, fed on her life force as the ice cored her out. She'd have been killed all because I didn't think to explain the plan and do the little goddamn checks!"

"Matt, she knew what you were doing. She's been through enough lessons that she damn well knew and she—"

"And she was still going to do it," I growled. "She knew it was likely to kill her, and she was terrified and she was still going to say nothing and do it because she knew we needed it!"

"Matt—"

"No!" I snapped. "I was pushing her too hard. I was pushing her and not talking to her as a person—just as a goddamn useful device, a dungeon-born, a part I needed to get the job done, not a bloody person—and I nearly killed her!" I sucked in a deep breath and jerked my head up, staring into the falling snow. The wildly crashing winds overhead sent it in all directions as distant howls rose, and I glared into the heart of the small storm above me.

I barely managed to choke off the stream of words before I said something I'd regret, and instead stomped down the emotions I was feeling.

"Fuck it, you want a job done right?" I muttered to myself. "You do it yourself."

With that, and ignoring the sense of Kelly and Aly hovering nearby, Griffiths and distantly others, I grabbed every fragment of mana I had, and I dove into myself, heading for my core.

Lightning danced and wove through me, roiling back and forth. And yet the madness of the storm externally, as it built second by second, was nothing to the one that I felt internally.

I could hear the distant undead screaming, the cries, even the moans and gnashing of teeth, the clacking of bone on bone…and bone on stone.

I could feel the cries building, and yet I conversely heard less and less of them, as the wind around me built to a howl and the temperature plummeted.

Inside, I tore along my mana channels at a horrific speed. The rings that I used to compress and contain, as well as purify my mana channels, squeezed me even tighter as I flashed through them, and the partially completed divine gates shimmered and seemed to stretch out as I passed them as well.

When I burst from the final channel into my core, I stared for a few seconds, getting ready as all around me I felt the storm roiling.

My core was no longer a spinning star made up of hundreds, possibly thousands of individual spires that reached out from the central vertical one of pure mana.

Where before they each reached out, dipping into the sea of passing mana and sucked free their own kind, drinking it down greedily, now in their place was a burning, spinning core of molten gold.

It was pierced through by spikes—spikes that crackled with power and that dragged in that same mana. But where once a hundred or a thousand spires of equal length had once stood, now four greater ones stood out—well, three in fact…three that were close to the same length. They were Lightning, Thunder, and Storm.

By far the longest of the three was Lightning. But even as I looked at Thunder, I realized that in forcing them into place, I'd increased my affinities through a kind of mad pressurized injection, one that could have just as easily killed me.

Rereading the original "congratulations" message about forming my Divine core, I winced, seeing that line about *"Through extreme methods, instead of meditation, you have surged ahead, scouring your path clean and..."*

Clearly the extreme methods paid off, considering I was now able to use Thunder at eighty-seven percent, which I'd been nowhere near before, but still...

That Lightning was at a hundred and seventeen percent, Storm at a hundred and seven, and then Thunder at a solid eighty-seven was incredible.

As soon as I saw them and knew it, I realized how close I'd come to massively fucking up. And then, as I saw the wobbling, unstable spin? I knew I wasn't out of the woods yet.

The first spire was Lightning for me now, no longer "pure" which had been there. And then, moving down, if that was at "north" essentially, then the other two were slightly forward and at southwest and southeast.

The fourth "leg" of the spires was the weakest of the four. Although at first glance it seemed they were all massive, it was significantly shorter.

Cyclone stood at fifty-three percent. I desperately needed that to grow—I knew instinctively—seeing the unstable wobble that having such a shorter "main" leg was imparting.

I could feel the ice, the snow, and the storm crashing in all around me now, even as the two converters sucked in power and made it available to me.

Lightning danced from one spire of the core. Thunder rolled on another. The pressure that came from the storm built, and I winced, realizing that this, in part, was my issue, and the storm itself caressed me.

Inside and out, I felt the conflicting, complementing forces building. I forced breaths out, trying to equalize the pressure that was filling me...before cursing.

I wasn't strong enough to manage the mana I could sense was coming. The storm was...it was too much, too much for me right now. As soon as I realized what was happening and that I needed to use all these forms to balance out my evolution, I felt the change as another prompt appeared.

Your current evolutionary position is: *Thunderstorm*: 47%

Increase your capacity to reach the next level of Evolution.

39% > 47%...

I blinked, then stifled a curse. Why had it risen? Well, that was fucking obvious, wasn't it. I'd learned something important.

Why hadn't it risen *much*? Well, that was obvious as well: I'd learned a truth, but I'd not put it into practice yet.

I drew a deep breath and reached out, dragging my mana up from my core and out into the world all around me. First, I mentally formed it into a net, one that was entirely made of Air mana. As I fed it out, it was like I was unreeling ten spools of wire, or whips.

They were drawn out into the world almost joyously. The tips flicked out into the darkened sky and then were drawn up to vanish into the clouds above.

As they went, I saw other forms of mana being briefly illuminated. Fragments of Air and more flashed past close enough that the pure Air mana felt it, and it tried to connect.

Fragments danced and spun in eddies all around the lines that extended. Then as they continued to vanish into the darkest parts of the sky, now lost to my eyes but still visible to my mind, I took a deep breath and flexed my fingers, imagining the streams of air as lines of a net, one that was suddenly full of branching tributaries.

Each of the lines, ten in all—one from each fingertip—suddenly released a single line, two-thirds along their length, and extending to the right, unwinding and spooling out.

The wind whipped around, my own Air mana both adding to the strength of the storm, and yet remaining separate…a rider instead of the horse.

Long seconds passed until the first streamer touched the next line along, and the link was formed. Less than a heartbeat after the first, the next connected as well. From there, it was a blur, the connections forming in no time at all.

Some lines had two or more connections; others had none. But that was fine.

The fractal nature of mana was helping as here and there more mana stuck to the pure Air that I was holding out.

To my eyes, all of existence had now been revealed to be impregnated with mana to my eyes. And as the storm broke above me—the howling wind and the frantic sleet, the driving hail and the swirling snow fell—I saw more.

The storm had picked up ten thousand different forms of mana in its travels, and until it blew itself out—the Air combining with too many other forms to continue to blow—it would continue to collect them. Just one in a series of storms that battered this isle over and over at this time of the year.

Now, with my net in place, as a second branching line slid out from the main lines again, higher, reaching and bonding over and over again, the pattern repeating, I started to feed.

The Air mana was the easiest to collect, Air to Air without issue. Then came the Water.

More and more the storm was simply that: a veritable lake of Water that was suspended over literal miles of storm. It in turn was contaminated, that Water bonded to Air, to Earth, to Death.

Ice mana was, I now knew, simply "dead Water"—Water with the life-giving heat of the Fire snuffed out.

That meant that as more and more of the Air was caught and stripped away, the other half of the mana in question was left stuck to my net.

As Water and Air mixes were broken, the Air was fed into the net, elongating and helping it to stretch and continue to grow. The Water more and more frequently caught up with Death, and now, having lost the Air mana that had kept it in motion, stuck to the net, slowly seeping downward.

The Air strings grew slowly more and more visible. Ice formed across them; Water ran along and over them in building waves. And then, at last, came the real power.

The updraft of air, the cold front, meeting the limited heat, the power of the storm and its wildness, was all in a delicate balance, one that was virtually on the verge of explosion at the best of times. And then, as my net reached as far as I believed I could hold it and still feed this form out?

I unleashed it.

Lightning is Air and Fire. A large enough level of Fire to the Air mix would result in a literal firestorm, but there was no need for that, not here.

No, what I needed was the literal power of the *storm*. I needed it. Although I could, with only a little nudge, spark it over the edge into a much more massive storm, I suddenly realized, for now what I needed was that power itself.

I needed to rip its beating heart out and feed my fledgling dungeon on it.

I started to force the air around me, twisting so that the winds that had danced and surged in all directions, now clear to me as a pattern, were easy to manipulate into a new rhythm. And as soon as I saw it, I did it.

Spiraling around in a faster and faster rotation, the howl of the wind grew deafening, screaming past. In seconds, the slipstream was enough that even here, in the eye of the intensifying storm, I could sense it.

The snow that had been building all around me, resting atop my battered armor and forming a creaking layer across my arms, cold-welding my gauntleted hands to the top of the converters, began to slide sideways.

It broke away, as on all sides the winds began to rage with increasing power. I felt the much more limited Fire that was all around, in infinitesimal specks, begin to match up as well.

This was my focus, as the ice and wind rose, as the water streamed from what were rapidly becoming webs of glittering power, flowing into the walls of the cyclone that built around me. The Fire rose and I dug deep, augmenting it with my own mana. The first flare of Lightning sparked to life, illuminating the storm-wreathed interior. I fed streams of pure Fire mana along the heart of my connections, unleashing it in sudden bursts that flared and filled the darkness.

I opened my eyes, staring at the webs of power that led from me into the storm as I felt myself lifted from the roof, sucked upward.

More strings and streamers slid free, arcing out to touch more of the net, creating an incredible, wonderful, *terrible* lattice of potential power.

Jez Cajiao

Bones flashed past and fragments of the undead. They were small at first, but as I climbed into the center of the storm, so, too, did they. I felt the others there, watching me. Their silence was all that I could hope for, as there was no space in my mind to help, to respond or to do anything else, as I shifted the nets back and forth. I felt the storm sucking the Fire from me, my Lightning building in strength, even as I felt the tingling caress of all the other forms so close by.

Seconds turned to minutes. It reached a crescendo; power rumbled all around me as the storm reached its apex. Then I did what I knew I had to do—what I had felt so many times before, and what I should never have tried, was my mind not so filled with the storm's majesty as it was.

I flexed the strings of Air surrounded by Water, the Fire that poured through them, the Earth that had been broken free and fed into forming Thunder mana. I arced my back and the tendrils of power flexed in rhythm. My hair blew this way and that, and that stupid, stupid cloak snapped in the wind...

Then I ripped it all *free*.

CHAPTER FORTY-TWO

Hundreds of lines whipped backward into me, every one of them with tens of thousands of fragments attached. The sudden overwhelming flood of mana, like a spiderweb skein of potential and possibilities, was torn down into my body, and I dropped.

I flew as fast as I could. The few dozen meters I'd flown up in my rapture was almost enough to prove my undoing, as the sudden vacuum of mana tore the heart out of the storm, creating a secondary effect that dragged more and more mana inward.

The forms raced in toward the center. The rolling booms of Thunder formed and Lightning exploded inward. Fractal patterns illuminated the land for miles on all sides.

I landed hard; the roof buckled under the impact. I slammed both hands down atop the pair of converters, my body now blazing like a fallen star with the massed mana that I possessed.

This was it—the most dangerous part, the part that could make it all a failure, or a win beyond our dreams.

I opened wide and I screamed. The fragmented mana inside me, filling my channels like the worst sludge imaginable, burst forward. A vortex of power thrust upward, displacing the incoming mana, and formed a new crescendo of impacting mana...

Then, with the last of my mana, with all the mana all around me in flaring, battling confusion, torn asunder and running wild...I formed a single path of power, a point from the manically writhing storm's heart high overhead...and I separated it all out and down, leading directly to me.

For a split second, there was a terrible silence, a void that encompassed me. And then the scattered Fire, Earth, and Air mana coalesced into a thunderbolt that outshone the sun.

It screamed down, crashing into me, pounding into my upturned face, and roared through my mana channels and out.

The Lightning and Storm converters accepted it. They tore it from me in greedy gouts. A surging power that should have vaporized me instead contributed to my growth as I sensed more than saw the counter of my evolution blurring.

Power seemed to stream through me forever, and conversely, it was over in a heartbeat. The incoming nuclear barrage dropped to a mere tsunami, then a flood, before finally a trickle.

I blinked and crashed to my knees. Steam rose from me; my mana bar glowed with a fierce blue-white light shot through with gold. I stared at my hands, where they were braced against the roof below.

The tiles shimmered with absorbed heat; the plastic ran like the water that cascaded to the ground on all sides.

I blinked, seeing the last of it as it fell, the rumble as a literal lake's worth of water rained on all sides from a now cloudless sky.

It thundered to the ground; waves roared in all directions away from the heart of the storm and me...and *still* I glowed.

I could feel it: my mana, my power surging, bounding around inside of me...too much for me to hold, and yet not enough to make a real difference as the dungeon on all sides around me screamed with change.

I focused, my armor battered and broken, my sword invested, but not yet awakened. I hissed as the power rose in me, a hundred thousand mana and more surging.

The white and gold flooded from me into it. The blue permeated my body and left me shaking.

The power roared through me and into my equipment, and I did the only thing I could, triggering my Soul Forge ability, and using it to feed some of the power into the blade, using the pathways it opened for me, and then, risking it all, I offered a fragment of my own soul up as well, creating a deeper bond.

I saw it then, a latticework of potential, even as the power bled free of me. I gasped for breath, the world around me whiting out in a flood of power.

The sword.

I needed the sword.

I focused on it, feeling it strapped to my back. What I'd believed was the maximum that the weapon could handle suddenly became clear to me as a fragment only.

I had no time, no time to create anything special, not that would be planned or considered. Instead, I poured everything I had, including ten points of Divine essence, into the blade. It shimmered with the pressure, before I finally pitched forward, crashing to the roof beneath my fingers, and laid there for long seconds, panting.

My breath was hoarse, my heart thundering, and the roof all around me felt...rubbery, soft and pliable in a way I was really sure that roofs shouldn't be. I forced myself up, blinking in shock. What I'd believed was me losing touch with the world through my own power was revealed as anything but.

The white light that had risen on all sides was the dungeon, the forming of the southern dungeon's defenses, and my God, had there been more mana than I thought.

I struggled to my feet, the roof giving slightly under me, and I forced myself into the air. I hovered a few feet from the surface, staring out across the steadily revealed citadel, before letting loose a sigh.

We'd done it.

What had been the roof of the main customer service building for the Eurotunnel was no longer plastic and glass, with a little artistically placed metal and stone only where it was unable to be avoided.

No longer was the area between it and the distant tunnel entrance mud and churned earth.

No more was the roof a mere twenty meters above the ground.

Now I hovered above a building that had surged upward while I'd been lost within my own personal daze of mana forms.

The citadel—for that was what it was now, a citadel in truth—stood thirty meters from the ground at its highest point. The building was square where I stood, but below that, where once the walls had simply risen in a straight line, a blocky building with a slightly overhanging top, now a stone-walled cube that would have been loved by any medieval knight loomed.

That was, in turn, encircled by thick walls that soared ten meters into the air, with a simple path that wound around it on the inside, with outward-leaning buttresses and crenelations that would make it a beast to scale.

The building was simple, with almost nothing in the way of flourishes, carvings, or improvements that any architect would have demanded. But the one thing that the citadel did bring to the world was strength.

I could feel the thickness of the walls from here. They'd been reinforced by meters of solid stone, clad in steel. And that wasn't all.

There'd been no space for the traps that Drak had suggested, not in the highly limited budget that we had available. But what there had been enough for was the nexus gate, set into a wall, facing out toward the singular main gate that in turn exited from the citadel.

It was over half done. And wonder of wonders, there'd been enough to build two of the winding paths to drain the undead as well.

I checked, and found that the crystals were gone, not a single fragment remained, and the dungeon core itself was shivering from the overload and shock.

Kelly, when I reached out to her was…well, she was almost manic, her mind and Aly's the same, practically fried by the backlash of power.

Checking that they were all right, and carefully disentangling myself from the pair as they word-vomited about how incredible the power had been, I reached out to Griffiths.

He was on the ground, cradling his head in his hands and panting hoarsely. All around him, the others were the same—dozens of people who had been shocked to the core by the literal power that I had just torn out of the storm and through the dungeon.

Jez Cajiao

On all sides were stunned and reeling people. Before I permitted myself to speak to the others, to go to them and accept the cheers and the disbelief—as well as what I hoped would be a little more cheerfulness than they'd exhibited earlier—I allowed myself a single notification.

Your current evolutionary position is: *Thunderstorm*: 74%

Increase your capacity to reach the next level of Evolution.

47% > 74%...

You have plateaued. You know the change that you must enact, and can no longer evolve until this change has been made.

Be ready, Thunderstorm, for once this evolution has begun, it cannot be stopped nor reversed.

Be ready for what is to come...

With that particularly ominous and clearly directed message read, I dismissed the prompt, and then headed inside for an overdue talk about magic with Emma.

I landed by the single door, but decided to check the nexus gate before entering, seeing as it was only a few meters to the side.

It was recessed into the wall, the section around it clearly cut out already—by Aly, if I had to guess. Although it gave the room for an arched portal sunk about eight inches into the wall, currently the stones that formed its outer frame were little more than knee height.

They were laced with various veins of precious metals; runes slowly sank into the rock as a gentle trickle of mana continued into it. I paused, tracing one of them with a finger, curious, before shaking my head and vowing not to allow myself to be so easily distracted.

The stones looked half melted, almost as if it'd been formed from molten rock, with cobblestone pressed into it, then allowed to cool. The running paths that slid between each stone lit with faint script that shimmered with the light as they were seemingly carved by invisible hands.

Each stone as it was completed was ringed in a spiraling script that started at its heart and then ran out until it reached the passing "streams" of semi-molten rock, where alternating scripts took over.

All in all, it was both fascinating and concerning, mainly because it showed that there was an entire language of magic that we had absolutely no clue about. And that it could be used to form linkages across space?

Most of the tech that we'd seen or had hinted at wasn't that far in advance of humanity's. Sure, it tended to use mana-based crystals instead of electricity, but that was a small change, and we were already factoring in those differences.

This, though? It was an order of magnitude different, and that was...concerning.

Mainly because I still harbored a deep-seated and oh so fucking cherished desire to rip the throats out of the fucking Cinthians.

Dismissing that and the tiny growth of the portal, I turned my back on it and headed for the door, checking and finding that Kelly and Aly were still a bit out of it. The pair had fallen back on a list of jobs they'd made earlier, going step by step to ensure that the little mana they had left was spent as frugally as possible.

I smiled, wondering just what state they looked in Newcastle, remembering how frazzled Aly had been the first time I'd done this, and moved through the main doors, passing a handful of figures venturing outside.

More than anything, the fact that five minutes or so ago there'd been a literal blizzard building, along with a typhoon or cyclone or whatever summoned by me, and that now the dungeon was humming with life, the snow gone for at least a mile in all directions and the skies clear, was madness of the highest order.

I jogged up the stairs, passing a couple of spaced-out and stunned bystanders, before finally finding Emma sitting with Jo in the makeshift hospital.

"Hey." I offered, stepping in and closing the door behind me, seeing the way that Emma wasn't willing to meet my eyes. "How's the patient?" I asked Jo.

"I'm fine, which is more than you'll be if you try talking over my head," Emma muttered, making Jo smile and me sigh.

"You're just such a little bundle of joy, you know that?" I asked her.

Almost despite herself, she smiled, then straightened. "I know what I did wrong," she said instead, and I nodded.

"Tell me."

"I should have told you about the issue with the Ice."

"So you knew about it?" I asked her, and she looked at me like I was an idiot. "Talk to me, for fuck's sake, Emma," I growled.

"I knew it was going to hurt," she admitted. "I thought I could handle it, and then when I was up there…"

"It felt like you were drowning without touching anything?" I asked.

She shook her head. "The cold was already in me, and I just couldn't make my mana move," she said slowly. "It was like even my mana was frozen, and there was nothing I could do to get it to come out, to do as I needed it to do."

"For me"—I slid onto a chair, shaking my head at Jo as she made a subtle "do you want me to leave" gesture—"it was Water. I was terrified of it. Had it at four percent at first, I think. Damn, I can't even remember…seems like forever ago."

"How were you scared of Water but liked storms?" Emma asked, and I shrugged.

"I don't know, if I'm honest," I admitted. "Hell, it doesn't even make a lot of sense to me right now, I mean—" I scratched my chin, thinking. "You been on holiday much?" I asked, deciding to take it from a different angle.

"As much as I could afford," she said. "Had a job in Dubai for a year, and saved up all year so that we could go away for as much of the winter as possible."

493

She smiled. "One advantage of these…" She tapped her chest. "Means we could go out whenever we wanted and not spend anything besides taxis home. There's always some guy wanting to buy you a drink at the bar, especially when they see you're twins."

"Okay, so you spent much time in the sea?" I asked, and she nodded again. "Right, well, I *hated* the water. Just plain hated it, like to a level that I can't explain. Not drinking it, not bathing—all that stuff is totally fine. Go in the shower and wash my body? All cool. Same for the bath…can be nice and relaxing. Water runs through my hair? Little feeling in my gut like I ate something that doesn't agree with me. If it runs down my face?" I shook myself.

"It made me want to vomit every time, like really lose it all, throwing up my goddamn toenails, that kind of sickness," I admitted, before smiling at the look of confusion on her face. "Now, I went to Crete not long ago with Chris, and I'm laying back in the water. He's talked me into going in deep enough that I'm up to my shoulders, and I'm all right…not happy, but okay, doing my best to keep calm."

She nodded, and I glanced at Jo, who was also following along.

"So there I am, and Chris…as much as he plays the big dumb fucker, you know that's an act, right?" Jo nodded, while Emma was clearly unsure, and I snorted. "Before he was the size he is now, he played different games to make it seem he wasn't very bright. Truth is he's an absolute legend. See, he knew about my issues with water, always has. We've been mates forever. He made me go out, and stood by my side.

"He helped to support me, to float, and then propped me up—making sure that nobody could see, so that I wasn't embarrassed as well—and then he supported me for a few minutes to just float there, in the sea, staring up at the sun." I shook my head. "Two weeks we were there, and for an hour a day, a few minutes at a time, he made me do that, him supporting me constantly, so that I wasn't as scared. So I could try and get over things. *That's* the kind of a friend he is. Never once mentioned it ever again—no taking the piss, no wind-ups…nothing. He knew it was a genuine issue for me, and he just helped as best he could."

"Right?" Emma said, not understanding.

"The thing is, that when I sat and worked with my mana, and I focused on that, on feeling it, on working through the feeling and fighting to accept that I damn well need the bloody Water? I improved my affinity." I smiled, seeing the confused look on her face.

"That's possible?" she asked.

I nodded. "It's not easy," I warned her. "I had to find the parts where the Water and I matched that I didn't freak out over, find the points of commonality, then where I enjoyed it. There must be some for you, right?"

"I…" She looked embarrassed; then, seeing we were waiting, she sighed and nodded. "We went away, the four of us to Lapland. Met Santa…the works. Then we were supposed to go skiing, and I faked hurting my leg to get out of it. Ended up staying in a lodge for the entire week while the others were skiing, relaxing in the hot tub and watching them fall over out the window."

"Why'd you go if you hate the cold so much?" Jo asked softly.

"Jenn loved it." Emma shrugged. "She wanted to go, so we went. She doesn't mind the heat, but she's generally happier in the pool or at the swim-up bars. I'm a full-on sun worshipper, stretched out in the hottest part of the day with my tits out and telling the sun to have a go if it thinks it's hard enough."

"And getting people to buy you drinks?" Jo asked knowingly, getting a grin from Emma at that.

"They cost me four grand, and I probably saved that in about a month of having them done." She winked, making me shake my head and look away as she deliberately made her chest bounce.

"I don't need to know." I sighed. "Women like you cost me a fortune."

"Hey, if you're stupid enough to buy me a drink, I'll take it." She shrugged. "We all know it's a game. You're buying us drinks to try and talk us into how nice a guy you are or whatever, interest us with how rich or cool you are. We're there for the free drinks. If you manage to talk us into hanging around long enough, maybe you get sex, maybe you don't. Maybe we make you buy us dinner first. Maybe we're not interested or we're just looking for a friend." She shrugged again. "Most of the time, though, it's all part of the game. You want sex, and we want attention...and not to waste our money if you're stupid enough to pay for everything."

"You make it sound so transactional." Jo shook her head.

"It is." Emma looked almost surprised at Jo's attitude. "They want something, and so do we."

"What about your husband?" Jo asked, and Emma shrugged.

"Sure, we love each other, but it started out as me liking his looks and his biceps, and he liked my tits and ass. A few days into fucking and partying and sure, there's something a little more building. A few months? Great, we fell in love. At first, though? I wanted attention, some dick, and not to pay for my drinks and dinner. He wanted to fuck me, and was willing to buy me those drinks and dinner. We both got what we wanted."

"Damn, that's cold." I shook my head. "And that brings us back to the point of this little conversation, though."

"Oh?" she asked.

I nodded. "We need to sort your fear of the cold out," I said. "Or at least lessen it."

"You think it's that easy?" She sighed. "Believe me, it's not, all right?"

"There's ways," I assured her. "Okay, now you're a Bloodwytch, right?"

"Yeah?"

"Did you get any class quests?" I asked her, and she winced.

"Maybe?"

"Emma, there's no time to be coy. Did you get a class quest?" I repeated.

"Two." She sounded annoyed. "Two seconds...I'll look for them."

Taking a few minutes to find them, she hesitated again and then started to read them out.

Congratulations!

You have begun your journey as a Bloodwytch! To fully harness the power of blood magic, you must master its various aspects. Continue to research, experiment, and create to unlock the true potential of your class.

Remember, the path of a Bloodwytch is one paved with sacrifice, be that your own, or that of another...

Complete this quest to receive a boost to your Blood and Storm affinities.

- **Offensive Blood spell: 0/1**

- **Utility Blood spell: 0/1**

- **Blood Ward spell: 0/1**

Example: Create a new utility-based blood magic spell that doesn't solely focus on dealing damage. This could be a spell for tracking, information gathering, or manipulating the environment using blood.

Upon completion of this quest, you will gain:

- **+10% to Blood affinity**

- **+5% to Storm affinity**

- **Unlocked: Blood Resonance passive ability (Increases the potency of blood magic when using your own blood)**

The second one was what I was looking for, more or less, but I had to admit, the first was cool, if slightly fucking terrifying.

Congratulations, Storm Caster!

You have demonstrated your potential to harness the raw power of the tempest. To truly master the storms, you must expand your repertoire of spells and deepen your connection to its elements.

Continue to research, experiment, and create to unlock the true potential of your class.

Remember, the storm bows to those who prove their worth...

Complete this quest to receive a significant boost to your elemental affinities.

- **Lightning spell: 0/1**

- **Wind spell: 0/1**

- **Precipitation spell: 0/1**

- **Area Control spell: 0/1**

Create three new spells that harness different aspects of storm magic. Focus on controlling winds, manipulating precipitation, and affecting a wider area with your storm powers.

Upon completion of this quest, you will gain:

- **A total of 60% increase to your affinities, which you can distribute among up to four different elemental affinities of your choice.**

- **Unlocked: Storm Synergy passive ability (Increases the potency of combination spells using multiple storm elements)**

She'd shared it as much as she could remember. And that the description and style of the prompts was as different as it was from mine made me wonder whether she was reading them accurately or not, but fuck it, it gave me what we needed at the end.

"You've still got access to both of these quests, right?" I asked. "You've not cancelled them, or completed them yet?"

"When the hell would I have the time to complete them?" she asked me in confusion. "Matt, we've had a day here or there, that's it. Since I found 'safety' with you guys, all I've done is run from one fight to another. There's never enough time!"

"Ask me for anything but time," I quoted, then shook my head at the look on her face. "Never mind, it's an old quote. I can't even remember where it's from. Look, I know what you're feeling, but believe me, you need to make the time, and I say that as someone that occasionally finds an hour here or there and that's it."

"I'll try," she said doubtfully.

"You will," I agreed, then smiled. "Mainly because you and I need you to, and right goddamn *now*."

"Now?" She blinked.

"Right now," I repeated. "You and me, we're going to get you the basics of some new spells in place, and then you're going to spend those affinity points on improving yourself to the point you're useful."

"Well, thank you so much for that." She rolled her eyes. "So what you're saying is that I'm useless now?"

"Nope, you're great and all, but that you're totally incapable of casting the one spell that might really help us out unless it warms up? That's an issue," I said. "Not going to sugarcoat it. You having a storm management and calling spell is something that we desperately need. That you've got it but can't use it? That's not just annoying, that's a fucking waste."

"Great, well, that makes me feel even better about myself," Emma snarled, throwing her arms up in frustration. "I'll just get over myself then, right?"

"Yeah, you will," I agreed. "Emma, if I was talking to Jenn or any one of a hundred other people, I'd approach this differently. But you're a hard-ass and we both know you prefer the direct route, so this is where it is. We need the power to defeat the undead. I can maybe—and I fucking mean maybe—build enough power to fight their leaders head-on, one against two of them. And bear in mind, they're supposedly as powerful as I am, or near enough.

"I *might* be able to fight them alone...I might not. But you and the others don't have the kind of powers that are needed to go toe-to-toe with them. Not yet."

"So it's all on you," she said.

"Maybe," I admitted. "Maybe not. Because for me to be able to go all out and stand a chance against them, I need to be out of the rest of this fight. I need to hold myself back to be ready for them, because you sure as shit know they're going to do everything they can to make sure that I'm at my weakest before we fight each other.

"They're going to throw every single body they have at us, to try and overwhelm us. They're going to make sure I've used every drop of mana I have, and they're not going to show up until then," I finished.

"So what do you want me to do?" she asked after a brief pause.

"I want you to fight by my side," I said clearly. "Emma, you're a pain in the ass. You're miserable half the time and acerbic the rest, with a double helping of challenging shite thrown in for good measure. And fuck, it pisses me off saying this, but you're also the one person I've met in all of this with anywhere near the potential that I have for the Storm. I need you, the dungeon needs you, and if you want a chance to ascend, this is it."

"What?" she asked, clearly caught off guard.

"You have the potential to be as strong, if not stronger than me, Emma," I said. "You need the fucking discipline, you need the push and the goddamn desire to be all that you could be, rather than just sitting back and just doing what you have to."

"I do more than what I have to!" she snapped.

"Really?" I asked. "Prove it—prove you've got what it takes."

"Then what?" She asked, "What do I get?"

"Besides a chance at being immortal?" I cocked my head to the side. "Besides the chance to keep your sister, those you love and your friends safe you mean? Yeah, I can see that might not be enough to motivate you, so you tell me." I shrugged and waved my hands, anger surging in me. "Come on, Emma, you tell me what it'll cost to buy your help!"

"Fuck you, Matt," she snapped, turning on her heel and storming out.

"Fuck you too," I snapped back, before shaking my head and holding my hand up as Jo opened her mouth. "I know," I ground out. "God's sake, I know, Jo. I need her."

"Then give her a minute to sort herself out," Jo said softly. "Matt, I've got no idea why the pair of you piss each other off the way you do, but fuck me, you really do rile each other just by breathing wrong."

"She's always out for herself," I snarled, before scrubbing at my face with both hands and sighing. "Gods, I know I need her, but why the hell couldn't it be Jenn who had the affinity? Or one of the brothers?"

"Because they'd never have manifested it, Matt," Jo said. "We're who we are for a reason. You and Emma are two of the hardest and most volatile people I've ever met, and you're as alike as two peas in a pod."

"I'm nothing like her," I said coldly.

"Matt, if you both had to speak through a voice synthesizer in a dark room, I'd not be able to tell you apart," she snapped right back. "The difference is that you have the dungeon and you have a fuckload more of earlier trauma on your soul, I'd bet. Her?

"We've talked about it. When she was young, she and her sister were dressed up and made to play at pageants and apply for advertising jobs, right up until her dad got so stoned he beat an agent for not getting a contract. That meant they, as they were kids, were suddenly just as blacklisted as the dad.

"That meant less money coming in, and because he was an addict by then, who needed his fix, that meant less food on the table. They went from having anything and everything they wanted to being the breadwinners of the family at a very early age.

"As soon as they could escape him, they did, but they were still known in the industry for having him attached. That meant fewer chances and them having to work harder, even as kids, constantly worrying that he'd show up and fuck it all up."

"I thought you said less trauma," I muttered, hating the thought of two little kids dealing with that.

"They had a damn good life at times as well...don't get me wrong. All the holidays, all the toys...then nothing. A feast or a famine, one where they either spent the money and got everything they wanted, or they found he'd beaten them to it and was coked off his tits. The easy jobs dried up by the time they were in their teens, and the only work, thanks to his actions and his aggression, was work

499

they weren't willing to take. Porno shoots were arranged, *by him*, and when they refused to star in them at literally sixteen, with him trying to lie that they were eighteen, they turned their back on him and the whole world.

"Feast or famine, Matt—they grew up hard. Jenn held onto the last of their optimism, but Emma didn't. She instead did everything she could to protect her sister and shield her from the harsher realities. I don't know what happened to break Emma but knowing what I do of her, it was bad.

"That's a hint of why she's the way she is. You, from what you've said, were orphaned and put into care. Some of the homes you went to were bad, some were good. In the beginning and at the end, you were loved. They weren't. Instead, they were a commodity. And so when you ask Emma why she's as cold as she is? That's why."

"Shit." I sighed. "I need to talk to her, but…"

"But you both rile each other up, all the time. As I said, Matt, if you were made to sound the same and I couldn't see you, I couldn't tell you apart. You've both had a shitload of trauma and some good, but it doesn't surprise me in the slightest that the most fucked-up people I know are the ones with similar powers."

"Yeah, well…" I sighed. "Shit, Jo, we need her, and handing this kind of power to her scares the shit out of me."

"And it scares her as well…more than you know, I think," Jo said. "She's the same as you are in so many ways. I think I know you enough to know that you're doing this for the right reasons, and not that you want power."

"And yet the first question she asked when I told her that there was a chance to get this power was to ask what she got in return." I groaned, rubbing at my eyes.

"It came out wrong," Emma said from the door, in a quiet voice.

"What?" I whipped around, having missed her return entirely.

"It came out wrong, okay?" she snapped, before taking a deep breath. "Matt, what I *meant* wasn't 'what's in it for me.' It was what do I get? What do I become? You're the Lord of the Storm…so what? What do I become? I'm not taking the role of concubine, all right?"

That last was said with an attempt at a smile, one that failed, and I returned it as well as I could.

"I wouldn't expect you to," I said. "I'm sorry, Emma. I thought you meant…"

"I know," she admitted. "That's why I was so angry. Not because of what you said, but because I'd said it so wrong and then… Fuck's sake, Matt, what's the deal, okay? What do you need from me and what would I become? I don't want to be like you. Sorry, but it's true. I don't want a dungeon. I don't want to be the one that everyone looks to, who everyone just trusts will sort it all out. I don't want to be a god."

"You think I do?" I asked.

She shook her head. "At first, I did. Now? Not so much." She moved to sit on the ground near me again and I sat too, as calmly as I could.

"Emma, you've got the potential—I think—to become a Storm Lord, or maybe a Storm Lady…I don't know, I don't get the whole thing myself. Sometimes I think I've got it figured out and then bang, the exact opposite. Anything I do seems to change the rules every friggin' week, and for all we know, we're only understanding a fraction of it. If we had a fairy, maybe that would be different, and we're working on alliances to get us information more than anything else." I took a deep breath.

"I'm rambling." I sighed. "I'm stressed, I'm tired, and I just had the power equivalent of a nuclear reactor run through me. And I'm sorry, Emma. How about we just start again, please?" I asked, and she nodded.

"I'm going to leave you kids to it," Jo said with a smile. "Anything you need me to do before I go…messages to pass on?"

"Tell Griffiths, Kelly, and Aly that we need to harvest every point of mana we can from the undead," I said quickly, relaxing and checking the system, only to find the ladies were still in full-on manic mode. "When they calm down, explain that I need more converters on the roof here, two more Storm, one more Lightning, and a pair of Thunderstorm and Cyclone ones." I took a deep breath, then went on. "And we need a Water in here…"

"Not here. This is my triage room." She shook her head.

"Fine, next door. And an Ice." That made Emma's eyes open, and I nodded at the look. "We're going to practice, and they're all important. Once those are done, we don't need anything else until the fight is going full-blown, so leave us out of anything else unless you really, *really* need us, okay?"

"Are you going to summon the converters…?" Jo asked, because obviously I could at any time.

"No," I said. "We're going to be practicing, and I don't have the time to fuck about with the levels of mana we have or working out the levels that are coming in. They can do them when they can afford to."

"How important are they?" she asked.

"Right after the nexus gate."

"So…more important than troops?"

"Pretty much," I said. "They'll have to assess and see what they decide. I've got no clue how many dungeon-born have been summoned, so I leave that up to them."

She nodded and then left.

I bit my lip, then turned back to Emma. "I'm sorry for pissing you off."

"I'm sorry for being a bitch," she replied. "I thought we were starting again?"

"We are."

"Then I wasn't a bitch and you didn't piss me off." She made a throwing away motion with one hand. "So, what's the plan?"

"Meditation and private lessons."

501

Jez Cajiao

"Well, when someone offered me that last time, my husband wasn't happy, so just to be clear, there's no 'open wide and suck out the magic juices,' right?"

She said it with a grin, and realizing that it was a joke and an olive branch rolled into one, I smiled in return.

"Not at all…" I pretended to be shocked. "Though you'll need to be naked, bent over, and touching your toes…"

"Ha!" She snorted.

"Seriously, this is going to be a bit hard to explain, mainly because I barely understand what I'm doing as well, but here goes." I smiled. "So…"

CHAPTER FORTY-THREE

"Now spin it!" I called to her, standing on the far side of the room. A gout of flames rolled from my right hand as a spinning localized storm in her left hand whipped my flame apart. "Spin it faster!"

"I'm trying!" she snarled.

She really was.

A full day had passed, maybe longer, and the pair of us were battling thundering mana migraines—not from draining ourselves to the dregs as I'd brought them about in the past, but instead because I'd made us both work with what we had for hours at a time.

The effort had paid off, though, as her mana pool was so small and mine was so needed, that we'd literally been alternating using meditation to refill and then going again since Jo had left the room.

She—with my help—had managed to get another lightning spell (Cascade of Crackling Whispers), a precipitation spell (Weeping Heavens), and an area control spell (Hidden Water's Rising) all down in short order.

It was the fourth and final spell that was causing her the delay. The wind was fighting her, and try as I might, I couldn't get her to manipulate it right, until we introduced an element of real risk.

It didn't sit well with me, but as she pointed out, at some point you had to get in the ring and spar with a real opponent.

I had lessened my fire spell as far as I could make it, and as near as I could tell it was a very, *very* weak version of Dante's Dragon's Breath.

Essentially, I was creating a flame and then pushing it out from my palm in a sort of flamethrower effect.

I'd created the spell deliberately weak for training, and although it could still give a nasty burn, there was little chance of more than that.

I also had plans for an evolution of the spell that would bring a massive improvement to it, but I didn't dare play with that now.

So, instead, I was basically vomiting a thin blast of fire from my right palm, and she was constraining it with a tornado in her own, one that seemed to be fighting her all the way.

"It wants to grow!" she snarled. "You know how hard it is to keep it to this size?!"

"Master it!" I snapped. "It's *your* spell, not the other way around! Either control it or stop wasting my time!"

We were both tired, and to make matters worse, the assault on the citadel had begun. Our friends and the dungeon-born were outside, fighting for their lives, and we were in here, playing at magic tricks.

"Fuck it!" she growled. "Here!"

She yanked her hand back, then slammed it forward in a kung-fu counter I almost recognized, before the spinning wind spell suddenly contracted and shot forward.

It hit my flaming extension and snuffed it out in a heartbeat, then picked me up and hurled me into the wall behind. I crashed into it, then right through. Plasterboard fell and bracings cracked as I hit the ground and rolled a dozen meters to hit the wall on the far side.

It had been a general internal wall in a public building. It wasn't meant for hundreds of kilos of semi-armored lunatic to be pitched at it in a fit, and it showed.

I groaned, shoving myself off the wall and to my feet, shaking my head muzzily, but grinning already, raising one hand to wave off the inevitable apologies...and found that I didn't need to.

Emma took one look at me, then went back to reading a prompt that only she could see, smiling wildly.

"Fuck's sake," I muttered, walking over and stepping back through into the smaller room we'd been in. The plasterboard and bracings were a mess; the room I'd been catapulted into was clearly supposed to be a bunkroom, and it was empty, weirdly. Then I shrugged, thinking of course it was—we were at war.

The plaster dust was someone else's problem for now.

"What did you get?" I asked her, and she waved me away absently.

"You okay?" she checked, clearly distracted.

"Yeah."

"Good."

That was all she said, still reading, and I sighed, settling myself on the ground, then stretching back out to lie flat, breathing deeply and focusing on my own quests for magic.

Crafting the signature spells of the Apprentice [Arcanist] is a hurdle that many sapiens fail to clear, as each spell completed not only limits the paths available to the mage for their future growth, but is also correspondingly more difficult.

Choose to create three separate spells of any two of the following categories to reach Apprentice Rank as an [Arcanist]. Alternatively, create a single spell in each category to receive an increased boost to your selected affinities and a bonus magical item:

- **Animation: 1/1**
- **Blood: 0/1**

- **Divination: 0/1**
- **Elemental: 1/1**
- **Enchantment: 0/1**
- **Mental: 1/1**
- **Rune: 0/1**
- **Temporal: 0/1**
- **Spatial: 0/1**
- **Summoning: 0/1**

I'd earned the animation and elemental spells earlier already, and although the fire one was also an elemental one, it was weak as hell, for now.

I'd managed a mental spell as well—not by intention, but instead by literally fucking around as much as possible trying to help Emma with her own spells. I'd found that Energy, which was itself a mixture of Fire and Lightning, was a very different beast.

I'd tried to push my mana out to her, thinking to form a bond to let her use some of my mana, when she was really starting to struggle at one point. I'd discovered the mana form of Energy, as that was in part what I was trying to give her. And then, as I experimented, I ended up discovering a mental spell, as I tried to push it into her.

She got one too, in that she discovered a similar spell, but its defensive variant as she pushed against me.

It really wasn't helpful to either of us at this stage, but her Bloodwytch class was really good at defensive counters like this, considerably better than my own, and it'd counted toward her blood ward requirement, so that was a relief.

Either way, though, I was sick of fucking around with magic in a small room, while outside people fought and died.

When I glanced at her, she blinked and shook her head, before groaning and sliding to sit on the floor again, her back to a still standing wall.

"You all right?" I prompted.

"Yeah," she admitted. "Got the quest...got the sixty percent to spread across my affinities."

"Good!" I exclaimed. "So?"

"So I'm trying to decide where to spend them." She shrugged.

"Ice," I said firmly. "I'm sorry to be a dick, Emma, but you need to level that out at least slightly."

"And I am, okay? But if I dump all my points into that, does that fix it or fuck it?"

"It fixes—" I started, then stopped as she shook her head.

"You said loads of times that we need to plan for the future, right?"

"Yeah?"

"Well, if I invest all sixty percent into my Ice, does that not just make me a one-trick pony, and shit in the summer?"

"Why...?" I started the ask, then shook my head. "You're thinking it'd change your class and you don't want to be a Cryomancer?"

"Well, yeah?" She shrugged. "I've not even started with my blood magic yet, and if I change to it...I mean, I know Kilo's got some kick-ass spells, but it's not really something that I want..." She gestured to the outside world in a general sweeping motion. "I know I need to, but I'm looking at it and trying to figure it all out, because Ice is Death and Water, right?"

"Yeah?"

"Well, my Death is minus four. What if I boosted that by sixty?"

"You'd get fifty-six. But—"

"But if Ice is Death and Water, and my Water is fifty-eight, would that not give me a higher level for Ice *and* Death, if I invest it at the bottom of the triangle? If I invest it in the component, will that not increase the end product automatically, meaning I gain twice as much?"

I opened my mouth...then closed it. "I don't know," I admitted. "I don't know, but I think...okay, fuck it, can you invest a little and then more?"

"What do you mean?"

"I mean can you put, say, ten percent into Death and take it out of the minuses, and then add more in once we've seen the effect? Or is it locked out once you've invested a little in there?"

"I don't know," she said. "Don't you?"

"Emma, I'm making this shit up daily." I groaned. "Believe me, if I knew, I'd tell you."

"Does Dante know?"

I paused, then nodded vigorously. "Good point—dammit, good point!" I closed my eyes and dove into the dungeon sense, then out of the room, searching for him.

"Matt?" Aly groaned, appearing next to me a heartbeat later. "Tell me you're ready to take a hand!"

"No, I need Dante," I admitted. "How bad is it?"

"Bad," she said. "Go to Griffiths, get an update and decide. But Matt, we need you...if not now, then soon. *Very* soon."

For the first time in what felt like forever, I allowed myself to reach out, to open my senses, and I felt it instantly.

The world around us was being drowned in Unlife mana. As I flew up and through the building's walls, I erupted into empty air, before jerking to a halt, staring in horror.

The battle was *not* going well.

Where we'd created killing fields, ready for the fight, with wide-open spaces and plenty of room to cut the enemy down, they'd countered it with sheer mass.

The open area between the wall and the tunnel was gone. In its place, there was a roiling sea of undead. Atop our walls were a small number of defenders, ones who were being slowly overwhelmed by the rolling mass of the undead. And beyond them?

The outer walls that we'd built to stop the undead getting out and any reinforcements getting back in for them were lost.

The dead had simply piled up against the wall and stood atop each other, climbing steadily higher on a base of broken bones until they could walk over it.

Atop the citadel stood two dozen defenders, all firing guns or magic. But the wave that was cresting was more than they could take down.

"Griffiths…" I started, flashing to his side and getting a grim look.

"Tell me you've got some good news for me," he demanded.

I hesitated. "How bad is it?"

"We're losing the walls," he said matter-of-factly. "Third time. But this time, my reserves are too low to retake them, I'm betting. If you can't add something to the fight, then we're going to pull back and hole up behind the next-stage defenses."

"Next stage?" I asked, then saw he meant the main doors.

"It's *that* bad?" I asked, aghast.

"Matt, we've been fighting for nearly a full day, against an enemy that doesn't need to rest, that doesn't care if it loses a thousand bodies to each of ours, and that then picks our own dead up and sends them against us! You see that?"

He gestured at a pile of shattered bones that had to have been a hundred figures strong. "That used to be some kind of an amalgamation, a troll or something, three meters tall. You see the wall?"

Right behind it, there was a section of gleaming spotless wall, but on either side was a blackened patch that made it clear that the original section had been stripped out and replaced by the dungeon's magic.

"We're fighting hard, but unless we get some reinforcements and damn soon, we're falling back," he said grimly. "I need fighters. I need mana or I need magic tricks—I don't care which. But if you give me just one of those, I can hold the wall a little longer."

"And without it…"

"We're falling back to the keep and fighting room to room," he said. "Make a decision, Matt: save it for the big bad and let us all die here, or start taking a hand. We've got no tricks left otherwise."

I paused then cursed, sliding free of the dungeon sense.

"Fuck, fuck, fuuuuuck!" I snarled, rolling to my feet. "Dammit, we're losing the walls! Talk to Dante, find out for yourself, then do what you need to do and get your arse on the roof. I need that fucking storm!"

With that, I was out of the door, charging across the ground, sensing the distant figure of Aly as she swooped in through the dungeon sense, aware of my presence.

"What happened?" I asked aloud, focusing so that I could hear her response.

"Too many of them, not enough mana." She grimaced. "We can't finish summoning the defenses or build the nexus gate without more mana, and we can't get that without fighting them. There's a load of it right there to claim, but we can't claim the bodies while the enemy is in contact with them."

"So you're battling them on the walls..." I paused to stare out through the dungeon sense, before I exited into the more populated areas, and double-checked what I thought I'd sensed.

They were there—Unlife mana converters sunken into the walls on all sides and sucking in the Unlife mana greedily. Checking the system, I could see that a third of the mana that was being harvested from both the deaths of the undead and their general existence was being used to summon reinforcements for our side and replacement ammunition.

The rest was being funneled into the nexus gate, which in turn stood at ninety-seven percent. Though, if the walls fell and the enemy got too close, that would freeze.

As it was, the gate was being protected by...fuck's sake. Robin and eleven others were gathered in a semi-circle around it, protecting it from harsh bloody language no doubt, instead of being on the wall where...

"We made Robin and her team leave the walls to protect the gate," Aly said quickly, apparently seeing the look I was giving her. "We're so close, and Kell is ready," Aly assured me. "But that last push means that we're losing the walls..."

I could see that as well. The defenders on the walls were backing into smaller and smaller groups, groups that were falling one by one. The undead were swarming up and over, the first of the skeletons crashing to the stone floor on the inside of the courtyard.

Dozens died before the first survived its landing, rather than shattering on impact. As soon as that happened, the area around it winked out of our control, preventing anything being summoned there.

"Matt, we're losing the area!" Aly cried, already diverting more mana from the nexus gate project to more fighters, this time clearly going for brutality and cheapness over capability or intelligence as a quartet of orcs appeared.

The first of them saw the incoming enemy, let loose a bestial bellow, then raced forward, weapon raised.

"Fucking hell!" Aly screamed, presumably seeing something I missed with them. "Goddammit, Kell!"

I missed whatever the issue was, already exiting the dungeon sense, finding myself braced against a wall. I forced myself to stand straight and head for the door.

I ran for it. The door banged open a heartbeat ahead of me hitting it and a short woman staggered in, half carrying a much taller one as I desperately dodged them.

"Matt, get out there and fix this shit storm!" Jo snapped at me, before dragging her unconscious burden out of the way.

I started running again, seeing the injured on all sides in here. The main room I was in now was the last before the exit, and a group was gathered by the door, weapons drawn, ready to fight.

"Make a hole!" I called, running for the door. The mixed group of humans and dungeon-born got the hell out of the way.

I burst into the courtyard. Before I'd taken a breath, I was hit with the cacophony of battle: the cries of the wounded, the roars of the fighters, the drumbeat of heavy fire, and the snap and sizzle of magic.

Explosions boomed on all sides, throwing undead into the air as some kind of rolling detonation trap went off, making it clear they'd managed at least a trap or two after all.

From above, ice suddenly rolled out, cascading across the walls, thrown predictably by Kilo. Undead that were cresting the crenelations suddenly found themselves encased in gleaming waves.

Fresh explosions rang out as someone finished reloading their shotgun. The fléchettes tore lines in the undead that sent bone fragments flying.

Fire, thunder, earthquakes—all fought for my attention. For a split second, I reeled with it all. Hell, on one side, I saw something I'd not seen in what felt like forever, as one of Kelly's puppets slammed fists like barrels of steel down atop the undead rhythmically, shattering bones into splinters. I'd had no clue she could even summon them remotely through the dungeon.

I could see it was exactly as Griffiths had feared: a thousand years of dross and death, barely ambulatory corpses that were driven with only hunger at their hearts. The elites hadn't even taken the field yet, and we were on the ropes. And worst of all, I saw in the distance, watching us, a figure atop a collection of bones.

I could feel the power and the hatred radiating off it, and yet... I could also feel that the enemy, my *real* enemy, still hadn't even arrived.

This was a little boss. A sub-boss sent to watch over the fight and to provoke me, was my guess. As I launched myself into the air, I decided that if it meant I got enough of a reprieve to finish the gate, then it'd be worth it.

I arced upward, twisting as I searched the surrounding area, seeing with my own eyes instead of the mixture of the dungeon's senses. It was worse than I thought.

It wasn't just that the elites hadn't taken the field. The more standard variations were drawn up in ranks at the very back, showing that although the dross wasn't in fact endless, we really weren't out of the shit, even if we could destroy all of them.

"Fine," I growled, coming to a halt and facing the figure in the distance, where it stood atop a pile of bones. "You want to provoke me? You want to see what I can do? Let's fucking play."

I felt the others gathering around me in the dungeon sense and I took a deep breath, twisting slowly as I searched internally, checking my limits.

I was at three-quarters roughly of my available mana, just a hair under eight thousand points, and *damn*. That was a lot of mana, and more than enough for what I had planned. First and foremost, I needed to not get bogged down in the minutiae of the battle. The enemy was coming over the walls because there were so many of them, and they were literally walking over their broken fellows.

If we could absorb them, then their advantage would be lost. That'd break the attack in its tracks. But we couldn't absorb them while the enemy was in contact with them.

The solution to that needed to either be the eradication of all the undead, or just to lower the level. Nice and simple. I focused, sliding into the dungeon sense as I lifted both arms dramatically. I drew a long ring around the outer walls, half a meter from the wall to five meters out.

I mentally tagged the entire line; then, sinking into the earth, I drew out a section that extended five meters out, five meters down, and ran all the way around it.

"It won't work," Griffiths said in my ear through the dungeon sense. "We can't affect anything within contact of the undead and there's too many of them. Their influence is solid, and it's too deep to eat away at the ground as well."

I nodded that I understood, and continued to outline it all, moving the line of influence to absorb as close to the surface as possible, before stopping.

A meter from the top was where I lost the connection, and in three places, I found that something similar had already been tried. The earth, as frozen as it was, resisted.

Stone and structural supports, all judged too deep to bother with in the first pass of absorption, now defied us, and I saw why they'd given the attempt up already.

That was fine, though.

The issue was the solidity, and that when people had tried to absorb it before, they'd done it on a much smaller scale.

We had more mana than we'd had earlier to play with. I could see the vanishing bones that ringed the surviving fighters, the wash of Unlife that burst free at each kill, and the general absorption of the undead's eternal miasma.

The issue now was that we didn't dare spend it, because we desperately needed it for the nexus gate. And even as I checked, I saw the gate's creation faltering.

A warning flashed up, counting down from ten. The failure of the gate's formation due to enemy presences would render it unstable, and unusable in ten minutes. All that mana, wasted.

Plenty of time.

I nodded to myself, a plan in place, and I spoke quickly.

"Absorb the ring. Summon orcs to face the undead and set them free. Spend what you have reserved for the gate, and beyond that, minimal investment. Clear the walls and get ready. As soon as the dross falls, they'll launch the real attack."

"What about him?" Griffiths asked.

"He's here to see what I can do," I said. "Time to share."

With that, I flashed through the air toward him, squinting as details resolved. The air was filled with a cold grey drizzle—not quite snow, but too cold for rain...that kind of slushy crap that builds on everything. As I picked up speed, I fired off an examination of the enemy.

Wraith Lord	Undead Creature

Wraith Lords are leaders of the undead, minor lordlings that, although not granted true power, are still fearsome enemies. They know that the majority of their kind understand only pain, fear, and lust, and they regard them with a hatred that is barely held in check by their own avarice.

As a naturally occurring Wraith Lord, there are no curbs upon the depravities nor hatred that drive this creature. In its past life, it committed crimes so heinous that in death the very earth rejected it at the earliest opportunity.

Wraiths are generally the souls of those who know that the great beyond would judge them harshly: murderers, rapists, and worse. Each wraith is unique, yet their power must come from another, forcing them into subservience that they hate almost as much as they hate the living.

Ability:

Plague! Wraith Lords, like all undead, are comprised of the decaying forms of the once living. Once per day, at a cost of 90% of the Wraith's life force, they may create a plague that will infect the living and the dead alike, draining the living of life, forcing them all to rise and serve the Wraith; area affected and effective time is determined by the health invested.

Ability:

Shield! Wraith Lords are more magically active than most and have the Ability to form that magic into a simple shield.

Ability:

Command! Wraith Lords retain much of the cunning they had in life, allowing them to act as leaders of their lesser brethren.

Ability:

Deathbolt! The Wraith Lord fires a bolt of necrotic energy across the battlefield, dealing 5-50 damage depending on the target.

Ability:

Wither! The Wraith Lord expels a harsh breath, drenching the area around it in the cold of the grave, before ripping this breath back into itself, and tearing the life force from those that were caught in the area of attack spell. This life force can be used to either heal itself, or raise additional minions from the bodies of the recently deceased.

Jez Cajiao

Ability:	
Grasp of the Grave! The Wraith Lord designates an area to hold, reaching through the veil that separates life and death, and forcing other undead to join it, reaching their limbs through to try to capture the living, dragging them through to feed upon.	
Weaknesses: Fire, Light, and Life Magics	
HP: 5000/5000	
Stamina: 0/0	
Mana: 2957/3800	
Speed 7/10	
Level: 19	
HP: 5000/5000	**Special Abilities: 6/6**

I snarled in recognition. The damn thing stared back at me, no past memories to drive it into a similar hatred, bar the entire real hatred of all existence.

It waited until I'd covered more than half the distance to it, barreling over the smaller mounds and knolls and approaching the distant hill, before it revealed the little surprise it had for me. And boy was it a doozy.

That massive pile of bones it was atop?

They slid together to form a *fucking dragon*.

CHAPTER FORTY-FOUR

"Oh, you want to play it like that, do you?" I snarled, focusing on the massive creation. I fired off a single Incinerate…to test the waters, as it were.

I needed to know a lot of things, but first and foremost, was it magically resistive?

The scream that came from the wraith as its crotch was superheated to a thousand degrees was satisfying, and revealed that no, it was not resistant to fire at the very least. As it writhed and screeched, the dragon roared and launched itself and its master into the air.

Wings that were clearly magical beat the air—great patches of midnight black dotted with stars stretched between bones that whistled and sang like death's own organ player.

The rib cage that the wraith was perched atop must have come from a whale or similar, it was so huge, and the neck from a giraffe or dino. The head? That wasn't hard—a T. rex had "donated" it. And the sheer sacrilege of knowing that a bone that was capable of being returned to life, if I could pull off the trick I managed with the trikes, was being wasted like this?

No. No, that I wasn't fucking having.

I cast two more Incinerates, almost disgusted by how easy it was, how simplistic it was. Each flared into being where the wings joined to the body; the bones there glowed cherry red, before charring.

I dismissed the spell, the wraith hunched over and hissing still as it recovered—it wasn't as if there was blood to boil in there, after all—and the bones of the shoulders creaked and screamed, the icy drizzle hitting them.

Then I cast it again, a few inches farther out onto the wings.

The superheated and already warping bones exploded, the strain too much for them, and the wraith screeched. It launched itself from the back of its creation as the bone dragon suddenly twisted and dived for the ground, barely avoiding the lashing tail.

And that was when I arrived.

Jez Cajiao

My sword was in my hand already, glinting as I hacked through the wraith at waist height. I arced around, sneering as it bellowed and screamed, casting out a barrage of necrotic bolts as I followed it down.

The wraith impacted the stone of the hilltop with a sodden crash. Bones shattered and bits flew loose, reaching up with one barely functional arm as I swept in, raising my blade to lop off its head...

Only to see the triumphant glare in its eyes as the hood fell back!

The first warning I had, as the mist rolled out from its body—thin and waspish, shimmering and filling the world with a sensation like nails on a chalkboard—was the sudden silence. Then, a heartbeat later, it was the dimness as the sky was hidden above me.

I glanced up on reflex as I lifted from the ground, flying back to escape the unravelling mist...only to see a second dragon, with another wraith on its back, bearing down on me from above. Its talons reached greedily, its mouth open wide and a hellish green glow screaming at me.

I swore, twisting and rolling—that goddamn fight had been too easy—and fired off a single blast of lightning into the open mouth that tried to follow me.

It hit the green smoke and vanished without a trace. The dragon seemed to surge suddenly faster as it arced around, teeth snapping a meter to my left as I jinked right.

Necrotic bolts flashed through the air. I dove, flipping over, and headed for the ground as the air around me was torn by their passage. Trees, dead and clawing at the sky in desperate last gasps, flashed past. I rolled again, crashing through a half dozen small branches on my way.

I'd barely pulled up—cursing that I'd had neither the mana nor the time to fix my fucking armor—and another dragon was before me. They'd boxed me in!

I dove again. This time my right foot scraped across the withered grass—I went that low—only to feel the tip of an outstretched claw rip scales free of my armor.

I was jerked back upright, the line of my flight ruined. I flipped around, catching myself and forcing mana into my flight to bring myself to a dead halt. I glared after the fucker, seeing the way that the wraith atop its back was twisting around and peering back at me.

I unleashed a Lightning Bolt into its back and then stared, before pushing off hard.

The bolt had hit—there was no doubt about that. But the magic did...*nothing*? It'd cascaded across its clothing and then sank into the dragon, seeming to feed it!

They weren't resistant—they were *feeding on it*! I had no clue how the fucker had managed it, but the lightning I'd sent at them so far had been absorbed and was fueling a surge in their power.

I dodged another necrotic bolt, then glared at the fucker on the ground. The broken wraith had thrown that one, and clearly it was thinking to take me unawares.

Immune to lightning, eh? Well, we knew judging from the charred mess that had been its crotch that they weren't immune to *fire*. I unleashed a new Incinerate spell, aimed at its head, and had the satisfaction of seeing its withered head blacken and burn.

Dead.

"Oh, so that's how you want to play? You want to fuck with me?" I muttered, staring at the others as the nearest dragon whipped around, the turn hard enough its passenger was pressed into the bony spine. "All right, let's fuckin' do this…"

I checked my mana, then nodded. I had enough for this, and it wasn't like the big boss was here, right? I double-checked. Nope, no sign of him—still a vague sense of distance and a weaker signal across the Channel, but that was fine. Even if he could fly as fast as these dicks were, it was an hour or more from there to here.

I checked for both of them and nodded to myself. They were arcing around, lining up for me. One went high, its wings beating hard as it went for height. The other came right at me.

I pointed my left hand at the oncoming dragon, led it with my finger in a finger gun, and then ostentatiously pulled the trigger and went "bang."

At the same time, I summoned an Atomic Furnace a meter wide and round, right in the middle of the dragon's head, and held it for the full second.

That was it—a full second.

And by the time that last one hundredth of a second passed and the spell winked out, the dragon had been cored out all the way down its length.

The skull—a priceless fucking T. rex skull…the genuine article—rained down in fragments, the front half that had been outside of the area of effect unable to survive the rear half being superheated to gasses and shards.

The undulation of the spine as the wings beat meant that half the neck entered the area of effect, vanishing into shattered bits that exploded in all directions, and half didn't. The shoulders? They were in the "down" position as that area passed through. But the wraith? *Oooh*, bad luck there, sir!

The wraith's head and shoulders rose into the orb just as it began to fragment, the constrained heat unleashed and washing out in all directions.

Its head burst into flames. The robes flashed to ash. The upper body alternatingly chargrilled and detonated as moisture and liquids met superheated air, and boom.

The rest of the dragon didn't even need to be hit.

It just came apart and collapsed into a thousand pieces in the air.

I turned my back on the collapsing figure then and pointed my sword up at the wraith on the back of the third and final dragon as it started to cast.

Spells rained down, and I launched myself after it, twisting to roll around the bolts. I flashed through the air, pushing hard. The wraith had gone from cackling

515

and clearly enjoying itself, here to spring a trap, to panicking with its balls in a vise.

It flipped over. The head of the dragon came around in a great arc, its mouth opening wide. For the first time, I got to see its breath attack in action.

I twisted aside at the last second. Sickly green flames roared past me, leaving a dead and burning track across the earth.

The dragon whipped its head back and forth, throwing the flames into my path and forcing me to abandon the attack run, adjusting out to fly wide. Glancing back at it, just as I was twisting to come around for another pass, I yelped and dove sideways through the air.

The dragon's neck was far too goddamn long and flexible as it tracked me. The flames rolled through the air just where I'd been about to fly a half second before.

Jerking back and forth, I managed to make it through the gaps left by the dragon's casting, and emerged on the far side, shooting into clear air as the breath weapon was released.

My cloak was gone—what was left of it, anyway—the armor singed. I felt strangely weak as I sucked in a breath of fresh air, but I'd made it out.

Looking back, I saw a faint mist draining from me, falling toward the dragon as it rushed after me, jaws open wide. I glared back, realizing that as close as I'd come to the damn fire, it'd still managed to latch on at least slightly.

"You want me?" I snarled, pulling up and stretching my arms and legs out as wide as possible, offering the largest surface area I could to the onrushing wind. "Then have me!"

I shoved backward with my mana, rocketing in the opposite direction, passing through my own falling life force and feeling like I'd just had a cold shower as I went through it.

Then the dragon's head was opening before me, the wraith on its back casting a spell...

I rolled, sword slashing out and around, hilt held in close in a two-handed grip, tip out at a forty-five-degree angle.

I passed by the side of the jaw closely enough that I saw the cracks and remaining fragments of stone that the bone had somehow been freed from. I saw the teeth, black and grey, looking more like stone than bone. I saw the missing area, the sections where the skull had been unable to reconstitute, where it'd shattered and been repaired by magic alone.

Then I was past. The blade cut through the neck with a sound like an elastic band under pressure being lopped through. The twang and releasing energy filled the air as the body collapsed into its separate parts.

The wraith launched itself free of the back. Hands like talons reached for my face, a maw that stretched open with skin like melted candlewax splitting.

A brighter man than me would have thought of a better solution.

A smarter man would have come up with a better line.

A man with any kind of goddamn sense wouldn't be flying through the air, bloody freezing in the middle of winter, fighting necrotic dragons and wraiths.

This man, however, managed to get out a single line as the stupid fuckin' wraith realized at the last second that when your opponent is holding a sword angled at you, and you are both flashing past each other with inches to spare, the time to try to give your opponent a struggle-cuddle was not right then.

"Shish-kabob, motherfucker!" I rammed the blade into the top of its head, out through the bottom, then into the top of its chest and through.

The hilt probably did the most damage, all things considered. It was a cruciform design, and having that rammed through your body lengthways at around ninety miles an hour would be memorable only for the observers.

The victim...not so much.

"Gah!" I spat out bits of the wraith as I arced around in the air, staring back at the disintegrating creature, before coughing and hacking more up.

Rising to a halt in the air, I stared down at the mass that was still streaming in toward the citadel. My height now made it look more like ants attacking a child's toy.

I couldn't help it. Holding my hands out to the side and turning gently in the air, I called out: "Are you not entertained?"

The "real" undead army still stood back, waiting. From my new vantage point, I could see what I'd missed closer in. There were entire armies coming to play from the south, marching up out of the water in battalions, their bodies streaming water and with great ragged lines with what had to have been thousands missing.

Tens of thousands remained, though, and out to sea? A massive form, one of three, rippled through the water, its back held clear of the water and a salty spray hanging in the air as it swam closer.

There were masses of creatures hanging from its back, and as it closed on the beach, it turned, and they leapt free, plunging beneath the wine-dark sea. They had *transports*.

Beyond it, the other two were swimming back out to sea, clearly on a run to reload and deploy, dammit.

The army that was about to overwhelm us was only a fraction of the true forces. And if we didn't deal with it right goddamn now? We were fucked!

I twisted in the air and launched myself as fast as I could at the distant citadel, reaching out as I did.

"Tell me you dug out those trenches!" I sent to the others, getting various versions of affirmation. I dug deep into myself for my go-to spell.

Lightning.

More specifically, Lightning Bolt!

I overcharged it and channeled it as I drew close, lashing out and punching it into the ground, carving a path through the mass of bones that the undead were climbing atop.

517

Jez Cajiao

Then I started pushing harder and faster.

I looped around the citadel, fast.

The first pass cut down deep. The second carved its way through to the ground, bones and undead detonating. I drained my own mana to the dregs, attempting a third pass.

On the fourth, when the ground shook but had yet to fail, I did what I kept telling myself I'd not do, and I used blood magic, driving my health into the spell to power it.

Blood streamed from my eyes and ears; it gushed from my nose and mouth, roiling through the air, forming symbols that burned and glowed around me.

The very life that was contained in my blood sparked and danced, and the blood lightning burned deep.

Cracks were the first signs of the breech. Then the creaks, the booms of the frozen earth failing. And then, first in pieces, before seemingly all at once, the entire section collapsed inward.

A five-meter-by-five-meter hollow section was revealed in the earth as the massed undead fell. Thousands of truly dead and thousands more of brain-dead and utterly vacuous creations collapsed inward. The earth buried them as they killed each other in their thrashing.

Skulls were knocked free and shattered, limbs lost to the darkness. Bones broken and tumbling, gnashing faces lost beneath their comrades' flailing feet.

It wasn't enough, though.

Not on its own.

There were still at least seven thousand undead on the field. The loss of a mere two thousand that had been ringing the walls was nothing in the grand scheme of things.

Certainly not to a foe that had no concept of or concern for issues of morale.

What it did mean, though?

It broke the wave that was pouring over the walls.

The undead that were used in this assault had only one thing going for them: their numbers.

They were the weakest of the weak. The soldiers who were already there, both dungeon-born and human, numbered less than a hundred, and they'd already killed nearly five thousand of the enemy today.

Dozens were killed by the minute in the underground paths, where the enemy were being harvested.

Hundreds more were killed in great spells. It'd never be known in truth how many had started the fight, but the rough estimate was over *twenty thousand*.

It cleared the wall of reinforcements, though, and thanks to the new forces that had been unleashed by Aly upon the walls to cover the retreat of the humans and more valued dungeon-born?

It was enough, just.

I landed in the courtyard, coughed, hawked, and dragged my hand across my face, then spat. Blood sprayed on the ground before I blinked through the red haze, trying to focus.

The nexus gate was a handful of meters away. I strode forward, staring at it. The last of the undead nearby was bludgeoned back to death with...

I blinked and wiped at my eyes again. Then, as the first spark of life flared in the nexus gate, I laughed.

It started as a disbelieving chuckle, then went to a shuddering, shaking convulsion, before erupting into a belly-shaking, booming exultation.

"KELLY..." I roared into the rain-streaming sky. "I LOVE YOU!"

It was an orc—dozens of them, in fact—all the common variant. They were armed with their signature weapon that Kelly had gifted them with in the dungeon, when they'd been summoned to act as training mobs.

We knew they were aggressive dickheads, and we knew as well that we didn't want to just lose our people in their first "real" fights, but they needed an enemy that would fight, and fight for real. So, Kelly had taken an unusual household item, and she'd supersized it.

What the orcs had been gifted to fight their enemies with was an eighteen-inch-long, seemingly fairly firm—*very* veiny—dildo. It even came with a suction cup on one end.

Apparently they were designed to be attached to the wall, and she'd never rescinded the order that the orcs be supplied with this "weapon."

I'd just realized that was what Aly had been cursing Kelly about before. As I looked around at the hundreds of shattered undead on all sides, obviously they'd proved to be viable weapons.

I wouldn't want an orc running at me with one and planning to put it to good use, that was for sure.

For good or ill though, they'd made the most of it. The nearest of the orcs moved toward me, huffing something at its companions.

I dragged some more blood out of the corner of my eye and stared at the hulking figure, ready to fight it, only to blink in surprise as it sank to one knee before me, head down, and laying its weapons on the ground in apparent supplication.

"Master," it ground out. "What you have the people do?"

"Defend this place," I ordered after a second's pause. "Protect the other dungeon-born and destroy the undead."

"Master." He nodded again, then swept up the two dildos he'd apparently been dual-wielding—gods, I was never going to live this one down—and he roared to the others, shaking his...weapons in the air for emphasis.

Then he was off and running, others appearing in waves behind him.

He made it to the top of the wall in a few bounds, barely pausing to touch the steps that ran up the side, then launched himself over and into the oncoming undead.

"Oh well, he's toast," I said to myself philosophically, before frowning and bracing myself against the wall, as I slid into the dungeon sense.

As I suspected, I found Aly, Kelly, Griffiths, and a dozen others waiting. Predictably, it was Aly who answered the question before I could ask it.

"Fifty mana." She grinned. "Twenty-five to summon them, twenty-five to provide them with basic armor and a 'cultural weapon' each."

"My God," I whispered. "How many can we afford?"

"A lot," she said. "We got so hung up on the more advanced units being the best, that we forgot that numbers have a quality all their own. We should thank the undead dickhead for that at some point."

"And with the break in their forces, we've gotten enough space to summon them." Kelly sighed. "How badly did that go, Matt? Have you still got any mana?"

"I'm down to blood." I winced. "My mana is gone, but that's life. I'll start meditating now, if you can—"

"Nexus gate is activating!" Aly grunted.

"It's not us!" Kelly snapped.

I twisted, pushing off the wall I'd just leaned against, and drew my sword.

A small figure jumped through, looking like a half a meter tall lizard in a jumpsuit. It landed, swept a handheld device around in a sharp arc, then spotted me and squeaked.

It was bipedal, mainly with a bright-green patterning that ran from its nose, back across its head and down its back, leaving the mouth, neck, and front of its collar area covered in tiny creamy white scales.

Its eyes were hourglass and bulging, like a goat's, but overall it reminded me of a gecko that had gained technological competency. Certainly that impression was born out by the handheld scanner that was clicking like crazy, twin antennas that came from either side waving in frantic warning.

"Zdhhhuo!" it squeaked. "M'halo I'm Zaporrr!" Then it spun and dove for the nexus gate, vanishing through it, before a half second later, the connection snapped off.

"Well, fuck." I grunted, before stepping up and laying a hand on it, locking the gate down to only authorized access. "Damn, I'd forgotten about that."

"What was that?" Griffiths asked as I slid into the dungeon sense again, the job done.

"We were warned when we set the gate up that if you didn't lock it, others would come looking, basically trying to explore and loot. We might get a trading partner step through at random, or we might get technologically advanced pirates. No way to know." I sighed. "Doesn't matter, though, first because it's now locked and nobody can get through without the key, and second because I think we gave that little guy a heart attack."

"Probably…bet he's learned a valuable lesson about exploring," Kelly agreed. "Okay, you get to meditating. We'll start the next phase."

"Converters," I reminded her tiredly. "I need the converters as soon as we can afford it."

"On it," she assured me. "Go. We need to know we can call you in if we need to."

"I agree." Griffiths grunted. "It's not good for morale when people see their most powerful spells have so little effect compared to yours, but the knowledge that we've got a living god on our side—even if you're just a baby one—is a hell of a counter. Rest, and we'll do what we can."

"Will do." I sighed, straightening. "Any word from Chris and the others?" I asked, then shook my head. "I know I can look, but…"

"They made it," Aly assured me. "Their gate is in progress, and they have the crystals ready. The gate freezes and won't continue construction when it's in transit, so they had to wait until they were solidly in place, but we're hoping that it can be moved once it's finished. If not…" She shrugged.

"It's fine, Matt," Kelly assured me. "Go rest."

"Shit, I need to talk to Dante…" I started to say, then shook my head. "You know what, I don't. Emma needs to talk to him. Now that the gate's open, send him through with the first wave and tell him to find her."

"Will do."

I didn't even note who said it, just that it'd be done. I nodded, marching back into the citadel, headed for the room that Emma and I had been working in.

CHAPTER FORTY-FIVE

Twice more I was called out, returning each time to what was increasingly becoming a meditation chamber. Once back, I sank into a dream-like fugue of magical research, experimentation, and meditation in between.

Emma and I were joined by Dante, and then by Kilo as time rolled on. Others came and went, but as the converters were built and the walls around us shifted, connectors growing almost organically upward to link to the converters on the roof, the area became more and more uncomfortable for those who weren't aligned as we were.

Kilo and Dante moved out to the periphery, taking an east–west line without discussion, and their respective converters grew behind them. Five Ice converters were created directly behind Kilo, and another five Fire behind Dante.

They were soon joined by a ring of four Water studded between the Ice, and four Air behind Dante. A gap was left to the sides rather than have the opposing converters too close. In the center to either side of me were twin Lightning converters, with Storm on either side of Emma.

Finally, to bring balance to the room, a pair of Earth converters were summoned behind us both.

It came to a grand total of twenty-three, and at fifty thousand a pop, it was well over a million in mana—which seemed insane, considering how much we'd been scrabbling for mana only a day ago.

Now, as the sun set on the second full day of fighting, I was with my small group, working on my magic, and trying my hardest to figure out the combination, as they did the same with their own.

Emma and Dante had found that increasing your lower elemental numbers did have an effect on the higher, but it wasn't, as we hoped, linear.

Despite me telling her to invest it in Ice, she'd invested all sixty points into her Death affinity, taking her from minus four to fifty-six. Although it had increased her Ice affinity as well, it'd not been as far as we wanted. At fourteen percent, she'd had no chance with the spells I needed her to be able to cast, not in the winter, and now, when she'd invested all the points in Death—she'd admitted it was her Bloodwytch class nudging her, and she'd trusted it—she'd reached forty-five percent instead.

It was a lot better, but considering we needed it to be in the sixties? It might as well have been nothing. Linking to the converters here and now, with the air as cold as it was, meant that she'd pull down a storm that was certain to convert into a blizzard, and that would not only kill her, but when it got out of control—as it would on her death—it'd probably detonate and kill everyone in the area.

Since then, she'd thrown herself into her studies with a desperation that bordered on insanity, making me order her in the end to get three hours' sleep, or I'd refuse to let her help at all.

Once she was gone, I'd taken a few minutes to myself, going to the toilet, not for need, but just to sit and brood. A hollow coldness filled my chest as I thought about how stupid it was of me to allow her to make that call herself.

My evolution had been gradually ticking, but not increasing up and over, moving from Thunderstorm to Cyclone in a steady, step by step route as I essentially worked on my magic. That meant that I was missing something and we were essentially doing crazily intensive research and experimentation in here, while outside our people fought for their lives.

There was a butt-load of things we didn't know still. Hell, I got the feeling it was *always* going to be like that. But the last six hours had come with some seriously impressive gains.

First and foremost, we'd discovered that although the main list had a hundred different forms of mana on it and prepopulated with your affinities to them, it didn't have all of them.

The list was simply there to show the first one hundred you interacted with, and they in turn could help you work out most of the others.

As a perfect example, I had some exposure to Lightning mana, which filled in that slot, but for whatever reason none to Pressure.

Pressure was a part of the Storm, though, and after a lot of careful figuring out, we'd found the real issue I had with Water, or one of them at least.

As well as why I goddamn hated flying in planes and I always had such issues with my ears. Scuba diving? Hard pass.

Basically, when you figured out a higher tier form of mana, you needed to learn the combination of the lower factors. If it was, say, Ice?

It was made up primarily of Death, seventy percent as near as we could tell, to thirty of Water.

That seemed a bit weird, considering it'd warm up and then the Death vanished and it became just Water, but that was what the numbers worked out at.

Cyclone, which was what I was working toward, was a three-part form of mana, and from what we could gather, if the mana was equal, split into thirds, then my Pressure affinity was truly shit.

It'd have had to be around minus thirty-nine, if that was the case. That would have made storms a nightmare for me, literally, as the pressure changes would have reduced me to tears from the pain repeatedly. So I knew it wasn't that bad, but it sure as shit wasn't a high score to drag my one hundred seven percent Storm and ninety-one percent Air down to an average of fifty-three percent.

It wasn't, fortunately; it was seven percent, and thankfully I'd still had the forty percent affinity boost I'd been awarded earlier, which I'd been saving in the hope that I could do this without it, and then spread it out… But it wasn't to be.

I spent the forty percent affinity boost all on Pressure, and after a few seconds of wanting to vomit my toenails out, I finally managed to pop my ears again, and sighed.

Then I glanced at my marker for the evolution and scowled.

Your current evolutionary position is: *Thunderstorm*: **74%**

Increase your capacity to reach the next level of Evolution.

74% > 74%…

You have plateaued. You know the change that you must enact, and can no longer evolve until this change has been made.

Be ready, Thunderstorm, for once this evolution has begun, it cannot be stopped nor reversed.

Be ready for what is to come…

That meant that to improve my chances of evolving, I needed to increase my affinity still further. And the best way that I knew to do that was through acclimatization and study.

Spell crafting as a group wasn't easy. You'd be deep in the zone of tweaking a path of mana and suddenly one of the others would shout something—they'd figure something out or they'd ask for help—and bang, you needed to start all over again thanks to the distraction.

It was worth it in some ways, though, because the handful of breakthroughs that I did manage were significant, with one of them triggering a minor cascade effect through the dungeon ability I'd unlocked a while back. That in turn helped the others, as tiny changes, points of congruity and potential were hinted at to them, leading them to take additional steps, until finally;

Crafting the signature spells of the Apprentice [Arcanist] is a hurdle that many sapiens fail to clear, as each spell completed not only limits the paths available to the mage for their future growth, but is also correspondingly more difficult.

Choose to create three separate spells of any two of the following categories to reach Apprentice Rank as an [Arcanist]. Alternatively, create a single spell in each category to receive an increased boost to your selected affinities and a bonus magical item:

- **Animation: 1/1**
- **Blood: 1/1**
- **Divination: 0/1**
- **Elemental: 1/1**

- **Enchantment: 1/1**
- **Mental: 1/1**
- **Rune: 1/1**
- **Temporal: 0/1**
- **Spatial: 0/1**
- **Summoning: 1/1**

First, thanks to Emma's instinctive knowledge bequeathed from the Bloodwytch side, she was able to teach me a relatively simple spell in that tree, one that she figured out simply by touching a patch of blood on the floor. It involved sucking the life from the blood and leaving it a blackened, crusted-over patch on the ground. It barely made a difference to her, considering she'd been at full health when she'd figured it out, mainly out of curiosity.

For me, though, having lost some of my life force, to enable me to draw on the life stored in my blood to in turn power my magic? It was going well. The blood that would have normally been sucked up and absorbed into the dungeon, powering maybe a point of mana, if that, was instead channeled to me, and I tore the life from it. It was more efficient. It was a cool healing spell, even if Vampyric Feast was a shitty name if I needed to sell it to anyone. But the one downside I could see right now was that the damn spell was useless here, when the only people I could rip the life from to fuel my spell were on my side.

The second discovery was a little better. I'd managed to create an enchanted item, a true one, even if entirely by fucking mistake.

Dante and I were working on Fire magic, discussing patterns he said "resonated with life better" and Emma, who'd just returned from a brief forced nap, had suggested that the pattern he was drawing was wrong.

With her greater control over blood, she took a little from her finger and drew it on the only surface that was available, the floor.

I'd summoned a sheet of metal, six inches on a side, and we transferred it to that, worrying that if someone looked in on us, they'd find the air warped by magic, and us all staring at a bloody scrawl on the floor.

Then, as she tried to explain what was wrong and what was right, mainly through a general "feeling" from the blood, adjusting it until she was happy, I fed a little of my regenerated mana into the blood, thinking that the way the blood had started to crust on one side was because it was colder, that side being closer to the Ice converters that Kilo was working with.

I wondered whether I could keep it from coagulating with a little extra mana so that Emma didn't have to cut herself again, and boom.

Instead of giving that bit of life to the blood, the plate flashed silvery; the blood sank into the steel and converted to what looked to be a drawing, and yet felt like crystal. And the notifications went wild.

Apparently we'd discovered the runic symbol for life, one of the basic elemental forms, and when you channeled a little mana into it, it bathed the area in Life mana.

It wasn't hugely helpful. It didn't really "heal" per se, as it instead promoted your body to heal naturally, and the fucker needed fresh blood to create more. But once we'd absorbed it into the dungeon, we realized that we already had access to a handful of other such symbols.

I drew a little blood out of my hand with the help of a scalpel, and wrote one of the other symbols with the Life one attached to it.

Channeled a little mana into the bloody plate again, and boom.

As the symbol was the one that the dungeon had always shown as an identifier on the doors that we created to seal access unless you had a token?

We'd basically created a marker that said, in runic script, "Life-Seal."

A few minutes of fucking around, and a rather risky experiment later, and we had a doorway that the undead couldn't cross.

We grabbed one of them, dragged them inside and locked it in a box with that symbol ringing the open exit.

The only issue was that as the undead tried to cross it, a seal appeared, like a force field, and it was shoved back bodily. That was great in theory, but in practice would cost a fucking insane amount if we were to scale it up to try to seal places off permanently.

It was a discovery, though, and it qualified for the rune component of the spell list I needed.

I had no clue about divination, temporal spells or spatial, but a little flexibility was all that was needed on my part to create a new summoning spell.

The first one I had, the only one until I created my own, was Summon Demon. That came with a whole host of knowledge that although weirdly specific was also helpful when you looked at the runic language as a whole.

The eldritch symbols it used were very different from the ones that we had access to, but they were highly effective. When we moved outside into the courtyard and I made a smaller circle, instead of the massive one that I'd used before to summon the bigger fucker, it summoned a correspondingly smaller demon.

The price it cost to summon the fucker wasn't significantly smaller, at eleven hundred mana. Instead of the full seventeen hundred mana that got us a twelve-meter-tall monstrosity, the smaller amount of mana got us a three-meter-tall, multi-armed, flat-faced thing with a mouth in its chest full of grinning teeth.

Multiple eyes dotted the head and shoulders. Four arms that ended in bone blades gleamed. And as soon as it oriented on me, I sent it over the wall to fight and kill the undead.

As a summon to help the fight, it was a washout. The damn thing lasted less than a minute before being pulled down and torn apart. As a proof of concept, though, it worked, and I gained the spell Summon Ventling, which did the job.

That left me three spells that I had no clue where to start with, but the others had all made significant gains on their own.

Dante had created three animation spells for Fire and Earth, Fire and Air and pure Fire, creating different types of elemental, each of which created great holes in the enemy's forces when he unleashed them. His elemental spells were pure Fire-based ones, spells that only a pyromaniac like him could have come up with. And they, too, erased entire sections of the battlefield, making it very clear that Fire as a weapon was a lethal one to the undead.

Lastly, he created three runic traps, plates that when stepped upon by the undead—we figured out the Death symbol, but still no luck with Unlife, but it worked—each created holes in their ranks.

We had a few minutes of comic relief, flinging them as far out over the enemy as we could, skimming them like stones on a lake.

We eventually gave up on such boring munitions as grenades, instead creating a metal ball with a core of sulfur, a thin line of inscribed Fire symbols and a Death sensor on the outside. Then the new fragmentation grenade was surrounded by tightly packed, blunt fléchettes.

Throw it out and as long as nothing dead touched it, no reaction.

A rotting foot coming down on the wrong section—boom…instant release. As a general weapon of war, it was too indiscriminate, too dangerous as we might be walking past and a bit of Death mana might touch it, and boom. But right now, when each one that was summoned could be thrown and have it detonate a heartbeat after summoning? It worked.

The other two were similar in design, and yet were close enough in form to enchanted items that they fulfilled the marker for both.

He was granted the rank of apprentice and immediately started swearing over the requirements for the next level.

The knowledge he unlocked came with a spell that was called Volcano, and yeah, summoned the earth to vomit molten lava across your enemies, which we all liked.

Mainly because he summoned it under a marching battalion of undead elites as they entered the field. They were wiped out in a heartbeat, and we all immediately went back to researching new ways to fuck shit up.

In the end, as the enemy godling finally revealed himself, I'd made a load of little steps in progress along the route to magical power, and fuck all steps along the path to "real" power as it pertained to a Divine being.

I genuinely was starting to feel I was hosed.

"Matt, it's time." Chris opened the door and winced at the wall of magical discharge that drifted free. "Shit, man, how the hell do you stay in here?"

"I stay because it's helping," I said sourly. "Or it was. What the hell are you doing here?"

"Kelly pulled us all in," he said. "The elites took the field, reinforcements arrived, and the fight's going all out. No time like the present to get out there and be counted."

"Who has the dreadnought?" I climbed to my feet and led the others from the room as he fell in by my side.

"You remember Arend-Jan?" He quirked an eyebrow.

I frowned. "The farmer?"

He nodded. "He's one of the most solid people I've ever met," Chris said. "Seriously, Kelly asked him to come and get the dungeon rolling, make sure we had a solid income, and keep the area being stripped—and he'd doubled it inside three hours of reaching me. I was just damn glad to hand it over."

"How the hell did he do that?" I asked, stunned.

"Moved it slightly, then spent a small fortune setting up a collection of converters. They each feed the next in line and make use of the same theories behind the undead leaking Unlife." He shrugged. "I get the basics, but you'll need to talk to him about it."

"I will." I sighed. "If we win."

"Well, look on the bright side. If we don't, no more stress or having to sleep in uncomfortable places!" he offered.

"No more sex, booze, and good food," I countered.

He winced. "Yeah, there is that."

"So, fill us in." I noted a set of stairs by the wall that hadn't been there earlier and that now made for a much easier path to the roof than the rungs in the wall people had been using before.

"The undead dickhead arrived about an hour ago—just appeared…walked out of a mobile portal, it looked like—and started gathering up all the bones."

"He can open portals?" I groaned. "Fuck's sake, of course he can."

"Yeah, personal ones. Not very big if what he used was anything to judge by. But there's also the fact that there were only two of them to step through before it closed, so maybe it just wasn't that he needed to waste the power."

"Go on," I said after he paused.

"There's good and bad news there, which is why I was sent to get you," he admitted. "First, the good…"

"Give me the bad."

"So the *good* news is that the army finally pulled its finger out of its arse and came to help." He ignored me. "They've got some skilled people and they're really kicking arse."

"Good, but?" I climbed the stairs, heading for the roof as he directed.

"The bad news is that as the fuckers arrived so goddamn late—Kelly thinks they did it deliberately to try to arrive when we were weak but could be either saved or overrun, depending on how things looked—they're on the outside."

"Outside?"

"We can't get to them," Chris said. "We've not got the forces to cut them a path to get to here. And if we did, we'd lose so many in doing it, that even if most of them survived, we'd be left at a net loss."

"Well, fuck," I snarled. "How many of them are there?"

"About five hundred." He shook his head. "Too many for it to be a token gesture, and not enough to make a real difference. Not that it's going to be much of a consolation when they're all dead."

"And Mike?"

"He can reach us through the dungeon. He also said Peterbilt, the commanding officer, is a wanker and not to be trusted. He clearly has an agenda, and a small team that are dangerous, but below him are a bunch of damn good soldiers. Says we need to find a way to use them, because we seriously need that kind of a force as allies."

"Any ideas?" I asked as I strode out onto the roof.

"Matt, good man," Griffiths called, speaking louder to make up for the crash and boom of magic, and the general roar of battle below us. I walked over to him and got a clap on the shoulder as I came to rest by his side, staring out at the field of screaming death and marching corpses that surrounded us. "Chris filled you in?" he asked, looking and sounding tired as he straightened and twisted, grunting as something shifted in his back.

I nodded slowly as I stared at the grey mass below and before us, surging forwards even as great rents were torn in their ranks with explosive magic. "We're surrounded, the bad guy is here with his mates, and the reinforcements finally arrived—too few, too late, and too untrustworthy."

"Basically." He agreed grimly. "Two other groups arrived before them, and we made room inside the walls for them as they fought their way through. Though one is mightily pissed at you, it seems."

"Joy. Who and why?" I asked.

"A band of roaming Scepiniir, first of all. Seems they were promised a convoy of boxers, all armed to the teeth, so long as they helped in a fight, and they've come to collect."

I looked down and saw a section of the wall was being manned exclusively by the humanoid cat people. On either side of them were orcs, but judging from the looks both parties were giving each other, there was a hell of a rivalry going on.

"I said we'd give them a single boxer provided they came and acted as scouts, or two if they brought more than fifty of their people," I corrected. "My plan was to have them scour the countryside and hunt down any pockets of undead, defeating them in detail, or just acting as scouts so we weren't surprised."

"Well, they found the undead, though that wasn't hard, and there were a hundred and seven of them." He shrugged. "To their credit, they've been kicking arse for the last few hours. But the way things are looking, they'd be long gone if it wasn't for the orcs."

"Why the orcs?"

"They're naturally occurring Scepiniir, as near as we can tell from questioning them. They just woke up in a group, a hundred of them close together, and over a few weeks found more of their kind, while losing plenty to natural and unnatural attrition. They know little about who they are as a people. I've got no fucking clue how they got here, but there were a handful of older ones with them in the beginning that died off. No clue what their real story is, but that's not important. What is, is that they don't have *any* issues with the orcs.

"The orcs, in turn, don't have any racial memories. A few have started to develop their own minds, but most are still mindless cannon fodder. That means that neither views the other as an issue from racial memories or external knowledge. As it is? They're either going to become the best of friends or the worst of enemies. They fight like nobody's business and are keeping score. See that?"

He gestured to a high platform that stood a dozen meters back from the wall with a pair of Scepiniir and a pair of orcs on it.

"They're the judges, and they're keeping a tally of which side kills more. Not sure what they win, but even if it's just bragging rights, I'm loving that competition."

"Nice. Does that mean the orcs are less of dicks than we thought?" I asked.

"Not really, they're still dicks. But in seeing them with the Scepiniir, it might be that they're more or less manageable, provided you give them an outlet and a reason to not hate you."

"Okay, so that's all well and good, but…"

"The other group is there." He pointed to a small contingent of apparently identical, massively muscled human soldiers in form-fitting, scale-like armor.

"Who the…" I started.

"Kaatachi and Akuba sent them," he said.

"There's…fuck me, there's what, ten of them?" I gasped in horror. "Where's the rest?!"

"Best you speak to Kelly," he said.

I braced myself, then slid into the dungeon sense, finding her waiting for me.

"Kelly, he…" I started, and she nodded.

"I know and I heard," she said. "It took days to make contact. And as Leilani said, they were at war already. They took Zeus's Master Bolt and agreed to come when we called, but only if they could get their people out of their current rolling fight. Akuba sent her honor guard, their most elite forces to help, and they promised to come. But their portal shut down about two hours ago. They're still alive, but that's all we know."

"How do we know that and—" I shook my head. "Fuck, I should have given it to Emma."

"No, we need a lot more power and we need an alliance," Kelly said. "They're the best choice for us, both in terms of strength and affinities, and they needed us as well. That we gave them the bolt now, and they could use it to turn the tide, when we could have kept it or sold it to them as Leilani was selling them ammunition for a massively inflated price? We made allies, Matt, and that was what we need the most."

"And we know they're alive?" I asked woodenly, staring out of the dungeon sense at the massing undead before us.

"Wouldn't *you* know?" she asked.

I glanced at her in confusion, then cursed and pulled up the notifications, discarding all that were useless—kills, magic details, increases in a point here and there because of the sheer effort and focus. All great news normally, but not what I needed now.

WORLDWIDE ANNOUNCEMENT!

THE LORD OF DUST, SECOND LORD OF THE PATHEON OF THE STORM, HAS PUBLICLY ACCEPTED HIS TITLE AND IS NOW A MEMBER OF A FLEDGLING HUMAN PANTHEON!

KNOW THIS! THE ONLY LIMIT ON YOU IS THAT WHICH YOU PLACE UPON YOURSELVES. GROW, ADVANCE, *LEAD*!

WORLDWIDE ANNOUNCEMENT!

THE FIRST LADY OF THE MONSOON, THIRD LORD OF THE PANTHEON OF THE STORM HAS PUBLICLY ACCEPTED HER TITLE AND IS NOW A MEMBER OF A FLEDGLING HUMAN PANTHEON!

KNOW THIS! THE ONLY LIMIT ON YOU IS THAT WHICH YOU PLACE UPON YOURSELVES. GROW, ADVANCE, *LEAD*!

Now that was fuckin' weird. I vaguely remembered a notification and chatter around me, though I'd just been pissed at the time it wouldn't go until I'd acknowledged it.

Clearly that'd been these two, not a single one and I'd been so deep in the fugue state of spell working that I'd blanked it all out at the time.

There wasn't anything else. No details as to who they were or how they'd managed to get the two of them to ascend out of the single Zeus's Master Bolt, nor if they were still alive or not. But I did know that when I'd killed Dickless, that had sparked another worldwide notification, so I had to guess if they were dead, Kelly was right, I'd know.

Focusing on them, much as with the affinity screen, a little concentration provided a new screen that was set with a space for ten "Lords and Ladies of the Storm." I stood at its head; they both stood a full rank beneath me, marked as "fledgling." There was also an affinity list attached to them. I had no time to fuck with that, but I did see "threat level" next to them with a small symbol I couldn't understand.

Focusing on it, and then on mine, I got a popup that explained that my own threat level was "significant"—which was nice—and theirs…was "minor."

The power levels weren't shown for humans and standard people as a comparison, so I had to just hope that was still okay, because there was less I could do about that right now than I could about the moon.

And shouting my hatred of the moon randomly was…well, it wasn't a good look if you didn't want to be thought crazy.

Damn the moon.

"So?" Kelly prompted, and I nodded, banishing the screens.

"They're alive, but that's all I know," I admitted. "They sent their honor guard?"

"The group down there," she agreed, and I looked down at the party of ten, where they were getting ready to join the fight. "They're good—they're lethal, in fact. All fighters and all mages as well. If we weren't so up shit creek, I'd have said they were a wonderful help. But as it is?"

"We need an army," I said grimly.

"We need an army," she agreed. "Our forces are ready at the northern dungeon. We shipped everyone through to there, but I didn't want to bring them until it was, well, time."

"And it is now?" I asked, before glancing out across the field and seeing what was coming. "Oh shit, it is now."

The sight before me made it horrifically clear that we were dealing with another godling, because there was just no way that anyone with a "normal" level of power was going to be raising the kind of creatures he was working on.

"Kelly, you deal with our people with Griffiths. Shit…" I groaned, hating that half the people on the roof were in the "real" world and half weren't.

I could totally understand the urge. When you were seeing through the dungeon sense, everything had a strange feel of unreality, even now that the system was so much more advanced than it had been.

It made for a goddamn awkward situation for me, though.

"Kelly, I love you," I said. "I need to be out there, though. I'll see you soon…and you're in charge." With that, I sent her a mental peck on the lips, then released the dungeon sense and stepped back into my own body.

"I need to get out there," I said to the group around me. "Griffiths, you're in charge of the local battle. Kelly is in charge overall. If I die, she's the boss. Got it?"

"Got it," he agreed distractedly, having already been barking orders as I'd been inside talking to Kelly. "You taking care of those?"

"Gonna do my damn best," I hedged, and he nodded, understanding.

Over the last day, we'd seen that the enemy were collecting their dead and moving them back from the fight in massive piles. They'd been keeping a token undead by them, always in contact, clearly to prevent us absorbing them into the dungeon.

Whichever asshole Dungeon Lord had told them about that little trick and counter was going right to the top of my shit list, I'd decided.

That they'd done it was a sensible course, though, as it both prevented us from summoning as many forces at their expense as we could have, and it lowered the Unlife concentrations around the walls that we were harvesting from.

That being said, as the links between the nexus gate were established now, we really didn't need as much of the mana from local sources as we had.

The other sites, primarily Heathrow, were working to produce crystals. They were then in turn being shipped through the gate regularly to us, and that had replaced harvesting locally as the main source of mana.

As such, we'd basically just accepted that it was keeping some of their forces occupied, as in the last day the shift had occurred from the dross, as we called them—the low-level, naturally occurring and weak as shit undead—into the *real* undead.

The same kinds that we had used for ages were now being unleashed upon us. Corpse lords, wraiths, advanced and apparently experienced soldier undead were now teamed with other, much more dangerous variants.

Banshees circled us high overhead, their screams bringing weakness and occasionally death. Stumbling zombies scratched and bit, bringing infections that turned our own fighters against us. Skeletal harpies flashed past, latching onto the unwary and yanking them from the wall to fall to the ground with painful consequences, or from the roof with fatal ones.

Another dragon had appeared, though on a run to try to clear the wall, it flew too low and too predictably, Dante reduced its head to ash.

That made it sound like it hadn't been a threat, but it'd already made two strafing runs, ones that had resulted in the deaths of hundreds on the walls, as had they just ran, the undead would have taken the walls anyway.

Instead, the dungeon-born had suffered horrific losses, more being summoned by the minute and thrown against the oncoming hordes to retake the wall, and then to battle it out with the next wave.

Back and forth, the war had gone, with incredible fights and acts of magic on both sides. But when they pulled out the big guns, it came to us to counter each time.

Now, the undead god was showing that the collecting of the bones hadn't just been to keep them away from us. Three distinct forms rose, with parts being siphoned off to the left and right. An eerie green glow suffused the growing abominations. I examined each in mounting concern, starting with the central figure.

Battlefield Colossus	Undead Amalgamation

The Battlefield Colossus is a monstrous fusion of thousands of fallen soldiers, their bodies and spirits bound together by dark magic and the will of an undead god.

Standing over twenty meters tall, this abomination is a grotesque patchwork of human, dungeon-born, and bestial remains, bound together with a will to cause as much destruction as possible. Weapons and armor protrude from its flesh at odd angles, and multiple faces contort in eternal agony across its surface.

The Colossus embodies the collective trauma and violence of the prolonged battle. Its movements are accompanied by the screams and whispers of countless tormented souls. The creature's singular purpose is to continue the slaughter that created it, driven by an insatiable hunger for more bodies to add to its mass.

Ability: *Absorb Fallen*: The Colossus can assimilate the bodies of fallen combatants, healing itself and growing in size and strength. For every 100 bodies absorbed, it gains 1000 HP and increases its damage output by 5%.

Ability: *Legion of Limbs*: The Colossus can extend dozens of arms in all directions, each wielding a different weapon. This allows it to attack multiple targets simultaneously within a ten-meter radius.

Ability: *Wail of the Damned*: Once per hour, the Colossus can unleash a terrifying howl that combines the anguished cries of all souls trapped within it. This causes fear and confusion in living creatures within earshot, potentially stunning them for several minutes, or until, as is likely, their death.

Ability: *Siege Form*: The Colossus can reshape its lower body into a battering ram or siege tower, allowing it to smash through fortifications or elevate smaller undead troops over walls.

Ability: *Soul Siphon*: By focusing on a single target, the Colossus can attempt to tear out their soul, dealing massive psychic damage and potentially killing them instantly if they are of sufficiently weak spirit.

Ability: *Undead Nexus*: The Colossus acts as a conduit for necromantic energy. While active, it passively enhances the strength and regeneration of all undead within a fifty-meter radius.

Weaknesses: Life, Fire, Lava, and Light Magics

HP: 50,000/50,000

Stamina: N/A (Tireless)

Mana: 10,000/10,000

Speed: 4/10 (Slow but with enormous reach)

Level: 5	
HP: 50,000/50,000	**Special Abilities**: 6/6

"Oh, that's not good," Chris said as I read out the details of the biggest, as it rose to tower over the battlefield. Hundreds of bodies slid to mound upward, as if reaching for the sky in hatred.

"Neither is this," I whispered, before reading out the second, as it appeared, already moving, winding back and forth. The bodies that lay piled in their hundreds nearby stuck to it. Bones shifted, disconnecting and reconnecting at different angles, growing only to two meters in height. But in length?

The Eternal Coil	Undead Amalgamation

The Eternal Coil is a massive serpentine construct, currently stretching for dozens of meters, and growing by the second, it is composed of countless interlinked corpses. Its body is a nightmarish fusion of human, dungeon-born, and animal remains, scaled with fused bone and metal. The creature shall encircle the battlefield. Should it be allowed to complete its terrible construction, it will settle into constantly devouring its own tail in an endless cycle of death and rebirth.

Guided by the soul of an ancient dragon, the Eternal Coil embodies the cyclical nature of conflict and the inevitability of death. Its presence pollutes the surrounding land, sea, and air with necromantic energy.

Ability: *World-Encircling Grasp*: The Eternal Coil can extend its body indefinitely, allowing it to constrict and crush entire fortifications or armies. Any section of its body can act independently, making it nearly impossible to truly pin down or surround, once it has grown to its full size.

Ability: *Miasma of Decay*: The creature constantly exudes a toxic fog that corrodes the living and bolsters the undead. Living beings caught in this mist suffer constant damage and risk becoming infected with a necrotizing plague.

Ability: *Ouroboros Resurgence*: If a section of the Eternal Coil is severed, it can regenerate by consuming part of its own body. This allows it to recover from seemingly fatal wounds, though at the cost of temporarily reducing its overall size and power.

Weaknesses: Life, Fire, Lava, and Light Magics

HP: 20,000/20,000 (spread across its entire length)

Stamina: N/A (Tireless)

Mana: 15,000/15,000

Speed: 6/10 (Deceptively fast for its size)

Jez Cajiao

Level: 5	
HP: 20,000/20,000	Special Abilities: 3/3

"Oh shit."

The Hydra of Lerna	Undead Amalgamation
The Hydra of Lerna is a grotesque fusion of multiple corpses, forming a serpentine body with nine heads. Each head represents a different race from the battlefield: human, orc, kobold, Scepiniir, and various other creatures. Standing at ten meters tall, it's smaller than the other amalgamations but no less deadly.	

Inspired by the mythical Hydra slain by Hercules, this undead version retains the creature's infamous regenerative abilities. It embodies the tenacity of the fallen and the ever-renewing nature of conflict.

Ability: *Regeneration*: When a head is severed, two more grow in its place unless the wound is cauterized by fire. Each new head represents a different fallen warrior, potentially granting new abilities and knowledge.

Ability: *Poison Breath*: Each head can exhale a cloud of necrotic poison, dealing damage over time to living creatures and corroding inorganic materials.

Ability: *Shared Consciousness*: The Hydra can perceive its surroundings through all of its heads simultaneously, making it nearly impossible to surprise and allowing for complex tactical decisions.

Weaknesses: Life, Fire, Lava, and Light Magics

HP: 20,000/20,000 (divided among the heads and body)

Stamina: N/A (Tireless)

Mana: 5,000/5,000

Speed: 5/10

Level: 5

HP: 20,000/20,000	Special Abilities: 3/3

"Okay, how about we call it a draw?" Chris suggested, and I snorted, recognizing the quote.

"You're not the black knight, you're a dumbass in tinfoil, and we've not lost any limbs," I pointed out.

"Yet," he countered glumly. "Man, why the hell did you have to start a fight with a bloody god, eh? I mean, shit, man."

"We have an advantage." I squinted as I reviewed the details.

"What's that?" he asked as the three forms hulked and grew, their bodies being formed through ongoing magic that was clearly draining the undead godling.

"Well, what's the point of all of this?" I asked.

"To kill us?"

"What's his aim, specifically?" I asked.

"To use your skull as both a sex toy and gumdrop holder?"

"Griffiths?" I asked, turning my back pointedly on Chris.

"To kill you," the soldier replied.

I nodded. "And mine is to kill him, and protect our people," I said softly. "I think he's counting on his creations to fight me."

"And us?" Chris asked.

"He's alone." I nodded at him. "He's had a couple of other undead dicks with him, the 'lesser' gods, but he's almost exclusively used to dealing with minions...*replaceable* minions."

"And we're not replaceable," Chris said firmly, then he winced. "That kinda sounds like he's got the advantage still, dude."

"Not really." I smiled. "I'm betting Dante and a few friends could take out the hydra. How many mages do we have now?"

"Thirty-seven." Griffiths nodded. "I see your point. As much as he nearly overwhelmed us at the beginning with the weakest and least valuable undead, in terms of experience given for defeating them...now we've spent the last day leveling up. A full day of around-the-clock battles has been enough to launch even the most basic of mage-wannabes all the way to their class choices."

"Dante?" I called, turning and finding him literally right behind me. "Shit, man, don't creep up on me!" I gasped, jerking back and shaking my head. "Dammit!"

"What?" He grinned.

"See the hydra?" I asked.

"Hard to miss it, to be honest."

"Think you can kill it?"

"Alone or with help?"

"Can you do it alone?" I asked, then shook my head. "No, do it with a party of ten. The faster it's dead, the faster you can turn your attention to the other two and help there."

"I can do that," he assured me.

"Griffiths, the snake?" I asked, and he nodded.

"Heavy fire, explosives, and solid effort should get us through, though don't expect the butcher's bill to be light," he agreed. "Do I get mages?"

"Ten," I said.

"I'll see it done."

"That leaves us the big fucker." Chris nodded, shifting his shoulders.

"No," I corrected. "That leaves *you* the big fucker. Take the honor guard, the remaining mages, and anyone else Griffiths can spare. You fuck that shit up, and I'm taking on the bony bastard."

"Sounds like it's time to put our game faces on, people," Griffiths called out.

"Time to fuck up his Tuesday." Chris extended a fist in my direction, and I tapped my own against his, glad I'd finally had the time to fix my armor earlier today.

I was going to need it.

CHAPTER FORTY-SIX

There was no time like the present, I decided, stepping up to the crenelations, only to have a hand grab my wrist and tug me back.

I twisted, glancing into Emma's face.

She glared at me.

"What?" I asked her, genuinely confused and trying my best to be polite.

"What about me?" she ground out. "We've spent days working on my magic, getting me to the point that I can nearly summon the storm, to the point I could be useful, and now you're just forgetting all of that and fucking off?"

"Can you fly?" I asked her coldly, pulling my sword off my back and shucking it out of its sheath, casting the leather scabbard aside. Clearly I wasn't going to need that for a while.

"You know I can't," she responded flatly.

"Can you summon a storm?" I tried again, hating that she was forcing this confrontation, but if it had to happen, it was better over here and now.

"No." She looked furious that I would ask aloud what we both knew. "I'm not strong enough. There's too much Ice here—"

"Then you need to help where you can." I swallowed hard. "Emma, I'm sorry, but I've got no time for this. We'll work on your affinities in the future."

With that, I stepped up onto the ledge and launched myself into the air, the whipping of the wind as gravity released its hold on me enough that I missed whatever else she said.

I'd needed her—dammit, we'd *all* needed her—and she'd ignored what I'd asked her to do, and she'd gone her own way.

I was infuriated, and I also damn well understood it, because it was her future on the line, and her class. Something that she was gifted because it was "her" to an absolute degree had guided her to that, which made it almost impossible to disagree with.

Regardless of my conflicted feelings, I was grimly sure we were going to lose people, good people, because she'd done what she wanted to.

As I lifted into the air now, a second figure lofted across the way from me, flying to position itself between me and the goddamn rotten bastard Balthazar.

I recognized him instantly, as much as I'd never seen him before, and I didn't bother wasting the mana on reading his details. He was the second or third Lord of the Unlife Pantheon, a minor godling...much as I had been until recently. That meant that either he was still there, or he'd managed to ascend to a higher level to join me—I'd been the first to reach this level of power only a week or so ago—but in either case, I was gonna have a fight on my hands.

Frankly, though, I had neither the time nor the interest in learning more about him. He'd kept his mouth shut, following along after that asshole Balthazar, and if that wasn't enough? He was defending him now.

I picked up speed, hurtling through the air at him, sword extended and making it abundantly clear that either he fucking moved, or he was getting introduced to the world's most painful reverse enema.

He did that same, crouching down atop his dragon's back motion, and extended a sword that looked to be carved out of midnight. Dots and sparkles in the blade made it look like the starry night had been captured within.

The dragon was bigger than the others. Where they'd had rib cages the size of large cars, this thing was closer to the size of a bus, with four legs like tree trunks, two sets of wings that beat in tandem, driving at me with eager speed, and spines that ran down its back like...

I twisted, rolling and slashing with my sword even as I fired off an Incinerate at the godling on its back—only to find that the spines that ran down its length, long and curved from the back of the monstrous head to the tip of its tail, weren't spines.

They were arms, skeletal arms that held curved swords: daggers for the shorter areas, great curved things like longswords for the larger, and khopesh for the talons of each feet.

Its head twisted, snapping at me. Twin, seemingly fixed in place, forward-reaching "horns" were revealed to be swords as well.

I carved through the first sword to reach for me, dodging the second, and slashed at the side of the dragon, before firing off another two Incinerates at the godling, and cursing as he grinned back at me.

We passed each other in a flash. His emaciated hand reached out to try and grab at me. All I saw, the speed was that high, was a pair of feverish eyes sunken back into a cadaverous skull, wispy hair plastered back by the wind of its passage, and teeth bared in hatred.

It huffed out a cloud of foul and noxious green and yellow mist at me. I spun, the blur of my sword whipping me around enough that I avoided most of it.

I pulled up, the wind screaming in my ears. That goddamn cape flapped around me as I twisted, wrapping itself around one arm, then practically being torn free as I frantically changed direction, cursing internally.

The fucker had nearly got me with a sucker-punch, I saw instantly, as dozens of harpies, all having been hidden behind the massive monstrosity, were revealed and closing on me.

I spun and cut, flinging out Lightning and Incinerate spells with desperate abandon, in a world of flashing teeth and claws, wings and screeching hatred, only to burst into the clear on the other side, and double down.

I threw myself at the leader. If I could take him out now—if I could do it before the dragon could turn around, before the bastard could finish his unholy creations, and before the harpies could close again—then this was over.

I'd covered more than half the distance. The last of the fliers were coming in from all sides now, but where banshees soared toward me, hands raised and foul mouths agape, my people made their presence known as well.

Of the seven banshees headed for me, three fell from the sky with headshots, their skulls detonating into shards. Two more took high-powered rounds to the chest or body, either being shattered and tossed away, or injured enough that they fell.

The last two, though, unleashed their unearthly wails. I gritted my teeth, a rapidly summoned lightning shield crackling into being around me.

Incinerate took care of both of them. A heartbeat later, the shield was dismissed, but they were achieving their master's desires. Every single point of mana wasted on these fuckers was a point not being spent on fighting him. I looked back, glaring as I saw the dragon closing on me again.

I judged the distance between me and the boss, and then between me and the dragon, then snarled in frustration. More banshees, conveniently hidden ahead, lifted into the air, hands outstretched. A shimmering wall of twisted sound formed a shield between me and their god.

Fine…that was fine, though, because I'd spent…eleven hundred mana.

Eleven hundred mana of ninety-five hundred. I remembered Ramnik telling me that her version of Wrath of the Heavens cost her six hundred mana, and it took a full minute to cast. My advantages in magic told me that with my particular build, it'd cost me significantly more to cast it, but it'd be correspondingly more lethal—and it'd take ten seconds to cast.

I glanced at the enemy god. I checked back at the other enemy god and his rapidly closing dragon, and then at the enemy before me, rising to try to cut me off.

Well, it wasn't like there were rules about not dual casting, right?

I pulled up, heading for the clouds, ignoring the crescendo that the enemy god's summoning spell was building to, and I mentally designated two spots as the target areas.

The first? The enemy god, Balthazar. I placed a solid target over that fucker's figure, even lost as it was in the middle of roiling clouds of necromantic magic.

The second? Well, that was easy. I put it on a space just at the point everything blurred into the clouds overhead, angled back to come from the direction of the citadel and set it to arrive in, oh… eleven seconds' time.

Then I headed right for it.

541

Picking up speed, I flashed past the first target zone, driven higher overhead and out of a direct attack range for anything but magic. I was betting that a rain of goddamn flaming rocks would be a lot harder to absorb.

The shields of the banshees withered away as I passed them. Instead, they responded to my proximity with a howling barrage of hatred. Their unearthly wails caused surging flares of pain, confusion, disorientation, and then, coming on the back of it all, a feeling like I was suddenly weaker than a kitten.

Mana started to stream from me, being sucked literally out of my body and falling like a mist to the hungrily gasping mouths below.

Then I was past. The siphon cut off as I shot back out of range. Behind me, I could distantly hear and sense the sudden unleashing of a barrage of spells. Glancing back, I cursed.

The spells were all well and good, Dante and his lunatics unleashing hellfire on the enemy, but right behind me was the dragon, its mouth open wide and a bright-green glow emanating from the depths of its throat.

Shadowy forms granted it unnatural depth and shape, making it appear more than the bone and make-believe madness I knew it to be. And yet...

I rolled to the side just in time, then up, feeling the sudden G-forces as I pulled as hard as I could... Then I gibbered in terror, as the first of the meteors, summoned by my Wrath of the Heavens spell, phased into existence, rocketing back along my path as I lifted into it.

The clouds encircled me. Grey, cold air suddenly cut off the rest of the world, and shadowy forms flashed past, going in the other direction.

I grinned. That fucking dragon was in for a surprise...then I burst from the lower cloud cover into a patch of clear sky above it...

And my stomach dropped out.

I wasn't the only one with a surprise for their enemy.

***

"Fire!" Dante screamed joyously, as all around him almost a dozen mages unleased their spells at once. Meteors, fireballs, frozen shards of ice a meter across, acid green missiles, and darkly sinister bloody crystal forms flashed through the air, rising and falling in a great wave that crested, then slammed into the hydra.

It was still incomplete, and Dante was hoping—he was fairly sure, in fact—that if he could hit it with more damage than it could sustain, the mana being poured into it to give it life would be lost.

If he and the others could just do enough damage to it that the unholy ass-wipe couldn't finish it and ran out of mana? That was going to be a win, and he, Dante, the soon-to-be Lord of Firestorms, would prove his worth and become a god!

Then, once he was there? He'd drag Ashley kicking and screaming into immortality. And when the entire world knew that he was a literal god...then, maybe he'd be brave enough that he could propose to her.

Life was incredible at times.

***

"Kill them, you goat-fucking, ball-gobbling bastards!" Mike roared at the soldiers all around him. "Get it stuck in!"

They were surrounded. What had been five hundred an hour ago was less than two now, and they were being taken out with terrible speed.

Corpse lords were bad enough. Wraiths were a nightmare he'd happily spend the rest of his day summoning and shooting in the face when he was back home. But the banshees?

They'd dropped out of the low clouds and had attacked in waves, one after the other. Their terrible wails sucked the strength from him, never mind those on all sides.

The shakes that they brought as they passed overhead, harvesting the mana and life force of those on the ground, caused trembling hands and dry mouths. Arms were robbed of the strength to even lift their rifles, let alone aim and fight in a pitched battle. And still they fought on.

The only alternative was death.

The limited few spellcasters who they'd had in the army had been driven mad in minutes. The combination of the massed undead armies, the theft of their mana, and the constant attack runs had sent them over the edge. Two had listened, apparently, to voices only they could hear, and had unleashed fire and acid upon their own side.

Another had just broken down, collapsing catatonic, while the majority screamed and gibbered, flinging spells in random directions until their companions took them out.

As battles went, this was an absolute clusterfuck.

***

"Onward!" Chris roared, sprinting through the massed ranks of the dead, fifty others with him. The head of the wedge cut its way into their enemy with blunt force, sheer aggression, and determination.

Their mages had unleashed hell, literally: massed magical fire used like an artillery bombardment to clear a path, followed by sheer muscle. Now they were pounding their way through what was left, and they were doing it!

By his side, Robin lifted her mace and roared something stupid about Matt into the air, and a surge of hope and joy rose in Chris. No matter the losses he'd suffered—the pain, the dismay, and the heartbreak—no matter the terrible days and nights filled with fear and terror, he knew that he was where he was supposed to be.

543

He was what he'd always been meant to be as well: a solid soldier, a fighter doing what was needed to protect those who needed it.

He triggered his Primal Shaman main ability. The armor clinked and shifted, special panels designed to allow for his expansion moving, as his voice deepened to a bestial roar.

The battle madness rose in him; his blood sang with twinned joy and terror. He roared in challenge, hearing the mingled exultation and madness that rose from half a hundred throats behind him in response.

He was home.

***

"Launch, launch, launch!" Griffiths roared, as a dozen shoulder-mounted, carefully checked and assessed, ASM rocket launchers unleashed their payloads. They were spaced along the wall, a wall that had been painstakingly cleared by the orcs.

Those mad bastards had demanded the right to stay there, even alongside his own soldiers who knew they had a solid chance to explode and take out a section of the damn wall with them. Yet, against all the odds, they'd worked!

Ten rockets streaked across the battlefield. Three were taken out by enemy action; spells flashed out and tore their delicate systems apart, great explosions filling the air.

Two more failed in mid-flight. In one, the chemical rocket simply cut out and the ballistic trajectory suddenly flattened, then nosed downward to introduce itself to a massed charge of the undead in an orgy of fire and shrapnel.

The other simply detonated. A cloud of fire and shrapnel appeared without anything from the enemy being near it.

Five, though? Five hammered home into the almost complete skeleton snake, and by the gods, did they make their presence known.

The detonations were huge. Bones and shadowy tissues were flung free and the snake-like creation, three-quarters formed, was suddenly rent into uneven, smoking chunks.

The majority of it sagged, collapsing inward, before sloughing apart. The magical tether of sickly green energy that had been streaming from the undead asshole snapped, then surged. The power lashed out as the impotent godling howled in fury and pain.

"Reload!" Griffiths bellowed. "Reload and fire at will!"

The head and a small section of the snake remained intact. But as the tether released fully, the energy that had been inside it thrashed, then exploded outward.

Sections nearby that had been part of its body shuddered and twitched. The head twisted frantically, latching onto a small part that was within reach.

There was a flare of light; the fragment of the body collapsed into bone dust. But the head and a short section of the attached body surged brightly with recovered power.

"Hit it again!" Griffiths roared, lifting the grenade launcher and unleashing repeated fire into the oncoming waves of undead.

The impact triggers in the grenades went off as each slammed home. He kept firing, walking them across the enemy lines.

A corpse lord reared up, howling in challenge as it triggered one of its signature abilities. Power gathered to raise the damaged and previously eliminated undead on all sides at the cost of its own life...and then it took a grenade to the face.

The magic released was a wave—undirected, wild—before being sucked up as the banshees raced across the battlefield, harvesting power.

Griffiths turned, tracking them, then blanched as he realized that they weren't just stripping their enemies of power. They were harvesting life and magic from everything, both sides of the field—the living and the dead alike were being drained. Then they arced around in waves and released it as they passed their master, allowing him to suck it in and channel it into his monstrous remaining creations.

"Snipers!" he shouted. "On the fliers! I want them taken down, and hard!" The words were barely out of his mouth before an emaciated figure darted into view to his left, thrusting both hands out in the direction of the next wave of incoming fliers.

"Catherine! What the hell are..." He started, only to grunt as the pressure that had been pushing down on them, coming on all sides from the Banshees, suddenly lifted.

"I can't keep their attention for long!" The nethermancer cried out, and Griffiths swore, realizing that was exactly what she was doing.

The attention of the banshees, of dozens of them, had changed from being spread across the entire battlefield, to just one person.

What he was feeling now, an urge to run and hide, to vomit, to sink to his knees and wish it would all go away, was only the leakage from their terrible focus on her.

"Fire!" He roared. "Take them down!"

Three fired, then four more, bullets lashing out and ending the fliers, but it took multiple hits most of the time, and even as a handful of fireballs lashed up from somewhere below, he knew it wouldn't be enough.

"Soul Eater!" Catherine cried suddenly at the lead banshee as it screamed, diving for her. A blast of energy leapt from the young woman's outstretched hand, purple fire and bright white light combining in twisting ribbons that punched into the creature.

Its scream—its counter attack—died instantly, the flight path ruined as it convulsed, arms thrashing, before something, something dark and twisted, was ripped free of the creation.

The banshee collapsed, its strings cut, falling from the air. It was suddenly rendered down to a collection of bones and rotting flesh, no more life in it than a mop, as the darkness was dragged through the air to Catherine in a flash.

She… she *ate it*.

Griffiths stared, before shaking off the shock, seeing more incoming as Catherine fell to her knees, shaking and convulsing. "Fuck, someone get her out of here!" He roared, before turning to direct others.

That was all he needed, a damn baby-mage dying on his watch, especially one that might come back and damn well haunt him over it.

"Ready!" another of the launcher team nearby suddenly bellowed, lifting his ASM to the shoulder, taking aim…then shrieked as a banshee that had come under fire toppled from the sky. It came on in a screaming rush, arms outstretched, passing between fire like a hero through raindrops, tumbling out of control, its body half shredded.

"Don't…!" That was all Griffiths had the time to say, as the soldier, seeing the horrific creation headed straight for him, fired on instinct.

The rocket shouldn't have activated. It *shouldn't have*. The minimum range hadn't been covered. It shouldn't have had the chance to even begin its arming process, and yet…and yet it was live.

It slammed into the tumbling hellion and exploded a handful of meters from the launch tube, right in front of the soldier.

The backlash scoured the nearby orcs and other defenders from the wall. Shrapnel tore through them, flames and a wall of sound and disorientation sending them reeling.

Then the undead were there. Those not affected by the actual blast were unfazed by it, streaming into the gaps and taking down dungeon-born and human alike.

Griffiths pushed himself up, his ears ringing. The world around him shimmered in and out of focus. He pressed at one ear, trying to get the pressure to equalize and pop again… And then he was fighting, ramming the barrel of his handgun into the ear of the banshee that had come out of nowhere to latch onto him, dragging him across the roof.

He fired, blowing its brain out, and then crashed down, hitting the far crenelation and bouncing off, stunned. The world spun as two more banshees blacked out the sky overhead…and dropped a corpse lord in.

The massive construct landed hard. Its hands lashed out with terrible speed. One clamped down atop the back of a kobold's head, then yanked it upright, flipping the stunned dungeon-born out over the side. Another flicked out to the left, a bone whip uncurling and latching onto the next victim.

Griffiths lifted his gun, squinting drunkenly as the world split into two unequal parts. He hurriedly closed one eye, opening fire and emptying the magazine in the direction of the corpse lord's head.

It staggered, fragments of the skull shattering, but the majority remained intact, shots whipping past to vanish into the darkening night.

Then the slide locked back, empty.

Griffiths reached down, fumbling a mag free and then dropping it, slurring out curses as he dragged another out and then tried to slot it in…as the empty was still seated.

"Damn… you…" he muttered, blinking owlishly. His concussion made the world reel back in and out of focus, as the corpse lord backhanded the gun from his grip.

His wrist snapped, and the gun sailed out over the side to vanish into the maelstrom below.

"Well, fuck," he managed to force out, as the massive construct raised a foot and slammed it down, hard.

***

The world had dissolved into a screaming, frantic blur. The hundreds of banshees that had been waiting, hidden from sight by the clouds, had begun their runs, tearing across the battlefield, one after another in great lines.

They spread panic and confusion as they wailed and streaked past overhead. Each successive pass drained their victims of mana and life, even as they made it harder and harder to face them, to focus.

Light surged on the battlefield as the goblin Luminaries fought back, sudden surging clean white light that seemed to bring hope…until the banshees descended, swamping them.

I slashed right and left, flashing across their lines again and again, taking down a handful here and there, but they were too fast. The closer I got to their master, the more they bunched up and unleashed their sonic wails, forcing me away.

The farther back I got, the fewer and fewer of them I could fight, making less of a difference to the battle—about as useful as a chocolate fireguard.

I wasn't out yet, though, because as near as I could tell, I'd managed to kill that fucker that had been right behind me as I entered the clouds… I pulled up the notifications—a horrifically risky thing to do in literally the middle of a fight—and checked.

"Fuck!" I snarled. No kill notification for it, not yet, but the dragon was toast. It was spread across half the battlefield, and…

I flipped, lopping off the head of a banshee that had been closing on me and hoping for an opportunistic kill. I spiraled desperately, shifting direction on a whim and hacking at anything that came too close, even as I searched.

Bones…bones were everywhere, but the dragon had been massive. It'd been driven to the ground by meteors; there had to be a trail…

There!

The shower I'd unleashed toward the big boss had done damage—not to him, but to his colossus. It'd moved into his way protectively, and the explosions, the devastation, and the sheer nuclear levels of damage had left it a scant third of its original size.

The asshole himself was now only working to maintain and try to finish two of the monstrosities, I saw; at some point I'd missed that. But the snake was…dead? No. Broken though, certainly.

I looked at it, seeing it in chunks, smoking and trying to reach other sections of its own battered form. The damn thing was crippled but trying to reform itself. For a split second, I almost went after it; then I shook my head.

It wasn't my job.

Was it Mike's? Griffith's? I couldn't remember, but it was someone's. And despite the way I could see the others were being slowed and even driven back, I couldn't help them.

Instead, I latched onto the one thing I could do.

I could kill gods.

Launching myself in the direction of Balthazar, I searched the ground frantically, finally spotting a trio of banshees gathered around a single corpse lord, one that looked…wrong.

It was half hunched over, frozen in place but glowing green with a sickly fog wreathing it. Without thinking about it, I changed direction and streaked at it.

They didn't see me coming—not in time, at least—and the dozens of banshees between my target and me lasted seconds. Some dodged, believing I was attacking them. Others attacked me and were cut from the sky.

Some detonated. Some tried to unleash their mind-altering effects: clouds of silvery smoke, pestilential breath, miasmic hisses and shrieks that promised the deaths of all I loved. All were tried, and all were ignored.

I focused so fully on my goal that nothing else existed for long seconds but him, me, and the blade I swung.

I crashed into the ground on the near side of the quartet. The sheer momentum drove me through to the far side. My blade whipped around at chest height to carve the stolen life from them all.

The corpse lord was massive. Bones like an elephant's were layered over and over: dual rib cages fused together, twin shoulders that had held two pairs of lethal arms—all shattered as the blade cut through from point A to B mercilessly.

They all disappeared in a cascade of bone, and then I launched myself into the air again, twisting and seeing that I was running out of chances.

Lights flared back at the keep, and I ignored them, twisting my back to it, desperate not to lose my night vision as the clouds rolled in heavier, bringing a cold wind and driving rain.

Two thousand, eight hundred and forty-seven points of mana left.

Not enough!

I needed more. I needed to drain the converters, but that would be a minor boost, at best! I launched myself forward, lifting my blade and drawing across my left palm in a fast motion, slicing the flesh in a hope that it'd take the blood from there instead of my goddamn eyes.

I needed them!

I flicked the blood free. Then, taking a breath, I triggered my full-on demon summoning spell, aiming at the ground behind Balthazar and shouting out the trigger words. "DEMON…I summon thee!" I roared. And wonder of wonders, the blood was ripped from my palm, making me gasp in pain as my health dropped from three and a half thousand—or close enough—to half that.

I needed my goddamn mana more than my health though, I knew.

Besides, I had a health potion, and there were more back at the…keep.

"Fuck!" I snarled, seeing the flaring lights, and finally realized what I was seeing and hearing—the distant flashes, the booms, the detonations and the feelings of "rightness" that periodically washed out, that I'd not even noticed consciously.

The keep was under attack. They were fighting for their lives there, while I was pissing around with the fucking undead! I twisted, hammering mana into my flight ability, and tore through the air. The keep was surrounded.

On all sides, the defenders had fallen back. They fought with their backs to the walls, trying to retreat inside. The air on all sides was filled with banshees that were screaming over and over again, pummeling the remaining defenders with the shock waves of their terrible abilities.

I couldn't even make a difference, I knew, not really. The demon was already coming through, as I glanced back, hands reaching out of a hole in the earth that led to another plane, ringed in slowly spiraling symbols that bled hellish light into our world.

The screams of dying, tortured souls filled the night as the demon levered its way out of its realm and into this one. And as one of the nearby banshees, that had been defending their master, turned and attacked it—

I had a chance!

I had a chance to get him, if I turned my back now and flew at the bastard, all in, and yet… yet… I turned back to the keep, seeing my people falling.

Dying.

It was all going wrong.

We were losing, I knew. Despair rose in me as I hesitated, knowing where I should go, where I had to go…even as my friends were falling.

Then the impossible happened, as the light of a fresh portal opening flared to life.

The portal burst with bright white light; then blue, reds, and golds flashed, before finally crackling lightning burst forth to scour a path from the portal clear of the enemy.

A pair of figures strode through.

Backlit by the portal, they were featureless in the night until one of them lifted a spear high and roared into the night in challenge.

CHAPTER FORTY-SEVEN, THE LAST CHAPTER

Hundreds of fresh troops raced through the portal, streaming forward in a double line that split to flow around the first to arrive. They ran two abreast, each holding a spear in one hand, with their opposite palm lifted and a spell already flaring to life above it. I blinked and then grinned as a figure I recognized yelled orders in a language I didn't.

The effect was clear, though. A barrage of spells flashed out, taking the undead on all sides and smashing them from their feet.

More than half of those targeted were killed outright. Those that survived were killed by the second barrage, or the third.

Again and again, for ten launches, the double line fired, clearing the undead back all the way to the wall. And then the light of fresh summons appeared behind them.

Orcs stepped out of the firefly light, straightening, screaming, and then raced forward, their clubs held high.

The pair of humans who had come to our aid leapt into the air then, arcing out toward me, even as I twisted around and bore down on Balthazar.

The demon was half clear of the hole between our realities when the banshees attacked, hitting it with wave after wave of screams. My summon roared in challenge and heaved itself all the way through, snatching a figure from the sky and tossing it contemptuously into its mouth.

The banshee vanished with a wail. The sound of bones splintering beneath long teeth was audible through the battle suddenly as the banshee's song faded, then burst back into frenzied life as they redoubled their efforts.

The demon launched itself to meet them, clawed hands passing through the air as they dodged and screeched.

I called out an order to it. "The creations!" I yelled. "Kill *them*!"

It didn't need the words, not to understand them, not really. I knew it as I knew how to summon the monstrosity; all it needed was its master to order it, and it would understand.

If I'd been able to speak it, I could have yelled it in Swahili, and it'd have understood.

As it was, though, I launched myself at Balthazar, who snarled, then threw up a shield, twisting and dodging aside, forced to abandon his creation only half complete.

Waves of spells launched again and again into the hydra. A misshapen lump that was all that had been finished so far, with Dante hammering each head with powerful flames as they were destroyed, making sure that they couldn't reform.

Chris was already carving a great section of the colossus free, even as it tried to awaken fully. The honor guard and the volunteers who had gone with him were cut down to half by the desperate battle, but still battling gamely on.

The demon launched itself onto the back of the colossus, biting down and tearing a section of it free, yanking back and spitting it out, then vomiting fire into the freshly revealed chest cavity.

The fire gouted through it, then began to burst free, dripping and gushing from a hundred places. The humans and their allies on the ground cried out and dove aside, but I had no time to deal with that or anything else.

Balthazar had changed his mind, clearly, and when he'd realized he couldn't back up fast enough, he attacked instead. He lifted a staff, pointed it at me, and unleashed a noxious yellow flame in a great gout. I rolled to the side, hurling a lightning bolt back at him, only to have him roar with laughter as the lightning hit, then crackled into nothingness, the last vestiges appearing to pour into him.

"Fool!" he screeched. "You think I haven't studied you? You think, all this time, surrounding yourself with my minions, I wasn't there, watching, waiting and learning! I know all there is to know of you!"

"You are a worm!" came a shout from behind me, as Akuba and Kaatachi struggled into the air, clearly having to fight to fly, and yet still game enough to try and damn well fight an enemy god while learning. Twin bolts of lightning flashed past me to crash against his chest, before breaking apart and filtering in as he laughed.

"Fools!" he repeated. "Come! Feed me more of your power!"

Seeing the lack of an effect, and the distance, the pair stopped throwing lightning then, instead focusing on their flight, and I attacked, moving in close with my sword whipping through the air.

Three times, the two of us launched ourselves at each other; three times, my sword crashed into his staff, sending great cascading waves of sparks falling free before the other pair were close enough to help.

I lunged at him, sword stabbing, then moving wide to enable them to attack from his sides as well…only to be blindsided by a banshee as soon as my attention was elsewhere.

It latched onto my back from behind, lunging forward, and screeched directly into my face. For a second, I lost all grip on reality. The banshee exploded even before I could instinctively hit at it, bursting into fragments as it used all its power up in a single frenzied attack.

551

I tumbled senseless through the air, all sense of reality broken for long seconds; the pull of the earth now seemed to come from all different directions at once. Coming to myself at the last moment and focusing, I forced my mana into myself to fly…and found that my inner ear was lying about which way was up. I crashed into the ground at an angle and tore a great furrow through the shattered undead.

Laying there dazed, I stared up as Kaatachi and Akuba battled, flashing in and out—one with a spear, one a shield—deflecting and striking in perfect tandem. Balthazar pulled in the last of his banshees to protect him, lashing out over and over with great blasts of fire and black necrotic energy.

Great shields of what looked like water and blackness roiled in and out, deflecting the necrotic energy, but the pair were obviously already outclassed.

I pushed myself to my knees, the world rolling. I fell sideways but forced myself back up, shaking my head. Then I desperately shoved my helmet up and aside, barely managing to get it out of the way before I vomited.

The world flared with light and then dimmed. My ears were telling me I was still rolling over and over, and yet I knew I was kneeling, on all fours. As I looked up, something caught my eye.

Ahead of me, there was movement, but in the madness all around, I couldn't make it resolve.

Somewhere beyond it, two towering figures fought.

The demon I'd summoned and the partially reconstituted snake-like construction fought for primacy, staggering.

The snake rose up, now at least fifteen meters long. It was wrapped tightly around the demon's chest, and it reared back, its mouth opening wide.

"Inside!" I coughed out, then vomited again, spitting the last of the foul mess from my mouth as I forced myself to one knee, then my feet. "Through!"

The demon knew what I meant. Compelled by the summoning spell, it spun, disregarding the lethal threat, and then leapt for the hole in the world it'd entered through.

For whatever reason, the hole hadn't shut, and now that hole provided an escape route for the demon…and a pit for the snake.

As the snake clamped down, the demon's head vanishing into the maw with a vicious and short-lived crunch, the pair disappeared from this realm, and the portal snapped shut behind their tumbling bodies.

I reeled drunkenly, and finally managed to focus on the sight before me as it drew closer.

A bright-blue cat. A goddamn *cat*?

I blinked owlishly, trying to make sense of it, before lifting my left hand and pointing at the cat, which in turn stared at me, sitting primly in the boneyard.

"I…know you?" I asked, then shook my head, wincing as pain flared. "I know you!" My right ear suddenly popped and crackled, the sound of cartilage reforming. The pressure abruptly rose, then seemed to vanish as it equalized. The sudden nausea rose again, then dropped like a stone, giving me a second of relief, before it surged once more.

"Foolish kitten."

"Fucking cat!" I groaned as it clicked. "Thor!"

"I am."

"You're a fucking menace!" I grunted, closing my left eye to help me focus.

"Get ready."

"Ready for what?!" I ground out, then gasped. The world crashed back into more or less focus; the fight was still going on overhead. "Dammit!"

"Be ready!" the cat snapped, and I glared at him.

"For fucking what? Christmas!?" I crouched. My head spun and my mana was low, but damn, I knew what I had to do. The undead had forgotten about me, and I might get one chance, just one...

I started to summon a Lightning Bolt, then snarled and dismissed it, focusing instead on an Incinerate as I knew he'd just absorb it anyway.

"Foolish kitten!" Thor snarled. *"You bat at prey with your paws but pull back your claws!"*

"My claws..." I glared at him as I rose to my full height. "He's immune to lightning!"

"Wrong!"

"I saw it!" I snapped. "I saw it with my own eyes!"

"They lie!"

"You're a fucking cat who's been hiding all this time! You don't even know what we're fighting for!"

"For prey."

"SURVIVAL!" I roared at him. "We're fighting to survive!"

"Fight to kill. Fight to win!" he snapped back. *"Use your claws!"*

"I'm trying!" I shouted at the furry little shit, who suddenly reared up and placed both paws on my shoulders.

I blinked at the wrongness of that—a cat that was, yeah, as big as a small dog, but no more, suddenly able to do that—until the eyes before my own banished everything.

I suddenly saw the fight with Daedalus, the way that I'd been able to block his attacks, the force that I'd surrounded myself with, and the great storm that I'd drained into a killing beam.

Then it was gone, and so was the cat. I sagged to my knees again, gasping. My mind felt like every memory had been slapped around and shoved back in backward.

I twisted, searching quickly, but the goddamn cat was definitely gone. And in moving fast, the world spun and reeled again, but at last my brain seemed to catch on a 'minor' detail. My goddamn bag!

Reaching down, I fumbled at my belt, finding the bag of holding on the second attempt. I yanked a potion out, the most powerful healing one I had, and a mana crystal. I downed the potion, dragged the mana from the crystal, and gasped as my battered bones, my abused mana channels, and my shaken brain were all suddenly snapped back to full strength and doused in clarity.

Then I grimaced as a distant voice came to me.

"Be ready."

"You furry fuckin' turd," I muttered, unable to believe that little shit had chosen now of all times to return, while half convinced that all that I'd just seen might have been a hallucination.

There was a sudden glow of light on the crown of the distant citadel, and I gasped as I saw the power dim, then flare to greater and greater brightness as it built, before I recognized the sudden feeling, and what had to be happening.

"What...? Wait, Emma... no!" I cried in horror as I realized the only one who it could be, even as a shriek sounded above me, and laughter rang out.

I glanced up, then back to the citadel, then snarled as I heard the voice in my mind.

"Be ready!"

Cursing, I forced myself upward. My sword, somehow still clutched in my right hand, flashed up to point at the heavens entirely on instinct.

Lightning flashed and thunder rolled in the distance. The clouds that I'd sensed flaring and congregating suddenly seemed to bang and crash against one another, as more and more power flashed out from the distant citadel.

The converters atop the roof were brightly lit, pulsing in tandem as each was drained, channeling their power and everything that the dungeon had to hand, into the frail and distant human form of a young woman atop it.

She screamed in agony and terror, a sound that rolled across the world—or so it seemed. Then a bright flash of power whipped upward into the sky as she unleashed the stored mana.

"NOW!"

I didn't need the prompt. I reached up with my own ability, forcing an ionized path through the air to the clouds above, already roiling and overloaded with power.

As the path was opened, the clouds responded. The burgeoning lightning, the power of a small, but still incredibly charged storm, thundered down, slamming into the tip of the sword, then filling me.

I screamed in triumph, in pain, in furious pleasure and determination. The void that I'd created between myself and the storm above served to draw in the power, all of it that Emma must have gathered atop the dungeon, that she'd fed upward.

The storm had taken that energy; it'd funneled it back and forth, using it to build upon the energy that it already held. The Water mana, the Fire, the Ice, the Lightning—each and every form of mana that roiled back and forth in the storm had been shocked and chained.

How she'd done it, I didn't know—hell, I barely felt that she had. But the elements seemed to twist into me, dragged downward along the path of power as the sky connected to the ground, using my sword to feed it into me as the conduit.

I launched myself into the air, travelling back up the path of the storm even as the clouds above faltered. The power of the storm was ripped free of it, channeled down my sword and me, building and scouring me from the inside out. I felt cored, like an apple, and yet filled to bursting as more and more mana flooded me than I could hope to contain.

Always in the past—heh...those many, many times I'd done this—I'd fed the power into the dungeon, using it.

Now, instead, the storm had been supercharged by the dungeon. I'd been filled with mana that was perfectly attuned to integrate with me, the dungeon's lord.

The clouds on all sides were unraveling. The wind slackened as mana continued to stream into me, feeding me, making my form tingle as more mana than I could ever hope to constrain tore along my mana channels. The power I was holding was enough to destroy me in an instant... if I hadn't already tempered myself through my ascension to divinity. As it was, I was still pushed far past where I'd ever dreamt I could reach, and I screamed, my body heating to the point that my skin and bones should already be turning to ash.

Balthazar hung there. He'd been speaking, staring down at Kaatachi as he hefted his shield, determined to protect Akuba, his love. The sudden cacophony of the storm had silenced his gloating, his evil villain monologuing, and the sudden bursts of rising sunlight shone through what had been cloud cover.

I rose, staring at him in abject fury over all that he'd done to me and mine, and what he'd planned to do next. I distantly felt the others as that furry little shitbiscuit guided them somehow as well.

The mana slackened off. For a split second, the balance was disrupted. Then a pillar of pure Fire mana was unleashed by Dante into the air, rocketing it upward in a fountain of brilliant power.

On the far side of the battlefield, his opposite knelt, one arm wrapped around a deep wound in his stomach, holding his entrails in, even as Kilo unleashed everything he had into the sky in a burst of coordinated Ice mana.

Both streams twisted and joined the storm, pouring into me, forming a connection between me and their mortal casters. I dragged the mana down, feeling the spark that flared within coalescing into a fresh neutron star.

The clouds around me petered out, even as below me, Dante dug deeper.

His form flashed from a human wielding fire, into a physical personification of the element of Fire itself. He burst into living flames, raising his hands and sending that fire streaming up in greater and greater quantities.

Kilo saw him, saw what he was doing, and he dug deeper as well, grabbing something within him and pushing past it, breaking a barrier that he'd never knew even existed.

Jez Cajiao

As the streams of Fire and Ice rose behind me, pouring inward, meeting the Air that surrounded me, the Water that even now cascaded in its last run from the shredded clouds overhead, I dragged in a deep breath, and I *knew*.

DOMINION ESTABLISHED

The message that printed across my soul was confusing, or it should have been, anyway. Instead the meaning was clear as I 'felt' the world around me in a way I'd never imagined.

The air, the water, the fire and the earth were all simply... mine.

The mana that had been gifted to me, that had been fed out to permeate everything on all sides, was attuned to me in a way that it never could be, to anyone that wasn't both a dungeon lord, and a god.

As such, I realized that 'dominion' was entirely goddamn accurate.

Balthazar stared at me as I flashed through the air toward him. My eyes glowed so bright, it was like I'd become the soul of Light itself instead of as I was, the fury of the storm made flesh.

He snarled and thrust both hands out, glaring at me as he switched his target, throwing a great gout of necrotic black and yellow energy from his left, and sickly green fire from his right. They raced toward me, obscuring him from my sight.

I stared, my resolve forming into an iron-hard ball of determination in my gut. "No," I said.

I made no gesture, cast no spell; I simply refused to allow this.

His spells were *failures*. They were corruptions of the mana that I, too, could use. Their Unlife was made of Life and Death; their necrotic fire was Fire and Death. They travelled through *my* air. They used *my* fire. They drew on *my* water to create the life that they perverted into this form.

The incoming spells from the Lord of Unlife simply...failed.

The component forms of mana broke free. The unusable mass of mana scattered while that which could be used—the Life, the Death, the Water, the Fire, the Air...it all streamed forward to feed me.

As the spells collapsed, the sneering form of the lord of liches beyond them was revealed. And that sneer poured off his face, as he saw that instead of being destroyed by his attack, I too was being fed by my enemy.

I opened my mouth and dragged in a deep breath.

Twisting, he tried to dive aside, fleeing as he saw that something had changed, and failed.

The beam of lightning that I unleashed was different from anything I'd ever channeled before. The sound that accompanied it was like a void in space. And as the blast hit him, he shrieked, lifting both hands and trying to conjure a shield between him and me, one that simply...unraveled.

The blast punched its way through the still-forming shield, then into him, boring into his forehead and through with a power that I'd never felt.

The life that had been animating him was ripped free and snuffed out, and the force that he'd granted to all his creations vanished at the same time.

His body fell, slowly at first, then with growing speed as he came apart. Everything from the lower jaw down was now lifeless and crumbling to dust. And from the jaw up?

It seemed to have been erased from existence.

On all sides, the crash as thousands of boney creations simply collapsed was incredible. But it was nothing compared to the chime that shook me, balls to bones.

WORLDWIDE ANNOUNCEMENT!
THE FIRST LORD OF THE STORM HAS DESTROYED HIS OPPONENT, THE FIRST LORD OF UNLIFE, IN A PITCHED BATTLE, ROUTING HIS FORCES AND CASTING DOWN ALL OPPOSITION! KNOW THIS! THE ONLY LIMIT ON YOU IS THAT WHICH YOU PLACE UPON YOURSELVES. GROW, ADVANCE, *LEAD*!

I stared at it, knowing that it was only the first of the announcements and that a shitload of decisions would have to be made, but for now, it was done. I batted it aside, fighting to see through the fucking things as they blinded me.

The next immediately replaced it. I couldn't help but stare at it…and the flickers that indicated updates being made to the notification, as others added their surrender to the notification.

Congratulations, First Lord of the Storm!
You have eliminated the majority of your enemy's forces, annihilated two of its chief lieutenants and its primary intended source of reinforcements, as well as destroying utterly the opposing god, Balthazar, First Lord of the Pantheon of Unlife.
The remaining forces of the Pantheon wish to sue for peace. What say you?
Will you accept their vassalage, or continue this war, to the knife?
All enemy forces save two, Petr, Lord of Darkness, his Dungeon Fairy Sin and their bonded Dungeon #91, and Sari, Mistress of the Sea, have added their unconditional surrender.
Petr offers conditional surr—

"No. They all surrender unconditionally, or they die," I whispered, staring out across the fields of the dead. "No negotiation. They obey, they kneel, or I'll come for them."

Jez Cajiao

**VERY WELL, DUNGEON WARMANCER, FIRST LORD OF THE
STORM, AND OVERLORD.
YOUR VASSALS AWAIT YOUR ORDERS. CONGRATULATIONS
ON YOUR ASCENSION. BE READY FOR UPGRADE IN 3... 2... 1...**

That was when the notifications went mental, and the world flared like the white rabbit had been caught with its dick in the plug socket.

As it all crashed in, I'd had a split second to think, "Well, at least I've gotten through the fight without being rendered unconscious." And then the mana that had been powering my flight, my abilities and more, was suddenly turned on me, flashing through my body and beginning my new "upgrade," as the system decreed it.

Minor issue—I was forty meters in the air at that point.

"MOTHERFUCKERS!" I tumbled from the air. The divot I plowed in the bones that covered the field was the least painful of the changes I was encountering.

THE END OF BOOK 7

Jez Cajiao

THANK YOU

Hi everyone! Well, that's the Age of Expansion complete! Hopefully you've all enjoyed it? I know it was good for me to return to this world, I'd honestly missed it.

At the minute my intention is that I'll take a little time off after I finish Age of Conquest to allow my brain to recover from the mass of melted mulch it feels like!

Then? Well then I'll be back to UnderVerse! Now, I'm going to need to read the story over again from scratch, and then I'll write it, so if I'm planning on starting it (as I am) around the end of 2024 or beginning of 2025, that means I won't expect to be done writing book 8 until at least March, possibly the end of April, so don't expect it to be out until around June, I'm afraid!

Book 9 should be back to the usual release schedule of around 3 months after that though if that helps!

Then, well I'll be back to this! Rise of Mankind is intended to finish at book 10, and that'll be on my Patreon around 3 months before release, because there I can share the unedited version! I'll be writing the final 2 Rise of Mankind, then returning to UnderVerse for the final 3 in that series as well then, so expect all of my extant stories to be complete by the end of 2026.

Once all of that is done? Well, there's a lot of tales left to tell, and maybe, if you look hard enough, you'll find a hint here and there of what's to come.

For now though, I just hope you've enjoyed the ride so far, and please, if you did? Leave a review or a rating. You'd be amazed at the difference two minutes of your time makes.

Thank you all for your support, and your trust.

-Jez
07/10/2024

PATREON

By the time this launches in November? Some of my Patreon supporters have already finished book #8, and have access to a secret project. So, if you want to read it perhaps 4-6 months ahead of release? Come join us on the dark side!

HOWEVER: I do want to point out one thing everyone, the app stores on apple and android platforms have enforced a 30% mandatory percentage goes to them of any purchasing done through there. So the app store Patreon subscription has increased by that amount automatically, PLEASE sign up through the website instead, it's still Patreon's website, but the increase doesn't apply there.

There's several of those wonderful supporters out there that I have to thank personally as well; ASeaInStorm, Mischa, Kevin, Lex, Simon, Jordan, Grant, Daviculus and Steve thank you all!

https://www.patreon.com/Jezcajiao

Jez Cajiao

RISE OF MANKIND 8: AGE OF CONQUEST

By Jez Cajiao

The divine war is over, but humanity's greatest battle is just beginning...

In the aftermath of a divine level conflict, Matt and his people need to unite a fractured world against a rapidly closing invasion. The Orcan are coming, and only a united front stands a chance against their savage might.

But unity is a hard thing to achieve in a world still reeling from apocalyptic change. As Matt strives to forge alliances and build a coalition strong enough to face the looming threat, he finds that humanity's old vices—greed, ambition, and short-sightedness—may prove deadlier than any alien force.

With time running out and options dwindling, a fateful decision is made. The Age of Conquest has begun.

Now, Matt and his people have to navigate a treacherous world where yesterday's allies could become tomorrow's enemies. He'll need to master the delicate balance between diplomacy and force, weighing the cost of peace against the price of victory.
In a world where dungeons shape the land and power can corrupt even the noblest intentions, can Matt unite humanity before it's too late?

Or will the Age of Conquest spell the end of mankind's rise?

Note: This is a Dark Fantasy Epic LitRPG. Expect graphic violence, strong language, and morally complex themes. Reader discretion is advised.

Preorder on Amazon

THEFT OF DECKS

By Lars Machmuller

When the deck is stacked against you? Change the game!

In the frontier town of Isarn, Chase will never be more than the lowly Darkborn thief he is. Banned from training, banned from acquiring better cards, if the Lightborn had their way, he'd be banned from life itself.

He's not alone though, and the one thing he and his friends have is determination. Losing a hand to a brutal punishment only fueled his obsession to get access to his own amazing, reality-bending cards.

That is the path to power and a future for them all. Nobody cares where you came from when you're rich enough. For now, though, they're facing both established powers, churches and age-old prejudices. It's time to get to work, and if the Lightborn won't share and play nice?

Sometimes the only way to get dealt a better hand is to steal the whole damn deck!

Buy on Amazon

Jez Cajiao

QUEST ACADEMY

By Brian J. Nordon

A world infested by demons.
An Academy designed to train Heroes to save humanity from annihilation.
A new student's power could make all the difference.

Humans have been pushed to the brink of extinction by an ever-evolving demonic threat. Portals are opening faster than ever, Towers bursting into the skies and Dungeons being mined below the last safe havens of society. The demons are winning.

Quest Academy stands defiantly against them, as a place to train the next generation of Heroes. The Guild Association is holding the line, but are in dire need of new blood and the powerful abilities they could bring to the battlefront. To be the saviors that humanity needs, they need to surpass the limits of those that came before them.

In a war with everything on the line, every power matters. With an adaptive enemy, comes the need for a constant shift in tactics. A new age of strategy is emerging, with even the unlikeliest of Heroes making an impact.

Salvatore Argento has never seen a demon.
He has never aspired to become a Hero.
Yet his power might be the one to tip the odds in humanity's favor.

WANDERING WARRIOR

By Michael Head

A divine quest to deliver justice.
One year to accomplish his mission.
After nineteen planets, there's something different about this one.

James Holden has reached the maximum level there is for a human. That's perfect, since he's the only one of his kind. A wandering warrior, without control of his destination, tossed between universes by gods who've failed to tell him why. James is the lone Judge on a new world in need of someone to balance the scales. He isn't afraid to do so with extreme prejudice. As the Chief Justice, he has to right the wrongs the innocent can't fix themselves.

As James quickly discovers, the roots of corruption run deep. Guilds choose to protect themselves rather than the people. Monsters roam the wilderness unchecked. Judgment is usually a decision between right and wrong, but nothing is ever that simple. This time, being the strongest human won't be enough to punish the guilty. James might have to recruit some new blood, even if he prefers to work alone.

On his twentieth world, he is going to win, no matter the cost. James will have to find a way to break past the limits of the system if he's going to have a chance at making a difference.

Buy on Amazon

Jez Cajiao

KNIGHTS OF ETERNITY

By Rachel Ní Chuirc

When Zara awoke in chains she thought she'd gone mad.

She was Zara the Fury - mistress of flame and fear. Her name was whispered
across the land, from ramshackle taverns to the royal court. Even the heroic
Gilded Knights thought twice before crossing her path.
She was feared—*respected.*
Now she was curled up on a dirt floor on her fiancé's orders. Valerius, leader
of the Gilded, mocks her cries for help. And the kingdom is on the brink of war
over the missing Lady Eternity…
But that wasn't why Zara thought she had gone mad.
The reason why is that the last thing she remembered was blood, an arcade
screen, and the gun that changed everything.

**But no chains can hold the Fury, and when she gets out?
The world is going to *burn.***

<u>Buy on Amazon</u>

SCARLETT CITADEL

By Jack Fields

Gormon Hughes is 19, thin as a broom, and has—not for the first time in his life—been swept into the path of trouble. Poor, recently heartbroken, and indebted to the sort of people who file their teeth into needle points and devour wriggling bloated spiders for fun, Hughes sets his sights on salvation.

That salvation is the Scarlet Citadel, a wealthy organization of pageant fighters, monster hunters, and secret keepers. With the aid of strange oracles, rare good fortune, and a unique power that bubbles like champagne in the core of Hughes' being, he must join the Citadel and advance himself.

But the ladder of progression is harsh and dark. The rungs are slippery.

And falling means disaster…

Buy on Amazon

Jez Cajiao

BATTLEFORGED: CONQUEROR

By M.H. Johnson

Battleforged: Conqueror

It was time for Eric to show what one man with a few dozen oversized warthogs and an extradimensional storage space can do against an army of bloodthirsty orcs who think the Northeastern United States is already theirs.

Join Eric on a wild ride of non-stop action and deadly peril as he shows the entire world what happens to a Necromancer's enemies when they dare to threaten the people he loves!

Buy on Amazon

FACEBOOK AND SOCIAL MEDIA

If you want to reach out, chat or shoot the shit, you can always find me on either my author page here:

www.facebook.com/JezCajiaoAuthor

<u>OR</u>

We've recently set up a new Facebook group to spread the word about cool LitRPG books. It's dedicated to two very simple rules;

1: Let's spread the word about new and old brilliant LitRPG books.

2: Don't be a Dick!

They sound like really simple rules, but you'd be amazed…

Come join us!

https://www.facebook.com/groups/LITRPGLegion

I'm also on Discord here: **https://discord.gg/u5JYHscCEH**

Or I'm reaching out on other forms of social media atm, I'm just spread a little thin that's all!

You're most likely to find me on Discord, but please, don't be offended when I don't approve friend requests on my personal Facebook pages. I did originally, and several people abused that, sending messages to my family and being generally unpleasant, hence, the author page:

www.facebook.com/JezCajiaoAuthor

I hope you understand.

Jez Cajiao

LEGION

Okay everybody, if you've not yet seen or heard, well, the secret is out! My wife Chrissy, and our friend Geneva and I have launched the Legion Publishers! We're taking on new authors, as well as experienced ones, focusing primarily on the LitRPG side of things, but we're open to anything really, with one very clear rule that guides our company:

Don't be a dick.

That's it. Our contracts aren't hidden behind layers of legalese, you can find them here:

https://www.legionpublishers.com/legioncontract

If you want to reach out and ask any questions, get an idea of the support we offer, and possibly become part of the family? We'd love to hear from you, just tap the link and fill in the form:

https://www.legionpublishers.com/contact-and-submissions

Hope you're having a good one!

-Jez, Chrissy and Geneva

LITRPG!

To learn more about LitRPG, talk to other authors including myself, and to just have an awesome time, please join the LitRPG Group

www.facebook.com/groups/LitRPGGroup

Jez Cajiao

FACEBOOK

There's also a few really active Facebook groups I'd recommend you join, as you'll get to hear about great new books, new releases and interact with all your (new) favorite authors! (I may also be there, skulking at the back and enjoying the memes...)

https://www.facebook.com/groups/LitRPGlegion/

https://www.facebook.com/groups/GamelitSociety

https://www.facebook.com/groups/LitRPG.books

https://www.facebook.com/groups/LitRPGforum/

Made in the USA
Las Vegas, NV
08 December 2024

13586645R00315